3 Glittering Regency Romances

SCANDAL AND MISS SMITH
by Julia Byrne

RAKE'S REFORM
by Marie-Louise Hall

REBECCA'S ROGUE
by Paula Marshall

*First published in Great Britain 2001 by
Harlequin Mills & Boon Limited,
Eton House, 18-24 Paradise Road, Richmond, Surrey, TW9 1SR*

THE REGENCY RAKES © by Harlequin Enterprises II B.V. 2001

The publisher acknowledges the copyright holders of the
individual works as follows:

Scandal and Miss Smith © Julia Byrne 1997
Rake's Reform © Marie-Louise Hall 1997
Rebecca's Rogue © Paula Marshall 1998

ISBN 0 263 82830 1

106-0101

*Printed and bound in Spain
by Litografia Rosés S.A., Barcelona*

SCANDAL AND MISS SMITH

by

Julia Byrne

Dear Reader,

Regencies are my very favourite romances. Like most fans I started with Georgette Heyer and have been hooked ever since. The greatest appeal for me is the opportunity to travel via imagination into a time and place that was elegant, exciting, extravagant. At least for the privileged few. Unfortunately, my ancestors sprang from struggling countryfolk, but that's another story.

My Regency heroes are strong, protective and honourable but also a product of their times with the natural arrogance that comes to those born to command. Until they meet the heroine, be she spirited or gentle, who will temper their arrogance with tenderness and love. The journey my characters take to achieve their happy ending is, for me, an endless fascination with the human spirit.

I hope you enjoy this journey into the past as much as I enjoyed creating it.

Julia Byrne

Chapter One

'Thanks to your lordship's unwarranted and selfish reluctance to assume the sacred charge laid upon you three years ago, I have been forced to take matters into my own hands. Not without considerable inconvenience, I might add.'

There was no reply.

Phoebe would have been surprised if an answer had been forthcoming, since she'd addressed her strictures to the portrait of a long-dead Deverell that was hanging over the mantelpiece in the library into which she had been ushered ten minutes ago.

She knew the gentleman immortalised by Lely was a Deverell. He possessed the same raven-black hair, lean, aristocratic countenance and ice-cold sapphire eyes that characterised every generation of Deverells. Phoebe studied the portrait with a jaundiced eye and decided she had become rather tired of that particular combination of colouring and feature. The occasional blonde or redhead would have broken the monotony somewhat. It might at least have infused some badly needed warmth into the family bloodlines.

Unfortunately, Deverells bred true, no matter what new blood was introduced into the family. In fact, they had probably looked exactly like the gentleman in the portrait when they had crouched over fires and worn mammoth skins. Doubtless the mammoths had been

rendered easy prey by the same piercing, basilisk stare
that arrowed down at her from the painted canvas.

Phoebe had had a great deal of experience with that
stare. And with Deverells in general. Which was why
she was busily rehearsing the opening lines of a speech
destined to be delivered to her employer, the Honourable
Sebastian Alexander Deverell, newly created—for services to the Crown that were of an unspecified and
mysterious nature—Baron of that name.

The reason for the creation of a barony to grace the
younger son of an old, distinguished family whose present head was an Earl was only the latest mystery
surrounding Deverell. Despite the rumours abounding in
the *ton*, Phoebe knew next to nothing about the man.
According to family lore, he had sailed off to India at
a young age and had remained there for several years,
after which he had travelled throughout the East, engaging in whatever shadowy activities had resulted in his
new title.

At any other time, Phoebe might have found such
highly rewarded patriotism reassuring. Even comforting.
Quite conducive to a measure of peace of mind, in fact.
But comfort, peace of mind and other such necessities
for a well-ordered existence had vanished from her life
the day Deverell's aunt had hired her to take up the
position of governess to his orphaned nieces and nephew.

Two years of living on the edge of disaster had ensued;
the minions who were supposed to answer her queries
and lend assistance when required failing dismally to do
either. Nor had the trenchant letters she had been sending
post-haste to Deverell since his return to England three
months ago elicited a more satisfactory response.

The only alternative, as far as Phoebe could see, was
a verbal assault.

Her attack on the gentleman in the portrait was not
the first such speech she'd rehearsed. She had begun the
practice a week ago, when she'd reached the conclusion
that she either handed over control of the younger

members of the family to their uncle and guardian, or presented herself at the gates of Bedlam in a state of babbling witlessness.

The opening lines of her speech had rapidly become less civil as her meeting with Deverell loomed closer, with the result that, after a journey to London fraught with adventures of nightmarish proportions, Phoebe was feeling extremely *uncivil*.

Not to say desperate.

She quelled that last thought immediately. Dramatic emotions such as desperation were no help at all when dealing with Deverells. One had to remain calm and in control of oneself.

Phoebe lifted a hand to her head to assure herself that she still appeared calm and in control of herself, even though her stomach persisted in performing such acrobatic feats as somersaults.

Her old-fashioned bonnet seemed to have remained in place. Its nondescript fawn hue did not show her light brown hair, brown eyes and fair complexion to advantage. That knowledge, borne in on her when she'd inspected her appearance prior to leaving Grillon's Hotel for Deverell's town house, had caused a pang in her secretly fashionable heart. She had sternly suppressed it. Governesses were expected to look plain and unremarkable. They were supposed to fade into the background.

In this case, she reflected, casting a glance at her surroundings, such a task would not be difficult. Her severe chocolate-brown pelisse not only matched the bookshelves lining most of the wall space, but also blended in rather well with the commodious sofa and armchairs grouped in a cosy arrangement about the fireplace. If she sat on one, she would probably disappear altogether.

A rueful smile curved her lips as she ran one gloved hand over the back of a nearby chair. Clearly, one of the rumours about Deverell was true. He appeared to

have made a fortune in India. The rich brown leather
beneath her fingers was the finest Cordovan, heavy
drapes of dark gold velvet, tied back with brown and
gold silk tassels, framed the long windows, and the floor
was covered by an exquisite Oriental rug into which her
half-boots sank to a positively decadent degree.

The rug wasn't the only object of beauty in the room.
Jade statues and antique urns loomed from pedestals or
from behind glass-fronted cabinets; a heavy globe on a
gold inlay and ebony stand graced the corner near
Deverell's solid mahogany desk; and on the desk itself,
illuminated by a shaft of sunlight, a graceful Psyche held
aloft a branched candelabra.

Phoebe found herself staring at the sculpted figure
with fascinated interest. Its creator had not believed in
covering the female form in anything but the flimsiest
of draperies, but what struck her was its setting. The
flowing lines of the statue were so fragilely feminine, a
waterfall in pure white marble, frozen forever in time,
that it should have looked out of place in such a darkly
masculine room. The fact that the statue looked perfectly
at home on the desk raised some equally interesting
questions about its owner.

She frowned and returned her gaze to the painted
visage above her. The saturnine features reminded her
that she was not here to be distracted by statues.

'On the contrary,' she informed the portrait sternly,
'I am here to condemn your lordship's utterly incomprehensible behaviour in the strongest possible terms.'

'How very unfortunate,' drawled a deep male voice
from the doorway behind her. 'The third Earl was notori-
ously profligate, but condemnation a hundred and fifty
years after the event seems a trifle unfair. Even for him.'

Phoebe spun around with a startled gasp. And went
completely still.

The gentleman standing in the doorway, one hand
resting on the door knob, black brows raised in faintly
mocking enquiry, was unmistakably a Deverell. The

height, the careless arrogance in his stance, the midnight-dark hair were all as she had expected.

What startled her wits into temporary paralysis were his eyes. Instead of the hard sapphire orbs she had anticipated, she was transfixed by a glittering aquamarine gaze that was as changeable and mysterious as the sea; blue one moment, green the next, shot through with shards of gold.

She had never seen eyes like them.

'Miss. . . Smith, I believe,' he murmured, coming into the room and pushing the door closed behind him.

The latch slid home with a decisive little click that succeeded in snapping Phoebe out of her trance. She opened her mouth.

'And this,' he continued, eyeing her attire, 'is, I presume, Lord Pendleton's idea of a disguise.' One black brow went up. 'Dear me. I must have sounded more than normally disapproving if he thought my tastes ran to buttoned-up Puritans.'

Phoebe felt her mouth drop open further. She blinked. 'I beg your pardon, my lord?'

'Ah, but the voice is very good.' A lazy smile curved Deverell's mouth as he came closer. He began to walk around her, circling her slowly while he made a comprehensive sweep of her person from her bonnet to the tips of her brown suede half-boots. 'Melodious and refined, with just a hint of provocative huskiness. Pen is to be congratulated.'

'What. . .? Pen . . .*who*?'

Phoebe shook her head in an attempt to recover her senses. It was not easy. Trying to keep track of Deverell while he circled around her was making her positively dizzy. So was the sudden breathlessness she was experiencing at his close proximity. She couldn't understand it. She was used to Deverells staring down at her. They did it all the time. But this particular example of the species was rather taller than the rest.

And larger.

He finally came to a halt directly in front of her, but Phoebe's relief that he'd stopped moving was short-lived. Up close, he towered over her. And, she noted with some annoyance, she couldn't even see past him to the door. Far from rejoicing in the slim willowy build of the rest of his family, Deverell looked as if he'd spent his years abroad engaging in hard physical labour.

His shoulders were intimidatingly broad and the excellent tailoring of his coat of dark blue superfine did nothing to disguise the formidable proportions of the body beneath. Tightly fitting buckskins adhered faithfully to the long, powerful muscles of his thighs, and his topboots appeared to be on the extremely large side.

His size was not the only difference, Phoebe saw, as her bemused gaze travelled upwards to rest on the strong planes and angles of his face. Polite society would have deemed him handsome, but, allied to that powerful build, on him the chiselled Deverell features took on an edge that sent visions of medieval knights and crusading warriors flitting through her mind.

There was nothing romantic about the visions. The warrior studying her with a coolly assessing intelligence gleaming in his blue-green gaze was straight off the battlefield. There was no obvious gore, but the classical nose looked as if it had been broken at one time, and a small scar curved around the angle of his jaw. Two deep grooves were carved on either side of his mouth, and while its thin, almost cruel, top lip was familiar, the lower one was disturbingly sensual and strangely compelling.

Phoebe gazed up at it and felt a very odd tremour somewhere deep inside her. A medieval warrior. As fierce in love as in battle.

'Miss Smith? Are you quite all right?'

'Uhh. . .' Phoebe wrenched her gaze upward and encountered a sardonic gleam that had her straightening her spine with an almost audible snap. 'Oh. Yes. Of

course I am, my lord. Um. . .you were saying?' She
could have sunk through the floor.

'Lord Pendleton,' he repeated dryly. 'He is to be congratulated. When he told me about the latest
establishment catering to a gentleman's every whim, I
confess it held no appeal for me. But I do believe, my
dear Miss Smith, that you could change my mind.'

'I could?' Phoebe searched vainly for the rapidly
unravelling thread of the conversation.

'My fantasies don't run to the peculiar or overly
exotic,' he explained when she frowned. 'On the other
hand, there was no need to get yourself up as a governess.
I hate to disillusion you, but, as a disguise, it is really
quite hopelessly inadequate.'

'Disguise? But. . .'

'And couldn't you have come up with a more
diverting. . .er. . .*nom de boudoir*, than "Smith"?'

Shock hit her heart like a small velvet fist. Her breath
caught. Her knees wobbled. She forgot about medieval
warriors and the strange statements issuing from
Deverell's lips. She even forgot her speech. One thought,
and one thought alone, reverberated inside her head.

He didn't believe Smith was her name!

But he couldn't know. . . She had used Smith for several years. He couldn't possibly know. . .

'Smith *is* my real name, sir,' she managed at last,
hoping the warmth staining her cheeks was not too visible beneath her bonnet. It seemed to be but a faint hope.
The critical assessment lingering in his eyes sharpened
abruptly to a knife-edged interest that set her babbling.
'And I do not have the least idea of what you are talking
about. Clearly I have come to the wrong house.
Although, when I asked for Lord Deverell, your butler
did not so much as blink. However, if you would kindly
direct me. . .'

'Oh, you're in the right house,' he murmured. 'So
there's no need to continue the charade.' He took a step
closer, his gaze narrowing further when Phoebe promptly

retreated. 'But surely you're not going to run away. Did Pendleton send you here only to have you vanish after you'd proven his point? How very disappointing. I can provide several inducements for you to stay, you know.'

'Stay? Point?' Phoebe took a deep breath and decided she was dealing with a lunatic. 'Sir, this has gone on long enough. If you are indeed Lord Deverell, which I doubt, you obviously belong in Bedlam. Of course, it is quite possible that I made my way there this morning and am experiencing some sort of delusion. In which case you are another inmate, which does not surprise me in the least. However, you do not appear to be overly irrational, so perhaps you would be kind enough to fetch someone in authority so the mistake may be rectified.'

The intent look vanished from Deverell's face. He laughed softly. A low growl of amusement that sent a series of nerve-tingling ripples down Phoebe's spine. She couldn't have said why, but that deep purr sounded distinctly dangerous.

'I can assure you, Miss Smith, that you're not presently in the madhouse. A Deverell's house is often unconventional, but madness hasn't overtaken the family. At least, not yet. Now perhaps if we start—'

But the word family had a galvanizing effect on Phoebe's senses. Drawing herself up to her full height, she launched into a diatribe that bore no resemblance whatsoever to any of her rehearsed lectures.

'Well, madness may not have overtaken the family, sir, but it is about to overtake *me* if I do not receive a more satisfactory reply to my petitions than mealy-mouthed put-offs from your man of business, and injunctions to use my own judgement from your secretary.' Her voice rose. 'Not to mention the total absence of any reply from *you*!'

'Uhh—'

She levelled a finger at him before he could elaborate. 'You, my lord, are about to take charge of your nephew and nieces whether you want to or not. *I* have had enough!' She shook her finger vigorously. 'Enough, I say! Do you hear me?'

'I hear you,' Deverell said mildly, eyeing the finger waving back and forth in front of his chest with great interest. Phoebe flushed and lowered her hand. He brought his gaze back to her indignant countenance, made another thorough survey of her costume and a smile of unholy amusement crept into his eyes. 'Ah-ha. You're *that* Miss Smith.'

Heat almost lifted her bonnet off her head. 'Furthermore, my lord, while you may consider the behaviour of your family to be unconventional, others may find it scandalous, shameless and downright shocking. And at whose door will the blame be laid when scandal erupts, as will surely happen if nothing is done?' Infuriated anew at this rhetorical question, she abandoned finger-shaking and began to pace. 'At the governess's door, that's whose! Well, I will not have it, my lord.'

She turned at the window, skirts flying. 'I have my future to think of. My living to earn. I will not tolerate the situation a moment longer!' She fetched up abruptly in front of him and returned his look of amusement with a ferocious glare. 'Do you understand me, sir?'

'Well, I didn't at first, but I think I'm beginning to see a glimmer of light.'

'I can't tell you how reassuring I find that information. Perhaps, now, you will refrain from circling me, weighing me up and looking me over as though. . .as though I was a horse for sale at Tattersall's!'

'I shall refrain immediately, Miss Smith. Believe me, even in those hideous clothes, the last thing you resemble is a horse.' He grinned.

The sudden change wrought to his stern features momentarily halted Phoebe in her tracks. She could, however, see nothing remotely contrite in the expression. 'I do not resemble anything other than what I am. Really! I cannot imagine what you must have been think—'

She broke off, staring at Deverell as a dreadful suspicion filled her mind. A muscle quivered near his mouth once and was ruthlessly stilled.

'Oh, my goodness!' Her eyes flew wide. Her reticule fell from suddenly nerveless fingers. 'Lord Pendleton. . .establishment. . .gentlemen's whims. You thought. . .*Oh, my goodness!*'

This time her knees did buckle. Fortunately for her dignity, Deverell seized her arm before she actually hit the floor and steered her over to the sofa. Phoebe sank onto it without a murmur, her stunned gaze fixed on his face as he sat beside her.

'You thought. . .? You really thought. . .?'

He raised a brow encouragingly.

With a heroic effort, Phoebe plastered a hideously bright smile onto her face. 'Goodness me, my lord, no doubt you thought I had met Lord Pendleton at some function or another, although I must tell you that I've never been to London before and—'

'No, don't spoil it,' he murmured, smiling back at her. 'You've no idea how refreshing it is to meet a female of practical sensibilities who neither feigns ignorance nor goes off into exaggerated hysterics at the mention of a gentleman's. . .ah. . .conveniences.'

'Conveniences!' Her smile vanished. 'But I *am* ignorant. That is, I am not precisely acquainted with— Ohh!' She blushed wildly when he burst out laughing. 'Oh, you are quite shameless, my lord. How dare you discompose me like this! I can only suppose you *are* mad if you mistook your nieces' governess for a. . .a. . .'

'Barque of frailty?'

She glared at him.

'Bird of Paradise?'

Phoebe arose in her wrath. Before she could annihilate her tormentor, he rose also and took her hand in a strong clasp. Her breath promptly deserted her. She stared at the long fingers wrapped around her own and wondered wildly if she was embroiled in some demented sort of nightmare.

'Miss Smith, I do most sincerely apologise for not immediately remembering who you are. Please allow me to explain. You see, my friend Lord Pendleton decided to enliven what he refers to as my "deadly boring existence" by challenging me to fault the. . .er. . .gentility of some females of his acquaintance. I was expecting the first one this morning and—'

'The *first* one? Good heavens! How many—? I mean. . .oh, no!' It was a wail of despair.

His aquamarine eyes gleamed with silent laughter. 'Aha. I was right. A female of practical sensibilities. How could it be otherwise when you've been out in the world earning your living?' Then, as her face turned stormy, 'But before you apostrophize me as being quite beyond the pale, Miss Smith, please recall that parading Incognitas through the house was Pendleton's idea, not mine.'

Phoebe was having trouble recalling her own name, let alone any ideas. Never had she been assaulted by so many emotions at one and the same time. Shock, outrage and dazed disbelief jostled about in her brain until she could scarcely think. Not to mention the uneasy feeling engendered by Deverell's remark about earning her living. Just what sort of a living did he think she'd been earning?

Several pithy words on the subject rose to her mind. Unfortunately, before she could utter them, she made the mistake of looking up. Wicked humour still gleamed in Deverell's eyes—and, to her horror, Phoebe was seized by a wild and irresistible urge to laugh back. She choked instead.

'This *is* a nightmare,' she finally gasped, snatching her hand from Deverell's as if he were the devil incarnate. Her fingers felt all warm and tingly. The circumstance only added to her agitation. 'I can't possibly be standing here conducting such an improper conversation with you, my lord!'

'A very proper attitude for a governess, Miss Smith,

but quite unnecessary at the moment. As I said a minute ago, I prefer your frankness.' He cocked a quizzical brow at her. 'Nor can I believe that you haven't attracted a gentleman's attentions before, even under more conventional circumstances.'

Phoebe sank back to the sofa as if her legs had turned to water. 'Well, yes, but. . .'

These were attentions? They were certainly unlike the attentions she had indeed attracted before— *they* had caused her to lose two previous posts, but—

'I don't understand *why*,' she almost wailed.

'Then you don't spend a great deal of time studying a mirror,' he said softly. 'I find you. . .intriguing.'

Her eyes widened before her gaze went to the large gilt-framed mirror hanging on the opposite wall. The drab reflection staring back at her made her wonder again about his sanity. *'Me?'*

He smiled.

Annoyed at the startled squeak that had emerged from her throat, Phoebe scowled back at him. 'Sir, your existence must indeed be boring if you find anything to intrigue you in your wards' governess. Nor did I come here to discuss— What *are* you doing?'

The demand was uttered in an even higher squeak as Deverell resumed his seat and, without so much as a by-your-leave, captured her chin with one large hand. He turned her face towards him, his grip gentle but quite inescapable.

'I see you're now determined to throw the governess at me at every turn,' he murmured, his slow survey of her features causing her heart to leap into her throat. It stayed there, fluttering.

'Why is that, I wonder? Do you hide behind her, Miss Smith? Is that why you disguise yourself in colours that dim your own?'

'C-colours? I'm as colourless as this costume, sir.'

He raised a brow.

'I. . .I mean. . .everything's brown.' She gestured

helplessly. 'Bonnet, hair, dress, pelisse. Even my shoes. Brown, brown, brown.'

'You forgot your eyes,' he said, gazing straight into them.

Phoebe swallowed. 'They're brown, too,' she whispered. 'Plain, ordinary brown.' And she couldn't tear them away from his. He's casting a spell on me, she thought. Some exotic, eastern spell that made her wonder if she was drowning. Drowning in a deep blue-green sea. She could scarcely hear him over the rushing in her ears, but his words stroked over her nerves like warm silk over bare flesh.

'Plain? Ordinary? With those long lashes? Oh, no, Miss Smith. There's fire within.' His mouth curved lazily. 'Amber flames that could singe a man if he wasn't very careful. And when you remember propriety the fire darkens and goes still, waiting behind a haze of smoke, hiding secrets.'

'S-secrets? No, I. . . That is. . .we should both remember propriety right now, sir.'

He ignored this feeble attempt to distract him. 'And while you may try to imitate a brown wren by your costume, your hair is every shade of fawn and sunlight and honey ever imagined.'

'Oh, my good— I mean. . .how very poetic, my lord, but—'

'As to the rest, your complexion is flawless, your mouth a perfect bow that defies the governess no matter what words she utters, and—' he turned her head to the side '—although that little chin is nothing less than determined, your profile is really quite exquisite. No, Miss Smith, to the discerning observer you are anything but plain and ordinary.'

She was now also anything but calm and in control. Deverell's low, caressing tone made her feel flushed all over. She had never had such things said to her. She should not be listening to them now. But protest was

the last thing on her mind. On the contrary. She wanted
to hear more.

It was shocking! It was scandalous! It was horrifyingly
delicious.

'My lord. . .'

'Relax, Miss Smith,' he said, his tone suddenly so
curt that she started. He removed his hand. 'I didn't
mean to alarm you.'

Phoebe took a steadying breath and realised she hadn't
been breathing for what felt like several minutes. 'I am
not alarmed,' she informed him, sounding distinctly
rattled.

'No? I suppose that's why you just lost every vestige
of colour in your cheeks.' He got to his feet with a rather
abrupt movement and crossed the room to a small table
on which reposed a crystal decanter and several glasses.
'Stay there. I'll pour you a restorative. And perhaps, in
future, you might be more cautious about calling on a
bachelor without escort of maid or footman.'

'Maid! Foot—'

The terse words stunned her into silence for as much
as ten seconds. Then enlightenment dawned. She stared
at Deverell's back and didn't know whether to succumb
to outrage or relief. Had he said all those shockingly
exciting things to her merely to teach her a lesson? Who
did the man think he was? *Her* guardian?

She eyed him for a moment longer in fulminating
silence and then decided it was safer to let the matter
drop. Something told her a protest on the grounds that
she was a mature woman of four-and-twenty, and a mere
governess besides, would go unheeded. And lesson or
not, Deverell's description of her had left her decidedly
unsettled. She had never met anyone like him before in
her life.

Not even another Deverell.

Frowning, she watched him pick up the decanter and
a glass and realised she was holding her breath again.
The delicate vessels looked in imminent danger of shat-

tering in the grip of those big hands. But the only sound that disturbed the stillness was the polite plink of liquid against crystal. Everything remained intact.

In fact, the only things in danger of shattering, Phoebe discovered, were her nerves. It was not a reassuring thought. Her frown deepened. Why had this particular Deverell so easily overset her composure when the others had not succeeded in doing so?

It was not the outward differences in him. The superficial contrasts of eye-colour and a more powerful physique might engage the interest momentarily, but surely not fluster one. They didn't explain the fluttery sensations still lingering inside her, or the fact that she'd forgotten every precept of proper behaviour and modest demeanour that had been drummed into her head since childhood. Good heavens, she had even forgotten her speech. Calmness and control had been things of the past. It had been Deverell who—

Phoebe stopped right there, eyes widening as the flickering candle flame of puzzlement in her brain roared into a sudden blazing inferno. Stunned, she raised a hand to her face, her fingertips brushing the place where Deverell had held her captive for those few heart-stopping seconds. She could almost feel his touch there still, the steely strength in his fingers, the careful restraint of his hold.

He was a man in complete command of both his physical power and whatever emotions lay hidden behind the glittering colours of his eyes. The emotions were there, almost palpably intense, but controlled by a force of will she'd never before encountered.

The notion was enthralling. Utterly, insidiously, enthralling.

Control and restraint were, as Phoebe knew only too well, completely foreign concepts to Deverells. Although they were all dissimilar in personality, they shared one trait; no matter what mood they were indulging in at any given time, they could be counted on to indulge it to the hilt. A Deverell who understood control, therefore, was something of a rarity.

She had just reached that interesting point in her ruminations when the object of her study turned and met her gaze. It was like taking a hit from one of the prize-fighters Gerald was always talking about. All the breath seemed to leave her lungs. She watched Deverell start towards her and was shaken by a most unaccountable desire to leap to her feet and flee.

Why hadn't she seen the powerful restraint in him before? It was in the way he moved, with a lithe, predatory grace that was riveting. It was in the firm line of his mouth, and the piercing assessment in his eyes. She was reminded once again of a medieval warrior—one who was deliberating the chances of storming a citadel.

Phoebe shivered, then gave herself a mental shake. Fanciful nonsense, she scolded herself, as he bent to scoop up her abandoned reticule on his way across the room. He hadn't really looked at her as if he intended to discover every one of her secrets. Those unusual eyes appeared so light and piercing only because his face was tanned; a legacy of his years in India, no doubt.

Her head jerked up as she realised Deverell had closed the distance between them and was standing beside the sofa. He was watching her from beneath half-lowered lashes and, as her eyes met his, she wondered abruptly if he'd ever been like the others, and if so, what price he had paid to acquire that cool veneer.

A very high one, she decided, and shivered again. She knew then the real difference that set him apart from his family. This man had looked danger in the face—and survived.

And to think she had come here to lecture him.

Phoebe blinked. What on earth was she about? She *had* come here to lecture Deverell. She'd been lecturing Deverells for two years. True, they seldom paid any attention to her homilies, but she'd never let one intimidate her before.

Feeling as if she was seizing her wits with both hands, she took the glass he was offering her, placed it firmly on the small fluted table beside the sofa and rose to her feet.

'I am not in need of a restorative, sir,' she stated in her sternest governessy tones. 'And it is past time we returned to the purpose of my visit. I can understand you delegating the care of your wards to others while you were out of the country, but that circumstance no longer applies.'

Deverell's brows shot up. He glanced down at her discarded brandy, aimed a narrow-eyed look at her face that rivalled the portrait above them for sheer intimidation, then tossed her reticule onto the sofa.

'Perhaps you should sit down again. Miss Smith. Something tells me this is not going to be a short visit.'

'Did you expect it to be?' Phoebe resumed her seat, waiting with primly folded hands while Deverell seated himself opposite her. The dangerous stare had gone, she was thankful to see. Now he just looked annoyed. For some reason she found the expression unexpectedly reviving.

'Since your mind seems fixed on my wards, yes,' he said, leaning back and crossing one booted foot over his knee. He rested his elbows on the arms of the chair and sent her a faintly menacing smile over the tops of his steepled fingers. 'However, let us get business out of the way first, by all means. Don't think I'm not happy to make your acquaintance, Miss Smith, but if you wanted to complain about the brats' behaviour, wouldn't a letter have been less trouble than a journey from Sussex?'

'Less trouble for you,' Phoebe retorted, feeling better by the minute. 'And I did write you a letter. Several letters! In fact I have sent you eight letters in the past three months!'

Deverell frowned. 'Ah, yes. I recall. I had to pay for them.'

'Well, if you'd extended me the courtesy of a reply to the first one,' she pointed out, 'you would not have been put to the expense of receiving the other seven!'

'You mean I wouldn't have been put to that expense if you'd accepted my secretary's initial reply,' he shot back. 'Mr Charlton attends to all the correspondence from Kerslake Park. I'm sure he wouldn't have been so remiss in his duties as to ignore your reports.'

She ground her teeth. 'Oh, yes, he replied, my lord. No doubt as instructed by you, with more useless injunctions to use my own judgement. If I'd used my own judgement, sir, I would have abandoned your charges months ago. The only reason I didn't is because I expected you to visit Kerslake Park shortly after you returned to England.'

'Good God, did you? Why?'

'Why?' She stared at him in astonishment. 'They're your brother's orphaned children, sir. Surely the smallest degree of family feeling—'

'Miss Smith, I have no family feeling. You'd best know that now, before you get carried away on this tide of sentiment. As for my late, unlamented brother, I imagine he took even less interest in his offspring than I do.'

'But—' Quite nonplussed, Phoebe found all her well-rehearsed arguments deserting her. She had been prepared for reluctance on Deverell's part, but his outright indifference to his nephew and nieces managed to deflate her wrath before she'd fairly got started.

The thought of her probable future if she remained in her present post, however, had her rallying. Reminding herself that she needed Deverell's co-operation, she tried a sympathetic smile.

'Well, I know that family relationships are not always felicitous, sir, but—'

'Yes, I imagine you've encountered several examples of infelicitous family relationships in the course of your career, Miss Smith. The sorry details of which were no doubt recounted to you by the males in the situation.'

Her mouth fell open. A second later she blushed hotly. 'That has nothing to do with the case,' she stated, resisting the urge to wriggle under his unnervingly penetrating gaze. 'I was referring to my own family, sir. I, too, was orphaned at a young age and had to—' She stopped dead.

'Please go on, Miss Smith. You had to—?'

The enquiry was delivered smoothly, but Phoebe found herself gripping her hands together.

'Your aunt, Lady Grismead, was given all the relevant information about my background when she hired me,' she finally replied after a taut little silence. She felt another blush burn her cheeks and silently cursed both Deverell and the strange effect he was having on her. 'The point I wished to make, sir, was that my relatives were always punctilious in their duty, and, if I am independent now, it is because I wish to be, not because of any neglect on their part.'

His brows snapped together. 'You can hardly claim my brother's children are neglected, Miss Smith.'

Phoebe swallowed. It was quite impossible, of course, but the temperature in the room seemed to have fallen by several degrees.

'I am not claiming any such thing, sir, but there is more to caring for children than providing them with servants to see to their physical needs. Besides, Gerald and the girls are hardly children anymore and—'

'There are also others apart from the servants living at Kerslake Park,' he interrupted curtly. 'If I recall, my Uncle Thurston can't be dislodged short of a volcanic eruption, and isn't there some sort of cousin to chaperon the girls? Clara. . .'

'Miss Pomfret,' supplied Phoebe. 'Yes, she's there, but I have to tell you, my lord, that Mr Thurston Deverell left before I took up the position of governess. He is presently residing in Harrogate.'

'Harrogate?' To Phoebe's relief, the ice in his eyes

was replaced by genuine, if irritated, surprise. 'What the devil's he doing there?'

'According to Miss Pomfret, he said Harrogate was the most distant watering-place from Sussex he could find, and that nothing would induce him to set foot in Kerslake Park again while his nephew's whelps were in residence.'

'Good God!'

'Precisely, my lord.' She smiled with grim satisfaction at finally eliciting a proper response. 'Since you care nothing for your family, you are obviously unaware that Gerald is turned eighteen. In fact, he will be going up to Oxford at the start of the Hilary Term, but how long he remains there is quite another matter. The boy is uncontrollable.

'As for Theodosia and Cressida, they will be presented next Season and will no longer require a governess. However, I have no intention of remaining in charge for so much as another day, sir, let alone several months, so—'

'So you came up to London to tender your resignation, Miss Smith. Is that it?' He uncrossed his legs and leant forward to fix her with a smile of relentless determination. His voice lowered to a note that made the smile seem positively benign. 'That is most unfortunate. You see, I have no intention of accepting it.'

'In-deed?'

Her minatory tone had surprise and then narrow-eyed speculation replacing his smile. Phoebe was rather pleased to see the rapid changes of expression cross his face. For one dizzying minute she might actually get the upper hand with a Deverell.

With that delirious thought in mind, she delivered her *coup de grâce*.

'I'm afraid you will have no choice, sir, when Grillon's Hotel sends to ask what you intend doing with your unchaperoned wards.'

Chapter Two

His wards were in London?

Sebastian stared at the small, triumphant figure opposite him and decided that Miss Phoebe Smith was in need of a sharp set-down. Unfortunately, she did not appear to be the type of female to stay down once she'd been set there. She hadn't even looked overly alarmed when he'd been waxing lyrical about her disturbingly lovely face. More than a little stunned perhaps, but not overly alarmed. He'd had to put that word on it to put some distance between them.

Keeping his hands busy hadn't been a bad idea either.

Sebastian frowned. He wasn't accustomed to needing an excuse to draw back from a woman. An experienced hunter, he knew the advantages of retreat, but it had always been an orderly manoeuvre, carefully planned and executed.

It had never been necessary to employ the strategem because he'd been a breath away from thrusting his fingers into the silky fawn and gold mass coiled primly at the nape of her neck, and finding out if freeing her hair from its tight confinement would have a similar effect on the passionate little creature held in check by the governess.

To make matters worse, he was finding the governess just as appealing. She was so delightfully disapproving.

The thought was unexpectedly pleasant.

Sebastian's frown vanished. The challenge of melting that disapproval into sweet feminine surrender would, he mused, prove far more interesting than exposing Pendleton's high-flying ladybirds for the rapacious harpies they were. It might even ease the restlessness that had been plaguing him lately. A restlessness not even his sculpting could alleviate.

He would need to move slowly, of course. The delectably disapproving Miss Smith was not a complete innocent, even if she did look as if she was scarcely out of the schoolroom herself. She'd known precisely what he'd been talking about when he'd mistaken her for a Cyprian, and she'd been within an Ames' ace of sharing the humour of the situation with him. But she had obviously survived an unpleasant experience or two, hence her attempt to render herself as unattractive as possible.

It would be his pleasure to change her mind. Not to mention her wardrobe.

Unfortunately, before he could implement the various schemes for Miss Phoebe Smith's re-education that were flitting through his brain, he had to put an end to her foolhardy intention of giving him her notice and disappearing from his life after leaving his brother's brats on his hands.

That thought was not so pleasant. And, he reflected, eyeing her grimly, the cause of it did not even seem to realise the danger she was courting in threatening him. Certain matters would need to be made clear right from the start.

Such as who was in charge.

Sebastian rose and walked over to the fireplace to prop one broad shoulder against the mantel. He folded his arms across his chest and fixed his visitor with a disapproving frown. It wasn't a difficult task. He was experiencing a quite irrational surge of frustration at the thought of the three objects in his path.

'Do you mean to tell me you went to the unnecessary expense of bringing my wards to London with you?' he demanded. 'That action was rather improvident, Miss Smith. If my memory serves me correctly, Kerslake's estate is almost under the hatches.'

His quarry looked annoyingly pleased with herself. 'Oh, there was very little expense involved, my lord. We came on the stage.'

Sebastian narrowed his eyes at her. The glare that had been known to cause grown men to quail seemed to have little effect. 'You travelled on the common stage? Unescorted?'

'Well, of course.' Phoebe bristled. She had never heard that the British population in India still lived in the dark ages, but perhaps she'd missed something.

'Really, my lord, you have some very antiquated notions of what is proper, do you not? I am not a green girl, and though it may be the custom in India for ladies to be chaperoned at all times, there is nothing improper in my calling on you on a matter of business, nor in travelling up to London by stage. And, as I keep on telling you, your wards are no longer children. Gerald is perfectly capable—'

'Yes?' he prompted when she fell silent.

Something in the silky anticipation in his tone stirred her temper.

'I was going to say, my lord, that Gerald is now of an age where he would be considered an adequate escort. That is, if he had any notions of responsible conduct. But I'm sorry to say that notions of responsibility and proper conduct have never entered his head. That journey, sir, is an experience I do not intend to repeat. In fact, it is a matter for astonishment to me that we're all alive to tell the tale.'

'That bad, was it?' he said with a mocking smile that made Phoebe grind her teeth. 'Let it be a lesson to you, Miss Smith. I suppose Gerald wanted to tool the horses. Driving a yellow bounder is the ambition of every would-be young whip.'

'No. Gerald did not want to tool the horses,' she

retorted through clenched teeth. 'He was perfectly happy with the guard's yard of tin, until the other passengers wrested it from him before we were all rendered quite deaf! It was Theodosia who drove for several miles, my lord. At the gallop! On a particularly winding stretch of road!'

His expression turned ironic. 'Well, you appear to be in one piece so I assume she didn't land the coach in a ditch. Be grateful.'

'Grateful!' Phoebe bounced to her feet in her indignation. 'For heaven's sake, sir, how can you dismiss Theodosia's reckless behaviour with such unbecoming levity and yet take me to task for not bringing a maid—?'

She swallowed the rest on a startled gasp as Deverell unfolded his arms, straightened and began to stalk towards her.

Phoebe sat down rather hurriedly. The action didn't halt his progress in the least. He leaned over her, propped one large hand on the back of the sofa and his other on the arm, caging her between them, and pinned her to her seat with a distinctly menacing stare.

'There is one difference in the consequences of those actions, Miss Smith, that I shall take great pleasure in demonstrating to you at a later date. As it is, unless several other members of Polite Society have taken to posting about the country in stagecoaches, I hardly think the knowledge that Theodosia drove one will be bruited abroad. I suggest you put the episode behind you.'

'I would be happy to do so,' she managed, refusing to be cowed, 'but that is not all.'

It was all she was capable of for the moment, however. Phoebe stared up into the dangerous glitter in her captor's eyes and tried to remind herself that she was used to the Deverell glare. The reminder did nothing to calm her suddenly tumultuous pulse.

Heat and terror and excitement swirled around her in a strange kaleidoscope of blues, greens and golds. She felt like a moth, drawn helplessly towards the flames,

but before she could decide what to do about such a
perilous situation, Deverell's brows met in a dark scowl
and he jerked upright as if she'd struck him.

Startled, Phoebe jumped a good three inches off the
sofa. She was immediately furious with herself. Her only
consolation was that her host didn't seem any happier.
Still scowling, he turned, strode back to his chair and
sat down. When his eyes met hers she could have sworn
she heard the clash of steel.

The reverberations seemed to echo in the silence for
several seconds. Determined not to lose the contest,
Phoebe continued to glare at him until, slowly, gradually,
she became aware of a new element in his frowning gaze.

Surprise. Puzzlement. As if *she*'d managed to startle
him.

Then, as her gaze wavered, as she felt uncertainty
shake her resolve, the intent frown vanished and his
mouth started to curve.

'I believe you were about to continue the tale of your
perilous journey, Miss Smith.'

The gentle reminder was all she needed to reanimate
her wrath. The spate of words jammed in her throat
spilled forth in a rush.

'Other members of Polite Society might not notice a
young lady driving a stagecoach, my lord, but some of
them—gentlemen to be precise—do attend prize fights.
I expect your response to the knowledge that Theodosia
prevailed upon Gerald to interrupt our journey so she
could also attend one, to elicit a more satisfactory
response than a metaphorical pat on the head!'

He seemed to consider the matter. 'I doubt it,' he
finally pronounced judiciously. 'For one thing, I hardly
think Theodosia was entirely truthful if she told you she
attended a mill. She may have given you the slip with
that intention, but females are not admitted to such
events.'

'That circumstance, sir, had been anticipated. She
dressed in some of Gerald's clothes.'

He smiled soothingly. 'Well, in that case, you have nothing to worry about.'

'What?' For a moment Phoebe could only stare at him. 'That might have been true had nothing untoward occurred,' she finally gasped. 'But, although I don't like to be put into the position of having to tell tales, in this instance Gerald led his sister into danger. Apparently someone in the crowd took offence at a remark she made and an altercation started, in the course of which her cap fell off. She was unmasked immediately. According to Gerald, it was only Theo's punishing left that enabled them to escape.'

He raised a brow in surprised approval. 'Sounds as if she gave a good account of herself.'

Phoebe could hardly believe her ears. 'Is that all you have to say?' she all but shrieked.

'Calm yourself, Miss Smith.'

'Calm myself? Your niece takes part in a common brawl and I'm supposed to calm myself? Theodosia may be utterly ruined! What if someone noticed the fracas and recognised her? The Deverell features are not exactly unremarkable, you know.'

'Yes, there's no need to glare at me as if I'm responsible for the Deverell features. I assure you, they've been a source of considerable irritation to me, also. But to put your mind at rest, I doubt if anyone of influence was present at an obscure mill held in a small country town. Be assured, however, that I will instruct Gerald that, if he wishes to reach a respectable old age, he won't take his sisters to any mills on your way back to Kerslake.'

'I do not intend to return to Kerslake,' Phoebe declared in a voice that shook with the effort of holding onto her temper. 'So the enormous effort of instructing Gerald will not be necessary.'

'Sarcasm does not become you, Miss Smith.'

'Perhaps you'd prefer to hear the details of Cressida's elopement instead,' she suggested, not moderating her sarcastic tone one whit.

'Not particularly. But I can see you're going to enlighten me anyway.'

'I certainly am,' she declared in a tone as menacing as anything a Deverell could produce. 'Let us see how much amusement you derive from the information that Cressy ran off last week with a man from a company of play actors.'

He looked thoughtful. 'Not a great deal, I should think. Especially if you expect me to go after the runaways.' His eyes gleamed. 'You see, I'd be obliged to disappoint you, Miss Smith, and I have the distinct impression you don't take disappointment silently.'

'Disappoint— You mean. . .your own niece. . .' She swallowed the other disjointed utterances trying to escape her lips and made a grab for her rapidly disintegrating wits. 'Then how fortunate that I don't have to suffer a blow of such magnitude,' she said with spurious sweetness. 'No doubt you'll be overwhelmingly relieved to learn, my lord, that Cressida was returned within twenty minutes of her departure.'

He burst out laughing. 'Twenty *minutes*?'

Phoebe glared at him. 'Apparently she spent that time describing their future life to her suitor. The knowledge that Cressy intended to join him on the stage was enough to cause him to turn his gig around, restore her to her family and flee.'

'Hmm. I can see how that circumstance would overset you. You probably thought you were getting rid of one of the brats.'

'Getting rid of. . .' She stopped, dragged in a badly needed breath and tried again. 'Have you no proper feeling, sir?'

'I believe I've already answered that question, Miss Smith.'

'But you must have some family sentiment,' she cried, waving a hand wildly towards the portrait she'd been addressing earlier. 'You've got one of them on your library wall.'

He glanced briefly at the painting. 'Ah, yes. Another black sheep, But as you discovered for yourself, he doesn't talk back. Believe me, that's the only reason he's been permitted to take up residence here.'

'Good heavens!' Brain whirling, Phoebe sagged limply back against the sofa. 'This is beyond belief.'

He grinned. 'Why don't you take a sip of brandy? It might help.'

The suggestion brought her upright again. 'I do not need any brandy, sir. What I need is for you to pay attention to me.'

'Oh, I'm paying attention, Miss Smith, I'm paying attention. You've no idea how much I'm learning.'

She glared at him suspiciously for a moment, then decided to ignore that obscure comment. She was probably better off not knowing what he meant anyway.

'Fortunately, no harm was done on that occasion,' she said. 'However, the same cannot be said for some of Gerald's latest pranks.'

'Gerald? I thought we'd disposed of him.'

'I am referring to the events that occurred last Saturday evening, my lord. Gerald and his friends tied flags to all the toll-gates and signposts in the vicinity of Kerslake Park so that everyone for miles around saw them when they went to church the next morning.' The memory had her shuddering. 'It was the outside of enough. Every proper feeling was offended. In fact, poor Miss Pomfret swooned away as soon as she saw the first one.'

'Well, my opinion of Cousin Clara's good sense was never high,' he said dryly. 'But what caused such an excess of sensibility? Were they French flags? Navy flags denoting an outbreak of yellow fever, perhaps?'

She set her teeth. 'Where would Gerald get hold of French flags, sir? Or flags used by the Navy, come to that. They were—'

There was an uncomfortable pause. Phoebe knew she was blushing but now that she was launched on the tale, there was really nothing to be done except continue. With extreme caution.

'It was not the flags themselves,' she finally muttered, 'but what they were made of.'

Deverell regarded the rosy hue washing over her face with fascinated interest. 'Dear me. You positively alarm me, Miss Smith. I must insist that you put me out of my suspense immediately. What were the flags made of?'

'Well. . .' Phoebe began to feel rather desperate. 'They were lacy.'

'Lacy?'

She nodded.

He waited. He was probably capable of waiting until the proverbial crack of doom, she thought despairingly. Or until she became frozen where she sat. Her spine felt so stiff she wondered it didn't snap in two. She took a deep breath and was careful to address his cravat. 'They were ladies' unmentionables, sir.'

'Ladies'. . .unmentionables?'

Her gaze whipped back to his. 'Drawers,' she snapped, goaded.

'Ah.' His grin held pure male wickedness. 'In that case, Miss Smith, the real question is, how did Gerald get hold of so many. . .uh. . .items of intimate apparel?'

'I don't care how he got hold of them, sir. Nor did I ask. Gerald is not, strictly speaking, in my care. Not that anybody bothered about that little fact when the local magistrate became involved,' she added bitterly.

'The magistrate became involved in the unmentionables?'

Phoebe scowled quite ferociously. 'Sir, you will oblige me by not mentioning the unmentionables again. Fortunately, the father of one of the boys made sure they were removed. The entire episode, however regrettable, was, on the whole, regarded as a prank. Perpetrated by boys with nothing better to do with their time.'

'Quite harmless, in fact.'

Phoebe had a quick vision of the usual serene village

churchyard enlivened by carriages and gigs full of shrieking, moaning and swooning females, and had to bite her lip.

'Some people might consider it so,' she agreed carefully, unwilling to perjure herself any more than was necessary. When his lips twitched, she rallied herself and frowned reprovingly. 'What is not so harmless, my lord, is the consequence of Gerald joining a gang of dissatisfied tenants in poaching from their landlord, and then marching on the man's house when several were caught and arrested.'

'Good God!' The amusement in his eyes was replaced by sheer masculine disgust. 'Don't tell me Gerald was caught. What a clunch.'

'A clunch?' All desire to laugh vanished from Phoebe's mind. 'A *clunch*? Does *nothing* make an impression on you, sir? We are now talking about a criminal action! Do you wish to see your nephew shipped off to the Antipodes in leg-irons?'

He shrugged. 'It didn't do me any harm.'

She gaped at him, utterly speechless. Seconds passed. Phoebe's gaze fell on the glass of brandy set before her. Without a thought, she snatched it up and gulped down a healthy dose in the manner of one in dire need of revivification. She nearly choked as liquid fire hit the back of her throat, but at least the shock restored her voice.

'You were shipped off to the colonies in leg-irons?' she squeaked.

He studied her rather enigmatically for a moment, then rose and walked over to the mantelpiece again. He thrust both hands into his pockets and leaned against the cool marble. 'It wasn't quite as dramatic as that, Miss Smith. The leg-irons were a figure of speech, and some parts of India are quite civilised.'

'Oh.'

'And in justice to my father, I must tell you that in

those days I was what is commonly referred to as a hell-born babe.'

'Oh, my goodness.'

He smiled faintly. 'I'm surprised you haven't heard the tale.'

'No.' She shook her head, still dazed. 'Only that you'd gone to India several years ago.'

'Fifteen to be precise.' Something she couldn't decipher flickered briefly in his eyes. 'A long time.'

There was not a lot to be said about that. But as Phoebe looked at the faintly bitter set to Deverell's mouth, she felt impatience seep out of her to be replaced with an odd sense of empathy. Fifteen years. He must have been very young, she thought. Not much older than Gerald perhaps.

'Well,' she began on a calmer note, 'I must say that sending a boy to the far ends of the earth seems somewhat drastic. No doubt you found it quite upsetting at the time, my lord, whatever you may say now, which is all the more reason for you to ensure that a similar fate doesn't befall Gerald. I'm told he was not a robust child. Indeed, that was why he's been taught by the local vicar all these years. Miss Pomfret wished to protect him from the rigours of school and—'

'Cousin Clara is an idiot,' he interrupted, not mincing matters. 'School would have given Gerald some discipline. It's plain to see he's been allowed to run wild at home. The girls, too.'

Phoebe briefly considered pointing out that they were talking about Deverells and not more amenable mortals, then dismissed the notion. It would be difficult to win the argument when her opponent was a Deverell who had achieved self-control under what she strongly suspected had been extremely harsh conditions.

'Yes, well, that is what I've been telling you,' she pointed out. 'I regret having to admit defeat, my lord, but it is no use blinking at the facts. I cannot afford to be involved in a scandal—and so far it has only been by the merest stroke of good fortune that scandal has been avoided. Your wards need a stronger hand than mine. They need a man's guidance. They need a man's authority. They need—'

'Yes, yes.' He held up a hand. 'Please spare me the rest of the clarion call, Miss Smith. The plight of my orphaned wards leaves me singularly unmoved. As I told you before, I have no intention of accepting your resignation.'

Phoebe's sympathy vanished as swiftly as her earlier desire to laugh. 'Well, *I* do not intend to argue with you any further, my lord. Especially as nothing I say has any effect.' She rose to her feet. 'You may collect your wards from Grillon's or wait until the hotel sends a cry for help, as I assure you they will. Unless you intend to imprison me—'

'An interesting thought.'

'I am leaving,' she finished, pointedly ignoring this blatant provocation. 'Perhaps you would be good enough to instruct Mr Charlton to forward the requisite recommendation to Mrs Arbuthnot's Employment Registry. Good day, sir.'

Snatching up her reticule, she started towards the door.

'One moment, Miss Smith.'

The command was so soft that for a moment Phoebe wasn't certain she'd heard it. She paused, glancing back over her shoulder.

Deverell stood before the fireplace, his powerful frame seeming to take up all the available space. His eyes were narrowed and glittering, and intent on hers.

'Did all your previous employers provide you with a character?' he asked very gently.

Phoebe's lips parted on a shocked little intake of air. By what diabolical twist of logic had he thought to ask that home question? she wondered nervously. And how was she to answer it without tripping herself up with a lie?

'I have had only three previous employers, my lord.

The first, an elderly lady to whom I was companion, died quite suddenly. Unfortunately, she was the last of her family, but the parish vicar was kind enough to write a letter of recommendation for me.'

'And the others?'

She was silent.

'I thought so,' he murmured. 'Tell me, Miss Smith, what are your chances for immediate employment when you have only one recommendation that is second-hand and several years old?'

A rather unpleasant hollow sensation made itself felt in the pit of Phoebe's stomach. Lifting her chin, she turned fully to face him. 'Are you threatening me, my lord?'

'I was under the impression it was the other way around,' he said drily. 'No, Miss Smith, I'm not threatening you, but it occurs to me that we would both benefit from. . .re-negotiating the terms of your employment.'

The hollow sensation increased. Phoebe stood as if glued to the floor, conscious of a strange tightness in her throat. Ridiculous, she thought. Utterly ridiculous, to feel a pang of disappointment so sharp it suspended her voice and caused a hot prickling behind her eyelids. This had happened before. Why would Deverell be any different to the other males of her acquaintance?

'You mean *you* would benefit from blackmailing me,' she managed at last.

He shook his head. 'When you know me better, Miss Smith, you'll discover that I never waste time with blackmail or threats. I'm merely pointing out the possible consequences of your abandoning your responsibilities without proper notice. Although,' he added when she opened her mouth to protest, 'I understand why you did it.'

She shut her mouth again.

'Come.' Deverell held out a hand and smiled at her— a slow smile that seemed to tempt and beguile even as it pulled her already taut nerves tighter. 'Won't you sit

down again, Miss Smith? The solution seems perfectly
logical to me. I have no experience in looking after
youths or girls. You need a stronger hand to back you
up. Why don't we pool our resources?'

'Pool our resources?' Taken completely by surprise,
Phoebe could only stare at him. Her thoughts scurried
in several directions at once. Had she misjudged him?
It appeared she had, and yet there was a disturbing stillness in the way he watched her that reminded her forcibly
of a hunter waiting for its quarry to make a false move.

But what would become of her if she obeyed the
instincts urging caution and walked out of the house?
She had already left two positions under a cloud, and
had only obtained this present post because Lady
Grismead had been so desperate to obtain a governess
that she hadn't been fussy about a lack of recommen-
dations.

On top of that, there was the unpleasant fact that she
would forfeit half a year's pay if she left at once—
no small sum when her future was so uncertain. And
underlying everything, hovering in the back of her mind,
was an insidious desire to stay. She didn't want to leave.
Especially now.

Well, of course not, Phoebe assured herself, hurriedly
consigning that last thought to oblivion. It was quite
natural to want to stay. She had lived with her charges
for two years. She was, despite everything, quite fond
of them, even thinking of them sometimes as the younger
brother and sisters she'd never had. Given that, she could
at least listen to what Deverell had to say. If she didn't
like it, then she could leave.

Bolstering herself with this practical advice, she took
a small step forward. The next one was a little easier.
But when she resumed her seat on the sofa, she perched
right on the edge with her reticule held like a shield in
front of her.

'I'm not going to bite you, Miss Smith,' Deverell said,
sitting down and crossing one leg over the other.

Feeling foolish, she blushed. 'I will pay you the courtesy of listening to you, my lord. Although, I should warn you that even the prospect of applying for a position without the proper references is less daunting than whatever disaster your wards may inflict upon us at any moment.'

'Then we shall have to ensure that disaster doesn't strike us. Fortunately, I don't anticipate any trouble knocking Gerald into shape.' He returned her startled gaze with a bland smile.

'Er. . .no. I mean, I trust you're speaking metaphorically, my lord. Gerald indulges in his pranks from boredom, I think, not from any serious defect of character.'

He didn't appear convinced. 'I daresay. Is boredom Theodosia's and Cressida's excuse also?'

'Very likely, sir. They were hoping Lady Grismead would present them this year, but she still has her own daughter to establish, so the event was put off.' She frowned. 'I'm afraid they didn't take the delay at all well. In fact, if their antics continue, they might ruin their chances before the Season even commences.'

'I doubt it. They're twins, aren't they? Identical twins? Knowing Society's constant greed for anything out of the ordinary, they'll probably take London by storm, whatever their antics.'

Phoebe was about to debate this cynical assessment of the situation when Deverell continued. 'However, perhaps they might feel more inclined to accept a companion, Miss Smith, rather than a governess.'

'A companion?'

'Yes. You could take them about London, do a little shopping. No doubt my aunt knows other young ladies who have left the schoolroom, but won't be presented until next spring. They must do something with their days.'

'Yes,' she said slowly, struck by the notion. 'Quite a lot, I expect.' She nodded, considering. 'It might work.

Theodosia and Cressida are only seventeen, after all, and if Lady Grismead could be prevailed upon to introduce them to other girls in the same situation. . .'

'There will be no difficulty about that, I assure you.'

She regarded him doubtfully. 'If you say so, my lord. But I must still warn you that Cressy and Theo are not overly given to obeying my instructions or listening to advice.'

'They won't need to obey your instructions, Miss Smith,' he stated gently. 'They will obey mine, or find themselves banished to Kerslake and faced with the prospect of relying on their brother's generosity when they make their come-out next year.'

'But Gerald has nothing to be generous with,' she protested.

'Precisely. I, however, do.'

'Oh, goodness.' Phoebe gazed at him with a certain amount of appreciative awe. A second later, she couldn't suppress a wry smile. 'More of your "possible consequences", sir?'

The swift, slashing grin that crossed his face sent a wholly unexpected and not altogether unpleasant shiver down her spine.

'I'm glad you approve, Miss Smith. Consider, also, that our plot has the added advantage of removing any burden of blame from your shoulders should disaster strike despite our efforts. Mine are broad enough to withstand the blow.'

Phoebe's gaze fell to the shoulders in question. She was about to agree that they were certainly broad enough to withstand several blows, when the voice of caution intervened once more. She quickly rearranged her features into an expression of sober contemplation.

'Your proposition does seem to have some merit, my lord.'

'I would, of course, make the exercise worth your while,' he murmured.

Her spine stiffened immediately. 'The remuneration

paid me by the estate is more than adequate, my lord.'

'Adequate by today's standards, perhaps. But what future awaits you when your days as a governess are over?'

Phoebe suppressed another shiver. This one was definitely unpleasant. Genteel circumstances was the usual lot of retired governesses unless they were fortunate enough to receive a pension from affectionate and grateful former pupils. Genteel circumstances was also a euphemism for grinding, relentless poverty.

She reminded herself that such a dismal prospect was still a long way off. 'I suppose that depends on how provident one is during one's years of employment, sir.'

'A courageous answer, Miss Smith. But it takes no account of illness or accident or any one of a number of circumstances. On the other hand, if you accept my offer, I would settle a sum of money on you sufficient to ensure your future financial security.'

She frowned thoughtfully. 'That sounds like a great deal of money, sir.'

'I can afford it.'

Yes, but could she?

It was tempting, Phoebe mused. A large sum of money would, if she wished, enable her to open her own academy for young ladies. It would banish the ever-present spectres of uncertain employment, unpleasant employers and grim old age.

It would also put her under a considerable obligation to a man who, in the space of one short hour, had caused her to experience more baffling emotions than she'd ever felt before in her life. And none of them had anything to do with safety or security.

Phoebe took a firmer hold on her reticule. She would think about that later. 'I appreciate your generous offer, my lord, but I must decline.'

His eyes narrowed. 'You insist on leaving?'

'Oh, no. No, you misunderstood me. I would like to stay, but I must insist on receiving no more than the usual remuneration for a companion.' She glanced away, unable to meet the sudden frowning intensity in his eyes. 'You don't have to bribe me, sir. Despite everything I said earlier, I do care about your wards.'

'Yes,' he murmured after a moment's silence. 'That was perfectly obvious from the start.'

Startled, her gaze flashed back to his.

'As for payment, Miss Smith, shall we see how our arrangement works out? Naturally your living expenses will be included. And,' he continued smoothly, 'a more suitable wardrobe.'

Phoebe's jaw dropped. 'Wardrobe? Certainly not!'

'Why not?' he countered at once. 'Recollect that maids and footmen and the like are provided with their working clothes. You can't expect to accompany my wards around town in your present attire. This is London. They'd probably refuse to be seen with you.'

'Well, that is just too bad!' Affronted, she glared at him as if he was personally responsible for her drab costume. 'I can make up one or two gowns myself if you consider it necessary, but—'

He shook his head in gentle reproof. 'Not good enough, Miss Smith. You'll need morning dresses, carriage dresses, evening dresses—'

'Evening dresses?'

He ignored this startled interjection and began ticking off items on his fingers. 'Possibly a riding habit, a pelisse, gloves, bonnets—'

'But I already have—'

'Half-boots, slippers, reticules, a fur muff—winter is coming on, you know—a shawl for evenings at home, a warm dressing-robe, stockings—'

'For goodness' sake, sir!'

'And—' a gleam of sheer devilment came into his eyes '—last but not least, we mustn't forget unmentionables.'

'Ohh!' Phoebe leapt to her feet.

He laughed and rose also, uncoiling from his chair

with a lithe, unexpectedly swift movement that caused her to take a quick step back. Just for a moment, the sheer threat of his size rolled over her like a swamping wave. She'd never considered herself a delicate creature, Phoebe thought, shaken. It was a considerable shock to discover she could feel so small and vulnerable.

'Calm yourself, Miss Smith. I was only teasing you. Reprehensible, I know, but you were looking so outraged, the temptation was irresistible.'

'Try harder to resist it!' she retorted, still grappling with hitherto unknown sensations. When he burst out laughing again, she ordered herself to stick to the point. 'Sir, you must know it would be quite improper for you to provide me with such a wardrobe.'

He grinned down at her. 'What about a modified version?'

'A modified version?' she repeated weakly.

'Why don't we compromise, Miss Smith? I'll leave it to your discretion to decide on a suitable wardrobe, as long as I have final approval of your purchases.'

'That isn't a compromise,' she protested indignantly. 'And—'

'You could regard it as a loan if you insist.'

'A loan?'

'When your tenure as a companion is over, you could return the garments.' He smiled blandly. 'They could be donated to a worthy charity.'

'Well, I. . .'

Oh, goodness, surely she wasn't going to accept. She was certain it wasn't the wise thing to do, but her mind was quite unequal to the task of summoning any further protests. She was positively exhausted. Arguing with Deverell was worse than facing a combined assault by his wards. And surely if the clothes were merely *loaned*. . .

If only he wouldn't watch her with those wickedly challenging eyes. If only the expression in the blue-green depths gave her some hint as to what sort of bargain she

would be entering into. Despite having infuriated her
earlier, he now seemed quite sincere. Even reasonable.
The only trouble with that was, in her experience,
Deverells were only reasonable when they wanted
something.

But that 'something' was merely to have her take his
wards off his hands. Wasn't it?

Oh, dear, her imagination was running away with her.
All she had to do was make it very clear to Deverell
that she wasn't accepting anything from him that could
be misconstrued. Well, not accepting anything *permanently*.

'You're looking quite torn, Miss Smith,' he murmured, breaking into the myriad thoughts spinning
around in her head. 'Is it such a difficult decision?
Perhaps you'd like a written guarantee that
your. . .er. . .uniform will be forfeited at the end of our
arrangement.'

'What I'd like,' she stated, desperately gathering her
wits for a final rally, 'is a guarantee that you won't—'

He tilted his head slightly and waited.

'That there will be no—'

He raised a brow in polite enquiry.

'That I won't have to—'

He put her out of her misery. 'That you won't have
to listen to the sorry details of infelicitous family
relationships, Miss Smith?'

'Ohh. Yes.' Phoebe's pent-up breath escaped her in
a long sigh of relief. Why, Deverell or not, he could
be perfectly gentlemanly. What on earth had she been
worried about?

'No doubt it is immodest of me to mention such
things,' she confided in a relieved little rush, 'but I only
wished to make it perfectly clear that my acceptance of
a temporary wardrobe does not mean I will be amenable
to the distasteful advances that always seem to follow
such sorry details.'

A slow smile began in his eyes and crept to the corners

of his mouth. 'Miss Smith, you have my word of honour that if I am ever tempted to pester you with the sorry details of my family relationships, they will not be followed by advances of any kind.'

'Thank you, sir.' Phoebe rewarded him with the first real smile she'd felt like in weeks and held out her hand. 'In that case, I accept your offer.'

Something fierce flared in his eyes. Shaken once more, Phoebe almost withdrew both acceptance and hand. Before she could, Deverell's strong fingers closed around hers. For an instant she felt as if her entire body was captured, enveloped by heat and strength, then he gave her hand a brief, business-like shake and released her.

Phoebe ordered her heart back to its proper place. She'd been mistaken. She had *not* been captured. Deverell had *not* looked predatory, merely pleased. Her fingers were *not* tingling, merely warm. And the rest of her merely felt limp with relief that the interview was over.

'Good,' he said briskly. 'Now, the only question remaining, Miss Smith, is where you're going to reside.'

Chapter Three

'Far be it from me to agree with anything Deverell might say, my dear Miss Smith, but in this particular instance I must admit he is right. It would be highly inappropriate for you to live in his house. Highly inappropriate.'

Lady Grismead, her tall, commanding figure resplendent in sable-trimmed, violet silk, made the statement in her usual manner—as one pronouncing an immutable law. The fact that she was seated in the largest chair in the parlour at Grillon's Hotel reinforced the image of royalty deigning to address the peasants.

As did her ladyship's appearance, Phoebe reflected, nodding obediently. Despite gaining weight in her middle years, Lady Grismead was dressed in a fashionably high-waisted pelisse that, ruffled to within an inch of its life, emphasised an expanse of bosom that took imposing and majestic to new heights. A matching violet turban rested upon hair that was still rather defiantly black, and her Deverell eyes had lost nothing of their hard sapphire snap.

Phoebe had felt the effect of those eyes already. Having apparently received a note sadly lacking in details from Deverell yesterday afternoon, Lady Grismead had arrived at Grillon's at an hour far in advance of the usual time devoted to morning calls, for the express purpose of inspecting her young relatives.

They had not passed muster. As a result of a shopping trip when they'd been left to their own devices yesterday, Theodosia and Cressida were garbed in scandalously low-cut, bright gold muslin gowns that, thanks to a deficiency of undergarments, clung to every curve. Their matching bonnets were adorned with a wealth of multi-hued feathers that threatened to seriously endanger the eyesight of anyone in the immediate vicinity. Had they been inhabitants of the establishment patronised by Lord Pendleton, the clothes would have suited admirably.

Lady Grismead had taken one look and sent the twins upstairs to change.

Gerald had been likewise banished for permitting his sisters to purchase gowns totally unsuited to their youth and station, not to mention his straitened pocket. He was also instructed to remove the Belcher handkerchief knotted carelessly about his throat and to replace it with a cravat more suited to assisting his sisters' companion in her forthcoming house-hunting expedition.

To Phoebe's utter astonishment, the trio had obeyed, meekly filing up the stairs with no more protest than a few muttered grumbles. She could only suppose they'd been momentarily overwhelmed by an older, more intimidating version of themselves. When Lady Grismead took command, Phoebe expected her victims felt much like a blade of grass facing a lawn-roller in the hands of a determined gardener. One simply bowed to the inevitable.

She had done so herself. As soon as her charges were out of sight, it had taken her visitor less than five minutes to learn the details omitted from Deverell's sorry excuse for a note. Much to Phoebe's relief, no word of blame had crossed Lady Grismead's rather thin lips. Obviously, the events which would have horrified lesser families were water off a Deverell's back.

Her ladyship, however, was not ready to depart. She fixed Phoebe with an interrogatory stare and continued declaiming on the matter of where she should reside.

'Had Cousin Clara come with you, it would, of course, have been a different matter.'

Dragging her fascinated gaze from the lorgnette bouncing about on Lady Grismead's ample bodice whenever she drew breath to speak, Phoebe hastened to reply to the implied query.

'Miss Pomfret feared the journey would be too much for her health, ma'am.'

Her ladyship raised a delicately arched eyebrow. 'The truth, if you please, Miss Smith.'

'Well. . .I'm afraid nothing would persuade Miss Pomfret to have anything to do with Gerald after the. . .er. . .unfortunate episode with the flags. In fact, even as we started off, she was laid out on the floor in the hall, drumming her heels and screaming, because he'd tried to persuade her to accompany us.'

'Clara is a fool. Always was,' stated her ladyship, unwittingly agreeing with Deverell for the second time in as many minutes. 'More of a Pomfret than a Deverell from the day she came into the world. Of course, she's only a cousin in the third or fourth degree, so what can one expect?' Clearly this was the only allowable excuse for Miss Pomfret's behaviour. 'However, that is neither here nor there.

'I am astonished, Miss Smith, positively astonished, that Deverell has permitted his wards to remain in London. Had you applied to me, I would have advised most strongly against your plan. You are not familiar with the metropolis, and as I am fully engaged in taking Pamela about—'

'I hope Miss Grismead is enjoying the Little Season,' Phoebe interposed in a vain attempt to stem the tide.

'Whether or not Pamela enjoys herself is not the question, Miss Smith. This is her Last Chance.' The words were emphasised with ominous foreboding. 'She is five-and-twenty and not a single eligible gentleman has she encouraged in all these years.'

'Miss Grismead has not formed an attachment to *any* of her suitors, ma'am?'

Her ladyship bent a severe frown upon her. 'What has that to say to anything? You don't suppose I married Grismead because I had formed an attachment to him, do you?'

'Well. . .'

'Foolish sentiment,' dismissed her ladyship. 'I accepted Grismead's offer because he was in possession of a comfortable fortune and he never argued with me. You may have noticed, Miss Smith, that we Deverells like our own way.'

'Er. . .yes, ma'am.'

'Unfortunately, Pamela takes after me,' continued Lady Grismead, sublimely unconscious of any irony in the statement. 'And who must she now decide to marry but a poet. A poet, Miss Smith!'

'Oh, dear.' Phoebe could readily understand her ladyship's concern. 'Poets are usually impecunious.'

'That is not the problem. The problem is he *wishes* to be impecunious. Something about suffering for his writing, or some such fustian. He has cast off his family! His exceedingly wealthy and well-connected family. Can you imagine that, Miss Smith?'

'Well, actually—'

'Of course you cannot. No sensible person could. I have told Pamela that her father has been instructed to accept the next respectable offer made for her hand, whether she likes it or not.'

'What did she say to that, ma'am?'

'That she would rather starve in an attic with her Norvel than feast with anyone else. Did you ever hear such nonsense?'

'Well, as it happens—'

'You can see, Miss Smith, why I have no time to devote to Cressida and Theodosia. Whatever Deverell may try in the way of bribery and blackmail,' she finished darkly.

Phoebe's eyes widened. 'Deverell tried to bribe you, ma'am?'

'He had the temerity to remind me that Grismead's investments have suffered several losses over the years, and the possible consequences to Pamela's chances should such a fact be made known.'

'Possible consequences? Oh, my goodness!'

Lady Grismead eyed her with grim approval. 'I don't wonder at your shock, Miss Smith. And I know I may rely upon your discretion. After all, Kerslake's estate has suffered the same setbacks. It is too bad. Poor Grismead has had the entire responsibility for all our finances while Deverell was off making that disgusting fortune of his.

'And now he is rude enough to bribe me with the offer of a new wardrobe for Pamela to distract a possible husband from her die-away airs, as he put it. How heartless! Pamela is delicate. She always has been. But one cannot expect a man to understand anything.'

Phoebe's mind balked at the thought of anyone in possession of a Deverell parent being delicate. Fortunately, while she was racking her brains for a soothing answer, the door opened to admit Gerald and his sisters, with the news that Mr Charlton was that moment stepping out of a hackney and requesting the driver to wait.

'You are inspecting houses with Mr Charlton?' demanded Lady Grismead before Phoebe could respond. 'Upon my word, what does Deverell think he is about to send an inexperienced girl and his secretary to choose a suitable house?'

'I'm sure Mr Charlton will be very helpful, ma'am,' Phoebe murmured, refraining from reminding her ladyship that she had not been considered inexperienced when she'd been hired. She turned to inspect her charges.

Both girls were now properly attired in cambric walking dresses of gentian blue that suited their ebony locks and sapphire eyes to perfection. Being possessed of the aristocratic Deverell features and height, they were striking rather than conventionally pretty, and as their uncle had remarked yesterday, identical in every respect, even to the way they dressed; the single outward difference being the jaunty epaulettes adorning Theodosia's slim shoulders. Only the most alert observer might note from this small distinction that the twins possessed very different personalities.

'Besides, what do we need with a fashionable house, Aunt Ottilia?' demanded Theo with a distressing lack of respect. 'It's not as if we're going to be giving stupid dances and parties.'

'Yes. We don't really need a house at all,' put in Cressida. 'I, for one, would be happy in lodgings as long as they're within easy reach of the theatres.'

'I'm sure we'll find something to suit everyone,' Phoebe intervened hastily before Lady Grismead recovered from her shock at being so addressed and actually heard what was being said.

'Well! This is a come-about.' Gerald stared at his sisters in the liveliest astonishment. 'You've been moaning to Phoebe for months about missing the Season, and now you say parties are stupid. Girls! Featherbrained ninnyhammers.'

Cressida sent him a pitying look. 'We wanted to come to London, Gerald. The Season was only an excuse.'

'Yes, anyone who wasn't a ninnyhammer would have seen—'

'That will do, Theo.' Phoebe stood up in the hope that the gesture would lend her some authority. Interrupting Deverells engaged in combat was no easy task.

She had to admit, however, that the combatants made a riveting picture, Gerald's resemblance to his sisters, who were only a year younger, often causing strangers to mistake them for triplets. They usually caused a sensation wherever they went, although Phoebe had long ago discovered how very disconcerting it could be to see three mirror images every time she turned around.

No wonder she'd been struck by Deverell's unusual aquamarine gaze.

She pushed the surprisingly vivid memory hastily out of her mind. She'd already told herself she'd been quite wrong about his eyes. The strain of the interview had no doubt affected her normally sensible judgement. His eyes were probably plain green. Or perhaps hazel. Yes, hazel was a nice, non-threatening colour.

Feeling exceptionally pleased with this conclusion, she returned her attention to the battle now being waged in acrimonious undertones.

'Cressida, stop arguing with your brother. Gerald, perhaps you would step outside and tell Mr Charlton we shall be with him directly. I expect Lord Deverell has asked him to draw up a list of suitable houses and—'

'How typical,' stated Lady Grismead in the satisfied tones of one who could have predicted the outcome had anyone thought to consult her.

Phoebe forgot her squabbling charges and flushed guiltily at having ignored her ladyship for several minutes. 'I'm afraid I said much the same thing, ma'am, when Deverell suggested Mr Charlton's escort.'

'Did you, indeed, Miss Smith?' A rather thoughtful look crossed her ladyship's face. 'And what was Deverell's reply?'

'He said I should be grateful for whatever assistance he chose to give.'

'Hmm.' Lady Grismead appeared to consider the statement for a minute, then come to a sudden decision. She glanced at Phoebe's brown pelisse, shuddered, but stood up as one determined to sacrifice good taste for the sake of duty. '*I* shall accompany you, Miss Smith.'

'Oh, ma'am, I wouldn't have you put yourself out for the world. I'm sure between the five of us—'

'You don't expect the children to aid you in your endeavour, do you?' Ignoring the lightning-bright glares being aimed at her by three pairs of eyes, she gathered up her reticule and sable stole. 'No doubt Mr Charlton is an excellent secretary, but what does a man know about choosing a house? Besides, my carriage will be more comfortable than a hackney. Come along, now. Standing about chatting will not solve the problem of where you are to live.'

Having had the last word to say on the subject, her ladyship sailed out of the parlour in much the same manner as Boadicea going into battle. Only the spear and chariot were missing.

'You know what the problem is, don't you, Deverell?'

Lord Pendleton tossed aside the newspaper he'd been reading and lounged back in his chair at White's Club.

'You wish they'd hurry up and serve breakfast?'

'No, damn it!'

Sebastian looked up from the sheaf of papers he was perusing and frowned. 'As a matter of fact I do know what the problem is, Pen, so you can save yourself the trouble of telling me.'

It was clear Lord Pendleton intended to ignore this sage advice. He ran a hand through his already fashionably tousled brown locks and bent stern hazel eyes upon his friend.

'You're too accustomed to women falling all over themselves trying to please you. I dare say it has its advantages, but a man needs a little spice occasionally. Not to mention intelligent conversation.'

'I hope you're not referring to the succession of lightskirts who called yesterday. I wager the only time they show any signs of intelligence is when they're assessing the value of a piece of jewellery. As for gentility—'

'And there's another thing,' Pendleton interrupted. 'Your tastes are too nice.'

Sebastian snorted. 'Good God, Pen! You're not so desperate for a ladybird that you consider the denizens of Madame Felice's establishment suitably entertaining, are you? Set up a widow as your mistress if you want gentility, intelligence and reasonably priced entertainment.'

Pendleton cocked a brow. 'Is that what you're planning to do? I would've thought a high-flying Society wife who knows the rules would suit you better. God knows, there's plenty of 'em.'

Sebastian's eyes went cold. 'I never conduct my liaisons with married women.'

'Dare say you're wise,' Pendleton agreed, making haste to retreat from a suddenly precarious position. 'Not but what half of London isn't at it. Well, we'll have to think of something else. Not widows, though.' He shook his head and added darkly, 'Expectations. Before a man knows it, they want a ring on their finger.'

Sebastian thought briefly of the pretty young widow with whom he'd enjoyed a discreet arrangement until a week ago. She, too, had had expectations but, fortunately, she'd had the wit to see that he wasn't going to meet them and, with his good wishes for success, had turned her attention to a rich, elderly banker whom she'd recently met.

Not so fortunate was the gap her departure had left in his life. Pen was right about one thing. He'd become too accustomed to the gentle, softly spoken women of the East, who were trained from girlhood in the arts of pleasing a man. The hard-eyed, grasping courtesans and bored ladies of the *ton* filled him with nothing but distaste.

Trying to impress that fact upon his well-meaning friend, however, was no easy task.

'Don't think I'm not grateful for your. . .er. . .altruistic interest in my *affaires*, Pen, but—'

'Well, I have to do something,' Pendleton muttered. 'If it hadn't been for the sound investment advice you've been giving me over the past couple of months, I wouldn't be in a fair way to recovering the family fortunes. Probably be waiting for breakfast in the Fleet. If they serve it there, which I doubt.'

Sebastian grinned. 'You'd have to send out for dinner, too.'

'Yes, it's all very well to laugh, Deverell, but I was getting pretty desperate, I can tell you. Seems to me the least I can do is return the favour.' He intercepted a quizzical look and couldn't help but grin back.

'I'm not giving up, you know, just because we've eliminated wives, widows and ladybirds. There's still one other possibility. Wedburne told me only the other day about a little governess he's set up in a cosy house in St John's Wood. All perfectly discreet, and the poor girl is so grateful to be rescued from a life of teaching other people's brats, she's as happy as a cat with cream.'

Sebastian's grin vanished. 'You may oblige me, Pen, by contriving to forget about my current lack of a mistress. The situation is very temporary, I assure you.' He proffered the papers in his hand with something of a snap. 'What's more important is this new shipping prospectus. Read it!'

Pendleton's instincts for self-preservation finally took the hint. He forgot about mistresses or the lack thereof and, rather in the manner of a rabbit diving down a rabbit-hole, buried his nose in the papers.

Just as well, Sebastian reflected. He did not want to discuss the possibilities of making a governess his mistress. It was a little too close to the intention he'd all but formed yesterday. An intention that, since then, was making him increasingly uncomfortable. And he wasn't precisely sure why.

He'd lain awake last night, his hands folded beneath his head as he'd stared at the shadowy ceiling, and had reminded himself that Miss Phoebe Smith was no innocent young girl. Not only had she known what he was talking about when he'd mistaken her for a Cyprian, the little minx had almost succumbed to curiosity on the subject of numbers before respectability had got the better of her.

She'd also been earning her own living for several

years; had been clearly accustomed to dealing with the male of the species; and had seemed totally impervious to the threat of his displeasure. Instead, she'd been only too ready to lecture him on his shortcomings.

Obviously Miss Smith did not subscribe to the generally accepted view that governesses were seldom seen or heard outside the schoolroom.

But as soon as he'd convinced himself she was not without experience, he'd remembered the quick succession of emotions that had fled across her face when he'd momentarily intimidated her into silence. His satisfaction at the shock and startled feminine awareness in her eyes when he'd loomed over her had instantly coalesced into an almost uncontrollable urge to pull her into his arms and kiss her senseless.

The force of his desire had stunned him, but it hadn't been nearly as startling as the suspicion, when her defiance had shattered into an utterly unexpected vulnerability, that she hadn't been as experienced as he'd thought.

And the doubts, once insidiously planted in his brain, had proceeded to roll other pictures past his eyes. The starched-up costume that had gone far beyond subdued dressing. The ruthless restraint she'd used to bury the laughter in her eyes. The delicate colour that had tinted her cheeks when he'd commented on her name, and again when they'd touched on her past.

The contradictions had intrigued him. The image of her delicately etched profile had stirred the artist in him. And the memory of graceful movement and suppressed energy had aroused a damned inconvenient urge to discover the soft curves and slender limbs hinted at beneath the hideous clothes. To know how she would look, how she would feel in his arms, when freed of the restraints imposed by the governess.

All in all, he had not spent a restful night. Had the problem been caused by any of the other women he'd had under his protection over the years, he would have taken immediate steps to eradicate it. However, he'd doubted Grillon's Hotel would take kindly to admitting a short-tempered male into a lady's bedchamber at three o'clock in the morning.

No, the situation called for more subtlety than that.

And at that point, suddenly, inexplicably, plotting to free Phoebe of restraints and himself of frustrating nights had made him. . .

Yes, damn it. . .uncomfortable.

Sebastian frowned. He wasn't used to feeling protective about a woman. Blast it, he wasn't even sure just what sort of protection she needed. That flicker of vulnerability might as easily have been surprise; she'd certainly recovered her sharp tongue fast enough. He could assume she was innocent and abandon the chase, only to find Miss Phoebe Smith enlivening the existence of some other gentleman who was presently lacking a mistress.

Expecially as it seemed half the males in London were going about setting up governesses in cosy cottages.

What madness had made him agree to let his wards remain in town? He should have bundled the whole crowd back to Kerslake—forcibly if necessary—and found another widow. One who didn't come with complications. But no. He'd watched shock, defiance and doubt chase each other across an exquisite countenance and had proceeded to outsmart himself.

And now it was too late.

She was here. Or rather, out there.

Looking at houses.

With his secretary.

With a barely suppressed snarl that startled awake an elderly Viscount who'd been snoring comfortably nearby, Sebastian surged to his feet, scattering papers all over the floor.

'I'll see you later, Pen,' he announced, as his friend glanced up, jaw dropping in surprise. 'I've just remembered some urgent business that needs my immediate attention.'

He was out of the room and striding towards the street before Pendleton could do more than gape after him.

Phoebe was feeling extremely frayed around the edges. She was also beginning to question the wisdom of coming to London. If yesterday and today were anything to go by, she would be laid low with nervous exhaustion before the week was out.

And she didn't even believe in nervous exhaustion.

At the moment, the only thing keeping her from emulating Miss Pomfret's farewell performance was the calm presence of Mr Charlton. For some reason, the three Deverells had taken an instant liking to their uncle's quiet, fair-haired young secretary, while he in turn seemed to be thoroughly fascinated by Theodosia. He had scarcely taken his eyes off her all morning, but Phoebe was too distracted by Lady Grismead to worry about the possible ramifications of this new development.

After listening to her ladyship criticise every aspect of the house they were inspecting, as well as the previous four houses they'd visited, two of which in Phoebe's opinion had been perfectly suitable, she was more than ready to put an end to the entire business. But first, she had to locate her charges, who seemed to have vanished in three different directions.

'I say, Phoebe, Aunt Ottilia, this is the best place yet.'

Gerald's voice, wafting down from above, caught her attention. She looked up to see him leaning perilously over the railing at the top of the staircase, the upper flight of which descended to curve sharply around a small half-landing before continuing down to the hall. From Gerald's appearance, Phoebe could only deduce he'd been exploring an attic so far removed from civilisation it had never seen a broom or duster.

'It has the oddest little rooms up here, and look at this capital bannister.'

Before Phoebe could ask why they should look at a perfectly ordinary bannister that was clearly too broad for grace or beauty, a door leading off the half-landing was flung open with a crash. Cressida stepped forward to the balustrade overlooking the hall, hands clasped at her breast, gaze uplifted.

' "O, shut the door! / and when thou hast done so, / Come weep with me; / past hope. . .past cure. . .past help!" '

'Upon my word!' Lady Grismead stared upward as if she'd never seen her great-niece before. 'What on earth is the child talking about?'

'Cressy has a decided liking for drama, ma'am,' Phoebe began. 'Especially Shakes—'

The rest of her explanation was destined to go unheard. With what she could only consider to be typical Deverell deliquency, Gerald chose that moment to launch himself on a life-threatening descent to the hall using the bannister he'd just been extolling. At the same time, his sister flung out her arm in a dramatic gesture worthy of Mrs Siddons.

Phoebe squeezed her eyes shut as the inevitable sounds of collision rent the air. She opened them in time to see Gerald skidding onwards while Cressida, describing several turns at high speed, reeled sideways into the cupboard from which she'd emerged. She landed on the floor in a dishevelled but extremely vocal heap.

'You horrid little toad!' she shrieked. 'You did that deliberately.' Picking herself up, she rushed forward to continue her tirade just as Theodosia, following Gerald's example, whizzed around the angle of the staircase.

Another outraged shriek ricocheted hideously around the hall as Cressida was sent flying again. The sound had scarcely died away when it was followed by the quiet closing of the front door and a firm footfall.

Phoebe, still standing frozen with the expectation of

broken limbs or worse, had her back to the door, but everyone else suddenly assumed the appearance of stunned mutes. Even Lady Grismead was struck dumb. She stared past Phoebe, her eyes almost starting out of her head in astonishment.

'Good heavens!' she exclaimed at last. 'Deverell!'

By the greatest exercise of self-control, Phoebe resisted the temptation to close her eyes again and pretend she hadn't seen her charges risking life and limb in front of their guardian.

She turned and smiled brightly. 'Oh! Good afternoon, my lord.'

Deverell's cool gaze swept over the scene in front of him. 'Miss Smith,' he acknowledged. 'Good afternoon, Aunt. Edward, would you mind telling me why you appeared to be standing ready to catch my niece instead of preventing her from a hoydenish activity guaranteed to distress her companion?'

There was another dumbfounded silence while everyone digested this acid request. Then a rueful smile crept into Mr Charlton's grey eyes.

'I'm afraid I was not in a position to do anything but stand by, sir. Your niece was too quick for me.'

Theodosia tossed her head. 'I don't see why Gerald should have all the fun just because he's a boy. It wasn't in the least bit dangerous.' Having obviously been aware of Edward Charlton's interest all morning, she turned to him with a brilliant smile. 'Was it, Mr Charlton?'

Phoebe resigned herself to witnessing another victim fall prey to Deverell manipulation.

'I dare say you enjoyed yourself,' Mr Charlton said quietly, surprising her. 'But perhaps it wasn't quite as harmless a prank as you suppose, Lady Theodosia.'

To Phoebe's further surprise, Theodosia seemed to accept this mild rebuke without a blink. She beamed at her new admirer. 'Oh, how clever of you to guess who I am. No one can ever tell Cressy and I apart. How did you do it?'

'It wasn't difficult.' He smiled back at her. 'There really are several clues.'

'I'm happy to hear you say so, Edward,' Deverell put in with some asperity. 'Since you'll be in charge of my wards for the rest of the day.'

'What?' Phoebe looked up at him, startled. It wasn't a wise thing to do. She discovered she hadn't been wrong about his eyes, after all. There was nothing in the penetrating aquamarine gaze focused on her face that could be described as either nice or unthreatening.

'You and I have some shopping to do, Miss Smith,' he informed her before she could recover the breath that had mysteriously disappeared from her lungs.

He turned to his aunt. 'And you'll be wishing to go about your business, Aunt. In fact, I can't think why you're here in the first place.'

'Well! Upon my word, Deverell! If this is the sort of ungrateful manner you expect will reinstate you in your family's affections, you sadly mistake the matter. As for your note yesterday—'

'If I ever had any such expectations, madam,' Deverell bit out in a voice abruptly edged with the chill of an ice-tipped wind, 'they were forgotten years ago.'

Lady Grismead's already indignant colour rose. 'That was your own doing, sir.'

'Was it?' Deverell said cryptically. 'You may be right, Aunt, but in any event, I don't intend to debate the matter with you. I've arranged for any bills you incur at Cecile's to be forwarded to me, if you wish to take Pamela there for some new gowns.'

From the tight-lipped set of Lady Grismead's mouth, Phoebe fully expected her to toss Deverell's offer back in his face. Practicality, however, won over outrage. Her blue eyes flashing angrily, she turned on her heel and waited in imperious silence for Mr Charlton to open the front door.

'Thank you for your advice this morning, Lady

Grismead,' Phoebe ventured, hoping to smooth a few ruffled feathers.

Her ladyship paused at the top of the front steps and looked back. 'I hope I know my duty, Miss Smith. You and the girls may call upon me in a day or two. I shall send my carriage for you when I have your direction. Good day.'

'Well, really, my lord,' Phoebe began as the door closed behind Lady Grismead's rigid back. 'How could you—?'

'Does anyone care about *me*?' demanded Cressida from the landing above them, her throbbing tones completely drowning out the rest of Phoebe's lecture. 'Does anyone care that *I* could have broken every bone in my body? Does anyone care that—?'

'Stop ranting and come down here!' ordered Deverell in a voice that made everyone jump visibly.

Cressida blinked at him, her mouth open in shock.

'Here!' thundered Deverell, pointing at the floor in front of him.

'For heaven's sake, my lord,' Phoebe protested in an agitated undertone, 'Cressy is not a recalcitrant puppy.'

'You will kindly stay out of this, Miss Smith. You wanted a strong hand. You're getting one.'

'Yes, but—'

He ignored her.

'Thank you,' he said when Cressida, still stunned, obeyed.

Theodosia and Gerald moved at once to flank her in a show of unity that raised Deverell's eyebrows. All three stared at their uncle with varying degrees of resentment, rebellion and curiosity, but in Gerald's eyes Phoebe saw the dawning of the boy's half-reluctant, half-cautious respect for an older, more powerful male.

She swallowed her instinctive desire to intervene and waited.

'Now,' Deverell began in the tone of one addressing troops, 'you will accompany Mr Charlton and you will oblige him by not engaging in the type of activities that brought Miss Smith to the point of resigning her post.'

Three pairs of astonished blue eyes turned towards Phoebe. The trio then looked at each other, communed silently and shook their heads.

'You must be mistaken, sir,' Gerald said, appointing himself spokesman. 'Phoebe wouldn't leave. Why,' he added ingenuously, 'we've done far worse things since she came to Kerslake than we ever did when the other governesses were there.'

'Yes, one left after only two days,' Theodosia added helpfully.

Cressida, still brooding, contented herself with a baleful nod.

'Indeed? Am I to understand that only Miss Smith's strong sense of duty has withstood all your attempts to be rid of her?'

'Oh, no!' Gerald looked shocked. 'We'd never want to get rid of Phoebe. We like her.'

Touched, Phoebe smiled. 'Thank you, Gerald.'

Deverell slanted a brief, amused glance down at her. 'Good. Then it shouldn't be too much of a hardship to comport yourselves in a manner she would approve.' He let that sink in and turned to his secretary. 'Give me the keys to this house, Edward, and then take my wards away. They can visit the Exeter Exchange or some such attraction.'

'What's at the Exeter Exchange, Uncle Sebastian?'

Phoebe saw Deverell wince. 'For God's sake, Gerald, don't call me Uncle Sebastian,' he said with so much disgust in his voice that Gerald grinned. 'Sebastian or Deverell will do. As for the Exeter Exchange, they house an exhibition of wild beasts there. You should feel perfectly at home.'

'Wild beasts!' Cressida shrieked, as her brother chuckled at this sally. She clutched at her sister and lowered her voice dramatically. 'Did you hear that, Theo? He's going to throw us to wild beasts! Our own uncle! Oh, wicked, wicked world that condones such a dastardly act.'

'Try to contain your transports of delight,' Deverell ordered sarcastically, eyeing his niece with disfavour. 'Even I draw the line at inflicting you upon helpless wild animals.'

Incensed at this cavalier reception of her performance, Cressida straightened and resumed scowling.

'I'm sure between the two of us, your brother and I will be able to protect you from an untimely end, Lady Cressida,' Mr Charlton soothed, handing over a bunch of keys to Deverell. He cast a laughing glance at his employer as he did so and moved forward to open the front door again.

'Oh, Mr Charlton!' Phoebe exclaimed, belatedly remembering the main business of the day. 'The second house we looked at—'

'Leave it to me, Miss Smith,' Edward Charlton called back as he was swept through the doorway on a small tidal wave of Deverells.

'Oh, dear.' Phoebe gazed anxiously after the departing expedition. 'I do hope they don't contrive to lose him.'

'It's far more likely he'll wish to lose them,' Deverell retorted. 'Gerald and Theodosia seem comparatively rational, but what the devil is wrong with Cressida?'

'Well. . .' Phoebe turned back to him with a rueful smile '. . .I'm afraid she is much addicted to melodrama, sir. I think that's why her actor held so much appeal for her.'

'Hmm. Her heart doesn't appear to be irrevocably broken.'

'Oh, no.' Phoebe laughed. 'Mr Corby's unromantic behaviour in returning her to Kerslake and then driving away faster than when they'd departed quite tore the scales from her eyes. She discovered that, away from the stage, he was really a very ordinary young man.

'In fact,' she added thoughtfully, 'I'm not even sure he knew he was eloping until Cressy embarked on their excursion to the village carrying a large bandbox. Of course, I may be wrong. When Gerald dashed out of the house waving a duelling pistol, Mr Corby didn't wait around to explain.'

She thought Deverell might appreciate the picture she'd evoked of Cressida's actor fleeing the scene of his short-lived betrothal, but although he did indeed glance down at her, his smile was rather perfunctory and his gaze returned almost immediately to the open front door.

The prospect of a quiet street in a genteel neighbour-hood was pleasant enough, but, watching him, Phoebe had the strangest feeling Deverell was seeing something else entirely. Something far distant, she thought, in time and place.

Only when the silence was broken by the rattle of carriage wheels on the road outside, did she venture to speak, instinctively softening her voice. 'What is it, my lord?'

He half-turned his head as if, for a moment, though hearing her, he was still in that faraway time and place. 'I beg your pardon, Miss Smith. It was nothing. Merely, I was remembering. . .'

Remembering a pair of tiny, doll-like Deverells gazing up at him with identical solemn blue eyes from their cradles, and a little boy scarcely out of leading-strings who had pestered to be taken up on his uncle's favourite hunter for a ride, and the unexpected pleasure it had given his younger self to grant the treat.

Sebastian shook the memory aside and looked down at the gently enquiring expression on Phoebe's face. She couldn't read his mind, of course, but in the luminous golden brown glow of her eyes he saw something that looked very like understanding.

He frowned, the deeply rooted wariness that had seen him return to England relatively unscathed raising its head like an animal scenting the air. 'You were right yesterday, Miss Smith,' he admitted curtly. 'I hadn't considered the fact that Gerald and the girls are no longer children.'

'A quite understandable misapprehension, my lord. They must have been little more than babies when you left.'

There was a faint coolness in her tone as though she'd sensed his withdrawal and responded in kind. Sebastian found himself regretting the change even as he told himself Miss Phoebe Smith sensed far too much.

And yet, he'd almost told her of those long-forgotten memories, was conscious, still, that the impulse to let her draw closer, to allow her inside the invisible barrier of his defences, lingered. Even the legacy of rage and pain left over from a past that would forever remain unresolved, seemed, in her presence, to have faded to a faint echo.

'Yes,' he said slowly, 'the twins were still in the nursery. You know my sister-in-law died while they were quite young?'

Her wide gaze searched his for a moment. 'Miss Pomfret told me.'

He nodded. 'Perhaps things might have been different for them had she lived. She was. . .gentle. Far too gentle to cope with my brother. Theirs was an arranged match and very—'

He broke off, suddenly realising where the conversation was going. And then couldn't help laughing in rueful acknowledgement. 'Infelicitous, Miss Smith. But don't worry. I won't bore you with the sorry details thereof.'

His smile was returned with a brilliance that made him blink. 'Your sentiments do you credit, my lord, but you musn't think your wards have *suffered* from not remembering their mother. The situation seems to have had the effect of making them closer, perhaps, than other siblings.'

Sebastian hadn't been thinking any such thing. The wildly conflicting sensations aroused by Phoebe's smile simply didn't allow room for extraneous thoughts. On the one hand, he wanted to disabuse her mind of the naïve assumption that he'd ever entertain such mawkish sentiments, while at the same time protect her from that knowledge. The warm approval in her eyes was surprisingly sweet. He could have basked in it for a very long time.

Unfortunately, her smile also aroused a shockingly fierce urge to sweep her up in his arms and carry her up the stairs where he could bask in private. His resistance wasn't helped when the loud striking of a clock in the adjoining drawing-room reminded him that they were completely alone in the house.

'Yes, well, I shall bow to your superior judgement in such matters, Miss Smith,' he said, turning on his heel and striding purposefully towards the front door. There was still a rather imperative point to be established, damn it. *And* he'd made her a promise. 'Shall we go?'

Phoebe blinked. Really! What had caused such a snappish reply? Just when she was feeling quite in charity with the man, he turned around and behaved in a manner that was totally incomprehensible. As if she hadn't put up with enough from Deverells today.

Elevating her small nose, she sailed past the door he was holding open for her. 'As it happens, my lord, my judgement in such matters may indeed be relied upon. I have had a great deal of experience with Deverells, you see. Despite their various foibles and faults, they do care about each other.'

'I shall have to take your word for that, too, Miss Smith,' he retorted, locking the door behind them.

His true opinion was only too plain. Phoebe levelled her brows at him. 'It is surely obvious, sir. Look at Lady Grismead's kindness in accompanying me this morning.'

For some reason, this remark elicited a savage scowl.

'Good God! You don't really believe she came along out of kindness, do you?' Taking her hand, he clamped it down on his arm and began striding down the street.

Almost whisked off her feet, Phoebe had perforce to follow. She didn't make the mistake of reading anything gallant into the gesture. If she snatched her hand away, she was quite certain Deverell would simply continue walking.

That realisation, however, did nothing to lessen the stunning impact of sheer male power in the steely muscles beneath her fingertips, or distract her from the tension emanating from her escort. It was so forceful, she wondered the air about them didn't crackle like one of the new electricity machines she'd read about.

And suddenly, without knowing precisely why, she felt an urgent need to have him believe her, to have him see his family as she did.

'Well, perhaps not kindness exactly,' she temporised. 'But certainly Lady Grismead wished to be helpful.'

He sent her an impatient glance.

Phoebe frowned right back at him. 'You seem to forget, sir, that she cared enough about Gerald and your nieces to take over the hiring of a governess when all Miss Pomfret's candidates left, one after the other.'

'Yes, you have me there, Miss Smith. Since my aunt had the good sense to engage you in the first place, I suppose I'll have to forgive her for dragging you all over London.'

'I'm sorry if I appear sadly wilted,' she retorted, incensed all over again. 'But I could hardly refuse Lady Grismead's offer. And it wouldn't have hurt *you* to have shown a little gratitude. This isn't an easy time for her, you know. Your aunt is extremely concerned about Miss Grismead.'

'Understandable,' Deverell allowed with a sardonic curl to his lip. 'My pea-brained cousin seems to spend her time either swooning, drooping or languishing.'

'Well, it doesn't help to have you pointing out "possible consequences",' Phoebe scolded, warming to the subject. 'How could you, sir? Poor Lady Grismead is probably living in fear of having it known that their circumstances are severely reduced.'

He shrugged. 'It's none of my concern if my aunt chooses to lose sleep over the matter. I'm quite sure you don't intend to spread the news abroad and nor do I.'

'I didn't for a moment think you had any such intention, my lord, despite what your note might have implied. But does Lady Grismead know that?'

Deverell stopped short in the middle of the footpath, the look he cast down at her almost making her gasp aloud. For one infinitesimal instant, bitterness, violent rage, and the shadows of years-old pain seethed like a sea-witch's cauldron in the blue-green depths of his eyes before vanishing beneath the frozen surface.

'She should,' he bit out. And stepped away from her to hail an approaching hackney.

Phoebe stood motionless as the driver reined his horse in at the curb. She was scarcely conscious of breathing. Never had she seen such raging emotions in a man's eyes. Nor the icy implacability that had followed. The Deverell stare was a benevolent gaze by comparison.

A warrior, she remembered, with a small inward shiver. The trappings of civilisation were in place, even elegantly in place, she thought, eyeing the snowy folds of his cravat and the superb tailoring of the coat covering those broad shoulders, but underneath was a warrior. Hard, powerful, and dangerous.

Her mind whirled with questions as Deverell handed her into the hackney and seated himself opposite her. For a long time no one spoke. Phoebe's gaze remained riveted on the stern lines of Deverell's profile, illuminated by a pale September sun as he stared out of the window at the passing scene. His brows were drawn together in a frown, and she was startled by an impulse to reach out and touch him.

Was it because she'd caught a glimpse of invisible scars? she wondered. A warrior, yes, but alone. A law

unto himself. She suspected he'd been alone for a very
long time.

'How did you know we've been all over London?'
she finally asked softly.

Deverell shifted his gaze from the cab window to her
face. 'I had a copy of Edward's list of houses,' he said.
'And followed you.' He was silent for a heartbeat and
then a wry smile touched his mouth. 'When I learned my
aunt was with you, I thought you might need rescuing,
Miss Smith.'

'Oh. . .no, I. . .' Feeling oddly shy, she glanced away.
Then humour came to her rescue and she smiled back
at him. 'Do I really look so wilted, sir?'

He shook his head, reached out and took her hand.
'I'm sorry,' he said very soberly. 'I shouldn't have
snapped at you like that. I frightened you.'

'Not at all, my lord.' Phoebe lifted her chin, but her
heart was racing. His hand felt very warm and strong
wrapped around her smaller one. She suddenly noticed
how much room he was taking up in the hackney. He
was so big, so close, she could feel the heat from his
body. Perhaps that was the reason her pulse was jumping
about beneath his fingers. 'As I pointed out earlier, I am
quite accustomed to Deverells.'

He smiled faintly at that and released her. 'Some of
us are less easy to control than others, Miss Smith,' he
murmured, and returned to his contemplation of the
street.

With that enigmatic remark echoing in her ears,
Phoebe did likewise.

The rest of the short drive passed in a not-
uncompanionable silence. All was not serene, however,
inside her head. No matter how diligently she ordered
herself to take heed of Deverell's warning—if warning
it had been—her brain refused to co-operate. It was too
busy grappling with another problem.

Deverell's indifference to his family had not been
feigned yesterday in order to amuse himself by teasing

her—an explanation that had occurred to her once or twice since their meeting. Though his wealth put him in a position of some power, he was indeed estranged from them.

And she was very much afraid that she wanted to hear every sorry detail of the infelicitous circumstances surrounding the rift.

Chapter Four

Half an hour later, the dangers of listening to sorry
details had given way to the dangers of temptation—in
the form of the loveliest pelisse Phoebe had ever beheld.

Modish, high-waisted, with shoulder-puffs and a neat
upstanding collar fashioned to frame her face like a small
ruff, its soft ivory hue was beautifully set off by the
delicate gold-scalloped trim on collar, puffs and hem
and a row of tiny gold buttons marching down the front.
A large sable muff and a jaunty ivory bonnet, sporting
gold ribbons and a sable-tinted plume, completed an
ensemble that was both elegant and feminine.

And totally impractical, Phoebe told herself firmly.

She took one last look at the transformation reflected
in the mirror in Madame Cecile's fitting-room and shook
her head in genuine regret.

'Oh, but, ma'mselle, the fit, it is perfect. And see how
the trim brings out the gold in your hair.'

Bustling about, twitching a fold into place here and
stroking a sleeve there, Madame Cecile paused long
enough to inspect the curls she had insisted on freeing
from their usual tight knot at Phoebe's nape. 'Such pretty
hair, but ma'mselle must have been out in the sun without a bonnet or parasol.' The plump little modiste
clucked in disapproval.

'No, it's quite natural,' Phoebe murmured, marvelling

that soft ringlets framing her face could make her eyes appear so dark and large. And oddly vulnerable.

She frowned. She wasn't entirely certain she approved of vulnerable. 'The pelisse is very beautiful, madame, but—'

'Ah, you think the ivory too pale, perhaps? Not every lady can wear such a colour, but with ma'mselle's eyes and complexion—' Cecile broke off with an eloquent gesture. 'But come,' she insisted, beginning to prod Phoebe gently towards the outer room of the shop. 'We will show milord Deverell. He will decide.'

'What does he know about fashion?' Phoebe grumbled as she was propelled through the curtain separating the two rooms.

'Enough to know what pleases me, Miss Smith,' Deverell replied, turning from his contemplation of the street beyond the window. Something dark flashed in his eyes before his gaze travelled over her from her bonnet to the tips of her tan suede half-boots.

Phoebe had time to be thankful the late hour meant they were the only customers in the shop before he very slowly reversed the procedure.

'And the vision of you in that pelisse definitely pleases me,' he murmured in a soft growl that sent a series of tiny shivers rippling down her spine.

She stared back at him, wondering if her imagination was suddenly running riot or if the light aquamarine of his eyes really had darkened to a deep sea-green.

Impossible, she told herself hastily. It was only because he was watching her so intently. She wished he wouldn't. She wished he had waited outside. She wished he looked ludicrously out of place surrounded by gowns and fabrics and fashionable feminine knick-knacks.

It was as if an extremely large predator had somehow found his way into a chamber full of dainty treasures, she thought crossly. But instead of appearing in the least uncomfortable with his surroundings, Deverell conveyed the distinct impression that if the shop had been filled to overflowing with breakable objects, he would prowl among them without so much as brushing a single one.

The image of incredible masculine strength under such powerful control set off another ripple of sensation, this time from her throat to her knees.

'Is not ma'mselle a beauty, milord?' Cecile crooned, lovingly curling the sable plume so that it brushed Phoebe's cheek.

She started at the touch and sternly ordered her throat to unlock and her knees to cease trembling. From the gleam in Deverell's eyes she knew she was about to have the same argument that had ensued with every other article of apparel she'd been shown. She needed her wits about her.

'The pelisse is lovely, sir,' she agreed. 'For a young lady of fashion. Not for a companion.'

'Miss Smith, my nieces will be young ladies of fashion once they're let loose in here with my purse. Their companion most definitely cannot look like a dowd in comparison.'

'Mais oui,' confirmed Cecile, nodding vigorously. She cast a mischievous glance at Deverell. 'Milord is very right. He usually is, ma'mselle.'

'Is he?' muttered Phoebe, noticing this little byplay. She hadn't been much surprised to find that Deverell was on terms of friendship with his secretary. But a modiste?

A second later the likeliest explanation occurred to her. She promptly blushed bright scarlet.

'The pelisse is really, how you say, not fussy, ma'mselle,' Cecile began, hurrying to avert customer embarrassment. She fluttered her hands expressively. 'Most suitable. There are no ruffles, no bows or frogging.'

'It isn't that.' Phoebe sighed. And seeing genuine puzzlement on the modiste's face, she launched into an explanation in French, hoping to make the situation clearer.

It only took her seconds to realise she'd made the situation much worse. Cecile was now looking positively blank.

Exasperated, she turned to Deverell, only to see him wheel hurriedly towards the window. He seemed to be fascinated by a high-perch phaeton drawn up on the opposite side of the street, but there was a suspicious hint of movement about his shoulders.

Phoebe narrowed her eyes at him. 'The plume,' she stated very clearly, 'will have to go.'

'Plume? Go?' Cecile appeared more puzzled than ever.

'Plumes are provocative. Companions are not. At least, they're not supposed to be. My lord, will you kindly look at me when I'm addressing you.'

'My apologies, Miss Smith. I thought you were still arguing with Cecile.' Deverell turned, his eyes brilliant with barely suppressed laughter. 'Am I to understand that you've decided to bow to the inevitable?'

Phoebe glared at him. 'That's what we blades of grass have to do.'

He raised an eyebrow. 'I beg your pardon?'

'Nothing, sir.'

He grinned wickedly. 'If you say so, Miss Smith. Cecile, remove the plume and send it along with the other packages. One of the girls may wish to have it.'

'*Oui*, m'sieur. What shall I do with ma'mselle's old pelisse?'

'Send that along, too,' Phoebe instructed with another minatory frown at Deverell. 'This one is only being loaned.'

Shaking her head over the vagaries of customers, Cecile directed her minions to obey.

'And I still say this pelisse is highly impractical,' Phoebe added when she and Deverell were once again seated in a hackney and bowling along towards Grillon's. 'Whoever heard of wearing a white pelisse in winter?'

Deverell lounged back in his corner of the cab and

regarded her with lazily smiling eyes. Apparently, getting the better of her by purchasing several gowns for her use had put him in an indulgent mood.

'There's no need to create problems, Miss Smith. When the weather is inclement, you will naturally instruct your footman to send for your carriage.'

'Carriage? Footman? Oh, my goodness. Servants. I'll have to—'

'You will have to do nothing. Mr Charlton already has the matter well in hand.'

'Oh.' She mulled that over for a minute. 'Mr Charlton seems to be an excellent young man,' she observed at last.

'He also has political ambitions and has already attracted the notice of an influential sponsor, so you may cease worrying about his obvious attraction to Theodosia. In a few years, if he's still of a like mind and she's unattached, he'll be perfectly eligible.'

'Good heavens, sir. Do you ever miss anything?'

'Very little, Miss Smith.'

'Yes, well. . .' She eyed him narrowly. 'Not all of us are blessed with your powers of observation, my lord. Would you mind telling me what you found so hilarious about me trying to communicate with Madame Cecile in French? I am accounted quite proficient in the language, you know.'

'You may well be, Miss Smith. Cecile, however, is not.'

'Not? But she spoke with an accent.'

Deverell threw back his head and laughed. The sound bounced around the hackney for a full minute before he managed to control himself.

'Well?' Phoebe demanded when his laughter faded to intermittent chuckles. When chuckles seemed to be the only answer forthcoming, she scowled even more ferociously. 'I am, of course, delighted to afford you so much amusement, my lord, but I am still waiting for an answer.'

'Miss Smith,' he said, grinning. 'You are a delight. Madame Cecile, I regret to inform you, started life as Sally Mutworthy. After advancing by way of the streets to. . .er. . .more salubrious places of employment, she became the mistress of a French émigré from whom she picked up an accent and the odd phrase or two.'

'Oh. I see. And th—?'

She stopped, appalled. Good heavens! She had been about to succumb to a scandalous urge to enquire about the next step in Cecile's career. And if Deverell had had anything to do with said step. She must be going mad!

'No, Miss Smith,' he said smoothly. 'I've tossed some business Sally's way, but by the time I made her acquaintance she was already well-established in her new profession.'

Phoebe felt herself blushing again. Now he was reading her mind. This was what came of challenging a Deverell. She should have known better.

'Oh. I mean. . .I am not surprised, my lord. She has excellent taste. One could purchase an entire wardrobe there. In fact, we seem to have done so. How am I ever going to find the time to wear all those clothes? We will have to—'

He leaned forward and laid his hand over hers, successfully putting an end to her babbling. Phoebe stared at him, transfixed, her fingers quivering once beneath his touch before she went very still.

Gently, slowly, he wrapped his fingers around hers until she could feel her own pulse fluttering madly against his palm. His eyes, glittering in the shadows of the hackney, gazed straight into hers for a long long time. Then he raised her hand to his lips and held it there.

Phoebe jerked back immediately, her breath catching on a small startled gasp. He must have felt her resistance but he ignored her struggles, his gaze continuing to pin hers. Then he nodded once, lowered her hand and released it.

'You really are innocent, aren't you?' The words were spoken with absolute conviction.

Her lips parted. 'Well, yes. I mean. . .that is to say. . .'

'No, not ignorant. Innocent, Miss Smith. There's a difference.'

'If you say so, my lord.' She could scarcely get the words out. Her heart was beating somewhere in her throat and she felt as breathless as if she'd run all the way from Kerslake to London. 'But what has that to do with shopping. . .or anything?'

'Quite a lot, Miss Smith.' He sat back in his corner of the hackney, his gaze going to the window, eyes narrowing as he stared out at the gathering shadows of late afternoon. 'Quite. A. Lot.'

Phoebe looked down at her tingling hand and tried to restore order to her wildly disordered senses. The task took an inordinate amount of time. Clearly, something had put a swift and comprehensive end to Deverell's mood of amused indulgence. She couldn't imagine what it was.

The only explanation that occurred to her was that he'd been testing her in some way. Perhaps he wanted to make sure his nieces' companion was a woman of high moral standards. Although after yesterday's confrontation, she was rather inclined to resent any need for confirmation of the fact.

But then, if he'd been testing her, why was he now looking so grim? No, she amended, studying him cautiously from beneath her lashes, not grim precisely. More brooding, as if someone had just presented him with a totally unexpected and not altogether welcome solution to a puzzle.

There was no need to puzzle over what she should do next, however. This time she had no intention of asking for enlightenment. It was definitely safer to remain silent. Very silent.

*   *   *

Several days later, Phoebe followed her charges through the gates of Hyde Park, and decided it was quite possible she would survive the move to London after all.

They were settled in a pleasant house in the fashionable area around Grosvenor Square; Theodosia and Cressida had already struck up a friendship with another pair of sisters whom they'd met while shopping with Lady Grismead; and apart from such minor domestic upsets as Cressida scaring the wits out of the housemaid with a rendition of Lady Macbeth's most bloodthirsty speech, and Gerald falling asleep on the back doorstep after an overly-convivial evening with a new acquaintance, life had been relatively peaceful.

True, she was experiencing some moments of concern over Gerald's suddenly busy social calendar, but, in an abrupt reversal of her original plan, Phoebe was determined not to apply to her employer for assistance unless it became absolutely necessary.

Her decision had not been influenced by his odd behaviour at their last meeting. Well, not entirely. After a period of calm reflection, she had come to the conclusion that Deverell had indeed been testing her. After all, she'd come to her post without proper letters of recommendation—which only went to prove that he was not so uncaring of his wards as he appeared.

Unfortunately, this happy exercise of logic had been overturned as the days passed. Not only had Deverell failed to call upon them at their new abode, he hadn't even sent to enquire as to how they were settling in. The omission had at first surprised, then disappointed her. Both reactions had given her a rather nasty jolt.

It was fortunate, she'd told herself sternly, that she'd been so summarily reminded of his indifference to his family. Otherwise, she might have been in danger of changing her mind about him. Or of thinking about him several times a day.

Phoebe frowned. She had finally succeeded in putting

Deverell out of her mind, and she was not going to let
him sneak back in now.

'Phoebe, look! Several ladies are riding in the Park. It
isn't fair that Deverell has permitted Gerald to purchase a
horse while we have to walk.'

So much for keeping Deverell out of her head.

'I don't think your style of neck-or-nothing would suit
Hyde Park, Theo,' she said, studying the riders trotting
sedately up and down the Row a few yards to their right.

'I don't know why we have to walk here at all,'
Cressida grumbled. 'I wanted to visit the theatres.'

'Mr Charlton kindly escorted us to the theatre the
other night,' Phoebe reminded her.

'Yes, and it was all very exciting, but I want to *act*.'

Phoebe suppressed a shudder.

'Gerald says he's going to buy a phaeton. Why can't
I have a phaeton, too?'

'I'm going to be the greatest dramatic actress the
world has ever—'

'Ladies can drive just as well as gentlemen,
you know.'

'I'm sure once Mr Kemble hears me, he'll—'

'There's Gerald now,' Phoebe interrupted hastily. She
waved with enthusiasm. It wasn't easy fielding complaints and unsuitable ambitions; Gerald had appeared
in the nick of time. 'And see,' she continued, 'he's on
foot, as we are. Who's that with him?'

'I think it's Mr Filby,' Theodosia said, momentarily
diverted. She studied Gerald's friend with a critical eye
as the two young men approached. 'Gerald says he's all
the crack, but if you ask me, he looks like he belongs
in a Fair.'

Cressida giggled. 'What do you think will attack him
first, Theo? The points of his collar or that bunch of
flowers he has in his buttonhole?'

'Hush,' commanded Phoebe, not feeling greatly
inclined to share her charges' mirth. Mr Filby had been
the gentleman who had deposited Gerald on the back

doorstep at an ungodly hour two nights ago. Adorning his rather plump person with every extravagance of male fashion, which included a waistcoat of palest rose embroidered with blue and purple unicorns frolicking in an improbable forest of greenery, did not predispose her to alter an already unfavourable opinion.

'Phoebe!' exclaimed Gerald. 'We're devilish pleased to see you. Some enterprising rogue is selling ices over there by the hedge. Has a deuced clever box with ice beneath to keep them frozen. Dare say it'll melt before long, but Reggie and I thought we'd sample a few. Only trouble is, we can't hold more than two at a time. Oh, forgot! You haven't met m'friend, Filby. M'sisters and Miss Smith, Reggie.'

This offhand introduction made Phoebe wince. Mr Filby apparently shared her view. After favouring each twin with a polite nod precisely calculated for young ladies not yet out, he bowed low over the hand she felt obliged to offer him.

'Reginald Filby at your service, ma'am. Very happy to make your acquaintance. Told Gerald he should present me, but didn't mean him to do it in such a shambling fashion. Feel I should apologise.'

Phoebe retrieved her hand. 'Please think nothing of it, Mr Filby.'

'Well, actually,' he contradicted, still apologetic, 'must think of it. Can't have the Earl of Kerslake going about flinging careless introductions right and left. Not the thing. Been trying to give him a few hints, but he ain't one to take advice, is he?'

'Indeed, Mr Filby.'

Her agreement seemed to cast Filby into deepest gloom. 'Told him so the other night when he kept drinking Blue Ruin,' he said dolefully. 'Told him better stick to ale. Told him he'd regret it.' He shook his head. 'Seems to be the sort of thing a fellow has to learn for himself though. M'father warned me, too, when I was

Gerald's age, but did I listen? No. Sick as a cat for two days.'

He continued to look so downcast about this apparently unavoidable male rite of passage that Phoebe couldn't help smiling. Her disapproval quite melted away. Clearly, Gerald had managed to reach a state of disgraceful inebriation without any assistance.

'Fortunately, Gerald seems to have recovered a great deal sooner, sir,' she said, instinctively dispensing comfort.

He cheered up somewhat at this. 'Amazing powers of recuperation,' he agreed. 'Even woke up long enough to tell me the way to the garden when we couldn't rouse your butler.' He lowered his voice and leaned closer. 'Thought you might prefer him on the back doorstep rather than the front, ma'am.'

'Very considerate of you,' Phoebe approved, hiding another smile.

'No need to fear Gerald might become addicted to the bottle, though. Told me he wasn't going to touch the stuff again. Seems to be more interested in ices now.'

This ingenuous observation proved correct. Phoebe looked around to discover that while she and Mr Filby had been chatting, Gerald and his sisters had descended upon the ice-vendor's cart and were arguing about how many ices were needed to quench the apparently hideous thirst engendered by strolling in the park on a mild September afternoon.

Phoebe sighed. She was about to step forward to do her duty when a sudden tingling between her shoulder blades made her turn her head. She found herself gazing straight into Deverell's glittering aquamarine eyes as he stood watching her across a stretch of lawn.

Her heart tripped. Her breath caught. Every nerve in her body pulled taut as if awaiting a signal to stand or flee. He was still several yards away, but the impact on her senses of his intense masculinity was enough to suspend every faculty.

It was his size, she told herself, more than a little
frantically as he started towards her. She'd forgotten
how big he was. How powerfully built. Really, there was
something not quite civilised about such raw masculine
strength, and yet all the politely behaved, medium-sized,
civilised males within view promptly faded to insig-
nificance.

'Good God, it's Deverell!' announced Filby. 'Wonder
what brings him here? Never walks in the Park. Rides
sometimes. Very handsome black. Temperamental,
though. Wouldn't like to throw a saddle over him
m'self.'

Phoebe experienced a strong desire to order Mr Filby
to cease chattering. It was very distracting when she was
trying to recover her wits. Never had she had such a
reaction to a man's sudden presence. Her senses seemed
to have become almost unnaturally acute. Her heartbeat
thundered in her ears; the scent of newly clipped grass
stung her nose. Even the breeze took on an almost tangible form. She could have reached out and touched it
as it brushed her cheek in passing.

It was all most unsettling.

So was the intent gaze Deverell subjected her to when
he reached them.

He inclined his head slightly. 'Good afternoon,
Miss Smith.'

Fortunately for her scrambled wits, he didn't wait for
an answer. After taking in her new cream muslin gown
worn with a frilled spencer of bronze silk shot with
green, he shifted his attention to her companion. 'Filby,
isn't it?' he enquired with a distinct lack of cordiality.

Filby promptly bowed with the flourish of a born
Tulip. 'Your servant, sir.'

Deverell merely looked at him. 'I hear you've put my
nephew's name up at your club.'

'Oh, that. Yes.' Mr Filby smiled happily, apparently
under the impression he was being thanked. 'No trouble
at all. Do Gerald good to acquire a little polish. One's

always a bit raw when one first comes to Town. Dare say you remember how it was, my lord.'

'No, I don't.' The words fell into the balmy afternoon like hailstones. 'I didn't acquire those particular memories.'

'Oh.' For a second Mr Filby looked taken aback, then whatever he'd heard in the way of rumours seemed to stir in his brain. 'Oh, yes. Yes, indeed, sir. Quite so.' He subsided, clearly crushed by the suspicion that he might have committed a social solecism.

'How *very* kind of you, Mr Filby,' Phoebe said warmly, finally recovering her voice. She bestowed a beaming smile upon him. 'I assure you Lord Deverell is most grateful to be saved the exertion of doing the same thing.' She turned a look of heavy meaning on her employer. 'Aren't you, my lord?'

He raised a brow.

Phoebe glared at him. This was too much. Not only was Deverell making mincemeat of her wits after ignoring her—*no*! Ignoring his wards—for the better part of a week, he was also being rude to the one gentleman who had taken Gerald under his wing.

'Pay no heed to him, sir,' she advised, turning a smile that had more than a suggestion of gritted teeth about it on the unfortunate Mr Filby. 'He's a Deverell. They can be exceedingly difficult at times.'

'Er. . .' Filby cast a wary glance from her smile to Deverell's face and began edging backwards. 'Yes. Um. . .that is, dare say you wish to consult with Miss Smith, sir. Be happy to assist by walking with your nieces. Take a toddle around the lake, you know. Your very obedient servant, ma'am.'

He retreated at speed, scurrying towards the shelter of the crowd about the ice-vendor's cart.

'Well!' Phoebe turned on Deverell, ready to deliver a pithy lecture on the subject of manners. She encountered a scowl that reminded her of their almost silent parting some days ago. Obviously his mood hadn't improved in the interim.

' "Difficult", Miss Smith?' he queried before she could start.

'Exceedingly,' she repeated with relish. 'Not only that, sir, but you will have to cease this habit you've developed of fobbing your wards off on to others. First it was Mr Charlton the other day, and now poor Mr Filby.'

'*Poor* Mr Filby?' His scowl darkened. 'He didn't look to be in a particularly unfortunate position a moment ago. In fact, you both appeared to be enjoying a most enthralling conversation.'

Phoebe blinked. 'Enthralling? Mr Filby was good enough to set my mind at rest about G—I mean, about a certain matter, sir, and—'

'You mean about Gerald drinking himself under the hatches two nights ago at Limmer's.'

'Oh.' The wind of righteous indignation whooshed out of her sails. 'You know about that.'

'Yes. And about Gerald applying to Edward as to how to hire a box at the theatre. Did you expect Edward to pass the matter over to me, Miss Smith? He was only too happy to join your party under the guise of assisting Gerald with the arrangements.'

This barrage of information undermined Phoebe's wrath still further. 'I was referring to their excursion to the Exeter Exchange the other day,' she said in weak accents. Good heavens! First Deverell pulled her nerves in two different directions; now her mind was being jostled to and fro as well. Had she misjudged him yet again?

'I have been a little concerned about Gerald,' she admitted, sending him a fleeting sidelong glance. The rather grim line lingering about his mouth made her feel positively guilty. 'But Mr Filby, at least, seems harmless enough.'

'Filby's all right,' he said impatiently. 'Good family, comfortable fortune which he doesn't show any signs of wasting. Gerald won't come to any harm with him—unless he tries emulating Filby's taste in clothes, of course. Then he'll have me to contend with.'

Not sure if he was jesting, Phoebe tried a tentative smile. It seemed to have about as much effect as a pin striking steel armour.

'Er. . .quite so, sir. And if you've been keeping an eye on him—'

'I know what Gerald's been doing, Miss Smith. I haven't been dogging his footsteps.'

'Well, I wouldn't expect you to, but—'

Before she could clarify the matter, a young, male voice hailed her from the Row.

'Good afternoon, Miss Smith. Capital day, isn't it?'

Deverell turned.

Phoebe couldn't see his expression, but her youthful acquaintance suddenly changed his mind about stopping to chat. Giving a hasty wave, he rode on, scarcely giving Phoebe enough time to call out, 'It certainly is, Lord Bradden,' before he departed at a fast trot.

'His mother,' she informed Deverell succinctly when he turned back to her, 'is your aunt's closest friend. We met them at Lady Grismead's yesterday.'

For all the notice he took of this statement, she might as well have saved her breath. His eyes glittered down at her from beneath frowning black brows. 'I permitted my wards to remain in London for one reason only, Miss Smith. That reason was not dictated by duty, mawkish sentiment or any of the other dozen reasons you can doubtless come up with. Do you understand me?'

'I understand you're in no mood to be even marginally polite, sir. To me or to anyone. No wonder Gerald displays such a lamentable want of conduct, if this is the sort of example set by other male Deverells. However, if you expect me to believe that you permitted your wards to remain in London because I threatened to leave, you will be sadly disappointed. A mere governess would have no influence on you, my lord.'

'You'd be surprised, Miss Smith,' he said grimly. 'Come on, let's follow my wards and that idiot, Filby, around the lake. I want to talk to you and if we continue to stand here, every fool in London will feel free to interrupt us.'

'The graciousness of your invitation leaves me breathless, sir. Or was it a summons? Whichever, I decline. I refuse to walk about Hyde Park with a man whose face resembles a thundercloud.'

To her utter astonishment, a reluctant smile started to dawn through the tempest.

'Miss Smith,' he said, shaking his head, 'you have a talent for confounding me at every turn. Does nothing intimidate you?'

'Is that what you were trying to do?' she countered, deftly dodging the question.

His smile turned rueful. 'Believe it or not, no.'

'Oh, I see. You only wished to terrify poor Mr Filby and Lord Bradden.'

He narrowed his eyes at her. 'Why do I have the feeling you're enjoying this?' he asked with a faint hint of menace. 'You know I won't dismiss you and you're making the most of it, aren't you?'

Phoebe smiled sweetly up at him, suddenly realising that, despite his terse speech of a moment ago, she *was* enjoying herself. It was no doubt reprehensible of her, and extremely improper behaviour for a governess, but sparring with Deverell was positively exhilarating.

She was about to continue the exercise when, without any warning whatsoever, he seized her by the arm and yanked her behind a stout oak.

'What in the world—? Will you kindly explain why I am being manhandled in this fashion, my lord?'

'It's Pendleton, driving his new greys.' Deverell seemed totally oblivious to her indignant splutterings. 'If we're fortunate, he didn't see us, but if he hails me, for God's sake don't tell him you're a governess.'

She stared at him. 'Have you run mad, sir? I *am* a governess.'

'Not any more. Now you're a companion.'

'Well, of all the— What has that to say to anything?'

When he didn't answer, Phoebe made a concerted effort to gather her scattered wits and tried again. 'I thought Lord Pendleton was your friend.'

Deverell spared her a quick glance. 'He is.'

'Well! If you go to these lengths to avoid conversing with your friends, I'm surprised you favoured poor Mr Filby with any discourse at all.'

His gaze snapped back to hers before she'd finished, his eyes fierce, glittering, and this time wholly focused on her face. Phoebe felt a jolt in the pit of her stomach; whether it was caused by fear, excitement or both, she wasn't sure.

'It was a near-run thing, if you must know, Miss Smith. Filby may consider himself fortunate that I didn't pound him into the grass.'

'Pound him—' Her voice failed her entirely. Then returned with a vengeance when his lips curled in a smile of diabolical satisfaction. 'You *have* run mad.'

'Very likely. Ah, Pendleton's gone. Let's get the devil away from—'

'Miss Smith! I say, Miss Smith! It *is* you! How happy I am to see you here.'

'Good God!' muttered Deverell. He sent an exasperated glance past her shoulder. 'How many more of your acquaintances are going to waylay us?'

'Well, if we hadn't been hiding from *your*—'

Phoebe turned on the words and felt her lips freeze in mid-speech. Wild notions of dashing around to the other side of the tree darted through her mind. Failing that, she would have been happy to dive into a flower bed and take her chances with the insect population.

The gentleman standing before her was the last person she wished to see. Tall and extremely thin, with a long neck and slightly hunched posture that had always put her forcibly in mind of a depressed crane, the soberly clad individual stood regarding her with a half-hopeful, half-anxious expression on his rather cadaverous face.

'Tobias Toombes,' he announced, looking rather more hopeful than anxious when she didn't immediately disclaim any knowledge of him. 'The curate at Upper—'

'Oh, yes, Mr Toombes, I remember. How. . .how very surprising to see you here.'

Toombes broke into a pleased smile that revealed a row of very white, tombstone-like teeth. 'I came up to Town to see my esteemed patron, Lord Portlake,' he confided in a hushed tone such as he might have used at a burial. 'I was, if you recall, Miss Smith, in London on a similar errand two years ago when that dreadful scand—'

'Yes, indeed,' she interrupted quickly. 'I did request the vicar to convey my farewells.' Aware of Deverell beside her, listening to every word, she racked her brains for something else to say—preferably in the way of another farewell.

Nothing particularly clever occurred to her. Especially when Toombes took her hand in a bony clasp.

'How very like you, my dear Miss Smith,' he intoned, pressing her fingers painfully. He lowered his voice. 'That you would think to send a farewell at such a time. I was never more shocked in my life to hear what had befallen you. What you must have suffered! Mr Dorridge told me the entire story, but I *know* you could not have been at fault, whatever ill-natured gossip may say.'

'Well. . .'

'If there is anything I can do for you. Anything at all. . .'

'You're a little late,' Deverell interposed in a voice that sent Phoebe's heart leaping into her throat. Suddenly noticing that Toombes still held her hand, she snatched it back.

'Oh, my goodness, how very rude of me. My lord, may I present Mr Toombes, the curate of. . .um. . .that

is to say. . .thank you so much for your kindness, Mr
Toombes. . .but I'm employed by Lord Deverell now as
governess to his nieces. No, not governess. I mean companion. Yes, companion. Isn't that right, my lord?'

Deverell raised a brow. 'You seem to be somewhat
confused about the matter, Miss Smith.'

'Yes, well, these things can get very confusing,
can't they?'

'So it seems.'

'My lord.' Toombes was bowing with great ceremony.
'Please allow me to apologise for approaching Miss
Smith in this unorthodox manner. My surprise at seeing
one whom I thought had been cast friendless upon the
world—'

'Where did you say you were from?' Deverell interrupted with blunt despatch.

Phoebe groaned silently and raised her eyes
heavenward.

'Upper Biddlecombe, my lord. I am the curate there,
but thanks to the kindness of my most illustrious patron,
Lord Portlake, I am shortly to be presented with the
living.' He turned to Phoebe and bowed even lower than
before. 'Miss Smith, may I be so bold as to ask if I may
call upon you to discuss such a momentous change in
my circumstances? I—'

'Oh, Mr Toombes, I wouldn't wish to delay your
return for the world. Think of your parishioners, sir.
How they must be missing you. Besides, I feel it would
not be proper in me to be entertaining visitors at my
place of employment.'

'Oh, dear. Yes, yes, you are right, Miss Smith.'
Toombes looked momentarily discouraged at this set-
back, but then bared his teeth again in a very determined
smile. 'But I shall be in Town for a few days and shall
hope for another chance meeting. Do you walk in the
Park every day?'

'No, she doesn't, Toombes, so don't bother lying in
wait.' Deverell took Phoebe's arm in a firm grip. 'Shall

we continue on our way, Miss Smith? We have a great deal to discuss. I'm sure Mr Toombes will excuse us.'

'Oh, certainly, my lord, certainly.' Toombes started bowing again, then realised he was bowing to empty air. 'I shall look for you again, Miss Smith,' he called plaintively as she was marched away.

'Don't even think about looking back,' Deverell ordered, as she went to do just that. 'He's an obnoxious mushroom who doesn't need encouragement.'

'I was merely trying not to be rude,' Phoebe retorted, trying instead to think of a way to avoid the questions rattling almost audibly in the air around her. After one glance at the implacable determination on Deverell's face, she decided escape was the only solution. She could always come back for the twins when she'd got rid of him.

'And speaking of rudeness, my lord, I have had enough of it for one day.' She tried to yank her arm free. 'Our discussion will have to wait.'

'Oh, no, Miss Smith. You're not slipping through my fingers that easily.'

She yanked harder. 'I'm not trying to slip,' she muttered through clenched teeth. 'I'm trying to wrench.'

He stopped walking, brows lifting as he glanced down at his long fingers wrapped about her arm as if only now noticing the strength of his grip. She was released immediately.

'My apologies, Miss Smith.' He frowned at the way she flexed her arm. 'Did I hurt you?'

Deciding she was still in one piece, Phoebe patted herself down in the manner of a small, ruffled bird. 'Of course not, my lord. What is a bruise or two?'

He winced. 'Yes, I deserved that. I'm sorry, Miss Smith. It was certainly not my intention to hurt you.' His mouth twisted. 'Strange though it may seem, manhandling women is not something I do on a regular basis.'

Phoebe looked up at him, surprised, all notions of

escape arrested by the oddly bitter note in his voice.

'That doesn't seem strange to me at all, sir,' she said quietly.

His gaze rested rather frowningly on her face. 'Thank you. It's no excuse for my lamentable manners, but I've had an extremely busy and. . .frustrating week.'

He'd had a bloody awful week, Sebastian amended silently. And having the cause of it looking up at him with big, searching eyes wasn't improving matters.

So far, he had not discovered one single fact about Phoebe that he didn't already know. And as if that wasn't frustrating enough, images of supple slenderness, a sweetly curved mouth and deep brown eyes that glowed with golden lights one moment and held shadowed secrets the next, were invading his dreams with increasingly detailed frequency.

'At least you haven't been busy on your wards' behalf, my lord. Nothing disastrous has happened. Yet.'

Her words came to him through the fog of his thoughts. 'Depends what you consider disastrous,' he muttered. *He* knew what was disastrous. A man in dire need of replacing his last mistress because he had no intention of seducing an innocent girl who was, in a sense, under his protection, only to find himself utterly indifferent to every eligible candidate he'd encountered in a week of intensive hunting.

That was disastrous.

'Well, I suppose we can overlook Gerald becoming intoxicated,' Phoebe continued, her mind clearly on more elevated calamities. 'Mr Filby seems to think it won't happen again, and since Gerald is now too occupied to indulge in foolish pranks and isn't wealthy enough to be lured to those dreadful gambling houses one hears of, what else is there?'

Sebastian regarded her broodingly. 'Women.'

She blinked at him. 'Women? But Gerald hasn't met any women. Except for the twins' friends, of course, and he's shown no interest in them. It's just as well, really, since he'll be going up to Oxford soon.'

Sebastian clenched his jaw and prayed for patience. 'Then we have nothing to worry about, do we, Miss Smith?'

Tilting her chin, she glared at him. 'There is no need to bite my head off, sir. It was you who wanted this discussion, if you recall.'

'That is perfectly correct. There are, however, more subjects of interest than my wards.'

Her glare immediately turned mutinous. And defensive. And wary.

Sebastian watched the succession of emotions flicker across her face and clamped his teeth shut on a blistering curse. Wonderful! Now he'd scared her into total silence.

Damn it, he hadn't lost his temper, or even let it slip, in fifteen years, but as soon as he'd called on Phoebe, only to find himself obliged to follow her to the park where she seemed happy to chat with every second male in the place, his vaunted self-control had disintegrated under a cannon blast of sheer primitive possessiveness.

He'd been behaving like something out of a cave ever since. Such behaviour was not likely to win Phoebe's trust. And if he was to discover the source of the shadows in her eyes, her trust was essential.

Leashing the primitive beast inside him that strained to tell her what he intended to do and then set about doing it, he offered her his arm.

'On the other hand, Miss Smith, your devotion to duty is just what one would expect of you. Shall we go on? I believe my wards can't be too far ahead of us.'

She eyed him with such a combination of suspicion and scepticism on her expressive little face that Sebastian's sense of humour got the better of him. He smiled.

The peace-offering wasn't returned. She accepted his arm, still in silence, and started walking again, eyes front.

Swallowing this set-down, Sebastian matched her pace while he considered various strategies.

The silence continued.

'Capital day,' he remarked at last.

Her lips twitched.

'Obliging of Filby to take the girls off our hands for half an hour.'

She pursed her mouth into a prim bow that made him want to kiss her witless. That necessitated a few seconds in which to regain his control.

'Unfortunate name for a curate,' he observed after a moment.

She choked.

'Especially with those teeth.'

Phoebe broke into giggles.

Sebastian felt himself start to grin like an idiot. 'That's better,' he said. 'I thought I'd terrified you into permanent silence, Miss Smith.'

'Very unlikely, I'm afraid, my lord.' She sent him a droll look. 'After two years with Deverells, I'm beyond terror. Besides, I could never be terrified of you.'

The expression that flashed into Deverell's blue-green gaze mirrored her own surprise at the confident statement. But it was true, Phoebe thought, bemused. She had no trouble believing Deverell could be dangerous. He was perfectly capable of making her extremely nervous. But she knew, beyond any doubt, that she would never be truly afraid of him.

'I'm pleased to hear you say that. Miss Smith,' he said, almost purring the words. A gleam came into his eyes that caused a sudden, and, she feared, belated resurgence of caution. 'In that case, I'm sure you won't mind clarifying a small point for me. Where the devil is Little Puddleton, or wherever Toombes' unfortunate flock resides?'

'Upper Biddlecombe,' Phoebe mumbled. She searched for a distraction and had to concede defeat. 'A very obscure village in Dorset, sir. You wouldn't know it. Dear me, how did we ever wander so far from the subject of your wards? What was it you wished to discuss? Gerald's hectic social schedule? The fact that Mr Charlton is calling almost every day? Or—'

'Why don't we start with the dreadful scandal that apparently rocked Upper Biddlecombe two years ago?' he suggested smoothly.

Phoebe promptly stumbled over her own feet. When she glanced up, steadied by the steely support of Deverell's arm, she encountered a smile that could only be described as one of fiendish anticipation.

'What dastardly crime did you commit, Miss Smith, that caused you to be cast friendless upon the world?'

Chapter Five

'That remark, sir, was a gross exaggeration.' Phoebe shifted her gaze to a clump of rhododendrons and affected a tone of airy unconcern. 'You may have noticed that Mr Toombes tends to speak in flowery periods.'

When this defence elicited nothing more than polite but relentless silence, she scowled up at him. 'It's true I was dismissed from my last post, but it was due to a most unfortunate misunderstanding.'

Deverell's smile took on a faint edge. 'It usually is. Who misunderstood whom?'

She sighed. 'I'm afraid the squire's son forgot he was expected to offer for my employer's eldest daughter and. . .er. . .'

'Offered for you instead?'

'It was not the same sort of offer,' she said primly. 'But even though I told Mrs Dorridge I had no intention of listening to *any* offer, and had not encouraged the young man in the slightest, she had made up her mind that I was a scheming, ambitious, unscrupulous— Well, I won't repeat the rest.'

Despite the warmth of the sun, Phoebe shivered slightly when she remembered the last hideous interview with her enraged and threatening employer. Sensing the sharp glance Deverell gave her, she lifted her chin. 'Anyway, it's all in the past now. I can't offer any proof of my innocence, of course, but—'

'You don't need to, Miss Smith,' he growled. 'You're so damned innocent you shouldn't be allowed out except on a leash.'

'A *leash*! Well! Of all the—'

'What did you do to discourage the lout? Suddenly start dressing like a dowd and refuse to speak to him?'

She swallowed the rest of her protest. 'Er. . .yes.'

'Exactly as I thought. You little goose, didn't you realise he'd immediately take that as a challenge?'

'Indeed?' She had realised, of course—too late. 'Perhaps you can tell me what else I could have done, my lord.'

He immediately disarmed her with a crooked smile. 'Not a thing,' he admitted. 'I'm sorry, Miss Smith, I wasn't being critical, but I suspect it wasn't the first time a disaster of that nature had befallen you. Am I right?'

Phoebe blushed. 'I wasn't dismissed from the position prior to that,' she stated with great dignity. 'I resigned.'

He looked down at her. 'Because?'

'Because the master of the house decided he wanted an extra mistress,' she muttered. She winced at the indelicacy of the statement, but then decided if there was anything capable of shocking Deverell, she, for one, would be mightily surprised. A thought occurred that had her rallying.

'In any event, my lord, what is the use of me finally learning a lesson and dressing unbecomingly from the start, only to have you oversetting the scheme?'

'There's a slight difference, Miss Smith.'

'Oh? What, pray?'

'You now have a watchdog.'

A surprisingly thrilling little tremor shivered through her. The sensation was oddly disturbing.

'I would be grateful if we could avoid any more animal metaphors,' she said faintly. 'First I need a leash, now you're a watchdog. I'm perfectly capable of looking after myself, my lord. Or I would be if you'd leave my wardrobe alone.'

'I think we're beginning to argue in circles. But since we're discussing your wardrobe, would you mind telling me what happened to the flounces on that gown?'

'Flounces?' Phoebe's brain whirled dizzily as she tried to follow this leap in the conversation.

'That dress had flounces on the hem when it left Cecile's.'

'Good heavens, my lord, I had no idea you took such a. . .a keen interest in ladies' fashions.'

He smiled down at her, the glinting light in his eyes causing another of those strange little *frissons* of half-nervous excitement to shimmer through her. She wasn't sure why. His smile wasn't exactly wicked. It wasn't exactly threatening. It wasn't exactly. . .well, she didn't know what it was. . .exactly.

'If you must know,' she said, hurriedly pushing the question aside, 'I removed the flounces for the same reason I had that plume removed the other day. Flounces are frivolous.'

'Good God! Flounces are frivolous. Plumes are provocative. I had no idea a companion's life was so hedged about by rules and restrictions. What do you do for fun and excitement, Miss Smith? Sleep?'

Phoebe elevated her nose. 'I read novels, my lord. Or I used to,' she amended, abandoning dignity for the truth. 'Since residing with your wards, I've discovered that drama of some description seems to occur on a daily basis. The experience has taught me that I much prefer a quiet, uneventful life. Constant excitement can be extremely wearing, you know.'

'Wearing?' His voice dropped to a deep, husky note that made her feel as if she was suddenly enclosed in darkest velvet. 'Yes, possibly. But what about excitement in small doses, Miss Smith?'

'S. . .small doses?'

He smiled lazily. 'Well, to begin with.'

'Uh. . .um. . .'

'For instance, was I wrong earlier when I guessed you enjoyed turning the governess on me?'

'Ohh.' Phoebe blushed and silently berated herself. Goodness, for a minute there she'd thought. . .

She hurriedly consigned what she'd thought to oblivion. 'I see you've found me out, my lord. What can I do but confess?' Stiffening knees that had gone weak with relief, she smiled confidingly up at him. 'Perhaps I enjoy talking with you, sir, because I'm secure in the knowledge that you won't make any undesirable advances towards me. You see, I've never had that freedom before.'

There was a very odd silence.

'I hope I haven't taken advantage,' she queried, suddenly anxious.

'Uh, no, Miss Smith.' Sebastian eyed her rather curiously. 'Yes, I did promise not to pester you with the undesirable advances that follow sorry details of infelicitous relationships, didn't I?' *He must have been mad.* 'I take it you didn't consider the episode in the hackney the other day to be an advance?'

'Oh, no. I know you were only testing me.'

'Testing you,' he repeated carefully.

'Naturally you wished to be sure that your nieces' companion was a respectable female.'

He stared at her, fascinated. 'Naturally.'

'Well?' She looked up at him with a quizzical smile. 'Weren't you? Testing me, that is.'

Sebastian gazed down into guileless brown eyes and had to fight a sensation of drowning. God, a man could lose himself in those warm golden depths and not even notice until it was too late. He must be losing his mind. Thanks to that idiotic promise, Miss Phoebe Smith had just managed to completely flummox him. A state of affairs that he couldn't recall ever occurring before. Obviously, unsatisfied desire was a more serious problem than he'd supposed. First he'd lost interest in other women; now he was losing control of the situation.

'You could say it was something along those lines,' he murmured at last, completely incapable of disillusioning her.

'I thought so.' Phoebe pushed aside a sharp little twinge of disappointment. Really. What foolishness. She had no reason to feel disappointed. Deverell had turned out to be more understanding than she'd supposed. He'd believed her innocent of any wrongdoing—even if his remarks on the subject were less than polite—and he even seemed somewhat protective.

Not that she needed protecting, Phoebe told herself hastily. But just once in a while—only for a few minutes, of course—it was a nice, warm feeling to have.

'Thank you for believing in me,' she continued earnestly. 'I've always dreaded anyone finding out about. . .well, what happened. Most people tend to blame the governess in such cases, and there's really nothing one can do. Protests only make it worse.'

'You may not be able to do a great deal, Miss Smith; however, should I ever encounter the squire's son from Lower Fiddleton, he will apologise to you immediately or be torn limb from limb.'

Phoebe giggled. 'Upper Biddlecombe, my lord. Oh, dear, I suppose I should tell you that violent retribution is not the answer, but I must confess I would have found it rather satisfying to have *planted him a facer*, myself. Do I have that right?'

He slanted an amused glance down at her. 'You do. I take it Gerald has sullied your ears with boxing cant. How improper.'

'I believe you're teasing me, sir. No doubt you consider me *overly* proper, but governesses must be forever mindful of decorum. We have our reputations to think of, you know.'

'Indeed you do. So was it after the episode in Little Muddlecombe that you changed your name to Smith?'

Phoebe stopped walking so abruptly her hand fell from Deverell's arm. This time she felt no inclination to correct him. The soft, totally unexpected question sent shock racing through every nerve-ending. Her mind went blank. Her lungs constricted.

'I. . .I don't know what you mean, sir. My name *is* Smith. I told you. . .' Her voice dried up.

Deverell took her hand in a warm clasp, but made no move to walk on. 'Haven't I shown you that I can be trusted with the truth, Miss Smith?' he asked very gently. 'I am no fool, you know. Indeed, it would be plain to the meanest intelligence—'

'My lord,' she interrupted, shaken immeasurably by his sudden gentleness. She hadn't expected it. Hadn't known he was capable of it. And yet. . .

But even as an image of the sculpted Psyche in his library flashed before her mind's eye, even as the bitterness in his tone when he'd apologised for bruising her echoed faintly in her mind, words that would keep him at a distance were tumbling from her lips. 'I don't know what has given you the impression that— In short, sir, I can only repeat that Smith is my name. That *is* the truth.'

And it was, she comforted herself. More or less.

His intent, searching gaze held her captive for several seconds longer. 'Then I can only apologise for upsetting you, Miss Smith.' He released her hand and drew back. 'Shall we catch up to my wards? I believe they're just ahead of us.'

'By all means, sir.' It was all the answer Phoebe could manage. The slight coolness in Deverell's tone caused her throat to close up and her eyes to sting. The sudden sense of loss was piercing, a sharp pain in her chest, but what else could she have said? She'd made a promise of her own, and even though the promise had been forced, surely it had still to be honoured.

While her beleaguered brain was struggling with this ticklish question, they overtook the small animated party ahead of them. To her mingled distraction and relief, Phoebe was instantly surrounded by Deverells wanting to indulge in such diverse entertainments as a visit to a bookshop to purchase political treatises on the rights of women, and an excursion to Astley's Amphitheatre to see the equestrienne displays. Cressida was suspiciously quiet, but Phoebe was too beset to worry about this unusual state of affairs.

As they made their way back to the Stanhope Gate, where Mr Filby took his leave of them, she made sure there was always someone between herself and Deverell. It was a depressingly easy task. He seemed to have the same intention.

Phoebe felt so ridiculously low by the time they were standing in the street again that she didn't even raise her voice in protest when she heard Gerald pestering his uncle to take him to Jackson's Boxing Saloon.

'Perhaps some time next week, Gerald,' Deverell said brusquely as he turned towards her. 'Miss Smith, thank you for a most instructive afternoon.' He took the hand she held out before she thought better of it. 'No doubt we shall meet again soon.'

'No doubt,' she agreed, avoiding his direct gaze.

He raised her hand to his lips, dropped a kiss into her palm and released her. 'By the way,' he said softly, 'have your abigail sew those flounces back on your gown before we do.'

He turned and was more than halfway down the street before Phoebe managed to get her mouth closed again.

It was Cressida who brought her back to earth. 'What abigail?' she asked.

Phoebe made a concerted effort to pull herself together. It wasn't altogether successful. Her mind seemed suspended in the moment when Deverell had dropped that casual kiss into her palm as if. . .as if. . .

'Your uncle has a very odd notion of companions, Cressy,' she managed at last, abandoning any attempt at rational thought. 'I expect he meant the girl Mr Charlton hired to assist the housemaid. Come now. We'd better go home before everyone wonders why we're all standing about in the street.'

'You don't need me to escort you home, do you, Phoebe?' Gerald started edging away along the street. 'Think I'll take a look-in at the Pigeonhole. Fellow I met at Reggie's club took me there last night. Interesting place. I'll see you tomorrow. Perhaps we can go to Astley's.'

'Astley's? Well—'

But Gerald was already out of earshot.

'Oh, dear,' Phoebe said again, gazing after him. 'The Pigeonhole. Well, that sounds like a nice, harmless place. Perhaps they serve ices.'

'Never mind about Gerald.' Theo seized Phoebe's sleeve and gave it an urgent tug. 'I want to go to Hatchard's on our way home, Phoebe. Edward says they have an excellent selection of political treatises on all sorts of subjects, and—'

'"Edward"? Oh, dear.'

'I don't know why you bother with those pamphlets, Theo.' Cressida frowned at her sister. 'You only annoy people when you quote Mary Wollstonecraft all over the place. The theatre is where people listen. I'll sway thousands. Millions. I'll be famous. I'll—'

'Oh, dear.'

'We're going to Hatchard's, Cressy. The theatre can wait.'

Taking charge in a manner strongly reminiscent of Lady Grismead, Theodosia took hold of her sister and started off in the direction of Piccadilly.

Feeling quite incapable of protesting, Phoebe followed, only vaguely listening to the argument which continued unabated. The words 'persecuted' and 'suffering' wafted to her ears, but whether in relation to thwarted theatrical ambitions or oppressed females was not clear. Nor was she inclined to enquire. She wondered if Hatchard's had a nice, quiet room set aside for customers who badly needed peace and solitude.

She devoutly hoped so. It seemed to her that every

time she encountered Deverell she needed a period of calm reflection in which to recover.

The following morning, Phoebe found herself in possession of all the peace and solitude she could have desired. The breakfast table, usually a popular and lively place, was entirely devoid of Deverells.

Since the butler had been summoned from Kerslake Park along with a half dozen or so other servants, and had been with the family for years, Phoebe had no hesitation in questioning him about this departure from the normal.

'The young ladies have gone out, miss,' he said in answer to her query.

'Already? But it's scarcely nine o'clock. Did Gerald go with them, Thripp?'

'No, miss. I understand his lordship is still asleep.' Thripp pursed his lips and allowed himself a small frown of disapproval. 'Master Gerald. . .I mean, his lordship, did not retire until dawn.'

'Dawn! Well, I suppose we should let him sleep. Did the twins say where they were going?'

'Not in so many words, miss, but Lady Cressida mentioned something about being thrown out into the snow.'

Phoebe gazed towards the window in astonishment. Beyond the open casement, bordering green lawns and gravel paths, gaily coloured autumn blooms nodded in the sunshine. 'But it's the middle of September.'

'Precisely so, miss.' Thripp's tone lowered to a note of heavy foreboding. 'Her ladyship may have been rehearsing.'

'Rehearsing!' She looked back at the butler in dismay. 'Oh, no! The theatres! She wouldn't! Would she?'

Thripp had no trouble following these horrified utterances. 'That I couldn't say, miss. But I did happen to notice that Lady Cressida was dressed rather strangely.'

'Dressed rather— In what way?'

'She wore a cloak, miss, and was heavily veiled.

Before she lowered the veil, however, I caught a glimpse of her face.' Thripp paused for effect before continuing in a voice of doom. 'I couldn't be sure, miss, but I think her ladyship's countenance was painted.'

'Painted! Oh, my goodness, they *have* gone to the theatres. For heaven's sake, Thripp, why didn't you stop them? No, never mind,' she added when the butler turned a look of reproach on her. It was no use chastising Thripp. He was elderly and not overly blessed with quickness of wit. 'I know they wouldn't have listened. I'll have to go after them at once. Send the footman out to summon a hackney, if you please, while I fetch my pelisse and bonnet.'

'Yes, miss. Shall I send a message to his lordship?'

Phoebe hesitated, trying to push aside her worry so she could think. 'No, let him sleep. There aren't that many reputable theatres in London. I'm sure I'll find the girls quite quickly.'

'I hope so, miss, but I was referring to Lord Deverell.'

'*Lord Deverell*! No! Good heavens, no! He is not to be told about this. Do you hear me, Thripp?'

Inured by long association with Deverells to alarums and starts of a similar nature, Thripp merely nodded obediently and left the dining-room.

Phoebe took a moment to finish her coffee on the principle that she'd need the sustenance, before dashing upstairs to fling on her old pelisse and her bonnet. No doubt Deverell would object to her attire, but this wasn't the time to be fashionable. When she ran downstairs again, a hackney was at the door. She wasted no time climbing into it and directing the driver to take her to Covent Garden.

Thripp stood on the front doorstep as she was driven away, looking mournfully after her. Phoebe wished his expression was a little more encouraging. She also wished she had some company. Even Miss Pomfret's presence would be preferable to sitting alone with her worried thoughts, but although Deverell had summoned

Cousin Clara to Town with the servants, Miss Pomfret, in a rare Deverell-like display of defiance, had taken refuge in her bed, citing nervous prostration and thus delaying her arrival.

Still, she wasn't seriously worried, Phoebe assured herself. After all, Theodosia was with her sister, and they would probably have to wait to see the managers of the various theatres. She would soon catch up with her charges.

But she did not catch up with them.

Three hours later, footsore and weary, Phoebe stood in a tiny malodorous court in the middle of a maze of streets and decided it was time to take stock of her situation.

It was not good. For one thing she was exhausted. She had called first at the Theatre Royal, Covent Garden, where she'd learned that her charges had been turned away by a charming but discouraging Charles Kemble, who had recently taken over as manager from his famous brother.

Undaunted, she had then repaired to the Theatre Royal, Drury Lane where, according to Mr Alfred Bunn, the manager, the twins had received a lecture on the impropriety of young ladies of quality seeking a career on the stage. Disinclined to believe they had taken this to heart, she had proceeded to the Theatre Royal, Haymarket, by then wondering why managers couldn't think of anything more original in the way of names for their playhouses.

Apparently they couldn't think of anything original in the way of lectures either. Her charges, it seemed, had received similar homilies to Mr Bunn's at the Haymarket, the Lyceum and the San Pareil.

'And I'll tell you what else they heard at the other theatres, miss,' Mr Scott of the San Pareil had added. 'The young lady's acting skills are rather too limited to tragedy and she won't take direction. I'm sure she does very well in amateur theatricals, but even if her station in life didn't prohibit her from the public stage, she wouldn't suit.'

'Do you think she might have abandoned the scheme?' Phoebe had asked hopefully.

But to her dismay, Mr Scott had no such good news to impart. Cressida had declared her intention of applying to every theatre in London.

'And some of them, miss, ain't what you'd call genteel,' Mr Scott had called after her.

Phoebe had just discovered precisely what he'd meant. After visiting a succession of lesser playhouses whose productions, while of an inferior nature, were at least respectable, she had finally been confronted by a bevy of scantily clad females rehearsing a very odd-looking tableau.

And the owner of the theatre, a rather oily individual, had seemed to think *she* was looking for employment.

After ascertaining that the man had not encountered any twins that morning, Phoebe had fled. Unfortunately, she had not taken note of where she was fleeing. And now, she realised, looking about her with a shiver, she was quite alone and completely lost somewhere in the labyrinth of courts and alleys surrounding Covent Garden.

No, not quite alone, she thought, glancing quickly over her shoulder. There was no one in sight—indeed, the rickety buildings surrounding the court appeared utterly vacant, their windows, darkened by the grime of years, reminding her unpleasantly of so many empty eye-sockets—but she was being watched. She felt it. The scrutiny of innumerable eyes was palpable, like a chilling brush of air across her skin.

The accompanying silence was even more unnerving.

There had been noise. She remembered a child's wail, quickly hushed; the clatter of a tin somewhere in an adjacent alley; a slow creak that might have been the closing of a door. But now silence hung over the small court like a shroud.

Phoebe frowned and took a firmer hold of her reticule. This would not do. She couldn't stand here dithering all day while hair-raising tales of the crime abounding in large cities chased one another through her head. She would find a shop somewhere and ask for directions.

Two exits led from the court. An archway beyond which she could see another smaller, dingier court, and a narrow alley. She couldn't remember running along the alley on her way here, but it looked the more promising of the two.

She had taken no more than a single step towards it when a door banged open directly behind her.

Phoebe squeaked and whirled about, her heart in her mouth.

A gentleman—yes, unmistakably a gentleman— stepped into the open, a slim ebony cane tucked under one arm while he drew on his gloves, quite as if he was preparing for a stroll in the Park.

She blinked. Once. Twice. And still couldn't believe the evidence of her eyes. In fact, so unexpected was the sight of such gentlemanly elegance in these mean surroundings that several seconds passed before she realised that he, too, was staring as if unable to believe his senses.

When his expression registered, she found herself stepping back a pace, her initial hope that here was someone who might help her receiving a severe jolt. The frozen rigidity of his features was out of all proportion to their encounter. He seemed shocked beyond measure; as if he gazed upon the utterly impossible rather than the startling and unusual.

Had there been anyone else in the court, she would have instantly turned to them, no matter how unsavoury and ruffianly their appearance.

Phoebe took a shaky breath and told herself not to be

foolish. There *was* no one else, and at least he was a gentleman.

'I. . .I wonder if you could help me, sir.' Her voice trembled and she stiffened her spine. 'I was trying to find the. . .the Market.' Yes, that would do. She could take a hackney from there.

The gentleman frowned at the sound of her voice, his pale, almost colourless blue eyes narrowing on her face as he came closer. 'You're lost?' he asked, his voice oddly hoarse. 'Who are you?'

Phoebe shifted uneasily. 'Yes,' she said, ignoring his second question. 'That is, I left the Birdcage Theatre by a side door and must have taken a wrong turning somewhere and. . .'

She let the words trail off. The strange expression of shock had gone but the gentleman was now staring at her in a way that put her forcibly in mind of a collector savouring the imminent possession of a rare specimen. She wanted to shrink into herself, and yet the stranger hadn't threatened her in any way.

But even as this reassuring thought occurred to her, his gaze travelled over her drab costume in a manner that suggested he was coming to some accurate conclusions about her circumstances.

'You must have come from the country,' he murmured.

Phoebe took another step back, tales of simple country girls lured to places of ill-repute and never heard of again promptly darting through her mind. 'If you wouldn't mind directing me to the Market,' she said firmly. 'I would be very grateful. This neighbourhood is not exactly comfortable.' And nor are you, she added silently.

'The Market. Yes.' His gaze returned to her face and lingered, seeming to study each individual feature. 'How very extraordinary are the machinations of fate,' he murmured, and smiled. Quite a pleasant, unthreatening smile. She didn't know why she shivered.

'Sir. . .'

'Yes. Yes, indeed. The Market.' His smile turned faintly chiding. 'This is no place for a young lady. Most reckless of you, my dear, to venture away from the main thoroughfare.'

Phoebe was too busy straining her ears at a faint noise to object to his familiar mode of address. Had that been a shuffling footstep over to her left?

'But first—though I feel introductions are hardly necessary—perhaps we should observe the niceties. Viscount Crowhurst at your service, Miss. . .er. . .'

'Smith,' she said briefly, scarcely listening to him. Yes, that had been a shuffle. The feeling of being watched grew stronger, as though the watchers had pressed closer, or perhaps there were more of them.

Her companion seemed to have no awareness of danger at all. 'Smith,' he repeated slowly, thoughtfully. 'Ah. Yes. Yes, of course. It would be. And you were looking for a theatre, my dear?'

'Not precisely. Sir, I'm sorry if I seem impolite, but I'm employed by Lord Deverell and—'

'*Deverell*?'

The name exploded in the air with such force that Phoebe jerked back instinctively. For a moment she could only stare, her mind reeling beneath the flash of sheer hatred in Crowhurst's pale eyes before he swiftly lowered his lashes.

She shook her head, unable to believe what she'd seen. Surely she was mistaken. Infuriating though Deverell could be, he could hardly arouse such bitter enmity in three short months.

'I'm companion to his nieces,' she ventured, beginning to feel rather like someone groping her way through an impenetrable fog.

Crowhurst raised his eyes to hers again, his expression impassive now but watchful. 'Is that so, Miss Smith?' He seemed to dismiss the statement with a gesture. 'Well, that shouldn't present us with any problems. I

don't know how it comes about that Deverell has abandoned you in this sorry neighbourhood, but I hope you'll
allow me to escort you—'

He was cut off by the sound of heavy footsteps ringing
on the cobblestones of the alley. Already stunned speechless by Crowhurst's assumption that Deverell would
abandon a woman in an area patently worse than sorry,
Phoebe barely had the wit to turn, heart pounding, as
she braced to confront whatever new danger was about
to show itself.

A heartbeat later, Deverell strode into the court, a
black scowl on his face, his fists clenched, and an
expression in his eyes that gave Phoebe a glimpse into
the hell awaiting anyone who crossed him.

She had never seen a more welcome sight in her life.
Ignoring the waves of lethal menace emanating from
him, she flew across the court as if her feet had grown
wings. 'Oh, my lord!'

He caught her, his hands tightening almost brutally
around her shoulders. For an instant she thought he was
going to pull her closer, to pull her into his arms and
hold her. The impression was so strong she cried out,
stunned by the intense longing that swept through her
for him to do just that.

And then it was gone. With a stifled oath he swung
her to one side, leaving his right hand free. Before she
could blink he drew a pistol from his pocket and levelled
it with one smooth motion.

Immediately a sense of movement rippled through the
court. There was still no sign of life, but it seemed to
her that the invisible watchers took a collective step back.

'A wise precaution, my lord.'

Crowhurst strolled over to them, his cane swinging
gently from one hand. 'But the people here know me
and have a certain respect for my own weapon.' The
cane was swung again before being tucked under his arm.

'Sword-stick,' said Deverell, nodding. He lowered the
pistol to his side but kept it in plain sight.

'Yes. One doesn't venture into these streets unarmed unless one is a fool. Or ignorant of the dangers,' he added, glancing at Phoebe. 'Your. . .er. . .nieces' companion, I believe.'

Deverell's eyes narrowed.

'Yes, quite so. I was about to offer my assistance, but it now appears unnecessary. I'm Crowhurst, by the bye. I believe we met at the Waterbrooks some weeks ago.'

Phoebe gaped at him, astounded by the unctuous civility. She *must* have been mistaken a moment ago. No man could look like that—so filled with hatred one minute and then able to hide it so completely the next.

And yet, there was something. . .

'I'm obliged to you,' Deverell said shortly, reclaiming her attention. 'I'm sure you'll understand that my thanks must necessarily be brief.'

'Of course.' Crowhurst turned to Phoebe, his pale eyes boring into hers before she could avoid his gaze. 'I shall look forward to meeting you again, Miss Smith. Please be assured that I will not say a word to anyone. About. . .anything.' A faint smile curled his lips. He inclined his head, then turned and walked away.

Without so much as a glance at her, Deverell stepped back into the alley, drawing Phoebe with him. Dazed, her mind in a state of suspension, she stumbled after him down the laneway. Across another court. Along an alley so narrow the upper storeys of the houses almost met overhead.

Whispers hushed through the air behind them. She caught a glimpse of a face, pale, furtive, before a door was slammed shut. A pile of refuse appeared at her feet. She dodged it, then blinked, startled, when they stepped onto a wider street lined with shops and coffee-houses and light struck her eyes.

A hackney was waiting at the curb, its driver leaning down from his perch to peer anxiously into the gloomy tunnel from which they'd emerged.

'Ah, there ye be, gov'nor. I was gettin' a mite worried.

The rookeries ain't no place for the likes o'ye, even if ye are a sight larger than most. I see ye found the young lady.'

Deverell's pistol vanished into his pocket as smoothly as it had appeared. He yanked open the door of the cab, stuffed Phoebe unceremoniously into it and climbed in after her. 'Park Street,' he said curtly to the driver and slammed the door shut.

She suddenly realised he hadn't addressed one word to her since he'd come upon her in the court. One swift glance at his face told her why. He was furious. Savagely, relentlessly, furious.

Chapter Six

Silent, deadly, his rage lashed through the interior of the hackney, filling the small space until the air felt too heavy to breathe.

A fine tremor vibrated through Phoebe's limbs. The thought of explaining the situation was almost impossible. This was no mere fit of male annoyance. Deverell's brief moment of gentleness yesterday was as distant as the stars, nor was there any hint that humour would come to her rescue. If the rigid line of his jaw was anything to go by, only the most formidable control was keeping his fury leashed.

She did not, however, have a lot of choice. Deverell's nieces were still missing, and she was too anxious to remain silent.

Taking a deep, steadying breath, Phoebe lifted her chin. 'Theo and Cressy. . .?'

'Both at home.'

'Oh, thank goodness!' Relief coursed through her, making her sag limply back against the squabs. She straightened immediately. His voice had been as chilling as the frigid depths of the ocean, but in his eyes blue lightning flashed across the raging sea-green surface.

'I know you must be very angry with them, my lord, but—'

'Angry with them?'

'Yes, and it's perfectly understandable, but please

don't be too harsh with them. Remember, Theo and Cressy are not used to being disciplined or checked in any way and—'

'You think I'm angry with *them*?'

'Well. . .' She blinked at him, suddenly wary. 'Aren't you?'

A sound that could only be described as a snarl erupted from his throat. 'This may come as a surprise to you, Miss Smith, but at the moment the thought uppermost in my mind is not the twins' transgressions. It's you I'm going to strangle. As soon as I get you alone.'

'Me! But—'

'What in the name of God did you think you were doing, chasing after my nieces in that reckless fashion? You should have notified me immediately. But no! You'd rather put yourself in danger because you didn't bloody well think first!'

'There is no need to swear at me,' Phoebe said, tilting her chin still further. She promptly lowered it again when the lightning in his eyes seemed to leap straight out at her. He looked as if he might strangle her there and then. It was probably not wise to offer any inducement. Such as unrestricted access to her throat.

'And I did think,' she muttered. 'In fact, I was doing quite well until that dreadful man at the Birdcage kept pestering me to join his tableau.'

'You went into the Birdcage?' The words were enunciated with ominous precision.

'I went to all the theatres. And since they were situated on relatively busy streets, I didn't see anything rash in my doing so. Besides, I was in a hackney most of the time.'

'*God-damn it! The Honeypot isn't on a busy street and you didn't drive there in a hackney!*'

The cab slowed down. 'Everythin' orl right in there, guv'nor?' the driver enquired, poking his face through the hatch.

'Keep driving!' Deverell roared.

The man vanished.

Phoebe scarcely noticed that the pace picked up considerably. 'Honeypot? What Honeypot?'

'That theatre where you met Crowhurst,' he snarled. 'How did you get there? Fly?'

'Good heavens! That was a *theatre*?'

Deverell eyed the stunned expression on her face and half-raised his clenched fists. 'My God, I ought to give myself the pleasure of strangling you now. It would be extraordinarily satisfying.'

'Oh, no, I beg you will not,' Phoebe said hurriedly. She eyed his fists until he lowered them, then tried an appealing smile. 'Only think of the scandal, sir.'

This attempt at diverting him didn't have quite the result she'd hoped. He ground his teeth audibly.

'You think the discovery of your stabbed or strangled body in one of the most dangerous parts of the city wouldn't have caused a scandal? You little idiot! Even the girls had enough sense to avoid such places.'

'They did?' Phoebe's jaw dropped. 'You mean I searched for hours. . .'

Her defiance collapsed like a deflated balloon, taking her voice with it. She sagged back against the squabs again, torn between outrage and thankfulness that her charges were safe. 'Where did you find them, sir? *How* did you find them?'

Deverell sent her a look of grim meaning. 'After your visit to Covent Garden, Charles Kemble realised who the girls were and immediately despatched a message to me. I caught them at the Parisian, only to be informed that there was still another female running around loose. Edward took the twins home while I began the search for you. Of course, if I'd known you preferred the company to be found at the Birdcage and its ilk, I would've saved myself the trouble.'

Phoebe grimaced. 'You must know I wasn't there by choice.'

'Then why the devil didn't you send for me the instant you knew what had happened?' he yelled.

Shaken, knowing she was in the wrong but too overset to admit it, she yelled right back. 'I didn't want to bother you!'

'*Not bother me?* You came up to London for the express purpose of bothering me, Miss Smith. Why have a change of heart now?'

'Ohh. . . I. . .' Phoebe felt tears flood her eyes and turned her face away at once, horrified. Her swift burst of temper disintegrated as abruptly as if Deverell had struck her. And yet his question was entirely logical. She had to answer. She mustn't let him see. . . She mustn't let him know she'd been nervous about meeting him again, when she didn't know precisely why.

'I thought I would find the girls quite easily,' she finally managed, clenching her hands until her nails dug into her palms. She risked a glance at him from beneath her lashes and saw that his savage expression hadn't abated one bit. 'I'm very sorry you've been put to so much trouble, my lord.'

'God damn it, Phoebe, don't you dare apologise.'

'What?' She gaped at him, hastily blinking back another threatening tear. 'Why not?'

'Because I'd be obliged to forgive you and you're not getting off so easily.' His eyes narrowed abruptly on her face. 'Damn it, are you crying?'

She gave a surreptitious sniff. 'Of course not, sir. Why would I be crying when everything has turned out all right in the end? I am merely tired.'

He continued to eye her rather narrowly for a minute, then said in a milder tone, 'I'm not surprised. Perhaps next time you'll think twice before embarking on such an ill-considered action.'

'Yes, well, I dare say such a situation will not occur again.' She blinked away the last traces of moisture, thankful that both his rage and her tears seemed to have passed. Now if she could only get her insides to stop quaking. 'What do you intend doing with your nieces, my lord?'

'I haven't decided, although locking them away some- where for an indefinite period has a certain appeal.'

'They'd only break out,' Phoebe warned him. 'Besides, Lady Grismead is giving a dance party for them tomorrow afternoon. They can't possibly cry off at such short notice.'

'A dance party. To which you're taking them.'

'Well, of course.' Hoping this information wouldn't start another outburst, she summoned up an expression of earnest appeal. 'Dance parties are quite unexception- able, sir. Only very young girls who are not yet out, such as Lord Braddon's sister and Lady Yarwood's daughters, will be attending. It gives them an opportunity to practise various dances. Naturally, if there's a waltz, Theo and Cressy will be partnered by their brother.'

'If you can get him out of bed in time.'

She thought it prudent to ignore that remark.

Deverell continued to study her somewhat grimly for a moment. 'Lady Yarwood?'

'Yes, do you know her?'

He shrugged. 'We've met. I believe Crowhurst is some sort of connection of hers.'

'I doubt if Lord Crowhurst will be present at a party got up especially for young girls, sir.'

'He'll find a way to be there if he discovers you'll be attending.'

'What?' Phoebe's jaw dropped.

'You heard me.'

'I heard you, sir, but I don't understand your meaning. I'm sure Lord Crowhurst was merely being polite when he offered his assistance and—'

'Polite be damned. My arrival was the last thing he desired. You'd have seen it yourself if you hadn't been busy fleeing to me as if I was your last hope.'

'Oh-h-h!' Heat stung her cheeks, staining them a bright scarlet. 'I didn't. . . He wasn't. . .'

'You did and he was. He wants you, you little fool. Even in that ridiculous disguise.'

'I wondered when we'd get around to my clothes,' she muttered. When Deverell gave a derisive snort, she straightened her spine. 'I'm not a complete idiot, my lord. I mentioned your name almost at once in case Lord Crowhurst thought I was alone and friendless in London. Although, as it happened, he was a perfect gentleman even before I told him I was employed as your nieces' companion.'

'A fact he didn't believe for one minute until I confirmed it.'

Phoebe frowned.

'Don't bother trying to recall the words. The situation didn't call for any.'

'Oh, I see,' she retorted, stung to sarcasm. 'It was one of those male rituals that we females consider incomprehensible.'

'You don't need to comprehend it, Miss Smith. Just stay away from him.'

'I have no intention of encouraging Lord Crowhurst,' she declared. 'However, if I happen to see him again I can hardly cut the man dead when he offered to help me out of an extremely uncomfortable situation.'

Deverell's eyes narrowed again, but this time he didn't say anything.

Feeling as if she'd at least managed to uphold rational womanhood by having the last word, Phoebe shifted her gaze to the window. They were almost home, she was thankful to see. She would be glad to seek the sanctuary of her bedchamber where she could recover her composure away from rebellious wards and furious guardians.

However, as they swung into Park Street, a glimpse of a nursemaid and her two small charges staring agape at a passing dandy nudged another thought to the forefront of her mind. She remembered Crowhurst's odd familiarity and frowned, glancing across at Deverell.

He, too, was staring at the passing scene. Or, rather, scowling at it. The worst of his rage might have dissipated, but the hard line about his mouth and the deep furrow between his brows didn't invite polite conversation. It was probably unwise to continue with the subject of Crowhurst, but the question in her mind was strangely insistent.

'My lord?'

His gaze snapped to hers. 'What?'

She winced at the bitten-off syllable. 'I was wondering. . . Is there anyone in London who. . .looks like me?'

'I shouldn't think so, Miss Smith. I suspect you're unique.'

Phoebe didn't make the mistake of taking that as a compliment. Her own temper stirred. 'I mean,' she enunciated through set teeth, 'do I resemble anyone closely enough to invite comment?'

Her insistence deepened his frown, the gem-like glitter of his eyes turning sharply interrogative. 'The answer is still no, Miss Smith. Why?'

She shook her head. 'It's probably nothing, but when I encountered Lord Crowhurst, he gaped as if he couldn't believe his eyes and I—'

'It's more likely he couldn't believe your recklessness. Or his good fortune.'

She let that pass. 'No, it was more than that. I think you're wrong about Crowhurst, sir. The way he spoke to me, it was almost as if he knew me. Or. . .thought he did. It was really quite odd.'

'The only odd thing about this entire episode, Miss Smith, is that I've managed to keep my hands from your throat. Don't press your luck. If you wish to remain unscathed, you will give me your word of honour that you'll refrain from dashing off unaided if this sort of situation occurs again.'

'Well, if you lectured the girls the way you've been lecturing me, I shouldn't imagine—'

The trapdoor opened a cautious crack.

'We're in Park Street, guv'nor. Which house is it?'

Deverell's mouth compressed at the interruption, but he glanced out of the window. 'You can set us down here,' he ordered as a familiar door came into sight.

Thripp was standing on the front doorstep precisely where she'd left him hours ago, holding a bouquet of flowers. As Phoebe stepped down from the cab, she found herself entertaining the wild thought that the butler had been standing there so long someone had planted the flowers on him.

Obviously she was going mad.

'These were just left by a Mr Toombes, Miss,' Thripp informed her in mournful tones. 'There is also a note.' He handed it over.

'Oh, no.' Phoebe eyed the note with dismay before thrusting it into her pocket. 'How on earth did he find out where I live?'

'If his patron is Lord Portlake, it'd be easy enough to make enquiries,' Deverell said after paying off the hackney. He glared at the colourful array in Thripp's hands as if the flowers might house particularly noxious bugs. 'Thripp, I want a word with you.' Grasping Phoebe by the arm, he marched her into the house. 'But first I'll speak to my wards. Where are they?'

'Mr Charlton has them under guard in the drawing-room, my lord.'

'Under guard! Good heavens, Thripp.' Phoebe bent a reproving frown upon the butler. 'The girls are not felons. I'd better see them at once.'

She took a step towards the drawing-room, only to be brought up short by Deverell's long fingers tightening around her arm.

'You're not seeing anyone at present, Miss Smith,' he pronounced, using his hold on her to steer her smartly in the other direction. Phoebe found herself confronted by the staircase. 'Is Gerald up yet, Thripp?'

'I'm not sure, my lord.'

'Go and check. You may inform him that if he isn't
down here in five minutes, I will personally see to it
that his exit from his bed is immediate and unpleasant.'

'For goodness' sake, sir, Gerald is not to blame for
this morning's activities.'

'The speech I intend to make to my wards,' Deverell
said as Thripp departed on his errand, 'will be made
only once. And you don't need to hear it, Miss Smith.
You may retire to your room.'

'Retire to my room?' Completely forgetting that she
wanted to do nothing else, Phoebe stared at him, incredulous. 'Well, of all the arrogant decrees. Retire to my
room! I'm surprised you're not ordering me to bed without my supper!'

He looked down at her, eyes narrowing until only
a glittering aquamarine sliver was visible between the
midnight-dark lashes. His voice went very soft. Very
soft and very gentle. 'An interesting punishment, Miss
Smith. I shall keep it in mind. Rest assured, however,
that should I resort to such methods, supper will be
served.'

Phoebe's mouth fell open in shock. At least she
thought it was shock. It was difficult to be sure when
Deverell's precise meaning seemed to be lost somewhere
in the swirling fog invading her brain. His words said
one thing, but his eyes—

Before she could recover her thought processes, he
brought both hands up to cup her shoulders and draw
her around to face him.

'Now,' he said in quite a different tone, 'do I have
your promise that you'll let me know the instant one of
my wards goes off on some hare-brained start?'

Promise? She couldn't even think. Surely he hadn't
meant that *he* was going to serve—

But that thought, too, shattered when his hands closed
more firmly around her much smaller frame and he drew
her closer. At least her upper body moved closer; her
feet seemed glued to the floor. Phoebe stumbled and

almost collided with Deverell's chest. Instinctively her hands lifted to steady herself and she gasped aloud at the contact. Beneath the fine fabric of his coat he was rock-solid, as hard as the most fiercely tempered steel; but warm, and intensely alive.

'Your promise, Miss Smith,' he repeated in a voice so low anyone standing more than three feet away wouldn't have heard it.

'Well, yes. . .I suppose. . . That is. . .not all their starts are hare-brained, sir. At least. . .'

'No.' He moved his hands inwards. Very gently, inch by slow inch, his fingers smoothed up her throat to cup the back of her head. Using the slightest pressure of his thumbs, he tipped her face up until her gaze was caught by his and held, chained by the intent, wholly focused power of those light, glittering eyes.

'No hesitations. No conditions. Your word of honour, Miss Smith.'

'My lord, this is most. . .'

The words vanished on another gasp as his fingers widened, moving gently against the sensitive flesh of her nape. If she'd had the breath, she would have accused him of trying to intimidate her again, except that she wasn't intimidated in the least. Her acute awareness of the formidable strength in those big, powerful hands made her shiver helplessly, but the shivers weren't induced by fear.

Her gaze fell to his mouth. It really was a beautiful mouth, she thought distractedly. Utterly masculine, hard, fierce, and yet passionate. And so close. Another inch or two and his breath would bathe her lips. An inch closer than that and they could almost—

'Promise me, Phoebe.'

'Yes,' she breathed.

His hold tightened. For a fleeting instant she could have sworn a faint tremor passed through his fingers to the flesh heating beneath his touch. Then he stepped back, releasing her slowly until his hands fell to his sides. Bemused, she followed the movement, watching his fingers curl into fists so tight she saw his knuckles turn white.

'There,' he said, his voice intriguingly husky, 'that wasn't so difficult, was it?'

'Oh!' Suddenly realising he was no longer holding her, Phoebe grabbed for the stair-rail. What on earth had Deverell done to her? She couldn't remember when she'd last taken a breath. Her head was spinning. Her throat felt tight. She feared she might actually swoon— an action she'd always considered as idiotic as it was useless. Now it seemed not only a real possibility, but rather more useful than she'd suspected.

With an enormous effort, she dragged in a breath and focused her eyes on his cravat. 'If you don't mind, my lord, I think I'll. . .retire to my room. I feel quite. . .quite. . .'

'An excellent idea, Miss Smith. You must be exhausted.'

'Exhausted. Yes. Yes, that's it. Exhausted. Good day, sir.'

'Until tomorrow, Phoebe.'

'To—' Her gaze lifted to his. It was a good thing she was still hanging onto the stair-rail, she thought. Because the blue and gold flames blazing in his eyes threatened her senses all over again.

'There's no need to look so alarmed,' he said softly. 'I intend to see how my wards comport themselves. One taste of me looking over their shoulders and there shouldn't be any trouble for a few weeks.'

'Oh. Trouble. Yes. I mean, no. I mean. . .a very sound notion, my lord.'

With a sudden burst of energy, induced by sheer panic, she relinquished her grip on the stair-post, turned and fled up the stairs.

Sebastian watched her go, aware of a fierce elation roaring through his veins. The force of it startled him. He barely managed to stop himself letting out a primitive yell of triumph. He felt as if he'd just taken a giant step forward in the pursuit of something elusive, and yet indefinably precious. Something he wanted. . .no, *needed* to possess. A need that until yesterday he'd put down to physical desire.

But physical desire did not account for the other emotions he'd recently encountered. The discovery just now that his delectably disapproving Miss Smith was not indifferent to him was, in fact, the only bright spot in a morning that had seen him reel helplessly from violent rage to raw fear and back again. Emotions he hadn't felt since he was nineteen. He had not enjoyed the experience then, and he liked it even less now.

Damn it, that little wretch had played absolute havoc with his control yet again.

But now. . .ah, now, he understood why. If he hadn't been so distracted by his strange possessiveness yesterday he would have seen it then. He hadn't even known he'd been waiting, but from the moment he'd stood, watching Phoebe across a swathe of lawn, and realised that the softness, the sweetness, the gentle glow haunting his dreams were as real, as enticing, as the strength and humour and intelligence shining in her eyes, he'd known.

This was the one.

Sebastian stared at the now empty staircase and thought back. Had he sensed it from the tone of the letters Edward Charlton had mentioned? he wondered suddenly. The writer's name hadn't stayed with him, but had he known, somewhere deep inside himself, that Phoebe would come up to Town to confront him if no one replied to her missives? Known and waited because he had no intention of returning to the scene of his banishment?

He shrugged inwardly. It didn't matter now. She was his. The one woman with whom he wanted to share his life.

It wouldn't be that easy, of course. Because of his own shadows—and because he suspected her heart would follow where she trusted—he wanted her belief in his honour before he won her heart. And the trust of such a wary little creature would be hard-won. One wrong word or move and she'd probably assume he was going to offer her a *carte blanche*.

She would also be only too ready to throw that promise he'd made her in his face.

A slow, rather anticipatory smile curled Sebastian's lips as he turned away from the stairs and strode across the hall to the room where his wards awaited him. Phoebe hadn't realised it yet, but contained in that promise was a giant loophole. And he was going to make sure she slipped right through it—straight into his arms.

His smile grew as he wondered what his delectably disapproving Miss Smith's reaction would be if she knew he was about to change the terms of her employment yet again.

Quite some time elapsed before Phoebe found herself recalling the oddly mislaid fact that Deverell was her employer. Her strange forgetfulness was extremely worrying. For the first time in her adult life, emotions and physical sensation had completely taken over her well-ordered mind.

And she didn't know what to do about it.

Restless, she rose from the chair where she'd been sitting, waiting for her senses to return to something resembling normal, and walked over to her dressing-table. She hadn't even removed her bonnet, she saw, gazing at the solemn-eyed image staring back at her through the glass. Thoughtfully, she did so, tossing the drab brown hat aside. Her hair was a mess. Several tendrils had been freed from their severe knot when Deverell had touched her nape, his hands so big and powerful and warm and—

A rush of shimmering heat flowed through her, turning her knees to water. Phoebe sat down rather suddenly, nearly missing the rose brocade stool in the process. She righted herself, glaring at her reflection as she did so.

This was ridiculous. She was going to put a stop to it immediately. The first thing to do was face the truth. She was strongly attracted to Deverell. It was no use denying what was perfectly obvious. Despite all the lectures on the evils of unbridled passion she had received nearly every day of her childhood, she suspected she could have felt very unbridled indeed if Deverell had been intent on passion rather than promises.

Unfortunately, no great illumination resulted from an inordinate number of minutes spent in wondering why she was so powerfully drawn to him. His flashes of humour appealed to her; she was curious about the restraint she sensed in him and the shadows briefly glimpsed beneath the glittering surface of his eyes, but those qualities would hardly turn her brain to mush and the rest of her to trembling blancmange.

No, it must be a case of intense physical attraction. She'd been warned to guard against unseemly urges often enough by her family not to know that ladies were capable of such urges, even if she'd never experienced the phenomenom until now. After all, Deverell was different to every other man she'd ever met. For all she knew, that was all it took.

Or perhaps it was merely a resurgence of her girlish tendencies towards romance, also deplored by her relatives. Or the fact that she'd rather foolishly come to think of her charges as the family she'd always wanted but would probably never have.

'But the Deverells are not my family,' she told herself sternly. 'In fact—' remembering the note in her pocket and frowning thoughtfully '—unless someone of humble station, such as Mr Toombes, offers for me, marriage is not likely to be my lot in life. And since I wouldn't accept someone like Toombes anyway, the only romance I'm likely to encounter is between the pages of my books.'

No argument came to mind to refute that unassailable

logic. Phoebe ordered herself to forget romance and concentrate on the real problem: how to cure herself of such an unsuitable attraction.

Her first impulse was to insist that Deverell accept her immediate resignation, but no sooner had the notion occurred to her than she was overwhelmed with dismay. So little did she want to leave, that for a moment she found her traitorous mind entertaining the hope that if Miss Grismead was still unmarried by the start of the next Season, Deverell might need her to stay longer.

'And what good will that do?' she demanded scornfully of her reflection. 'You might find your employer interesting—well, all right, fascinating,' she amended as her image frowned in disapproval of this mild description. 'But nothing can come of it.'

'Are you sure?' asked an insidious little voice that seemed to come out of nowhere. 'He said you intrigue him and he can be quite charming to you.'

Phoebe stared at the glass, wondering if her mirrored self had actually spoken or if she was losing what few wits she had left. Not that it mattered; there wasn't anyone around to hear her talking to herself.

'He said that only once, and I'm not at all sure he meant it,' she argued. 'As for charm, well, you know what Deverells are like. They're perfectly capable of using charm if they think it'll work. Look at the way he extracted that promise from me.'

'But he didn't have to use charm. You'd have promised anyway.'

'*He* didn't know that.'

This gave her reflection pause. Phoebe took advantage of the lull to point out a few facts. They weren't particularly pleasant, but experience had taught her they were correct.

'Whether or not Deverell could ever be attracted to me doesn't matter. I'm his nieces' companion. And we know what happens when gentlemen develop an interest in governesses and companions. Marriage is not the first thought that pops into their heads.'

'Very true. But it might be the second.'

Phoebe gaped at the temptress in the mirror. 'Have you run mad?' she demanded. 'It wouldn't be the third. Or even the fourth, fifth or sixth. I have absolutely nothing to recommend me as wife to a man of Deverell's standing. Not only that, but if *any* gentleman were to offer for me, I'd be obliged to tell him my real name and why I changed it.'

Her reflection pursed its lips. 'A Deverell wouldn't care about that old scandal.'

'How do you know? You're not even sure precisely what happened.' She considered that. 'Nor am I. Besides, there are other matters to take into account. If I recall correctly, Deverell's barony is not a landed title. If he does marry, he's sure to choose an heiress to a large estate.'

Her reflection could do nothing but nod in reluctant agreement to this statement. Phoebe found the response so disheartening she immediately ordered herself to cease such an idiotic conversation.

How on earth had she got onto the subject of marriage anyway? She was supposed to be effecting a cure, not slipping further into fantasy. Instead of wondering what attracted her to Deverell, she might be more profitably employed in compiling a catalogue of his less appealing qualities. There were sure to be plenty. He was a Deverell.

This exercise, once started, proved reasonably successful. By the time she'd reached the end of a list that included arrogance, unjustifiable threats of strangulation and dictatorial tendencies, and had added the suspicion that he deliberately set out to addle her wits—quite unnecessarily—every time they met so he could have his own way, she felt a good deal better.

Quite able to return to her duties, in fact.

*   *   *

When a knock sounded on the door a short time later, she had even changed into one of the gowns Deverell had provided for her. The soft amber-coloured jaconet muslin skirts hushed gently about her ankles as she crossed the room to answer the summons.

She wasn't very much surprised to find the twins standing in the hall outside her room. What did bring a startled exclamation to her lips was the evidence that Theodosia had been crying, not her more dramatic sister.

'May we speak with you, Phoebe?' Theo asked in uncharacteristically subdued accents.

Phoebe blinked at her to make sure she'd got the right twin. Although, since Cressida's made-up face put her forcibly in mind of a badly constructed rainbow, it was difficult to be mistaken.

'Yes, of course, Theo.' She stepped back so the girls could enter. 'Oh, dear, I did ask your uncle not to be too harsh, but I can see he ignored me as usual.'

'It wasn't Uncle Sebastian,' said Theo, hovering around Phoebe as though she feared her companion was going to collapse at any moment. 'We knew what *he* was going to say. Can we get you anything, Phoebe? A mustard plaster? One of Dr James's Powders, perhaps?'

'Dr James's Powders? A *mustard plaster*? Why on earth. . .? Cressy, why are you holding on to me? I'm not about to swoon.'

'Are you sure?' Cressida queried, peering at her intently. 'Perhaps you should lie down. Do you have any smelling-salts? Is there anything we can do for you?'

'We'll even do your mending,' Theodosia offered. 'Should we dust the ornaments? Would you like me to arrange some flowers?'

'Perhaps we can make you some gruel.'

'Yes. You could sip it in bed.'

'Do you want us to read an improving sermon or something?'

'*An improving sermon!*' Phoebe gaped at Cressida as if she'd lost her wits. 'Has everyone run mad today? I can't believe your uncle even knows that improving sermons exist. Sit down and tell me precisely what he said.'

This command appeared to throw Theodosia into a pit of despair. She plunked herself down cross-legged on Phoebe's bed and propped her chin in her hands. 'Nothing we didn't expect,' she said dolefully. 'We should have thought of the consequences. We should have known you'd come after us. Why did he have to be inflicted with fluff-brained females?'

'Actually, he said pretty much what Edward said,' Cressida added. 'Except for that last bit.'

'Edward?' Phoebe glanced quickly at Theodosia. 'I see.'

Theo sent her a look of earnest appeal. 'We're truly sorry, Phoebe. I mean, we would have apologised anyway, because Uncle Sebastian told us to, but we really mean it.' She turned to her sister. 'Don't we, Cressy?'

Cressida nodded. 'We didn't think our going to the theatres would put you in danger, Phoebe.'

'I wasn't in that much danger,' Phoebe demurred, deciding to accept this rather ingenuous apology in the spirit in which it was offered. 'In any event, nothing untoward happened, so we'll say no more about it.'

She fully expected the twins to bounce back to their usual exuberant selves after this speech, but instead Cressy sat down next to her sister and the pair proceeded to stare dismally at nothing in particular.

'Has your uncle forbidden you to go out?' Phoebe queried after a moment, unable to think of anything else that would cast her charges so thoroughly into gloom.

'Oh, no,' Cressida said vaguely. 'He didn't even threaten to send us back to Kerslake, which we quite expected him to do.' She glanced sideways at her sister. 'It was Edward.'

'Oh. Well, I'm sure he won't remain angry for long, Theo.'

Theodosia sniffed. 'It isn't that, Phoebe. Edward was quite calm about the whole thing. But he said if women wanted to be given more rights and independence, then we had to be prepared to accept responsibility also, and. . .and be worthy of those rights. And. . .he was right.'

'Yes, he was,' Phoebe said gently. 'But nobody expects you to understand that immediately, Theo. Goodness, at your age most girls think only of gowns and parties, not of rights and responsibilities.'

'She only did it for me,' Cressida muttered.

'You see, Phoebe, Cressy needs something to do. I have my interest in the rights of women—Edward and I have the most fascinating discussions, you know—but Cressy isn't like me. She needs something different.'

'But acceptable,' Phoebe responded, smiling ruefully.

To her relief, this drew faint smiles in return. Dealing with contrite Deverells was an interesting experience, but it was also somewhat disconcerting. She should have known, however, that the twins would take even contrition to extremes.

'I really did want to be an actress,' Cressida said wistfully. 'But if there was something else. . .'

'Why not try writing drama?' Phoebe said, struck by sudden inspiration. 'You know you've always enjoyed the Gothic novels I borrow from the circulating libraries. I'm sure you could write one just as interesting.'

Cressida looked doubtful. 'Do you think so?'

'Of course I do. What's more, your uncle isn't likely to take exception to the scheme. Especially if you write under a *nom de plume*.'

'I suppose I could try it.'

'You could make Uncle Sebastian the villain,' Theo suggested darkly. She scowled. 'He certainly has the temper for it. Edward was just as cross, but he didn't threaten to strangle us and throw our bodies into the Thames.'

'Oh, goodness! Is that what your uncle threatened to do?' Phoebe thought of her own encounter with Deverell's temper and was stunned by a sudden return of her earlier gloom. She'd known he wouldn't really carry out his threat to strangle her, but the fact that he'd made the same threat to the twins made her wonder if, in his mind, she belonged in the same category.

Not only another fluff-brained female, but a nuisance. A troublesome duty. A responsibility he didn't want.

The thought was positively depressing.

'That wasn't all,' Cressida added. 'He said that if anything happened to you, we'd find ourselves on a ship to the Colonies so fast we wouldn't know where we were. Can ladies be shipped to the Colonies, Phoebe?'

'He didn't mean it, silly.' Theodosia frowned at her sister, but a moment later her frown took on a rather thoughtful aspect. 'But you're right. Uncle Sebastian did seem more worried about Phoebe than about us.' She looked at her companion. 'Isn't that strange?'

'Quite extraordinary,' Phoebe agreed glumly.

Her mood hadn't lifted by the time Thripp announced that dinner awaited them. As far as she was concerned, the only reason for Deverell's concern was that he would have felt in some way responsible if his nieces' antics had led to her being harmed. And since she'd been the one to put him in that position in the first place, it was no wonder he wanted to strangle all three of them.

Unfortunately for her low spirits, there was no diversion to be found at the dinner table. The girls were still contrite, and Gerald looked as if he hadn't slept for several weeks. Phoebe was quite sure she could detect early signs of dissipation in his heavy-eyed countenance. Something else for her to worry about.

All in all it was a very subdued party who adjourned

to the drawing-room and began a lacklustre game of Speculation. The tea-tray was brought in and ignored. Nobody argued when Phoebe decreed an early night was in order.

Chapter Seven

Fortunately for her equilibrium, a reasonably sound sleep did much to restore the balance of Phoebe's mind. She arose betimes, having convinced herself that her usual calm good sense had been overset yesterday by worry about her missing charges.

As for her strange attraction to Deverell: well, she had simply mistaken the novelty of enjoying a man's company—secure in the knowledge that he wasn't going to make any unwanted advances—for a stronger attraction. And she had to admit, annoyingly large and dictatorial though Deverell might be, there was something rather reassuring about those qualities when one found oneself in a potentially dangerous situation.

All she had to do, therefore, was maintain a polite and proper distance and avoid dangerous situations. Especially where gentlemen were concerned.

With this resolute goal in mind, she launched an assault on the gown she intended to wear to the dance party that afternoon. Unfortunately, thanks to the lectures she gave herself all through the exercise, she didn't remember Tobias Toombes's note until after a light luncheon had been consumed.

She was just in time to avert disaster. Mr Toombes had apparently decided that the violence of his feelings outweighed the tricky question of his calling on her at her place of employment. He had, he wrote with a determined hand, a matter of crucial importance to his physical and mental well-being to discuss with her. He would do anything in pursuit of a favourable outcome. He was sure her celestial sweetness would lead her to forgive his disobeying her veto on visits. If not, he would be happy to crawl to her on hands and knees in pursuit of this worthy cause.

Since Phoebe had never given him any reason to suppose that the well-being, physical or mental, of a gentleman who waited for fate to throw her in his path again was of the slightest interest to her, this very pointed note sent her into a frenzy of activity. Her charges were pushed and prodded out of the house a good half-hour before they were due to leave for Lady Grismead's— and a mere ten minutes before the hour appointed by Toombes for his visit—and told that a walk to the Grismead residence would do them good.

The walk was not one of unalloyed pleasure. She didn't know from which direction Toombes would come and at every corner expected to be confronted by the sight of him crawling pathetically towards her, bony hand outstretched. No such hideous vision assaulted her eyes, however, which left her free to lend an ear to Gerald's complaints that he'd wanted to try out his new phaeton, while her mind pondered ways and means of avoiding both Toombes's impending proposal, and Deverell's company.

She needn't have worried about Deverell. When they were ushered into Lady Grismead's drawing-room, there was no sign of him among the crowd of chattering damsels and the male relatives they had coerced or cajoled into accompanying them.

So much for keeping an eye on his wards' behaviour, she thought, irrationally annoyed by this evidence of neglect. She'd spent the last half-hour rehearsing a very cool, proper little greeting and he wasn't even here to receive it.

Then, as her eyes met those of a gentleman standing

on the other side of the room, her emotions underwent
an abrupt about-face. Elegantly clad in a plum-coloured
coat and pale pantaloons, his hand resting lightly on
the back of Lady Yarwood's chair, Crowhurst stood
watching her with the fixed stare that had made her
want to shrink into the background yesterday. The effect
hadn't diminished overnight.

'Ah, Miss Smith. At last. Now we can begin.' Lady
Grismead, resplendent in steel-grey silk, descended upon
them, cutting off all retreat. 'You will be happy to play
the pianoforte,' she informed Phoebe. 'So much easier
to practice the steps of a dance when there is music.'

'Yes, ma'am,' Phoebe agreed, abandoning at birth any
hope of leaving her charges in Lady Grismead's care
and making her escape. 'And I must apologise for our
lateness. We took a wrong turn and walked a little out
of our way.'

'A little?' muttered Cressida, handing her bonnet into
the tender care of a maid. 'More like miles.'

'You walked?' Her ladyship frowned. 'Extraordinary.
I am an advocate of genteel forms of exercise, Miss
Smith, but one cannot consider wandering, lost, about
the streets of London to be anything but unsuitable.'

'Worse than that,' Gerald grumbled. 'I wanted to try
my new phaeton.'

Phoebe quelled him with a look that would have done
credit to a Deverell and bent her mind to the task of
placating her hostess. 'No doubt we'll soon learn our
way about, ma'am. Goodness, I see you have quite a
crowd. One would think it the crush of the Season.'

She scanned the room, her eyes widening when she
recognised several familiar faces, Edward Charlton and
Lord Bradden among them. 'Gerald has even impressed
Mr Filby into service. How did you acquire so many
partners for the girls?'

'My parties are always successful,' pronounced her
ladyship in a tone that would have given pause to any
party considering failure. 'Even a simple dance party.

All it takes is organisation. Organisation, Miss Smith. Next time you walk, consult a map. The pianoforte is behind you by the window. You may begin as soon as you are ready. Theodosia, Cressida, come with me.'

Left summarily alone, Phoebe made her way to the pianoforte, wondering if a visit from Toombes wouldn't be preferable to an afternoon spent on tenterhooks, after all. If Deverell ever discovered Crowhurst was here, she'd never hear the end of it. As for Crowhurst, himself, though he showed no signs of approaching her, his pale, unwavering gaze was extremely disconcerting. She could only hope the afternoon would go off without incident.

For a while her hope seemed justified. With a great deal of laughter from the ladies and instructions from the male contingent, the dancers took to the floor, twirling their way through country dances, the quadrille, and even a waltz, those ladies not fortunate enough to be partnered by brothers or cousins pairing off with each other.

It was when the butler appeared with refreshments that the afternoon disintegrated with positively startling rapidity. Before she could rise from the piano stool, Phoebe found herself beseiged by males.

'Miss Smith—' Lord Bradden gazed at her with the earnest expression of a puppy anxious to please '—may I fetch you a cup of tea, or a glass of lemonade?'

'Miss Smith, do try one of these salmon patties.' Mr Charlton's smile was a trifle strained. He leaned closer under the guise of offering her a plate. 'Do you think Lady Theodosia seems rather quiet today, ma'am? I'm concerned that I may have been too harsh yesterday.'

'I say, Miss Smith, you must be fixed to that stool by now.' Mr Filby, a blinding vision in bright yellow pantaloons, a white satin waistcoat embroidered with gold hummingbirds, and a gold brocade coat of startling cut and hue, bowed with a flourish. 'Care to take a toddle around the room with me? Loosen up a bit, you know.'

'If anyone could toddle after being trampled upon by one's partners,' drawled a gentleman on Phoebe's other side. 'You positively astound me, Filby.'

At the sound of the light, mocking tone, Phoebe froze. She didn't know why, but quite suddenly she felt extremely cold.

Crowhurst must have had the same effect on Deverell's secretary. Mr Charlton glanced across at the older man, his fine grey eyes hardening. 'Miss Smith, I don't believe you've met Lord Crowhurst,' he said, his voice heavy with meaning.

Crowhurst's lips curled. 'Oh, Miss Smith and I are old friends,' he contradicted easily. 'I was, in fact, hoping to see her today. Allow me to congratulate you on your playing, my dear Phoebe. But I know you have many talents.'

A strained silence fell on the group. Phoebe suspected that one glance at her face would be enough to inform the others that Crowhurst was lying, or at least exaggerating, but none of them, she realised, was a match for the older man's cool assumption of friendship. Lord Bradden was far too young; Mr Filby, though three or four years older than Gerald, was still no match for a man close to Deverell in age; and Edward Charlton, while looking grim, was clearly aware that a public challenge might place Phoebe in an awkward position.

She was aware of it herself. Rising to her feet, she prepared to do the only thing possible. Abandon the field.

'Allow me to escort you to the refreshment table,' Crowhurst said, immediately divining her purpose. His gaze slid over her, lingering on her throat. The square neckline of her gown was quite respectable, but Phoebe had to resist a swift urge to tug it upward. 'That is, if you insist on cruelly abandoning your admirers, my dear.'

'I do,' she stated, feeling a flush of annoyance stain her cheeks. 'Furthermore, sir—'

She was pulled up short by the abrupt change of

expression that flashed across Edward Charlton's face. Alerted, her gaze flew to the doorway.

Deverell stood in the aperture, broad shoulders filling out a coat of burgundy superfine, long, powerful legs clad in breeches and topboots, one hand stuffed into his pocket, the other clenched by his side, and a scowl on his face that would have quelled the most besieged maiden looking for rescue.

Phoebe's heart did indeed trip and start to race. All in all, Deverell did not look like her idea of a gallant rescuer. In fact, she wouldn't have been surprised to learn that the hand clenched in his pocket was wrapped around a pistol. And yet, despite the ugly expression in his eyes as he stared at Crowhurst, despite the hard, unrelenting line of his mouth, she didn't feel quelled in the least.

Her lips parted as though she would call to him; she even took a step forward, as though pulled towards him by an invisible chain, before she recollected herself.

Oh, goodness! What was she doing? If anyone noticed. . .if he ever suspected. . . And he wasn't even dressed for the occasion. It was just like him to arrive in riding clothes when. . .

Her thoughts scattered like wraiths in a mist. Phoebe's heart almost stopped completely when Deverell's gaze flashed from Crowhurst to her face and the menace in his eyes disappeared. A slow smile curved his hard mouth. A rather pleased smile. It had the very peculiar effect of making her legs feel as if they were suddenly made of jelly. When he started towards her she had to put a hand on the pianoforte to steady herself.

'Good afternoon, Miss Smith. I trust I find you well?' Deverell took her free hand and bestowed a brief kiss on the inside of her wrist.

Phoebe nearly sank back onto the piano stool in a boneless heap.

'For goodness' sake, my lord,' she expostulated in a strangled whisper. 'What on earth do you think you are

about? Riding clothes! And you should be greeting your
aunt and Lady Yarwood, not— Oh, dear, now I have
five gentlemen. . .'

She glanced distractedly about her. Filby, Lord
Bradden and Mr Charlton weren't paying the least attention to her incoherent stutterings. They were too busy
goggling at the hard-edged looks being exchanged by
her infuriating employer and Crowhurst.

Images of snarling, sword-wielding warriors instantly
presented themselves to her beleaguered mind.

'Oh, my goodness. My lord, don't you think you
should greet your aunt before you. . .before you. . .?'

'Before I what, Miss Smith?'

With considerable effort she summoned up a glare.
'I don't know, sir, but Lady Grismead is your hostess
and—'

Deverell laughed softly and glanced down at her.
'Who do you think is footing the bill for this little gathering? If I greet my aunt, she's likely to go off in a fit of
apoplexy that I dared show my face here to remind
her of it.'

Fortunately for Phoebe's frazzled wits, she was spared
the need to answer this irreverent statement. A lady of
about her own age, a cap of feathery black curls and a
pair of sapphire eyes proclaiming her Deverell heritage,
chose that moment to drift into the room in a cloud of
palest blue muslin. Scurrying behind her was a thin,
gnome-like little gentleman of sparse hair and harassed
mien who, Phoebe deduced, could only be Lord
Grismead.

'There! Now your uncle and cousin have arrived. Will
you kindly take me to Lady Grismead, sir?'

'Are you sure you wish to be caught in the middle of
a confrontation between Deverell and his aunt, Miss
Smith? I'm reliably informed that it isn't a comfortable
position in which to be.'

Phoebe stiffened as Crowhurst's mocking tones smote
her ears again. Really! Didn't anyone have any manners

these days? There was Deverell treating his family as if
they didn't exist, and now Crowhurst apparently felt
quite at liberty to intrude on a private conversation whenever he heard one.

Momentarily forgetting that contact with Deverell had
a highly unsettling effect on her senses, she touched his
arm lightly. He promptly tucked her hand into the crook
of his elbow.

'There will be no confrontation, sir,' she informed
Crowhurst in her coolest tones. 'Gentlemen, if you will
excuse me, I have neglected my duties long enough.'

The three younger men, who until that moment had
been giving an excellent imitation of exhibits in a wax-
works, came to life with a collective start.

'Most obliging of you to play the pianoforte for us,
Miss Smith,' Lord Bradden said earnestly.

Mr Filby bowed. 'Your servant, ma'am.'

Mr Charlton aimed an absent smile at her, then turned
anxious eyes on his employer. 'Sir, you did grant me
leave of absence this afternoon.'

'Yes, Edward, I remember.' Deverell bestowed a
benign smile on the trio that had them all blinking like
astonished owls. 'Please continue to enjoy yourselves,
gentlemen. I'm sure the other young ladies will be only
too pleased to assist in the endeavour.' He led Phoebe
away, pointedly excluding Crowhurst from the request.

'Well!' After one glance at Deverell's expression,
Phoebe valiantly assumed the bright tone of one praising
a diligent pupil. 'That went off quite civilly.'

'Strive for the intelligence I've come to expect from
you, Miss Smith.'

She abandoned approval with unprecedented speed.
'Except for the glares you and Crowhurst were exchanging, of course. Would you mind telling me what that
was all about, my lord? Yesterday you were obliged
to him.'

'Yesterday I had more pressing priorities than feeding
Crowhurst his own sword-stick. As for today, you know

damned well what it was about. I warned you about
Crowhurst. Now are you convinced he wants you?'

'There is nothing more annoying than a person who
says I told you so,' stated Phoebe, nose in the air. 'Lord
Crowhurst certainly has a very odd manner, but even
though he behaved in that detestably familiar way, it
seemed. . .I don't know. . .almost natural.'

'It is natural, you little goose. The sort of naturalness
designed to fluster innocents like you by forcing an intimacy that doesn't exist.'

'I don't mean *that*,' she said impatiently. 'It was just
as I told you yesterday. He spoke as if. . .as if he *really*
believes he knows me well. Do you think he might be
a little unbalanced?'

'A convenient explanation,' Deverell said grimly.
Then, quite unexpectedly, he started to smile. 'But I must
say, my little innocent, you gave him a most delightful
set-down.'

'Set-down? What—?'

His eyes glinted down at her. 'You touched me. Of
your own free will. And that, my proper little governess,
was done perfectly naturally.'

Phoebe promptly snatched her hand from his arm.
'Obviously, a gentleman's mind exists on quite another
plane than that of a lady,' she said severely, conscious
of the hot colour sweeping into her cheeks. His little
governess, indeed! She might be little compared to a
Deverell, and no doubt the same applied to being proper,
but she wasn't *his*!

It was strange how that realisation made her feel quite
alone all of a sudden.

'A lower plane,' she clarified, shaking off these useless maunderings. 'I merely requested your escort, my
lord. And, I might add, I would not have needed to do
so if you hadn't been glaring at Crowhurst as if you
were about to call him out.'

'If what Edward discovered for me this morning is

more than rumour, Crowhurst needs whipping rather than a chance on the field of honour.'

'Good heavens!' Phoebe's eyes widened. 'You've been asking about Crowhurst? Whatever for?'

'I prefer to know my enemies, Miss Smith.'

'But Crowhurst hasn't done anything to you.' She tilted her head, considering that statement. 'For that matter, he hasn't done anything to me.'

'He shows every sign of pursuing a lady who is under my protection,' Deverell said with soft menace. 'He is a man whose reputation with women is not that of a gentleman. Have you forgotten precisely where you met him, Miss Smith? The Honeypot isn't a theatre that caters to the usual crowd of playgoers.'

'Oh, goodness!' Phoebe came to an abrupt halt near a bay window where several young people were engaged in animated conversation. 'No, I suppose not. Well, if the manager stages plays like that very peculiar tableau—'

She stopped, glaring, as Deverell started to grin. 'Yes, you may well laugh, my lord, but I found nothing amusing in having to talk my way out of a career as a sea-nymph!' She thought back and shuddered. 'As far as I could tell, their costumes consisted of fish scales painted on muslin and wrapped around their legs and very little else.'

'Nothing else, I expect,' Deverell said, a wicked light in his eyes. 'But although that creature at the Birdcage deserves a good thrashing for insulting you, Miss Smith, I can't fault his taste. You would make a delightful sea-nymph. Not for public edification, of course.'

'Not for—' Under Deverell's amused gaze, Phoebe struggled valiantly to recover her powers of speech. 'No, of course not. As if I would. . . Oh, goodness me, what am I saying? Really, my lord, this is a most improper conversation. I can't think how. . . Kindly remember where we are, sir.'

Good advice, she thought distractedly. *She* hadn't even remembered to keep a polite and proper distance.

Or to avoid perilous situations. Actually, now she came to think of it, perilous situations and Deverell seemed to go hand in hand. Immediate rescue was imperative.

'Dear me, where is Lady Grismead? Ah, over there on that sofa. If you'll excuse me, sir, I'll—'

'In a moment.' Deverell prevented her escape by the simple expedient of taking her hand in a gentle and totally unbreakable clasp. He contemplated their joined hands for a moment, then lifted his gaze to her face. All traces of wicked amusement had gone, leaving his eyes intent and wholly serious.

'I don't know what Crowhurst said that annoyed you,' he began. 'But next time you encounter him, Miss Smith, cut him dead. Letting yourself bandy angry words with him will only whet his appetite.'

This instruction—from one who took a fiendish delight in bandying words with her at every turn—incensed Phoebe so much she said the first thing that came into her head.

'Indeed, sir. In that case, I shall expect you to follow your own advice.'

'What the deuce does that mean?'

'It means that I expect you to support my statement to Crowhurst that you will not pick a fight with your aunt.'

His eyes took on an unholy gleam. 'What if she picks one with me?'

'Then I will expect you to conduct yourself in a manner worthy of your position, my lord.'

The gleam disappeared. 'In that case, Miss Smith, I wish to claim another concession. An answer.' He glanced quickly around the room then bent until he could speak directly in her ear. His voice lowered to a soft growl. 'Where the devil is the chemisette that belongs to that dress?'

'Oh. . . Well—I—' Phoebe stuttered to a halt, her mind going unnervingly blank. Oh, heavens! What was he doing to her *now*? Just because Deverell's mouth was two inches from her cheek was no reason to shiver. If anything she felt extremely warm—another reason why tiny shivers had no business chasing themselves around in her stomach.

'Yes?' he purred, straightening.

'You know very well where it is,' she retorted, recovering her wits with the safety of a respectable distance. 'The chemisette was very frilly so I took it off. However, before you say anything else, my lord, I intend to sew the wretched thing back on as soon as I return home.'

His mouth curved in a slow smile. 'Oh, I don't know. We wouldn't want to make a hasty decision, Miss Smith. That peach colour is really quite delectable against your skin. And it would be a crime to hide so graceful a throat.'

'Graceful! Yesterday you wanted to strangle it!' she squeaked, torn between indignation and the shivery sense of excitement still rippling through her.

'Yes,' he said, laughter, and something more intense, glittering in his eyes. 'But, you see, I would have strangled you very, very gently, Miss Smith. You wouldn't have been hurt at all.'

Phoebe nearly choked without the assistance of any hands around her throat. Before she could recover her breath to annihilate her tormentor—always supposing she could think of a lethal enough response in a matter of seconds—he fired another question at her with a speed that left her brain reeling.

'And while we're on the subject of yesterday, what did Toombes want?'

This was too much. Phoebe drew herself up to her full height and, ignoring the risk of a cricked neck, stared Deverell straight in the eye. 'Nothing that concerns you, my lord. You may be right about Crowhurst, although he hasn't— But that is neither here nor there. If Mr Toombes has any intentions towards me, you may be sure they're honourable. And that is the last concession

you are going to wring from me. I am going to sit with
your aunt and you, sir, will behave yourself.'

Snatching her hand free, Phoebe turned on her heel
only to be brought up short by Deverell's voice, still
soft, still amused, but with something beneath the gentleness that set her spine tingling.

'Remind me to tell you, Miss Smith, that you are not
my governess. That is to say, you are not the arbiter of
my behaviour.'

She would not answer. She would treat all such
remarks with dignified disdain. She would take refuge
in the small alcove behind Lady Grismead and, what
was more, she would take great pleasure in composing
a letter of application for the post of companion to an
elderly lady who possessed no male relatives, no male
friends and no male acquaintances. And as soon as she
found this mythical person she would—

'Ah, Miss Smith!'

Lady Grismead, one imperious finger crooked in
Phoebe's direction, promptly put a spoke in this
particular wheel.

'You may sit with us,' she commanded as one
bestowing a great favour. 'Lady Yarwood wishes to
compliment you on your playing. And I don't believe
you have met dear Pamela.'

Meeting dear Pamela was not high on Phoebe's list
of desirable treats, but after exchanging polite greetings
with Lady Yarwood, an attractive, fair-haired matron in
pale chartreuse silk, she found herself turning to
Deverell's cousin with an alacrity she told herself had
nothing to do with the fact that he'd followed her and
was greeting his aunt.

Fortunately, Miss Grismead showed every promise of
living up to her reputation. Draped limply over a small
sofa, she managed a wan smile in response to her
parent's introduction that would have led the uninitiated
to suppose she was in the last stages of a fatal decline.
Phoebe was not of their number. There was a determined

set to Miss Grismead's lips that looked all too familiar.

'You play delightfully, Miss Smith,' Lady Yarwood said, smiling kindly. 'But you must be quite exhausted. Do come and sit down. Ottilia tells me you're an excellent governess, but your charges are safely occupied with the other young people at present, so you may relax for a moment.'

'Miss Smith is most conscientious,' Lady Grismead stated, shifting her steely-eyed gaze from where Deverell was now conversing with Lord Grismead to her friend. 'And very properly behaved. I was pleased to see, Miss Smith, that you did not linger among the gentlemen. No doubt they were only being polite, but a lady in your position must always guard against attracting a certain type of attention.'

'Er—yes, ma'am.'

'Isn't that correct, Almira?'

'It certainly is.' Lady Yarwood looked anxiously at Phoebe. 'Please don't take this amiss, my dear, but I thought you seemed a little *distraite*. I hope Lord Crowhurst didn't say anything improper.'

'Oh. No, ma'am. That is. . .'

'Forgive me if I seem inquisitive,' Lady Yarwood murmured, apparently taking Phoebe's hesitation for embarrassment. 'But you must know that before my marriage I, too, was a governess. I know how very uncomfortable one can be made to feel on occasion. Really—' she turned to her hostess '—I can't imagine why Adrian would put himself out for us today. He doesn't call above two or three times a year, but there he was just as we were climbing into the carriage; when I told him where we going, he at once offered his services. Of course, Amabel and Caroline were positively in alt, but I think it very odd.'

'What does he want?' asked Lady Grismead in accents of grim foreboding. 'That is the question you must ask yourself, Almira. When a man offers to assist his family, you may be sure he wants something in return.'

Only the greatest exercise of self-control stopped Phoebe from glancing at Deverell to see if he'd heard this cynical pronouncement.

'Well, he did say he'd come to seek information,' Lady Yarwood continued, 'but that since he was going to attend your party, it might turn out to be unnecessary. It seems very odd to me. How did he know it might be unnecessary before he'd made his inquiries?'

Both ladies turned to contemplate the subject of this question as if an answer was to be found writ large on his countenance. Phoebe followed the direction of their gazes. A faint ripple of unease drew her brows together when she saw Crowhurst talking to Gerald. Not that there was anything wrong in that, of course, but judging by the expression of eagerness on Gerald's face, Crowhurst was putting himself out to be pleasant to the younger man.

Phoebe frowned again, annoyed at the instant suspicions wafting about in her mind. This was what came of listening to Deverell. Even if Crowhurst had nefarious intentions towards her, Gerald would hardly help in the endeavour. He might be young, but no one had ever accused a Deverell of being a fool.

Reflecting darkly on the influence one particular Deverell seemed to be wielding on her calm, well-ordered mind lately, she brought her attention back to the conversation that had resumed next to her.

'Not that I know anything against him, Ottilia, because you may be sure if I did I wouldn't have accepted his escort, Yarwood's cousin or not. But it can't be denied that since that unfortunate affair fifteen years ago, Adrian has suffered from very strange moods.'

'So I've heard.' Lady Grismead frowned portentously. 'I am not one to encourage maudlin behaviour in anyone, Almira, and in a gentleman it is particularly displeasing. One cannot deny, however, that the effect upon a young man of an unsuitable liaison is to be deplored by all persons of character. Especially,' she added with a darkling glance behind her, 'by their unfortunate families.'

This time Phoebe turned her head before she could stop herself. It couldn't have been clearer that Deverell, also, had been involved in an unsuitable liaison in his youth. He was utterly still, the expression in his eyes as he stared down at his aunt as cold and deadly as the unfathomable depths of the ocean.

Phoebe found herself clasping her hands together, almost in supplication. Oh, dear. He was going to take Lady Grismead's comment as condemnation. She wondered if he'd heard even a hint of the concern and regret in her ladyship's voice.

Her mind whirling with conjecture, conscious of an odd little ache in the region of her heart, she gazed up at him, silently pleading with him not to retaliate with a scathing response.

As if he sensed her gaze, Deverell turned his head. The cold expression vanished. And in its place dawned a light she recognised—and yet still couldn't name. The same light, she realised with a tiny jolt, that had puzzled her in the Park.

Her brows knit as she gazed up into the aquamarine eyes gleaming down at her from between midnight-dark lashes. The touch of wickedness she recognised. And amusement—as if his aunt's strictures, though annoying, hadn't truly enraged him. But the disturbing gleam held something else. Something warm, and. . .

She didn't know. And wasn't sure why her ignorance bothered her. In another man, that warmth alone would have rendered her wary, but Deverell had promised not to pester her with attentions.

And she trusted his word.

Why did that thought make her feel so low? Why, in fact, was she feeling inexplicably confused about so many questions at once that her thoughts seemed to be scurrying back and forth like extremely busy mice? Whatever had happened to Deverell in the past—

whether the unfortunate liaison had led to his banishment or not—was none of her business. But. . .

Not only Deverell but Crowhurst, too, it seemed, had been involved in an unsuitable liaison years ago. Was that the real source of the enmity between the two men? Had they been entangled with the same woman? But they'd only been introduced a few weeks ago; Crowhurst had said as much in that horrid little court.

Phoebe blinked, suddenly realising she was still staring over her shoulder at Deverell, and that the smile in his eyes was beginning to reach his mouth. That same pleased little smile that had curved his lips earlier.

Dismayed, she whipped her gaze to the front and addressed the first person she saw.

'I believe you take a keen interest in poetry, Miss Grismead. Have you—?'

The rest of Phoebe's question lodged in her throat as the conversation between the two older ladies ceased as abruptly as if a door had slammed shut. From the corner of her eye, she saw Deverell's shoulders begin to shake with silent laughter.

Oh, how like him! She had just sunk herself beneath reproach and he had the temerity to laugh.

'Pamela has more practical interests than poetry,' stated Lady Grismead in quelling accents. Passing over Phoebe's flushed countenance, she cast a gimlet-eyed glance behind her. 'Isn't that so, Grismead?'

Lord Grismead jumped like a startled rabbit and looked more harassed than ever. 'Oh. Yes. Yes, indeed, my dear. Mathematics, for instance. Really, she is quite—'

'A lady does not profess to understand complex mathematical equations.' Her ladyship's tone dared anyone to contradict her. 'It is not a talent valued by gentlemen.'

'Oh, I don't know, Aunt.' Deverell bestowed a brief glance of approval on his cousin. 'When the bills start rolling in, Norvel might be grateful for Pamela's talent with figures.'

'Well, as to that, Sebastian, nothing has been arranged, you know.' Lord Grismead blinked several times, his resemblance to a hunted rabbit becoming more pronounced than ever. 'That is, there has been no formal announcement or—'

'You will oblige me by changing the subject, Grismead. There will be no announcement until Mr Hartlepoole comes to his senses. And even then, the outcome is by no means certain.'

This provoked a response from an unexpected quarter. Miss Grismead, who until then had been watching the other occupants of the room as if their very animation was too much for the depleted state of her health, abandoned her air of exhaustion.

'Dearest Norvel is coming to see you tomorrow, Papa, and if you don't immediately send an announcement to the *Gazette*, it will be the meanest thing!'

'Now, my dear, you know Mama and I must think of your future, which is not likely to be felicitous if you're forced to live in penury. Nor is this precisely the time or place—'

'I don't care.' Miss Grismead pouted prettily, but there was a steely light in her blue eyes. 'If you don't send an announcement to the *Gazette*, then *I* will.'

'But, dearest, females don't send notices to the *Gazette*.'

'Well, I'll send it somewhere else then.'

Lord Grismead goggled at his daughter. 'Somewhere else? But—'

'Silence, Grismead. I will deal with this.'

His lordship subsided, his demeanour that of one long accustomed to being crushed between two determined Deverells.

Phoebe could only sympathise. On the other hand, she mused, his lordship must have known the fate in store for him. After all, he'd married a Deverell. Perhaps he'd expected his wife to give birth to a Grismead. But no. True to form, she'd produced a Deverell. Really, he'd been foolish to think otherwise. If *she* married into the family, she'd expect to produce a Deverell, too, and—

Oh, good heavens! Had her mind run completely mad? How could she possibly marry into the family? The only Deverell of suitable age was—

Her mind seized before she could finish the thought. Phoebe stared straight ahead of her, very much afraid that her countenance was taking on a distinct resemblance to Lord Grismead's. With an additional element of stunned stupefaction.

Mercifully, before anyone could notice her sudden paralysis, several ladies arrived to collect their various offspring. Suddenly the drawing-room was all bustle and confusion. She could only be grateful for the small reprieve. At the moment, she seemed to have no conscious control over herself at all.

To think of marriage and. . .

To think of marriage *at all*! Really, she'd reminded herself only yesterday to put aside girlish dreams for the reality of her life, but here was her well-ordered mind dashing down forbidden paths two days in a row.

What she needed was distraction. Immediately. The Grismeads were no help. Father and daughter were still arguing about impecunious poets; while Lady Grismead was farewelling her guests. Nothing would induce her to speak to Deverell again until she had her wits about her. That left Lady Yarwood.

And, suddenly, inspiration struck.

'Excuse me, ma'am.' Thanking Providence for the timely notion, Phoebe turned to Lady Grismead's friend. 'I can't help but wonder what sort of woman would trifle with a young man's affections. From the point of view of a governess of boys Gerald's age, of course,' she added mendaciously. 'The lady who caused Lord Crowhurst such pain, for instance. What did she look like?'

Fortunately, Lady Yarwood didn't appear to find anything odd in this request. She smiled and answered readily enough. 'I never saw her, my dear. The affair took place in the country. A fortuitous circumstance, I've always considered, for I believe she was already married and several years older than Adrian. Only imagine the scandal if such a liaison had been carried out under the eyes of the *ton*. As it is, her identity remains a mystery to this day.'

'I see.' Phoebe pursed her lips thoughtfully.

'In any event, it's long forgotten now.' Lady Yarwood smiled again and patted Phoebe's hand in her friendly fashion as she prepared to depart. 'I do hope you'll bring the girls to visit Amabel and Caroline one day, Miss Smith. Please don't think they must wait until Ottilia is available. You are very welcome.'

'I'm sure Miss Smith appreciates your concern, cousin.' Crowhurst approached, a faint smile on his thin lips. 'It must be a great comfort to her to encounter one who was once in her. . .er. . .position. Are you ready to leave? Not that I wish to hurry you, of course, it is just that one has so many engagements.'

'Then you should have said so, Adrian,' Lady Yarwood returned, with what Phoebe could only con- sider to be great self-restraint. 'I will fetch the girls immediately.'

Phoebe watched her ladyship cross the room, then turned a look of displeasure on Crowhurst. 'Were you trying to embarrass your cousin, sir, or me?' she demanded, too annoyed to remember Deverell's instruc- tions regarding the Viscount.

His smile held a touch of spite. 'You must pardon me, my dear Phoebe. A petty remark, wasn't it. But, you know, it was very naughty of you to go off with Deverell. And quite unnecessary.'

'I don't know what you're talking about, sir.'

'Oh, I think you do. You escaped me once before, my dear Phoebe, but not a second time.'

Seeing her eyes widen, Crowhurst seemed to realise he might have gone too far with that remark, because he wiped the unpleasant sneer from his face and replaced it with a smile. As far as Phoebe was concerned, the change wasn't an improvement.

'I don't believe I've given you leave to use my name, sir,' she retorted. 'I was grateful yesterday for your offer of assistance, but I would prefer you to address me correctly.'

His voice lowered to a sibilant whisper. 'Are you saying you want me to use your surname, Phoebe? Oh, no.' He shook his head. 'I don't think so. Not here. No, I don't think you'd like that at all.'

And with his mouth still curled in that sly smile, he bowed and walked away, leaving Phoebe with a mind once more whirling with surmise and conjecture.

None of the possible explanations for Crowhurst's enigmatic remarks were reassuring, but she wasn't, she saw, to be allowed the luxury of brooding over them now.

Lady Grismead, having despatched the last of her guests, returned to the drawing-room and the attack. Apparently considering Deverell and his charges capable of seeing themselves out, she commanded her now weeping daughter to adjourn to the morning-room.

Adding heartrending wails to her repertoire, Pamela obeyed.

Under the awed gazes of her younger relatives, her ladyship, undaunted by the rapidly increasing volume of the performance, prepared to follow. She paused with her hand on the doorknob and swept the room with a basilisk glare.

'It is all very well for Pamela to say she has a talent for managing finances,' she stated sternly. 'So has Deverell. But have we seen any advantage from it? Pray tell me that.'

No one was foolhardy enough to volunteer an answer. Indeed, since her ladyship swept out of the room on the words, Lord Grismead hard on her heels, Phoebe was not certain if she'd expected a reply. The question did, however, set up a new train of thought in her mind. She was seizing on it with an eagerness that bordered on the desperate when Deverell planted himself in her line of vision. He appeared to be torn between annoyance and amusement.

'I have to say, Miss Smith, that infuriating though our charges may be at times, they at least refrain from performances guaranteed to shatter the ears of anyone in the immediate vicinity. Are you ready to depart? Since my esteemed uncle has chosen to add his mite to the melodrama being enacted across the hall, there's nothing to stop us. Let's escape while we can.'

Phoebe was in no mood for flippancy. The past few hours seemed to have been filled with one disaster after another. And they could all be laid at the doors of the gentlemen involved.

She turned to their interested audience and took a leaf from Lady Grismead's book. 'Gerald, you will oblige me by escorting your sisters to your uncle's carriage and waiting for us there. I presume your carriage *is* downstairs, my lord?'

He raised a brow. 'Since I gave my coachman instructions to meet us here at four o'clock, it had better be.' He nodded to Gerald, who reluctantly withdrew with his sisters, then winced as several despairing shrieks reverberated across the hall before the door was closed again. 'Do you have any further orders, Miss Smith?'

Phoebe regarded the sardonic lift of his brows and glared at him. 'If your aunt is correct in saying you're a financial genius, my lord, it would better become you to assist your family than to make fun of them. It seems to me that Miss Grismead is sincerely attached to her poet and—'

'If Nermal, or whatever his name is, really wishes to marry Pamela,' he shot back, 'he'll cease this idiotic notion he has of cutting himself off from his family for no good reason.'

'But that is precisely what I mean!' she exclaimed.

Pleased at his ready understanding, she momentarily forgot her other tribulations. 'I knew you would comprehend the matter perfectly, my lord. First of all, you could give Lord Grismead a nudge in the right direction. Financially, I mean, and then you could speak to—'

'Have you lost your mind, Miss Smith?'

'No, of course not. Only think. It's much more likely that Mr Hartlepoole will listen to someone who really was estranged from his family for years. You could tell him how very uncomfortable it is.'

'You *have* lost your mind.'

Grappling with details, Phoebe waved this away as one absently brushing aside a bothersome insect. 'Really, I'm surprised I didn't think of it before. Just think how relieved and happy the Grismeads will be. It will heal the rift beautifully and—'

'I wonder if my aunt has a blue powder in the house.'

'Very likely. Now, would it best if you—'

'Yes, I believe you're right. Blue powders must work on Pamela, otherwise the neighbours would be forever complaining. Now, if I can only prevail upon my aunt to spare one, I'm sure you'll soon feel more the thing.'

That got through. Phoebe ceased contemplating the brilliance of her scheme and bent a severe frown upon him. 'You seem to forget, sir, that your aim is to have your aunt take charge of Theo and Cressy as soon as possible. She won't oblige you in that until Miss Grismead is suitably married. And if the only impediment is Mr Hartlepoole's intransigence, then the sooner he is convinced of the foolishness of his actions, the better.'

She didn't expect this admonition to be greeted with exclamations of delight, but the abrupt narrowing of Deverell's eyes sent a tingle of alarm down her spine. He went very still. The stillness of a predator about to spring.

'Do you know, Miss Smith, I'd forgotten how anxious you are to leave us. How very remiss of me. However, in case you're considering ways of escape, you may disabuse your mind of the notion that Toombes is a likely prospect. He'd drive you mad within a week.'

Phoebe's mouth fell open. 'Well! Really, my lord. This time you go too far! What I do about Mr Toombes is none of your business, although escape certainly has a definite—'

'Damn it, Phoebe, as your employer I have a right to know if you're considering accepting an offer from Toombes!'

His outburst momentarily stunned her into silence. Phoebe took a deep breath, contemplated the grim line about Deverell's mouth and decided she'd better answer.

'No, I am not!' she exclaimed, goaded. 'Not that I expect him to take any notice of me,' she added disagreeably. 'Like all men, he doesn't listen to anything he doesn't want to hear.'

Without a word, Deverell grasped her by the elbow and marched her over to the door, snatching up her pelisse from a chair near the piano where she'd placed it earlier.

'You won't be required to say anything, whether or not Toombes wishes to hear it,' he grated through set teeth as he propelled her down the stairs. 'From now on, Miss Smith, you will refer any offers, of any kind, from any gentlemen, to me. Is that perfectly clear?'

Phoebe clenched her own teeth. 'Perfectly,' she muttered. And refused to say another word all the way out to the carriage.

The Grismeads' butler looked enviously after them as they exited through the front door while the sounds of battle continued unabated from the floor above. Phoebe found herself in entire sympathy with Miss Grismead's piercingly uttered desire to send a notice to the *Gazette* at once. She would very much like to place an advertisement therein herself.

For the mythical male-free, elderly lady she'd imagined earlier.

Chapter Eight

Several days later, Phoebe had not changed her mind
about the advantages of a household free of gentlemen.
In fact, she told herself, rubbing salt into the wound, if
she'd remained at Kerslake, she could have looked
forward to such a household once Gerald was settled at
Oxford.

But no. She'd insisted on bringing Deverell's wards
to London and look what had happened. Instead of allevi-
ating all her problems, she now had a whole new set to
worry about. All of which had to do with males.

She never seemed to be rid of the creatures.

Coming down the stairs, she bumped into Mr Filby
on his way up to haul Gerald from his slumbers. She
tripped over Lord Bradden in the drawing-room. Mr
Charlton appeared to have taken up residence in the
library. Only the sounds of Mr Toombes's measured
tones wafting into the morning-room prevented a disastrous encounter in the hall.

She couldn't even take comfort from the fact that
Crowhurst hadn't called. Instead, he was bombarding
her with flowers that came attached with invitations to
dinner at a discreet coffee-house at a time of her choosing. As if he had only to ask!

Her bedchamber was the only place where she could
be guaranteed any peace and privacy. And even that
seemed to have been invaded by memories of her last

159

encounter with Deverell. For some strange reason, she was constantly beset by a desire to tell him that she wasn't at all anxious to leave his employment. It was very odd. Why should she care if he'd taken her helpful suggestions the wrong way? It was just like him, she'd fumed, pacing up and down in front of her mirror, to be the only gentleman to make himself scarce precisely when he was needed to oust the others. Typical Deverell behaviour.

Rallying her spirits with that stricture. Phoebe tried valiantly to oust him from her mind.

Her efforts had not been crowned by any great success when she ventured cautiously into the dining-room in anticipation of breakfast two days later.

She immediately perceived another problem. The room was mercifully free of gentlemen, but it was *too* empty. Phoebe eyed the vacant places at the breakfast table with foreboding. They did not augur well.

When Thripp tiptoed into the room after her and carefully placed the coffee-pot on the table, her uneasiness increased twofold. One glance at the butler's face aroused the unpleasant suspicion that another breakfast was about to be rendered hideous by disclosures she would rather not hear.

Phoebe fortified herself with a mouthful of coffee and braced for the worst. 'Don't try to break the news gently, Thripp. Tell me at once. Where are they?'

Thripp shook his head. 'That I couldn't say, miss, but I doubt the young ladies have gone to the theatres.'

'Well, that's a relief. I think. What makes you say so?'

'They prevailed upon his lordship to lend them his new phaeton, miss, which they would hardly do if they intended to pay frequent visits to theatres.'

'Gerald lent them his phaeton?' Phoebe contemplated her empty plate while she mulled over that bit of news. It wasn't reassuring. Theo was an excellent driver, but this was London.

'So I understand, miss. And very smart they looked, too, in their greatcoats.'

'*Greatcoats!*' Her head jerked up. 'Greatcoats? Thripp, ladies don't wear greatcoats.'

'Well, as to that, I couldn't say, miss, but greatcoats they were. With capes,' he added helpfully. 'Several capes. And large brass buttons.'

A variety of nerve-racking pictures chased one another through Phoebe's head. She didn't like any one of them.

'I don't suppose you managed to see what they were wearing under the greatcoats, Thripp?' she asked, hoping against hope that her sudden suspicions were too wild to be true.

'Nothing you could take exception to, miss,' responded Thripp, quite as one who was an expert on suitable fashions for young ladies. 'Very pretty gowns, I thought. Blue and yellow stripes.'

Phoebe's suspicions took a giant stride towards certainty. Several remarks passed by Theodosia on the subject of female drivers echoed ominously in her head. Oh, why hadn't she taken more notice of the twins' activities over the past few days? It was no use only now recalling hurried forays to the shops, and several meetings with other young ladies, conducted in hushed voices and accompanied by excited gigglings.

Distracted by the possible reasons why Deverell had formed no part of the male invasion, not to mention Gerald's increasingly haggard countenance, she'd been only too relieved that the girls were happily occupied. And now. . .

'Thripp, go upstairs and tell Gerald if he isn't down here in five minutes his exit from his bed will be even more unpleasant than what Lord Deverell had in mind for him.'

Thripp's countenance immediately fell into its usual mournful lines. 'His lordship has not as yet returned home, miss.'

'Good heavens! Where is he?'

'I couldn't say with any accuracy, miss, but his lord-ship has been very flush with the ready—' Thripp coughed discreetly behind his hand '—I beg your pardon, miss, I'm sure. That is to say, very well-heeled lately. If you take my meaning, Miss.'

'Oh, my goodness! Do you mean Gerald has been *gambling*?'

Thripp looked cautious. 'I believe his lordship has taken quite a liking to a place called the Pigeonhole.'

'The—*Pigeonhole*! Of course! Pigeons! For the plucking. Oh, how could I have been so foolish, so neglectful?' Abandoning all thought of breakfast, Phoebe leapt to her feet. 'I'll have to see Deverell immediately. Thripp, go and summon a hackney, and then send the footman out to search for Gerald. I don't care where you find him or what he's doing. Tell him he's needed at Lord Deverell's house at once!'

Wasting no more time, Phoebe dashed out of the room. She was still chastising herself several minutes later as she leapt into a hackney, pelisse half-buttoned and bonnet askew. What a dreadful mess she'd made of everything. She'd known what she was dealing with but, too busy brooding over Deverell, she'd forgotten the schemes his wards were capable of concocting.

On the other hand, Deverell was supposed to be applying a firm hand. He'd told her he was keeping an eye on Gerald. What was he about, to let an inexperienced boy throw money around in every gambling hell in town? And who had given Gerald the money in the first place?

She hadn't reached any satisfactory conclusions when the hackney arrived at Deverell's townhouse. Paying off the driver, Phoebe ran up the steps and wielded the knocker with violent force. The door was opened by a startled butler. Phoebe raced past him into the house as if pursued by demons and demanded its master.

'His lordship is Upstairs, Miss Smith,' intoned the guardian of the door in frigid accents. 'I will see if he can Be Disturbed.'

'Good heavens, does everyone in London spend half the day abed?' she cried. 'Tell his lordship he'll be extremely disturbed if he doesn't come down here immediately. His entire family will be disturbed. The whole of Society will be disturbed. In fact—'

'What seems to be the problem, Miss Smith?'

The calmly voiced query did not come from the butler. Phoebe looked up—and felt her throat seize in mid-sentence. Not that she didn't have plenty to say, she tried to remind herself, but it was, she suddenly discovered, impossible to deliver a tirade when its recipient stood two floors above her, dressed only in breeches, topboots and a shirt that, with sleeves rolled up and half-unfastened, exposed a good deal of tanned throat and powerful forearms dusted with a covering of dark hair.

Phoebe swallowed and wondered why the sight of Deverell interrupted in the process of dressing for the day should have the very peculiar effect of suspending every faculty.

He stepped forward to the head of the stairs, a faint smile curving his lips. 'Won't you come up, Miss Smith?'

'Come up?' She repeated the words. That is, her lips moved. She still seemed incapable of uttering a sound.

'You obviously have news of great moment to impart. Dawby, would you be good enough to bring some tea up to the studio for Miss Smith?'

Her gaze still fixed on Deverell, Phoebe moved towards the stairs as one in a trance. 'Oh, no. Nothing, thank you. I—'

She started to climb, her breath growing shorter with each step. It was no use telling herself the stairs were particularly steep. It was the way Deverell watched her that was rendering her both breathless and witless. She was too far away, at first, to see the expression in his eyes, which were shadowed anyway by the downward sweep of his lashes, but when she reached the landing there was no mistaking the intensity of his gaze.

Unable to meet it, she looked at his throat instead and found herself instantly transfixed by the pulse beating there. And lower still, just where his shirt was fastened was the veriest hint of the same dark hair that covered his forearms.

Phoebe felt a shiver ripple through every nerve in her body. She tried to tell herself that Deverell wasn't the first male she'd seen in a state of *déshabillé*. She'd once come upon Gerald *completely* bare-chested when he'd been swimming in the stream at Kerslake. But somehow it wasn't the same. Gerald was a stripling, a boy. Her only reaction had been to order him to don his shirt before he encountered Miss Pomfret and sent her into a fit of the vapours.

Deverell, on the other hand, was all adult male. At least a foot taller than her, broad and solid across the shoulders, all powerful muscle and sheer primitive masculinity. And she felt a shockingly primitive urge to draw closer, to lift her hand to his chest, to feel the strength and power she'd felt once before and could now see.

Oh, dear, such urges were definitely unseemly. Extremely unseemly. And it didn't help that she could feel Deverell's intent gaze on her as if he was about to *do* something unseemly.

Completely unnerved, Phoebe whirled about and scurried through the nearest open doorway. She immediately froze, squeezing her eyes shut. Oh, heavens! This was worse. She was probably in Deverell's bedchamber! What was she to do *now*?

She didn't stop to contemplate her options. Spinning about, eyes still tightly shut, she dashed back towards the hallway and cannoned straight into Deverell.

Heat enveloped her instantly. If he hadn't grasped her arms, she would have collapsed in a heap right there at his feet. The thought was so shocking, she didn't realise he continued to hold her a mere inch away until his breath stirred the curls at her temple.

'Did the sight of this room startle you so much, Miss Smith?'

Phoebe took a deep breath and opened her eyes. The triangle of his open shirt met her gaze; feathery black hair almost tickled her nose. She swallowed, wrenched her gaze upward and met a wry, heart-shaking smile that was totally unlike the fiendish grin she'd half-expected.

'I. . .that is. . .'

Her voice was a mouse-like squeak. She dragged in another breath and tried again. 'I shouldn't be here, my lord.'

Something glittered in his eyes behind the smile. She felt his hands tighten very carefully. 'This is precisely where you should be,' he murmured. And turned her around. 'Look.'

Phoebe obeyed, and then blinked as light and space bombarded her senses. They weren't standing in Deverell's bedchamber after all, but in a room that appeared to her astonished gaze to be filled with items of statuary in various stages of construction. Several finished pieces stood on pedestals against one wall, and in front of her stretched a long bench covered with a liberal coating of whitish dust and holding an array of tools whose purpose she could only guess at.

'Oh, my goodness.' Blinking again, she glanced down at the long fingers still wrapped about her upper arms. They, too, wore a coating of dust. She transferred her gaze to his face. 'You're a sculptor, my lord.'

He continued to hold her for a moment longer, looking down into her face. He didn't appear to be put out by her discovery, she thought. Or annoyed that she'd invaded his privacy. Rather, his eyes held a watchfulness, an almost wary stillness; every emotion carefully hidden.

Then as her awareness of him, warm and solid against her back, set her pulse tripping, he released her and moved away to a table holding a porcelain basin and ewer. Pouring some water into the basin, he began washing the dust from his hands.

'It's merely a hobby. I started years ago, whittling pieces from wood to pass the time.'

'Pass the time?'

He threw her a sidelong glance from beneath half-lowered lashes. 'It can be rather tedious waiting in the mountain regions of India for bandits to show themselves.'

'Oh.' So her initial assessment of him as a warrior had been accurate.

Unable, for the moment, to do anything except ponder that point, Phoebe watched him withdraw his hands from the basin, shake them and reach for a cloth that lay folded nearby.

Big hands. Powerful hands. The hands of a warrior.

And, she mused wonderingly, remembering the candelabra in his library, hands capable of creating delicate beauty.

'The Psyche,' she murmured, then blushed, recalling the statue's paucity of civilised clothing.

'Guilty, I'm afraid.' The corners of his mouth curled upward. 'I hope she didn't shock you, Miss Smith.'

Phoebe valiantly fought back a hotter blush. 'Of course not, my lord. Your Psyche is formed quite in the classical mode. A most accurate. . .er. . .rendering of the ancient Greek, um. . . That is to say. . .'

She subsided when Deverell tossed the cloth aside and strode towards her, a distinctly amused light in his eyes.

'Are you feeling overly warm in here, Miss Smith? There are a lot of windows, and it is a particularly sunny day. Perhaps if you were to move out of the direct light—'

'I am not overly warm,' Phoebe retorted, recovering somewhat under this goad. She assumed her primmest posture and levelled a disapproving frown at him. 'It is just—I'm not in the habit of conversing with a gentleman who hasn't taken the trouble to don his coat before receiving visitors.'

'But I didn't know you intended to visit,' he returned inarguably. He stopped in front of her and subjected her to a swift examination. 'And I hardly think your strictures are fair, Miss Smith, when you appear to have flung your clothes on in some haste yourself.' The words were followed by a slow smile. 'In fact, your bonnet is listing quite dangerously to the left. If you'll allow me. . .'

Phoebe just managed to prevent a startled gasp escaping her lips when Deverell's fingers brushed her throat. She stood still, every muscle rigid, as he placed her bonnet at the proper angle and began retying the ribbons.

He was obviously going to take his time about the task. She wondered why her heart seemed determined to leap out of her chest; why she couldn't breathe; why the feel of Deverell's fingers, warm and hard against her bare flesh made her nerves quiver like harp strings recently struck. He was only touching her neck, for heaven's sake.

But then he rested the backs of his fingers against the pulse beating wildly in her throat and she ceased thinking at all. A strange melting lassitude made her legs go weak and her insides dissolve. She wanted to lean on him, to feel his arms go around her, supporting her, holding her.

Oh, dear, this was beyond unseemly urges. She was crossing the line into unbridled passion. And it *was* dangerous. Her family had been right to warn her. Instead of raising her voice in protest, she could only gaze, mesmerised, into those half-narrowed, intensely glittering eyes, and picture his hands, fashioning, moulding, smoothing over the feminine contours of the statue he'd created.

No, not just picture them. *Feel* them. On *her*. Even though he hadn't moved an inch.

She trembled once, violently. Then, with an incoherent

whisper, wrenched herself away and fled to the other side of the room.

She found herself contronted by an array of statuary and at once began babbling. 'Good heavens, my lord, you *have* been busy! Marble, wood, clay. You're certainly versatile. What a very interesting statue of a child. It looks just like. . .'

The spate stopped abruptly as her mouth formed a silent 'oh' of surprise. 'It looks just like Gerald,' she finished slowly, turning to face him.

But Deverell was no longer watching her. He stood before the bench, fists thrust into the pockets of his breeches, apparently deep in contemplation of the block of ebony wood in front of him.

'It is Gerald,' he said curtly. 'As I remember him. Always pestering me for a ride.'

Eyes wide, Phoebe stared at the unyielding line of his shoulders and wondered uneasily what had brought about the demise of all traces of devilishness. He'd spoken so tersely, so dismissively. It could be in response to the possibility of her remarking on his work. She hoped so. It was bad enough that her nerve-endings still felt as if they were simmering under some invisible source of heat. If Deverell knew how shockingly she'd reacted to his touch, she would be forced to leave him. And. . .

She didn't want to.

'I see,' she managed, and turned to the statue again. Blindly, at first, her thoughts in a turmoil. But then her vision, strangely blurred, cleared, and she did see. More, perhaps, than Deverell realised, she thought, distress and embarrassment forgotten in the wonder of discovery.

She studied the upturned marble face, the chubby out-stretched arms, and felt something move deep within her. A little child wanting to be lifted, and yet there was something in the way the arms reached upward, something about the face. . .

Then she shifted slightly—or perhaps the angle of the

light changed—and the child's features seemed to alter, to harden, to show hints of the man he would one day become. And in that moment, Phoebe knew, with absolute certainty, that it was Deverell reaching out; that he was innocent of whatever scandal had seen him banished from his home; that he'd been hurt, terribly; was still hurt, by that banishment.

'You're very talented, my lord,' she murmured, hearing the huskiness of repressed tears in her voice. She cleared her throat, hoping he hadn't noticed, trying desperately to think of something else to say. What was the matter with her? Why did this particular man cause these strange emotions that tempted her to draw perilously close to the invisible line beyond which lay scandal and disgrace?

But even as the faintest whisper of an answer threatened to creep into her consciousness, she fought it back. She didn't want to face the reasons for her odd behaviour. She didn't even want to think about it. Now wasn't the time. Later she could put it down to overwrought nerves. Surprise that a warrior could also be an artist. Something she'd eaten.

Anything.

Right now the only line she was prepared to cross was that of employee telling her employer precisely what she thought of people who abandoned their responsibilities—

'Oh, my goodness! What on earth are we about? My lord, we can't stand here chatting about statues. We must go at once! At once, I say!'

Deverell turned to face her, his hands still thrust into his pockets. His gaze was rather searching, causing uneasiness to flutter again like tiny moths in her stomach, but his voice held a familiar sardonic note.

'I am, of course, only too happy to oblige you, Miss Smith. Not, however, until I know where we're going and why.'

'I'll explain on the way.' Phoebe glanced hurriedly

around the room. 'Where's your coat? Why is nothing ever where it should be? You'll have to send a message to your stables, my lord, and then—'

'No.'

She gaped at him. 'No?'

'No.'

'But. . .there isn't a moment to lose. Disaster will overtake us at any moment. Think of the scandal, sir! Think of your nieces' reputations! Think—'

'Aha. So that's the cause of this precipitous visit. I did wonder if I was to be called upon to rescue you from the estimable Mr Toombes, or even Crowhurst. How very disappointing.'

'What?' Phoebe shook her head as if trying to clear her brain. 'What on earth have they got to do with anything? I'm here because I think Theodosia may have started a club for female whips based upon the Four-in-Hand and—' She glared at him as he started to smile. 'There is nothing amusing about it, I can assure you.'

His smile widened. 'I dare say, Miss Smith. If I'm amused, it's because you're a constant source of delight to me. But surely your reaction is unnecessarily exaggerated. Theodosia may have spoken about a whip club, but she won't get far without a carriage.'

'She has a carriage, sir. Gerald's phaeton. And while we're wasting time arguing, the twins are driving to Salt Hill with heaven's knows how many other young ladies. Also in carriages.'

He shrugged and turned back to the bench to start putting tools away. 'Then, I dare say, if they adhere to the rules of the genuine Four-in-Hand Club, they'll eventually return.'

'Is that all you have to say?' she cried. 'Didn't you hear me? I said they're driving to *Salt Hill*! They intend to dine at a public inn. Imagine the spectacle they'll present! Good heavens, most of them aren't even out yet. Their parents will never forgive you.'

He sent her a look over his shoulder that clearly stated his indifference to parental disapproval.

'Well, if that doesn't move you, my lord, consider the fact that I'll give you no peace until you agree to accompany me.'

'A telling threat, Miss Smith.' His mouth curved wryly as he abandoned his task to lean casually against the bench. 'You know,' he mused aloud, 'I returned to London for some peace. Strange. I wonder what made me think such a commodity could be found here?'

'I have no idea,' Phoebe snapped with some asperity. 'Peace is not something one readily associates with Deverells. Now, will you send a message to your stables, sir, or shall I?'

'You realise, of course, that we may be setting off on a futile enterprise. Theodosia may be doing nothing more innocuous than tooling Gerald's phaeton around the Park.'

Phoebe considered the suggestion with a quick uprush of hope, only to dismiss it. 'I'm afraid not, sir. You see, I overheard the girls talking.' She wrung her hands in self-reproach. 'I know I should have taken more notice at the time, but it all sounded so far-fetched I didn't think anything could come of it. Theo was setting out some sort of rules and regulations. That they would drive to Salt Hill, just like the gentlemen's Four-in-Hand Club, in single file at a strict trot, with no overtaking. And they'd even wear the same sort of costume.'

'Good God!'

She nodded gloomily. 'I am very much blame, my lord. I'm fully aware of it. I can only hope that no one has met with an accident. If I recall correctly, only men with a great deal of experience in driving a team are admitted to the Four-in-Hand Club. Some even take lessons from professional coachmen. Heaven knows what we'll find. But,' she added hopefully, 'I've sent a message to Gerald to meet us here, so we'll have some help.'

'You can't imagine how that reassures me, Miss Smith.'

Phoebe hung her head. 'I'm very sensible of the patience you're exercising, my lord.'

'Hmm. First threats, now remorse.' Straightening, he strolled over to her and tipped her face up to his with one long finger under her chin. Amusement, and something that made her breath quiver, glittered in his eyes.

'Forgive me for saying so, Miss Smith, but you're more than a match for any Deverell. I'll accompany you—if only for the pleasure of seeing you cope with what is sure to be a shambles if the young ladies are indeed emulating the Four-in-Hand Club.'

Phoebe shuddered, but straightened her shoulders. 'We must save them from scandal, my lord.'

And while she was about it, she'd better do the same for herself, she reflected, taking a careful step away from his touch.

She was still expounding silently on this theme when Deverell, having left a message for Gerald with his butler, handed her up into his phaeton. The vehicle appeared to be fashioned more for speed than safety, a sight that heartened Phoebe somewhat. Deverell might appear to be less than concerned about the situation, but clearly he didn't intend to waste any time.

He had just walked around to climb up next to her, when the clatter of several wheels on cobblestones had them both turning their heads. Bowling up the street towards them came a bright yellow curricle drawn by two chestnut horses. Mr Filby, resplendent in a greatcoat with wide lapels of the same hue as his carriage, held the reins, and seated beside him, looking slightly rumpled, was Gerald.

Two or three more curricles, all crowded with young gentlemen, followed hard on their wheels.

Deverell watched the approaching cavalcade for a moment, then turned a narrow-eyed look on Phoebe. 'How many females did you say were in this club?'

Phoebe decided it would be prudent to keep her eyes lowered. 'Um. . .I didn't say precisely, my lord, but. . .several.'

'Several.' He muttered something indecipherable, climbed into the carriage and gathered up the reins. 'And several of Gerald's cronies have obviously entertained second thoughts on the wisdom of lending their various equipages to their sisters.'

'Er. . .it would seem so, sir.'

He continued to eye her for a moment longer, his lips set in a grim line. Then, without waiting for Mr Filby to come up with them, gave his horses the office to start.

Followed by the astonished stares of a number of passers-by, two youthful crossing-sweepers and assorted loungers and tradespersons, the procession headed out of Town.

'Don't worry your head about an outbreak of scandal, Miss Smith.'

The sound of Deverell's voice, abrupt in a silence broken only by the rapid rhythm of horses' hooves, shook Phoebe out of the gloomy contemplation of her probable future that had occupied her for the first few miles.

They were driving through some rather pretty country, the autumn hues of the trees and hedgerows painting everything in sight in warm russets and golds. The road wound through a small wood enclosing them in a dim, sun-dappled tunnel. Birds flew, twittering, between the branches, seeming to dart from sunbeam to sunbeam.

She hadn't noticed a thing.

'I cannot help but worry, my lord.'

'Unnecessary, I assure you. Thanks to your quick action in coming to me immediately, we'll overtake the little beasts before they reach Salt Hill.'

When she failed to take exception to this unloving description of the miscreants, he cast a quick glance at her face. 'And if they're decked out in identical costumes, as you say, they'll probably pass for pupils from a young ladies' academy. Taking driving lessons,' he added helpfully when she turned a look of scepticism on him.

'Without any teachers?'

'We were delayed.'

'How?'

'One of the horses threw a shoe.'

'And they went on without us?'

He grinned. 'They're pupils. They couldn't get their horses to stop.'

Adjuring herself not to respond to that wicked grin, Phoebe returned her gaze to the road. 'I don't think that will work, sir.'

'Why not? You're already wearing your governess costume. Again.'

When she once more refused the challenge, his voice changed. 'All right, Miss Smith, let's have it. What else is causing that line between your brows?'

Phoebe contemplated ignoring the demand, then decided that delivering herself of another lecture might keep her mind on her proper sphere in life. Despite all her strictures to herself, it still seemed possessed of a regrettable tendency to dwell on such inappropriate matters as the way Deverell's mouth kicked up at one corner when he smiled in that wry fashion, the brilliant intensity of his eyes, the strength of his hands as he handled the reins with easy competence.

'It you must know, sir, I am extremely worried about Gerald. If you didn't notice it before, the merest glance over your shoulder should tell you how haggard he's looking.'

'If you don't mind, Miss Smith, at this speed I'd rather keep my eyes on the road.'

'You told me you were keeping an eye on Gerald,' Phoebe pointed out. 'But this morning I learned from Thripp that Gerald is spending night after night at some dreadful place called the Pigeonhole.'

'Hmm. Gambling hell. St James's Square. Precisely what one would expect of a young fool.'

'I can see you're beside yourself with worry,' she observed with heavy sarcasm. 'It is not good enough, my lord. Poor Gerald could fall into the clutches of evil moneylenders at any moment. Be cast into the Fleet. Throw himself into the river! What will you do then?'

'You've been reading novels again, Miss Smith.'

'If you don't do something,' she threatened, sweeping over this accusation with magnificent disdain, 'then *I* will. I cannot stand by and watch Gerald ruin himself, even if I have to drag him out of that dreadful place myself.'

'If you go anywhere near the Pigeonhole, Miss Smith, or any other hell for that matter, I'll put you over my knee.'

Phoebe's mouth fell open. The action didn't seem to restore the air to her lungs. While she was still struggling with outrage, Deverell apparently forgot the dangers of driving at speed along a winding road and looked down at her.

'Phoebe.'

He waited until she glared back at him.

'You are worrying to no purpose,' he said very softly, and looked straight into her eyes.

Phoebe could only gaze back, her mind whirling. She could have sworn a full minute passed before Deverell released her from the spell of his gaze. Even then she could hardly think. She stared at the ribbon of road unfurling ahead of them and wondered how one direct look could deflate her wrath so thoroughly.

No answer seemed forthcoming, but that and every other consideration was abruptly forgotten when they swept around a bend.

The road ahead, empty of traffic only seconds ago, was crowded and congested beyond belief. Horses, carriages and people milled about in a seething kaleidoscope of confusion and noise.

Trapped in the middle of the turbulent sea of humanity
and horses was a large stage-coach, its driver standing
upright on the box, his mouth opening and closing, arms
waving frantically. Passengers hung out of windows or
shook their fists from the roof. Since no one could be
heard over the shrieks, shouts and equine squeals that
filled the air, their efforts were useless.

'Oh, my goodness!' Hands pressed to her mouth,
Phoebe stared in horror at the scene before her. Even
as she watched, one young lady, who had apparently
considered herself competent to drive tandem, managed
to free her carriage from the fray only to have her lead
horse turn in its traces and try to rejoin its fellows. She
promptly succumbed to hysterics while her pair
exchanged nips and uncomplimentary pleasantries.

'Oh, my goodness! This is impossible!'

'I'm surprised you know the word, Miss Smith.' There
was a suspicious tremor in Deverell's voice as he pulled
his horses to the side of the road. 'Here—' thrusting the
reins into her hands '—try to keep my greys from adding
to the disaster.'

'But what—?'

She didn't get any further. Before the enquiry was
fully formed in her mind, Deverell put his head in his
hands and laughed so hard he almost fell out of the
carriage. If she hadn't been fully occupied in preventing
the greys from backing into Mr Filby's curricle, Phoebe
was certain she would have given him a helping push.

'For goodness' sake, my lord, have you run mad?
Don't just sit there laughing! *Do something*!'

He straightened, still grinning. 'Have *you* run mad,
Miss Smith? Anyone fool enough to wander into that
pandemonium will be trampled underfoot.'

'I say, sir.' Gerald appeared at the side of the phaeton,
looking as frantic as Phoebe felt. 'What is to be done?'

'It's your phaeton, I believe.' Deverell turned a look
of sardonic mockery on his nephew. 'You rescue it. And
while you're about it,' he added, his gaze sweeping over

the crowd of young gentlemen gathering about Gerald, 'every one of you had better be prepared to pay compensation to the coach driver and his passengers. Unless you want news of this episode to reach the ears of higher authorities.'

As one his audience blanched.

A silence fraught with dismay followed.

'My lord, I don't think Gerald is quite up to this task.' Her hands still full of reins, Phoebe tried to put as much of a plea into the words as possible. She didn't *think* Deverell would abandon his wards to their fate, but she wasn't above a little pleading if it got results.

Apparently reaching the same conclusion, Gerald and his cohorts did their best to look pathetically guiltless.

Deverell's eyes narrowed slightly. He glanced from his nephew to Phoebe then, rising to his feet, leaned over and spoke very softly in her ear. 'You, my love, are going to be knee-deep in debt to me. Don't move from this spot.'

He sprang down from the phaeton, waded into the fray and started giving orders.

He tended to do that a lot, Phoebe reflected, struggling with a pair of edgy horses and even more turbulent nerves. On the other hand, she didn't know of anyone else who could cope with a disaster of this magnitude. Softly spoken threats and inappropriate, heart-stopping appelations were a small price to pay, she decided.

Besides, he hadn't meant it. He'd been infected by the madness of the moment. Who could wonder at it?

Chapter Nine

It was well past noon by the time the procession returned to Town, at a slightly more decorous pace than when it had started out.

Theodosia was the only female still driving. The other young ladies sat beside their grim-faced brothers and tried, earnestly or tearfully according to their wont, to explain that if the guard on the stage-coach hadn't decided to blow his yard of tin just when Miss Forsythe was trying to prevent her pair from committing the heinous crime of overtaking the carriage in front of her, the entire débâcle would never have occurred.

Their explanations fell on deaf ears. So, too, did Gerald's dissertation on the matter. From her seat in Mr Filby's curricle, Phoebe had seen Gerald gesturing and talking all the way home. Deverell had appeared deaf and blind to his nephew's efforts.

She could only be thankful she'd retained enough wit to shove the greys' reins into Gerald's hands when he'd emerged, more rumpled than ever, from the mêlée, so she could take refuge with Mr Filby.

Listening to that Tulip's ambitious plans to start a new fashion of greatcoats with lapels to match one's carriage was a lot less nerve-racking than listening to an account of the debt she owed Deverell.

Unfortunately, her reprieve was not indefinite. Mr Filby, after one glance at Deverell's countenance as he

178

alighted from his phaeton, very basely drove off the instant her feet touched the ground. Phoebe gazed after the rapidly disappearing curricle and reflected on the general cowardice of males.

Then she caught sight of Deverell herself, and Mr Filby's cowardice was instantly elevated to the status of strategic retreat. In fact, it would, she decided, be wise to follow his example while Deverell was occupied in directing Gerald to take the reins from his sister, and in making arrangements for the disposition of his own phaeton and horses.

Before the thought was fully formed, Phoebe was scurrying up the front steps and into the house. If fortune smiled upon her, she might even reach the safety of her bedchamber while Deverell was further occupied in lecturing his wards.

Fortune did not feel inclined to smile upon her that day.

'Miss Smith! I *knew* you would return. I knew I would be wise to wait. Your butler has been trying to tell me—'

'Oh! Mr Toombes.' Phoebe skidded to a stop in the middle of the hall, and stared at her visitor in dismay. 'Oh, dear, what else is going to—? That is, I didn't expect to see you still in Town, sir.'

'The gentleman insisted on waiting,' Thripp muttered, eyeing Toombes with disfavour. 'But what's one more gentleman cluttering up the house?' He sniffed and prepared to depart to the nether regions. 'London. I knew how it would be.'

The front door opened again.

Phoebe refrained from demanding why, if Thripp had known how it would be, he hadn't warned her, and braced herself for the addition of yet another gentleman into the house. If Deverell could be described as such.

As she turned, Theodosia and Cressida slipped past her like wraiths. It was quite a feat, considering they were still clad incongruously in greatcoats.

Deverell didn't try to slip anywhere. He took in the

situation with a lightning-swift glance and stopped less than an arm's length from Phoebe.

'Theodosia, Cressida, the morning-room. Now.'

The twins halted in mid-step. Clasping each other's hands, they changed direction.

'And take off those ridiculous coats.'

'But, Uncle Sebastian, they're part of the costume of the Two-in-Hand Club for Lady Whips.'

'The Two-in-Hand Club for Lady Whips is now defunct. *Off*!'

'My lord!' Toombes started bowing as though to royalty. 'No doubt you are wondering why I am here. My presence, when you are aware of Miss Smith's very proper notions on such conduct, has startled you. One can readily understand your surprise. I'm sure you did not mean to speak so harshly to these poor, innocent—'

This highly inaccurate description of Deverell's nieces came to an abrupt halt as the coats were removed. A stunned silence filled the hall as everyone blinked at the barrage of brilliant blue and yellow stripes thus revealed. The paralytic effect was not lessened by the addition of white cravats decorated with large black spots.

Deverell closed his eyes as if in acute pain. 'I know why you're here, Toombes.' Opening his eyes again, he waved his nieces towards the stairs. 'Go! I'll deal with you later. Miss Smith—'

'A wise decision, my lord.' Toombes beamed ferociously. 'I'm sure after a rational discussion with another gentleman of sensibility you will be able to perform the sacred duty of directing your wards' footsteps on to the proper path with patience rather than brutality and—'

'A rational discussion, Toombes?' Deverell's lips curled back, baring as many teeth as Toombes. 'If you're here to discuss Miss Smith's future, no discussion will be necessary. Rational or otherwise.'

'If, by that, sir, you mean you have no objection to my intentions, I am happy to hear you say so. However—' Toombes glanced at Phoebe, who was standing, frozen, as one waiting for the sword to fall '—although one does not like to keep a lady in suspense, I would prefer to make myself perfectly clear to you.'

Deverell narrowed his eyes. 'Clarification is certainly needed on several points around here. Very well, you can have five minutes.'

'Five minutes!' Toombes's smile disappeared. He struck an attitude. 'Sir, it would take me forever to describe the exquisitely elevated nature of my feelings for Miss Smith.'

'Then I trust you will refrain, because when five minutes have elapsed—'

'My lord.' Bowing to the pressure of the moment, Phoebe tugged frantically at Deverell's sleeve. This was no time for such extravagant luxuries as panic. She had to take action before Toombes was laid out insensible at her feet.

'Ah, yes, Miss Smith.' Deverell glanced down at her, a particularly fiendish light in his eyes. 'I hesitate to behave in such a brutal fashion, of course, but you may consider yourself banished to the drawing-room.'

'But, sir, I—'

'You heard Mr Toombes. He doesn't want to keep you in suspense.'

Toombes beamed again.

'But—'

'The drawing-room is right over here, Miss Smith.' He grasped her elbow.

'I know where it is,' Phoebe muttered through gritted teeth as she was marched inexorably forward.

When Deverell opened the door for her and showed every sign of thrusting her unceremoniously into the room, a change of tactics seemed called for. She lowered her voice to an urgent whisper. 'My lord, what are you going to say to Mr Toombes? No doubt you mean well, but pray remember that, even as my employer, it isn't your place to be receiving offers on my behalf.'

'It's either that or leave you to handle Toombes on

your own. I'm choosing the lesser of two evils, Miss
Smith. Comfort yourself with the reflection that you'll
now be hip-deep in debt to me.'

Smiling grimly, he propelled her over the threshold
and shut the door in her face.

Phoebe resisted the urge to thump the door panels
with her fist and, muttering, began to pace back and
forth across the carpet. After several passes, she finally
caught sight of herself in the mirror over the mantelpiece
and realised she was still wearing her bonnet and pelisse.

Removing the garments restored a measure of composure. Pacing wasn't going to help. She needed to
decide how she was going to deal with Deverell when
he'd finished with Mr Toombes.

She wasn't quite sure how she was going to go about
the task, but she was *not* going to behave as if she really
was hip-deep in debt to him. She would, of course, be
grateful if Deverell managed to rid her of her unwanted
suitor. She was extremely grateful that she hadn't been
left to cope alone with the abrupt demise of Theodosia's
Two-in-Hand Club for Lady Whips. But anything else
was out of the question.

She absolutely refused, for instance, to allow herself
even a *hint* of a tender feeling for a gentleman who was
so ungallant as to render an account whenever he was
asked to come to her rescue. Or even when he wasn't.

Not that the odd little sensations hovering around her
heart lately could be described as 'tender feelings'. No,
no, not at all. Naturally she'd been deeply touched by
the poignancy of the statue she'd seen that morning. She
admired Deverell for using his talent as an outlet for his
feelings rather than allowing bitterness to ruin his life.
He also had an appreciation of the ridiculous that
appealed to her, and there was that fleeting sense of
protection she'd experienced once or twice in his company, but—

Phoebe frowned uneasily at the mirrored reflection in
front of her. Protection, she reminded herself, wasn't all

she was capable of feeling in Deverell's company. He seemed to have the knack of arousing some extremely disturbing, not to say positively scandalous, sensations whenever he came too close.

She couldn't understand it.

Or didn't want to understand it.

The insidious thought flitted across her mind and was instantly quelched. There was nothing *to* understand. However unseemly her urges, she'd observed enough to know that without tender feelings such urges didn't last long. And she'd just finished telling herself that she didn't have any tender feelings for Deverell so—

The sound of the door opening had her mind going blank in a singularly unnerving fashion. Every thought, every stricture, every resolve vanished as if it had never been as Deverell strode into the room and shut the door behind him.

Phoebe turned slowly to face him—and was instantly beset by an intense longing to run to him, to fly straight to the warmth of his arms. He looked so big standing there, watching her. Big and powerful and, somehow, protective.

Which was really quite ridiculous, she thought distractedly, because he was the cause of her dilemma.

'My. . .my lord.' Somehow, from somewhere, she conjured up a bright smile. He mustn't know. That was the one clear thought in her head. He must not know.

What, precisely, he wasn't to know she wasn't prepared to admit.

'I've been waiting here on tenterhooks forever. You haven't strangled Mr Toombes, I trust.'

'No,' he purred, his lips curving in an anticipatory smile, 'that is a fate I'm reserving for you, Miss Smith.'

For some reason, this response restored a semblance of normalcy to the situation. Threats of strangulation were as nothing. She was becoming quite accustomed to them.

'Now, my lord, I know the morning has been. . .er. . .

fraught with strain, but there is no need to lose your temper.'

He began to stalk slowly towards her. 'I never lose my temper.'

Phoebe's jaw dropped. 'But you just threatened to strangle me. Not for the first time, I might add.'

'That's right. And I'm going to enjoy every minute of it.'

She skipped nimbly behind a chair. 'Quite out of the question, sir. Besides, I know you don't mean it. Your family might be fooled by such threats because they're inclined to dramatic utterances themselves, but you're a great deal more controlled than they are and—'

'If you think that, Miss Smith, you're even more innocent than I supposed.'

The chair began to look rather flimsy. Phoebe retreated to the far side of the sofa. 'Nonsense, my lord. Apart from your outburst in Covent Garden last week, which was quite understandable, you've always behaved with perfect control.'

'I'm all too aware of that, Miss Smith. That's another item you can add to the account.' He moved closer.

'I'm afraid I don't understand you, sir.' Phoebe side-stepped along behind the sofa and measured the distance to a small writing desk. 'Perhaps we should sit down and discuss the matter.'

'You seem to be more interested in dancing around the furniture.'

'I'm trying to avoid being strangled,' she retorted with some asperity. 'It is not a practice I approve of, sir.'

He halted his advance and eyed her consideringly. Phoebe took the opportunity to dart across to the writing table. It wasn't as solid as the sofa, but it was wider.

'You deserve to be strangled,' he growled. 'Just what would you have done if you'd returned here, alone, to find Toombes waiting for you?'

'I'd have sent him about his business precisely as you did.' She paused and thought for a moment. 'Er. . .how did you send Mr Toombes about his business, sir?'

The fiendish gleam came back. 'I told him the truth about your position here.'

'What!' Phoebe's eyes widened. 'What truth? My position here is perfectly respectable.'

'You and I know that, Miss Smith, but Mr Toombes, I'm sorry to say, seemed not to approve of the fact that you've visited me, unescorted, on two occasions before most people have left their beds. And when I pointed out that Lord Portlake, not to mention the worthy parishioners of Little Muddleford, wouldn't understand how it came about that you allowed me to purchase your clothes, he—'

'Good heavens! You didn't have to tell him *that*!' Phoebe's voice soared. 'What did you think you were about? Are you trying to ruin every shred of reputation I have left?' Forgetting her present danger, she took an agitated turn in the small space behind the table. 'Not that I care what Toombes thinks of me, but—'

'I am, of course, relieved to hear you say so, Miss Smith.'

'Yes, that's all very well,' she retorted, coming to a halt so she could glare at him. 'But what if he goes to Lord Portlake with the information that you're providing your nieces' companion with her clothes?'

'Perhaps I should also explain that Toombes left here with the additional impression that if he so much as lets your name pass his lips in future, it will be the last thing he'll ever say.'

'Oh, my goodness.' Phoebe put a hand to the desk and wondered why, when she was absolutely certain Deverell would never strangle *her*, she didn't have the same assurance about Mr Toombes's continued good health. 'Really, my lord, you can't go about threatening people like that.'

He quirked a brow. 'You did want to see the last of Toombes, didn't you?'

'Well, yes, but—' After a futile effort to gather her

thoughts, she abandoned the attempt to bring her tormentor to a sense of his inappropriate behaviour. Such attempts were seldom crowned by success when dealing with Deverells anyway. 'I don't think I wish to know what you said to the twins,' she muttered.

'A wise decision, Miss Smith. However—' he took a deliberate step towards her and fixed her with a narrow-eyed stare '—what *I* wish to know is why you didn't see fit to inform me that this house is being overrun by males and that Crowhurst has been sending you notes capable of making you appear extremely worried, not to say frightened.'

'Thripp!' she exclaimed, flushing. 'Really! How dare he tell such tales? He's as bad as the rest of you Deverells. I am *not* frightened of Crowhurst. Merely, I thought if I ignored his notes he would eventually desist.'

'Indeed.' He took another step forward. 'And has he?'

'Well. . .' Suddenly realising she was being stalked again, Phoebe scuttled to the end of the table. She discovered, too late, that an overzealous housemaid had placed a chair at an inviting angle to the desk—right behind her.

In front of her, Deverell loomed.

Phoebe stiffened her spine. 'These things take time, my lord. Patience. Resolve.' She raised an admonishing finger. 'One must stand by one's guns. Hold the line. Um. . .'

'Never mind the rest,' he ordered, coming right up to her. 'Miss Smith, you and I are going to come to an understanding.'

'We are? I mean. . .' She raised her finger higher. '*You* must understand, my lord, that—'

'Miss Smith,' he interrupted again, very gently, 'if I hear one day that one of Toombes's parishioners has strangled him in the middle of a sermon, I will be most understanding. My understanding, however, does not extend to you placing yourself in awkward or dangerous situations with the male half of the population.'

Phoebe pursed her lips. 'Well, actually, my lord, I believe the proportion of population is not quite half and half. In fact—'

'Obviously words aren't going to do the trick,' he muttered. He caught her still-raised hand and tugged.

Phoebe squeaked, stumbled, and found herself landing in a disordered heap against Deverell's chest. Stunned, she gazed mutely from their clasped hands to his face.

'Allow me to remind you once again, Miss Smith, that you are not my governess. As a matter of fact, at present, you are not anybody's governess.'

'Yes, I know that, my lord, but—'

'And I'm beginning to believe that your talents as a companion are rather limited. So far this morning I've been compelled to spring my horses out of Town, engage on a battleground that would cause Wellington to blanch, deal with my wards and set an idiot vicar straight on one or two crucial points. All without giving vent to the famous Deverell emotions, Miss Smith.'

'Yes, I know that, too, sir, but. . .'

'Even a controlled Deverell, Miss Smith, has his limits.'

'But—'

He circled her waist with his free arm and drew her even closer. Phoebe tried frantically to remember what she'd been about to say. She couldn't seem to think at all. A shivery sense of excitement was racing along every nerve-ending. Her heart fluttered somewhere in her throat. Her breathing halted.

She watched, mesmerised, as he lowered his head until their lips were less than an inch apart.

'And before you remind me of it, Miss Smith, I know this is not part of our agreement, but keep in mind that no sorry details of infelicitous relationships have recently crossed my lips.'

His mouth closed over hers with devastatingly gentle mastery.

A thrilling, utterly shocking torrent of excitement

poured through her. Sweet, melting weakness followed. Every muscle went limp. She felt his arm tighten across her back, supporting her, holding her locked against him. Heat and strength enveloped her, wrapping her in a mindless haze of increasingly dizzying pleasure as his mouth moved slowly on hers.

Her lips parted on a tiny yearning sigh and suddenly the pressure was no longer gentle. His mouth was hot and hard and fiercely demanding; the arm across her back like iron.

He stroked his tongue across the tingling curve of her lower lip, but even as pleasure burst inside her in streamers of heat, Deverell broke the kiss, jerking his head back so abruptly she felt as if she'd been picked up and tossed about by a wildly eddying whirlwind, only to be as swiftly dumped back to earth. She had to cling to him, her face pressed to his coat, until the room and her senses stopped spinning.

He held her like that, his arm around her waist, his free hand still wrapped about her smaller one. Almost as if they'd been dancing, she thought dazedly, raising her head at last.

Except that her breasts throbbed where they'd been crushed to the hard planes of his chest. She felt unutterably soft and vulnerable and yielding inside. And she doubted the fierce expression glittering in his eyes was to be found in any ballroom.

She drew in a shaky breath, suddenly, overwhelmingly conscious of his much greater strength, of her own softer femininity, and he loosened his hold enough to put an inch or two of space between them. His hand remained at her waist. Big and powerful, it burned like a brand through her gown.

She didn't know why he kept it there. Fleeing from the room wasn't an option. Her legs wouldn't have carried her.

'Well, Miss Smith—' his voice was low, and strangely husky '—at least I didn't strangle you.'

'No.' Phoebe struggled desperately to think, to follow his lead. If he could shrug off a kiss, then so would she. She could collapse later. 'You showed great. . .self-restraint, my lord.'

He smiled at that. A slow smile that made her tremble inside.

'You have no idea, Miss Smith.'

'No. I. . .I mean. . .am I now out of debt, sir?'

For the first time since she'd known him, Deverell seemed to hesitate. His gaze shifted to her mouth. Very slowly he bent his head and brushed his lips lightly across hers. 'No,' he murmured.

And, releasing her, he turned and strode out of the room.

Phoebe was left staring after him, her mind a complete blank. She didn't move for several minutes. Then, quite abruptly, she put out a hand and lowered herself to the chair behind her. Her other hand lifted to touch her mouth.

What had she done?

The answer was all too evident in the tingling heat and softness of the lips beneath her fingers. She had allowed Deverell to kiss her. She hadn't raised her voice in protest for as much as one second. She had *wanted* him to kiss her.

That was scandalous enough. What was infinitely more devastating was why.

Phoebe groaned and leaned forward to rest her elbows on the desk. She lowered her brow to her clasped hands. Hiding her face, however, did nothing to disguise the truth. The answer could no longer be ignored. The moment of revelation could no longer be pushed aside to wait until later. She had done a very foolish thing. She'd done the most foolish thing a governess could do.

She had fallen in love with her employer.

When had it happened? she wondered, raising her head to stare blankly into space. When Deverell had rescued her in Covent Garden? At Lady Grismead's dancing party? When she'd discovered the statue of Gerald in his studio that morning?

Or earlier, in the Park, when he'd almost tempted her with gentle persuasion to tell him all the secrets of her past?

'Oh, what does it matter?' she exclaimed, leaping to her feet and pacing restlessly to the window and back. She'd had this conversation with herself before. Nothing but disaster could come of such a situation. If she had any sense of self-preservation, she would go upstairs and pack as fast as she was able.

Phoebe stopped pacing and dropped onto the chair again. It was a lowering thought to discover she hadn't any sense at all. Obviously she was more like her mother than she'd been told, because she was actually contemplating throwing away everything, including her reputation, for a love that was unlikely to be reciprocated and could only lead to scandal and disgrace.

That was if Deverell really wanted her. *Truly* wanted her. He might have kissed her, but then he'd all but informed her she should be grateful he hadn't strangled her instead.

This reminder caused a kindling light to dawn in her eyes. If Deverell had sworn undying devotion after that kiss it would be one thing. But no—typical infuriating male—he'd talked of debts. She *should* go upstairs and pack. It would serve him right to be left to cope with his nieces, and Gerald's gambling, and the Grismeads, *and* Miss Pomfret, because that lady would have to be summoned immediately from Kerslake.

But even as she rose and stalked over to the door, Phoebe knew she wasn't going to carry out any revenge. In fact, she admitted gloomily, while one part of her mind was busy ordering herself to dash off a letter to Mrs Arbuthnot's Employment Registry, the other half was issuing reminders that she still had a lecture to deliver to the twins.

And she really should look closely into Gerald's activities.

Then there was the fact that Miss Pomfret's last letter had contained ominous mention of the restorative tonic that had failed in its purpose.

A responsible companion simply couldn't abandon her charges at this point.

But she would not go to Deverell again. Oh, no. If she mentioned Gerald's troubles to him, there was no saying where the debt would end up. Over her head, no doubt. And until she managed to discover some sort of cure, she would be all too willing to drown.

Phoebe sighed and opened the door. For the first time she wished she knew more about the scandal that had sent thunderous reverberations echoing through her own family. She'd known her mother had been cast off; that her father had become a recluse. She'd listened for most of her life to warnings and reproaches every time her behaviour was less than exemplary. But she didn't know the hideous details.

Perhaps she should write to her aunt and ask. Hideous details might help her avoid a path that could only lead to more scandal and recriminations.

She was just wondering why that thought should put Crowhurst into her head, when the front door bell rang with a particularly urgent-sounding summons.

Still deep in thought, Phoebe absent-mindedly waved Thripp away and crossed the hall to answer it herself. She was speedily snapped back to full attention when Lady Yarwood hurried through the aperture.

'Miss Smith, you're home. Thank goodness! I came as soon as Caroline told me what was afoot. If only she'd mentioned it earlier. But perhaps it is not too late.'

'My dear ma'am, please don't fret yourself.' Gathering her wits to cope with this relatively minor calamity, Phoebe ushered her breathless visitor into the drawing-room. 'You've come about Theodosia's club, I expect. Really, it is too bad. Those dreadful girls! I'll summon them downstairs immediately to apologise for putting you out like this.'

'You mean they're here? Safe?' Lady Yarwood sank onto the sofa and fanned herself with one hand. 'Thank heavens.'

'Yes, indeed.' She turned to the butler who had followed them and was watching her with mournful disapproval. 'You may take that look off your face, Thripp. Nobody cares if I answer the door on the odd occasion.'

'What if it'd been Mr Toombes again?' Thripp demanded in sepulchral accents. 'Or that fellow sending notes?'

'Yes, I'd like a word with you about that,' Phoebe retorted. 'Later, if you please. In the meantime, you may ask Lady Theodosia and—'

'No, no, don't bother them, Miss Smith.' Lady Yarwood sat up and straightened her bonnet. 'If Caroline's news was precipitate, I'm only too happy to hear it.'

'Well, as to that, ma'am, if Miss Yarwood was referring to the first meeting of a certain club for young ladies, she was quite correct. Thanks to Lord Deverell, however, the first meeting was also the last.'

'His lordship told me to keep an eye on all the gentlemen running in and out of this house,' Thripp declared, Deverell's name apparently stirring him to animation. 'Just as well, if you ask me. Someone should know what's going on around here.'

'Yes, well, Lord Deverell already has quite enough to do.' Phoebe waved Thripp away and sat down beside her visitor. 'It was very good of you to come, ma'am, but I can assure you that the girls are indeed safe. All of them.'

'All?' Lady Yarwood blinked at her in dismay. 'How many were there?'

'Six or seven,' Phoebe admitted, shuddering as she remembered her first sight of the disaster. 'If it hadn't been for Deverell— But never mind that. You may be thankful, ma'am, that Miss Yarwood had the good sense not to take part in such an ill-considered romp.'

'Believe me, Miss Smith, Caroline is as silly as any young miss with more hair than wit. It was only her brother's refusal to lend his phaeton, and his representations on the matter, that convinced her to come to me in the first place. I dashed around here at once.'

'Oh. Well. . .' Phoebe hesitated and looked down at her hands. 'You. . .er. . .didn't think to go directly to Deverell, ma'am?'

'Perhaps I should have done so, Miss Smith, but I do know something of the strained relations between Deverell and his family. It occurred to me that if his intervention was necessary, you would have more influence when it came to persuading him to set things right.'

Phoebe felt herself turning pink. 'I. . .beg your pardon, ma'am?' she asked weakly.

'Perhaps I'm wrong, my dear, but from the way Deverell's attention scarcely left you the other day— except when he was glaring at any other gentleman who looked as if he might venture too close—I received the distinct impression that his interest in you was more than that of an employer.'

'Oh, no. Surely you're mistaken, ma'am.'

Lady Yarwood gave her a thoughtful look. 'I don't think so, my dear.'

'But—'

She stopped, anything as useful as rational thought beyond her. Tremulous hope, niggling doubt and an awareness of harsh reality jostled about in her head until she scarce knew what to think.

'Nothing but disaster could come of such an interest,' she finally managed.

'I see you believe you have reason to say so, Miss Smith. And I must admit that when Yarwood first showed a hint of interest in *me*, I was considerably incensed, having already suffered one nasty experience.

But remember, not all men prey on vulnerable females.'

'I dare say not, ma'am, but Deverell has never shown a hint. . . That is. . .' She blushed fierily as the memory of his kiss returned in full force. 'Well, *that* wasn't what I would call a *hint*,' she blurted aloud before she could stop herself.

Lady Yarwood laughed delightedly.

'Oh, dear, I shouldn't have said that.' Phoebe wrung her hands. 'What I meant was, that Deverell has never *said*. . . Indeed, he promised at the outset. . .'

Again her words tangled in her throat. He'd promised, yes, but suddenly a giant omission from that promise loomed large in her mind.

'Yes, I made it very clear to Yarwood that there would be no undesirable advances if he wished me to join his employ,' her ladyship said drily. 'It didn't take him long, however, to discover that *his* advances would be far from undesirable to me.'

'Oh, dear.' Phoebe wrung her hands again.

Lady Yarwood leaned over and stilled her writhing fingers. 'There, my dear, I didn't mean to distress you. I may be quite mistaken in Deverell's interest. Although,' she added shrewdly, 'perhaps you should ask yourself if he would have chased after his nieces at Ottilia Grismead's request.'

'He refused to do so at my request, ma'am. I had to threaten him.'

Her ladyship looked amused again. 'I doubt there are many people in this world who have threatened Deverell and managed to escape unscathed, Miss Smith.'

This remark, though clearly intended to reassure, had the opposite effect. Phoebe sank immediately into gloom.

'Yes, ma'am,' she agreed sombrely. 'I doubt it, too.'

Lady Yarwood bestowed a last pat on her hand and rose to her feet. 'In any event, whether Deverell is interested in you or not, Miss Smith, I hope you know I would like to stand your friend. If you need assistance or advice at any time, please don't hesitate to come to me.'

'Thank you, ma'am.' Phoebe rose, also, and tried to paste a polite smile on to her face. 'You're very kind.'

'Not at all.' Lady Yarwood gathered up her reticule and moved towards the door. 'I know precisely how difficult your situation can be. And Deverell, unlike everyone else in his family, is a great deal harder to read than Yarwood ever was.'

For the second time that day, Phoebe was left staring at the drawing-room door while she contemplated her visitor's parting remark.

It was not, she discovered after a moment of intense examination, altogether discouraging. She, herself, knew that Deverell was harder to read than the rest of his family—and in his dealings with others, it was perfectly true. But, she realised with a quick little uplift of her heart, he had shown her several different sides to his nature. Annoyance, anger, laughter, understanding.

And although she'd always been aware that he possessed the arrogance of a warrior completely sure of himself, this morning she'd seen the vulnerability of a boy unjustly banished from his birthright.

This morning she'd looked into his soul.

Had he meant that to happen?

Phoebe pondered the question for quite some time before she rose and walked over to the door. A new decisiveness was in her step. She might be more foolish than ever. She might be putting a rather desperate sort of faith in Lady Yarwood's opinion. She was definitely risking the destruction of her reputation, and the possible devastation of her heart.

But she knew she couldn't leave Deverell without knowing why he'd allowed her that glimpse of his soul.

Chapter Ten

Despite the improvement in her spirits, Phoebe did not spend the night in restful slumber.

For once, Deverell wasn't wholly to blame for this state of affairs. After Lady Yarwood had left, she had thought to distract herself by concentrating on her charges, her first task being the delivery of a stern lecture to the twins on the differences between the freedom enjoyed by gentlemen of the *ton*, and that allowed young ladies.

Theo and Cressy had watched her with close attention throughout the homily, but Phoebe was left with the impression that they had not listened to a single word. When she ran into Gerald outside the girls' bedchamber, however, her vague suspicions were forgotten. Gerald had been marched down to the drawing-room and ordered to render an account of his recent activities.

He had been all reassurance. There was nothing to worry about. No, no, not a thing. Yes, he had been keeping rather odd hours lately, but everything was all right and tight. Anyone would look pale after spending so much time indoors, but a run of luck had to be pursued. There was absolutely no need for her to concern herself—and could she possibly inform him if a minor could draw up a Will?

Phoebe had been so stunned by this mind-numbing

question that Gerald had made good his escape while
she was wondering if she'd heard him aright.

By three o'clock the following afternoon she was still
fretting over the question, and was further thrown into
anxiety when Mr Charlton was shown into the drawing-
room and immediately demanded to know what was this
nonsense about Gerald needing to draw up a Will before
he'd reached his majority.

'For I don't mind telling you, Miss Smith, that I'm
seriously concerned,' he went on, accepting Phoebe's
offer of a chair. 'I'm all too aware that Gerald has been
gambling every night for the past couple of weeks. God
knows what sort of company he's fallen into.'

'Oh, dear.' An anxious frown creased Phoebe's brow.
'You don't think he's been so rash as to accuse someone
of cheating, do you, sir? What if there should be a duel?
Gerald has never engaged in such a thing in his life.'

'We can only hope not,' Mr Charlton said heavily.
His tone held out no hope at all. 'But you know what
Deverells are like. Try as I might, I can think of no other
reason why Gerald would express this sudden desire to
draw up his Will. It's not the sort of thing he'd normally
consider.'

'No.' Phoebe thought for a moment, then cast a fleeting glance at her visitor. 'I take it, you haven't told Lord
Deverell of your suspicions, sir?'

Mr Charlton looked a little self-conscious. 'Er. . .no,
ma'am. In light of yesterday's events, I hesitated to bring
Deverell's wrath down upon Gerald before I have all
the facts. Gerald is very close to his sisters, however.
Perhaps, if we were to ask them. . .'

His suggestion was cut off as the drawing-room door
opened to admit the sisters in question. They greeted Mr
Charlton with every sign of pleasure, and had scarcely
sat down when Lady Grismead, a wilting Pamela in tow,
sailed into the room. She did not waste time.

'Never have I been so mortified!' she declared, sweep-

ing Mr Charlton from her path with a puce silk-clad arm
as he rose politely. She appropriated his abandoned chair
and fixed her nieces with a fulminating eye.

'Perhaps you can tell me,' she began ominously, 'why
it comes about that every young lady in London is this
minute explaining chipped paintwork and dented carriage doors to their fathers.'

'Well, Aunt Ottilia, you see—'

'And stripes! How could you, Theodosia? If the
gentlemen wish to make fools of themselves by dressing
in blue and yellow striped waistcoats, that is one thing.
Deverells do not emulate such fashions.'

'But, Aunt Ottilia, we wore dresses.'

Her ladyship shuddered, then proceeded to chastise
her nieces in no uncertain terms. Her main grievance
seemed not to be the fact that Theodosia had started
the Two-in-Hand Club for Lady Whips, but that she'd
allowed incompetent drivers to join the ranks.

Shaking her head at the predictable unpredictability
of Deverells, Phoebe was about to retire to the window-
seat to wait out the storm when the door opened yet
again. Gerald and Mr Filby strolled into the room, took
one look at its occupants and promptly began to retreat.

'Gerald!' Phoebe darted forward, raising her voice to
be heard above the din created by arguing Deverells.

'Can't stop now, Phoebe,' Gerald said hastily. 'Reggie
and I are on our way to Manton's Shooting Gallery. Just
stopped in to collect my pistols.'

This statement, delivered in a tone of airy unconcern,
was enough to cause Phoebe to grasp Gerald's coat with
both hands and haul him bodily back into the room. The
thought crossed her mind that had it been Deverell she'd
been trying to haul, the tactic would never have worked.

She instantly dismissed such useless meanderings.

'Just for once,' she told Gerald in minatory accents,
'you can stay here and help entertain your aunt and
cousin. And I believe Mr Charlton has something to say
to you.' She turned to Filby with a determined smile.

'Mr Filby, I have been wishing since yesterday to hear more about your brilliant idea of coat lapels to match one's carriage. Shall we sit over there by the window?'

No fool, Filby began to look hunted. Unfortunately for him, his manners precluded any other action but compliance. He followed her to the window-seat, his demeanour that of one approaching a designated place of execution.

'See you have quite a crowd,' he began with rather desperate chattiness as Phoebe seated herself. 'Bit hard on the ears, so many Deverells at once. Not that Miss Grismead ever says much. Seems to prefer draping herself over the furniture. Always wondered, y'know, if she actually has any bones.'

Phoebe smiled despite herself. 'An interesting theory, Mr Filby.'

'Once had a bet on it at White's,' he confided, looking more at ease. 'But no one could think of a way to prove anything one way or the other.'

'Indeed, sir.' Phoebe firmly suppressed the urge to laugh and turned an uncompromising look on him. 'I believe the Betting Book at White's is not the only form of gambling enjoyed by some gentlemen.'

'Well, if you mean Gerald,' said Filby, apparently deciding to take the bull by the horns, 'no need to worry he'll end in the River Tick. Inherited Deverell's talent for mathematics. Never loses.'

'Never?' Phoebe's brain reeled. She'd been so beset by visions of Gerald signing away Kerslake Park to some monster who preyed on green boys from the country, and in despair challenging said monster to a duel, that she'd never even considered the alternative.

Perhaps Deverell was right. She *had* been reading too many novels.

'Soon be rich,' Filby added, not without a touch of pride. 'Well, richer than he is now. Never seen anything like it. Figures the odds before you can say knife. Wants to repair the family fortunes, you know.'

'Well, I'm sure that's very commendable,' Phoebe began, still coping with this reversal of every plot she'd ever read. 'But, in that case, why would Gerald wish to draw up his Will? And why is he going to Manton's?'

'Oh, nothing in that. Everyone goes there. Well, not ladies, of course, but. . .'

'Mr Filby, has Gerald accused someone of cheating and demanded satisfaction?'

He began to look hunted again. 'No, no, nothing of the sort. Other way about. I mean—' he gasped as one going down for the last time '—all an unfortunate mis-understanding.'

'Oh, good heavens! Then there *is* going to be a duel!'

'Shouldn't mention such things to ladies,' Filby yelped frantically. 'Only send you into a fit of the vapours.'

'Mr Filby, it seems to be you who is having a fit of the vapours, but let me assure that I will immediately join you in the exercise if you don't tell me everything you know. Right now!'

Filby blinked several times in an agitated fashion, then capitulated. 'Told Gerald he shouldn't play at the Pigeonhole,' he whispered, as if anyone could have heard him over the voices of Deverells *en masse*. 'Full of Sharps and Flats.' Heartened by an encouraging nod, he continued. 'Trouble was, once everyone at the proper clubs realised how good Gerald was, they'd only play a few games at a time with him. One thing about Sharps, they always think tonight will be the night they'll fleece someone, so they continue to play. But Gerald didn't get fleeced.'

'The Sharp turned into a Flat?'

'Very neatly put, ma'am. Rather well-heeled Sharp, though. Didn't seem too concerned about losing, at first. Usually when that happens they cast about for another victim, but two nights ago he suddenly accused Gerald of cheating.'

'Oh, my goodness!'

Filby nodded soberly. 'Very nasty business. Ain't likely a Deverell's going to take that in the face and walk away. Took three of us to keep Gerald from beating the fellow to a pulp. Creech—that's the Sharp—challenged him at once, and Gerald accepted. I'm one of his seconds,' he added, sinking into gloom. 'Offered immediately. Nothing else to be done.'

'Oh, yes, there is something else to be done,' Phoebe announced trenchantly. 'I understand the first duty of a second, Mr Filby, is to effect a reconciliation.'

'Already tried it,' Filby answered. 'Very obstinate fellow, Creech. Seems determined to put a bullet in Gerald. Wouldn't apologise, even when I pointed out that Gerald couldn't have cheated because they were playing with the House cards. Surprised he didn't challenge *me* when I said that. Not the thing at all.'

'But did you also point out that Gerald is a minor? I'm not perfectly certain about such things, but surely any gentleman would hesitate to shoot a boy Gerald's age.'

Filby shook his head. 'Tried that, too. Creech told me he'd never withdrawn from an affair of honour and he wasn't going to start now.'

'You mean this dreadful creature has fought duels before?' Phoebe gazed at Filby in dismay while hideous visions of Gerald's lifeless body being carted into the house flashed through her mind. 'Then there's nothing else for it. Gerald will have to go to Deverell.'

Filby so far forgot himself as to sink his chin into his cravat. 'Won't do it, ma'am. Suggested it m'self, but he refused point-blank. Seems Deverell likes to go about strangling people. Doesn't sound too likely to me. Haven't heard of any corpses lying about, for one thing, but Gerald seemed very certain.'

'Oh, for goodness' sake, of course Deverell doesn't strangle people,' Phoebe exclaimed, quite exasperated. 'Although, after this, he'll probably make an exception in Gerald's case.'

After this unanswerable conclusion, a rather melancholy silence descended upon them. Phoebe tried vainly to think of a way to extract Gerald from his obligations without involving Deverell in yet another disaster. Mr Filby appeared to have sunk into a mindless torpor.

'You said you're *one* of Gerald's seconds,' she finally recalled. 'Who's the other?'

'Crowhurst,' Filby answered glumly. 'He was playing at the next table that night. Good of him to offer, I suppose, but he hasn't been particularly helpful.'

'Perhaps not to you, Mr Filby, but surely he wouldn't refuse a lady's request.'

Filby frowned. 'I don't know, ma'am. I know you and Crowhurst are friends, but to tell you the truth, he's not quite. . .'

'Lord Crowhurst exaggerated when he called us friends,' she interrupted hastily. 'I hardly know the man, but—'

Before she could explain the situation further, they were interrupted from an unexpected quarter. Miss Grismead floated up to them, obliging Mr Filby to rise to his feet. Under his fascinated gaze, she crumpled slowly and gracefully onto the windowseat, transforming herself into a limp heap of pale blue muslin.

'Miss Smith,' she breathed in accents that would have led anyone to believe her next words would be her last, 'I wonder if I might have a word with you?'

Only too happy to take a hint, Filby swept a magnificent bow. 'Must pay my respects to your mother, Miss Grismead. Your very obedient servant, Miss Smith.'

'We shall continue our conversation later, Mr Filby,' Phoebe said with heavy meaning. But Filby was already making good his escape.

Not that he was going far, Phoebe consoled herself, as she watched him fall into the clutches of Lady Grismead. She heard her ladyship demand his expert opinion on the proper costume for a Ladies' Driving

Club and decided Filby would still be within easy reach
when she'd finished with Pamela.

When she turned to her visitor, Miss Grismead fixed
her with a soulful gaze and managed the enormous effort
of clasping her hands together. 'Miss Smith, I must and
will speak with you. You're my Last Hope.'

'I am?' Phoebe blinked at her, momentarily distracted
from Gerald's problems.

'Yes, indeed. I know you are aware of my situation.
How could you not be, when Papa so brutally refused
to countenance my betrothal to dearest Norvel the other
day? In front of *everyone*!'

'Well, I don't think he refused precisely, Miss
Grismead. He seemed to think—'

'It is all of a piece,' stated Miss Grismead, waving
away anyone else's thoughts on the matter. 'But I was
struck, Miss Smith, by your sympathy. By your courage
in mentioning the Fatal Word in front of Mama. By
your—'

Phoebe gazed at her, mesmerised. 'Fatal Word?'

Miss Grismead glanced about the room, assured herself that no one was listening, and leaned closer. 'Poetry,'
she whispered.

'Oh. That Fatal Word.'

'I knew in that moment you'd been Sent.'

'Sent?'

'To aid me in my affliction.'

'Well, actually, I came up to London to demand help
on my own account, but—'

'Yes, I know. From Deverell. You see. It is all Meant.'

'Meant?'

Pamela nodded. 'Deverell will never listen to me,
Miss Smith, but if *you* ask him to help us, he won't
refuse.'

Phoebe started to wonder if she'd missed something,
somewhere along the line. 'Naturally, I'd be happy to
help you in any way I can, Miss Grismead, but—'

'*Thank you*, Miss Smith, thank you. I knew I could

depend on you.' Pamela rose to her feet. She managed the task so gradually that Phoebe held her breath, expecting her visitor to collapse back onto the seat at any moment. So fascinated was she by the procedure, she completely failed to comprehend that Pamela considered her task done.

'I knew you wouldn't refuse to exercise your influence to ensure the Happiness of one who will be Forever Grateful.'

'Influence!' Phoebe's pent-up breath rushed out in a startled whoosh. By the time she'd recovered, Miss Grismead had drifted back to the sofa where she appeared to fall asleep. Phoebe was not fooled. She had just been struck by the unpleasant realisation that Miss Grismead's languishing pose gave her plenty of opportunity for observation.

Heat stung her cheeks as she wondered what, exactly, Pamela had observed to cause her to say practically the same things that Lady Yarwood had said yesterday? Had she betrayed herself in some way before she'd even been aware of her own feelings for Deverell? But even if she had, surely Deverell hadn't done anything to cause two such diverse personalities to assume she had any influence over him?

Phoebe gripped her hands together, fighting a whirling torrent of emotions while her mind see-sawed dizzily between alarm that she'd made a public spectacle of herself, and a quite improper hope that Deverell wasn't indifferent to her.

Hope, she discovered to her shock, even a tiny, tremulous hope, was stronger than any amount of alarm. It took several minutes of severe self-chastisement before she managed to drag her mind back to more important matters. She had to prevent Gerald's untimely demise on the field of honour. And she would also try to persuade Deverell to help Pamela.

She wanted to see him reconciled with his family, she realised, with a little pang of her heart. She didn't want

him to be alone anymore. He had stopped being a
warrior. Now it was time he. . .

Before she could finish the thought, the door was
flung open with a flourish, and Thripp ushered Deverell
into the room.

Phoebe's entire body went rigid. She went hot all
over. She was positive she was one big blush. Every
thought in her mind vanished, leaving only the memory
of his kiss. The warmth and gentleness; the strength of
his arms; the fierce demand of his mouth on hers in the
instant before he'd wrenched away.

Dismayed, trembling, suddenly realising that all conversation had been momentarily suspended, she whipped
her head around to face the window, fighting the sensations aroused by his arrival. Given the choice, she
would have fled from the room, but what would
everyone think?

On the other hand, she couldn't stay here, gazing
rudely out of the window when the drawing-room was
full of visitors. What if Deverell ignored everyone else
and approached her as he'd done at Lady Grismead's
dancing party? Every eye would be upon them. Everyone
would think what Pamela and Lady Yarwood were
already thinking.

Completely unnerved by the possibility, Phoebe leapt
up and scurried over to take cover in the crowd. Collaps-
ing onto the chair next to Mr Filby, she pressed a hand
to her middle. A futile gesture, she thought despairingly.
It was going to take more than a shaking hand to still
the butterflies dancing a reel in her stomach.

'Cressy, perhaps you might ring for some tea,' she
managed distractedly, breaking into that damsel's conversation with Mr Filby.

'Yes, of course, Phoebe.' Cressida glanced at her
uncle, then gave her a sweet smile that had alarm bells
jangling once more in Phoebe's head. She felt more like
an insect on a pin than ever.

'Glad you came over,' Filby muttered out of the corner

of his mouth. His furtive manner had her mind struggling back to Gerald's plight. 'Got something to say. Better say it quick. Deverell's chatting to his secretary, but no telling when that might change. After all, he can talk to Charlton any time, can't he?'

She resisted the urge to scream. 'Do you have an idea, Mr Filby?'

He nodded. 'Brilliant notion. Can't think why it didn't occur before. Deverell won't give me the time of day. Will only strangle Gerald.' He paused and beamed at her. '*You'll* have to tell him.'

'*Me!*' She stared at him. 'Oh, no, not you, too, Mr Filby.'

He blinked. 'Beg your pardon, ma'am?'

'Oh, dear. What am I saying? Really, I hardly know. . . Please take no notice, sir.'

'All a bit much,' he said with perfect understanding. 'Shouldn't have suggested it. Bit alarming, isn't he? Rather large. Can quite understand why you wouldn't want to be strangled either, ma'am. Better try Crowhurst first.'

'Yes,' she agreed weakly, quite unequal to the task of explaining her incoherence. 'Perhaps you're right, Mr Filby.'

'No hurry,' he assured her, rising. 'Meeting's not for another two days. Insisted that Gerald have time to practise. Only fair.'

'Oh, my goodness.'

'Must go. See Deverell wishes to speak with you. Very obedient. . .'

He was gone before the last words were out.

'What a very strange effect I seem to have on Filby,' Deverell observed blandly as he approached. He turned Filby's vacated chair slightly towards her and sat down, one arm resting along the low curved back. 'Why do you suppose that is, Miss Smith?'

She shook her head, not risking even the most fleeting of glances at him. She didn't need to look at him to know that his hand was resting only inches from her shoulder, that his gaze was fixed unwaveringly on her face. She could feel the heat and intensity in him as if they were actually touching.

'Hmm. I see I've put myself beyond the pale.' His voice lowered, sending a shiver down her spine. 'Aren't you even going to greet me, Phoebe?'

'Good afternoon, sir.' Her own voice showed a distressing tendency to squeak. Phoebe cleared her throat and sat up straighter. 'Did you wish to consult with me about something?'

'Nobody would remark upon it, if I did, you know.'

Her gaze flashed to his.

He smiled, but those aquamarine eyes were watchful. 'That's better. Would you mind telling me why you're behaving as if I kissed you in front of my entire family yesterday, instead of privately?'

'For goodness' sake, my lord! You must have run mad!'

His smile turned wry. 'An unnerving possibility.'

'No, not because of *that*!' She gestured wildly in her agitation. 'What if someone had heard you just now?'

Deverell obligingly followed the direction of her hand. 'Gerald and Filby have escaped, Theodosia and Edward aren't paying the slightest attention to anyone else, and my aunt is arguing with Cressida about which theatre to attend tomorrow night. Pamela appears to be the only one interested in our conversation, and that's probably because she's hoping you'll persuade me to cast a vote in Nermal's favour.'

'Norvel,' she corrected faintly. 'And how did you know that, sir?'

His lips twisted. 'I know my family, Miss Smith. However, before you embark on a futile course of action, I wish to apologise to you.'

Phoebe's mouth fell open. She instantly clamped it shut again.

'Deverells do apologise on occasion,' he murmured, a wicked smile lighting his eyes.

'Yes,' she agreed, by now quite distracted. 'Bowls of gruel.'

A quizzical brow shot up. 'I beg your pardon?'

'Nothing, my lord. I mean. . .' She made a heroic effort to pull herself together. 'Every time Theo and Cressy apologise, they offer me bowls of gruel or mustard plasters. Heaven knows why.'

'Probably fell into the habit with Cousin Clara,' he suggested drily. He hesitated, then seemed to choose his next words carefully. 'I'm afraid I can only offer my regrets that I've made you uneasy in my company, Miss Smith. It was inexcusable of me to take my frustrations with my wards out on you.'

'Frus— Oh. Yes. Yes, I see.'

'I doubt it,' he muttered, then, raising his voice, 'it would have given me great pleasure to have despatched them back to Kerslake yesterday. Unfortunately, I'm unable to do that.'

'No, my lord. Er. . .why not?'

He met her gaze. 'And abandon you to your fate, Miss Smith? Or have you leave?'

'Oh,' she said again. 'Yes, I suppose I did threaten you, sir.'

He laughed softly. 'You did. But don't let your conscience bother you. There have been. . .compensations.'

Oh, dear, how was she to take *that*? Now her heart didn't know where it was supposed to be. It was probably safer to leave it in the vicinity of her feet, whence it had plummeted as soon as Deverell had implied he'd kissed her out of frustration with his nieces. But then, what compensations was he referring to? So far, all she'd done was involve him in one imbroglio after another. Something he didn't seem to appreciate.

Especially as no one in his family seemed to appreciate him.

But he was wrong, she thought, intercepting a fleeting,

keen-eyed glance from Lady Grismead. She was sure her ladyship would soften towards him, given the chance.

And she was going to see that he received that chance, Phoebe vowed again. She knew what it was like to be isolated through no fault of one's own. He shouldn't have to endure his aunt's disapproval, when a simple favour might put things right. He shouldn't have to spend his life fashioning statues, whose pleading arms wrenched at her heart.

If she did nothing else for him, she would heal the rift with his family.

'Compensations,' she repeated brightly, as though suddenly struck by the notion. She avoided the amused gleam in his eyes and gathered her thoughts in the manner of a general mustering troops. 'Well, I'm pleased to hear you say so, my lord. That is one thing about Deverells. They're seldom boring. I'm sure as you come to know your family better, you—'

'I wasn't talking about my family, Miss Smith.'

'Well, I was!' she retorted, cross at this lack of co-operation. 'Whether you like it or not, my lord, you do have a family. I. . .' She hesitated and her voice softened. 'I know you were treated harshly in the past, but surely your father's actions can't be laid at the Grismeads' door. If you would only offer to help—'

The faint smile in his eyes vanished abruptly beneath a layer of ice. 'I have no intention of assisting any member of my family in the follies they choose to commit, Miss Smith.'

Phoebe heaved an exasperated sigh. 'My lord, it is no use trying to make me believe you are heartless. You aren't.'

'Indeed?'

'No. You'll always assist your family, even if you don't particularly like some of them.'

His eyes narrowed. 'Why would I do that?'

'Because you are a man of honour, sir. Don't bother trying to convince me otherwise. I know better.'

'Do you? What makes you so damn certain of that?'
His voice was even more frigid than his eyes.

Phoebe took a deep breath, as though she was about
to plunge into those icy depths. 'Because you think your
family believes otherwise, and that hurts you,' she all
but whispered.

The silence hanging between them almost vibrated
with the echo of her words. Sebastian stared at Phoebe,
buffeted by so many conflicting emotions he could only
hold himself savagely in check while the storm howled
within him. The sensation was stunningly similar to the
one he'd felt when he'd been confronted by his father
all those years ago. The sudden sense of vulnerability,
the frustration, the helpless rage at having the hurt place
deep inside him stripped bare.

But. . .this time. . .there was something else. Something that held him here, waiting. Something that warred
viciously with his desire to draw Phoebe closer. Something that goaded him to see how far he could push her
blithe certainty, even while the fear that he could push
her too far sank icy claws into his gut.

The conflict was so intense, so agonising, he had to
glance away from her before he could speak.

'You're mistaken, Miss Smith.'

She shook her head. 'Actually, you know, they don't
consider you dishonourable in the least.'

'Oh?' He looked back at her, one brow raised. 'You
have an intimate acquaintance with their innermost
thoughts as well as my own?'

'No,' she said softly, ignoring his sarcasm. 'But I do
know Deverells, and I shouldn't think Gerald and the
girls have given the matter a moment's thought. They
would have been far too young when you left England
to have had an opinion on the subject. As for the
Grismeads, you intimidate them. You see, instead of
chastising you, your years away have made you very
much stronger than they are. They know it, and they
know you know it. That's why they're so wary of you.'

She smiled with sudden mischief. 'You also take a delight in giving your aunt apoplexy, but she is still ready to approve of you if you'd only give her the chance.'

That smile went straight to his heart. She hadn't even taken his bad-tempered denials into account, Sebastian realised. She was far too busy trying to convince him that his family no longer considered him a disgrace. *She* believed in him, and that was that.

He went utterly still as the knowledge sank into the dark place in his soul.

Phoebe believed in him. Without any evidence to the contrary.

The raging conflict within him abruptly coalesced into a surge of desire so violent he almost shook with it. His hand clenched hard around the back of the chair. He didn't dare move a muscle. It took every ounce of self-control he'd learned over the years not to reach out, drag her into his arms and make her his here and now.

He'd known she was necessary to him, but this sudden savage desire. . .this *need*. This yearning to sink into her warmth and belief in him so he'd never be alone again— he'd never felt anything like it. His body ached with wanting her, but it was more than that. His heart. . .his very soul. . .hungered.

God damn it, he was starving for her.

Shaken, Sebastian managed to unlock his clenched jaw so he could speak. 'My aunt doesn't approve of anything, Miss Smith.'

She tilted her head slightly, the mischievous gleam taking on a touch of provocation. 'Why don't you try it and see?'

The challenge dragged a reluctant laugh from him. 'I did say, didn't I, that you're more than a match for any Deverell? Little did I know how true that was.'

She clasped her hands. 'Then you'll do it?'

'What, precisely, is "it", Miss Smith?'

'Merely what you do so well, sir.' Her mouth curved in a way that deepened the tiny dimples at its corners.

'Intimidate Mr Hartlepoole into behaving sensibly and assist the Grismeads out of their financial quagmire.'

Sebastian took a deep breath. 'Is that all?'

She nodded.

'And what do I receive in exchange?'

For the first time, since he'd startled her out of her nervousness, she began to look wary. 'Er. . .your family's gratitude?'

He started to smile. Damned if he was going to be the only one suffering here. Leaning closer, he deliberately lowered his voice. 'Not enough, Miss Smith.'

She looked more wary than ever. 'Um. . .the knowledge that you've done the right thing?'

'Still not enough.'

'Well, I don't know what more you expect, but—'

'Keep in mind that, despite your little speech on the subject, I'm not doing this for my family but for quite a different reason, and I'm sure the answer will come to you.'

Phoebe swallowed, immediately rendered speechless. A shivery sense of excitement raced through her body as though tiny bubbles of heat were sizzling in her veins. Everything tingled, even her fingers and toes. The tremulous hope that Deverell wasn't indifferent to her was both thrilling and terrifying.

Thank goodness she hadn't mentioned Gerald's predicament to him, she thought inconsequentially. She was already drowning in those intense, glittering eyes. When they lowered to her mouth and lingered there for a heart-stopping moment, it was almost as if he was kissing her again.

'Yes,' he growled very softly when his gaze returned to hers, 'you know the answer, Miss Smith.'

She swallowed again. 'I don't think. . .'

He smiled slowly. 'There's no need to think. The details will have to wait until a more convenient time anyway.' He rose, still watching her from beneath half-lowered lashes. 'I shall report back to you, Miss Smith, when my tasks are done.'

Phoebe couldn't summon the breath for even the briefest of farewells. She watched Deverell bow to his aunt—while sending a glinting sidelong look at her that plainly told her he was adding the courtesy to her debt—and leave.

Before the door was fully shut, her thoughts were whirling around and around like ribbons on a maypole. She couldn't seem to catch hold of any one of them. The arrival of Thripp with refreshments went almost unnoticed. She was aware of Theodosia dispensing tea and cakes, but it was like watching everything from another place.

What was she to do? What was she to make of Deverell's remarks?

She felt torn, unbearably torn, between her belief in his honour and the painful awareness that the most honourable man in the world might not offer anything but a *carte blanche* to a governess whose past was still largely shrouded in mystery. She had no dowry, no land, no prospects, and a family who refused to publicly acknowledge the connection. What else was she to think?

And yet he'd said she was innocent.

Phoebe felt her heart constrict so sharply her lips parted on a silent cry of pain.

There *was* one other alternative. One she hadn't considered until now. One that filled her with so much desolation she couldn't bear it.

If an honourable man had no intention of marrying her, he wouldn't offer anything at all.

He might tease her because she'd persuaded him to go against his personal inclinations in assisting his family. He might even kiss her because he'd been driven to the edge of his control.

But he wouldn't ruin her.

The realisation that she wouldn't care about being ruined occurred and was dismissed. It no longer had the power to stir so much as a ripple. She loved him. She would accept an offer of any kind, for as long as Deverell wanted her. Because when love was placed on the balance, the consequences weighed nothing.

Unfortunately, despite several hours spent in contemplation of the subject after the guests had departed, she couldn't think of a way around the situation. Knowing that Deverell had been unjustly punished for suspect conduct in the past, precluded her from trying to tempt him into definitely scandalous conduct now.

Even if she'd known how to deliberately tempt a man against his more honourable inclinations.

All she could do was treasure every moment she spent with him in the months she had left. To gather memories and store them. To hold them in her heart against the time when she'd have to leave. There was really no other option.

The prospect was so depressing, it was almost a relief to turn her mind to the problem of how she was to approach Crowhurst.

Chapter Eleven

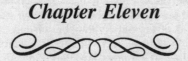

In the end it was all quite simple. She sent a message to Crowhurst, asking him to call on her the next day on a matter of business, and when he arrived she stationed Thripp, already forewarned, in the hall.

At least, it was meant to be quite simple. Her plan should have worked. Unfortunately, she had forgotten that she wasn't dealing with a gentleman.

'You'll have to pardon me if I seem a little surprised by your invitation, Phoebe,' Crowhurst began to say as he sat down on the chair she indicated. His pale brows rose slightly when Thripp departed, leaving the drawing-room door wide open and remaining in plain sight in the hall, diligently polishing the stair-rail.

'And in view of the fact that Deverell has informed me that the next note I send you will be my last, isn't it a little indiscreet for us to be meeting under the roof he's providing for you, and under the eye of a butler who's engaged in a task more suited to the under-housemaid?'

'No doubt you're accustomed to noticing such nuances, my lord,' Phoebe retorted before she could stop herself. 'You may also have noticed that it is Lord Deverell's wards who live under this roof. They, or rather one of them, is the reason I asked you here today.'

Crowhurst smiled mockingly. 'Yes, I can appreciate that you'd prefer some privacy.'

She took a deep breath, determined to ignore the implied insults. 'I wish to speak with you about Gerald, sir. About his forthcoming engagement with a certain Mr Creech, to be exact.'

Crowhurst's eyes narrowed. He watched her for a few unnerving seconds, then sat back and crossed one leg over the other. 'I take it Filby has been busy. You'd better get rid of the butler, Phoebe. Or close the door.'

'Thripp is completely devoted to Gerald,' she informed him. 'If he does hear anything, it will go no further. Besides,' she added, descending from these lofty heights, 'I've already informed him of the situation. He knows I'm trying to save Gerald.'

She didn't add that Thripp had threatened to go to Deverell with the tale if she didn't succeed.

'How very heroic of you, my dear,' Crowhurst drawled. 'I wish you every success.'

Phoebe straightened her spine. The interview was not going as she'd planned, but she refused to give up. 'Success, sir, may depend upon you. Mr Filby has already failed in his attempt to bring about a reconciliation, but there's still hope. This Creech person may listen to an older man.'

'You expect me to visit him?'

'Will you not do so, sir?' She leaned forward, clasping her hands. 'The fact that Gerald has never fought a duel in his life, and is still a minor, must weigh heavily on a gentleman acting as a second. Surely you'd wish to do everything in your power to bring about a happy resolution.'

Another silence fell as Crowhurst seemed to consider both her and her words. His expression never changed, but Phoebe felt her skin start to crawl under his appraising stare.

'A happy resolution,' he repeated. 'That, my dear Phoebe, might take considerable effort on my part. I believe. . .' He paused and smiled faintly. 'Yes, I really do believe that if I help you, some recompense will be in order.'

Phoebe rose at once. 'Then this interview is at an end, sir. Good day.'

'You think so?' he snarled suddenly, coming to his feet. His hands clenched and unclenched by his sides. His lips drew back in a grimace of rage as he glared at her.

The transformation from mockery to menace was so swift, so unexpected, that Phoebe's entire body jolted. She backed away, putting her chair between them, the similarity of the situation to the one two days ago when she'd retreated from Deverell's wrath striking her with stunning force.

The same circumstances; two such different men. How could anyone think Deverell dishonourable, she thought, angry and hurting for him, when men like Crowhurst existed?

'Do I have to call Thripp to show you out?' The ice in her voice, born of anger and contempt, seemed to throw Crowhurst off stride for a moment. He shook his head, as if he hadn't expected her to respond like that, and made a visible effort to control his fury.

'We haven't finished, Phoebe.'

'We never started, sir. I was labouring under the misapprehension that, as Gerald's second, you would wish to assist him. I see I was mistaken. There's only one thing to be done, and I should have done it in the first place. Go to Lord Deverell.'

The expression that flashed into his pale eyes had her hands gripping the chair tightly, but his voice was still controlled. Sibilantly soft, it slid over her nerves like ice-water over bare flesh. So might a snake speak, she thought, before striking.

'Why do you think I'm reluctant to serve you in this regard, Phoebe? Go to Deverell, by all means. Pour out the tale of Gerald's woes. I'm sure you'll find he's already aware of the situation and intends to do nothing about it.'

Her hands gripped the chair tighter. 'What do you mean?'

'It's all quite simple, my dear. Ask yourself who would have reason to desire Kerslake's death. Who will benefit from the likely outcome of this duel? Who, indeed, is in a position to arrange for such a challenge to be issued in the first place?'

Phoebe stared at him, shocked speechless. 'You're mad,' she whispered at last. 'Deverell has no reason to want Gerald dead. Why should he?'

'Why? There's the title for a start. Then—'

'But Deverell has his own title.' Still reeling from Crowhurst's insinuations, she shook her head. 'He's wealthy, he. . .'

'Ah, yes. Wealthy. Riches he acquired as a result of exile. Do you think even wealth such as Deverell's would influence a man bent on revenge against the family who banished him in the first place? As for his title: what's a new barony against an earldom several centuries old? I think you'll find, Phoebe, that when the evidence mounts up—'

'That evidence may weigh with you, sir,' she retorted, abruptly restored to her wits. 'But as has already been made perfectly clear to me, you and Deverell are entirely different. Kindly take your leave. I will strive to forget that this conversation ever took place.'

'Strive to forget it?' he hissed back, taking a step forward and speaking so quickly the words almost slurred together. 'Do you think to fob me off so easily? Do you think I'll forget you asked me here to assist a Deverell? Do you think you can crook your finger and I'll come running, even while you're living under another man's protection? Go to him, then. See who's right and who's wrong. See—'

'My lord, for goodness' sake. . .' From the corner of her eye, she saw Thripp move towards them.

'You come to London to haunt me. You set up house

with Deverell. The one man you knew it would kill me to see you with. You—'

'My lord, *please*. . .'

Crowhurst stopped. He glared at her, his eyes unfocused, staring blankly at something—or someone—only he could see.

Phoebe swallowed and tried to think of something to say. She'd been rendered totally off-balance by Crowhurst's attack. Not only the unexpectedness of it, but the extent of his rage was beyond what was reasonable. Clearly he wasn't entirely sane. Especially on the subject of Deverell.

And it was all too obvious that, in his frenzy, he'd mistaken her for the lady with whom he'd had that long-ago affair. She didn't know what to do. All she could think about was the fastest method of getting him out of the house, and yet she couldn't help feeling a sense of pity.

Glancing past Crowhurst, she motioned Thripp to remain in the hall. 'Look about you, sir,' she said, gesturing to their surroundings. 'Do you see any sign of Deverell living here? I'm companion to his nieces, nothing more. Nor do you do yourself—or, indeed, the lady you once cared for—any credit by insulting me like this.'

'Do you think I care about that?' he muttered. The fixed glare was fading, but he continued to stare at her with a kind of brooding purpose that was even more disturbing. 'I haven't cared about anything since you left.'

'My lord. . .' Phoebe took a deep breath and tried to instil as much gentle firmness into her voice as possible. 'I'm very sorry for your pain, but. . .I'm not who you think I am.'

He seemed not even to hear her. 'I know who you are,' he grated and, turning on his heel, walked out of the house.

*   *   *

Several hours later, Phoebe had forgotten all about Crowhurst and his problems. Indeed, she was so worried about Gerald, who hadn't put in an appearance all day, she even managed to prevent her heart from somersaulting more than once or twice when Deverell at last strolled into the drawing-room.

She stopped pacing to scowl at him. 'My lord! At last! Where have you been? Didn't you receive my notes?'

'All three of them,' he replied, crossing the room to her. A wry smile curved his mouth. 'I'm willing to do a lot for you, Phoebe, but being in three places at once is impossible. Even for me.'

'But I haven't asked you to be in three places at once! Really, my lord—' She stopped, her indignation vanishing under the impact of his wicked smile. That same smile that at once puzzled and disturbed and excited.

Wrapping her arms across her waist, she took a firm grip on her elbows. It was better than flinging herself at him and taking a firm grip on him, which was what she really wanted to do.

'*Where* have you been?' she demanded, forcing her mind back to the matter at hand.

'I,' he said virtuously, 'have been obeying the first of your orders, Miss Smith. I've been engaged with Nermal.'

'Oh, my goodness,' she uttered weakly. 'You didn't call him "Nermal" to his face, did you?'

Deverell tilted his head while he considered the matter. 'Actually, now I come to think about it, I don't remember calling him anything at all. I merely pointed out a few facts.' He regarded the way she was holding on to herself and raised his eyes to her face. 'I take it you don't wish to hear about the interview?'

'No. Yes! I mean. . .not now, my lord. Something much worse than Nermal's stubborn— Oh, heavens, now you've got me doing it. I mean, something much worse than Mr Hartlepoole's—'

'Phoebe. . .' His voice lowered and went dark. A large hand was laid across her lips. 'Hush.'

Phoebe went utterly still. Even her breathing stopped.

'Unless,' he continued very softly, 'the girls have taken up scientific experiments that threaten to blow up the house while we're in it, I really don't care what has happened.'

She tried to take a breath and felt her lips brush against his fingers. Tiny shivers of sensation coursed through her body, tightening her throat and turning her knees to water. She made an inarticulate sound and he lifted his hand. But only to trace the line of her jaw with one long finger, to stroke the curve of her ear, to retrace the path to her chin. He tilted her face up to his.

'If. . .if only that was all,' she managed to say, amazed she could speak at all. She'd never known that a light caressing touch to her ear could cause such a quivering in the pit of her stomach. She focused desperately on Deverell's cravat and tried to recall why she'd summoned him. 'It's Gerald.'

'Gerald?'

'He's engaged himself to fight a duel with a dreadful man called Creech.'

Deverell smiled faintly and lowered his hand. 'Yes, I know.'

'You know?' Phoebe's gaze flashed up to his. The faint echoes of sensation quivering inside her abruptly stilled. '*You know*! Then what do you intend to do about it, my lord?'

'I've already done it,' he said calmly. 'Creech has been. . .ah. . .persuaded to acknowledge the rashness of his challenge by apologising on the field.'

'Oh, thank goodness!' Phoebe's stunned expression changed with lightning speed to a brilliant smile. 'Now Gerald will be able to cease pretending that he hasn't been worried out of his mind for the past few days.'

Deverell didn't seem unduly moved by the prospect. 'Not quite. You, Miss Smith, will behave towards Gerald as if nothing has happened. It won't hurt him to lose a few nights' sleep over the matter. He's as much at fault for being cozened into playing in an out-and-out Hell in the first place.'

'Oh.' Her smile lost some of its brilliance. 'You want to teach Gerald a lesson.'

'Precisely.'

'Well, I suppose your intention is admirable, my lord, but—'

This time he captured her chin on the edge of his hand. 'I thought I asked you to trust me, Phoebe.'

'I do trust you,' she retorted, valiantly striving to ignore the resumption of dancing butterflies in her stomach. 'But how was I to know you were even aware of the situation?'

'There were any number of people at the Pigeonhole that night who were only too ready to apprise me of it,' he said drily. 'If anyone should have remained ignorant of the situation, it was you.' His brows met. 'Don't tell me Gerald ran to you for help.'

'No, of course not.'

'Then it must have been Filby. No wonder he fled yesterday. Damn it, I ought to seek him out and throw a real scare into him for upsetting you like this.'

'It wasn't Mr Filby's fault. He tried to persuade Gerald to confide in you, but because you're forever threatening to strangle your wards, Gerald refused to do so.'

'So now it's my fault?' A faint smile edged his mouth. The fist beneath her chin stroked briefly, gently.

'Well. . .' She swallowed, intensely aware of the size and warmth of his hand. She didn't know whether she was supposed to ignore his touch or object to it. When his knuckles stroked down her throat and back again, she shivered and rushed into speech.

'Threats of strangulation are not conducive to happy relationships, my lord. It is one thing to strangle bandits in India. I dare say they were trying to rob you at the time. It must have been vastly inconvenient, but—'

'There's nothing for it,' he murmured. 'I see I shall have to kiss you again.'

'Oh. Oh. Well. . .'

'If you have no objection, of course.'

'Objection?' she squeaked. She felt herself blushing wildly as his other arm went around her, drawing her closer until she was nestled against him. . .melting against him, she realised in wonder, her softer curves accommodating themselves to his bigger, harder frame as though they'd been lovers forever.

The thought made her tremble. Somewhere in the back of her mind she couldn't quite believe her own recklessness, but she knew she was going to grasp the moment and hold on tight. Her voice was barely a whisper. 'Well. . .as you pointed out yesterday, my lord, no sorry details of infelicitous relationships have recently crossed your lips.'

The smile in his eyes was suddenly heart-shakingly tender. The hand beneath her chin uncurled to cup her face. 'My sweet, trusting, innocent little Phoebe. How did I ever live without you?'

Fortunately for her scattered wits, he didn't seem to expect an answer. He lowered his head and with the same irresistible, utterly overwhelming mastery that had rendered her helpless yesterday, covered her mouth with his.

Phoebe found herself drowning in sensation instantly. Heat and excitement, deliciously thrilling, poured through her from her head to her toes. Her lips parted, her arms lifted to cling to him, and this time. . .this time when his arms tightened in response, when his mouth hardened on hers in fierce demand, he didn't draw back, leaving her dizzy and bereft.

His tongue caressed her lower lip, gently, insistently, as though preparing her for his deeper claiming, and then he was tasting, touching, possessing every soft, hidden part of her mouth, coaxing her into a hesitant response until she was kissing him back as deeply, as passionately, until she lost all awareness of anything but their embrace.

When he lifted his head aeons later, she was limp and trembling in his arms, her heartbeat wild, her breasts deliciously crushed against his chest, a strange insistent ache throbbing through her lower body. She sorted the sensations out one by one and then was suddenly flooded with the knowledge of Deverell's violently leashed desire. Every muscle in his body was rock-hard with tension.

Her eyes flew open. She gazed into the golden flames blazing in his aquamarine eyes and felt herself melting all over again. Not even the crushing strength of his arms, or the frankly intimidating male arousal pressed against her had the power to restore a semblance of caution.

'Phoebe.' He kissed her again, briefly, her name a whisper against her lips, and then pressed his mouth to her temple. His heart thudded, powerfully, against her breast. 'Don't be afraid. I want you, but—' His breath shuddered out and his arms tightened. 'Just give me a minute.'

'I'm not afraid,' she breathed in the same hushed tone.

'You're trembling.' He drew back to look down into her face.

She blushed at the raw hunger in his eyes. He made no effort to disguise his need, continuing to hold her so closely she could feel the faint vibration of muscles held rigidly in check. And yet she'd spoken the truth. She wasn't afraid. Her awareness of the fierce restraint in him was as thrilling as all the rest.

Only one thought had the power to disturb her.

'It's just. . .when you kissed me yesterday. . .' She faltered, then met his gaze openly. 'You're not angry, or frustrated, today, are you, my lord?'

His mouth curved. 'I think under the circumstances, Phoebe, you might call me Sebastian.'

'Oh.' She felt herself turning pink again. 'You're not annoyed with anyone, are you. . . Sebastian?'

He bent and brushed her mouth with his, a half-groan, half-laugh escaping him. 'I didn't know until now that the sound of my name had the potential to drive me mad. Phoebe—' He held her impossibly closer. 'No, I'm not angry, or annoyed. And as for frustration, I think I can survive another day or two of it.' The rueful laughter that sprang into his eyes was as swiftly banished. 'Phoebe, you do know, don't you, that there's no debt between us? That I was only teasing you the other day?'

She smiled on a dizzy rush of happiness. *He cared.* He cared about her feelings.

'Of course I do,' she assured him. And added confidingly, 'Crowhurst said much the same thing, you know, about favours and recompense, but he meant it. The difference was glaring.'

And so, without any warning, was Deverell. The hands that had been lightly stroking her back abruptly ceased their movements. He seized her by the arms and stepped back a pace.

'Crowhurst was here?'

'Yes, but—'

'What gave Crowhurst the idea he would be welcome in this house?'

'Well. . .I sent for him.'

'*What?*'

She winced. 'Please, my lord. I have had quite enough of gentlemen yelling at me today.'

His voice immediately went ominously soft. 'Crowhurst yelled at you?'

Phoebe began to perceive that whatever Deverell might have felt before, he was now *very* seriously annoyed. She set herself to rectifying the situation. 'He wasn't himself, my lord. Or, perhaps he was,' she amended, recalling Crowhurst's erratic behaviour.

'Make up your mind. Whether Crowhurst was himself

or not may be the deciding factor in whether he continues to exist at all.'

She ignored this growled threat. 'Do you know, sir, I believe Lord Crowhurst must be quite unbalanced. Not only has he constantly mistaken me for someone else, but he actually had the temerity to imply that you were somehow involved in Gerald's duel.' She gazed up at him anxiously. 'Perhaps you'd better have a word with him, my lord. If he were to spread it about that—'

'I'll have a word with Crowhurst, all right.' He released her, but only to clench his fists. 'Several words. Unlike you, Miss Smith, who will never speak to him again if you wish to avoid the inconvenience of being unable to sit down for a week.'

Phoebe's eyes widened. 'Now you're threatening to beat me? Well! Of all the— I was only trying to help Gerald.'

His teeth met. 'I'm aware of that.'

'All I did was send Crowhurst a note—' She stopped, abruptly recalling something else her earlier visitor had said. 'And that's another thing, my lord. Did you threaten Crowhurst with retribution if he sent me any more notes, because if you did—'

'Yes?' Deverell didn't appear to move, but suddenly he was looming over her, eyes glittering. 'If I did, Miss Smith?'

'Nothing,' she said, metaphorically retreating with as much dignity as possible. 'I have no wish to receive notes from Crowhurst, but since I needed to see him I had to send *him* a note. You must know he's one of Gerald's seconds. How else was I to speak to him about the situation?'

Deverell continued to loom. 'You weren't supposed to speak to him about anything,' he grated. 'But just so I have all the pertinent facts, where did this interesting conversation take place?'

'In here, of course.'

'Crowhurst was in here? Alone? With you?'

'Thripp was in the hall the entire time and the door was open.'

There was a moment of menacing silence. Deverell continued to study her with ominously narrowed eyes. Then he scowled.

Phoebe rewarded this evidence of self-restraint with a brilliant smile. She was far too hasty.

Deverell reached for her. His hands, big and immensely strong, closed around her shoulders.

'I don't know how you manage to drive me straight to the edge,' he muttered, dragging her not entirely gently into his arms. 'But right now I don't particularly care.' His mouth came down on hers.

A tidal wave of male passion and outrage washed over her. Phoebe trembled under the impact. Deverell wasn't so much kissing her as staking a claim. From a deep well of feminine awareness, she recognised the difference instantly and responded to it, clinging closer, yielding the moist secrets of her mouth, letting him know she was his.

And as if her response was all he'd been seeking, he gentled at once. His arms tightened, but they cradled her. He broke the kiss, but only so he could trace the curve of her throat with warm lips. She trembled again as his mouth nudged aside the lace-trimmed neckline of her gown to caress the soft skin beneath, and he murmured something she couldn't understand, nor barely heard over the pounding of her heart.

'You're mine,' he whispered. 'Only mine, Phoebe.'

'Yes.'

The word was lost in his kiss as his mouth returned to hers. He began to stroke her, his hands caressing the curves of her waist and hips, until she felt his fingers come to rest just beneath her breast.

She shivered in almost unbearable anticipation. Then he moved his hand upward and enclosed one soft mound with the sureness of absolute possession.

Phoebe cried out softly and clung to him. Liquid

warmth unfurled inside her, the muscles in her thighs
went soft. She was helplessly adrift on a sea of the
sweetest pleasure she'd ever known, and yet caught, held
safe, in the arms of the man she loved.

Even when he raised his head and looked down at his
hand cupping her so intimately, she made no protest.
She blushed. She trembled inside and knew he felt it.
But she had never felt such a sense of rightness as the
warmth of his touch.

'You trust me.' He sounded awed, as if he'd just
discovered the most priceless treasure in the world.

'Absolutely,' she whispered.

He raised his eyes to hers. Something fierce blazed
in the blue-green depths for an instant. Desire was blatant; she thought she recognised glittering triumph; but
behind it was something so dark, so vulnerable, that she
made a tiny sound of protest.

'It's all right,' he said swiftly. And releasing her,
cupped her face in his hands. The breath he drew in was
audible. 'Phoebe, I—'

The drawing-room door opened with a crash.

'Phoebe! You must read this at—whoops!' Theodosia
started to retreat.

Flushing with confusion, Phoebe tried to back away
from Deverell. He promptly prevented her escape by
seizing her hand.

'It's all right, Theo,' she managed to say when he
whipped his head around and fixed the intruders with
slitted eyes. 'Come in.'

'No, it's not all right,' Deverell all but snarled.
'Go away.'

Theo giggled. 'Sorry, Uncle Sebastian, but from the
look on Phoebe's face, I suspect the moment is lost.'

'I'll be the judge of that. Vanish.'

'Really, my lord.' Phoebe tried to summon up a
reproving frown. She suspected the effect was sadly
ruined by the bright colour staining her cheeks. 'Is that
any way to speak to your wards?'

'Yes.'

She frowned even more severely.

'You're not still angry with us for starting a driving club, are you, Uncle Sebastian?' Cressy gazed at her uncle with an air of innocence that didn't fool Phoebe for a minute.

She stared at the twins more closely. They didn't appear to notice anything odd in the fact that their uncle was holding their companion's hand in a particularly possessive grasp, and showed no inclination to release it. Their eyes were certainly sparkling with excitement, but it didn't seem to stem from any anticipation of scandal.

Phoebe's wits reeled. What lost moment had Theo been talking about? Surely her charges didn't suspect she was willing to become Deverell's mistress?

'Be assured,' Deverell responded in a tone that wouldn't have reassured anyone in possession of their senses, that this latest crime puts the Two-in-Hand Club for Lady Whips in the shade. Leave.'

'But we haven't told you our news.' Theo waved a thick wad of paper under his nose. 'Cressy has written a melodrama.'

'I'll be the first lady playwright.'

'We're going to show it to Mr Kemble at once.'

'I'm sure he'll wish to produce it.'

'But if he doesn't, well take a copy—'

'In the first instance,' Deverell interrupted in crushing accents, 'Cressida is not the first lady to write plays. And in the second instance, as much as I'd like to be rid of you, you will not pester Kemble, or anyone else, with anything.'

'But, Uncle Sebastian, you don't understand. I'm going to write plays instead of acting in them. I'll be famous.'

'Unlikely.'

'I'll sway millions.'

'The theatres only seat thousands.'

'That is quite enough, my lord.' Phoebe tugged at her hand. This time she succeeded in freeing herself. The fact that she did so only because Deverell chose to release her wasn't lost on her. 'Cressy, I would be delighted to read your play. Perhaps I should do so before you take it to Mr Kemble. I consider myself something of an expert on melodrama, you know.'

Out of the corner of her eye she saw Deverell start to grin. While the twins conferred in excited voices, she turned and fixed him with a minatory stare. 'And I believe you have several other people to visit today, my lord. Now that our discussion is finished, you mustn't let me keep you.'

'Our discussion is far from finished,' he growled in a low voice. 'But you're correct. I still have Grismead to see and a long-overdue account to settle with Crowhurst before I can be sure of your undivided attention.' He recaptured her hand and raised it to his lips. 'But I'll be back, Miss Smith, be certain of that, at which time I intend to see we have some privacy. I have a very important question to put to you.'

The sudden cessation of chatter had Phoebe glancing at the twins. They were watching the proceedings with bright-eyed interest.

'Well. . .I cannot imagine. . .that is. . .'

'Don't let your melodramatic imagination run away with you while I'm gone,' he murmured against her fingers. 'It's a very straightforward question, requiring a very straightforward answer.'

His brilliant aquamarine eyes smiled straight into hers for a heart-stopping second, then he pressed a lingering kiss into her palm, released her and left.

Phoebe gazed after him, suddenly floating so high on a bubble of happiness that she scarcely noticed the twins' scurrying out of the room after him.

Deverell wasn't going to offer her a carte blanche. His intentions were honourable. There could be no other explanation for his words or his actions. If he'd intended to make her his mistress, he would never have spoken or behaved with such frank purpose in front of his nieces.

And with that thought whirling through her mind, she finally realised what had continually puzzled her about that very wicked, very inviting smile. She'd seen the warmth and amusement, she'd seen the devilish invitation to share his humour, but she hadn't recognised the intimacy or the promise in his eyes.

The promise of a man of honour, she thought wonderingly. The impossible seemed to have happened. She didn't know how it had happened. She didn't know what Deverell saw in her that placed her above ladies of wealth and beauty and position, but he wanted her. He cared about her feelings; about her reputation. He might even—

Oh, did she dare to hope for so much? He might even grow to love her as she loved him.

Phoebe hugged herself and executed a small skip of uncontained excitement. For the first time in her life, the future was full of hope and promise. For the first time, she dared to believe that the fantasy she'd dismissed several days ago might come true. The impossible really had happened.

Deverell was going to ask her to become his wife.

Her euphoria lasted until she sat down to a solitary meal in the dining-room. Gerald still hadn't returned, and the girls were attending a concert with Lady Yarwood and her daughters, thereby allowing their companion a free evening.

It was a pity she didn't want a free evening.

Phoebe studied the silent, empty room and wished she'd thought to pay a visit to Hatchards. The latest calf-bound novel from the Minerva Press would be preferable company to the doubts that were beginning to crowd into her head.

Not she doubted Deverell's intentions. Not for a minute. But he'd practically expressed those intentions before she'd put him in full possession of the facts. And three pertinent facts were now staring her most unpleasantly in the face.

Her circumstances were perfectly suited to becoming a mistress.

A wife was another matter.

Before Deverell said another word, she would have to tell him the truth.

She would have to do more, Phoebe told herself, a sharp ache already piercing her heart at the thought. She would have to point out every disadvantage, every possible repercussion, every drawback to a marriage between herself and Deverell. She would have to do it even if he loved her—and he hadn't said a word about love.

He *wanted* her. She had no doubt about that. The memory of the fierceness of his embrace and the heated demand of his mouth on hers caused tingling little shivers of sensation to dart about inside her every time she thought about it.

But he was a Deverell. When Deverells wanted something, they tended to go after the object of their desire and worry about the consequences later. If he married her and later regretted it, she knew the heartbreak would be unbearable.

Because she loved him, she would have to bring about the possible destruction of her dreams.

Phoebe sighed and pushed her unfinished meal away. She propped her chin on her hands and stared unhappily at the window. Dusk had fallen, shadowing the garden in shades of grey. She could vaguely make out her own reflection in the glass. Doom and gloom emanated from her like a shroud that threatened to engulf her entire surroundings. The destruction of her dreams seemed all too imminent.

When Thripp opened the door, she turned with a sense of foreboding.

He carried a small white envelope. The logical explanation seemed to leap out at her from the shadows.

She wasn't going to have to explain things to Deverell after all. She'd forgotten he was more controlled than the rest of his family. He'd already had second thoughts.

'This was just delivered for you, miss.' Thripp glanced down at the note he held, but made no move to give it to her.

Phoebe braced herself and straightened. She held out her hand. 'Thank you, Thripp.'

He didn't move. 'It's from that Crowhurst fellow.'

She frowned. 'How do you know?'

'After all them notes, miss?' Thripp indulged himself with a most unbutler-like snort. 'I'd know his hand anywhere.'

'Oh. Well. . .' She tried not to let her spirits revive too much with the small reprieve. 'No doubt he wishes to apologise for his very peculiar behaviour today. I'm sure Lord Deverell won't object to me reading it.'

Assuming his most mournful expression, Thripp handed over the note.

Phoebe ripped open the envelope and drew out the single sheet of notepaper. Its message was brief. She had to read it twice, however, before the meaning sank in. When it did, she leapt to her feet, sending her chair crashing to the floor behind her.

'Oh, dear God! Oh, my goodness! Thripp, what—? Where—? Oh, heavens, what are we going to do? Crowhurst has kidnapped Gerald!'

'Knew that note boded no good.' Thripp nodded several times. He seemed more satisfied at his own acuteness than appalled at this latest calamity.

Phoebe was too busy scanning the note again to pay attention. 'He says if we wish Gerald to remain alive, I'm to come to the Black Mole Inn on Hounslow Heath before eight o'clock tonight. Alone. He gives directions on how to find the place.'

'His lordship isn't going to like that, miss.'

'*I* don't like it, but what choice do I have? Gerald's

life could be snuffed out at any moment. Good heavens! This must be why we haven't seen Gerald all day. Crowhurst must have kidnapped him this morning in case I refused to. . .er. . .repay him if he prevented Gerald's duel.'

'Why would he do that, miss? He didn't know you were going to ask for help. Any road, even if you'd gone off with Crowhurst all meek and cosy, Master Gerald would still have a tale to tell.'

Phoebe stared at him in dismay. 'Perhaps Crowhurst doesn't intend to keep Gerald alive. He seemed to be quite irrational earlier, but now—he must be insane, and there's no saying how such a mind works.' Her own was racing. 'He even accused Deverell. . . But what if it was Crowhurst who arranged for that awful man to challenge Gerald?'

'So the innocent young lady'd be forced to ask for the villain's help,' Thripp concluded knowledgeably.

When Phoebe blinked at him, he gave a discreet cough. 'Mrs Thripp likes to read them news pamphlets, miss. You've no idea what some folks get up to. A right disgrace it is and no mistake!'

'Good heavens!' Her mind remained suspended for a moment on the image of the Thripps poring over scandalous halfpenny pamphlets before she managed to wrench it back to the present.

'I'll have to obey Crowhurst's instructions, there's no question about that. But if he thinks I'll tamely succumb to his threats, he's very much mistaken.'

She thought for a moment longer. 'Thripp, while you instruct Gerald's groom to bring the phaeton around, I'll write a note to Deverell. Tell the footman he's not to rest until he's delivered it into his lordship's own hands. Oh, dear. . .' She wrung her hands and glanced at the clock on the mantelpiece. 'Crowhurst might be insane, but he's not entirely stupid. It's past seven now and I have to be at this place by eight.'

'Aye.' Thripp nodded gloomily. 'Just the time when

his lordship has likely gone out for the evening. Henry'll have to search for him all over, and by that time who's to say where you'll be?'

His words were an all-too-accurate reflection of her own fears. Phoebe scowled at him. 'Let's not sink to the level of your pamphlets, Thripp. If Deverell has already seen Crowhurst, which seems likely since Crowhurst has resorted to threats, he may still be at the Grismeads'. If not, try his clubs.'

'Aye, miss.'

'And I'd better leave another note for the girls. There's no saying when I'll return.'

She wouldn't say 'if', Phoebe told herself, as Thripp hurried away to summon Gerald's groom. Of course she would return. When Crowhurst saw that she'd followed his instructions to come alone, she might even find an opportunity to help Gerald escape. Even if she didn't, Deverell would come after her, she was sure of it.

If only she could be as certain that Gerald was still alive. Her fear for his safety was all too real. Crowhurst would soon realise—if he hadn't already—that he could hardly release his bait without serious repercussions to himself.

Pushing the chilling thought aside, Phoebe raced into the drawing-room. Her hands were shaking, but she managed to pen the note to Deverell and stuff it into an envelope.

The clatter of carriage wheels outside the window told her the phaeton was ready. She scribbled a hasty note to the twins, thrust the missives into Thripp's hands and threw on the bonnet and pelisse a maid had fetched for her.

As she dashed out into the night she could only hope and pray that Deverell wouldn't be too far behind her.

Chapter Twelve

Hounslow Heath was not a comforting place to be in broad daylight. By night, for a lone traveller, it was eerie in the extreme. One tended to see footpads and highwaymen lurking behind every bush. When Phoebe finally drew up outside a small inn crouched by the side of the track in the meagre shelter afforded by a few stunted trees, she released a huge sigh of relief.

A curricle and pair drawn up to one side of the building was the only indication that she was in the right place. The lantern over the door was unlit, and the sign creaking in the wind was so grimy, only the most keen-eyed observer would have discerned the figure of a small, sly-eyed creature. In the faint glow from the downstairs windows, Phoebe decided the creature was a black mole.

The inn named for the animal did not appear to be the most well-run hostelry. No ostler came running to hold the horses. No host was bustling through the doorway with offers of refreshment.

She began to regret having left Gerald's groom a mile or so back where the rutted lane, leading to the track she herself had followed, left the main road. Mindful of Crowhurst's instructions, she had thought it safer to come on alone. The groom had argued vociferously, but Phoebe had been adamant. They had already taken several wrong turns, having passed the ill-defined lane in the darkness before the moon had fully risen. Jem had been ordered to hold the lantern and keep a look-out for Deverell.

She wondered what time it was. Sending up a prayer that she wasn't too late and that Deverell was hard on her heels, she tied the reins and climbed down from the phaeton.

The door of the inn opened as her feet touched the ground. Hazy golden light spilled into the yard. The illumination didn't improve the scene. Turning, she saw that an attempt had once been made to pave the yard, but now tufts of grass poked up between the stones and weeds grew in wild profusion. Leaves and refuse blew and eddied across the small space every time the wind gusted.

Phoebe shivered in the cool breeze and started to chafe her arms. She froze in mid-gesture as Crowhurst strolled through the open doorway, a smile of triumph twisting his features.

The memory of her first encounter with him flashed through her mind. She shivered again and glanced around her. At least, then, she'd been in the middle of a city. The Black Mole seemed to be situated in the middle of nowhere.

'Ah, Phoebe, my dear. I was beginning to wonder if you'd been so foolish as to ignore my instructions.'

'Where is Gerald?' she demanded without preamble.

Crowhurst smiled again and gestured to the doorway behind him. 'Won't you come in? We may as well discuss the situation in comfort, don't you think?'

Ignoring the question, Phoebe swept past him into the inn. She halted at once, transfixed by dismay and a spine-tingling silence.

Comfort was not the word she would have used to describe the interior of the Black Mole. The door opened directly into an evil-smelling taproom that hadn't seen a broom or mop for years. Several seedy-looking individuals were seated around the solitary table. Their eyes bored into her with avid interest. A tankard clunked as it was put down on the table. One of the men made a remark beneath his breath and was answered with coarse snickers.

Crowhurst ignored the crowd. 'In here,' he said, opening another door off the taproom.

Thanking providence that she didn't have to walk past those men, Phoebe followed Crowhurst into what was clearly a private parlour. It was no less gloomy than the taproom, lit only by a branch of candles on the centre table, but at least it was cleaner and a fire burned in the stone fireplace opposite the window.

She crossed to it, holding her hands to the warmth. The flames seemed to have little effect on the chill sweeping through her body.

'I must apologise for these crude surroundings, Phoebe.' Crowhurst closed the door and crossed the room towards her. 'But the Black Mole has been rather convenient for my purposes over the past few years. Out of the way. No one asks questions. And we won't be staying long.'

Phoebe raked him with a scornful gaze. 'You would seem to have a taste for low company, my lord. First that grimy little theatre, and now this.'

He laughed. 'Always the haughty madam. But I'm no longer a boy to be kept dangling at the end of one of your strings.'

'Gerald,' she prompted coldly.

He raised a brow at her lack of response to his comment, then indicating the wooden settle by the fire, seated himself at one end and picked up a glass of wine from the table beside him. Phoebe remained standing.

'Still playing cards at White's, I expect,' he murmured casually, raising his drink to contemplate the reflection of flames through the dark liquid.

She stared at him.

He smiled and lifted his glass to her before taking a sip. 'You didn't think I'd really kidnap Gerald, did you,

Phoebe? That would have been a very foolish thing to
do. And far too much trouble.'

'You lied?' She almost whispered the words. Her
brain struggled to take them in.

'Indeed. You see, I'd been watching Gerald today in
pursuit of my original scheme. An exhausting process,
I must say. First I trailed him to Filby's, then Tattersall's,
then Manton's. Then he and Filby must needs lunch at
a coffee-shop, and visit Filby's tailor. I knew he hadn't
been home all day, and the idea of setting a trap for you
by claiming he'd been kidnapped occurred to me. Once
I saw him settled at White's, I doubted he'd ruin my
plans by making an inconvenient appearance before you
left London, so—' he spread his hands '—here we are.'

She could only continue to stare at him, incredulous.
'And you think you'll get away with this?'

He lifted a shoulder. 'Why not? By the time anyone
realises the truth, we'll be long gone.'

The comment had a rather nasty ring of truth. Phoebe
took a steadying breath and tried to think past the quick
jolt of fear spreading ice through her veins. Somehow
she had to prevent Crowhurst from taking her further
afield. The Black Mole was unprepossessing, but she
was safer here where Deverell had a chance of finding
her. If she could just manoeuvre for some time.

'What was your original scheme?' she asked, her mind
scurrying to think of ways to keep him talking.

He hesitated, then shrugged again. 'I don't mind telling you, since you won't be going back to Deverell
anyway. As soon as I realised the duel I'd arranged
wasn't going ahead, I formed the notion of making a
more overt attempt on Gerald's life.'

'You wanted to kill *Gerald*? *Why?*'

'No, no,' he said irritably. 'Of course I don't want to
kill Gerald. Don't you see? If an attempt had been made
on his life, everyone would've thought Deverell was
behind it. He would have been imprisoned. At the very
least disgraced. He'd have left England again.'

'No,' she murmured, shaking her head. 'No one would believe Deverell capable of harming Gerald.'

Crowhurst sent her an impatient glare. 'They would after I'd reminded everyone of the old scandal. It's common knowledge that Deverell has no love for his family, nor they for him. And then, you see, you would have been mine, and *he*'d have been punished for trying to take you from me.'

The gloating satisfaction in his voice momentarily deprived Phoebe of speech.

'Why did you change your plan?' she finally asked, hoping he couldn't hear the faintness in her voice.

His air of triumph dropped from him like a cloak. He turned to her with an almost boyish eagerness that made her want to cringe. A combination of fear and pity roiled inside her, making her feel sick to her stomach.

'I thought you wouldn't like it if Gerald got hurt, Phoebe. Even though I wouldn't have killed him, I'd still have had to make it look like a real attempt on his life. That was when I thought of the kidnapping scheme. I knew you'd come.'

'My lord, surely. . .' Dear God, how did one reason with a disordered mind? 'Do you honestly think you'll get away with this? Deverell will come after me, but it's not too late if you'll only—'

'Let him come after you!' Crowhurst shot to his feet and flung his glass into the fire with a violence that made her flinch. The glass exploded, sending sparks hissing up the chimney and illuminating the sudden viciousness of his expression.

Phoebe remembered Lady Yarwood's comment about Crowhurst's moods and tried to force herself to stillness. Her ladyship hadn't known the half of it. Nor was the memory going to help her now, she thought, glancing at the door. Had he locked it? But if she tried to escape, Crowhurst was close enough to catch her. And she doubted those men outside would lift a finger to assist her, even if she screamed.

'I don't mind killing *him*,' Crowhurst snarled. 'You'd like us to fight over you, wouldn't you, Phoebe? You always played one of us off against the other. How many were there? Two? Three?'

Trembling inside, she put a hand to the back of the settle to steady herself. 'Sir. . .' She swallowed and tried again. 'I am *not*—'

'No!' He cut her off with a jerk of his hand and, frowning, took a few agitated steps towards the window. Again she saw him try to master his rage. 'I know! I know. Not her. Keep forgetting.'

'I'm sure. . .I'm sure that's quite understandable,' she faltered. 'It's clear I very closely resemble the lady you once loved, and. . .I'm sorry for that, but—'

He wasn't listening. 'Not her,' he muttered, peering through the glass.

Phoebe's heart leapt as she heard a faint noise outside. Had Crowhurst heard? Could he see anything but their own dim reflections?

'Not her,' he continued to mumble. He turned and started back towards her. 'Look the same. Yes, that's it. Exactly the same. She's you.'

Ice water flowed down Phoebe's spine. She stopped straining her ears for sounds beyond the window. 'Who?' she whispered.

Crowhurst halted and peered at her in the hazy light. 'Your mother,' he said as if surprised she should ask. 'Just like her.'

'My *mother*?' Phoebe dropped to the settle as if her legs had turned to water. Scenes from her childhood whipped through her mind with a speed that left her reeling. Suddenly several things began to make sense. 'You were in love with my mother?'

'Her name was Phoebe, too.'

'No.' She shook her head, still dazed. 'Charlotte. It was Charlotte.'

'That's what her family called her.' Crowhurst dismissed the name with a gesture. 'We used her middle name. She said it made her feel like another person. Not hedged in by that puritan family of her husband's. Phoebe. Like you.'

'And Deverell?' she whispered, staring at Crowhurst. 'Was he. . .? Did he. . .? But you met him only weeks ago. Was that a lie, too?'

'We never met. She kept us apart. But he took her from me!' he shouted suddenly. 'She ran off with him. She was supposed to leave your father for *me*. But she chose him. She chose Deverell.'

'Not quite, Crowhurst.'

'Oh, thank God! *Sebastian!*'

Her cry was lost beneath the crashing of the casement against the outside wall. Before the echoes had died away Phoebe leaped from the settle, darted around Crowhurst and flung herself at Deverell as he came in through the open window.

He caught her as he straightened, holding her close for a moment before drawing back to look down at her face. His gaze, dark and concerned, swept over her. 'Are you all right, little love?'

She nodded. It was all she could manage. A rush of relieved tears sprang to her eyes. She blinked them away, and was opening her mouth to speak when she found herself abruptly thrust to one side.

Crowhurst launched himself at Deverell, his lips drawn back in a snarl of rage.

Before Phoebe could so much as gasp, Deverell took one step forward and lashed out with his clenched fist. The full strength of his body was behind the blow. Crowhurst's jaw cracked under the impact. He went down in a sprawl of arms and legs and lay there, groaning.

'Oh, good heavens.' Phoebe unglued her hands from her mouth. 'He's just lying there. Do you think you've broken his jaw, my lord?'

'Very likely.' Deverell didn't appear to be unduly dismayed by the prospect. He stepped over his victim and stalked towards the door. He opened it and subjected the occupants beyond to a flint-eyed stare.

Phoebe felt the sudden stark silence from where she stood.

Deverell shut the door without a word and waited until the faint murmur of conversation started up again.

Obviously, Crowhurst had been right when he'd said no one asked questions at the Black Mole. Phoebe glanced at him and immediately went rigid. 'Sebastian!'

Deverell drew a pistol from his pocket with a deceptively casual movement. 'Don't bother looking around for your sword-stick, Crowhurst. It's over by the fire and I'll bring you down before you can take one step towards it.'

'Bastard!' Crowhurst's voice cracked but apparently his jaw was still in one piece. He could speak. Crawling to a chair, he pulled himself painfully to his knees, then to his feet. 'I'll see you ruined for this. I'll see you both ruined. She came to me. She came to *me*! I didn't force her.'

'Depends on how you look at the situation.' Deverell nudged the settle closer to the fire with one booted foot. 'I seem to recall being told quite recently by a certain governess that blackmail is a form of threat.' He beckoned to Phoebe. 'Come here, love. You're shivering.'

Phoebe obeyed, reflecting on the very peculiar effects of shock. The gentler note in Deverell's voice and the careful way he seated her—while holding a gun in his other hand—was having a strange effect on her nerves. She began to wonder if she was growing slightly hysterical.

'I didn't blackmail her,' Crowhurst repeated. He eyed Deverell for a moment, then his features twisted into a look of cunning. 'She came to me to avenge her mother!'

'What?' Phoebe's eyes went wide. She snapped back to life. 'What *are* you talking about, sir? You wrote me that dreadful note. I can produce it right now!'

'Sweetheart—'

'Don't you know?' Crowhurst burst out. 'Your mother killed herself when Deverell abandoned her. Her family cast her off. She couldn't stand the loneliness and disgrace and—'

'God damn it!' Deverell roared. 'Will you shut up, Crowhurst!'

'It's all right,' Phoebe said quickly. She glanced up at him and felt her heart turn over at the glittering rage in his eyes. 'I knew my mother had been cast off. I was going to tell you, but. . .'

Oh, dear God, what a way for him to learn the truth. Would he ever believe that she was going to tell him everything at their next meeting?

'I was going to tell you,' she repeated. 'Everything. That my name is really Phoebe Everton-Smythe and—'

'I know, love.' She saw his eyes narrow as he controlled his anger. 'I heard Crowhurst ranting while I was prising the window open, and put most of it together. Until tonight, I don't think any of us knew all the facts. We'll talk about it later.'

'Will you tell her the truth, Deverell? That you only want her because you were forced to give up her mother and your family shipped you off to India to avoid the scandal.'

'In the first place, Crowhurst, I neither abandoned Phoebe's mother nor was forced to give her up. She was having an affair with my brother, not with me. Unfortunately,' he added into the stunned silence that greeted his announcement, 'on the evidence at the time, my family thought as you did.'

Both his listeners continued to stare at him, speechless. Crowhurst looked as if Deverell had struck him again. Phoebe had already received so many blows to her senses that she could scarcely think. The sweeping sense of relief washing over her was immediately followed by another stronger wave of foreboding.

She'd been wondering how Deverell could ever love

the daughter of the woman who had caused so much pain in his life. She was still wondering. Charlotte Everton-Smythe hadn't broken his heart, but she'd been the unwitting cause of his banishment.

'Your brother?' whispered Crowhurst. His face had turned a sickly pale colour.

'Yes. Your revenge has been for nothing, Crowhurst.'

'He arranged for that man to challenge Gerald,' Phoebe murmured.

Deverell nodded, glanced down at the pistol in his hand and returned it to his pocket. 'That threw me for a while. Crowhurst's obsession with you made it obvious that you closely resembled a past lover, and taking into account my brother's series of affairs and Crowhurst's enmity towards me—despite the fact that we'd never met—it seemed all too probable that he and Selwyn had been rivals. When he inveigled Gerald into playing at the Pigeonhole, I thought he was trying to revenge himself on Selwyn's son by ruining him.'

He turned to Crowhurst who was now slumped in brooding silence. 'But it was me you were after, wasn't it, Crowhurst? The only trouble was, you didn't have the guts to tackle me personally, so you decided to strike at me through Gerald. Quite a neat scheme, but you should choose your tools more wisely. Creech crumpled as soon as I told him you'd been seen together.'

'You can't prove anything from that,' Crowhurst said sulkily. 'I dare say I've been seen with everyone who's played at the Pigeonhole.'

Deverell appeared unperturbed by the claim. 'Quite true. But men who make a living by fleecing young sprigs from the country aren't noted for their superior intelligence. Creech not only admitted that you paid him to accuse Gerald of cheating, but added the interesting fact that you promised him swift passage out of the country and enough money to live on for several years if Gerald was fatally wounded. Then you would've sat back and waited for Society to remember the old scandal.'

Crowhurst's already pale face turned a ghastlier hue. He plucked at his sleeve with shaking fingers. 'What are you going to do?'

'Strange though it may seem, I have no wish to ruin you. I can even sympathise with your desire to wreak vengeance on my family.' His expression hardened. 'I spent several years harbouring similar fantasies. But you made a fatal mistake when you involved Phoebe in your schemes.'

'I wouldn't have hurt her. I just wanted her back.'

Deverell's eyes flashed with such savagery even Phoebe gasped. He strode forward, yanked Crowhurst up by the collar of his coat and slammed him against the wall. His voice lowered, each word emerging with deadly clarity.

'Phoebe is not her mother. Do you understand me, Crowhurst? She is not yours. She never will be.'

Crowhurst stared at Deverell as if mesmerised. 'Not mine,' he whispered obediently, and then his face crumpled. 'I loved her,' he choked. 'And now she's dead.'

'Oh, Sebastian.'

He silenced her with a look. 'She died a long time ago, Crowhurst.' He released the other man and stepped back. 'Unfortunately for both of us, she died before she could right a few misconceptions.'

Phoebe couldn't tell if Crowhurst had heard that last remark or not. He crumpled to the floor and stayed there, utterly beaten. She looked up at Deverell, her eyes widening at the grim set of his mouth, and wondered what was going to happen next.

The answer came from the vicinity of the window.

'I say, Uncle Sebastian, what on earth is going on here? Is Phoebe safe?'

She blinked in astonishment. 'Gerald? Is that you?'

Deverell turned in time to see his nephew swing one

leg over the windowsill and clamber into the room.

'Of course it's me,' he said. 'You feeling all right, Phoebe? You look a little pale. No need to. Thought I'd better come and tell you I haven't been kidnapped.'

'How. . .very considerate of you,' Phoebe uttered in faint accents.

'We had, however, already deduced that useful fact,' Deverell added. 'May I ask how you found us?'

Gerald grinned. 'Got home to find the girls in an uproar over Phoebe's note. Bad decision to leave one,' he tacked on, sending her a reproving frown. 'Took me ten minutes to calm everyone down.'

'But I wrote that note so they *wouldn't* worry.'

Deverell raised his eyes heavenward.

'Anyway,' continued Gerald, correctly interpreting this expression, 'I followed Phoebe's directions. She was driving my phaeton, of course, so I had to dash off a note to Reggie.'

'Good God! Don't tell me you brought Filby with you.'

'Very obedient servant, sir.' As if at a signal, Filby's head and shoulders popped up at the window with the suddenness of a plump, particularly fashionable jack-in-the-box. He beamed at Phoebe. 'Very happy to see you, ma'am. No trouble at all to bring Gerald. Curricle took only a minute to harness. Sorry to be a little delayed just now. Had to tether the horses. Gerald's, too. Looked as if they might wander off. See you left your phaeton down the lane with Gerald's groom,' he added chattily, turning to Deverell. 'Don't blame you. Yard's getting a bit crowded.'

Phoebe couldn't help it. She had to succumb to the madness of the situation or go mad herself. Her peal of laughter earned her a glare from Deverell that threatened to set her off again.

'It was very gallant of you and Gerald to come to my rescue, Mr Filby,' she finally managed. 'Won't you come in?'

Filby eyed the windowsill with a dubious expression, then looked down at the pale blue pantaloons he wore beneath his greatcoat. 'Might use the door, if no one minds,' he chirped, and vanished as suddenly as he'd appeared.

His place was promptly taken by the twins. Phoebe blinked at them and wondered if she was losing her mind. She heard Deverell swear comprehensively.

'What the devil are they doing here?' he demanded of his nephew.

Gerald scowled fiercely at his sisters. 'I thought you promised to stay in the curricle until Reggie and I discovered what was afoot.'

'You have discovered it,' Theo pointed out inarguably. 'And we're tired of sitting there, doing nothing.' She hopped nimbly over the windowsill, followed by her sister, and glanced about with interest. 'Besides, we heard Phoebe laugh so we knew she was all right. You are, aren't you, Phoebe?'

'Gerald,' began Deverell before she could answer, 'if you wish to survive until tomorrow, you will take Filby and your sisters and—'

He was interrupted by the sound of horses' hooves entering the yard at a smart trot. At the same time Filby pushed open the parlour door.

'Strange set of company Crowhurst keeps,' he remarked, strolling into the room. 'Think someone else has arrived, by the bye.'

'Surely not,' Deverell said sarcastically. 'I could have sworn we're all here.'

Filby turned a look of polite enquiry on the figure still crouched on the floor. 'You expecting anyone, Crowhurst?'

As though emerging from a deep trance, Crowhurst started and managed to push himself upright again. His voice was not the one to answer Filby, however.

'This cannot be the place. Look at it. You, my good man. Are you the innkeeper? You should be ashamed of yourself. And who are all these slovenly persons? Get rid of them at once! Disgusting! Sitting there drinking while villainous crimes are going on under their very noses. I've a good mind to summon the nearest magistrate.'

'Good God!' muttered Deverell.

Before he could enlarge on the theme the door was flung open, narrowly missing Mr Filby. Lady Grismead sailed into the room, followed by Mr Charlton.

'Bloody hell,' growled Deverell. 'I thought I left you explaining finances to Grismead, Edward?'

'Kindly moderate your language, Deverell.' Lady Grismead came to a halt in the middle of the parlour and swept the occupants with a single gimlet-eyed glance. 'I,' she announced with awful meaning, 'have come to find out what is Going On.' She let her gaze rest on Deverell. 'If you think, sir, that you can receive an urgent summons while in my house and dash off without an explanation, you may think again.'

Deverell sighed. 'Nothing is going on, as you so succinctly put it, Aunt. Miss Smith found herself obliged to leave town and requested my escort.'

'Indeed? I suppose that is why Mr Charlton and I encountered a groom skulking in the lane, and why there are carriages everywhere one looks.' She paused to let this sink in, then softened her tone.

'I am not quite a fool, Sebastian. Mr Charlton and I hastened to Park Street and found Miss Smith's note. It was clear she was in a great deal of danger. And although I dare say you are capable of managing any number of unpleasant situations, there are some that require the Presence of a Woman. You,' she added, with the air of one throwing in a clincher, 'have been extraordinarily helpful to us today; now I wish to return the favour. That is what families are for.'

While her nephew was swallowing this piece of worldly wisdom, she turned to Phoebe. 'Perhaps you will enlighten me, Miss Smith.'

Predictably, everyone except Phoebe started to talk at once.

'All an unfortunate misunderstanding,' Filby stated positively.

'Crowhurst told Phoebe he'd kidnapped me,' Gerald informed his great-aunt. 'Of course, he was lying, but—'

'Phoebe didn't know that,' Theo put in, glancing anxiously at Deverell. 'It wasn't as if she ran off with him.'

Cressy nodded emphatically. 'She was duped.' She glanced around, spotted Crowhurst and turned on him with such ferocity that he shrank. 'Villain! Blackguard! You knew if you put a limit on Phoebe's time, she wouldn't be able to check the truth of your story. I hope Uncle Sebastian spits you on the end of his sword.'

Gerald rolled his eyes. 'Cressy, Uncle Sebastian isn't wearing a sword.'

'Well, I hope he shoots you full of holes.'

'Please, Cressy.' Phoebe's voice wobbled as laughter threatened to overtake her again.

'Leave this to me, Miss Smith.' Lady Grismead took charge. 'No one will be riddled with holes, Cressida. I do not approve of violence. However—'

As the full force of the argument about what to do with Crowhurst began to rage about her, Phoebe subsided. She was only too happy to let her ladyship have her way. She was starting to feel rather shaky. The result of too much excitement, no doubt. She slumped a little on the settle and felt Deverell glance down at her.

Mr Charlton claimed his attention before he could do more than touch a gentle hand to her cheek.

'Sir, do you want me to get rid of Crowhurst for you? It's the least I can do since I'm here.'

'No, what I want you to do is get rid of everyone else.'

His secretary winced. 'I claim ignorance of your wards' intentions,' he pleaded hurriedly. 'And I'm sorry about bringing your aunt along, but when you walked out leaving me with Lord Grismead, I doubt a juggernaut would have stopped her.'

Deverell grinned unexpectedly. 'You're forgiven. But only because you had enough sense to leave Grismead, Pamela and Nermal in London.'

'Pamela and Mr Hartlepoole,' pronounced her ladyship, overhearing this and abandoning the argument, 'are engaged in composing a notice to be placed in the *Gazette*. Thanks to Deverell,' she added graciously. 'However, poor Grismead is probably worrying himself into one of his dyspeptic fits, so—'

'Aunt,' interrupted Deverell firmly, 'if you really wish to repay me for knocking some sense into that idiot poet and advising Grismead on financial matters, would you please take the girls back to London? Gerald and Edward will accompany you. And Gerald's groom, of course. You'll be perfectly safe.'

Her ladyship frowned. 'What about Miss Smith?'

'She'll be perfectly safe, too.'

'Hmm. You do realise, I suppose, that Miss Smith has been through a most harrowing experience.'

'No, really, I'm—'

'I realise it,' Deverell said with unaccustomed patience. 'Don't worry, Aunt. We won't be far behind you. I have one more matter to make clear to Crowhurst, after which I'll take Phoebe home.'

Lady Grismead considered this statement for a few moments, glanced at Phoebe, then gave a brisk nod. 'I see Miss Smith trusts you implicitly, Sebastian. No doubt we have been wrong about you all these years. You shall tell me the truth tomorrow.

'As for you, sir—' her ladyship swept a basilisk glance over Crowhurst, who seemed to be trying to make himself as small as possible '—if I see your face in town in the near future, I shall make it clear that your predilection for unsavoury theatrical productions renders you unfit to be received by all respectable persons. I trust you understand me.'

'Good heavens!' exclaimed Phoebe, startled. She looked up at Deverell. 'How did she discover that, sir?'

'I'm afraid I made the mistake of warning Grismead after Crowhurst attended my aunt's party,' Deverell answered in the same low tone. 'Obviously, she prised the story out of him.' He bent and covered her tightly clenched hands with one of his. 'Just a few more minutes, sweetheart, then—'

'Uncle Sebastian, do we really have to go with Aunt Ottilia?' Cressida bounced up to them with so much energy, Phoebe felt like a wilted leaf in comparison. 'I know Theo is happy to go off with Edward, but I want to hear precisely what happened. Think what a tale this could make. I could write—'

'Wouldn't do,' stated Filby, coming up to them with the air of one anxious to quit his surroundings. He peered worriedly at his sleeve and flicked off a cobweb. 'Heroine rescued before she's been ruined. Nephew full of gig. Wicked uncle turns out to be the hero. No good at all. Are you ready to depart, Lady Cressida?'

'No good, sir?' Cressida drew herself up. 'What, pray, do you know about melodrama?'

Filby appeared completely unaware of her outrage. 'Well, m'mother likes to put on amateur theatricals at our Christmas house-parties and—'

'She does?' Cressy clasped her hands. Her scowl vanished.

Still inspecting his coat, Filby nodded. 'Thought you might be interested. Lot of fun. Often acted in them m'self.'

'You have?'

'Tell you all about it on the way home. You ready, Gerald?'

'A moment, Gerald.' Deverell bent, picked up Crowhurst's sword-stick and handed it to his nephew. 'Send this around to Crowhurst's lodgings tomorrow, will you? And see if you can stay out of gambling hells until you go up to Oxford. If you're serious about repairing your fortunes, I'll help you, but—'

'Oh, will you, Uncle Sebastian? That would be—'

He was propelled through the doorway by Mr Charlton. As everyone departed, arguing about which carriage to occupy, Deverell's gaze rested for a moment on Filby and Cressida.

'A match made in heaven. Why didn't I see it before? Do you know, Phoebe, I believe I may have underestimated Filby.' He turned and smiled down at her. 'I must have been preoccupied at the time.'

'No doubt, my lord,' she responded demurely. She glanced at the open window. 'Have they really all gone? I don't wish to sound ungrateful, but being rescued by an entire phalanx of Deverells is rather overwhelming.'

'I trust you'll that find one Deverell can do the job quite as well,' he replied solemnly, and walked over to the window. 'Hmm, we're not safe yet. Gerald and the girls seem rather anxious about one of the wheels on Gerald's phaeton. You didn't collide with anything on your way here, did you, Phoebe?'

'Of course not, sir.' She smiled faintly. 'Fortunately, the road was free of stage-coaches.'

'Fortunate, indeed. Ah, at last. They're going.'

He closed the window and latched it before turning to Crowhurst. The smile edging his mouth vanished. 'And as far as I'm concerned, we've had enough of your company, too, Crowhurst. Before you leave, however, let me make it clear that, like my aunt, I don't wish to encounter you for some considerable time. I suggest you take an extended tour abroad for reasons of health.'

Crowhurst merely nodded dejectedly and shuffled to the door. He didn't even glance at Phoebe.

Deverell watched his progress through slitted eyes. He waited until Crowhurst reached the door, then spoke. His voice was quiet, ice-cold, and utterly convincing.

'One more thing, Crowhurst.' The other man paused. 'Come near Phoebe again and I'll break your neck.'

Phoebe's eyes widened. If Deverell had threatened to strangle Crowhurst, she wouldn't have taken much notice. She had no trouble at all picturing him snapping Crowhurst's neck in two without even thinking about it if he so much as looked sideways at her.

Crowhurst knew it, also. He shuddered, glanced back fearfully into eyes that glittered with all the deadly chill of a naked blade, and hurried away.

For a moment silence filled the small room. Then Deverell took two long strides towards her, snatched her up and, yanking her bonnet off with jerky, impatient fingers, wrapped her in a crushing embrace. He pressed his face to her hair; his heart thundered wildly against her breast.

'God! I never want to go through anything like that again as long as I live,' he muttered. 'I kept telling myself that Crowhurst wouldn't hurt you. At least not immediately. But I couldn't be sure.'

'I knew you'd come.' Phoebe clung to him as desperately, absorbing the reassuring warmth and strength of his body. 'But I was so scared, Sebastian. He was going to take me somewhere else.'

'It's over now.' He relaxed his hold a little and drew back to trace the line of her cheek with gentle fingers. 'However—' his hand stilled '—it may not have happened in the first place if you'd confided in me. Perhaps you can explain, Miss Everton-Smythe, how it comes about that a daughter of one of Yorkshire's most starched-up families is masquerading under the name of Smith and earning her living as a governess.'

'Precisely because they are so starched-up,' she said drily. 'When I decided I'd had enough of reprimands and reproaches and being treated like an unpaid drudge, my family decided they wanted nothing to do with such an ungrateful person. In fact, they said I'd probably end up like my mother, and made me promise to drop the Everton name so no one would connect me with them, or be reminded of the scandal she caused.'

Deverell's eyes narrowed. He released her, shoved his hands into his pockets and took a few steps away to stand staring into the fire.

Phoebe sank back to the settle, feeling abruptly bereft. She had the distinct suspicion that the next few minutes were not going to be pleasant.

'It suited me, too,' she ventured. 'I had my living to earn, and a governess with a scandal attached to her name doesn't find employment easily.'

He turned his head to frown at her. 'Damn it, the scandal wasn't of your making. Perhaps you didn't mind changing your name, but what the hell was your father about to cast you off like that?'

'My father died several years ago. Although he probably would've done the same thing,' she added after a moment's thought. 'The Everton-Smythes are so puritanical they refuse to attend the Assemblies at Harrogate or York. Dancing can lead to improper behaviour, you know. Even to smile is a crime. As for coming to London— Well, you can imagine what they think of the Season.'

'I don't give a damn what they think of the Season. If they didn't isolate themselves, someone else besides Crowhurst might have recognised you and we might've put everything together a lot sooner.'

'Perhaps,' she said doubtfully. 'I suppose my father was only too thankful to keep the scandal contained. Even I didn't know the details until tonight. When my mother left, he banned all mention of her name, and sent me to live with his parents.' A wry smile touched her mouth. 'For a short time I believed it was so his mother could take the place of mine, but I soon learned it was because I resembled Charlotte so closely.'

'He couldn't bear to be reminded of her?'

Phoebe shook her head. 'Only because she'd brought shame on the family. First by her affairs, obviously, and then. . .her suicide.'

His expression gentled. 'Did you know she'd killed herself, Phoebe?'

'I. . .wasn't sure,' she said painfully. 'I was only nine when it all happened, and although I knew my mother had done something terrible—sensed it, as children do—it was soon made very clear that I wasn't to ask any questions.'

He studied her rather thoughtfully.

'It didn't change my life to any great extent,' she went on, shifting under that steady gaze. 'She was always rather distant. I didn't know her very well.'

'We both seem to have been somewhat unfortunate in our parents,' he observed, looking back at the fire.

'So it seems, sir, if you were punished for your brother's actions.'

One corner of his mouth kicked up. 'You're showing great self-restraint, Phoebe. I'm sure you wish to know how that came about.'

She ducked her head to hide a quick smile. 'Every sorry detail, I'm afraid.'

'That won't protect you, you know.'

Her head snapped up again. Before she could decide if he was referring to the promise he'd made her, he continued speaking.

'My brother was several years older than I and my father's favourite. Only the most iron-clad evidence would have convinced him that Selwyn could do anything wrong. And all the evidence pointed at me.'

'But. . .you couldn't have been more than nineteen or twenty.'

He shrugged. 'I was wild. Even by Deverell standards. You think Gerald's prank with the unmentionables was shocking. Well—' he sent her a glinting, sidelong glance '—I wouldn't have wasted time with the unmentionables, but spent it with their owners.'

'Oh.' She levelled her brows at him. 'Indeed, sir.'

He grinned unrepentantly. 'To put it bluntly, Phoebe, I, too, was involved in. . .er. . .liaisons, the only difference being that the women concerned were unmarried. Unfortunately, Selwyn's mistress began to want more than an illicit affair. Probably because her husband had cast her out, as we now know.

'Selwyn, of course, had no intention of disillusioning my father, and risking his own position, by leaving his wife and becoming embroiled in what promised to be a scandal of epic proportions. The result was a series of increasingly impassioned letters, addressed, to avert suspicion, to the Hon. S. Deverell instead of Viscount Kerford, as Selwyn was then styled.'

'What happened?' Phoebe prompted when he fell silent.

He shrugged. 'The inevitable. One can only assume that your mother was suffering from extreme distress to have behaved so rashly. Since Selwyn and I shared the same initial, far from averting suspicion, a barrage of letters addressed so simply in a feminine hand could mean only one thing as far as my father was concerned. That I was causing trouble again. He opened them and, since endearments rather than names were mentioned, all hell broke loose.'

'But you must have protested your innocence. And surely your brother didn't allow you to be punished so terribly for his wrongs.'

'Protests didn't do much good when I couldn't prove anything. As for Selwyn—' his mouth twisted '—there was no love lost between us. Imagine a Deverell determined to hide his true nature behind a façade of pious respectability, and you have Selwyn. Whenever the two of us were alone, I scorned him for his hypocrisy. I might've been wild, but it was out in the open and Society be damned.'

'Also just like a Deverell,' she murmured.

He smiled reluctantly. 'Yes. I'm afraid I also had more than my fair share of Deverell pride. If Selwyn wasn't going to confess, then I wasn't about to accuse him. And when my father refused to believe me without proof, I ceased trying to convince him.'

Phoebe shook her head. 'That was very foolish of you, my lord.'

'I didn't think so at the time.' He hesitated, then added, 'I did try to trace the lady who'd written the letters, but by the time I'd beaten her whereabouts out of Selwyn, she was dead. He didn't tell me her real name anyway, only the one she was using by then, which is why I didn't make the link between you until tonight.'

'Your brother provided for her?'

'No, he'd abandoned her along with everyone else, but he knew where she was living. One wonders why desperation didn't send her to Crowhurst.'

'No wonder his mind became disturbed,' Phoebe mused aloud. 'She preferred death to running off with him.'

'Perhaps he wasn't offering marriage in the event that your father divorced her,' Deverell suggested drily. 'Apart from the fact that she'd had other lovers, she must have been several years older than him and would always be associated with scandal. Not insurmountable drawbacks in a mistress. A wife is another matter.'

Phoebe glanced fleetingly up at him. 'Precisely my own words, sir.'

There was a rather charged silence. Phoebe could feel Deverell's gaze on her, but she kept her own eyes lowered, even when he reached out a hand to her.

'Phoebe. . .' He drew in a breath and let his hand fall back to his side. 'You must be tired, little one. We'll talk further tomorrow. I'll ask the landlord to fetch you a glass of brandy while I bring my phaeton to the door. It'll warm you before we start out.'

Phoebe felt her throat tighten for some inexplicable reason. She nodded and managed a small, rather wobbly smile.

It seemed to do the trick. Deverell strode to the door. He paused for a second to study the empty taproom.

'It's a lowering thought,' he observed, 'that I had to come in through the window in case that crew in here were in Crowhurst's pay, while my aunt swept the place clean with a few well-chosen words.'

He sent her a swift grin over his shoulder and walked into the other room. Phoebe could hear him summoning the landlord. She bent to pick up her discarded bonnet, crushing the ribbons between tense fingers.

She had absolutely no idea, she realised, of Deverell's thoughts on the situation now that the past had been laid bare. Apart from that brief, fierce embrace, his present manner was that of a concerned friend. And although he'd used that most precious endearment, he had never, even earlier that day, mentioned anything about being in love with her.

Of course, there had hardly been time for a discussion on the subject, but they were alone now. What had happened to the very important, very straightforward question he'd wanted to ask her as soon as they had some privacy?

Phoebe gazed unseeingly into the fire and remembered her earlier doubts. It was no use repining, she told herself. Nothing had changed—except that Deverell was now aware of her unsuitability as a wife, which saved her the trouble of pointing out that fact. She should be grateful to be spared the duty.

And she was, after all, still willing to become his mistress. No doubt her heart would be shattered some time in the future, but she wouldn't think about that right now. She might not even have to worry that he wouldn't make any sort of offer at all. He *knew* she was willing to become his mistress. Of course he knew it. She'd responded to him without reservation only that afternoon, before he'd so much as hinted at marriage.

Well, she simply wouldn't act like a woman who expected a marriage proposal. The task shouldn't be difficult. Up until several hours ago, she hadn't had any such expectations.

Nodding at the logic of her reasoning, Phoebe sat up straighter and arranged her features into an expression of calm composure. She wondered when Deverell would be back so she could get her performance over and done with.

Chapter Thirteen

Deverell was back in two minutes, a very thoughtful look on his face.

'Phoebe, little one, are you certain you didn't collide with anything on your way here? Or run over something on the road?'

Phoebe blinked up at him, distracted from the bracing speech she was delivering to herself. In her fragile state of mind, she was inclined to take umbrage at his question.

'Well, I know I was extremely worried about Gerald, my lord, but I think I would have noticed a collision. Why do you ask?'

He didn't immediately enlighten her. Instead, a slow smile started to spread across his face. 'Those devious, diabolical little Deverells.'

Phoebe eyed the smile with foreboding. 'What have they done now?'

'I should have made sure they climbed into the right carriages. Gerald has very kindly taken my phaeton and left his for us.'

'Good heavens. Why would he do that?'

'Probably because he knew his days would be numbered if he damaged mine.'

When she only continued to stare at him in bewilderment, he elaborated.

'You may recall, my love, that I thought Gerald seemed anxious about his phaeton.'

'I don't think I want to hear this.'

'Gerald, no doubt with the connivance of his sisters, has splintered the cotter pin on each wheel. As soon as we hit the first pothole in the road, we'll find ourselves sitting in it.'

'He *what*? Why——? Oh, this is too much! Just wait until I see him again. I'll——' She stopped, her eyes widening as the full force of their predicament struck her. 'What on earth are we going to do, my lord?'

'Not a great deal, I'm afraid. It's some distance to the nearest town where I'd be likely to find a wheelwright, and even if I was willing to leave you here while I made the trip on the landlord's cob—which I'm not—I doubt the gentleman would be willing to return with me at this hour.'

'But——'

The landlord appeared in the doorway before she could voice even one of the protests whirling about in her head.

'Yer horses're stabled, me lord, and the wife's lighting a nice fire upstairs.'

'Fire? Upstairs?' Phoebe stared from one man to the other in horror. 'But. . .you're not suggesting we stay *here*!'

'Why not?' The landlord appeared to take offence at her tone. 'The room up yonder's as good as this 'ere. The last owner had 'em built on for himself,' he confided to Deverell. 'Thought him and his rib was a cut above, if ye take me meaning, sir. But *I* says a bedchamber's there to make money.' He grinned ingratiatingly, displaying several gaps between his teeth. 'There's even a bolt on the door, so ye'll be reel private, like.'

'Not to mention solvent in the morning,' Deverell remarked, treating the landlord to a hard stare. 'Which is when you'll be paid.'

'Oh, aye, sir. Wotever yer honour wishes. And I hope

yer both has a very good night.' Chuckling, he withdrew.

'Oh, my goodness.' Phoebe sagged limply against the back of the settle. 'Whatever are we going to do now?'

Deverell raised a brow. 'Take over the landlord's best bedchamber. What else?'

'How can you be so calm about this, my lord?' Her voice soared to a note the great Catalani would have envied. 'Don't you understand? If we stay here all night, you'll be placed in a compromising position!'

He stared at her as if she'd suddenly expressed a desire to fetch the wheelwright herself. 'You're worried about *me* being in a compromising position?'

'Of course I am. What else would I be worried about?'

'Your own position?' he suggested.

She dismissed her own position with an agitated wave. 'This is terrible! Just when everything was going so well; when everyone will know you were unjustly accused and. . . We must *do* something, my lord.'

'Before you manage to whip yourself into a real fit of the vapours, Phoebe, let me remind you that no one knows we're here.'

'Your aunt does,' she wailed, not in the least mollified by this unhelpful remark. 'And your wards. And Mr Filby. And—'

'Please.' He held up a hand. 'Spare me the list. If we leave early in the morning, everyone concerned will think we got home tonight.'

'But—' She paused, frowning. There was a flaw in there somewhere, but she couldn't put her finger on it.

A second later the thought fled from her mind. Deverell strode forward, a look of determination on his face, and scooped her up off the settle before she realised his intention.

'However, if I'm going to be in a compromising position, I might as well take advantage of it,' he muttered, and carried her out of the room.

Phoebe could have sworn her heart stopped. She flung one arm around his neck in an instinctive reaction to suddenly finding herself in motion while several feet off the ground. Her other hand still clutched her bonnet. 'My lord, wait! Are you sure you know what you're doing?'

He grinned. 'Positive.'

'But. . .' After several futile attempts, she found her voice again. It sounded very small. 'Well, then. . .what *are* you doing?'

'Carrying you up to bed so I can make love to you.'

'Oh.' Her heart did stop. 'Oh, my goodness.'

'Don't worry, love,' he murmured, and smiled straight into her hugely rounded eyes. 'This only puts things forward a little.'

'Things? Oh, yes. Things.'

She searched vainly for something else to say. Nothing came to mind. It didn't matter because her breath had stopped, as well. All of a sudden Deverell seemed bigger and more overwhelming than ever. The easy way he carried her up the stairs was daunting enough; she could also feel every powerful shift and surge of muscle against her softer form.

The rhythmic movements began to render her unaccountably weak inside, but at the same time she was gripped by a wholly unexpected feeling of apprehension. Deciding to become a man's mistress was one thing. The actual physical act was something she hadn't exactly thought about until this very moment.

Now it seemed to be all she could think about, as she was carried into a bedchamber at the top of the stairs and set down before a small fire. A branch of candles, their flames reflected in the brandy bottle beside them on the mantelpiece, was the only other source of light in the room. A large, comfortable-looking four-poster seemed to take up most of the space.

Phoebe glanced at it and started to shiver inside.

Deverell strode back to the door, closed and bolted it, then turned to face her across the bedchamber. 'Ah, I see the landlord had the happy idea of bringing the brandy up here,' he observed, glancing past her. He came forward and picked up the bottle. Glasses clinked.

Struggling for the same casual aplomb, Phoebe burst into speech. 'I can't tell you how pleased I am that you're finally reconciled with Lady Grismead, my lord, and. . . Oh!' She took the glass of brandy he handed her. 'Thank you, sir.'

'I've recently discovered that life holds a lot more promise if you're not continually looking back,' he murmured. He replaced the bottle and turned so that she stood side-on to him, her shoulder brushing his chest. She knew he was watching her. He lifted a hand to briefly touch a curl that had come loose from its tight knot. 'You taught me that, Phoebe.'

For some strange reason the low, husky note in his voice made her shiver even more. 'Oh?'

'Yes.' He reached down, gently prised her tense fingers open and removed her bonnet from her grasp. 'You won't need this, little one.'

She watched as the bonnet went sailing onto a nearby chair.

'And I think you'll be more comfortable without your pelisse,' he went on, still in that low, almost soothing tone. He began undoing buttons with one hand.

Phoebe held her breath, torn between an impulse to stop him and a trembling awareness of his fingers moving downward between her breasts. She didn't *dare* breathe. The thought of him touching her there again made her legs shake. She began to wonder if she could stay upright.

The last button slipped free. Deverell pushed the folds of material aside and pressed his hand, just for an instant, to the softness of her stomach. Even through her gown and petticoat, the heat of his touch burned her. There was something primitive about the gesture; something intensely possessive.

Phoebe's hand shook. Brandy sloshed dangerously close to the edge of the glass. She brought her other hand up to steady it, suddenly realising that he'd been talking softly the whole time he'd been unfastening buttons and she hadn't heard a word.

'I. . .I beg your pardon, my lord?'

His smile sent more shivers chasing one another down her spine. 'I said, when I first returned to London I thought it would be amusing to sit back and watch my family tumble into the pit of financial ruin yawning at their feet. I didn't even have to lift a finger to bring it about. They were doing such a good job of it, themselves.'

'But you ch—'

Her throat seized when he shrugged out of his coat. He flung it across the chair and loosened his cravat. The strip of snowy muslin went the way of the coat. Phoebe followed its progress, then looked back in time to see him hook a finger in the neck of his shirt and yank it open.

A touch of indignation seeped into the maelstrom of emotions whirling about her head. If he wanted to converse, that was perfectly all right with her. In fact, it might help her regain her balance. But how were mistresses supposed to carry on an intelligent conversation while clothes were casually being removed right and left?

'You changed your mind?' she managed to say, racking her brain to recall the thread of the discussion.

'No,' he murmured. 'You changed my mind.'

'I. . .I might have given you a new slant on the situation, sir.'

'Let's just say, then, that your view of the situation put a new slant on it for me.' He began pulling his shirt out of his breeches.

Phoebe decided that if she wasn't to faint right then and there, drastic measures would have to be taken. She glanced down at the brandy in her hand, raised the glass to her lips and took an indecently large sip.

Heat spread through her veins almost instantly. She stopped shivering. At least outwardly. Her shivers were replaced by tiny internal flutters that were surprisingly

pleasurable. She eyed the brandy with approval and took
a larger mouthful.

The glass was gently removed from her hand and
replaced on the mantel.

'Sweetheart.' Deverell tipped her chin up on the edge
of his hand. She was piercingly aware of the heat radiat-
ing from him; of the fact that his shirt hung open,
revealing the powerful planes of his chest and the rigid
muscles of his stomach.

'I want you more than my next breath,' he said softly,
'but not if it makes you so nervous you have to toss
brandy down your throat. Nothing has to happen here
and now. Would you rather I spent the night downstairs?'

'Downstairs?'

His smile was crooked. 'If I climb into that bed with
you, little one, I don't think I can trust myself not to
make you mine every way there is before morning.'

For a moment the words stunned her. Then, just as
abruptly, Phoebe was flooded with their meaning. He
wanted her. His desire was tightly leashed, but it was
there, straining against the barriers of his formidable
control, apparent only in the narrowed intensity of his
eyes and the taut, waiting stillness of his body.

Despite his gentle tone, despite the wry amusement
in his smile, he really *did* want her that badly.

And suddenly she thought of the way everyone was
always wanting something from *him*. Protection, money,
rescue. It didn't matter what. She thought of the way
his family had ignored him for years. She thought of the
statue of a child with its arms outstretched.

And she thought of the way she loved him, with all
her heart and mind and soul.

What good was that love if uncertainty made her hesitate to give freely the one thing he wanted from her?
What good was it if she hesitated to take whatever he
was offering of himself? Love, she discovered in that
moment, transcended everything. Her upbringing, her
own innate caution, a woman's vulnerability—all were

powerless against the overwhelming need to give.

She smiled up at him, filled with the same sense of rightness she'd felt that afternoon, and lifted her hand to touch his wrist with gentle, questing fingers. 'Sebastian. Please stay with me.'

His hard warrior's face lit with a smile that almost took her breath away. For a fleeting second she saw the boy he'd been. Passionate, reckless, wild, but with a rock-solid sense of honour that had been forged in fire, making him the man he was today. The only man she would ever love.

'Phoebe,' he whispered, and bent to brush a gentle kiss across her lips. 'Don't be afraid. We're going to be perfect together.'

She lifted her mouth, wanting more, and with a half-stifled groan he thrust his fingers into her hair and kissed her with a fierce ardour that sent arrows of pleasure darting down her thighs. She felt her hair tumble down as pins went flying, and a delicious sense of freedom raced through her.

'I've been wanting to do that forever,' he muttered, breaking the kiss to run his fingers through the honey-brown tresses. His hands were shaking, she realised in bemusement. 'It's like silk. The finest, softest silk.'

With another muffled exclamation, he untangled his hands from her hair and started undoing the ribbon beneath her bodice. Phoebe scarcely noticed. She was no longer worrying about clothes being removed. She gazed with fascination at his bare chest, its covering of thick, dark hair drawing her fingers like moths to a flame.

He shuddered heavily as she flattened her hands on him. 'Yes, sweetheart. Touch me. I've been wanting you to touch me for weeks.'

Her eyes widened and he smiled in rueful acknowledgement of her effect on him. 'Didn't you know?' he asked. 'I've wanted you since that first day. That first second.'

'Even when I was wearing those old clothes?' she asked, smiling with a hint of mischief.

'All I have to do, little one, is look into your eyes and I want you.'

'Ohh.'

His mouth curved, she thought with tenderness, but his eyes were glittering, intense. He bent to kiss her again, long and hard and deep. Until her arms went up around his neck and she was pressing so close she could feel the quiver of muscles under relentless control. A heady sense of feminine power went through her. He made her tremble with longing; she'd never dreamed she could have the same effect on him.

Then, with a muttered imprecation, he drew back, whipped his shirt off and turned her around to unfasten the tiny buttons that ran down the back of her gown. She heard fabric tear.

'Bloody hell, do there have to be so many of the damn things?'

Phoebe giggled. Her laughter faded, however, when Deverell turned her again and pushed her gown down to her waist. It obligingly fell the rest of the way to the floor. But it wasn't the fact that she was standing there wearing only her petticoat and chemise that caused amusement to change to awed wonder.

He was the most beautiful male she'd ever seen. Tall and perfectly proportioned, his shoulders and arms hard with muscle, his chest deep and wide, and covered with the dark pelt of hair that made her fingers itch to explore the fascinating new territory spread before her.

'You're beautiful,' she whispered, utterly enthralled.

He shook his head, slowly, as though barely hearing her. The heat of his gaze almost seared her skin. With one finger he traced the ribboned edge of her chemise before slowly freeing the laces.

Phoebe trembled as he lowered the straps. In another second she would be as bare to the waist as Deverell. She felt herself blushing and squeezed her eyes shut.

The thought was shocking. It was positively scandalous. But the thrilling excitement pouring through her veins prevented even the smallest protest.

Cool air brushed over her, she heard him say something, his voice so hoarse she couldn't make sense of the words, then she cried out in stunned pleasure as his big, powerful hands closed around her soft flesh, cupping her, shaping her, stroking her. The sensation was indescribable, sending tingling streamers of heat from her breasts to a place deep inside her that throbbed with a longing she'd never felt before.

'Sebastian. . .' Her legs quivered with the effort to stay upright. 'I can't. . .stand. . .'

She was swept off her feet before the next word was out. Phoebe's eyes flew open as Deverell carried her to the bed and lowered her gently to the mattress. He stood looking down at her, his aquamarine eyes brilliant, glittering, reflecting the moonlight filtering through the window beside the bed.

When he bent to remove her petticoat, leaving her in her stockings and bunched-up chemise, Phoebe wondered how it was possible to feel utterly abandoned and wicked, and blush all over at the same time. Despite the excitement and longing pouring through her, she flexed her knee in an instinctive attempt to shield herself from that intense gaze.

'It's all right, sweetheart. My lovely Phoebe.' His voice was shaking almost as badly as his hands, Sebastian realised. God! If he didn't stop looking at her, he'd fall on her like a ravaging warlord intent on taking the spoils of battle.

But she wasn't the spoils of battle. This was his innocent, trusting Phoebe. He'd barely reassured her about their future, hadn't said a word about anything other than wanting her—a totally inadequate description for the grinding, wrenching need tearing at his gut—and still, she lay there, gazing up at him with a fascinated wonder that threatened to rip his precarious control to shreds.

He wrenched his gaze away from the sight of her lying there waiting for him, and sat down on the edge of the bed to yank off his boots. It was no use worrying about the things he hadn't said. He could hardly speak, let alone string the right words together. He felt as if he was going to explode if he didn't sink into her warmth and softness. He could give her all the right words and reassurances later.

He hauled off his second boot and tossed it after the first, then froze when Phoebe reached out a hand and touched his arm.

When she ran questing fingers up to his shoulder and flexed them to test the strength there, Sebastian knew he was going to go mad. The knowledge didn't prevent him from shifting to face her so she had access to his chest. He watched her lips part in a delighted smile as she touched him, saw the innocent feminine appreciation in her beautiful eyes and nearly groaned aloud as the ache in his body intensified to the edge of agony.

'You're so hard,' she said wonderingly.

He drew in his breath sharply as one little finger stroked across a male nipple.

'I'm aware of that fact,' he muttered through clenched teeth. 'Painfully aware of it.'

'Sebastian?'

'Don't worry about it.' Surging to his feet, he wrenched open his breeches. 'If you don't wish to receive the shock of your life, my innocent little governess, I suggest you shut your eyes.'

Phoebe smiled happily up at him. 'I'm not completely ignorant, Sebastian. I have seen statues of males, you know, and—' Her eyes blinked wide. 'Oh, my goodness!'

His ragged laugh sounded as if it had been torn from him. He lowered himself to the bed beside her and gathered her into his arms. She came willingly, but he could feel her trembling.

He brushed his knuckles gently over her cheek. 'There have been several times when I've wanted to silence you, Phoebe, but not, believe me, by terrifying you.'

'I am not terrified,' she informed him, blushing so rosily he could feel the heat beneath his fingers. 'It's just that. . .well. . .you're very large, aren't you? All over, I mean.'

Despite the need clawing at him, Sebastian couldn't help himself. He grinned. 'You're worried about the discrepancy in our sizes?'

Phoebe blushed again. 'Well, it is rather pronounced.'

'Phoebe, sweetheart. . .' He bent to kiss her. 'My innocent darling, do you really think I'd do anything to hurt you?'

'Of course not, Sebastian, but—'

'You've given me so much of your trust. Can't you trust me in this, too?'

She sounded indignant. 'It isn't that I don't trust you, Sebastian. But. . .well. . .one can hardly ignore the evidence of one's eyes.'

'Oh, God.' He rested his forehead against hers, unable to decide whether to laugh or swear. What other woman would stop proceedings at this point and expect an explanation that was utterly beyond him? 'Just trust me, darling. *Please.*'

He felt her hesitate, then she relaxed and curled against him, snuggling closer. Sebastian groaned softly and bent to kiss her throat, at the same time pushing her chemise lower. 'Lift up, sweetheart. Let me get this off you.'

The softly growled command sent a tremor of mingled excitement and apprehension through her. Phoebe obeyed, then went very still as he stripped her chemise and stockings off and let his gaze travel over her naked body.

His chest expanded on a ragged indrawn breath. He touched one finger, just the tip of one finger, to her throat. As if he didn't quite trust himself with a firmer caress, she thought wonderingly. Then he laid the flat of his hand against the pulse beating wildly in its small hollow and she trembled in uncontrollable response.

Such big, powerful hands. Such gentleness. The contrast made her melt and then shiver with excitement. When he moved his hand to trace the small bones below her throat, her flesh pulsed with heat where his touch had been.

He bent his head to retrace the same path with his mouth. Phoebe gasped as his kisses went lower. Her breasts felt flushed and heavy, the tips aching. Then he closed his mouth over one rosy crest and she cried out sharply at the sudden, piercing pleasure.

'Yes,' he growled against her throbbing flesh, and she shuddered at the raw sound of his voice.

'Sebastian. . .' Her own voice was barely audible. 'I feel so. . .'

'Yes,' he said again. 'Tell me, sweetheart.'

Tell him? she thought dimly. *Tell him?* She could hardly speak. She felt his hand stroke down her body until his fingers tangled in the soft triangle between her legs and all the muscles in her lower body seemed to dissolve.

'*Sebastian!* Ohh, I thought. . .I felt unbridled passion when you kissed me, but this. . .is beyond anything.'

'Not yet,' he grated. 'But it soon will be.'

Her eyes flew open at the stark promise in his voice, then widened even further at the savage look of arousal on his face as he watched his hand caress her so intimately. His touch was still achingly tender, but the expression in his eyes held all the fierceness of a warrior; the muscles beneath her hands were coiled springs waiting to unleash the full force of his passion.

He was holding himself in check by the merest thread, she realised. Every tendon was rigid with self-imposed restraint. And, in that fleeting moment of awareness, she knew his restraint was costing him.

The last remnants of nervousness vanished. All that power. All that power, leashed, held in check. For her. She shivered in helpless response to the thrill of anticipation coursing through her.

'I want you,' she whispered, stunned by the truth of her words. Not even her own boldness shocked her. The sensations he was arousing with the gentle, insistent touch of his hands and mouth swept her beyond anything but the strange throbbing emptiness only he could satisfy. 'Oh, Sebastian, I love you.'

'*Phoebe*. Oh, God, sweetheart, I can't wait any longer for you. I have to have you. I won't hurt you, darling, I swear. I'll be so careful. . .'

Not even aware of what he was saying, knowing only that he couldn't bear to frighten her, Sebastian pressed her legs further apart and lowered himself over her.

She made a soft whimpering sound of pleasure and longing when his weight came down on her that threatened to send him straight over the edge. He paused, teeth clenched, feeling sweat break out across his back as he fought for control.

She lifted her hips beneath him in an instinctive seeking movement that was so utterly female, so unbearably arousing a harsh groan tore from his throat.

'Phoebe, don't! Be still, little one. Let me. . .' He raised himself on his forearms to look down at her and felt as if the breath had been kicked out of him.

Her lashes fluttered upward. She gazed up at him, her lovely eyes cloudy with desire, her lips soft from his kisses, her hair a silken fan against the pillow. He remembered that he'd wanted to know how she would look in his arms. Now he did know. Small and soft and heart-wrenchingly vulnerable.

Dear God, how did the sight of such fragile delicacy arouse him to almost crazed desire? The violence of his own need shook him to his soul. And yet something—was it the utter trust in her eyes?—managed to leash the wild hunger straining to break free so he could enter her slowly, lead her gently into an intimacy that had to be new and frightening in its very intensity.

'It's all right,' he whispered when she made a small frantic sound and clung to him. He gazed deeply into her eyes, willing her to relax, to accept the intrusion of his body. 'I won't hurt you, love. Just be still.'

'Sebastian? I don't think. . .'

'Shh. Relax, darling. Yes, that's it. *That's it*. Oh, God, *Phoebe*—'

Phoebe gasped as he thrust forward, possessing her completely. Her nails bit into his shoulders. He hadn't hurt her, but the thrilling anticipation and excitement was abruptly swamped by the shock of his invasion. She vaguely realised that Sebastian had gone rigidly still, holding her in a grip of iron while her body struggled to adjust to his. His heart pounded against her breast with a violence that would have terrified her if she hadn't been so caught up in the incredible sensations of joining with him.

'Are you all right?' he asked, sounding as if his teeth were ground together.

Phoebe managed a small nod and relaxed her grip on his shoulders. In truth, she was beginning to feel more than all right. The feeling of being invaded was passing and a delicate quivering sensation was taking its place. She tried a tentative movement and almost fainted as a piercingly sweet ripple of pleasure coursed through her.

His arms tightened so convulsively she squeaked. Then he lowered his head, buried his face in her hair, and began to move with a restrained power that brought all the thrilling excitement rushing back.

Phoebe clung with all her strength, eager now to follow wherever he led. Her entire world narrowed to this moment; this man who held her with such fierce tenderness; this act of total surrender of all that she was. The intimacy was shattering, tearing apart any preconceptions she might have had and overwhelming her with the reality of feeling him all around her, inside her, enveloping, sheltering, possessing.

Sweet, hot tendrils of pleasure began coiling inside her, tighter and tighter, until the tension was almost unbearable, until she cried out in intolerable need. And, as if her cry snapped some invisible leash, Deverell's control exploded in a passionate assault that sent her hurtling into ecstasy. If she hadn't been held so fast in his arms, she would have flown into a thousand pieces.

Amazement, helpless delight, love so intense she could hardly bear it, streaked through her in the instant before she was swept into a torrent of exquisite sensation, pleasure throbbing through her with every pulsing beat of her heart, filling every part of her, taking her to the edge of consciousness. Dimly, she heard the harsh sound that erupted from his throat. He held her as if he would never let her go, shuddering against her, whispering her name over and over in a litany of passion, until he sank heavily onto her, crushing her into the bedding.

Phoebe came back to herself very slowly. She felt as if she was sinking into a soft, endless sea. All her bones seemed to have melted. An incredible feeling of lassitude flowed over her. Vaguely she was aware of questions floating somewhere in the back of her mind, but it was too much trouble to think about them. Too much trouble to speak. The moment was too precious.

Lying with Deverell like this, still holding him within her body, feeling his weight over her, sheltering and warm, was almost sweeter than what had gone before. She had never known such a complete and utter sense of belonging. Whatever happened in the future, whatever life held for them, she would always be a part of him. As he would be part of her. Forever.

'Sebastian,' she murmured, and let the sweet lassitude take her into sleep.

His name roused Sebastian from the torpor of satiation. He withdrew as gently as possible, knowing she had to be tender, and gazed down at her.

She was already deep in slumber, her lashes delicate silken fans against her cheeks, her lips still rosy from his kisses and softly parted.

A wave of protective tenderness swept over him, making his body clench and shudder violently in reaction. The intensity of emotion stunned him. Phoebe had taken the pain and emptiness from his heart and filled it with something he'd never known before.

Tenderness.

Until she'd burst into his life, he hadn't known he was capable of so much feeling.

He thought about waking her and telling her how much she meant to him, but she looked so fragile. She was probably exhausted. And he was, after all, the one who had exhausted her. He could wait until morning.

Gathering Phoebe close to his side, he pulled the covers over them and lay back against the pillows. She felt sweet and warm in his arms. Sebastian smiled as another thought occurred to him.

Tonight he had turned his delightfully disapproving Miss Smith into a creature of fire and passion. She had responded to him with an innocent sensuality that had set his senses reeling.

But more importantly—she had given him her heart.

Making a silent vow to cherish her gift for the rest of his life, he fell asleep, feeling at peace for the first time in years.

An early morning mist still hovered in the air when Phoebe settled herself on the seat of Gerald's phaeton and watched Deverell climb up next to her. Around them the trees hovered, insubstantial shapes in the seamless grey of mist and sky. The Black Mole crouched, an unlikely harbour in the stillness.

'It's certainly a relief to be on our way,' she remarked chattily as he gave the horses the office to start.

She winced at the inanity of the remark, but decided that if Deverell required anything more in the way of

witty conversation at this hour he shouldn't have woken
her before dawn in a fashion guaranteed to addle her
wits for the rest of the day.

And then, she remembered, having reduced her to a
deliciously limp state, he'd dressed, bounded downstairs,
whistling, and appropriated the entire inn.

Phoebe had been inclining towards a hazy sort of
indignation until the landlord's wife had appeared with
breakfast, the makings for a hot bath, and the news that
her spouse had fetched the wheelwright and repairs were
underway.

They had both been fully occupied ever since.

'Oh, I don't know,' he said now, sending her a wicked,
sidelong glance. 'I'm going to have some rather fond
memories of the place, myself.'

Phoebe tried to look severe and failed dismally. The
task was impossible when she was blushing. And she
seemed to have run out of chatty responses. In fact, now
that she and Deverell were alone, she found it difficult
to think about anything except her uncertainty about the
immediate future.

The trouble was, she reflected, she didn't have any
experience at being a mistress. She'd been touched by
Deverell's thoughtfulness in ensuring her privacy this
morning, but that was at an isolated inn. What was going
to happen when they returned to town?

She cast a quick glance at his profile and decided that
since she didn't know the rules of mistressly behaviour,
he would have to explain them to her.

'My lord?'

He grinned. 'Yes, Miss Smith?'

Despite herself, Phoebe giggled. 'Oh, dear, I suppose
that did sound absurdly formal after. . .after. . .'

'After you spent the night lying naked in my arms?'

'*Sebastian!*' She felt herself turning an even brighter
shade of pink. 'I did not. . . Well, I *did*, but. . .'

He laughed and covered her hands briefly with one
of his. 'I'm sorry, darling, but when I'm confronted by

the prim and proper Miss Smith, I can't resist teasing her. What is it you wished to ask me?'

She took a deep breath. 'Well, I was wondering what we are to do now. I mean, you might wish to spend another night. . .um. . .that is to say. . .'

'You're perfectly correct, my love. I will wish to spend another night making love to you. Every night, in fact.'

'Ohh.' She was momentarily distracted as a tingling echo of pleasure rippled through her. When his mouth curved, she hurried into speech again.

'Yes, well, that is precisely what I mean. But you can't very well visit me at Park Street. What would Theo and Cressy think? Especially if you were to stroll around without your shirt on as you were doing this morning. Not that I wish to live in another big house,' she added hastily, in case he might think she had mercenary tendencies. 'No doubt you are thinking of a little cottage somewhere. I'm sure it will be quite delightful.'

There was a rather ominous silence from the figure beside her. Too anxious to notice anything amiss, Phoebe broached her greatest concern. 'And perhaps—only if the occasion were to arise, of course—you might give me a. . .a suitable recommendation?'

Deverell hauled on the reins so abruptly, Phoebe almost found herself hurtling from her seat. She looked down, fully expecting to see sparks fly as the horses skidded to a jarring halt. Wood shrieked hideously against wood as he yanked on the brake.

'*What?*' he roared.

The pair in the traces promptly took exception to his tone.

'God damn it to bloody hell!'

The next few minutes were spent in a lively tussle with Gerald's horses.

When Deverell finally got them calmed down, secured the reins and turned an enraged countenance on her, Phoebe was put forcibly in mind of black thunderclouds hurling bolts of aquamarine lightning. It finally dawned on her that she was in a great deal of trouble. The only good thing about the situation was that they were still sitting in the carriage. At least he had to keep his voice down.

'A recommendation?' he repeated with deadly inflexion. 'As *what*?'

'A. . .a governess, of course,' she ventured. 'I mean. . .I couldn't very well ask for a recommendation as a mistress, because I'm not terribly experienced at it yet, and besides, Sebastian, even if you tired of me, I would never want to belong to another man anyway, so a recommendation wouldn't be. . .'

He made a strangled sound of frustration and clutched at his head.

Phoebe eyed him anxiously. 'Oh, dear. Are you all right, sir?'

'No, I am not all right, Miss Smith. I am rapidly going mad. And you are the cause of it.' He straightened, took hold of her shoulders and gave her a none-too-gentle shake.

'Phoebe, you little idiot. After last night, what insanity makes you think there'd ever come a time when I wouldn't want you? Not only as a mistress, damn it, but as a *wife*!'

Her jaw dropped. 'A wife?'

Her reaction seemed to enrage him all over again. 'What the devil did you think I meant yesterday when I said what I did in front of the twins?'

'Well—' Her brain reeled dizzily. 'I did think. . .*then*. But after last night, you must know how ineligible I am, and. . .' She looked up earnestly into his furious countenance. 'Indeed, Sebastian, you said it yourself. Someone associated with scandal is not suitable as a wife.'

'I didn't mean you, damn it!' He closed his eyes, then opened them again to fix her with a glare that made her feel as if she'd been transfixed by one of the lightning bolts.

'Phoebe, I will put up with my aunt's managing ways and my wards' peccadilloes. I will tolerate Pamela and that dim-witted poet. I will even refrain from strangling Filby. But I will not accept idiocy from you! Is that clear?'

'But. . .' She faltered, eyes wide with anxiety and tremulous hope. 'Sebastian, are you sure you're not just doing the honourable thing because we were placed in a compromising position last night and everyone will—?'

'I don't give a damn for Society's opinion,' he interrupted roughly. 'You know that.'

'Yes, but you care about your family's opinion.' She gave him a gentle smile. 'And, although I doubt Lady Grismead would wish to welcome a daughter of Charlotte Everton-Smythe into the family—especially as I have absolutely no expectations—she'd still expect you to do the correct thing.'

'Sooner or later, Phoebe, you'll learn that the day I do what my aunt considers proper will be the day they discover the earth is flat, after all. Why the hell do you think I made love to you after discovering we were stranded? Because I knew if I asked you to marry me last night, you'd start babbling about obligations and compromising positions, even if I'd convinced you that I couldn't care a snap for a scandal that had nothing to do with you.'

There was a short silence while she digested this speech. Then Deverell smiled dangerously and leaned closer. 'As it is, my love, thanks to my forethought, you do not have a choice. Fortunately for me, you do care about Society's opinion, therefore you have to marry me.'

Phoebe eyed the pleased triumph on his face with a disapproving frown. 'Are you threatening me with possible consequences again, my lord?'

'Yes.'

She took a deep breath and grasped her courage with both hands. 'Why?'

'Why?' He scowled at her. '*Why?* Because I love you, God damn it. Why the hell else would I want to marry you?'

As a declaration, this thundered avowal of devotion left much to be desired. Its effect, however, was potent. Phoebe flung herself into his arms, so deliriously happy she couldn't speak. She rained fervent little kisses over his face instead.

Deverell's response was instant. His entire body went hard. He pulled her into a crushing embrace, but instead of kissing her as she'd expected, he wrenched off her bonnet and buried his face in her hair, holding her so closely she could feel every heartbeat, every breath. Her own breath caught in wonder when she realised he was shaking.

'Phoebe, I love you,' he said hoarsely. 'I love you so much. You must believe me. Until you stormed into my life, believing in me, trusting me despite all you'd been told, I didn't know what need was. I didn't know trust like that was possible. Now I'd fight the entire world to keep you.'

'Oh, Sebastian.' She clung closer, instinctively giving, instinctively reassuring. 'You'll always have my trust. Just as you'll always have my love.'

'Sweetheart!'

He drew back for a moment, gazing down into her face as though making very sure. And then his mouth came down on hers with an urgency that made her senses swim. But even as she trembled and melted against him, he gentled, kissing her so deeply, so slowly, with such intensely possessive ardour, she felt as if he was filling her with all the love in his heart, as if, with just that kiss, they would be joined for all time.

The moment was so sweet, so tender, Phoebe felt tears of happiness fill her eyes.

She blinked them away as Deverell drew back to smile

down at her. 'God, you give yourself so completely. If you knew some of things—darling, you're so innocent sometimes, you scare me.'

She shook her head. 'If I was that innocent,' she said, gently reproving, 'I would have believed Crowhurst last night.'

Without warning, the hard edge of power returned to his face. 'That's when I knew I'd do anything to keep you, Phoebe. Your trust awed me. Humbled me. What Crowhurst said was pretty damning, if you didn't know the truth. Especially as *he* believed what he was saying. And I know it shook you to hear about your mother like that.'

'The only thing I feared was that you'd once loved her,' she whispered. 'But I knew if you had, you would never have abandoned her.'

'You're the only woman I've ever loved,' he said, gazing deeply into her eyes. The truth reverberated in his words, irrevocable, unchangeable. 'You're the only woman I ever will love.'

Phoebe's face lit with a smile that was radiant with love and so much happiness she could have soared into the cloudy sky and flown on the wind. 'In that case, sir, I can face any amount of Aunt Grismeads and doubtful Deverells. Let us be off.'

Sebastian laughed out loud, catching her mood. He released her and bent to untie the reins. 'My love, you're forgetting two things. One, my wards were obviously aware of my intentions and last night decided to hasten the inevitable conclusion in their own ruthless fashion. And two, my aunt is a Deverell. Not only that, at present she's a grateful Deverell. What does that tell you?'

'That you think you'll be able to do precisely as you like while her gratitude lasts,' she answered, exchanging her smile for a severe frown.

The frown didn't seem to have much effect. He grinned down at her, his eyes glittering with an expression that reminded her vividly of the passion of the night. 'Precisely. We'll get married today. You see, I also had the forethought to procure a special licence.'

'*Today?* But—'

He leaned over and silenced her with a kiss as they started off.

Several minutes later, Phoebe emerged from the embrace, flushed and flustered. 'My lord! Kindly keep your attention on the road when you're driving. I do not wish to end up in the ditch.'

'Ah. I wondered where she'd gone. Now you see why we mustn't delay our nuptials a moment longer than necessary, my love. I need my delectably disapproving Miss Smith to keep me in line.'

Phoebe pondered that for a moment, then pursed her lips. 'Clearly a difficult task lies ahead of me,' she concluded. She nodded, her prim expression belied by the laughter dancing in her eyes. 'However, you will be happy to know, my lord, that I have considerable experience in dealing with Deverells.'

'And last night you added to your talents in that direction,' he murmured.

'*Sir!*'

'I beg your pardon, Miss Smith. What I *meant* to say is that you're perfectly placed for the task.'

When she sent him a mischievous sidelong look, his mouth curved in a smile of heart-wrenching tenderness. 'Right where you are now,' he said softly. 'In my heart.'

The sun broke through the mists as they turned onto the main road to London, lighting their world with golden promise.

RAKE'S REFORM

by

Marie-Louise Hall

Dear Reader

I've always loved the Regency period for its contrast between severe, cool elegance and riotous living. A glimpse of a tall, white town house, a painting of a sleek thoroughbred horse, a cavalry sabre in a museum are enough for me to start speculating upon the lives of the characters who might have owned them.

The inspiration for my hero and heroine in Rake's Reform came when a friend asked me what any sensible woman could possibly find attractive in an elitist, chauvinistic, unprincipled Regency rake. Wit, exquisite taste, total self-confidence, physical toughness, courage and a good dash of danger and passion, was my short answer. This book is the fuller version.

After all, let's be honest here, if you had been at the Duchess of Richmond's famous ball upon the very eve of Waterloo, and there seemed every likelihood that Brussels and all Europe would fall to Napoleon's army upon the morrow, who would you have chosen to dance with in what might well have been your very last waltz? Some good, reliable, stolid old Captain Dobbin type, who would never compromise your honour, or a wickedly handsome rake who made you laugh and would sweep you off your feet before making some very improper suggestions? I'd wager the latter, because even if sensible women don't care to admit it too loudly, bad boys are simply more fun, which is why the Regency rake will never be out of fashion.

I hope you enjoy the book as much as I did writing it.

Marie-Louise Hall

Chapter One

The courtroom was small, crowded, but utterly silent as the judge, resplendent in his crimson, put on his black cap and began to intone the words of the death sentence. Above in the gallery, a young woman sat as still and as rigid as the ashen-faced boy who stood in the dock, his hands clenched upon the wooden rail.

Miss Jane Hilton stared disbelievingly at the judge, her hazel eyes ablaze with anger beneath the wide brim of her black straw hat. This was nothing short of barbarism. This could not be happening! Not in England! Not in the supposedly civilised, well-mannered England of King William IV in this year of 1830. And she was not going to let it happen.

She was on her feet before she had stopped to think.

'How can you?' Her question rang out in the hushed room. 'What crime has this child committed? Any farmer or labourer in this room could tell you that a rick of poorly cured hay may heat to the point where it catches fire without any assistance.'

There was a murmur of agreement from the more poorly

dressed onlookers as every head in the lower part of the courtroom turned and looked upwards, including that of her guardian, Mr Filmore, who regarded her first with astonishment and then with tight-lipped fury as he gestured to her furiously to sit down and be silent. The judge's hooded eyelids lifted as he, too, stared at her with bloodshot blue eyes.

'Silence in the court, madam, or I shall have you removed from the building,' he roared.

'I shall not be silent!' Janey retorted. 'I know Jem Avery is not guilty of arson. On the morning and at the same time as he is supposed to have set the rick alight, I passed him upon the road some five miles from the Pettridges Home Farm yard.'

'Indeed?' The judge's bushy white brows lifted. 'I trust you acquainted the defence counsel with this—' he paused '—alleged meeting.'

'Of course I did, but—' Janey began.

'M'lud?' The defence counsel stepped forward and said something in an undertone to the judge. American, unstable and prone to female fancies were the only words which Janey caught, but it was enough, combined with the smug smile of her guardian, to tell her why she had not been called as a witness.

'It seems your evidence was deemed unreliable,' the judge said, lifting his head again to look down his long nose at Janey. 'So I must ask you a second time to be silent.'

'I will not!' Janey repeated furiously. 'I have seen better justice administered by a lynch mob in St Louis than I have here today.'

'Then perhaps you had better go back there,' the judge

sneered, earning sycophantic smiles from both defence and prosecution counsels, who were already surreptitiously shuffling their papers together. 'Gentlemen,' he said laconically to two of the ushers who stood at the back of the gallery, 'remove that woman from the courtroom.'

'I suppose I should not have lost my temper.' Janey sighed heavily a few minutes later as she stood next to her maid upon the steps of the courthouse, attempting to push strands of her flyaway fair hair back into the rather workmanlike chignon in which it was usually confined. 'But that judge is a pompous, port-sodden old fool!'

'Yes, miss,' Kate agreed as she handed her the wide-brimmed hat which had become dislodged from Janey's head during her somewhat undignified exit from the courtroom between the two ushers.

'It makes me so angry, Kate,' Janey went on as she rammed the hat down on her head. 'Jem Avery has never hurt a soul in his life. The worse he has ever done is poach a rabbit or two to prevent his family from starving. I know he did not fire that rick, though Mr Filmore gave him reason enough in the way he treated him! It is monstrous to even suggest he should hang.'

'I know, miss,' Kate said sympathetically. 'And there was not a Christian person in that room who did not agree with you.'

'Then why didn't they all get up and say so!' Janey said, her American drawl more pronounced as it always was when she was angry. 'Why don't they demand a retrial?'

'Because that's just not how it's done here, miss. People don't dare make a fuss, for fear they'll lose their places or trade if they're in business. You have to know someone,

one of them. . .if Jem were a Duke's son, then it would
be different.'

'I know,' Janey said gratingly as she retied the grey
silk ribbons on her hat beneath her pointed chin. She was
almost as angry with herself as she was with the judge.
After four years in England, she should have known better
than to expect an instant public protest. Kate was right.
That wasn't how things were done here in this genteel
and ancient English cathedral city, where the law was
enforced to the letter and property valued above lives.

She glanced upwards at the serene, awesome spire of
the nearby cathedral, which seemed almost to reach the
grey November clouds, and sighed. Even the buildings in
this corner of England seemed to have that air of superior
certainty which she had encountered in so many of her
English acquaintances.

God in his Heaven and everything and everyone in their
proper place, including Miss Jane Hilton, colonial nobody,
she thought, feeling a sudden overwhelming homesick-
ness for the handful of ramshackle timber dwellings strung
out along a muddy track, half a world away. That had
been the nearest to a town she had known, until her
parents' death had forced her to return to St Louis, where
her grandfather had found her.

The log cabins in which she had spent her childhood
had had no attractions with which to rival either the medieval splendour of the cathedral or the exuberant prosperity
of the timbered Tudor merchant's houses that clustered
about its close. And the people who had lived in them
had often been rough and illiterate. But they would not
have condemned a boy like Jem for the loss of a hayrick,
which had in all probability set alight by itself.

No, she thought, Lilian, her parents, the Schmidts, the Lafayettes and the rest would all have been on their feet with her in that courtroom—and one way or another the judge would have been made to see reason.

She shut her eyes, seeing them all for a moment as if they were stood beside her. Her mother, fair, calm and beautiful, even with her apron besmirched with smuts and her sleeves rolled up. Her father, weathered and strong as the trees he had felled with his own hands to make the clearing that they had farmed. Proper Mrs Schmidt, looking askance at red-haired Lilian, who was as tough as the trappers she allowed to share both her cabin and her body. And Daniel, quiet, brown-eyed, brown-haired Daniel Lafayette, who had moved through the forest as silently as their Indian neighbours.

Daniel, who had been her childhood sweetheart and the first to die of the smallpox that had swept through the small frontier community. And with all the innocence and intensity of a fifteen-year-old, she had thought nothing worse could ever happen to her. And then her parents had become ill, and she knew that it could.

She shivered, remembering the sound of the earth being shovelled on to their rough wooden coffins by Lilian who, since she had had the smallpox as a child and survived it, had taken on the responsibility of nursing the sick and burying the dead.

'Miss?'

She started, wrenched back into the present by Kate's voice.

'They'll commute it, surely—give him transportation, won't they?' Kate said hopefully.

'I don't know,' Janey said flatly, swallowing the lump

which had arisen in her throat. Hankering for the past and feeling sorry for herself was not going to help Jem. This was not Minnesota, this was England. Green, pleasant, and pitiless to its poor. And if she was going to save Jem's neck, she had to think clearly and fast.

'They wouldn't hang him, they couldn't,' Kate added with a distinct lack of conviction. 'He's just a child, really.'

'I know,' Janey replied grimly. 'But everyone is in such a panic of late because of the labourers' riots in Kent and Hampshire that they are seeing the threat of revolution everywhere. If you had heard Mr Filmore and his fellow magistrates at dinner last night, you would have thought them in danger of being carted off to the guillotine at dawn. They see harshness as their protection.'

'But it's not right!' Kate's blue eyes brimmed with unshed tears. 'If Mr Filmore had not dismissed him, this would never have happened. I don't know how we're going to break this to Mrs Avery, miss.'

'Nor do I, but I promised I should call and tell her of the verdict as soon as it was known,' Janey said grimly. 'Where's the gig, Kate?'

'That way, around the corner—I paid Tom Mitchell's boy to hold the pony out of the master's sight, like you said,' Kate replied.

'Thank you—I'd better go before Mr Filmore arrives and tries to stop me,' Janey said as others began to trickle down the courthouse steps. 'Can you stay here and see if the warders will let you see Jem for a moment, or at least get a message to him that I will do everything I can for him? I saw Jem's uncle, Will Avery, over there. I am sure he will give you a lift back to Pettridges if you ask him.'

'Yes, miss,' Kate agreed. 'Miss—you'd better go. There's Mr Filmore.'

With an unladylike oath acquired from Lilian, Janey picked up the skirts of her grey gown and pelisse coat and ran.

'Be careful, miss,' Kate admonished from behind, 'that leg of yours is only just healed. You don't want to break the other one.'

'Jane! Jane! Come here at once!' Janey increased her speed a little as Mr Filmore's rather shrill tones overlaid Kate's warning. But flicking a glance over her shoulder, she slowed a little. Mr Filmore's overinflated idea of his own dignity would not allow him to be seen chasing his ward down the street.

There would undoubtedly be a scene when she returned to Pettridges Hall, she thought resignedly as she scrambled into her gig and took up the reins. Not that she cared. While her grandfather had been alive, she had done her best to turn herself into the English lady he had so wanted her to be, out of affection for him. But she had no such feeling towards the Filmores, and what they thought of her had long since ceased to matter to her in the slightest.

Five months, she thought, as she cracked the whip over the skewbald pony's head and sent it forward at a spanking trot. Five months, and she would be twenty-one, and she would have control of her fortune, her estate—and would be able to tell the Filmores to leave Pettridges.

Heads out, extended necks flecked with foam, the blood bays pulled the high-wheeled phaeton along the narrow lane at full lick. Bouncing from side to side on the rutted surface, the wheel hubs scraped first the high stone wall on one side then the other.

'You win, Jonathan! I still consider this contraption outmoded and damned uncomfortable, but I will grant you it is faster than anything in my carriage house. So, slow down!' the fair-haired man, sitting beside the driver, gasped as he held on to his tall silk hat with one hand and the safety rail with the other. 'We'll never make that bend at this speed and if there's anything coming the other way—'

'You're starting to sound like my maiden aunt, Perry.' The Honourable Jonathan Lindsay laughed, but he pulled upon the reins and began to slow the team of matched bays, who were snorting and sweating profusely. 'For someone who was cool as a cucumber when Boney's old Guard came on at Waterloo, you've made an almighty fuss for the last twenty minutes about a little speed.'

'At nineteen, one has not developed the instinct for self-preservation one has at thirty-two,' Perry said, sighing with relief as his dark-haired companion brought the bays down to a trot. 'And I can assure you, I was far from cool. . .' A faraway look came on to his fresh ruddy face. 'Is it really fifteen years ago? I still have nightmares about the sound of the damned French drums as if it were yesterday. And at the time, I didn't think either of us would see our twentieth birthdays.'

'No.' Jonathan Lindsay sighed. 'Neither did I, and sometimes I begin to wish that I hadn't—'

'Begad! You *have* been bitten by the black dog!' Lord Derwent said, giving him a sharp look from his brown eyes. 'What the devil is up with Jono? First, you announce you are giving up the tables, next, that you are going to bury yourself in the country—' He stopped and gave a theatrical groan. 'You have not been spurned by Charlotte?'

Jonathan shook his fashionably tousled dark head.

'Or Amelia, or Emily Witherston?' Perry frowned as Jonathan's craggily handsome face remained impassive. 'Tell me it is not that ghastly Roberts girl—'

'Margaret? Allow me some taste!' His friend sighed again. 'I have not fallen in love, Perry, and I have not the slightest intention of doing so!'

'Then what is chewing at you?' Lord Derwent persisted in asking. 'Go on like this and you will be in danger of becoming positively dull.'

'Exactly!' Lindsay sighed again, checking the bays as he looked ahead and saw a small ragged-looking child swinging precariously upon one of the gates that interrupted the run of stone walling here and there. 'Don't you feel it, Perry, creeping in from all directions since the old king died? And it'll get worse if Wellesley steps down for these reforming fellows—'

'Feel what?' Lord Derwent looked at him blankly.

'Dullness, respectability, worthiness and rampant hypocrisy! You can't enjoy an evening in a hell without these new Peelers turning it over. And as for society— the most innocent flirtation sends young women into a simpering panic, and let slip the mildest oath and the mamas look at you as if you have crawled out of the midden! Conversation is all of profit and industry, new inventions and good works—everyone fancies themselves an archaeologist or scientist or writer—no one confesses to idleness or sheer self-indulgence any more. I begin to think old

Bonaparte was right—we're becoming a nation of shop-keepers with a tradesman's morality—damnation, I am even beginning to feel that I should be doing "something useful" with my life!'

'But you do. . .you do lots of things. You hunt and fish, and you're damned good company at the club—'

'Amusements, Perry, that's all,' Jonathan said gloomily. 'Amusements of which I am beginning to tire.'

Lord Derwent's brow furrowed. 'Well, you're a Member of Parliament. That's useful, ain't it?'

'Parliament! I rarely visit the place and I've made *one* speech in five years—and that was for a wager to see if I could make old Beaufort's face go as purple as that young Jewish fellow's waistcoat.'

'Caused more of a stir than most, though.' Derwent laughed. 'When I read it in *The Times*, I thought you'd become a raving revolutionary. If every landowner gave land to his labourers for their use, we'd all be penniless and I doubt they'd bother to work for us at all!'

'One can hardly blame them,' Lindsay answered drily. 'The price of bread is up, wages are down, and the common land has been fenced in for sheep. Their work is being taken by machines in the name of profit and the poor relief has been cut to subsistence.'

'Well, at least they're spared all that nasty dusty work—and the farmers do well out of it,' Lord Derwent said lightly. 'All the clever chaps tell me that the health of the nation is dependent upon the creation of wealth—'

'And also, it would seem, upon the creation of paupers,' Jonathan said glancing towards the pinched face of the child as they passed him.

'The lower orders have always gone without when

times are hard, they're used to it. A bit of hunger toughens 'em up and keeps 'em grateful for what they do get. They're not like us, Jono, they don't have the finer feelings—look out!'

But Lindsay had already reined back the bays almost to their haunches as they rounded another bend, made blind by the gable end of a cottage built into the wall, and almost collided with a pony trap slewed across its width.

There was no sign of its driver. The reins were looped loosely about the post of a small gate to one side of the cottage, and the skewbald pony was nibbling at a weed growing in a crack in the wall.

'Damned silly place to leave it!' Derwent announced loudly. 'All Curzon Street to ninepence that it's driven by a woman.'

'The Rector's wife or daughter, I'd wager,' Jonathan agreed wryly, glancing at the weathered straw hat with a plain ribbon trim that lay discarded upon the seat of the trap. 'Calling upon the downtrodden and irreligious with some tract, no doubt. Jump down and move it, would you, Perry? Or we'll be here all day. There's a field gate a bit further on—put it in there while I pass—'

'Must I?' Lord Derwent looked down doubtfully at the chalky mud of the lane. 'It took my man hours to get this finish on my boots.' His face brightened as he noticed that the tiny downstairs window of the cottage was open and leant across to pick up the whip. 'No need, watch!'

He stretched out the whip and rapped upon the window sill. 'I say, you there, would you like to earn a shilling—?'

'Go away! Go away!' A woman's voice, choked with sobs, replied. 'You're murderers! All of you!'

'Murderers! I assure you, we are no such thing!' Perry shouted back cheerfully. 'All we want is for someone to move this trap—surely you have a good strong lad—'

The woman's sobs became a low keening wail.

There was a bang as a door was thrown open. A moment later, Janey was at the gate. Tall and slender in her grey gown and white apron, she glowered up at them, as she settled a grubby-looking infant more firmly upon her hip.

'Can you not just go away?' The voice was low, educated and furiously angry with the faintest of accents, which puzzled Lindsay for a moment. He had heard that accent before, but where? His brows furrowed for a moment. And then he remembered. Jack de Lancey, the young American officer who had served on Wellington's staff at Waterloo before being mortally wounded.

'Whatever is the clergy coming to? She sounds like a colonial,' Perry hissed in an all-too-audible whisper at the same moment.

'Perhaps that is because I was born in America and spent the first sixteen years of my life there,' Janey snapped. She was in no mood for condescension from a pair of aristocratic dandies who were probably incapable of tying their own cravats. 'Now, if your curiosity is satisfied, will you please go away!'

'With pleasure,' Lord Derwent moaned, 'but this—' he wrinkled his nose distastefully as he gestured to the trap '—this vehicle is in our way.'

'You have my permission to move it!' she retorted, brushing back a strand of dishevelled fair hair from her face with her free hand. 'Unless you would prefer to hold the child? I thought not!' she said scathingly as her hazel eyes blazed across Derwent's horrified face. 'It might spoil your gloves!'

'But surely there is a lad—' Derwent said.

'Not any longer! You hear that woman weeping—she has just heard that "her fine lad" is to be hanged for the firing of a rick, which he was not even near—'

'Hanged! Bigod!' Lord Derwent's fair brows lifted. 'Damned inconvenient timing, but I suppose he deserves it.'

'Deserves—' Her voice came out of her throat as a hiss of contempt. 'Do you think anyone deserves to die for the price of a hayrick, when his employer is a mean-minded cheat who will let men, women and children starve to death? Is hanging a just punishment for such a crime?'

'Should have thought of that before he set fire to the rick. Common knowledge that arson's a capital offence,' Lord Derwent drawled.

'He did not fire the rick!' Janey found herself almost choked with rage. If they did not go soon, arson would not be the only capital offence to be committed of late. She could easily murder the pair of them. 'I do not know how you can be so complacent! So arrogant!' she said fiercely.

'Quite easily, really. Someone has to support the rule of law, you know.'

'The trap, Perry?' Jonathan interposed quietly, speaking for the first time when he saw Janey's free hand clench upon the crossbar of the gate as if she were intending to rip it off and hurl it at Derwent like a spear. 'Now, if you would not mind?'

'Must I?' His companion's answer was one sharp

glance that sent Lord Derwent down from the box in a moment.

The hazel eyes followed Derwent, and the soft rose lips silently framed an epithet that the Honourable Jonathan Lindsay had never heard from a lady, and certainly not from a Rector's wife. His cool blue gaze flicked to the hand she had put up to push away another stray strand of hair from her eyes, leaving a smudge of soot upon her slanting cheekbone. No ring upon the slender fingers— the daughter, then?

A pity, he thought. With her great angry dark eyes, slanted dark brows and wide, soft mouth, she was all passion and fire, a veritable Amazon. Quite unlike the insipid blue-eyed misses who were English society's current ideal, but put her in Paris and she'd have 'em falling at her feet. If she had been married, country life might have proved more entertaining than he had expected, but he had a rule of never seducing unmarried girls. There were some depths to which one could not sink, even to relieve boredom.

And then, with a start, he realised that those extraordinary hazel eyes were fixed upon his face, regarding him with a coolness that he found distinctly disconcerting. He was not accustomed to women looking at him as if he had just crawled from beneath a stone. Possessed of a large fortune, and good looks since the age of sixteen or so, he had always been the recipient of frank admiration, dewy-eyed adoration or thinly veiled invitations from females of all ages.

'Lord Derwent is not as unkind as he sounds, I assure you,' he said, wondering why that cool dark gaze should make him feel as if he should apologise to her. After all, why should he care what she thought of him?

'No?' The fine dark arch of her brows lifted as she glanced to where Lord Derwent was somewhat ineffectively coaxing the unwilling pony away from the weed in the wall. 'Perhaps I misjudged him. . .perhaps he is merely stupid.'

'Derwent is far from stupid. He is overly flippant at times,' he said tersely, knowing that it was equally true of himself. 'It has been a habit of his for so long he no longer notices himself doing it.'

'Flippant!' Her voice was as contemptuous as her stare as she looked at him a second time, taking in the studied carelessness of his Caesar haircut, the immaculately tailored grey topcoat that emphasised the broad width of his shoulders, leanness of his waist and hips, the glossy perfection of riding boots that did not often have contact with the ground. 'If you think that an excuse, then you are as despicable as he is.'

Her gaze came back up to his, defiant and decidedly judgmental, he thought. She might as well call him a dandy and a plunger and have done with it as look at him in that fashion. Well, if that was how she wished it—

'Oh, no, I really cannot allow you to insult Derwent in such a fashion,' he drawled and returned her scrutiny with a blatancy which sent the colour flaring in her cheeks. 'I'm worse, much worse, I assure you.'

'That I can well believe,' she replied, involuntarily lifting her free hand to the little white ruff collar at the neck of her grey gown to be sure it was fastened. And then, aware that his mocking blue gaze had followed the gesture, she let her hand drop swiftly back to her side and lifted her chin to glare at him again.

'But I do have my saving graces,' he said, drily feeling
a flicker of satisfaction that he had succeeded in disconcerting her. 'A sense of humour, for instance.'

'Really?' Her faintly husky voice was pure ice as her
gaze blazed into his eyes. 'I cannot say I find hanging a
source of amusement.' Hitching the infant more firmly
upon her hip, she made to turn away.

'Wait! My apologies. You are right, of course—hanging is no laughing matter.' He found himself speaking
before he had even thought what he was going to say.
'This lad who is to be hanged—if you tell me his name
and circumstances, I might be able to do something. I
cannot promise, of course, but I have some influence as
a Member of Parliament.'

'You are a Member of Parliament?' There was astonishment in her voice and in the wide hazel eyes as she turned
to face him again, and, he noted wryly, deep suspicion.

'Difficult to believe, I know, but it is the truth,' he
drawled.

'For a rotten borough, no doubt.' she said, half to
herself.

'Positively rank, I'm afraid. My father buys every vote
in the place,' he taunted her lightly. 'But the offer of help
is a genuine one.'

She regarded him warily for a moment. There was no
longer mockery in either the blue eyes or that
velvety voice.

'You mean it?' she said incredulously. 'You will
try—?'

'My word on it,' he said, wondering how he had thought
her hair was mouse at first glance. It was gold, he realised,
as a shaft of weak sunlight filtered through the clouds. A

warm tawny gold, like ripe corn under an August sun. And it looked soft. Released from that tight knot, he would wager it would run through a man's hands like pure silk.

'His name is Jem, Jem Avery, he's fourteen years old and he was sentenced at Salisbury Assizes, by Judge Richardson.'

Jonathan jerked his attention back from imagining the circumstances in which he might test his own wager and gave her his full attention. 'Fourteen? That does seem harsh,' he said slowly.

'Yes. Fourteen. They seem to think that to make such an example will quell the discontent amongst the labourers and prevent it spreading to Wiltshire,' she said flatly, as his blue gaze met and held hers for a moment. 'You really will see what you can do? You will not forget?'

'No. No.' He shook his head, quite certain that even if the unfortunate Jem slipped his mind, his advocate was not likely to do so for a week or two at least. 'You have my word I will do what I can.'

'Why?' she asked suddenly. 'You are a stranger here and can have no interest in what becomes of Jem.'

He shrugged his shoulders. 'Must be my altruistic nature. I can never resist a distressed damsel, so long as she is passably pretty, of course,' he added self-mockingly.

'I am not distressed, sir! I am angry!' she snapped with a lift of her chin. 'And neither am I passably pretty!'

'No,' he said, after a pause in which his gaze travelled over her face, taking in the breadth of her brow, the fine straight nose that had absolutely no propensity towards turning up, the clean, strong upward slant of her jaw-bone from the point of her lifted chin, and that wide, generous mouth, 'you are not passably pretty.'

'I am glad you realise your error—' she began to say, wondering why she felt such a sense of pique.

'Any man who considered you merely passable would be lacking in judgement and taste,' he interrupted her lazily, his eyes warm and teasing as they met her gaze. And that was true, he thought, with a touch of surprise as his gaze dropped fractionally to the decidedly kissable curve of her mouth and then lower still to the perfect sweeping lines of her body beneath the plain grey gown.

Janey stared back at him. He was flirting with her. This laconic, drawling, society dandy was flirting with her! He was looking at her as if he wanted to kiss her, touch her. . . The image that arose in her mind was so shocking, so devastating, that she could do nothing for a second or so but stare back at him helplessly. And then, as the corners of his wide, clever mouth lifted imperceptibly, and the clear blue eyes dared her to respond, the breath left her throat in a small exasperated sigh.

'Have you no sense of propriety?' she found herself blurting out and then frowned as it occurred to her she had sounded all too much like Mrs Filmore.

'Afraid not,' he answered with a complete lack of apology. 'I blame it upon a youth spent in hells and houses of ill-repute, not to mention the houses of the aristocracy and Parliament, of course.'

'Oh, you are quite impossible!' In spite of herself, in spite of everything, she found her mouth tugging up at the corners.

'You can smile, then?' he said lightly. 'I was beginning to wonder if you considered it a sin.'

'No.' She sobered, feeling guilty that for a second or

two she had almost forgotten Jem. 'But I cannot say that I much in the mood for merriment at present.'

'No.' The hint of mockery, of invitation, left his face and voice as he glanced at the cottage. 'That is understandable enough in the circumstances. You have not told me where I might send word. The Rectory?'

'No, Pettridges Hall,' she said with inexplicable satisfaction, having overheard his comments about the likely owner of the trap through the open cottage window. 'I have no connection with the Rectory and no fondness for reforming tracts.'

'I am delighted to hear it,' he said without the slightest trace of embarrassment. 'Especially since it seems we are to be neighbours. I have just become the new owner of Southbrook, which I understand borders the Pettridges estate.'

'You have bought Southbrook?' Janey's face lit as she looked at him with unhidden delight. 'That is wonderful!'

The dark brows lifted, mocking her faintly. 'I am flattered by your enthusiasm to have me for a neighbour.'

'It is not for you in particular, sir, I meant merely that it is wonderful that Southbrook has been bought at last,' Janey said, and knew as she caught the flicker of amusement in the pale blue eyes that she had spoken just a little too quickly to be completely convincing either to him or herself. 'The land has lain idle so long and there are so many men in the village who desperately need work.'

'I stand corrected,' he said drily. 'Though I feel honour bound to confess that I did not buy the estate from any sense of philanthropic duty. I accepted it in lieu of a card debt after the owner assured me it was no longer his family home. We are on our way to inspect the property now.'

'Oh, I see,' she said, her voice flat again suddenly. 'You are not familiar with the estate, then?' she asked, thinking that he and his companion would undoubtedly take one look and return to town forthwith, as had all the other potential purchasers.

'Not yet. Why?' he asked sharply. For a moment she considered warning him about the leaking roof, the broken windows, the last five years of complete neglect that had followed upon twenty of inadequate maintainance, but then she decided against it. There was always a chance that he might see beyond Southbrook's failings to its original beauty and decide to restore the estate.

'Oh—no reason,' she replied, carefully giving her attention to the child in her arms who was beginning to grizzle and wriggle. 'I'm sorry, what did you say?'

'I asked whom I should ask for?'

'Janey.' Stupidly, for no reason she could think of, she answered with the name with which she had been known to family and friends for the first sixteen years of her life. 'Miss Hilton, Miss Jane Hilton, I mean,' she stammered slightly as the straight black brows lifted again.

'Jane,' he repeated it with a half-laugh. 'Plain Jane.'

'Yes,' she said defensively. It was a jest she had endured more times than she could count from her guardian's son and daughter. 'What of it?'

'Nothing.' Again his narrow lips curved. 'Somehow I did not think you would be an Araminta or Arabella, Miss Hilton.'

'Jono! Are you coming through or not?' Lord Derwent called impatiently.

'I must go. I think your trap would be better there by the gate, but if you wish—'

'No, your friend was right, it was a stupid place to leave it,' she admitted ruefully. 'I was thinking only of how to break the news to Jem's mother. I am sorry for the inconvenience.'

'It is of no consequence.' He smiled at her as he gathered up the reins. 'Good day, Miss Hilton, I shall send word as soon as I can.'

'Thank you, Mr—' she began to say and then realised she did not even know his name.

'Lindsay,' he called over his shoulder as he sent the bays forward, 'Jonathan Lindsay.'

She stood staring after him in disbelief. That was the Honourable Jonathan Lindsay? That laconic mocking dandy had made the passionate speech, demanding better conditions for the labouring poor that she had read in the paper? Surely not! And yet he had offered to help Jem, a boy he had never met.

For a moment, as she watched the phaeton disappear down the long winding lane, she felt like chasing after it and begging him to take on Southbrook. If she were honest, it was not only because a humane landlord would make such a difference to so many in the village, but because he had made her feel truly alive for the first time since she had arrived in England.

'Miss, miss. . .' The child who had been swinging on the gate came and tugged at her skirt. 'Have you brought us something, miss? I'm hungry—'

'Yes, Sam. Some broth, some bread and some preserves,' she answered, still staring after the phaeton, 'and some gingerbread, if you promise to be a good boy for your mother.'

She broke off, frowning as she watched the little boy who was already running for the door, his too thin arms and legs flying in all directions. Even with what she could persuade cook to let her have from the kitchen, they were not getting enough to eat, nor were at least half a dozen other families in the village.

As farm after farm took to the new threshing machines, there would be more men out of work this autumn—and she could do nothing, since she had no control of her estate, nor access to the fortune left her by her grandfather until she was twenty-one. And five months was far too long for Sam and the other families, who would starve and freeze this winter. There was nothing she could do, nothing—heiress she might be, but she was almost as powerless as poor Jem in his prison cell.

Biting her lip, she adjusted the child on her hip again as she limped slowly up the little herringbone brick path to the cottage door. As ever when she was tired, the leg she had broken a year ago had begun to ache. But there was no time to think of that now, not when Mrs Avery stood in the doorway, her face grey and desperate.

'He'll be so scared, miss, so frightened,' the older woman blurted out. 'I'd rather it was me than him.'

'I know,' she said helplessly.

'I've got to go to him, miss.' Mrs Avery caught her arm. 'I've got to!'

'I will take you tomorrow, I am sure they will let you visit,' Janey said huskily as she guided the other woman back into the little dark room, where the other four Avery children were huddled upon the box bed, pale and silent. As she looked from one thin, pinched miserable face to another, the rage in her bubbled up afresh. If Jonathan Lindsay failed them, she would not let them hang Jem! She would not! Not even if she had to break him out of gaol herself.

Chapter Two

'Great God, Jono!' Lord Derwent broke the lengthy silence which had ensued after the phaeton drew up before the edifice of Southbrook House. 'You took this in lieu of ten thousand? I should not give five hundred for the whole place! The park is nothing but weeds, the woods looked as if they had not been managed in half a century and as for this—' he gestured to the ivy-masked façade of the house '—look at it! There is not a whole pane of glass in the place, and what the roof is like I hate to think. . .'

'Perfect proportions, though,' Jonathan Lindsay said thoughtfully as he, too, surveyed the house. 'See how the width of the steps exactly balances the height of the columns on the portico. Come on, Perry, let's look inside now we're here.'

Knotting the ribbons loosely, he leapt lithely down from the box.

'Do we have to?' Derwent groaned.

There was no answer. Jonathan Lindsay was already striding across the weed-choked gravel of the drive.

*   *   *

'You are not *serious* about intending to live here?' Lord Derwent pleaded an hour later, after they had inspected the house from attic to cellar. 'It's damp, dusty and—' he paused, shivering in his blue frock coat '—colder than an ice house in December.'

'Nothing that someone else's industry will not put right,' his friend said absently, as he stared up at the painted ceiling of the salon adjacent to the ballroom. 'This ceiling is very fine, don't you think?'

'It might be,' Lord Derwent said unenthusiastically, 'if you could see it for dust and cobwebs. I'm sorry, Jono, but I simply can't understand why you would wish to reside here when Ravensfield is at your disposal.'

'I never shared my late uncle's taste for Gothic fakery, you know that, Perry.'

'Yes, but it has every convenience, it's in damned good hunting country and the agent runs the estate tighter than a ship of the line: you wouldn't need to lift a finger from one year end to the next. Local society's not up to much, I'll grant you that, but it won't be any different here.'

'Oh, I don't know.' Jonathan smiled. 'I thought the neighbourhood showed some promise of providing entertainment.'

'You mean that extraordinary young woman?'

'Ah, so you thought she was extraordinary, too,' he said, as he began to walk slowly back towards the entrance hall.

'Extraordinarily rude,' Lord Derwent replied huffily. 'It is scarcely my fault some idiot boy is going to get himself turned off, but she looked at me as if she'd have preferred to see me in a tumbril on the way to Madame Guillotine.'

'I'm sure you misjudge the fair maiden—I think she'd have settled for a horse whipping,' Jonathan said drily.

'I don't!' Derwent said with feeling. 'I can't think why you offered to help.'

'No, not like me, is it?' Jonathan agreed, deadpan. 'I must have succumbed to this fever for worthiness.'

'Succumbed to a weakness for perfect proportions, more like,' Derwent said darkly, 'and I'm not referring to the portico.'

'Ah, Perry, you do know how to wound one's feelings,' Jonathan said, grinning. 'But you must confess, she was very easy on the eye.'

'And to think that, only two hours ago, you were telling me that you were going to give up women along with the tables.' Derwent sighed. 'But I'll wager you'll get not that one past the bedroom door, Jono. These radical females are all the same—they only give their affections to ugly curates or long-haired poets who write execrable drivel.'

'No gentleman could possibly accept such a challenge.' Jonathan laughed. 'So, what are your terms?'

'Triton against your chestnut stallion,' Lord Derwent said after a moment's thought.

'Triton!' Jonathan's dark brows rose. 'I'd almost contemplate marrying the girl to get my hands on that horse before the Derby. Are you so certain of my failure?'

'Positive. I chased after a gal like that once. There I was, in the midst of telling her about my critical role in defeating old Boney and waiting for her to fall at my feet in admiration, and all she says is "Yes, but do you read the scriptures, Lord Derwent? Spiritual courage is so much more important than the physical kind, don't you think?"'

'Poor Perry.' Jonathan sighed. 'It must be a sad affliction to lack both good looks and natural charm—' He
broke off, laughing as he ducked to evade a friendly blow
from Derwent.

'And,' Derwent went on, 'she'll never forgive you for
not saving her arsonist. You said yourself the local men
were determined to make an example, so they're not likely
to listen to a newcomer to the district, not even you, Jono.'

'Who said anything about local men?' Jonathan smiled,
a wide slow smile. 'We are going to get some fresh horses,
and then we're going straight back to town and I am going
to see the Home Secretary.'

'The Home Secretary! He wouldn't intervene on behalf
of an arsonist and thief if his mother begged him on
bended knee. And you are not exactly in favour with the
government after that speech—the front bench did not
appear to share your sense of humour.'

'Oh, I think he'll lend a sympathetic ear,' Jonathan
drawled. 'Remember I told you I was involved in a bit
of a mill with the Peelers when the hell in Ransome Street
was raided? Well, if I hadn't landed a well-aimed blow
upon one of the guardians of the law, our esteemed Home
Secretary would have found himself in an extremely
embarrassing situation.'

'Great God!' Derwent cried. 'You mean you are going
to blackmail the Home Secretary to win the admiration of
some parson's daughter! It'll be you on the gallows next.'

'Blackmail—what an ugly word.' Jonathan grinned.
'I'm just going to seek a favour from a friend. And she's
not the parson's daughter, her name is Jane Hilton and she
resides at Pettridges Hall,' he added, his grin widening.

'If she's not a clerical's brat, she must be a poor relation or a companion and they're as bad,' Perry said huffily.

'You know the people at Pettridges?' Jonathan's blue eyes regarded him with sharpened interest.

'Hardly describe 'em as acquaintances, but their name's not Hilton, so she's not one of 'em,' Derwent said lazily. 'I met the offspring last season: sulky-looking lad who talked of nothing but hunting and a distinctly useful little redhead that Mama was doing her best to marry off before she got herself into a tangle of one sort or another. Now, what the devil was the name—ah—Filmore, that's it. They must be comfortably off, though—Pettridges wouldn't have come cheap. My father told me old Fenton never spared a penny when it came to improving the place.'

'Fenton? I don't know the name.'

'Well, he was something of a recluse. He was a cloth manufacturer, worked his way up from millhand to owner and dragged himself out of gutter by clothing half the army and navy and, if the rumours were true, half Boney's lot as well.

'By the Peace of Amien he'd made enough for a country estate and respectability, even had an impoverished earl lined up for his daughter. But she reverted to type and ran off with her childhood sweetheart, a millhand. Fenton was furious. He never saw her again and cut her off without a penny. Affair made him a laughing stock, of course, and he never made any attempt to take part in society after that.' Derwent sighed. 'Damned waste of a fortune and a pretty face by all accounts. Wonder who did get his money? They say he had one of the biggest fortunes in South-west England.' Then he brightened. 'I think I might look into it, Jono. You never know, there might be a great-niece or something, and I might land myself an heiress.'

Jonathan laughed. 'He probably left it all to the Mill Owners Benevolent Fund for Virtuous Widows, Perry.'

'Probably,' Derwent agreed gloomily. 'I suppose it will just have to be Diana, then. My father has told me he wants to see his grandson and a generous dowry in the family coffers before next year is out or he will discontinue my allowances, and tell the bankers to withdraw my credit. You don't know how lucky you are being the youngest son and possessing a fortune to match those of your brothers—it spares you no end of trouble.'

'Yes,' Jonathan said beneath his breath, 'and leaves you no end of time to fill.'

Janey sat in the window-seat of the morning-room, the copy of Cobbett's *Register* in her lap, still at the same page she had opened it at half an hour earlier. She stared out at the gravelled sweep of drive that remained empty but for the gardeners, raking up the fallen leaves from the beeches that lined the drive. Surely Mr Lindsay would send word today, even if he had been unsuccessful. It was eight days now, and time was running out. In five days' time Jem would be led out from Dorchester Gaol and hanged.

She dropped her eyes unseeingly to Mr Cobbett's prose. At least she had not told Mrs Avery, at least she had not raised false hopes there—

'Jane! Have you heard a word I have said?'

She started as she realised that Annabel Filmore had entered the morning-room. 'I'm sorry,' she said absently, 'I was thinking.'

'You mean you had your head in a book as usual,' the red-haired girl said disparagingly as she studied her reflection in the gilt-framed mirror above the mantelpiece. 'Mama says so much reading and brainwork ruins one's looks,' she added as she patted one of her fat sausage-shaped curls into place over her forehead.

'You need not worry, then,' Janey said, not quite as quietly as she had meant.

'I have never had to worry about my looks,' Annabel said blithely, utterly oblivious to the insult as she turned upon her toes in a pirouette to admire the swirling skirts of her frilled pink muslin. 'Just as well, with Jonathan Lindsay coming to live at Southbrook.'

'He is coming!' Janey's face lit up. 'When?'

'Oh, in a week or two, I think Papa said,' Annabel replied carelessly still admiring herself in the glass.

'A week or two!' The brief flare of hope she had felt died instantly. A week and all would be over for Jem. No doubt the promise had been forgotten as soon as made. So now what was she to do?

'Yes, but whatever has Jonathan Lindsay to do with you?' Annabel asked, suddenly curious as she turned to look at Jane. 'You have gone quite pale.'

'Nothing, I met him in Burton's Lane a few days ago,' she said tersely, Mr Cobbett's *Register* fluttering unnoticed from the lap of her lavender muslin gown as she got to her feet. 'That's all.'

'That's all!' Annabel's blue eyes widened in exaggerated despair. 'You meet the most handsome man in England in Burton's Lane and you did not say a word to anyone!'

'I did not think him so very handsome,' Janey said, not

entirely truthfully. 'He was a little too much of the dandy for my taste.'

'Not handsome!' Annabel groaned and flounced down upon a sofa. 'When he is so dark, so rugged—and that profile! Why, he could be Miss Austen's Darcy in the flesh.'

'That is not how I see him,' Janey said, half to herself, as an unexpected image of his face, chiselled, and hard, lightened only by the slant of his mouth and brows, and the lazy amusement in the cool blue eyes, came instantly into her mind. Oh, no, she thought, Mr Lindsay was definitely no Mr Darcy. He was far too incorrect—far too dangerous in every sense.

She doubted he was afraid of breaking conventions, or anything else for that matter. In fact, strip him of his dandified clothes and put him in a suit of buckskins and he would not have been so out of place among the backwoodsmen among whom she had grown up. Whether or not someone would survive on the frontier was the yardstick by which she always found herself assessing people; in Mr Lindsay's case, she found her answer was a surprising 'yes'.

'It's so unfair that you had to meet him in Burton's Lane instead of me,' Annabel complained as she toyed with one of the flounces on her gown. 'You should have invited him back here. Do you have any idea of how hard I tried for an introduction when I was in Town last Season?' Then her sullen round face brightened. 'Mama will not possibly be able to refuse to allow us to be introduced now he is to be a neighbour.'

'Your mother would not allow you to be introduced to him? Why ever not?' Janey asked, curious in spite of herself. The son of an Earl, even if he were the younger could usually do no wrong in the eyes of Mrs Filmore.

'Because of his reputation, ninny,' Annabel explained patiently, as if she were speaking to a child. 'He is the greatest rake and gambler in England; at least, that is what Miss Roberts told Mama. She said that there were a dozen husbands with cause to call him out, if duelling had not been banned, and another twenty wives who would willingly give their spouses cause to do the same.

'And she told me that he quite broke Araminta Howard's heart—and very nearly her reputation. Miss Roberts says he cares for nothing but his pleasure—' Annabel's lips parted upon the word and she gave a little shiver.

'I can scarcely believe that of the man who made the speech that was printed in the paper,' Janey said, feeling a peculiar distaste about hearing of Jonathan Lindsay's apparently numerous amours.

'The speech about the poor!' Annabel gave a shriek of laughter as her brother entered the room, and came to lounge sullenly against the mantle. 'Piers! Piers! Jane admires the speech Jonathan Lindsay made on behalf of the poor.'

'Then, once he has settled in, we must be sure to call so she can congratulate him in person,' Piers drawled, an unpleasant smile on his rather too-plump mouth. 'I am sure he will be delighted with her admiration.'

'Oh we must—we must—' Annabel spluttered into helpless incoherent laughter.

With a resigned sigh, Janey bent to pick up the *Register* and made to leave.

'Where are you going, dear coz?' Piers stepped in front of her.

'Somewhere a little quieter,' Janey said, staring back into Piers's rather bulbous pale blue eyes. 'Will you stand aside, please?'

'Papa wants you in the library,' Piers answered without moving. 'He is none too happy about the food you've been doling out in the village. Quite choleric, in fact, says he won't have the estate's money wasted upon the undeserving poor who do no work.'

'And yet he does not mind keeping you in funds,' Janey said mildly.

'I am not poor,' Piers said frostily, his heavy features taking on an expression of hauteur.

'Undeserving was the adjective I had in mind.' Janey smiled. 'Now let me pass, if you please. Perhaps you can convey my apologies to your father? I have other more pressing matters to attend to this morning.'

'Like reading this insurrectionist rubbish!' Piers snatched the *Register* from her, crumpled it into a ball and threw it into the fire.

'How dare you!' Janey hissed. 'That was mine, you had no right—'

'I had every right, dear coz,' Piers sneered, catching her arm as she went to turn away. 'You know Papa will not have that paper in the house. And now you are coming to the library, as Papa wishes.'

'Let go of me!' Janey said warningly.

'No.'

'Very well.' Janey brought her knee sharply upwards in a manoeuvre which no well-brought-up young English lady would have known.

There were definitely some advantages in a frontier upbringing, she thought, as she saw Piers's eyes bulge, and he crumpled into a groaning heap upon the floor.

'Jane! What have you done? You have killed him!' Annabel flew to her cursing brother's side.

'I fear not,' Janey said unrepentantly. She picked up her shawl from the window-seat and turned for the door, a smile upon her lips. A smile that froze as she found herself looking over her guardian's shoulder, straight into Jonathan Lindsay's blue eyes.

How long he had been there, what he thought of her after the scene he had just witnessed, were of no consequence for the moment in which their gazes locked. She only knew that she felt a ridiculous surge of happiness that he had not forgotten his promise to her. He had come.

'Jane!' Mr Filmore, who had seemed transfixed, apart from the trembling of his moustache, finally found his voice in a tone of thunderous disapproval. 'I cannot think what you have to smile about! Brawling like some tavern slut! Has the money your grandfather spent upon your education, the effort Mrs Filmore has expended, counted for nothing?'

Janey made no answer, but stood, head held high, her gaze fixed upon a point somewhere over the rather short Mr Filmore's head. She had a very good idea of how the conversation would progress. Mr Filmore never lost an opportunity to remind her of her failings, her lack of gratitude for the belated, but expensive, education lavished upon her by her grandfather.

Or the fact that she had been discovered, at the age of fifteen, living in a boarding house in the care of a woman who thought little of hiring herself out along with the beds, a woman who taught her the very useful manoeuvre she had just tried out on Piers. And upon receipt of that information, Jonathan Lindsay would no doubt decide to discontinue their acquaintance at the earliest opportunity, she thought, her happiness evaporating into a sudden bleak emptiness.

'Have you ever had the misfortune to witness such behaviour before, Mr Lindsay? I should wager you have not!' Somewhat to Janey's surprise, Mr Filmore turned to address his visitor before berating her further.

'No.' Mild contempt edged Jonathan Lindsay's voice like a razor. 'But then, neither have I seen such provocation before, being accustomed to the company of gentlemen.' He looked pointedly at Piers who, after being assisted to his feet by his sister, strode out of the opposite door without so much as a word to any of them.

Janey's hazel gaze flashed back to his in grateful astonishment. She had not expected to find an ally in the aristocratic Jonathan Lindsay.

Holding her gaze, he gave her the briefest of smiles. A smile that made her heart stop and skip a beat. Suddenly, the imminent lecture to be endured did not seem such an ordeal.

'If you knew my ward, sir, you would know my son is blameless in this matter,' Mr Filmore said huffily. 'We make allowances, of course—she has never been quite herself since her betrothed died so tragically last year.'

'Allowances!' Janey's hazel eyes took on a greener hue as her temper rose.

'Jane,' Mr Filmore said firmly, 'do not let us have another scene. You do not want Mr Lindsay to think you unbalanced, do you?'

'That is not an error I am likely to make,' Jonathan said coolly. 'In my opinion, Miss Hilton is perfectly balanced.' He put the slightest emphasis upon the last word, and Janey felt her insides contract as his blue gaze skimmed downwards from her face to the sharp curve of her waist emphasised by the tightly fitting bodice of her lavender gown. 'And it is a delight to see her again.'

'Again?' Mr Filmore said, looking down his sharp thin nose. 'I was not aware you had been introduced, Jane.'

'We met by accident, last week,' Janey said dragging her gaze from Jonathan Lindsay's face. A delight. Was that true?

'In Burton's Lane,' supplied Annabel with deliberate malice. 'That's where the family of that boy who fired the rick live.'

'Not for much longer, if I have anything to do with it.' Mr Filmore was curt, disapproving. 'I might have known you were gallivanting about the countryside again, dispensing largesse to all and sundry.' He drew himself up. 'If it were not for me, Mr Lindsay, Miss Hilton would not have a penny of her money left by the time she is of age.'

'Oh, Papa, I am sure Mr Lindsay does not wish to be bored with our little domestic disagreements.' Annabel came forward, all smiles, swaying flounces and bouncing curls, as Janey stood, momentarily stricken, wondering whether Mr Filmore could evict Mrs Avery without notice. 'And you have not introduced me yet.'

'There is hardly any need,' Jonathan said, with a smile that did not reach his eyes. 'I know you by sight, Miss Filmore, and by reputation.' His mouth curved a little upon the last word. 'You were in Town last Season, were you not?'

'Yes, how clever of you to remember,' Annabel simpered, fluttering her eyelashes. 'I did not think you would have noticed me amongst so many.'

'Oh, you are impossible to ignore, Miss Filmore,' Jonathan said drily as his eyes flicked over the pink frills. 'Quite impossible.'

'Oh, Mr Lindsay, you are such a flatterer,' Annabel said, twirling one of her red curls coyly about her finger. 'Is he not shameless, Jane?'

'Utterly, I fear,' Janey agreed mildly, the corners of her mouth curving in spite of everything. Only Annabel, whose vanity was overwhelming, could possibly have taken what he had said as a compliment.

'Jane,' Mr Filmore said frowningly, as he glanced from Lindsay to Janey, 'have you entirely forgotten your manners? Go and order some refreshment for our guest.'

'Of course,' Janey said demurely. 'If you will excuse me?' She waited for Jonathan Lindsay to step aside.

'A moment, Miss Hilton.' He touched her arm as she made to pass him, stopping her in mid-stride. She stared down at his long elegant fingers, so brown and firm upon her thin muslin sleeve just above her wrist. It was the lightest, politest of gestures. There was no need for her pulse to beat wildly at the base of her throat, no reason at all for her breath to stop in her throat. And it was ridiculous to have this feeling that her whole life had been leading to this moment, this man's touch upon her sleeve.

Dragging in a hasty breath, she jerked her gaze upwards to his and found him staring at her speculatively.

'Yes?' Her voice was almost, but not quite, as steady as she would have wished it as his gaze held hers and she caught the gleam of amusement in the indigo depths of his eyes. No doubt he was used to women reacting to him in such a fashion and that piqued her. She did not want to be like the rest. . .not to this man.

'That matter we spoke of—'

'About the gardens of Southbrook, you mean?' she interrupted him warningly, willing him with her eyes to understand that she did not want Jem's case mentioned before Mr Filmore.

'Yes,' he said after a fractional hesitation, 'the gardens.'

'You will find the camomile seat at the foot of the waterfall,' she went on hastily. 'Sunset is the best time to sit there, the light turns the water to rainbows—' She stopped, as close to blushing as she had ever been, as his brows lifted quizzically and he smiled at her in a way he had never done before, a wide slanting smile that reflected the warmth in his gaze.

'Rainbows at sunset?' he said with gentle mockery. 'How very romantic for a Radical.'

'It was merely an observation—you really do get rainbows—' she said tersely as Annabel giggled.

'Then I shall go there this very evening.'

She exhaled with relief as he lifted his fingers from her arm. He had understood. But then he understood everything far too well, she thought wryly as she took a step back from him.

'Rainbows!' She heard Annabel snort as she left the room. 'I swear Jane is becoming more fanciful by the day.'

Chapter Three

The orange disc of the sun was just slipping below the distant horizon of the downs when Janey stepped out of the woods. A few feet ahead of her was an apparently sheer cliff, out of which sprang a small torrent of water, which foamed and sparkled as it tumbled into the shadowy pool some forty feet below. Above the noise of the water, she could hear the frantic excited barking of a dog; glancing down to the edge of the pool, she saw Jonathan Lindsay, throwing sticks for his liver and white spaniel into the calm end of the pool.

Cautiously she began to descend the narrow zigzag of a fern-lined path that threaded down the cliff, thinking ruefully that it would have been easier if she had been as close a follower of the fashions as Annabel and, hence, would have been wearing a skirt that skimmed her ankles rather than the ground.

The roar of the falling water drowned out the noise of her approach. It was the spaniel who sensed her presence first, dropping its stick at Jonathan's feet and raising its head to bark furiously.

'Hello! I was beginning to think you were not coming, or I had misunderstood you,' he called up to her as he turned.

'No, you understood perfectly,' she shouted back, wondering why it was that seeing him should give her this peculiar feeling of instant well-being. 'I am sorry to have kept you waiting,' she said as she drew nearer, 'it was more difficult than I had expected to get away.'

'You are still in disgrace, I take it?'

'For all eternity, I suspect,' she said with feeling, her guardians having waxed long and lyrical about her out-rageous behaviour.

'Wait, I'll help you—the path has collapsed there.' He came forward, hands outstretched to help her down the last drop of two feet or so.

'Thank you,' she said after a fractional hesitation, and put out her hands to rest them on his shoulders as his hands closed about her waist. It would have been ridiculous to refuse. As ridiculous as it was to feel so afraid of touching him. Daniel had lifted her down from a thousand such places when they had roamed the great forests on the long trail west, looking for firewood and berries.

'Ready?'

'Yes. . .' The word dwindled to nothing in her throat as she glanced down into his blue, blue eyes and everything seemed to stop: time, her heart, her lungs—even the roar-ing, cascading water.

For a second, no more, he stared back at her. Then, with a flicker of a smile, he lifted her down. Staring at his snowy linen cravat, she waited for him to release her waist, and then she realised that he could hardly do so until she removed her hands from his shoulders, where they seemed to have become fixed.

Snatching her hands back, she pulled out of his grasp, took two steps back and dragged in a breath. She had danced with several men, even been kissed upon the mouth once by Daniel, but she had never, ever felt anything like that sudden irrational sense of belonging, of wanting to touch, hold on and never let go—

Get yourself in hand, girl, she told herself impatiently, as he regarded her a little quizzically with a half-smile hovering upon his wide mouth. Sure, he was handsome, but he had not found their proximity in the least bit earth-shaking—but then, no doubt, he was used to simpering society misses falling at his feet. She took another breath and lifted her chin, preparing to be as cool, as ladylike and as English as she knew how.

'Do you always look at man like that when he touches you?'

His dry question almost made her gasp. No one she had met since she had come to England had ever been so direct, so outrageously intimate. How *dare* he ask such a thing! And then she almost laughed—if he wasn't going to play by society rules, then neither was she. . .she would be what she was, a colonial who did not know how to behave properly.

'Only when they have dishonourable intentions.' She gave him a blithe smile as she spoke and had the satisfaction of seeing surprise flicker across his face.

'Alas, you know me so well already.' He inclined his head to her, his blue eyes sparkling with laughter. 'But at least you did not slap my face; I suppose I should be grateful for that.'

'I have never cared for overly trodden paths,' she said

as they walked side by side towards the camomile seat.

'Oh, sharp, sharp, Miss Hilton, I am wounded to the quick.' He put a theatrical hand to his breast.

'Not so much as Piers was,' she said sweetly, thinking it would do him no harm to be reminded that she was very capable of defending herself.

'True,' he agreed wryly, and then frowned. 'You are limping. Have you hurt yourself?'

'It's nothing. I broke my leg in a fall almost a year ago and it still aches sometimes,' she answered, as she sat down gratefully upon the springy cushion of herbs.

'Horses can be dangerous beasts, can they not?' he said as he seated himself beside her. 'I broke a collarbone once, and that took long enough to mend.'

'Yes.' She let his assumption go. She did not want to have to explain about the accident, or Edward, just now. She was having trouble enough coping with his disconcerting nearness and the knowledge that she was as susceptible as any society miss to Jonathan Lindsay's very considerable charm.

'So is that why you like to come here often, because you do not care for the overly trodden paths?' he asked a moment later, giving her a sideways glance.

'How did you know I come here often?' She paused in the act of crushing a sprig of the camomile between her fingers, wondering if the herb's calming properties would have any effect upon her heart, which had begun to race from the moment he had sat down beside her.

'This—' he patted the springy camomile, his fingers a scant half-inch from her thigh '—has no need of weeding, someone has been doing it, and—' he reached into his pocket with his other hand and produced a glove worked with the initials J.H. '—I found this. You, Miss Hilton, have been trespassing for some time. Have you not?'

'Guilty, m'lud.' She released the breath that had caught in her throat as she accepted the proffered glove and his fingers momentarily brushed hers. 'It was the one place I could be sure of escaping my guardians and—' she glanced across the pool and upwards to where the tall pines clung to the edge of the cliff above the waterfall '—there is something about it which reminds me of home.'

'Home?' His straight brows lifted as he looked about him, from the sparkling spill of water to the wild untidy tumble of ferns, brambles and once-cultivated shrubs, long since gone wild. 'I cannot say this puts me in mind of the grounds of Pettridges Hall.'

'I meant America,' she said, still staring across the pool. 'This reminds me of the Kentucky Trail and where we settled in Minnesota. Sometimes, sitting here watching the water and listening to the wind in the trees, I can almost believe I am back there—that if I turn around quickly enough I will see my father hitching up the team or my mother coming out of the cabin to call us in for dinner—' She broke off, wondering why on earth she was confiding such thoughts to him.

'You miss your life there?' There was the faintest note of surprise in his voice. A note she recognised all too well in carefully educated English voices, when she made the mistake of speaking about her past.

'Yes, I do,' she said with a sharp lift of her chin, telling herself that she was a fool to think that he might be different from the rest, that he might just understand. 'America has a great deal to recommend it. England does not have a monopoly upon natural beauty, Mr Lindsay.'

'While you are resident in England, that is a subject upon which I shall have to disagree with you,' he said, bending down to pick up the stick that the ever-hopeful spaniel had dropped at his feet.

'Then I suppose it would be churlish to argue—' she said after the slightest intake of breath. 'Do you always flirt so outrageously, Mr Lindsay?'

He straightened, threw the stick and then turned to look at her, his eyes sparkling. 'Only with women whom I find interesting or desirable.'

'And into which category do I fall, Mr Lindsay?' she asked, surprising herself with the apparent uninterestedness of her tone.

'Both,' he said softly after a moment, his eyes suddenly very dark as his gaze dropped to her mouth, and then lower still to the fullness of her breasts. 'Very definitely both.'

His voice had lowered to a velvety depth that made her skin prickle and grow tight, as if his hands had followed his stare, and she found herself staring back at his face, the wide slanting line of his mouth, his long clever fingers as he toyed with a piece of camomile.

Her mouth and throat grew dry as his gaze came back to her eyes and she knew that he meant it and that they had just stepped off the safe ground of light-hearted flirtation into some decidedly dangerous waters—for her, at least.

She swallowed and stared down at the glove in her hands. 'Good,' she said, as matter-of-factly as she could manage. 'I should hate to be merely desirable.'

He laughed, dissolving the tension that had been almost

tangible. 'I do not think you could ever be "merely" any-thing, Miss Hilton.'

'You are doing it again,' she murmured, lifting her gaze to watch the spaniel heave itself out of the pool and shake the water from its coat.

'What?' he said innocently as he studied her detachedly, thinking that he had been right. She was not pretty: her fine nose was too straight, the upswept line of her jaw too clean and sharp, her forehead a fraction too high, her mouth too wide and feline. Oh, no—no insipid, dainty, English rosebud, this—more a lioness, lithe, fierce and very beautiful.

'Flirting,' Janey replied, putting a hand to her face, ostensibly to push back an errant strand of fair hair, but in reality to shield herself from the piercingly blue gaze that was making her feel decidedly uncomfortable.

'And you are not?' he mocked softly.

'No. I have no talent for it,' she said tersely, wishing that she were not quite so aware that, if she moved a matter of an inch, his shoulder would touch hers. 'All I asked you—'

'—was whether or not I found you desirable?' He laughed. 'If that does not constitute flirting, Miss Hilton, I don't know what does.'

She shrugged, determined not to fall into another of his verbal traps as she glanced at him with what she hoped passed for indifference. 'I was simply curious.'

'I should be happy to satisfy your curiosity whenever you wish.' He grinned at her and quirked a dark eyebrow. 'You only have to say the word.'

He was wicked. Quite impossibly wicked, she thought,

the corners of her mouth lifting despite all her efforts to look stern.

'The word is no,' she said a little too emphatically.

'Pity.' He was almost sober suddenly. 'You would not reconsider if I told your hair was the colour of gold, your eyes as dark and mysterious as that pool, that I shall die if I do not kiss you—'

'No!' She laughed, but got up abruptly and almost ran to where the dripping spaniel had dropped its stick, before adding, with all the lightness she could muster, 'but before you expire, do tell me of any last requests and I shall be happy to see they are carried out.'

'Heartless—heartless,' he reproached her softly as he watched her bend lithely and throw the stick with an easy competency not often seen outside of Mr Lord's new cricket ground. 'How can you be so heartless at sunset, beside a waterfall of rainbows?'

'I daresay I have not read enough of the latest novels,' she said as she watched the spaniel plunge into the shallows of the pool again. 'But it is beautiful, isn't it? I shall miss coming here.'

'Why should you miss it? So far as I am concerned, you may come here whenever you wish.'

She started as his voice came from immediately behind her shoulder. He had moved as silently as an Apache warrior across the muddy grass until he was a scant pace behind her. She turned, and then wished she had not as he met her gaze. She felt her heart leap and race beneath her ribs as if she had suddenly found herself between a she-bear and its cub. It was ridiculous, she told herself, ridiculous to think he had meant that nonsense about kissing her, ridiculous as this soaring feeling of happiness because he seemed to like her.

'That is very good of you, but I should not like to intrude.' Her words came in a rush.

'I should count your presence an advantage rather than an intrusion.'

His voice was soft, warm, like his blue eyes as he sought and held her gaze. 'So promise me you will come here again, whenever you wish?'

Annabel had been right, she thought wryly. He was seductive, far more dangerous than any of the trappers she had encountered while staying at Lilian's boarding house in St Louis. And this was no polite invitation from one neighbour to another to visit his garden. Any well-bred young lady would refuse such an invitation without hesitation.

But then, she wasn't a well-bred young lady, she was Janey Hilton, colonial and daughter of a millhand. And Janey Hilton was tired of a life that held no more danger and excitement than taking a fence on her horse. . .tired of trying to behave like an English lady and being constantly reminded that she had failed.

'Thank you, I will,' she said, holding his gaze steadily.

'You will? Alone?' He could not quite hide his surprise.

'Yes,' she replied with a calm that she was very far from feeling. 'It is a very special place for me.'

'And for me—now.'

It was her turn to be caught off-guard by his sudden unexpected seriousness; she let her gaze drop to the ground.

'Why is it so special for you? Because it reminds you of home?' he asked as he, too, dropped his gaze, and flicked a stone into the water with the toe of his top boot. 'Or did you meet with your betrothed here? No—don't answer that,' he said as he heard her sudden intake of breath. 'I had no right to ask such a question.'

'No, you did not,' she agreed, staring at the ripples that spread out from where the stone had sunk, wondering how they had come so far so fast. It was, she thought, as if they had known each other for years, not a few minutes.

'The answer is no,' she said quietly. 'Edward would never have considered meeting me in such a place alone, even if I had suggested it—he would have considered it far too improper. He was always very concerned for my reputation. He was a curate and very principled.'

'They usually are, until it comes to getting a lucrative living or catching an heiress,' he said cynically.

'That is unfair. He was a good man. He did a great deal for the poor and he cared for me, not for my money, I am sure of it.' But was she? The words sounded hollow, even to her own ears. Of late, she had begun to wonder about Edward, wonder if he was all she had once thought him. . .wonder if he would have been so prepared to over-look her shortcomings, or quite so supportive of her efforts to improve conditions for the poorer families in the village if she had not been her grandfather's heir.

'I am sorry,' he said as he watched her face. 'Cynicism becomes something of a habit.'

'Like flippancy?' She gave him the ghost of a smile, remembering their first encounter in the lane.

'I am afraid so.' He smiled back at her ruefully. 'But—'

'Jem!' she interrupted him sharply, horrified that for these few minutes she had forgotten the very reason she had come to meet him 'Oh, have you had any success?'

'No, I am afraid not.' He looked away as he answered. 'I had hoped to call in a favour from the Home Secretary and obtain a pardon for him, but—'

'He refused,' she said flatly. She had not realised, until this moment, just how much trust she had placed in him or how much she had hoped she would not have to put her other plan into action.

'Not exactly.' He shook his head. 'The government fell shortly after I reached town. Wellington has resigned and, unfortunately, we have a new Home Secretary.'

'But couldn't you ask the new Home Secretary?'

'Melbourne?' He shook his dark head a second time. 'Lord Melbourne does not hold any affection for me. I was a friend of his wife, Caroline Lamb, and of Lord Byron, you see.' Then he gave a wry smile as he saw her blank expression. 'You don't see. . .you were probably playing with your dolls then.'

'I was more likely helping my mother deliver a neighbour's child or my father harness the oxen,' she said shortly, feeling as if a chasm had suddenly opened up between them as she saw shock ripple across his face. She had been a fool to think him different, a fool to think that he might like the real Janey Hilton.

'I suppose it must be a very different life for young women who live on the frontier,' he said after a moment of silence.

'Different is something of an understatement.' She was brisk. The use of the word 'women' rather than 'ladies' had not escaped her after four years in England. 'You have to grow up fast on the frontier, Mr Lindsay,' she added sharply, as he opened his mouth to say something. 'Just as the sons and daughters of labourers must in this country. Now, if you will excuse me—' she turned abruptly from the pool '—I really must go back, before I am missed.'

'Wait!' He strode after her. 'I did not mean to upset you and I am truly sorry I have not been able to do more for Jem.'

She stopped and turned to look at him, and to her surprise found that she believed him.

'It is not your fault.' She sighed. 'And I am very grateful that you at least tried to help him. You haven't upset me. . .it is not your fault that you are a—' She faltered, struggling for the right words.

'A patronising, arrogant society dandy who has never had to step outside of his gilded and well-padded cage?' His dark brows lifted quizzically.

'I should not have put it quite so rudely,' she said a little ashamedly.

'No, but you thought it.' He grinned at her.

'True,' she confessed ruefully, 'and I apologise for it.'

'Then will you allow me the honour of escorting you home? It will be absolutely dark in the woods.'

'Oh, there is no need,' she protested politely. 'I shall be perfectly safe. I am not afraid of the dark—it is not as if you have bears or Indians in England.'

'I insist,' he said and turned away momentarily to whistle to the spaniel.

'You insist?' Her brows lifted and so, for no reason, did her heart as he returned his attention to her. 'Then I suppose I have no choice in the matter.'

'None,' he said, offering her his arm.

It was politeness, she told herself, as she put out her gloved hand and tentatively let her fingers rest upon the sleeve of his coat and they began to walk towards the cliff path, falling easily into step, nothing but ordinary politeness. There was no reason for her pulse to race, her heart to pound. No reason at all.

'No, Tess! Down!' His exclamation as they halted at the base of the cliff path came too late for her to avoid the spaniel's enthusiastic greeting as it caught up with them and transferred a considerable amount of mud, water and pond weed from its coat and paws to the skirts of her black wool pelisse.

'I am so sorry—she's still very young and gets rather out of hand,' he apologised. 'Lie down, Tess!'

Tess shot off up the cliff path.

He muttered an imprecation under his breath and then turned to her. 'I hope she has not done too much damage—I have a handkerchief somewhere.'

'It really doesn't matter,' she said, laughing as she watched the spaniel turn and come back down the path again, so fast it turned a somersault at the bottom as it tried to stop at its master's feet.

'Idiot dog!' He laughed, too, as Tess put her muzzle upon the toe of his boot and gazed up at him soufully, the very picture of man's loyal and obedient friend. 'She was the runt of the litter and is terrified of guns. I should have knocked her upon the head at birth—still should, I suppose—'

'But you won't,' she said with a certainty she did not stop to question.

'No.' He gave a half laugh. 'As you have obviously perceived, a tender heart beats beneath this grim exterior.'

'I should not have called you grim,' she replied, giving him a brief sideways glance. 'A little weathered, perhaps.'

'Thank you.' He inclined his head to her in a mocking bow. 'Dare I allow myself to be flattered?'

'I do not think you have any need of my flattery. I suspect even the youngest son of an Earl receives more than enough.'

He laughed again. 'That was definitely not complimentary, Miss Hilton, though I am afraid it was all too true. Have you always been so brutally honest with your friends?'

'Yes,' she said sweetly. 'I find real friends always prefer honesty to pretence.'

He smiled and conceded her the victory with the slightest nod of his head. 'I had better go first,' he said, gesturing to the rocky beginning of the cliff path, 'then I can help you over the difficult places.'

'Thank you,' she acquiesced politely with a fleeting smile. She had climbed this path a hundred times without mishap and, in her childhood, rock faces as sheer as the one the water tumbled from, not to mention trees. Daniel had always got her to do the climbing when they had been looking for bird eggs—of the two of them, she'd had a better head for heights.

But that had been a different world, a different life, she thought, as he turned and held out his hands to her after scrambling over the first few boulders. English ladies were expected to be fragile, helpless creatures, and for once, as she put her hands into his and he smiled at her, she found she did not particularly mind furthering the illusion.

The path was steep enough to preclude much conversation and they climbed mostly in a companionable silence, with Tess padding quietly behind them.

He had been right. It was almost pitch black once they entered the woods. Out of old ingrained habit, she paused, listening and cataloguing the sounds in her mind and relaxing as she heard nothing but the natural chorus of the wood at night: the cooing of wood pigeons, the flutter and swoop of an owl, the squeal of a shrew and the rustle of leaves beneath Tess's paws as she nosed around their feet, seeking a scent. It was only as she went to move forward again that she realised he had also halted and was listening.

'Sorry—' he turned his head to smile at her in the gloom '—I've never walked into a wood at night without stopping to listen since my troop was ambushed in Spain.'

'You were a soldier?' She was surprised. He was so unlike the army officers who dined with the Filmores from time to time.

'Briefly, in my misspent youth.' He shrugged as they walked on. 'I did not particularly enjoy the experience. The Peninsular War was savage enough, but Waterloo— that was simply a slaughterhouse, and killed any remaining hankering to cover myself in military glory. I decided twenty was far too young to die and resigned my commission the moment we were sure Napoleon was beaten.'

'You were six years older than Jem is now,' she said flatly.

'I know.' The self-mocking tone left his voice. 'And I wish to heaven there was something else I could do. . .I feel as if I have failed you.'

'No. No,' she protested, knowing she had been unfair. 'At least you tried to do something for Jem, which is far more than I expected of a—'

'A worthless rake and a dandy?' he supplied wryly.

'That is what you thought me at first glance, is it not?'

'At first glance, perhaps. But I could not count anyone who made the speech that you did to Parliament entirely worthless, Mr Lindsay.'

'Speech?' He looked at her blankly for a moment.

'The one defending the rights of the labouring poor.'

'Ah—' he stumbled suddenly upon a tree root '—that speech. There is something, perhaps, you should know— I am no radical, Miss Hilton. I sit on the Tory side.'

'Why?'

'Why?' He echoed her question in astonishment, as if he had never considered any other possibility. 'Well, because my father did, and his before him, I suppose,' he said after a moment of silence.

'That's the worst reason I have heard yet,' she said drily.

'Thank you,' he said with equal dryness.

She sighed. 'Oh, well, I suppose it is not the label which matters, it is what you say. And you said all the things I should like to, except that you did it a great deal better than I ever could—'

'I doubt that. I suspect you would make a formidable advocate of any cause, Miss Hilton.'

She sensed rather than saw his smile in the gloom.

'And is that what you thought of me at first glance? That I was formidable?'

'No. My first thought was that I should like to take you to my bed.'

'Really, how strange. . .' she said after a moment, biting her lip to stop herself from laughing. He was impossible. Quite impossible. But did he really think he could shock her so easily when she had lived most of her sixteenth year in a St Louis boarding house?

'Strange?' He sounded faintly piqued by her reaction. 'No man would think so, I assure you.'

'That was not what I meant,' she replied, after the most fractional of hesitations. 'I thought it was strange because I was wondering whether or not I should like you to be one of my lovers.'

'One of your lovers!' He halted so abruptly that she found herself dragged backwards. 'Great God, how many have you had?'

'Not nearly so many as you, I fear,' she lamented. 'There are so *few* men that I find both interesting and desirable.' She could hardly keep the bubble of laughter out of her voice.

For a moment he stared down at her, trying to discern her face in the darkness, and then started to laugh. 'I have just been hoist with my own petard, have I not?'

'You should not have tried to shock me,' she said as they started to walk on again.

'I am beginning to think that is impossible,' he said, shaking his head. 'But, do you know, what shocks *me* most, Miss Hilton, is that you came to be betrothed to some milksop of a curate. What did the poor devil die of? Heart failure?'

'No.' Her expression became closed and the laughter left her face abruptly. 'And he was not a milksop!'

'I am sorry.' He held her arm more tightly as she tried to walk ahead. 'I did not mean to intrude upon your grief and I had no right to say that of a man I have never met.'

'No,' she said as they fell into step again, 'you did not.'

'I suppose he would have helped you in your efforts to save Jem and succeeded, most like,' he said sourly, and then wondered what the devil was wrong with him to behave so mawkishly.

'I am sure he would have pleaded for Jem to be treated mercifully,' she said a little too quickly, then realised that she was not sure at all any more. There was something that nagged at her, something that had been at the edge of her mind since the day of the accident, but she could never quite remember what it was, what they had been discussing in the minutes before the staircase in the Tower had collapsed.

They walked on in an awkward silence, each sunk in their own uncomfortable thoughts. And then, quite suddenly, they stepped out of the darkness into the comparatively lightness of dusk that turned Pettridge Park to every hue of silver and grey.

By mutual, unspoken consent they both halted in the shadow of a large beech at the edge of the Hall's garden. Pools of light shone out from windows of rooms in which curtains had not yet been drawn. Glancing up, she could see Mr Filmore, reading beside the drawing-room fire, Annabel playing the piano, and Piers leaning lazily across its lid.

'It does not seem you have been missed,' he said as a maid suddenly appeared at the window, and the scene was abruptly blotted out by a sweep of lined brocade.

'No,' she agreed succinctly as she remained staring at the curtained window.

He stared at her, studying her face in the dusk. For all her sharpness, her apparent self-confidence, her fierce honesty, she suddenly looked so very young, vulnerable, wistful and alone that he wanted to take her in his arms— though for very different reasons to those he had had until a moment or so ago. But now—now he was getting distinct twinges of conscience about his pursuit of Miss Janey Hilton, and about what the consequences might be for her.

'I had better go back,' he said. 'Your guardians might think it a trifle odd for me to be walking alone with you in the dark.'

'They'd think you odd for choosing to walk with me at all.' She gave a slightly ragged laugh.

'Then they have no taste,' he said softly.

'All these compliments, you could turn my head, Mr Lindsay.' She strove to sound light.

'Like this?' He lifted a hand and placed his palm against her cheek, turning her face and tilting it upwards so she found herself staring into his shadowed face.

'I was speaking metaphorically,' she said a second— or was it minutes?—later. She did not know. She only knew that her face was burning beneath his hand, and that the world had seemed to stop again the moment he had touched her.

'Really? How stupid of me not to realise,' he mocked her softly and himself for being such a fool as to think she did not know the rules of the game. But there was no hurry, he told himself as his hand dropped away. Janey Hilton was like a rare vintage wine—she should be enjoyed slowly.

'You had better go in, Miss Hilton,' he said as she remained motionless.

'Yes,' she agreed, 'but I cannot until you let go of my arm.'

'Of course,' he said, but still did not release her.

She swallowed. 'Is there something else, Mr Lindsay?'

'Jem?' he said, not knowing where or how the sudden anxiety had arisen in his mind, but only that she had been too quiet upon the subject. 'You have not any wild or reckless schemes for his rescue in mind have you?'

'No,' she said. It was not a lie. Wild and reckless simply would not do. It was going to take careful planning to save Jem. And a miracle to save herself from falling in love with Jonathan Lindsay.

'Good.' He exhaled and let go of her arm. 'Because this is England, and in England, the rule of law is upheld mercilessly.'

'You need not tell me that,' she said, half-relieved, half-disappointed that he had believed her so easily.

'And neither need I tell you, I hope, that such strategies as exchanging clothes with the prisoner, or copying keys with wax and the like, only work in the pages of fiction.'

'I know.'

'Then I'll say goodnight.'

'Goodnight.' She turned and began to walk towards the house.

'Wait!' he called softly after her. 'How are you to get in?'

She stopped, turned and looked back at him. 'Why, through the door, Mr Lindsay. You did not think I was going to climb the ivy in my petticoats, did you? If I had meant to do that, I'd have worn my buckskins.'

'Breeches?' He sounded shocked again, she thought with a smile.

'Buckskins are what the Indians wear, men and women—' she began to expound, and then laughed. 'Never mind, Mr Lindsay, I'll explain another time. Goodnight.'

'Goodnight, Miss Hilton.' His voice floated after her as she walked across the drive. And she was aware of him standing in the growing darkness, watching her, until the moment the great front door swung shut behind her.

She stood for a moment in the dimly lit hall, a half-smile on her lips. Worried as she was about Jem, and the estate, somehow, she had the absurd conviction that everything would be all right now Jonathan Lindsay had come to Southbrook.

Outside, at the same moment, Jonathan Lindsay frowned. He was feeling unaccountably guilty and it was not an emotion he was accustomed to. The trouble was, he liked Miss Janey Hilton, liked the way she looked at him, liked her cool directness and the way she smiled. He swore silently. What the devil was wrong with him? He was thinking like some greenhorn. She was just another woman, another conquest to be made. . .wasn't she?

He turned away without answering his own question, whistled to Tess and strode back into the woods.

'Jane! There you are!' Mrs Filmore, her ample figure tightly upholstered in cherry silk, greeted Janey majestically from halfway up the broad flight of stairs. 'I have been looking all over for you. Mr Filmore has relented. You may come down and join us—when you are suitably dressed, of course.' She frowned as she glanced derisively at Janey's besmirched pelisse.

'I'd rather go to my room, thank you.' Janey gave Mrs Filmore her most benign smile. 'I've been walking in the gardens and I am rather tired.'

'Walking alone in the dark!' Mrs Filmore gave a long-suffering sigh. 'Really, Jane dear, you cannot go on like this. A little eccentricity in the first throes of grief is allowable, but poor Mr Grey has been dead almost a year now—though the ordeal you suffered would be enough to turn anyone's mind.'

'There is nothing wrong with my mind.' Janey sighed as she began to climb the stairs. 'And I should prefer it if you and Mr Filmore would stop implying that there is to anyone who cares to listen.'

'Well,' Mrs Filmore snorted, drawing herself up to her full, rather limited, height, 'would you rather that I had explained to Mr Lindsay that your extraordinary behaviour this morning was learned from the female brothel-keeper with whom you lived for the year following your parents' death?'

'Lilian was not a brothel-keeper,' Janey retorted. 'She owned a boarding house.'

'A boarding house! A wooden hut where men drank liquor, and women sold their services.' Mrs Filmore gave a theatrical shudder. 'If I had been your poor dear late grandpapa, I should never have brought you back here.'

'Sometimes, Mrs Filmore,' Janey muttered as she began to climb the stairs, 'I wish that he had not.' But she knew that was not true, not any longer. It had not been true from the moment Jonathan Lindsay had first smiled at her.

'About time, Jono, where the devil have you been?' Lord Derwent said complainingly as Jonathan entered the library of Southbrook House. 'This place is freezing, and I've been ringing for ages for your man to bring some more wood for the fire. Had to put some books on—only Mrs Radcliffe,' he added as Jonathan frowned. 'Didn't think you'd miss those.'

'Probably not,' Jonathan conceded, as he stepped up to the fire and held his hands out to the blaze, 'but I'd rather you did not burn any more. The reason the servants have not answered is because the bell wires are all in need of replacement. You will have to go to the door and shout.'

'Shout? Didn't think of that,' Lord Derwent grumbled, leaning back in a creaking chair upholstered with well-worn green leather and putting his feet up upon the brass fender. 'And where have you been?' he asked as his brown gaze took in Jonathan's muddy boots.

'Playing in the garden and walking in the woods,' Jonathan said with a grin, sitting down in the opposite chair.

'Playing in the garden! Walking in the woods on a November evening!' Lord Derwent scowled, his fastidious nose wrinkling as the wet and muddy Tess pushed against his boots in an effort to get closer to the fire. 'And to think we could have been at White's, or eating Wilkin's steak and oyster pie.'

'Woods have their compensations,' Jonathan said, 'in the very delicious shape of Miss Hilton.'

'What!' Lord Derwent's feet dropped from the fender to the floor. 'You've not had an assignation with Miss Hilton already! How the deuce did you manage that?'

'Very easily.' Jonathan laughed. 'I do hope you've told your horseman to get Triton fit for me, Perry. Winning this wager is going to be easier than beating you at cards.'

'After you've failed to save her arsonist?' Lord Derwent shook his head. 'I'll believe it when I see it. A walk in the woods is one thing but—' he made an eloquent gesture '—is quite another.'

'I haven't failed yet. We are going back to Town.'

'Hurrah!' Lord Derwent's countenance brightened immeasurably.

'As soon as we have dined.'

'Tonight?' Lord Derwent groaned. 'But it's just started to rain.'

'There's not much time and I want to see Caroline Norton.'

'Caro Norton.' Lord Derwent looked at him in surprise. 'I thought it was all over between you years ago.'

'It was. But we have retained a fondness for one another.' Jonathan smiled. 'Melbourne is besotted with her and, where he might not do me a favour—'

'He will do anything for the beautiful Mrs Norton,' Lord Derwent said slowly, 'and Mrs Norton will do anything for you.'

'Exactly, Perry, exactly.' Jonathan laughed. 'I don't know why I did not think of it before.'

'Probably because you haven't been thinking clearly since you first saw that female,' Lord Derwent muttered darkly. 'If it wasn't for her, you'd not have contemplated taking on this place for a moment.'

'What did you say?' Jonathan said, lifting his gaze from the flames of the fire into which he had been staring.

'Nothing.' Lord Derwent sighed dejectedly. 'I'll go and shout for Brown.'

Chapter Four

The chalky Roman road stretched like a pale ribbon ahead, in the pallid dawn light, as Jonathan Lindsay urged his tired horse on. The long ride from London had left him cold, hungry and impatient to see Jane Hilton's face when he told her that he had succeeded in saving her arsonist.

He checked his horse as the road dropped steeply down into a hollow lined with hawthorns and scrub. He let the animal come down to a walk, glad of the respite from the biting wind that had cut through even his many-caped topcoat and caused him the loss of a new beaver hat. For a county so soft and pleasant in summer, Wiltshire could be damned bleak in winter, he thought, especially the edge of Salisbury Plain.

But then, as he rounded a sharp turn, all thought of the weather left his head. A fair distance ahead of him was a female rider, a rider he recognised more by instinct than any logic.

'Miss Hilton!' His shout was lost in the wind. For a moment, as she brought her horse to a halt, he thought she had heard him. But then, as he saw her dismount without so much as a glance behind her, he realised she was still oblivious to his presence.

'What the devil is she doing?' he muttered to his mount, which responded by coming to an uncertain halt itself.

He watched the distant figure with growing curiosity as she seemed first to address the hawthorns, and then cast her horse loose, shooing it away. Next she took her off her hat, threw it down and stamped upon it, and then cast herself down upon the chalky road to lie prone across its centre.

And then from behind him, he caught the sound of hooves and the clatter of a carriage wheel borne forward by the wind. Looking back along the straight road, he saw a dark chaise, one which seemed to have more than its share of guards and bars upon its windows. He stared at it disbelievingly as understanding came with devastating clarity.

Prisoners were being transferred from Salisbury to Dorchester for the hangings, the chaise would already have slowed for the steep descent into the hollow, and would certainly stop at the sight of a lady, apparently having fallen from her horse. And the hollow was a perfect spot for an ambush with its high banks and ample cover. An ambush. No he shook his head at his own thought. He had to be wrong. Jane Hilton might have a strong sense of justice, but surely she would not be so reckless, so foolhardy, not for the sake of some poacher's boy, would she?

He spurred his horse forward into a gallop as he answered his own question. The steep chalk track was slippery and he prayed his horse would keep its footing as it plunged and slithered towards Janey's prone form.

Hearing the rapid approach of hooves, Janey shut her eyes, praying that the chaise would be able to stop in time. If it didn't, it would run her over. But there was something wrong—the hoofbeats were far too light, too fast. There must be an outrider—why hadn't she thought of that? Supposing his pistol had not come from the Salisbury Gaol's armoury? She had been so sure she had arranged it so no one would get hurt.

She held her breath as she heard the horse and rider come to a slithering stamping halt upon the chalky mud, so near she felt the ground shake beneath her head as the rider dismounted. Then a moment later a hand was upon her arm, shaking her roughly, ignoring what she had hoped was a pathetic groan.

'Get up!'

She opened her eyes and stared in disbelief at the man bending over her. It was Jonathan Lindsay, his dark hair windswept, his eyes as dark a blue as his mud-bedecked top coat as he glared down at her.

'You!' She gasped with horror as he lifted her bodily to her feet, momentarily too astonished to resist. But then, as she heard the approaching rattle of the chaise, she began to struggle frantically.

'Go away,' she hissed at him. 'Please just go away, you will ruin everything!'

'And you will get yourself shot!' he retorted fiercely, dragging her forcibly to the side of the road, an arm clamped about her waist.

'Let me go! You don't understand—' She wrestled to free herself in vain.

''Ere, you! Let her be!' A burly looking man, his face

masked with a red and white kerchief, arose suddenly from the hawthorns and there were other rustlings from the other side.

'Get down, Will!' Janey half-sobbed as she heard the squealing of the chaise's brakes being applied at the top of the hollow.

'You heard her! Get down, damn you! Unless you want to end up on the gallows as well!' Jonathan reinforced the instruction. 'And leave the talking to me! All of you!' he added as he glimpsed the shadowy shapes of three or four others in the bushes on the other side of the road.

'Please, please help us, it's his only chance!' Janey turned her face up to his, her eyes pleading. 'Everything is arranged—there is a boat waiting at Poole to take him to France—'

'No. Absolutely not. There's no need.'

'There's every need,' she protested, struggling furiously to escape his grasp.

'Shut up! And keep your face hidden or we'll be the talk of the county!' As the chaise was almost upon them, he turned her against him, and held her face against the wall of his chest, so tightly she could hardly breathe, let alone protest.

'Trouble, sir?' the driver of the chaise asked, giving them a wary look and nodding to the guards to have their pistols ready.

'No, no—' Jonathan gave them a cheerful smile '—a small domestic disagreement—that's all—' he said grittily as Janey kicked him in the shin. 'On your way, there is no need to stop.'

'Have the same trouble with me own woman, sir.' The

driver grinned. 'A good spanking usually stops her nonsense.'

'Excellent advice, I am sure,' Jonathan grated out as Janey kicked him a second time. 'But, please, don't let us delay you.'

The driver grinned and whipped up his horses again, and the chaise clattered on.

'I hate you!' Janey spat out, jerking back from Jonathan as he released her. 'I hate you!' And then, as she stared after the chaise and saw the small pale face peering back at them from behind the barred window, she made a helpless gesture. 'Look at him!' Her eyes filled with tears and her voice broke as she gestured to the disappearing chaise. 'He is a child! Just a child.'

'And you are behaving like one!' he snapped. 'You and your—friends, you could all have been shot. The guards are armed!'

'I am not a fool! All their pistols have powder so damp they would not go off if you dropped them into a furnace!' she snapped, rubbing her hand across her eyes.

'How the devil can you be sure of that?'

'Because Will's cousin works in the armoury at Salisbury Gaol.'

'My God! How many of you are there in this conspiracy?' He groaned. And then shook his head. 'No, don't tell me that. I'm a magistrate and a Member of Parliament, for God's sake. I don't want to know.'

He turned suddenly to where Will was standing looking at them uncertainly. 'You, take the others and get out of here. This has not happened, I have not seen you, understand?'

'Yes, sir,' Will agreed sullenly, and four other masked

men all carrying staves stood up looking sheepish. 'But Miss Hilton—'

'I shall see Miss Hilton safely home. Now, go before anyone sees you here!'

Janey stared despairingly after them as they strode off across the grey-green turf of the down, moving with the long, ground covering stride of countrymen. Then she rounded upon Jonathan, her eyes blazing close with fury, her hands balled into fists.

'How could you! We could have saved him and you have ruined everything! Oh! I hate you! I wish that you were dead! I wish—' She broke off, incoherent with rage as she saw the amusement in his eyes.

Jem would die and he was laughing at her. She jabbed at him with her right fist, aiming straight for his arrogant, aristocratic nose.

'Temper, temper,' he said, as he ducked aside and caught her wrist. 'Didn't anyone tell you that ladies are supposed to slap—not deliver right hooks like a professional gentleman? Who taught you to fight? Surely not your namby-pamby curate?'

'No!' she seared, twisting to free herself. 'Let go of me! If Edward were here, you would not dare to treat me so.'

'If your milksop of a curate were here, I should hand you over to him with pleasure, but—'

'He was not a milksop!' she shouted, swinging at him with her other fist. A blow which he did not duck quite quickly enough, so her hand grazed his cheekbone. 'He was a good man! He helped people who were less fortunate than himself! He might not have had your wealth, looks and wit, but at least he made a difference to people's lives, which is something more than you will ever do!'

'A curate who practised what he preached.' His mouth curled derisively. 'He sounds too good to be true. Are you sure he did not merely have his sights set upon your inheritance?'

'That is a monstrous thing to say! But then, someone like you would never understand someone who puts others before himself!'

'And you do, I suppose? Were you really thinking of the good of those men who have just left by involving them in this hare-brained scheme?' He was scathing. 'If things had gone wrong, which seems more than likely, what do think would have happened to them? This is England, Miss Hilton, not the backwoods of America! There is no wilderness for fugitives to disappear into and make a new life. They would have been hunted down, tried and most likely hung.'

'I shared that risk,' she began defensively.

He gave a derisive laugh. 'A beautiful, young heiress is rarely judged the same as a labourer, Miss Hilton. You'd probably have got off with a plea of insanity—which I begin to think is not so far off the mark.'

'Yes. You're right, I know you are right—' she said miserably as she met his relentless blue gaze. 'But I had to do something—I had to try. Jem is innocent. I know he is innocent. And they are going to hang him. . .' Her voice cracked and she bit her lip to stop the tears she could feel welling up behind her eyes.

'No,' he said more gently, 'they are not going to hang him. I have a full pardon, signed by the Home Secretary, here—' he patted the pocket of his coat '—which, when you have done with assaulting me, I shall deliver to the Governor of Dorchester Gaol.'

'What?' She stared at him, her eyes very wide and glittering with unshed tears. 'You have a pardon?'

'Yes.' He smiled at her. 'Happy now, Miss Hilton? Jem should be home with his mother by tomorrow morning at the latest.'

'Yes, yes,' she said. 'It's wonderful. I don't know how you managed it.'

'Better perhaps that you don't,' he said with a smile as he thought of the beautiful Caro Norton and the flattery he had employed.

'I don't know how to apologise. Or how to thank you—' She broke off helplessly.

'I believe a kiss is customary upon such occasions,' he said matter-of-factly as he bent to pick up her hat from the ground.

'A kiss!' She stared at him, her hazel eyes wide, her heart racing faster than it had when she heard the chaise approaching.

'Yes.' He smiled as he straightened and pummelled her hat back into some sort of shape. 'Merely out of gratitude, of course.'

'Of course.' She did not quite succeed in matching his tone as he stepped up to her and placed the hat upon her head, standing so close she had to tilt her head up to see his face. 'So long as you understood it was for no other reason. . .'

'Perfectly,' he said cheerfully, his gaze never leaving hers as he crossed the satin ribbons and pulled them up beneath her chin and tied them into a bow. 'Why else would you kiss someone you hate?'

'Oh, t-this is r-ridiculous!' she found herself stammering as he stroked a strand of her dishevelled hair away from her mouth with a gloved fingertip. 'I can't just kiss you.'

'Why not?' He smiled in a way that made her want to murder him. 'I presume you know how, considering the legion of lovers you laid claim to the other day?' The amusement in his eyes was barely hidden.

Janey bit her lip. He knew, or was almost certain, she had lied. But she was not going to admit it, not so that he could laugh at her. She had made enough of a fool of herself for one day.

'And you must have kissed your curate upon occasion?' he added innocently.

'Yes, but only once!' she snapped. 'And that was like this. . .' Some lunatic irresistible impulse made her go on tiptoe and touch her lips fleetingly to the corner of his mouth.

Now who was shocking who? she thought triumphantly, as she heard the catch of his breath.

'I see,' he said after a moment of frozen stillness in which his hands remained immobile upon the ribbons beneath her chin. 'He did not do this, then?'

He let go of the ribbons and put his hands upon her shoulders, and drew her to him. She shut her eyes, knowing she had either just made the worse mistake of her life or—

'No.' The word was no more than a shaken breath as he brushed his lips over hers, once, twice before lingering in the gentlest of kisses.

'Or this. . .' he murmured, as he folded her into his arms and kissed her again in an entirely different way—a way she had heard Annabel boast to her friends of having experienced. A way that made her momentarily freeze with shock at the invasion of her mouth. And then she was lost, melted by the warmth of his lips, his tongue. Her lips softened, yielding to him completely. She pressed closer to him, instinctively seeking relief for this new aching heaviness in her breasts, her whole body.

He was hard, both mouth and body, hard against this feeling of softness that was drowning her, until she felt boneless, helpless, utterly female. Her gloved hands moved involuntarily against his caped coat; she wanted to be closer, closer than these layers of cloth would allow. She belonged to this man, wanted to be one with him. . .it was as if everything, the long hazardous journey to England and the last four years of loneliness and boredom had all been bringing her to this moment, this man. . .

This man who would undoubtedly laugh at her if she ever expressed such ridiculous sentiments, said a cynical voice at the back of her mind. To Jonathan Lindsay, society rake, this was probably nothing more than an opportunity for amusement and she, if she had an ounce of sense left, should never let him know it was anything more for her.

She withdrew abruptly from his embrace. He made no attempt to restrain her, but his eyebrows lifted as he met her wide dark eyes with a quizzical stare.

'Well,' she said, a little more shakily than she would have liked, as he continued to stare at her in silence, 'I hope you consider yourself properly thanked, Mr Lindsay?'

'No,' he said and smiled, a wide slow smile as he lifted a hand to stroke back a wing of hair that had blown over her face. 'Improperly, perhaps.'

He was so sure of himself, so practised, she thought,

so damnably composed and confident while she—she was dissolving beneath his touch like snow in sunshine, as probably had scores of simpering misses like Annabel, she told herself fiercely. Well, she would show him Janey Hilton was made out of different cloth!

'Well, if you are not satisfied, I suppose I could try again,' she said, as flippantly as she could manage while his fingers slid through the silky mass of her dishevelled hair and came to rest upon her shoulder.

His hand stilled and she heard the short, sharp intake of his breath as he stared at her, and she had to fight down the impulse to laugh. For all his sophistication, she could still surprise him.

'Thank you for the offer,' he said, very drily. 'But perhaps I should warn you, Miss Hilton, that I am not likely to be satisfied with a kiss and our surroundings are hardly appropriate for a more thorough expression of your gratitude.'

It was her turn to catch her breath. The darkness in his voice, in his eyes, and her body's instant response to the image his words aroused brought home to her quite suddenly that she was playing a dangerous game with a man who had long since thrown away the rule book. But then, she could hardly criticize him for that, when she had never even read it, she thought, the corners of her mouth lifting.

She lifted her chin and gave him a blithe smile. 'I suppose it would be rather uncomfortable. Lilian always said the outdoors was not to be recommended in winter.'

'Uncomfortable!' He gave a splutter of disbelieving laughter. 'Is that all you have to say?'

'What would you have me say?' she asked with deliberate innocence.

'A little outrage, some hot defence of your virtue would at least assist me in my attempt to behave like a gentlemen should towards a lady—' he said gratingly. 'And who the devil is Lilian? Was she your governess?'

'Not exactly. . .' Her mouth curved at the unlikely vision of Lilian as a governess. 'She was a friend. She looked after me when my parents died until my grandfather came for me. She kept a—lodging house in St Louis.'

'A lodging house. I see.' His brows lifted. 'And do I take it that Lilian also taught you the useful manoeuvre with which you laid Master Filmore low?'

'Yes, and a great deal more besides. I could have knocked you down, Mr Lindsay, the moment you set a hand on me, if I had wished to—but I guess I didn't want to. . .' she confessed with a shy, slightly uncertain smile.

'You didn't want to. . .' he repeated slowly, almost accusingly, as he wondered what was wrong with him. She had just about handed him an engraved invitation to seduce her. The wager with Perry was as good as won if her response to his kiss and her smile was anything to go by. So why did he feel so damnably guilty as she smiled at him, her eyes still soft, her lips still faintly swollen and dark from his kiss? It was not as if she were some innocent fresh from the schoolroom. By the sound of it, she had seen more of life than many women twice her age.

'No.' She shrugged, wondering why she felt as if she were gambling with her life. 'I suppose I must like you, Mr Lindsay, perhaps more than I suspect is wise.'

'Really?' He gave a brittle laugh, as her blatant honesty

caught him completely off guard. 'I cannot think why you should. You would do better to trust your first impression of me, Miss Hilton. You had me down as a dandy who cares for little but his own pleasure and amusement, did you not?'

'Yes,' she admitted a little ashamedly. 'But I know now I am wrong. You have gone to such trouble to save Jem.'

'An aberration in an otherwise conscienceless life,' he said scathingly. 'So save your halo for your beloved curate's blessed memory, it will not fit me.'

'I am not likely to mistake you for a candidate for sainthood,' she said with a half-smile as she caught the edge in his tone. 'And in case you are wondering, I am not some sheltered debutante who is likely to mistake a kiss for a declaration, nor am I seeking to entrap you.'

She turned away as she spoke and putting two fingers into her mouth she whistled to her huge black horse, which left off cropping the springy downland turf and came trotting up to her.

'Where the devil did you get that?' He could not quite disguise his opinion of the black gelding as it approached. It was practically a carthorse.

It was a carthorse, he amended as the gelding came up and nudged at Janey with its enormous head. It had to be a good eighteen hands and it had chest, quarters and legs that would carry a twenty-stone man all day without noticing. It was hardly a typical lady's mount, but then, he thought wryly, Janey Hilton was not a typical lady.

'Looks are not everything, Mr Lindsay,' Janey said a little defensively as she stepped forward to catch the horse's reins. 'He jumps like a chaser, but he's as mild as milk—and he could pull a wagon if he had to, which is more than that thoroughbred of yours could do.'

'I don't doubt it.' He smiled. 'I only wish I had had the sense to choose something like him when I went on my first campaign.'

'I still cannot imagine you as a soldier.' She stopped in the midst of bundling up the twenty yards or so of her trailing habit skirt over her arm and stared at him.

'Wellington told me once I had the makings of a good one,' he said as he put his hands about her waist in readiness to lift her up into her saddle. 'You don't have to look quite so astonished, Miss Hilton. I understand that, as far as junior officers go, I acquitted myself very well.'

'I don't doubt that.' She gave him a mischievous glance from beneath the rather battered and lopsided brim of her hat. 'For a dandy, you do have your compensations, Mr Lindsay.'

'I am pleased to here it.' With a soft laugh, he caught her by the waist with both hands and drew her close. 'I suspect you also have compensations for a radical, Miss Hilton,' he murmured against her ear before dropping the lightest, most frustrating of kisses upon her mouth. 'A theory I look forward to exploring. . .'

It was a statement of intent, she thought, her heart beating wildly as he lifted her into her saddle. And she should be outraged—not delighted that he still wanted to see her, even though Jem was saved and any obligation he had towards her more than discharged. She glanced down as he guided her foot into the iron and found herself wanting to reach out and touch his dark, tousled head. He looked up, as if sensing her thought, and smiled before turning away to catch his own horse.

She gathered up her reins and shook out her habit skirt,

then smiled as she watched him swing lithely on to the large grey's back. He rode like one of the trail scouts, she thought, totally at ease and at one with his horse. With his muddied coat, windblown hair and weathered craggy face he did not look in the least like the dandified society rake she had first encountered—in fact, an outsider might consider that she had had quite an effect upon Mr Lindsay's elegant and well-ordered life.

She gave a half-laugh at her own foolishness. It was madness to feel so ridiculously happy on a muddy, windy road at dawn in the company of an out-and-out rake who had treated her with complete impropriety. But then, perhaps, that was because she knew instinctively that he liked her as she liked him. They were two of a kind—she not quite a lady, and Jonathan Lindsay, though he was an aristocrat to his fingertips, not quite a perfect gentleman. If he had been, he would never have kissed an unmarried young woman.

Jonathan, turning in his saddle to ask if she was ready to set off, found his breath catching in his throat as she smiled at him, her face alight and quite startlingly beautiful beneath the fluttering brim of her hat.

'Shall we go?' he said after staring at her for a moment.

'I'll race you—' she laughed back at him over her shoulder, already nudging her horse into a trot down the steep hill '—from the bottom of the hill to the market cross in the village.'

She still felt elated as she strode into the entrance hall of Pettridges, tossing aside her hat and gloves, not caring how much noise she made. It was *her* house, after all.

'Rather unconventional time to ride, ain't it, dear Jane?'

A few days before, Piers's supercilious drawl would have destroyed her mood in a moment, but now she did not care in the slightest. She felt invulnerable to his taunts. Jonathan Lindsay liked her, liked her enough to ride to London and back to please her. So what did she care for the opinion of a louse like Piers?

She turned slowly to face him. He was lounging in the open doorway of the dining room, tapping a crop against his muddy boots.

'I felt like some fresh air,' she said coolly, 'as you did, apparently.'

'Oh, I've been riding all night, one way or the other.' He smiled unpleasantly. 'And what about you? Was it a satisfying ride?'

His gaze lingered on her face for a moment before dropping down with blatant insulting slowness.

Her chin came up, and she smiled. A deliberate, slow smile. 'Very, dear Piers, very.' She aped his tone and had the satisfaction of seeing his eyes widen in surprise. 'Now if you will excuse me, I wish to change before breakfast.'

Turning her back upon him, she swept up the skirt of her habit, and began to ascend the stairs.

'I do hope Mama and Papa don't find out about your extraordinary behaviour, Jane,' Piers called after her. 'They are already anxious about you after your little exhibition in the morning-room. People might begin to think you not quite right in the head.'

She halted to glance down at him over the polished mahogany balustrade. 'I am not a child anymore, Piers. Tell them whatever you wish, I am sure it will not do anything to change their opinion of me.'

'True, it could scarcely be lower,' he sneered.

'Then they will delighted to be quit of me and this house when I attain my twenty-first birthday, will they not?' She smiled and, not waiting for his answer, continued on up the stairs.

'Jane, dear, here you are at last, we've all been waiting for you.' Mrs Filmore's plump face was all benign smiles beneath her rather unnaturally black curls as Jane came into the dining-room for breakfast.

'I was not aware I was late. The clock has not struck the hour yet,' Janey said, startled as Piers leapt to his feet to pull out a chair for her. Ignoring it, she went around the table to sit beside Annabel, who gave her a speculative look.

'No, no, of course not, it is we that are early,' Mrs Filmore said hastily, shooting a glance at her husband, who was frowning at his kedgeree. 'It is just rather a special day—sad, of course, but life goes on. Poor dear Mr Grey, how you must miss him.'

'Edward?' Janey looked at them blankly. They had hated Edward Grey, hated her engagement.

'It is a year to the day, my dear—' Mrs Filmore's tone was reproving '—a year to the very day since that awful tragedy.'

'Oh.' Feeling more than a little guilty that, of all anniversaries, she had forgotten this one, Janey dropped her eyes to her Wedgwood plate.

'You can come out of your mourning, dear.' Mrs Filmore reached across the table to pat her hand. 'No one will think the worse of you for it now, nor of anyone who has already waited overlong to declare his affection for you.' She sent an adoring glance to the sullen Piers, who forced his thick lips into the semblance of a smile. 'He has suffered, too, my dear, seeing you every day, and not being able to speak, being so sensible of your loss. No wonder he has been a little out of sorts with you. But that's all forgiven and forgotten, isn't it, Frederick?'

'Forgiven and forgotten,' Mr Filmore intoned gravely. Janey looked from husband to wife in total disbelief. In the past, the Filmores' attempts to persuade her to become betrothed to Piers had been mostly made upon the basis that someone of her background should consider themselves fortunate in the extreme to marry a distant cousin of the Duke of Westminster. But to suggest that Piers was suffering from unrequited love for her and expecting her to believe it—she put a hand to her mouth.

'Surely you are not surprised, dear?' Mrs Filmore smiled at her. 'It would make us all so happy if you were to accept him.'

Janey did not doubt that. Not for a minute. 'Marry Piers?' she gasped breathlessly. 'I will not marry Piers. Not now! Not ever!'

'Why ever not, dear? It would be such a match for you.'

'Because—' Janey caught her breath and struggled to suppress the bubble of laughter rising in her throat. Because he is nasty, cruel, lazy and utterly despicable, she felt like saying. 'Because—' she hesitated, as Mary, the housemaid who was standing behind Piers, bit her lip to stop herself from laughing '—he's too fat and I simply cannot abide fat men.'

'Fat!' Mrs Filmore gasped. 'He is simply well built like myself. Besides, he could always reduce a little.'

'And he's too short,' Janey added, carefully deadpan. 'Perhaps you could stretch him a little, too? I expect one

of your numerous aristocratic relations still has the odd
rack or two tucked away in the family dungeon?'

Janey saw Mary turn hastily to the sideboard, her black-
clad shoulders shaking with suppressed laughter. It was
her undoing. She was utterly helpless to stop the laughter
that spilled out of her mouth.

'Marry Piers!' she spluttered. 'Oh, I should not marry
him to save my life!'

'That's as well—' Piers got up so suddenly his spoon-
back chair toppled backwards '—because you might not
be so lucky next—'

'Piers!' Mr Filmore's roar coincided with Mary giving
a gasp and dropping a tray of crockery and silver with
spectacular results.

Then all was bedlam, Mr Filmore storming after Piers,
Annabel bursting into sudden tears and Mrs Filmore leading her weeping from the room, pausing only to call Mary
a stupid girl and instruct her to clear up the mess.

'Sorry, miss,' the maid said timidly to her as Janey got
up and helped herself to bacon and eggs from the covered
dishes upon the sideboard, 'about the china.'

'It doesn't matter. Accidents happen.' Janey shrugged.
'Another five months and breakfast times will be more
peaceful, I promise you. What happened—did you trip?'

'Not exactly. . .it was just what Master Piers said—'
Mary hesitated and shook her head. 'Don't matter, miss,
I was probably just being stupid. I'll just go and get the
brush and shovel, if you don't mind?'

Janey shook her head and sat down to her breakfast.
Standing up to the Filmores had given her an appetite and
her head was too full of Jonathan Lindsay for her to give
any more thought to Piers's display of temper. She smiled,

her breakfast momentarily forgotten as she recalled the way he had looked at her, the way he had kissed her—

Oh, hellfire, she repeated one of Lilian's favourite oaths softly beneath her breath. She would not be foolish enough to fall in love with Jonathan Lindsay, would she? How could she fall in love with a rake, a dandy, an indulged aristocrat, when she had never fallen in love with Edward?

Good, kind, worthy Edward, who had shared so many of her ambitions for the village. Edward, who had loved her—or had he? Edward had been so eager to improve her, so full of helpful suggestions as to how she might mend the deficits in her education and manners so that English society would approve of her. . .unlike Jonathan Lindsay, who seemed to approve of her exactly as she was.

The thought brought another smile to her lips, and her breakfast grew cold as she let herself indulge in a day-dream of Jonathan Lindsay riding up the drive to demand her hand in marriage before the astonished gaze of all the Filmores. Then she sighed. Dreams were one thing, reality quite another. When and if the Honourable Jonathan Lindsay married, it would be to some aristocrat's daughter of impeccable blue-blooded pedigree. It would not be to Miss Jane Hilton.

Chapter Five

'Ah, awake at last! I was beginning to think you were going to sleep the clock round a second time,' Perry greeted the unshaven Jonathan cheerfully as he came into the morning-room and threw himself down upon a sofa. 'Not that I'm surprised. London to Dorchester in thirty hours in winter is damned good going, even for you. You should have made a wager on it.'

'I did.' Jonathan yawned. 'With Russell. And, speaking of wagers, I trust you have made up your mind to part with Triton.'

'I doubt she'll be that grateful for saving her felon's neck,' Perry said confidently.

'Gratitude, my dear Derwent, does not come into it. Shall we say, the attraction is decidedly mutual?'

'You've seen her again?' Perry looked at him in disbelief. 'When the devil did you find time for that?'

'A chance encounter upon the Salisbury road at dawn.'

'On the road at dawn!' Perry's brows lifted. 'What the deuce was she doing on the road at dawn?'

'Oh, being her usual extraordinary self,' Jonathan said

slowly. 'Tell me, Perry, do you think you have ever made a difference to anyone's life?'

'A difference?' Perry's brown eyebrows knitted. 'Wouldn't have thought so—' Then his face lightened. 'Parents, I suppose, were pleased to have me, son and heir and all that. But why the deuce do you ask?'

'No reason,' Jonathan said as he shrugged.

'You're not back on this being useful thing, are you?' Perry sighed. 'If you are, Jono, I am going back to Town. You're starting to sound like—well—one of those Reform fellows.'

'God forbid!' Jonathan laughed. 'But you have to move with the times, Perry, and reform is going to come, you know. You can't deny the cities like Manchester and Birmingham representation in favour of the counties for ever.'

'The day town tells country what to do is the day I retire to the family castle and pull up the drawbridge.' Perry sighed, fending off Tess as she tried to jump upon the sofa to lick his face.

'Has it occurred to you that that is just what I have decided to do here?' Jonathan said as the thwarted spaniel returned to sit upon his feet.

'You're not serious?' Perry stared at him. 'You're one of the clever ones, Jono, you always were. You're bound to get a cabinet post sooner or later and then you'd make your difference.'

'Nice of you to say so, Perry—' he smiled '—but I doubt it after that speech I made. Besides, I have difficulty in knowing which side I wish to be on these days—yes, Brown, what is it?'

He lifted his head as his butler came in after tapping at the door.

'A person to see you, sir. A William Avery, the local blacksmith, says he met you yesterday morning, sir.'

'Then show him in to the estate office. I'll see him there.'

'Yes, sir.' Brown retreated.

'Avery? What can I do for you?' Jonathan said as he entered the estate office, and saw the burly man whom he had seen with Miss Hilton upon the road standing at the window.

'It's a bit delicate, like,' Will said, turning his cap over in his large, weathered hands. 'But you seem to be a friend of Miss Hilton, and there's no one else I know round 'ere I can turn to. Doctor and Vicar, well, they're all mighty thick with the Filmores.'

'This concerns Miss Hilton?' Jonathan's expression of indifference left his face abruptly.

'Yes. It's about the accident she had last year.'

'The fall from a horse?'

'No, no, sir, when the staircase in old Fenton's Folly collapsed.'

'Fenton's Folly?'

'The tower, sir, the one on top of White Sheep Hill. Miss Hilton and Mr Edward used to walk there every Sunday after church. You can see the whole of the Pettridges Estate from the top of the tower.'

'Ah, I know where you mean now,' Jonathan said. 'That is how she broke her leg?'

'Yes, sir, and her fiancé his neck. The top landing gave way when they were on it. He fell from top to bottom of the central stairwell, she was saved by her skirts catching on a piece of broken timber. Trapped there for hours she was, poor girl, hanging over a void, until the search party found them.'

'My God! I had no idea,' Jonathan said. 'I thought it was a fall from a horse.'

'It always bothered me, you see, sir,' Will went on in his slow drawl. 'My uncle built that staircase and there was no better joiner in all Wiltshire. That timber should have lasted another fifty years easy, and it was only a week before it fell that Mr Piers asked me to check it over. Said he'd heard it creaking. I went over it with a finetooth comb and it was sound as the day Uncle put the last nail in. Not as much as a single wormhole from top to bottom.'

'Really, Avery?' Jonathan's brows rose. 'Are you implying the collapse was not accidental?'

'I don't know.' William Avery shrugged his massive shoulders. 'I never got a close look at it afterwards, what with having to stop Master Piers from rushing in like a bull in a china shop to save Miss Hilton. He nearly dislodged the timber before the rest of us could get a rope on her. If it hadn't been for Tom—he's a stonemason, so he's used to scaffolding and the like—well, she'd have fallen, too. To be honest, sir, I've tried hard to put it out of my mind—but when Mary told me what Master Piers had said—'

'Mary?' Jonathan said, bemused.

'My betrothed, though I'd be grateful if you'd keep that under your hat, sir, or she'll lose her post. She's housemaid at Pettridges, you see.'

'You have my word on it. What did Master Piers say?'

Will replied with a lengthy description of the previous day's breakfast at Pettridges.

'Hardly evidence upon which to hang an accusation of attempted murder,' Jonathan said drily when Will had finished. 'I think it would be better for you if you did not mention this to anyone else, Avery.'

'I know that, sir,' Will said. 'But I'd be a sight easier in my mind if I thought someone was looking out for Miss Hilton.'

'I am sure Miss Hilton is more than capable of looking out for herself,' Jonathan said with a smile, as he recalled the effective way in which she had dealt with Piers Filmore's churlishness.

'Maybe, maybe,' Will said slowly, 'but she's a bit inclined not to see what she don't want to, if you get my drift, sir. That curate. . .'

'What of him?' Jonathan asked with sudden interest.

'Well, all his fine talk and good works, it was only when he had an audience, if you know what I mean.'

'Indeed,' said Jonathan, after a moment in which his spirits inexplicably lightened. 'Thank you for the information, Avery. Now, if you will be so good, I have a great deal to do.'

'You will look out for her, sir.' Will turned back at the door. 'There's summat wrong, I can feel it.'

'I shall do my utmost to see that no harm befalls Miss Hilton,' Jonathan assured him.

'Thought you would, sir, and thank you again for what you did for Jem. T'was a good thing, even if it were only to impress her,' Will said with a grin, as Jonathan stared at him in astonishment. 'I might not have your learning, sir, but I ain't stupid, I saw the way you looked at her up

on the road. And we all wish you the best of luck, sir—
you'd have to go a long way to find yourself a better
wife. Good day to you, sir.'

'And good day to you,' Jonathan said weakly as Will
left. Damned impertinence, he thought and then laughed.
No wonder Miss Hilton was popular with her tenants.
Wiltshiremen appeared to be as outspoken in their soft,
slow way as she was. . .

'Trouble, Jono?' Perry asked as he knocked upon the
open office door some fifteen minutes later and found
Jonathan sat upon the circular rent table for lack of a
chair, staring out of the window.

'No.' Jonathan shook his head and laughed. 'Just some
rustic with a peculiar fascination for staircases. He seems
to think the Filmores harbour dark designs against Miss
Hilton on the basis of some altercation at breakfast yesterday and the accident she suffered last year.'

'Oh, is that all?' Perry laughed. 'I feared "Captain
Swing" might be about to raise his ugly head. I gather
from the paper the disturbances have spread all over
Hampshire. Apparently, the old Duke says organising the
militia to quell the rioters is the best fun he's had since
beating Boney.'

'I don't doubt it,' Jonathan said. 'Wellington has always
looked happier wielding a sword than the pen, though it
surprises me he is willing to do it against has own people
with such alacrity.'

'Now you are really starting to sound like one of these
Radical fellows.' Lord Derwent snorted. 'People who riot
deserve what punishment they get.'

'And people also deserve to eat,' Jonathan said absently
beneath his breath. Then, straightening, he sighed. 'You

don't think there could be anything in what that rustic said, do you, Perry? He didn't strike me as a fanciful sort of fellow.'

'Oh, you know what country folk are,' Perry said blithely. 'Where there is no mystery, they are sure to invent one. And, speaking of mysteries, have you taken a look at the lake lately?'

'No. What of it?'

'Seems to be disappearing,' Perry said laconically. 'Awful lot of mud, flapping fish, very little water and a frightful smell.'

'Damn!' Jonathan groaned. 'I suppose we had better go and take a look at the inlet.'

'We?' Perry's fair brows lifted and his nose wrinkled. 'Don't you have men to do that sort of thing?'

'I have not got myself an agent yet, let alone taken on any labourers. And Brown and the servants are already muttering darkly about the amount of extra work in making the house habitable, and supervising the joiners and builders. I can hardly ask them to go poking about in the undergrowth or they'll all hand in their notice.'

'Better go and change my coat, then,' Perry said unenthusiastically.

'Mmm,' Jonathan replied, still preoccupied with his thoughts. 'I'll meet you at the south end of the lake, that's where the feeder pipe is, according to the estate plan.'

'Oh, I didn't realise you are coming with us.' Annabel pouted at the very same moment as Janey rode up to join her and Piers in front of Pettridges Hall.

'It was Piers's suggestion,' Janey told her. 'And I think

he is right. Mr Lindsay might be my neighbour for some years to come.'

Her emphasis upon the possessive pronoun was not lost upon the brother and sister, who exchanged sour glances.

'Let's go, then,' Piers said sullenly. 'We'll cut across the park, shall we? I fancy a gallop. And Jane always enjoys a good ride, don't you? My American coz?'

'So long as it is in the right company,' Janey returned mildly, smiling inwardly as she saw Piers scowl. 'And I am not your coz.'

'But we'll have to jump the Wren's Dyke and two walls,' Annabel protested sulkily, 'and my new habit is bound to get splashed when we go through the river.'

'Oh, for pity's sake, Annabel, don't you think of anything but clothes?' Piers snapped. 'We are going across the park and that is an end to it. Understand?'

'Oh, very well.' Annabel gave in and set her heels to her horse's glossy side. 'Shall we say five pounds to whoever gets there first?'

'Ten,' Janey said quickly. Her allowance for the month had already been spent on paying the lawyers she had employed to defend Jem, and ten pounds would buy a substantial amount of bread for the families whose men had no work.

'So sure you will win, coz?' Piers drawled.

'Absolutely,' Janey said blithely and meant it. Brutus responded to the touch of her heel with his usual good-natured obedience and launched into a steady ground-swallowing gallop, leaving Piers and Annabel's highly bred horses plunging and rearing in excitement as they struggled to turn them in the right direction.

A few minutes later, as Brutus slithered and slid his

way carefully down a steep bank on the approach to a ditch, Janey glanced back over her shoulder. Annabel and Piers were taking the longer and more gentle slope. Janey laughed and took a handful of Brutus's mane for safety as his great quarters bunched for the leap over the ditch.

Having come late to side-saddle, she might never gain the perfection of Annabel's elegant seat, but when it came to the scramble and scrape of a fast cross-country ride, neither Piers nor Annabel could match her—but then, she thought wryly, they'd never had to literally ride for their lives with a war party of Indians on their tails.

The inlet pipe cleared, after a considerable effort and no assistance from Perry, who had taken one look and hastily suggested that he should go and look for some rods or something, Jonathan strolled back across the park, his coat slung over his shoulder, and his usually perfectly tied cravat hanging loose about his neck. He did not bother even to chastise Tess as she leapt up at him with a stick in her mouth. A few muddy pawprints, added to the mud with which his breeches and boots were already bedaubed, were going to make very little difference.

Taking the proffered stick from the spaniel, he brought his arm back and threw it in a lazy arc and then halted and shaded his eyes against the morning sunshine. It seemed he was about to receive his first callers.

His mouth curved up at the corners as he recognised the foremost of the three riders galloping across the park. A race by the look of it, and Miss Hilton was winning by a good quarter of a mile, riding as low on her horse's neck as a staff galloper delivering a despatch under fire. He grinned as the giant black scarcely broke stride to leap a fallen beech; the style might not be orthodox, but it was certainly effective.

'Miss Hilton! Over here!' he shouted through cupped hands, and then, snatching off his cravat, he waved it in the air to attract her attention.

A moment later she turned her horse in his direction and waved back.

Pink-cheeked beneath her veil, exhilarated, and for some reason, stupidly, ridiculously nervous at seeing Jonathan, Janey did not rein in until the last possible moment.

Then, without any warning, she was flying through the air, past the black's shoulder, almost beneath its plunging forelegs to somersault into an untidy swirl of black habit, white petticoat and windblown golden hair at Jonathan Lindsay's feet.

'Miss Hilton! Have you hurt yourself?' Letting go his coat and the cravat, he dropped to his knees beside her, his voice ragged with what she took to be laughter.

'I don't think so,' she said breathlessly after a moment's careful thought. 'Fortunately it rained a great deal last night, and the ground is very soft,' she said ruefully, as she pushed herself up to a sitting position and swept a loose tress of soft gold hair out of her eyes, unaware that in doing so she had transferred a considerable amount of mud from her gloves to her face.

'Good morning would have sufficed, Miss Hilton.' He grinned at her. 'You don't have to throw yourself at my feet.'

'It was not out of choice, Mr Lindsay—' She gave a slightly breathless laugh as his eyes met hers and she knew instantly that he had no more forgotten their encounter upon the downs than she had. Her heart drumming in a way that had nothing to do with her fall, she looked away as the black gave her a hefty nudge between the shoulder blades. 'It's no use saying sorry now, Brutus, you beast.' She twisted and pushed at the horse's nose. 'And now you've trodden on my hat!' she said exasperatedly as she began to disentangle herself from the hampering skirts of her habit.

'Come here, before he treads upon you as well.' He slipped an arm about her waist and straightened, lifting her on to her feet.

Her breath caught as she found herself standing almost as close as they had been the previous morning, and she felt his fingers feather out across her ribs, preventing her from drawing back and trapping strands of her waist-length hair, which spilled down over her back and shoulders.

'You are quite certain you have not hurt your leg again?' he said softly as he looked down into her face. 'You've gone very pale.'

'Have I?' Her voice shook a little as she let her gaze lift to his.

'And you have begun to tremble.'

'Have I?' She could find no other words as his eyes held her gaze.

'Yes.' He smiled, smiled in a way that melted something in the pit of her stomach. 'It must be the shock of your fall, no doubt.'

'No doubt,' she echoed, still unable to think of anything except his nearness, the weight of his arm about her waist, the way his mouth curved at the corners.

'You've got mud on your nose.'

'Oh!' Her hand began to lift and then fell as he dabbed gently at her face with the soft folds of his cravat.

'And here. . .'

He touched the fine linen to the corner of her mouth. A touch that left her body aching and heavy, yearning to be closer, to be kissed—

'And if mud becomes me as well as it does you, perhaps we shall start a new fashion,' he said with a lightness that did not match the darkness of his eyes as he drew back a little, leaving his hand only lightly upon her waist.

It did become him, she thought as she returned his scrutiny, noticing for the first time the degree of his dishevelment. There was no trace of the slightly effete dandy she had first taken him for. With his buckskin breeches liberally bedecked with mud, his thick dark hair windswept and his fine billowing linen shirt clinging to his broad shoulders where they were damp from perspiration, he was all lean, muscular strength.

'A slight problem with the lake,' he said drily, his brows lifting as he intercepted her gaze.

'Oh.' She felt her face colour and dragged her gaze from the open neck of his shirt. 'You have not taken on any labour yet?'

'I have not decided yet whether I shall remain here or sell the place on,' he replied without looking at her, his gaze going to the Filmores, who were approaching rapidly.

'Oh. I see,' she said flatly. She stepped back from him and gave her attention to the business of bundling up the trailing skirt of her habit over her left arm.

Aware that he was watching her intently again, she

found herself fumbling as she searched for the loop to slip over her wrist.

'Here.' He bent and offered her the fold which had the little black silk cord stitched to its underside.

'Thank you,' she said without looking at him. 'Whoever thought this was a sensible garment for riding can never have fallen off. What did happen, by the way? Did he put in a buck? It's not like him.' She was talking too much and too quickly, she thought, but she could not stop herself.

'Your girth broke—' He gestured to her side-saddle, which lay on the ground behind Brutus, who was cropping the grass placidly. 'You did not have a chance of staying on.'

'My girth broke—? But it was new only last month.' She frowned and then shrugged her narrow shoulders. 'Poor leather, I suppose. These accidents do happen.'

'Yes,' he said slowly.

'Well, at least it did not happen when we were jumping Wren's Dyke.' She sighed. 'But I shall have to speak to my horseman. I cannot understand it—he is usually so careful about such things.'

'Wren's Dyke?' he queried.

'It is a large bank with a hedge upon the top and a ditch on the far side. It runs along the boundary between the Pettridges and Southbrook estates.'

'Don't tell me any more, I don't think I want to know.' He exhaled audibly and then smiled at her, his eyes so warm that she felt her heart skip with a half-formed hope that she could not define. 'Why is it I have the feeling you are going to prove a very troublesome female?'

'Probably because I am one, or at least that is what I have been told since I arrived in England.' She smiled up at him and then sighed as the Filmores reined in beside them. 'And no doubt I am about to be told so again.'

But Piers and Annabel were all consternation and concern for her welfare, fussing over her, until Jonathan suggested firmly that they make their way to the house and find Lord Derwent and ask him to order refreshments, while he walked back at an easy pace with Miss Hilton.

'I'll take the saddle, if you care to pass it up,' Piers offered.

'Thank you,' Jonathan said. He strode over to the saddle and picked it up and walked back to Piers.

'Saddler ought to be shot,' Piers said disdainfully, as Jonathan handed up the saddle. 'New leather should not give way like that.'

'No—it should not.' The hesitation was infinitesimal, fleeting as the shadow that crossed Jonathan's face as he stared at the broken girth and thought suddenly of the broken staircase in the tower.

'I'll lead Brutus.' Annabel nudged her mare forward, coming between Jonathan and Piers. 'Jane is welcome to ride my horse in, if she wishes. I'd be quite happy to walk back with you, Mr Lindsay.'

I don't doubt it, thought Janey. But she managed to smile sweetly, and said that she would rather walk.

'Whatever you wish,' Annabel returned with an equally insincere smile from the back of her dainty flaxen-maned chestnut. 'I wonder if you could pass me Brutus's reins, Mr Lindsay?'

Reaching up to take the reins over the black's large head, Jonathan passed them to Annabel, who gave a slightly nervous laugh as the horse lifted his head and tried to nip at the foliage upon her hat.

'Behave, Brutus!' Janey hissed at the horse, who turned his head to look at her reproachfully.

'Brutus.' Jonathan gave a half-laugh as he looked at the horse. 'How appropriate.'

'Not in the least.' He's a lamb, and certainly not treacherous—hats are his only real vice,' she said a moment or so later as she and Jonathan Lindsay watched the Filmores trot away towards the house, Brutus dwarfing the chestnut mare.

'Eating them or standing on them?' he asked her with a grin.

'Eating, mostly.' She smiled back at him, wondering why it was she felt this irrational surge of happiness every time he looked at her.

'I suppose all that fruit is rather tempting,' he said as he watched Annabel Filmore's bobbing millinery confection disappear into the distance.

'If you like looking like a costermonger's barrow, I suppose it is.' Janey could not quite keep a thread of jealousy out of her tone. She knew that if Jonathan Lindsay came to prefer Annabel to her, she could not bear it.

'Tempting for horses, was what I meant.' His wide mouth curved as he glanced sideways at her. Then suddenly he frowned. 'Your girth—did you say it was new?'

'One month old,' she said. 'Why do you ask?'

'Oh, no reason.' He shrugged, deciding he was letting Will Avery's wild imaginings occupy far too much of his thoughts. Filmore had more than enough money of his own. And evil guardians plotting against their wards belonged in Gothic romances, not on sunny autumn mornings in Wiltshire.

But with her soft gold hair tumbling in disarray down her back, and her slender figure swamped by the voluminous skirt and petticoats of the muddy habit, he found himself thinking that the self-sufficient, self-composed, unshockable Miss Hilton looked uncharacteristically vulnerable. She could so easily have broken her neck if the girth had broken earlier.

The thought sent ice along his spine at the realisation that he was already fonder of Miss Janey Hilton than was at all sensible.

'What are you thinking?' she asked as she watched his face.

'I was thinking that you might have been killed.'

'But I wasn't—' she smiled at him, her dark limpid eyes full of unconscious invitation '—I suffered nothing more than a dent to my pride.'

'I know a cure for that. . .' His voice was soft as velvet as he reached out and drew her into his arms.

'Do you?' There was the slightest of shakes in her voice as she looked up at him, and her heart began to race. He was going to kiss her again. And she wanted him to. Very much. Too much—it did not matter that she knew his intentions were not in the least honourable. All that mattered was this. . .

She shut her eyes as he bent his head and kissed her. Kissed her mouth, her eyelids, her throat, kissed her as if he could not stop. Kissed her until she felt boneless, floating, anchored only by his hands, his mouth. She gasped, her knees buckling suddenly, as his fingers found the aching tips of her breasts beneath the layers of wool and linen.

He caught her to him, one hand spread against her back,

the other cradling her head against his chest. For a moment neither of them moved. She could hear his heart thumping as furiously as her own beneath his ribs, feel the rapid rise and fall of his chest.

'We had better go in,' he said slowly. 'The Filmores—'

'Yes,' she agreed. But still neither of them moved, except for his hand that had begun to stoke her silky fair hair, smoothing it back from her brow.

'Jono!' It was Lord Derwent's distant shout that broke the spell.

They jerked apart and turned as one to see Perry striding across the park towards them. 'Filmore said Miss Hilton had fallen. I thought you might need some assistance—' His voice tailed off as he looked from one to the other of them.

'My God!' he laughed good-naturedly. 'You both look in dire need of a large brandy and bed—' He choked off the last word as Jonathan fixed him with an icy blue glare. 'For Miss Hilton, I mean, best thing for nasty shock and all that. . .'

Janey's face went from ashen to scarlet as she realised suddenly that a considerable amount of the pondweed which had bedecked Jonathan Lindsay now decorated her habit.

'I've no doubt you're right, Perry,' Jonathan said coolly. 'Miss Hilton has been feeling a little dizzy.'

'So I saw.' Lord Derwent gave Janey a conspiratorial smile which increased her embarrassment.

'I'd be very grateful if you would go back quickly and reassure the Filmores,' Jonathan said, a distinct warning note in his voice.

'What? Oh, yes, see what you mean. Glad you weren't

hurt, Miss Hilton.' With the most unsubtle of winks at
Jonathan, Lord Derwent strode ahead of them.

By silent and mutual consent they began to follow,
walking side by side and falling easily into step.

But as they came close to the house, Jonathan halted
suddenly. Janey stopped and turned her head to look
at him.

'If we continue like this, we will undoubtedly create a
scandal,' he said slowly.

'Would you mind if we did?' she asked, lifting her chin
to look him in the eyes.

'No,' he said after a fractional hesitation. 'I am no
stranger to scandal, Miss Hilton. But perhaps you should
mind. Society will forgive behaviour in the son of an earl
that it will not countenance in a—'

'In a colonial of no breeding or consequence,' she interrupted him wryly as he hesitated again.

'An unmarried lady, is what I was about to say,' he
reproved her softly.

'A lady?' Her brows lifted as she held his blue gaze.
'Is that really how you consider me, Mr Lindsay?'

'You are generous, brave and honest, therefore I consider you a lady in every sense that really matters,' he said
with a conviction that made her heart flip over beneath her
ribs. 'Which is why I should not care to see you the
subject of malicious gossips. It would perhaps be wiser
if we took care only to meet in company in future.'

'So that we may discuss the weather or the last run of
the hounds?' she said with a sudden passionate anger that
surprised even herself. 'If that is being wise, I should
rather be foolish. At least when I am alone with you I
can be myself, rather than have to behave like some over-

sized wax doll without an opinion of my own or thought in my head except for the colour of my next new gown or the fitness of my horse! Every time I open my mouth upon any subject, the others all stare at me as if I am weak in the head.'

'The others?' he queried.

'The people whom the Filmores have deemed me fit to be introduced to, all of whom seem to care for nothing but fox-hunting and their family connections. And their rules, of course. Their endless rules!'

'Rules?'

'The unspoken, unwritten ones, which you only know you have broken when they get that look upon their faces!'

'That look?'

'You must know the one I mean,' she said bitterly. 'Down the nose, with the faintest suggestion of a superior smile. The look that says *I am an English gentleman* or *woman*, and *you are a colonial nobody* with pretensions above your station.'

'Ah, *that* look,' he said with a wry smile. 'They're not all like that, you know, and those that are. . .half the time I doubt they are even aware they are doing it.'

'Just as half the time they do not appear to be aware that their labourers are starving! And even if they are, then they do not show any concern! Why is it in England that, if you show any compassion, any feelings about anything at all, you are made to feel as if you have committed a crime?'

'All this fire and passion. Lord Byron would have adored you, do you know that?' he said softly as she paused for breath.

'I had the impression the only person Lord Byron

adored was himself,' she said tartly. 'Besides, I would rather you did,' she added, her anger evaporating suddenly into something approaching a plea. 'Adore me, that is.'

'Miss Hilton!' He gave a gasp of laughter. 'How the devil am I supposed to do the decent thing when you say things like that?'

'Not at all, I hope,' she said with total honesty as she met his gaze. 'And from what I have heard, except for the fact that I am not married, that will not exactly be a dramatic departure from your usual habits.'

He stared at her for a moment, and then his mouth curved slowly. 'Very well, Miss Hilton, I give in. I only hope you do not come to regret your victory and think an ageing cynic like me a prize not worth the winning.'

It was another warning, but it did nothing to dim her soaring relief. She knew that their flirtation would have to end at some point, but not just yet. It was the first real happiness she had felt since her arrival in England, the first time she had felt not quite so alone and as out of place as a square peg in a round hole.

'I should never make that mistake,' she said a little too quickly to achieve the faintly mocking note she had intended. 'And thirty-three or so is hardly what I should describe as ageing. You are only thirteen years older than me, Mr Lindsay.'

'Maybe, but closer, I suspect, to a hundred in experience, Miss Hilton.' He sighed.

She smiled sweetly and gave him what she hoped was a look of invitation. 'That could be remedied, could it not?'

'Not here and now—' He laughed after a sharp intake of his breath, and gave her a small push into the marble-lined hall. 'Behave, Miss Hilton, or I shall forget that I am a gentleman.'

'Oh!' Janey came to a sudden halt and gasped as she looked around her at the gleaming hall. 'I never realised this marble was pink-veined before—you have made such a difference to the house already.'

'Not me,' he said drily. 'The improvements are all down to Brown and the servants. Brown regards dirt, dust and cobwebs as enemies to be vanquished at all costs. And, having done that, he is now badgering me for more servants.'

'And will you be taking on more men?' Her carefully unconcerned question did not fool him for a moment, she realised, as he gave her a swift glance from beneath his dark lashes and smiled.

'I told you I have not made up my mind to stay yet. So don't start telling me which of the deserving poor I should employ.'

'I am sorry, I did not mean to pry into your affairs,' she apologised as the train of her habit slid unnoticed from her arm to pool upon the ground, and breathed an inward sigh of relief that he had not seemed to realise that her question had been based upon an entirely selfish desire to know whether or not he would be staying for some length of time.

'I need to think about it for a few more days, look at the quality of the land, the improvements needed,' he said after a short silence. 'There is no sense in throwing away money upon an estate that will never be profitable. That benefits no one in the long term.'

'I did not think profit was so important to you,' she said, without looking at him.

'There are a great many things you do not know about me.' There was a warning note in his voice again which reminded her that he was right. She did not know him, not really. 'And perhaps it is best you do not.'

'Oh, there they are!' Annabel's trilling voice came drifting down the stairs. 'I do hope you do not mind, Mr Lindsay, Lord Derwent has been showing me the ballroom. It is wonderful! A little gilt and paint and it would be as fine as any in London. How I should love to dance in it.' She sighed as she reached the foot of the stairs. 'I can imagine it now—' she twirled a few graceful steps, and turned to smile up at Jonathan '—can't you?'

'Vividly. But I am sure the reality would be better than the imagination,' Jonathan said drily. 'Obviously, I must give a ball.'

'Capital idea!' Lord Derwent said enthusiastically. 'The Hoares over at Stourton would be sure to bring a party, and then there are the Morrisons from Fonthill and the people at Wilton—'

'Oh, all the county will come if Mr Lindsay invites them,' Annabel said airily, posing gracefully with one elbow upon the newel post and giving Jonathan a flirtatious blue glance from beneath her eyelashes. 'I know I should never refuse *any* of his invitations.'

'Or anyone's,' Janey muttered beneath her breath.

'What did you say, Miss Hilton?' Jonathan said mildly. 'I did not quite catch it.'

'I said—I said a ball would be—fun,' Janey invented hastily, glowering at him, knowing as she saw the laughter in his blue eyes that he had heard her perfectly.

'Do you mean to come?' Annabel addressed her in

astonished tones. 'What of your leg? You have not danced since the accident.'

'Then perhaps it is time I started. I shall certainly come—if I am invited?' Janey replied, throwing a faintly challenging glance at Jonathan.

'You are the first upon my list,' he smiled at her.

'Then I shall be delighted to accept, Mr Lindsay.' Her face lit up as, ignoring Annabel's coy glance of invitation, he stepped over to her and took her arm. When he touched her, she did not care what Annabel, Piers or the entire British aristocracy thought of her.

Piers, sprawled in a chair in the morning-room, a large glass of brandy in his hand, looked up as they all entered the morning room.

'Piers! What do you think! Mr Lindsay is going to give a grand ball,' Annabel said excitedly, seating herself upon the chair Lord Derwent drew forward for her. 'We are all invited. And even Jane has agreed to come.'

'Is that true, Jane?' Piers frowned as he turned his head to look at Janey, who was laughing up at Jonathan Lindsay as he settled her upon the sofa and then sat down beside her.

'Yes, what of it?' Janey replied, her chin lifting as she met Piers's stare.

'Nothing, dear coz,' Piers drawled. 'I just wondered whether you are quite sure you are ready for society. It is, after all, scarcely a year since Grey died.'

'It is *more* than a year, as your mother so kindly reminded me but the day before yesterday,' Janey replied sweetly. 'And since your parents have gone to every length to prevent me from having a season, I am sure they will not begrudge me attendance at one ball.'

'Oh, of course not.' Piers gave her a benign smile. 'You do say the most extraordinary things, Jane. Mama and Papa only prevented you having a season because they were concerned, when you first came to this country, that you should not be made a laughing stock because of your lack of education and manners.'

'A deficit that they have obviously more than compensated for since,' Jonathan put in smoothly as he heard Janey's fierce intake of breath and saw the green glitter of anger in her hazel eyes. 'But then I suppose they had had plenty of practice in improving manners with you, Filmore.'

Piers's slack lips gaped like those of a landed fish and he went red with what Janey knew to be anger. Then he gave a ragged laugh. 'If I did not know you were such a jester, Lindsay, I'd call you out for that.'

'By all means,' Jonathan voiced his invitation with a smile that made Janey think suddenly of a mountain lion she had seen once, lazing with deceptive tranquillity in the sun on a rocky ledge. 'A jester like me will do anything for a little amusement.'

Piers's colour changed from red to white. 'Well, I would oblige you, of course,' he spluttered, 'but it's rather frowned on now, isn't it? And, what with you being a Member of Parliament. . .'

'Oh, pray don't let that stop you,' Jonathan drawled, his smile wider. 'It didn't stop Wellington, after all, and he was Prime Minister.'

Annabel gave a small stifled moan and went as pale as her brother.

'Jono!' Lord Derwent said with uncustomary sharpness.

'You will frighten the ladies with your teasing—Miss Filmore looks quite faint.'

'My apologies,' Jonathan said at once, his tone losing its edge. 'Derwent is quite right, I was merely teasing, Miss Filmore. And you, Miss Hilton? I trust you are not feeling faint?'

He turned to Janey, his mouth curving slightly at the corners as he saw that she had been struggling to suppress laughter.

She swallowed. 'Oh, no,' she said with careful sobriety. 'It takes rather more than teasing to alarm me, Mr Lindsay.'

'So I have observed,' he drawled, his voice like velvet as his gaze travelled over her face and came to rest upon her mouth. 'You seem to be quite fearless. Can I take it that you will not swoon into my arms at the sight of a mouse or spider, or the merest hint of thunderstorm?'

'You may depend upon it,' she said firmly, determined that she would not rise to his bait like Piers. 'But I am sure some lady will oblige you, should the occasion arise.'

'Really, Jane!' Annabel gave a little gasp of shock. 'You are as bad as—'

'Me?' Jonathan laughed as Annabel stopped in confusion. 'I rather fear you are right, Miss Filmore. I think Miss Hilton and I are a well-matched pair, don't you?' he added carelessly.

He could not have shocked Annabel more if his choice of words had been deliberate, but perhaps they had been, Janey thought, biting her lip as she caught the gleam in his blue eyes. He was wicked. Quite wicked.

'I should not have said so,' Annabel said tersely, 'but

then you are not so well acquainted with Miss Hilton as I am.'

'A lack I look forward to remedying,' he replied coolly, but his eyes were warm as they met Janey's gaze. 'Where shall we begin, Miss Hilton?'

'I thought we had begun, when we met upon the downs,' she returned blandly, deciding that two could play this game.

He smiled. A slow, slow smile that made her melt and pool inside and want to hit him in the same moment. 'The downs? Remind me?'

'Another time, perhaps—I should not wish to bore everyone else,' she replied hastily, knowing she had just been outplayed and what was more, she was blushing and she never, ever blushed.

'Oh, neither would I,' he replied innocently. 'I have absolutely no desire to bore anyone else, Miss Hilton.'

She caught her breath at the image his words brought to her mind. He was shameless, utterly shameless, and she was so far out of her depth that she was drowning. She stared at him helplessly, her lips faintly parted as she struggled to find a reply.

It was Lord Derwent who came to her rescue. 'Awfully nice weather for the time of year, don't you think, Miss Hilton?'

'Yes. Almost springlike,' she replied politely, glad that her voice was steady, even if her throat was dry and her pulse racing.

Jonathan shot Perry a glance and received a distinctly disapproving look in return, which startled him for a minute; then he smiled. No doubt Perry had just realised he was in severe danger of losing the wager and Triton.

He leant back against the sofa, his smile broader as he let his hand fall to his side and brush Janey's fingers.

If Perry thought he could make him feel guilty with a few stern looks, he was mistaken. Even if Miss Janey Hilton was not quite so unshockable as she liked to appear, it was not as if she was some innocent, protected miss, straight from the schoolroom, was it? If he had had any doubts that she wanted him as much as he did her they had disappeared as he felt her jolt at his touch. Oh, no, he was going to enjoy winning this wager. . .

Chapter Six

'Not quite the usual sort of girl,' Lord Derwent observed as he and Jonathan drove back from Pettridges, having taken Janey home in the carriage. 'Very pretty, though, and even my father could not complain at the size of her fortune.'

'If you have an interest, say the word,' Jonathan replied. 'I should not care to stand in the way of Miss Hilton's lasting happiness.'

'Me! Marry a Radical! And a millhand's daughter to boot!' Lord Derwent laughed. 'The family would disown me in an instant. But you surprise me, Jono—I did not think you'd give her up so easily. I had begun to think—'

'What?' Jonathan interrupted harshly.

'Well—that you were over Susanna at last,' Lord Derwent said tentatively.

'I was over Susanna the day she accepted that doddering old Duke's proposal,' Jonathan said coldly.

'Really?' Lord Derwent snorted. 'As far as I can see, she's had you wriggling on her hook these last six years. The minute you look twice at a marriageable girl, Susanna makes damned sure you don't look a third time. It's not just her husband she's made a fool of, you're not even the *only* one she deceives him with—'

'Enough, Perry!' Jonathan rasped.

Lord Derwent sighed. 'Someone has to say it—you've been rattling round like a loose cannonball ever since she jilted you for her Duke, and leaving a trail of wreckage in your wake. There's half a dozen young women with broken hearts in Town who would agree with me.'

'I have never misled any of the women you refer to. I told all of them I had no serious intentions. It is not my fault if they chose not to believe me!' Jonathan glowered and whipped up the horses to a faster pace.

'You're not exactly being as honest with Miss Hilton,' Lord Derwent said, frowning. 'It's obvious she's partial to you and when she finds out about the wager. . .'

'I see no reason why she should,' Jonathan snapped. 'Unless you are so unsporting as to tell her, Perry.'

'It's more a question of conscience than being sporting,' Lord Derwent said, sighing. 'You know as well as I do, we should never have made that wager. Not that calling it off is likely to make a difference to your pursuit of her, I suppose?'

'None. Pursuing Miss Hilton is proving far too enjoyable to give up.' Jonathan laughed. 'And conscience be damned—you're just worried that you're going to lose Triton.'

'Believe what you will. But I don't think I will be the loser this time, Jono—' Lord Derwent shrugged '—I can always get another horse.'

'Meaning?' Jonathan drawled, giving him a cool look as he hesitated.

'You might not find your self-respect so easy to regain,' Lord Derwent said, after clearing his throat. 'It's one thing to play games with the likes of Mrs Norton—she knows the rules—but Miss Hilton. . . Damn it, Jono, she's an unmarried woman and you could ruin her reputation.'

'She is quite aware of the danger,' Jonathan asserted with a smile, 'and I assure you, Perry, she does know the rules—she simply chooses not to play by them. However much the lady Miss Hilton appears now, I can assure you that she is far from some sheltered innocent. In fact, I rather suspect she enjoys living dangerously.'

'She will need to,' Lord Derwent muttered grimly beneath his breath as Jonathan whipped up the horses and sent them speeding through the rather dilapidated gateposts at the end of Southbrook House's drive, 'if she's foolish enough to fall in love with you.'

Late the following afternoon as the light was fading, Janey hurried back towards Pettridges Hall. Her grey pelisse and gown were soaked right through from a short icy shower. It had been silly to think that he might decide to walk to the waterfall on such a dull, damp November evening, sillier still to do so herself just because there was a remote possibility of meeting him. Shivering and calling herself every kind of fool, she increased her pace to a near run and decided to take the shortest route across the stableyard.

'Miss! Miss Hilton! Could I have a word?'

She halted in response to the hail from the harness room and retraced her steps.

'Does it have to be now, Iggleston?' she asked the head groom as she stood at the harness-room door, her arms wrapped tightly about her for warmth. 'I'm chilled to the bone.'

'It's your saddle, miss, it got left at Southbrook yesterday. Mr Lindsay has just brought it back and said you ought to change your saddler. But it wasn't Hobson's fault, miss. Look. . .' He held out the girth of her sidesaddle in his wizened, nut-brown hands.

Janey took it unseeingly, her heart and mood soaring, the cold forgotten as she wondered if he was as impatient to see her again as she was to see him. 'Mr Lindsay is here?'

'Aye, and Lord Derwent. The master invited them to dine. I took the message over this morning, miss.'

'Oh, I see,' she said wryly. So *that* was why Mrs Filmore had been so insistent that she still looked peaky after her fall and should rest and dine in her own room. It was not the first time she had been relegated to her room when eligible bachelors had been invited to dine. The Filmores' efforts to prevent her marrying anyone except Piers before she was twenty-one had only been exceeded by their efforts to find a husband for Annabel.

Given the nature and character of the men the Filmores had considered desirable matches, she had usually been more than grateful not to have to endure their company at the dinner table. But if her guardians thought she was going to retreat gracefully tonight, they were mistaken. Her father had taught her that you had to be prepared to fight for what you wanted—and she wanted Jonathan Lindsay. Wanted to see him, hear him, and be kissed by him again. . .that thought sent a spiral of remembered warmth coiling through her insides.

'Look at it, miss—' with a start, she realised Iggleston

was still talking about the girth '—a buckle might tear
through after a lot of use—but both of 'em together—
and new leather—' Iggleston shook his head in disbelief.
'I've never seen that happen in fifty years, miss. And look
how clean the edges are—that leather was scored, scored
more than three-quarters through. And it weren't like that
when I saddled up, miss, I swear it. No horse goes out
of this yard with a girth I would not trust my own neck to.'

'Are you saying someone deliberately cut the leather
so the buckles would give?' Janey said, her attention
caught now as she stared at the supple leather strap in her
hands. 'But who would do such a thing. . .?' Her words
dwindled as the answer came. Piers!

Piers, who had brought Brutus round to the front of the
house for her with unprecedented thoughtfulness. Piers!
It would be just his idea of a jest to see her go flat upon
her face in the mud. And he had chosen their route, had
knowingly let her jump Wren's Dyke with a girth that
could have broken at any moment. Some jest, she thought
furiously. He could have killed her!

And that would probably have amused him, she thought
grimly. Well, this time he had gone too far and she was
going to tell him so! In the last month there had been a
burr under her saddle, a dead rat in her bed and the
disappearance of her brooch. Until now she had bitten her
tongue, and let the matters go without comment, knowing
that a reaction would only give him satisfaction. But this
time she was not going to suffer in silence.

'I don't like it, miss, first that burr under your saddle,
now this.' The furrows on Iggleston's walnut face deepened. 'Who'd do such a thing?'

'I think I can guess,' Janey exhaled slowly as she

struggled to control her growing anger. 'And I suspect it was his idea of a jest.'

'A jest! There's only one here who'd be that stupid!' Iggleston said disgustedly. 'That burr were bad enough, but he's gone too far this time, and he needs telling so— if I were his father, I'd have taken a whip to him long ago. Do you want me to have a word with Mr Filmore?'

'No,' said Janey resignedly, 'he'd only blame you or me. I'll deal with it.' One way or another, she added beneath her breath as she marched towards the house, her anger burning inside her like a flame. She had had enough of the Filmores! Had enough of their superiority, their pettiness and their constant denigration of her and her background! And, most of all, she had had enough of Piers's practical jokes.

Once in the house, she picked up her grey woollen skirts and ran across the hall and up the stairs, still clutching the girth.

'Whatever is it, miss?' her maid asked, starting up from darning some stockings as Janey threw open her bedchamber door, dropped the leather girth upon the carpet, tossed her bonnet onto the bed and began to unfasten her sodden pelisse. 'No time for questions, Kate,' Janey said breathlessly. 'Can you get me some hot water to wash with, and get out the red silk dress? I have decided to dine downstairs after all.'

'The red silk. . .' Kate's blue eyes widened for a moment, but then she smiled. 'Yes, miss. It'll be good to see you out of those mourning clothes.' Still smiling, she hastened away to do Janey's bidding.

Some fifteen minutes later, Janey checked her reflection

in the looking glass. It did suit her, she thought, as she stared into the glass at the claret silk gown. She had ordered it especially for the dinner where her betrothal to Edward had been made public, drawing exactly what she had wanted for the dressmaker, remembering one of Lilian's simple cottons which she had always admired.

A frown furrowed her forehead. She had loved the gown from the first fitting—and Edward had been horrified by it. Edward had thought it made her look like a whore—though he had not said so in so many words. Unsuitable for an unmarried woman and even more unsuitable for a clergyman's wife, he had said in hushed tones. And then, seeing her disappointment, he had consoled her, telling her that she must not worry, in future he would assist her in the selection of her gowns.

That was the first time she had begun to wonder whether being married to Edward would be better than being the Filmores' ward. But by then it had been too late—Mr Filmore had risen to his feet and announced their engagement with stilted and wholly insincere words of congratulation.

She stared at her reflection in the mirror, wondering whether she should change into one of the more conventional frothy, frilly confections of pastel colours which Mrs Filmore had ordered for her when she first arrived in England.

She tugged a little at the deep pleated band of crimson silk which ran straight and very low across her breasts, leaving her throat and shoulders bare. She had forgotten this gown was quite so low, and, she thought with a tiny half-smile, how well it suited her.

Unrelieved by any contrasting colour, the glowing

wine-coloured fabric set off her pale skin, making it look luminous and pearly, and enriched the soft gold of her hair which, with little time for curling tongs, Kate had caught up in a simple knot embellished with a pearl and tortoiseshell comb, leaving a few simple spiral curls to frame her face. No, she decided with a lift of her chin, she did not care what the Filmores or anyone else thought of the gown, she liked it and that was all that mattered.

After one last adjustment of the neck and twitching out the full skirt, which belled out from the tight waist which came down to a little point, she turned away from the mirror and went to her dressing table.

Opening her jewellery box, she put pearl drops in her ears, and then frowned as she found her pearl necklace missing. Not again, she thought with a grimace, her anger surging again. Surely Piers did not think she would fall for the same trick twice?

'Kate?' She turned to her maid. 'Have you seen my pearls?'

'They're in their box, miss, I'm sure I saw you put them away last night,' Kate said, her round face creasing into a frown. 'Unless it was the night before?'

'They're not here now,' Janey said, taking out a gold chain with a single pearl drop. 'I must have put them down somewhere. Will you have a look for me while I am at dinner? I am late already. There—' she fastened the gold chain about her neck and turned a pirouette '—will I do, Kate?'

'You look beautiful, miss,' Kate said approvingly.

'Thank you.' Janey started for the door with smile and then hesitated. 'You would not happen to know what Miss Filmore is wearing tonight?'

'Just about everything but the curtain swags, miss,' Kate said with a wicked grin. 'Her mother's diamonds, the white lace with the blue overskirt and the yellow bows, miss, and she has her hair curled and dressed with lace, a Swiss Bodkin and blue feathers. Jeanne says she's out to make an impression upon Mr Lindsay since, apparently, Lord Derwent is as good as spoken for by Lord Ishmay's daughter.'

'I rather think she will succeed.' Janey laughed as her eyes met Kate's. 'I doubt he will have eyes for anyone else. Who else is dining tonight?'

'The Doctor and Mrs Hutton and the Reverend and Mrs Norris, I'm afraid,' Kate replied, her voice heavy with sympathy.

Janey sighed. 'Then I suppose I may look forward to a lecture upon the calming qualities of camomile tea and the inadvisability of concerning myself with matters out-side the home from Mrs Norris, and Mrs Hutton speaking to me as if I have lost my wits.'

'Least you'll have Mr Lindsay there,' Kate said a little enviously. 'From the way he handed you out of his car-riage yesterday, I'd say you had an admirer there, miss.'

'Really, Kate!' Janey said, going a little pink as she remembered exactly how Jonathan had lifted her down from the carriage, putting his hands upon her waist and letting her slide down the long lean length of his body, and holding her there far longer than was polite, until her breasts had grown tight and heavy, and her heart had begun to race. Just for a moment, an insane, glorious moment, she had known he had been tempted to throw all propriety to the winds and kiss her again in full view of Lord Derwent, the Filmores and the servants.

'Sorry, miss,' Kate grinned. 'You'd better go, you're late already.'

'Yes.' Janey turned for the door in a sweep of red silk and then swung back to stoop and pick up the girth.

'Whatever do you want that for?' Kate said, her eyes widening in astonishment.

'A gift,' said Janey with a grimace. 'A gift for Mr Piers.'

'They've already gone in, miss, the fish has just been served.' Dawson, the butler, greeted Janey outside the dining-room door. 'Shall I take that for you?' His impassive gaze dropped to the girth which Janey held at her side in one of her gloved hands.

'No, thank you, Dawson.' Janey smiled at him blithely. 'Just open the door for me, if you would?'

He did as she asked, but she hesitated on the threshold momentarily, feeling as dazzled by the dining-room's grandeur as she had when she had first entered it as a seventeen-year-old girl who had never eaten a meal from anything but a deal table close to the kitchen range.

There was a part of her that would never get used to this, she thought wryly, as her gaze flicked from the green silk-hung walls to the great polished length of the mahogany table that was so laden with German porcelain, Irish crystal and English silver that there was barely any wood left to be seen, a part of her that would never belong in Jonathan Lindsay's world of luxury and privilege.

'Miss?'

She started, realising Dawson was still holding the door. Taking a deep breath, she swept into the room in a rustle of silk, determined that even if she felt like an interloper, she was not going to look like one. It was her house, she reminded herself firmly.

'Good evening,' she said coolly and clearly as she was able, halting in front of the blazing log fire in the grate at the nearest end of the room.

Nine heads lifted and turned as one to look at her and all the men rose instantly to their feet. But there was no unison in their expressions. The Filmores looked annoyed, the Doctor and the Reverend and their respective spouses disapproving, Lord Derwent amused and Jonathan—

Far from the smile she had hoped for, Jonathan was simply staring at her, his eyes very dark in his frozen face, as if he had never seen her before, as if she were a creature from a different world. And to him she probably was, she thought, wondering if he thought her severe gown and simply arranged hair as unsuitable as Edward had.

She would never get things quite right, she thought despairingly. She did not belong. And for the first time since she had come to England, it mattered. It mattered because she wanted desperately to be a part of Jonathan Lindsay's world. But she never would—the Filmores had made that clear upon a thousand occasions. She might have money, but she would never be considered the equal of the people sat at this table, however hard she tried. She would always be the colonial, the millhand's daughter.

Jonathan exhaled the breath that had caught in his throat. He had become used to the way she hid her beauty beneath the dull grey and black gowns; now she had caught him as offguard as if she had drawn a blade from a scabbard. The dressmaker who had made that gown should be declared a danger to the public, he thought, as his gaze dropped from her face to the impossibly, wonderfully plain gown. If she wore it in town, it would set a new mode.

There was nothing to detract from the fierce beauty of her face, the surprising delicacy of her shoulders and arms. The tight bodice of glowing crimson silk highlighted the milky fairness of her skin, the darkness of her eyes and left scarcely anything to the imagination above her handspan waist. Feeling the distinct, uncomfortable stirrings of desire, he dragged his gaze upwards, trying to think of anything but the soft satiny swell of her breasts and how easy it would be to free them from the confines of that gown.

And then, as he caught her gaze again, he found himself startled by the bleakness in her dark eyes, a bleakness that puzzled him.

'This is very inconvenient, Jane. You will have to wait until another place has been laid.'

It was Mrs Filmore's cold remark that brought under-standing as he realised with a spurt of anger that neither of her guardians had any intention of making her late entry anything but embarrassing for her. They had not even made the slightest move to accommodate her at the table.

Janey's chin lifted. 'If I had known we were to have guests, I should have been here earlier. Unfortunately, no one thought fit to tell me.'

Her last remark hung in what seemed like endless silence as Mrs Filmore went a rather dull red.

'Oh, really, Jane,' Annabel drawled sweetly. 'I heard Mama tell you but two hours ago that we were to have guests.'

'I recall nothing of the kind,' Janey said tersely.

'No, no, of course you do not, you must not let it upset you, dear Jane, but perhaps it would be best if you dined in your room as you had intended. You do not look at all well.' Annabel was all cooing concern. But Jonathan caught the sideways glance she exchanged with the doctor, the raised eyebrows and the brief tap of her finger to her forehead. Not for the first time, he wondered how someone of such good business sense as old Fenton had displayed so little judgement in the selection of guardians for his granddaughter.

And by the look of her pale face and the shimmering rage in her hazel eye, Miss Hilton was thinking much the same and, he feared, was about to say so, which would only lend substance to Annabel's nasty little innuendoes.

'I must disagree with you, Miss Filmore,' he said lazily, just as Janey's lips parted to give voice to her anger. 'I have never seen Miss Hilton look better, and I am certain she feels very well indeed.'

Janey caught her breath as he smiled at her, the slanting, challenging smile that put an entirely different private meaning into his words. It was as well she was not over-given to blushing, she thought, as she smiled back at him and let her gaze drop to his lean whip-hard body before lifting it to meet his again.

'Thank you,' she said demurely. 'You are quite right, Mr Lindsay, I have rarely felt better.' And then she had to bite her lip to stop herself from laughing as she saw that the 'rarely' had struck home.

'I am gratified to hear it.' There was a flash of laughter in his eyes as he inclined his head to her in the briefest of nods before turning to Mrs Filmore. 'But perhaps Miss

Hilton should not be kept standing. There is space for another chair beside me.'

The hint of censure in his tone was barely perceptible, but it was there and it made her feel warm inside. It was wonderful not to feel utterly alone in this house that she had never come to think of as home.

'I suppose so,' Mrs Filmore replied irritably. 'Thomas—' she made an irritable gesture to the footman '—a chair for Miss Hilton and another place before the dinner goes entirely cold!'

Janey waited for Thomas to set the chair in place, and then walked slowly across the room towards Jonathan. At least he did not seem to disapprove of her gown, she thought, her spirits soaring as she felt his gaze follow her every step, every dip and sway of her hips beneath the rustling silk, every rise and fall of her breasts.

He was smiling at her, his eyes warm as she reached him. And then, as he drew out the chair the footman had placed beside him, he noticed the girth she held at her side, almost hidden amid the voluminous folds of the red silk skirt. His dark brows lifted in silent enquiry.

'After-dinner entertainment,' she murmured as he helped her be seated and the rest of the gentlemen sat down.

'I did not know your tastes ran in that direction, Miss Hilton,' he said with another lift of his brows as he glanced down at the leather strap again. 'Though I understand a little gentle restraint can add to one's enjoyment.'

For a moment she stared at him, not understanding. Then, as a memory of just why Lilian had thrown out one trapper into a rainstorm without so much as his shirt on came back to her, she felt a *frisson* of shock.

Which was exactly what he had intended, she realised, as she saw what was becoming a familiar teasing challenge in his blue eyes.

'That is not the sort of entertainment I had in mind,' she said with a determinedly bland smile.

'Pity.' He sighed in a tone that sent a melting heat through her body.

'And you should exercise a little gentle restraint upon your imagination, Mr Lindsay,' she returned, stabbing a fork into the plate of fish that had just been laid before her as she tried to take her own advice and failed. He was so damnably handsome in his dark coat and snowy cravat, and so close to her she caught the spicy clean scent of his cologne. So close that, every time he moved, the soft wool cloth of his coat sleeve grazed the satiny skin of her shoulder like a caress, making her whole body prickle and grow tight.

'I'm trying but it's very difficult,' he murmured, his breath warm against her ear, as he leant forward to pick up a glass. 'That gown is decidedly stimulating—to the imagination,' he added innocently, as she froze with the speared morsel of herring upon her fork.

'Are you utterly shameless, Mr Lindsay?' she said grittily as she lowered her fork to her plate.

'I don't know,' he said, his eyes suddenly very dark and smoky as he held her stare. 'Care to find out, Miss Hilton?'

Chapter Seven

It was more than teasing, she thought, her mouth and throat going quite dry. It was a most definite and improper invitation, and not one any gentleman should make to an unmarried lady at a dinner table before her guardians. The only response to it was to slap his face or laugh. . .or simply say yes.

She dropped her eyelids a fraction too late. She knew by the sudden fierceness in his face that he had read that last thought.

'Well?' he prompted silkily.

Janey laughed a little shakily. 'I think you have just answered my question, Mr Lindsay. But should I require a fuller answer at some other time, I will be certain to let you know.'

'Then I shall live in hope.' He laughed good-naturedly, dissolving the almost tangible tension that had flowed between them a moment before. 'Which is more than poor Derwent looks likely to do,' he added quietly. 'One more toss of the beauteous Miss Filmore's head and he'll lose an eye to that Swiss Bodkin.'

Janey glanced across the table and almost laughed aloud as Lord Derwent flinched from a particularly lethal toss of Annabel's over-ornamented head as she leant towards him confidingly.

'I am surprised she was not placed beside you,' she said, turning back to Jonathan.

'I dare say Mrs Filmore could not resist the chance of an elder son, even if he is nearly spoken for,' he whispered back. 'A circumstance for which I am deeply grateful. Miss Filmore is not to my taste.'

'Nor the fish, by the look of it,' Janey said as she toyed with her own food. 'Aren't you hungry?'

'The only appetite I have at this moment cannot really be indulged in upon a table,' he said, as his gaze held hers. 'At least, not in company—I doubt it would be considered polite.'

'I doubt it would be comfortable.'

He laughed, recognising her reference to their encounter upon the downs. 'Comfort is important to you, Miss Hilton, is it not? I begin to think that, for all those rather puritan gowns and radical views, you are something of a sybarite at heart.'

'Very probably,' she agreed mildly. 'I should do almost anything for crisp linen, French perfume, a goosedown bed, and hot water that I have not had to fetch and boil, Mr Lindsay. So would you, if you had spent any time on the trail in a wagon or in a cabin in the wilderness.'

'Anything?' His eyes held hers. 'That's a reckless offer, Miss Hilton. I might be tempted to purchase the contents of Bond Street tomorrow and throw them at your feet.'

'*Almost* anything, I said, Mr Lindsay,' she corrected him softly as the challenge and counter-challenge flowed between them again. 'And I am not reckless.'

'Aren't you?' His mouth curved as he studied her face intently. 'I think you are a gambler, Miss Hilton. I should wager you are as fond of risk as I am. The more I know of you, the more I am convinced that we are two of kind.'

'A well-matched pair?' There was an edge to her voice she could not quite suppress as she quoted his own words.

He frowned as he saw the bleakness in her eyes again. 'What is it?'

'Nothing.' She gave a stiff smile and looked away. 'I was just wishing—'

'Wishing what?' he asked.

That I was the Earl's daughter I could have been, a well-bred English lady, someone that you might consider for a wife instead of merely another conquest, she wanted to say, but couldn't. That was a cold truth she would face when she was alone, but not just yet. Just for now, she wanted to dream that there was more than desire in his eyes when he looked at her.

'Well?' he prompted softly as she stared unseeingly at her plate.

'I was wishing I was someone else,' she said, barely audibly.

'Then that is a wish I would never grant you, even if I had the power,' he replied softly in a tone that made her melt inside. 'I would not change anything about you, Miss Hilton.'

'Wouldn't you?' She turned her head to look at him again, her heart flipping over as he shook his head.

'No.' He smiled and lifted his glass to her. 'To perfection, Miss Hilton.'

She stared at him, feeling as she were drowning in the

blue warmth of his eyes as she met his gaze over the crystal glass. Don't, she wanted to say, don't make me fall in love with you. But what was the point? she thought with sudden wry self-honesty. It was too late—she already had. As Lilian had told her once, love was not a matter of choice, more like a horse bolting with you on its back: the only thing you could do was hang on for dear life and try and enjoy the ride before you got thrown off.

Why Jonathan Lindsay? she wondered, as she stared at his rakish face. Why did he have to be the man who could set her mind and body alight with a word, a touch, a smile. . .?

'Why aren't you wearing your pearls, Jane?'

She jolted at the sudden question from Annabel and put an uncertain hand to her throat. 'My pearls?' she said blankly.

'The ones your grandfather gave you,' Annabel said very markedly and slowly as if speaking to a child. 'Don't you like them anymore?'

'Oh, no, it is just that I have mislaid them,' she replied without thinking, too preoccupied to sense Annabel's trap.

'Mislaid!' Annabel said in horror. 'They are worth a fortune. You must have the servants search for them as soon as we have dined. Really, Jane, you are becoming so forgetful. You would not believe how many things she has lost in the last month, Dr Hutton—we turned half the house upside down looking for a brooch that she had pinned to a shawl she was wearing!'

'And do these instances of absentmindedness occur often, Miss Hilton?' Dr Hutton asked her gravely.

'No,' Janey said tersely, aware of Jonathan regarding her intently from beneath dark lashes and wondering if he was beginning to doubt her sanity—he certainly had more cause than the rest, given her attempt to rescue Jem and some of the outrageous conversations they had had. 'And it was not absentmindedness; someone took the brooch out of my jewel case and pinned it to the inside of the shawl without my knowledge.'

'Yes, yes, of course.' Dr Hutton exchanged a glance with Annabel, which made Janey wish to stab him upon his large gouty nose with her fork. 'You have not thought a change of air might do you good, Miss Hilton? Perhaps you are in need of rest.'

'There is nothing wrong with me that will not be cured upon my twenty-first birthday,' Janey said tightly, causing Jonathan to reflect with a smile that, while the Filmores might have the means to win the present battle, Miss Hilton was going to win the war, and meant them to know it.

'Which is some five months away, dearest coz,' Piers smiled at her. 'And, since this is England, not the colonies, you had best mind your manners until then, had you not?'

'And so had you, Filmore,' Jonathan Lindsay said very softly, and very succinctly, his blue eyes as cold as the crystal glass of chilled champagne he held in his hand, 'unless you would like to discuss the matter in a different manner.'

Piers's wine-flushed cheeks went suddenly pale and Annabel gave a slight gasp.

'Jono—it's against the law,' Lord Derwent groaned and then went very quiet as Jonathan's gaze flicked momentarily to him.

'Quite right, my lord,' Piers blustered. 'Much as I should like to take up your offer, Lindsay, duelling is frowned upon these days, especially by Members of Parliament.'

'Who said anything about duelling?' Jonathan said with a tigerish smile. 'I was thinking about a little boxing or horsewhipping, if you persist in treating Miss Hilton so ill-manneredly.'

'I hardly see that how she is treated is your concern—' Piers began.

'Really, Lindsay,' Mr Filmore broke in with forced cheerfulness, 'we are all friends here, are we not? You must not think my son was in earnest—Miss Hilton and my son are the best of friends and she is quite used to his teasing, aren't you, my dear?'

His dear! Janey almost gaped, so unaccustomed was she to hearing an endearment from the lips of Mr Filmore. As for being the best of friends with Piers—words momentarily failed her.

'Perhaps she is,' Jonathan answered before she could. 'But I am not,' he added in the same soft tones. 'A fact that your son would be wise to remember.'

There was an uncomfortable silence, filled only by the crackle of the fire, the scrape of silver against porcelain and the clink of crystal glasses. A silence in which Janey had to bite her lip to stop herself from smiling like an idiot as she saw the utter astonishment on the faces of the Filmores. They simply could not understand why Jonathan should choose to defend her.

Even the easy-going, kindly Lord Derwent looked startled and, she thought with a faint sinking feeling, more than a little disapproving. No doubt he thought his friend had gone a little soft in the head himself to defend a woman towards whom he had no obligation.

Lord Derwent cleared his throat and made a heroic effort to put the conversation on safer ground. 'Did I hear you say that you are to bring in the new threshing machines this winter, Filmore?'

'Yes, within the fortnight. It'll save us a small fortune in wages,' Mr Filmore said smugly. 'I'll be able to let ten men go at the end of the week.'

Beside him, Jonathan heard Janey's sudden exhalation of breath, saw the outrage written upon her face.

'Ten men!' Janey would have risen to her feet, if it were not for Jonathan's arm suddenly gripping her elbow, holding her down in her seat. 'You have laid off ten men at the beginning of winter! How could you do such a thing?'

'Very easily,' Mr Filmore said coldly. 'You should be thanking me for husbanding your funds so carefully. Would you rather I paid men to be idle all winter?'

'They need not be idle.' She fought to sound cool, controlled. 'There are fields that need new drains, hedges to be laid, copsing. The barn at Home Farm needs rethatching—'

'I do not need you to tell me how the estate is to be run,' Mr Filmore said glacially.

'Please reconsider,' she said pleadingly, struggling to control her temper. 'Please—more than half the families in the village depend upon Pettridges for their livelihood and so many men are without work already.'

'They are quite at liberty to look elsewhere for work,' Dr Hutton said.

'Exactly,' Mr Filmore agreed with a smile and lifted his glass.

'Where would you suggest they look?' Janey said

desperately. 'There is no work in the city mills or the factories these days because of the slump in trade and precious little in the country because of the enclosures and threshing machines.'

'There is always work if a man is willing enough.' Mr Filmore's lips pursed. 'I am certain the men I lay off will find something to do.'

'Undoubtedly,' Jonathan agreed drily. 'In Hampshire, I believe the labourers have taken up machine-breaking and rick-burning as a pastime.'

'And they will be driven to the same here,' Janey said fiercely, 'if something is not done to help them.'

'Then they will be punished,' Mr Filmore said coldly. 'Now, do be quiet, Jane, you are making yourself ridiculous as usual. Ladies understand nothing of these matters and nor should they wish to.'

'I understand you will see women and children starve to death.' Janie's hazel eyes blazed gold. 'Isn't it enough that you took away their common land, where they could at least keep a beast or two? Must you now take their livelihoods?'

'They can always apply for the poor relief,' the Reverend said, dismissively setting down his wine glass and taking a large mouthful of salmon.

'The poor relief!' Janey looked at his rotund figure contemptuously. 'I should like to see you live upon it for a week. A paltry pound or so of bread that does not even adequately feed one man for day, let alone a family for a week! I do not see how any man of intelligence can possibly regard it as an adequate substitute for a man's wages!'

'Oh, really, Jane, must you spout this Radical nonsense?' Annabel sighed. 'You will spoil all our appetites.'

'Quite,' said Piers, who had already cleared his plate and was finishing his second glass of wine.

'You need not worry upon my account,' Jonathan drawled, giving Janey a wicked sideways glance. 'Miss Hilton could never spoil my appetite.'

Janey found herself going pink, and looked down hastily at her plate.

'Nor mine,' Lord Derwent put in gallantly.

'I never took you for a Radical,' Jonathan said drily to his friend.

'I'm as much a one now as you are,' Lord Derwent grinned back at him. 'Who could fail to be converted when the cause has such a beautiful advocate?'

Far too many, thought Janey, as she saw the looks of disapproval exchanged by the Filmores with the Doctor and the Reverend.

'Oh, pray do not encourage her—' Annabel smiled lazily, winding one of her fat red curls about her finger as she glanced at Jonathan '—or she will be quoting Mr Lindsay's famous speech on behalf of the labouring poor next.'

Beside her, Janey felt Jonathan go very still. She glanced at him, puzzled. 'I doubt it.' He smiled, but it did not reach his eyes as he met Annabel's challenging stare. 'I hope Miss Hilton is far too sensible to take anything I say seriously. Isn't that so, Miss Hilton?'

'Yes.' The monosyllable dragged out of her suddenly tight throat. It was a warning, as clear as a peal of bells rung from a church tower, that he was out of her reach and always would be. What there was between them was a flirtation, which would have no permanence, no importance—to him.

Suddenly miserable, she stared down at her Limoges plate, counting the petals upon the pale pink roses on the soft yellow ground as she half-listened to him conversing with Annabel, who was talking brightly and effortlessly about horses, hunting and the weather—all approved topics for a lady, according to the book of etiquette Mrs Filmore had given her upon her arrival in England.

'Don't.' The sudden light touch of his fingers upon hers beneath the table made her head lift and her heart race.

'Don't what?'

'Worry so much,' he smiled at her, his voice tender. 'The men who are to be laid off will be well used to adversity; they will find a way through.'

'I do not think anyone ever becomes used to watching their children starve,' she said, half-glad, half-guilty that he had mistaken the reason for her sudden depression. 'I shall have to do something, I cannot simply let Mr Filmore turn those men off without trying to do something to prevent it.'

'Whatever you choose to do,' he said very quietly, as his hand closed over hers, 'promise me that you will stay within the bounds of law this time? No more hare-brained conspiracies?'

'Very well.' She sighed. 'But my attempt to rescue Jem was not hare-brained—it was very carefully planned.'

'So carefully planned that you would have been the one person easily identifiable,' he said drily. 'You must remember this is England, Miss Hilton, where the law will prevail, whether the cause is just or not.'

'Sometimes,' she said wistfully, 'I wish my grandfather

had never searched for me. Everything seemed much simpler in America.'

'That's another wish you cannot expect me to share, since I should have been denied the pleasure of your acquaintance,' he said gently.

'Is it really such a pleasure?' she asked a little distractedly, as he began to stroke her gloved hand with his fingers, tracing fine bones that seemed to become liquid at his touch. 'By taking my side, you will not endear yourself to your new neighbours.'

'You are the only neighbour whose opinion I care for and, I assure you, our acquaintance brings me nothing but pleasure,' he whispered as he slipped his thumb into the small aperture beneath the lowest button which ran down the inner seam of her gloves from elbow to wrist and began to circle her palm.

'And not just that kind, either,' he added with the flicker of a smile as he saw the sudden parting of her lips and the downward flutter of her eyelids at the shocking, startlingly intimate contact of their flesh. And then he laughed. 'Do you know, Miss Hilton, I think that is the first time I have made you blush?'

'I suspect it will not be the last,' she said a little shakily, wondering how so innocuous a caress could be so tantalising, so unendurable, that she drew her hand away abruptly.

'Oh, I think I can promise you that.' His voice was husky as she raised her eyelids and met his gaze again.

'I am not so easily embarrassed,' she retorted, more than a little cross with herself for being so transparently shocked by his remark.

'Embarrassment was not quite what I had in mind,' he said, his eyes glinting with amusement.

'Why else should anyone blush?' she asked with such directness and clarity that several heads turned towards them.

He stared at her for a moment, wondering if she were being deliberately obtuse in order to embarrass him and get her own back, but there was nothing in her gaze but innocent and genuine enquiry.

He cleared his throat, aware of Perry's raised brows on the other side of the table, and Mrs Norris on his other side, straining to hear with her mouth open and eyes almost out of their sockets. 'I really cannot imagine,' he lied, giving Perry a murderous glare as Lord Derwent clapped his napkin to his mouth in an apparent fit of coughing.

'And I was beginning to think you knew everything, Mr Lindsay.' Janey smiled at him. She still did not know what he had meant, but she knew he had lied and could not resist teasing him.

'Not quite, and nor do you, Miss Hilton, I think,' he replied slowly as he searched her mischievous, shining face with his gaze. For all her worldliness and unshockability, she was such an innocent in some ways. So passionate in her belief in fairness, truth and justice— and probably love, he thought with a sudden pang of conscience.

Perry was right—if he had an ounce of decency left, he ought to call the wager off and go back to town at the first opportunity before he hurt her, before things went beyond the point of no return. But then she smiled at him, her heart in her eyes and he knew it was already too late. What the devil, he thought with savage humour, as he reached out for his wine glass and drained it. He might as well be hung for a sheep as for a lamb.

'I trust you will not keep us too long, gentlemen,' Mrs Filmore said after the dessert had been cleared. 'Shall we withdraw, ladies? If you are too tired, Jane, you need not feel you must join us. You do become overtired so easily since your accident.'

Overtired of you, Janey felt like retorting. For a moment she was almost tempted to accept the offer of escape. The dinner had been a torturous mixture of delight in Jonathan's company and frustration that they were not alone. Her whole body felt aching and heavy and as tight as an overwound clock spring. But if she retired early, she would not see him again this evening.

'Stay,' he murmured softly as he pulled out her chair, making up her mind for her instantly. 'I shall do my best to see the gentlemen do not stay at the port over-long.'

'I am not in the least tired,' she said brightly as Mrs Filmore frowned at Jonathan, 'and I should not miss Annabel's new song for anything. She has practised it so very many times and at such very great length I swear I know every note by heart—and every wrong one, too,' she finished with a fluttery little laugh that was so exact a mimicry of Miss Filmore's that Jonathan had to bite his lip in order not to laugh. Vulnerable! Innocent! he told himself wryly, she was about as vulnerable and innocent as Wellington behind his lines at Torres Vedras.

'And what will your contribution to the evening's entertainment be?' Piers sneered at Janey from across the table. 'Nothing, I suppose, since you can neither sing properly nor play.'

'Oh, I thought I should recount a few of the tricks you

have played upon me of late, since you find them *so* amusing,' Janey retorted.

'I don't know what you are talking about,' Piers said and yawned.

'Then perhaps this will jog your memory?' She stooped suddenly to pick up the girth in both hands, and, stretching it out, she dropped it into the middle of the table.

The leather strap looked utterly incongruous lying amid the silver, crystal and porcelain. There was a faint gasp of surprise from the diners as they all looked from the girth to Janey, with expressions that ranged from horror to curiosity.

'What the deuce! You've spilt my wine and ruined my waistcoat!' Piers was the first to break the astonished silence.

'How very careless of me,' Janey said, with a complete absence of regret. 'You see—' she swept the table with a glance '—Piers thought it a great jest to score the leather so the buckles would break and I should fall from my horse. Is that not terribly amusing? He could have killed me, of course, but no doubt that would merely have added to his mirth.'

'*What*?' Mr Filmore, having recovered from his initial shock, gave a roar of outrage at the same moment as Mrs Filmore gave a gasp of horror and sank back into her chair, demanding to know how Miss Hilton could possibly make such an accusation against her son, who worshipped the ground she stepped upon. Mrs Norris and Mrs Hutton scurried to her aid, muttering loudly about ingrates and ill-bred young women.

Jonathan's mouth curved momentarily as he took in the scene and saw the alarm upon Perry's face. Perry still had something to learn about Miss Hilton's remarkable directness and her disregard for convention. But then, as Mr Filmore continued to roar at Janey, he frowned.

'Take it back! Take it back at once!' Mr Filmore shouted, his moustache quivering so that it looked as if it were about to take flight from his face. 'I have never heard such a nonsensical, insane suggestion in my life.'

'Nonsensical?' Janey pointed to the girth. 'Have you ever seen buckles pull through new leather in such a way? It was cut—scored nearly through with a knife. Look, if you do not believe me.'

Mr Filmore glanced at the girth and then leant forward to snatch it up. 'Ridiculous! It is bad leather and poor workmanship, that is all,' he spluttered, coiling up the strap rapidly in his hands as he saw Jonathan staring at it closely. 'Thomas—' he turned to the footman, who was trying hard to look busy clearing the sideboard '—take this away—see that it is destroyed at once so no one else is tempted to try and mend it—I shall have words with the saddler, of course.

'And you, Jane. . .' He shook his head in sudden, apparent grief after Thomas had taken the girth out of his hands. 'Your fancies are becoming ever wilder. What reason would Piers have to harm you? He holds you in the highest regard.'

'And pigs fly,' Janey drawled in a biting tone that caused Mrs Norris to gasp and Jonathan and Lord Derwent to exchange an amused glance.

'Really!' Mr Filmore shook his head once more. 'You see now for yourself, Dr Hutton, what I was speaking of.'

'Indeed,' Dr Hutton intoned gravely as he looked

assessingly a Janey, who glared back at him. 'A grave case, I fear. . .'

'A grave case of what?' Janey demanded, her American drawl pronounced as it always was when she was angry. 'Honesty? Piers detests me and has done since I set foot in this house, and anyone who disputes that is suffering from terminal hypocrisy!'

'Now, now, my dear—' the Reverend Norris decided to intercede '—why don't you let my wife take you to your room? You are obviously overwrought.'

'I am not going anywhere until Piers apologises,' Janey said, fixing the Reverend with a glance that made the hand he had lifted to put upon her arm drop back to his side. 'And I am not in the least overwrought, I am merely angry and with good reason, as Mr Lindsay can vouch, since I fell off at his feet.'

'Exactly so,' Jonathan said coolly. 'Miss Hilton has every reason to expect an apology for such a jest, if such an act can be considered a jest?'

There was sudden silence, then Dr Hutton laughed somewhat nervously. 'As Mr Filmore says, it was just bad leather, Lindsay. No sane person would do such a thing as a jest.'

'No sane person would even suggest such a thing!' Annabel said shrewishly, directing a stare at Janey.

'Are you suggesting I am losing my wits, Annabel?' Janey snapped in return, her hazel eyes glittering in her taut face.

'Hrrmph!' Mr Filmore cleared his throat and glanced at the doctor. 'Better to humour her, perhaps?' he muttered.

'Yes, yes,' Dr Hutton agreed with alacrity, giving Piers

a very obvious wink. 'Always better to humour the ladies, eh, Filmore?'

'But I didn't touch the blasted thing,' Piers began sulkily, glaring at Janey. 'If anyone's trying to murder you, it isn't me, though you make it tempting enough.'

'Murder is hardly the right word, Piers.' Mr Filmore gave a rather forced laugh as he saw Jonathan Lindsay and Lord Derwent exchange a look. 'My apologies to you all for this little domestic disagreement. This is all something of a storm in a teacup, gentlemen—but we must allow for these weaknesses in the fairer sex, especially in Miss Hilton's case.'

'Oh, apologise to her, Piers, and then we might all get to enjoy our evening!' Annabel interposed with sudden vehemence.

'Very well,' Piers said sullenly, giving his sister a glare before glancing up at Janey. 'I apologise, dear coz, for whatever wrong, real or imagined, that I have done you. Will that do?'

'I suppose it will have to, since it is the closest you are likely to come to admitting the truth, dear coz,' Janey said bitingly. Then, with an imperious nod to Mrs Norris, Mrs Hutton and Mrs Filmore, she said sweetly, 'Shall we withdraw, ladies? I should not like to keep the gentlemen longer from their port.'

'The ill-mannered, impertinent hussy!' she heard Mrs Filmore exclaim as she swept towards the door to the chorus of agreement from Mrs Norris and the others. 'Behaving as if she were already mistress here!'

And carried it off like a duchess, Jonathan thought with a grin as he hastened to open the door for her.

'Well,' he said as she glanced up into his face with

more than a little uncertainty as she paused at the door, wondering if he might be thinking what the others were saying. 'That was not quite the entertainment I had in mind, but it was very diverting, none the less.'

'I am glad you found it amusing,' she said with more than a little defiance, 'but do not expect me to apologise for my behaviour. Piers is—'

'The most unpleasant young man I have ever had the misfortune to meet,' he interrupted her softly, then, moving to screen her from the others with his back, he touched a finger to her lips. A fleeting, devastating, tender gesture that rooted her to the spot. 'I am on your side, Miss Hilton—I'd scarcely dare to be otherwise. And I shall come to your support in the drawing-room as soon as I am able. I fear you are going to be the subject of a concerted attack,' he added as Mrs Filmore began to advance, supported by Mrs Norris, with Mrs Hutton and Annabel fluttering in their wake.

'I have survived worse.' She smiled at him over her shoulder, as she walked on through the door. 'Apaches and bears frighten me, Mr Lindsay, but not Mrs Filmore and her cronies. What can they do? Lock me up in my room like some errant child?'

They could do exactly that—or worse, he felt like calling after her, as the nagging unease, which had been growing since Janey had dropped the girth upon the table, suddenly crystallised into a definite suspicion. He dragged his eyes from Janey's retreating back and turned back to the others. No, he told himself, as he looked from the moustached Mr Filmore to his overplump, silly wife, and then to Annabel and Piers. He was becoming as wild in his imaginings as that rustic.

The Filmores were just ill-mannered, narrow-minded bigots who thought that anyone who did not think or behave as they did was somehow weak in the head. To think they might be deliberately trying to make Janey look unbalanced and unfit to manage her affairs was to credit them with too much intelligence. And as for attempted murder—that was even more inconceivable. And what reason would they have? The Filmores had money enough, if rumour was to be believed. They did not need the Pettridges Estate badly enough to risk hanging for it.

But, none the less, he was not entirely reassured as he glanced after Janey and caught the flash of her red skirts as she disappeared into the drawing-room. He found himself wishing she were a little less fearless, a little more cautious in demonstrating her contempt for the Filmores—at least until she reached her majority. A great deal could happen in five months.

Chapter Eight

'Mr Filmore is engaged upon business and the rest of the family are not at home, sir,' Dawson informed Jonathan the following afternoon.

That was something Jonathan already knew, having seen the Filmore siblings and their mama in their carriage heading down Southbrook's long drive towards the house from his bedroom window. Instructing Perry to detain them for as long as possible, he slipped out of the back door as they had rung at the front, taken his horse and headed for Pettridges Hall at all speed.

'And Miss Hilton?' he asked. 'Is she at home?'

'I will enquire, sir.' Dawson headed ponderously for the library, while Jonathan impatiently paced the hall; scanning the portraits upon the walls, he was not surprised to find that the brass plates on the frames identified them as Filmores. A gloomy-looking lot, he decided, all hanging judges and horse-faced women.

Where was that damned butler? He sighed fiercely, the minutes seeming like hours. He had to see her—he'd scarcely had the chance for so much as a word with her in the drawing-room last night, what with Miss Filmore's caterwauling of Italian songs, and Hutton's determination to recount every run the local hunt had had in the last twenty years. No, not see her, he amended, with wry self-honesty, he wanted to be alone with her, be able to touch her—as he had ached to do the previous night.

'Sir?' Dawson had returned and informed him that Miss Hilton was in the library, and he was to go in.

Old Fenton had obviously had a taste for books or display, Jonathan thought as the library doors were shut behind him. The room was lined from floor to ceiling with row upon row of leather-bound volumes. For a moment he could not see Janey, and then her bright 'Good morning' caused him to look up to the very top of a rather unstable-looking library ladder, where she was bracing herself by her knees against the top rung as she flipped through a thick volume.

'Good morning.' His gaze skated over her as he spoke, taking in everything about her, from the neat knot of coiled hair upon the crown of her head, to the kid slippers, peeping out from beneath the hem of her moss-green pelisse gown. The gown could scarcely have been a more modest contrast to one she had worn the previous night. The sleeves billowed from the shoulder, then tightened to fit closely at the wrist; the tightly fitting bodice buttoned from her narrow waist almost to the little winged collar that framed her long slender neck.

But it made no difference. The unsatisfied aching desire to hold her, which had kept him awake half the night, returned in an instant. He wanted to drag her off the ladder, put his lips to the little white V at the base of her throat, undo those buttons, one by one. . .

'I'll come down,' she said, reaching up to replace the volume she was holding upon the top shelf.

A faint, barely audible groan came involuntarily from his throat as his eyes followed the lift and fall of her breasts beneath the constricting bodice.

Hearing him, she glanced down. The colour left her face. She had been aware of him watching her the previous evening, but then his hunger had been contained by the necessities of convention. This was different—they were alone, there was nothing to stop them—

'Oh!' she gasped as she trod upon the hem of her gown and her foot slipped.

'Miss Hilton!'

Grabbing at a shelf, she regained her balance as he lunged for the base of the swaying ladder and steadied it, amid a shower of pages from an old volume she had dislodged in the wild lunge to save herself.

He exhaled slowly with relief, leaning momentarily against the ladder, his forehead pressed against a rung, before he lifted his head to look at her again.

'Come down,' he said almost wearily. 'Please.'

She descended slowly, carefully, holding up her skirts with one hand, the side of the ladder with the other. She was shaking inside, not because of her near fall, but because of the way she could feel his eyes on her, following every dip and sway of her hips, every movement.

She stepped on to the floor and turned to face him and found him herself in the circle of his arms as he held either side of the ladder, and so close that the tips of her breasts grazed against his coat and became instantly hard. She drew in a rapid, audible breath and shrank back slightly against the ladder, something like the beginnings of panic fluttering in her stomach. It was one thing to tease, to dally with the idea of being his mistress, another to see the desire that flared like a flame in his dark eyes and know that they were alone and unlikely to be disturbed.

'You are very pale,' he said, after a moment in which his gaze burned across her face. 'Have you hurt yourself?'

'No. I—I did not sleep well last night,' she said tightly. She had not slept for longing for him. Those secret dissatisfying caresses during last night's dinner had left her tossing and turning until dawn, longing to be in his arms again, longing to be alone with him. But now that she was—she was suddenly, inexplicably afraid of the intensity written in his face.

'Neither did I.' There was a husky note in his voice that made her insides contract. 'I could not sleep for thinking of you in that red silk gown—and out of it,' he added, his mouth curving as he heard her faint, but sudden intake of breath.

She swallowed, her mouth and throat suddenly dry at the image his words conjured up in her mind, and wished that he would take her in his arms. When he held her, she forgot that she barely knew him, forgot that he did not love her, forgot that she could never hope to be more than his mistress.

'I was wondering if you might be able to think of any remedy for my insomnia?' he went on softly.

'Mrs Hutton swears by camomile tea—' she blurted at, her nerve breaking suddenly. 'You must be thirsty after your ride, I'll ring for some refreshment.' She was babbling but could not help herself. 'Some madeira— would you like—?

'I do not want any madeira,' he cut her off in mid-sentence, trapping her with his weight against the ladder. 'Or camomile tea,' he added thickly.

She lifted her gaze from the snowy folds of his cravat and looked up into his taut face, her heartbeat slowing to what seemed to her a deafening thump as his night-dark gaze held hers for a moment, before dropping to her slightly parted lips. She stared up at him, her back pressed to the ladder, her whole body unbearably tight with anticipation, with memory of his kisses, his touch.

'Well?' His voice was low, velvety, sending a shiver along her spine.

'Some brandy, perhaps?' she offered as a last-ditch defence with a wobbly smile. If he did not take her in his arms soon, if he did not touch her soon, she would scream—

'No,' he said almost tenderly, his lips curving a fraction. 'Just you.'

She made a small ragged sound of relief as he caught her to him, and kissed her. Kissed her almost roughly, crushing her lips beneath his, thrusting into her mouth, demanding instant and absolute possession with a fierceness that was echoed by his hands as they swept over her, moulding her back, the narrowness of her waist, the curve of her hips, the fullness of her tight, swollen breasts. . .

She gasped, her head tilting back, as his fingers found their aching peaks, drawing her into a spiral of piercingly sweet and unsatisfying pleasure, a pleasure intensified to an unbearable anticipation as his lips moved from her mouth, along her jaw, down the length of her throat in hungry, rushed kisses that heated her skin and melted her inside. She reached for him clumsily, her hand sliding across his chest and shoulders, seeking a way to touch him, to give him the pleasure he was giving her, but finding nothing but frustrating layers of wool and brocade.

'You are wearing too much. . .' he groaned, echoing her own thought as he began to pull at the buttons of her bodice. 'I want to touch you properly.'

Her eyelids lifted and, with a mixture of shock and anticipation so sharp as to be almost painful, she watched his fingers move down, parting the buttons, so impatient, so male and hard against the satiny softness of the upper curve of her breasts, so brown and weathered against the translucent lawn of her chemise.

This was utter madness. And she did not care. She did not care about anything while he was touching her. Her heart began to race crazily as the last button parted at her waist and his fingers lifted to the neck of her chemise, tugged at the ribbon that fastened the gathered neck, then with almost rough haste at the soft folds.

'You are irresistible. . .' he growled as he slid a hand beneath the green wool on either side of her waist.

'Am I?' The words were half a gasp as the heat of his hands seemed to burn into her flesh and she shut her eyes.

'Yes.' The word was hardly more than a low noise in his throat as he bent his head and kissed her. Kissed her throat, kissed the frantic beating pulse at its base, kissed the tight, tight swell of her breasts.

Her breath came in a startled groan as his mouth closed suddenly over an aching, coral peak. The rush of heat, of pleasure was so overwhelming, so unexpectedly intense that she clutched at his shoulders, her fingers curling into him as the floor seemed to sink beneath her feet. She had thought she understood desire, understood what it was to be touched by him, kissed by him, but this—this was almost frightening. She did not know if she wanted him to stop or. . .

The thought was lost as he sucked her into a whirlpool of fiery, all-consuming and unfamiliar need that had her reaching for his head, stabbing her fingers into his hair, dragging his mouth up to hers as she pressed against him, wanting to be closer, closer—

She made a sound of protest as he pulled back from her suddenly with an oath.

'Janey—' his voice was low, urgent, demanding her attention as she opened bemused hazel eyes '—listen.'

'Listen?' She looked at him blankly, her breath still coming in shallow gasps, her pulse racing. 'What is it?'

'Your guardian—looking for you—' There was a soft, almost despairing note in his voice as he looked at her. There was no other exit from the room but the one into the hall and, even if there had been time to repair the damage to her dress, it would make no difference. One look at her shining eyes, her reddened and swollen lips and her half-fallen-down hair tumbling about her glowing face, and any man with half a brain would know exactly what they had been doing.

He swore beneath his breath. What had possessed him? He had come here to warn her to behave with discretion and had behaved like the most impetuous of fools. My God! This should amuse them at the club, Lindsay caught like the greenest of flats with an unmarried girl!

'My guardian?' she repeated slowly, still too drugged with desire to register anything except him.

'And, by the sound of it, Dr Hutton, in the hall. . .' He sighed as he reached out and pulled her sleeves back up onto her satiny shoulders and jerked the gaping edges of her bodice together with rough haste, trying and failing to find buttons and loops that matched.

'What?' She stared at him in horror as she realised the full extent of their predicament. 'Filmore and Hutton?'

'I am afraid so,' he said resignedly. 'If you happen to know of a secret door in the panelling, now would be a good time to tell me of it.'

'No,' she said as she fumbled frantically with her buttons, half of which were undone, half in the wrong loops, 'but there is a perfectly good window. Come on!' She ran for one of the window-seats, knelt upon it and started to lift the heavy sash window. 'Help me,' she hissed at him as he stood staring at her.

'You can't get out of the window—it must be eight feet or more to the lawn,' he said, shaking his head.

'I assure you I can,' she said with some asperity. 'I've done far worse with an Indian upon my heels—now, come on!'

'Miss Hilton!' He dived for the window as she sat upon the sill and swung her legs out. 'Wait! I am not entirely without honour, you don't have to—*Janey*!' He reached for her, but was a second too late to prevent her from launching herself off the sill.

He swore again as she landed in a somewhat untidy heap upon the lawn, and then vaulted out after her as the handle on the library door started to turn.

Janey was already sitting up when he landed beside her on his feet, as neatly as an Indian brave dropping from the branch of a tree. Jonathan Lindsay was a man of many talents, she thought wryly.

'Miss Hilton—are you all right?' His voice was thick with anxiety as he bent over her.

'Perfectly.' She grinned at him as she scrambled to her feet and gathered up her skirts, displaying a most unlady-like length of silk stocking-clad leg. 'We'd better run before they come to close the window.'

She set off without waiting to see if he was following, running as fast as her encumbering skirts would allow, down the length of the house, keeping close to the wall, and stooping now and again to avoid being seen through the lower set windows.

She wouldn't have looked out of place amongst the rifle boys in Spain, he thought with a half-smile, finding to his surprise that he had to exert himself a little to keep up with her.

'I think we are safe enough now,' she said a few minutes later, as she halted and leant her back against the grey stone wall of the terrace, gasping in breaths of the raw November air.

'Thanks to you,' he said as he slumped beside her. 'You went down the side of the house like a professional skirmisher, Miss Hilton.'

'And you came out of that window like one,' she said with a slightly breathless laugh. 'But then, you have had plenty of practice, no doubt, at escaping irate guardians and husbands.'

'Now and then, in my ill-spent youth.' A wry smile flickered across his mouth, then he sobered as he glanced sideways at her.

'And what about you, Miss Hilton, where did you acquire your skirmishing skills—escaping compromising situations with your lovers?'

'No, Indian raids,' she said a little sharply.

'Indian raids!' He stared at her, his astonishment written upon his face. 'You mean your settlement was attacked by natives?'

'All the frontier settlements were attacked from time to time.' She shrugged. Sometimes, in this quiet part of civilised England, she found it difficult to believe as well. It had been a different world. 'I shot my first Indian at thirteen. . .'

Her voice trailed off as the memory came back suddenly, sharp and horribly clear. Her father had been crouched against the wooden wall of the cabin, trying desperately to reload his musket; the Indian, a painted, snarling giant with an axe raised for the killing stroke, and then the blood blossoming across the Indian's chest as the recoil from her musket had sent her tumbling backwards.

'I had to do it,' she said, more to herself than him, 'he would have killed my father.' She turned her head slowly to look at him, wondering why she had blurted it out to him, when she had never spoken of such things to anyone else in England.

Her grandfather had made it very clear, on the long voyage home, that the less she said to anyone about her former life the better. He had told her that the people he expected her to mix with would simply not understand, and he had been right. It had caused consternation enough when she had inadvertently mentioned eating at the kitchen table.

'You had to fight—at thirteen—a girl?' His voice was shocked, but his eyes were dark, compassionate, as he held her gaze. 'I saw women fight in Portugal—but I never imagined that you had had to do such things. Somehow, one always imagines America to be an extension of England. . .'

'You would lose that illusion the moment you stepped further west than Massachusetts,' she said, her eyes dark as she remembered the endless trails she had travelled with her father and mother. Trails that had taken her through the forests of Kentucky, over stony mountains and desert and across the endless, buffalo-studded prairies. 'No, it is not like England at all, Mr Lindsay. There are no fences, no walls, no boundaries—no one to tell you what you may or may not do—there are no limits except what a man imposes upon himself.'

'You make it sound like some sort of egalitarian paradise,' he said.

'Then I have not described it properly. The western frontier is more beautiful than you can possibly imagine, but it is also crueller—' She broke off again, remembering the extremes of heat and cold, the constant struggle to grow enough food for man and beast out of land that had never been cultivated.

'Your parents?' he asked tentatively as he saw the darkness in her eyes. 'Was that an Indian raid?'

'No—' she shook her head '—they died of the smallpox, together with thirty-five out of our forty neighbours. It kills more settlers than the Indians ever have or will. I have never felt so helpless or so afraid in my life. Indians you could fight—but the smallpox, with no doctor in five hundred miles—' she shrugged '—it was hopeless.'

'And then you went to live with Lilian?' he said, thinking that it was little wonder Mrs Filmore and her ilk held no terrors for her.

'Yes. With more than half the settlement dead, we decided it was best to go back to St Louis. Lilian had a little money put by and we set up the boarding house. We had no other means of making a living.'

'That is where your grandfather found you? In Lilian's boarding house? It must have been very hard for you.'

'In some ways, yes,' she replied absently. 'But Lilian protected me as if I were her own daughter. The trappers used to tease me about my book reading, my ladylike manners, and ask me if I were saving myself for some English lord—' She stopped, but a brief glance at his impassive face reassured her that he had not noticed her slip of the tongue. 'But on the whole they were kind enough.'

'And your plethora of lovers you told me about, were they kind enough?' he said mildly, watching her face.

'Lovers. . .' She looked away from him.

'Yes, lovers—tell me about them, Miss Hilton,' he invited softly, and she knew that he had not missed that slip of the tongue after all.

'I—I can't—' she exhaled heavily '—there weren't any.'

'I was beginning to wonder if you were going to wait until after I had seduced you to tell me that,' he said with a half-smile. 'You have not been playing entirely fair, Miss Hilton.'

'If I was not playing fair, Mr Lindsay, I should not have jumped out of the library window so that you might be saved from having to make me an offer!' she retorted hotly.

'You did not have to do that,' he replied gently. 'I am

not so devoid of honour as to have abandoned you to the gossips.'

'I know,' she said grittily. 'Why do you think I jumped?'

His brows lifted. 'Were you not in the least tempted to take advantage of the situation and net yourself an eminently eligible bachelor?'

'Oh, I was tempted—' she matched his mocking tone, but her eyes were dark, wistful, as she looked at him '—for a moment.'

'A whole moment! Thank you for the compliment,' he replied with a laugh and then sobered as his blue gaze met hers. 'Did you think we should deal so ill together?'

'I could not see how we would do otherwise.' She tried and failed to smile. 'You have made it clear enough that your intentions towards me did not include marriage. I should not care to be a resented wife who had been forced upon you, Mr Lindsay.'

His eyelids dropped for a moment, and then lifted. 'No, you would not, would you?' he said with a slow smile as he reached out to draw her to him. 'And yet you would be my mistress? Why is that?'

Because I could very easily love you, because I only feel alive when I am with you—The answer was in her eyes as she looked at him, but she forced a smile and shrugged her slender shoulders. 'The Filmores would probably say it is because I have lost my wits.'

'Then perhaps we are a pair,' he murmured and kissed her briefly upon her parted lips. 'Do you know, I almost find myself regretting our escape from the matrimonial mousetrap?'

'Almost, is not entirely flattering,' she said a little tersely.

'It is closer than I have come to considering marriage in a long time.' He laughed softly as he brought her closer against him, and rested his chin against the top of her head.

'Then I suppose I should thank the Almighty for my lucky escape,' she returned, her eyes sparking green fire as she tilted her head back to look up at him. He was playing with her, teasing when her heart was being twisted into a knot.

'Yes, you should.' He was sober suddenly, the mockery fading from his eyes, leaving them dark, empty. 'I am not the man you think me, Janey. I have few principles and less conscience. You'd do better to find yourself another curate to fall in love with.'

'No.' She shook her head. 'I'd rather have a man with a few good principles than one with a great many bad ones and so much conscience he considered kissing me a sin to be atoned for.'

'You are not making this easy, Janey. I am trying to do the honourable thing,' he sighed.

'Why break the habit of a lifetime?' she said flippantly, though she felt like she was gambling for her life. 'You seem to have survived well enough so far.'

'True.' He gave a gasp of laughter as she met his gaze with clear, challenging eyes. And then he hugged her to him, so close, so tight she thought her bones would crack. 'But I am not sure I am going to survive a liaison with you, Miss Hilton, not at all sure. . .'

That made two of them, she thought, her heart racing beneath her ribs. But she did not care. So long as it was not over, she did not care. So long as she could be with him, she did not care about anything.

'But we are going to have to be a great deal more discreet.' He sighed. 'I am not sure you even ought to risk seeing me alone at all at present.'

'Why?'

He hesitated for a moment. 'Look, I know this sounds ridiculous—but I found myself wondering last night if Filmore might be trying to retain control of your fortune and estate after your majority.'

'But how could he do that?' She stared at him.

'By having you declared unfit to manage your own affairs,' he said slowly.

'You mean, by saying I am mad. . .?'

'The whole family seem to go out of their way to try and give that impression. The business with the girth did not exactly help to counteract it.'

'No, I suppose not—' she laughed ruefully '—but I think you are reading much more into their maliciousness than there is. Piers always does something to make me look foolish every time we have a remotely eligible man to dine—the Filmores want us to marry, you see. And Mr Filmore seems to consider my fortune his son's birthright. I thought he would have apoplexy when my grandfather gave his blessing to my engagement to Edward. And now my year of mourning is over, he is trying to persuade me again.'

'So that's what they are about.' He gave a stifled laugh. 'I should have guessed. I take it you are not co-operating in their scheme?'

She gave him a speaking look of disdain. 'I have made it perfectly clear to Piers that I should rather die than marry him—' She broke off as he went very pale and still, his face frozen as he stared down at her.

'What is it? You look as if someone has just walked over your grave.'

'Nothing,' he lied, her words conjuring up a vivid picture in his mind of her tumbling from the supposedly rotten staircase and of the severed girth. 'But. . .' again he paused '. . .I know this is none of my business, but what happens to your inheritance, if you were to die before you marry or reach your majority?'

'It all goes to a charitable trust for the good of the village—at least, that is what I asked my grandfather to specify in his will,' she said after a moment of thought. 'So it would do Piers no good to murder me, Mr Lindsay,' she added with a smile. 'Though I am sure there are moments when he would like to.'

'You are sure?' He exhaled slowly with relief.

'Well, no,' she confessed, 'I have never actually seen the entire will. But I assumed he did as I asked.'

'Find out,' he said firmly, 'and do it discreetly—'

'Jane! Jane! Where are you, girl?' Mr Filmore's shout from the other side of the house made them both start.

'Damnation!' he swore softly as he caught her to him and pressed a swift kiss on her forehead before releasing her. 'The man is everywhere he is not wanted. You'd better go before he gets here. A few flowers in your hair and you'd pass for Ophelia in her mad scene—a fact that I am sure would not escape your guardian or be unwelcome to him.'

She laughed as she picked up her skirts. 'You make me feel like a heroine in one of Mrs Radcliffe's Gothics. You need not worry, I assure you I can defend myself from Piers Filmore and his father.'

'Yes, I suppose you can,' he laughed, but his eyes were serious as they sought hers. 'But this is not the American frontier—battles are not won and lost with a musket here. You will bear in mind what I have said? At least until you are sure of the contents of the will?'

'I'll try,' she replied blithely over her shoulder as she turned towards the terrace steps. The knowledge that he cared for her enough to be concerned had sent her heart soaring.

He watched her run up the terrace steps, a frown upon his forehead. She was so damned fearless and, for all her experience of life at its rawest, so innocent.

'Lindsay!'

He turned slowly to see Mr Filmore and a tall, slightly seedy-looking man in a black coat, which was shiny at collar and cuff, approaching rapidly.

'Filmore.' He returned the greeting easily and nodded to the stranger, waiting for the introduction that Mr Filmore neglected to make.

'What brings you here?' Mr Filmore demanded.

'A neighbourly call, that is all,' Jonathan said coolly. 'I gather I have had the misfortune to miss your wife and daughter, but your butler said I might find Miss Hilton in the garden.'

'You have not seen her, then?' Mr Filmore said sullenly.

'No, have you lost her?' Jonathan enquired innocently.

'Yes, and that is not unusual,' Mr Filmore huffed and turned to his companion. 'As I told you, sir—her behaviour becomes wilder by the day. Between you and me, sir, I fear a complete breakdown of her sanity is imminent. Mr Lindsay will vouch for how she assaulted my son—and he was witness to her hysterical accusations last night—'

'Oh, I should call Miss Hilton's behaviour last night entirely reasonable in the circumstances and, as for her assault upon your son, I should swear upon oath it was nothing but self-defence,' Jonathan drawled as he held the other man's gaze. 'But if you are really concerned, you must let me recommend a friend of mine. He attended the King's late father in his youth and has made a study of such maladies ever since. I doubt there is a physician in the country more expert in such matters. He'll be down for the ball, I'll send him over—'

'Oh, I am sure there is no need to inconvenience you, sir,' Mr Filmore said hastily.

'It will be no inconvenience—in fact, I shall insist.' Jonathan smiled, but it did not reach his eyes. 'I am sure you would not want people saying your ward received anything less than the best of care, Filmore. You know what ugly rumours can arise out of such things.'

'Quite!' Mr Filmore said tersely. 'But I fear Miss Hilton's beauty has caused you to look upon her behaviour with a far-too-indulgent eye. Now, if you will excuse me, sir, I have some business to attend to.'

'Of course.' Jonathan bowed. 'My apologies to your wife and daughter—I am sorry I have missed them.'

Janey flung open the ballroom doors that led off the terrace, shut them behind her, and then leant against them for a moment to catch her breath, her spirits higher than they had been since she had last galloped across the endless flower-bedecked prairie in the spring. He cared for her, she was suddenly sure of it. Her skirt in her hands, she waltzed her way across the polished floor, dancing with him in her imagination, reliving every touch, every kiss, every look from his blue, blue eyes, until she was dizzy and laughing, her hair flowing loose down her back.

'Jane! Whatever are you doing?' Mr Filmore's roar from the terrace door broke her daydream into pieces. 'You look like—a—a wanton!'

Her heart plummeting, she skidded to a halt, and looked up to see Mr Filmore, Dr Hutton and a man she had never met before at the terrace door, staring at her in stony disapproval.

She drew herself up to her full height and pulled together the upper edges of her bodice as she saw the stranger's cold beady gaze drop and linger there.

'I am practising,' she said coolly, 'practising for the ball. It is so long since I have danced, I thought it would be wise.'

'Practising! Half-naked!' Mr Filmore spluttered. 'You are a—'

'Now, now, Mr Filmore, we must remember, Miss Hilton suffered a dreadful loss in that terrible tragedy. It is enough to disturb anyone's power of reason,' Dr Hutton put in hastily.

Janie exhaled heavily. 'Dr Hutton, I broke my leg last year, not my brain, and I should have thought even a physician of your calibre could tell the difference. My powers of reasoning are quite intact. My gown is unbuttoned because I became hot while dancing,' she continued coolly, as Dr Hutton's mouth opened and no sound came out. 'And now, if you will excuse me, I shall go and find some refreshment. Dancing is such thirsty work, is it not?'

Head high, she dropped them the most mocking curtsy she could manage and headed for the door.

'Come here! Come back here! Dr Pearson has come especially to see you,' Mr Filmore shrilled after her.

'He need not have gone to the trouble, I am quite well,' she said blithely over her shoulder, before shutting the door behind her with a satisfyingly final click.

'You see—what more evidence do you need, gentlemen?' Mr Filmore demanded triumphantly.

But Dr Hutton and Dr Pearson exchanged a doubtful look.

'I am not sure—not sure at all,' Dr Pearson said. 'Not now this Lindsay fellow is going to involve the King's physician—I have my reputation and my practice to think of.'

'Your reputation, sir, is that you will do whatever is required for a sufficient fee,' Mr Filmore snapped ill-temperedly. 'But perhaps you are right—perhaps we had better wait a little until Lindsay has lost interest. By all I hear of him, it should not be long before he eschews the country life for Town.'

'You are sure he will lose interest?' Dr Hutton said tentatively. 'He seemed to be very taken with her last night. I do not think he would be a good man to make an enemy of, Filmore.'

'Of course he will lose interest!' Mr Filmore snorted. 'Lindsay and a millhand's daughter! I think we are safe enough there, Hutton, don't you?'

'I suppose so,' Dr Hutton agreed without great enthusiasm.

Chapter Nine

'Well, you were right, Jono,' Perry said as he strode into the drawing-room at Southbrook. 'I took a quart or two at the local hostelry. That seedy-looking fellow you saw at Pettridges is a doctor—of a kind. He's from Town, apparently—and, the landlord's daughter tells me, Filmore is paying his bills.'

'Ah, I was afraid of that.' Jonathan sighed.

'You really think Filmore is trying to get her inheritance,' Perry said, frowning.

'Yes, I do think so. I think he came up with this scheme for retaining control of her estate when it became clear that she would never consider marriage to the inimitable Piers.'

'Hadn't we better do something about it?' Perry said.

'I think I may have done enough to stop him already. I made it clear enough to him that I suspected what he was about. If I know Filmore, he will not risk a scandal.'

'Mmm,' Perry said doubtfully as he dropped into a chair beside the fire, causing the spaniel that had been occupying it to give a muffled yelp and scrabble clear.

'But if he's prepared to go that far to get her money—supposing he goes further, Jono?'

'Murder?' Jonathan grimaced. 'It has crossed my mind, Perry, especially when I saw that damned girth and remembered what that rustic said. But I think Filmore was as surprised by the business of the girth as we were. And I cannot see Filmore risking his neck for her fortune, not when the family has money of its own.'

'Perhaps he doesn't anymore,' Perry said thoughtfully. 'By all accounts, Master Filmore was playing very high last year at the tables—and losing a great deal more often than he won.'

'Yes—you could be right. I think I shall look a little closer into Mr Filmore's affairs.' Jonathan frowned as he stared into the fire. 'And I think we will take a look at that staircase in the Tower. I'll ask Avery to come with us—he could probably tell if it had been tampered with.'

'And Miss Hilton? Are you going to warn her?'

'I have hinted to her that Filmore might be trying to get her declared unfit to manage her affairs and she should be careful in her behaviour—but as for the possibility of murder? If I tell her that, she will probably confront Mr Filmore the next time she sees him. At best, such accusations would only increase his case about her mental state, and, at worst—'

'It might provoke him into acting,' Perry finished heavily.

'Do I think Lindsay will make Annabel an offer?' Piers gave a derisive snort as he replied to his mother's hopeful question at the breakfast table the next day. 'About as likely as snow in June, I'd say. He might be an arrogant swine, but he's not half-witted.'

'Thank you kindly, brother dearest.' Annabel gave him a withering glare.

'Don't fret, my dear. . .' Mrs Filmore beamed at her daughter '. . .I think Piers is quite wrong. What other reason would he have to call so soon after coming to dine?'

'Oh, for heaven's sake, Mother!' Piers groaned. 'Can you not see? It is as plain as the nose upon your face— it is not Annabel he has taken an interest in—it's your delightful ward. Isn't it, my lovely coz? He never takes his eyes off her the whole time he is here.'

Janey sighed and put down her fork. 'If you say so, Piers, who am I to argue?'

'Who, indeed?' Mrs Filmore snapped. 'As if Mr Lindsay would consider a match with Jane! Really, Piers, I think you have must have taken too much brandy last night.'

'That would be nothing new,' Annabel muttered.

'I did not say he meant to *marry* her.' Piers directed a glance at Janey. 'He probably knows he does not need to. . .since half her girlhood was spent in a brothel.'

'Piers—' Annabel gave a stifled little splutter upon a mouthful of bacon '—you should not say such things.'

'Why not?' He laughed and raised his wine glass to his lips. 'It's true, ain't it, my beautiful cousin?'

Janey went white and put down her coffee cup with a shaking hand as she fought back the impulse to hurl the hot liquid into Piers's mocking, sneering face. Piers had an unerring instinct for hitting upon her weakest point. But after Jonathan's warning about Mr Filmore's attempts to make her look unbalanced, she was not going to give him the satisfaction of seeing that he had done so, not if it killed her. She exhaled slowly, before looking up, and gave him her sweetest smile.

'No, it was a boarding house. But I should not expect you to appreciate the difference, Piers—that would require a mind capable of thought. And in the six months I *was* there, I was treated with greater respect and kindness than I have ever known in this house since my grandfather died. Now, if you will excuse me, I have an appointment to keep in Salisbury. I shall take the gig and Kate will come with me.'

'Have you Papa's permission?' Annabel asked, her small pointed tongue flicking out of her mouth like a snake as she licked a crumb from her lip. 'He said last night that none us must venture abroad until the unrest in the countryside has been quelled.'

'Oh, I doubt he will mind my going.' Janey smiled. 'Do you think so?' Jonathan Lindsay had issued her the same warning, out of what she was sure was genuine concern for her safety, insisting she must not even think of walking to the waterfall on her own. A request she had agreed to reluctantly because it was their only opportunity to meet alone.

Annabel looked almost embarrassed for a moment and did not answer the question.

'And you'll miss Mr Lindsay, if he calls at his usual hour,' Piers drawled.

'Good, then I shall have him all to myself,' Annabel said archly. 'Aren't you afraid I shall steal your admirer, Jane?'

Janey's gaze travelled slowly, from Annabel's over-curled and over-beribboned head to her pink silk gown, which was also decorated with ribbons, beads, lace and fringing. She shook her head and smiled, a slow, confident smile. 'No,' she said with a quiet certainty, 'I am not at all afraid, Annabel, but by all means consider yourself at liberty to try, should Mr Lindsay call.'

Mrs Filmore's gasps of incoherent outrage followed her out of the dining-room as she made her exit. Once outside the door, she laughed aloud. If war was what the Filmores wanted, war was what they were going to get!

'I don't like this,' Kate said as Janey drove the gig smartly through the small town of Hindon. 'It's too quiet. Where is everyone? There's no one in the fields, no children playing. And look at The Lamb—' she pointed to the coaching inn '—they've still got all the shutters on the windows. I think we ought to go back.'

'I have to see my solicitors,' Janey sighed. 'It's the only way I might be able to stop the Pettridges men from being caught up in the disturbances. But if you don't want to come, Kate, you don't have to—your mother lives near here, doesn't she? Why don't you wait there for me?'

'You can't go to Salisbury on your own, miss, it's a good ten miles from here. And it's hardly light yet.'

'Yes, I can,' Janey said firmly. 'Now let's go and ask your mother what is going on.'

'Miss! Miss!' Kate came running out of her mother's small redbrick cottage some five minutes later, her round face white against her red hair, her blue eyes brimming. 'They've gone to break the machines at Pyt House Farm, four hundred men, and they've got hammers, and pitchforks and iron bars, and my father's gone with them. But that's not the worst of it. My brother, Harry, he's run after him. He's only ten, miss—he'll get himself killed, I know he will. Mother says the squire has already sent to Hindon for the Yeomanry cavalry.'

'Four hundred,' Janey repeated. That had to be an exaggeration. But if it was anything like that number, she knew the authorities would react with a heavy hand, for fear of real insurrection.

'Yes, miss,' Kate said tearfully. 'And Harry's with them.'

'How long ago did he leave?'

'A half-hour or so.' Kate hiccuped.

'Then get in,' said Janey, making an instant decision. 'It's three miles to Pyt House. If we are quick, we might catch them before they get there, though how we're going to find Harry amongst four hundred, I don't know.'

'He'll show up, miss—' Kate managed a watery smile '—his hair's the same colour as mine.'

'Well, that's something.' Janey tried to smile back at her as she backed up the gig and flicked the whip over the pony's head. 'We'll find him, Kate.'

Jonathan reined in his horse in front of Pettridges Hall just as the sun broke through the early morning mist. He scanned the windows, hoping that he might see Janey and be able to signal to her to meet him at the stables without encountering the Filmores. A hope that was dashed as he saw a twitch of the yellow morning-room curtains, and the flash of Annabel Filmore's carrot-coloured curls.

He swore and sighed as a moment later the door opened. Fixing a polite smile upon his face, he dismounted. So much for getting to see Janey alone; now he would have to endure an hour of taking tea and Mrs Filmore's conversation. He sighed again. At least he would be able to see Janey, even if they could not really talk—or touch. Then he brightened. He could still suggest a ride, if the weather stayed fine. It shouldn't be too difficult for Janey and himself to lose Annabel and Piers Filmore.

Annabel came tripping down the steps to meet him in a frothing gown of pale lemon, bedecked with cerise ribbons, which also adorned her head. The overall effect was rather as if she had been dropped in a giant trifle, he thought uncharitably. But then, all women had looked grossly overdressed to him since he had met Janey. He reluctantly dragged his thoughts away from the direction of Janey in her clothes and out of them, and made his bow to Annabel.

'Why, Mr Lindsay, we did not expect to see you so early,' Annabel trilled at him. 'And it is such a cold morning. You must come in and take some refreshment. Dawson—' she turned to the butler who was hovering at the open door '—see that Mr Lindsay's horse is taken care of.'

Jonathan followed her into the morning room, making occasional answers to her observations about the weather and the progress upon the plans for the ball. His heart sank as he saw that only Mrs Filmore was in the room, netting a purse in a combination of particularly lurid colours that he suspected could only have been chosen by her daughter.

'Mr Lindsay! How lucky!' Mrs Filmore greeted him. 'We've just been looking through my daughter's sketchbooks and were about to put them away, but now you will be able to see them—I shall ring for some tea, and then we will settle down to enjoy them. Annabel is so clever with her drawing.'

'And Miss Hilton?' Jonathan asked casually, after some fifteen minutes of leafing through the leatherbound drawing-books of sketches that had long since become indistinguishable to him. 'What is she doing this morning?'

'Oh, she's gone to Salisbury—'

'I really don't know—'

Annabel and her mother spoke at the same moment.

'Salisbury?' Jonathan stared at them. 'Then I presume Mr Filmore and Piers are with her?'

'No. They are out shooting,' Annabel replied. 'Papa did tell us we must all stay at home, but Miss Hilton ignored him as I am afraid she usually does.'

'You mean she has gone alone!' Jonathan stood up so abruptly he nearly knocked over the occasional table beside the sofa.

'Well, yes. . .' said Mrs Filmore uncertainly, as his blue eyes held her accusingly.

'And no one even tried to stop her, I suppose,' he said bitingly. 'Have none of you read the papers these last two days? The whole countryside is upon the edge of revolt. Anything could happen to her!'

'I do not see how we could have prevented her,' Mrs Filmore said huffily.

'At the very least your husband and son could have gone after her—when did she leave?'

'About an hour ago,' Annabel sighed.

'Then you will excuse me if I take my leave,' he snapped, made his bow, and strode out of the room.

*   *   *

What optimism Janey had had about finding Harry died as they were forced to a halt in the village of Fonthill Gifford because the way was blocked by more men than Janey had ever seen gathered together in one place before. A murmuring, growling mass of ragged, angry men, clutching every kind of weapon from broom handles to pitchforks. In their midst, looking like a vessel afloat upon a stormy sea, was a prosperous-looking gentleman, standing upon a cart and struggling to make himself heard. She recognised him as John Benett, who owned the Pyt House estate and was the Member of Parliament for the county.

As she watched, wondering what to do next, one of the labourers was hoisted up upon the shoulders of his fellows.

'All we want is two shilling a day so we can feed our families. If we don't get it, we'll break your machines.'

John Benett's response was to begin to read a newly issued Royal Proclamation against rioting, which was received with derisive jeers. And not a man moved as he resorted to threats that the army would be used to stop them.

'We'll have broke the machines and gone before the Redcoats get here,' the labourers' self-appointed spokesman shouted at Benett.

There was a roar of agreement and the mob began to move.

'Wait!' John Benett shouted. 'I'll give five hundred pounds to any man of you who will inform upon ten others! You may have it now, this very moment!'

If he was prepared to part with five hundred pounds, why not give them their two shillings a day for an honest day's work? Janey felt like asking him.

'Don't you mean thirty pieces of silver, Benett?' the spokesman returned fiercely. 'You keep yer five hundred, you'll find no Judases here!'

There was another roar of agreement from the crowd as they began to flood away in the direction of the farm.

'I can't see him, or Dad, anywhere.' Kate sighed as she scanned the fast-thinning crowd.

'No,' Janey said. 'What a fool that man is! He could not have said anything more guaranteed to make them angry than to offer them money to inform against their own.'

'Aye!' Kate's pretty face contorted with dislike. 'Just because we're poor, the gentry think we have no honour or feelings!' And then, glancing at Janey, she added hastily, 'I know you're not like that, miss. You're different.'

'Well. . .' Janey sighed '. . .the Filmores would probably tell you that's because I'll never pass for the gentry, and,' she added, glancing at the furious and red-faced John Benett, who was striding up and down his cart barking orders at his agent, 'I can't say I particularly wish to, if he is an example of it.'

'Miss! There he is!' Kate stood up suddenly in the gig and pointed. 'I saw him—Harry!'

'Come on, quick, before we lose him.' Janey leapt down and knotted the reins about a gatepost.

Clinging to each other, they tried to push their way to where they had glimpsed Harry, but the weight of men behind them carried them the wrong way.

'Out the way, you two,' a burly man said without rancour as he pushed them to one side, 'you'll get hurt here—' Then he swore. 'Kate, what in the good Lord's name are you doing here? You get yourself home at once!'

'But, Dad—'

Janey, glimpsing Harry a few yards away, left Kate to make the explanations. Picking up her skirts, she began to run.

'Harry!' she shouted, but knew the boy had not a chance of hearing her amid the general clamour. And, no matter how hard she tried, he remained a little ahead of her, his bright red head bobbing amid the now-running crowd. Why did women have to wear skirts? she thought fiercely as she hoisted hers up further to try and get more speed, and then she tripped and fell on the cobbles. By the time a kindly shepherd had hauled her to her feet, she had lost sight of Harry and Kate and lost her hat.

The mob swept her forward again, out of the village and down the track to the farm. It was impossible to turn back down the narrow, thickly hedged lane—there was no choice but to go forward.

'Harry!' she shouted again, hopelessly, as she caught sight of the boy.

And then all was bedlam as the crowd swept into the yard, breaking down the locked gate, climbing the walls. Janey pressed herself into the corner of a wall, for lack of anywhere else to go. The expressions on the faces of the men breaking into the barns with their iron bars scared her. This was no peaceable protest, this was months of suppressed anger and fear spilling out.

'That's broken the blasted machines!' someone shouted minutes later. 'That'll show Benett what we think of his wages!'

'And about time!' A man whom Janey took for a

quarryman, judging by the dust upon his clothes, agreed noisily beside her. 'Tuppence a day! That's what they want us to work for! Tuppence!'

'Aye, and it'll not be long before that's all he wants to pay us!' a smocked labourer said, pushing a stave into the quarryman's hand as there was a crackling that Janey recognised as musket fire.

She stood up from where she had been crouching. 'Get out of here!' she shouted at the quarryman and the labourer, who both stared at her as if she were a ghost. 'That's musket fire. The Yeomanry are here—and they'll have you in this yard like rats in a trap.'

The labourer turned his grey head. 'She's right—they'll catch us here like we had the French at Hougemount—'

'The woods,' Janey said desperately. 'Tell everyone to head for the woods—'

She broke off and lunged forward, catching Harry's arm as he came skittering across the yard.

'Hey, let go of me!' Harry struggled and wriggled.

'No!' Janey said, hauling him almost off his feet. 'Your sister is looking for you, and if we don't get out of here, we are very like to be hurt. So do as I say.'

'She's right, lad.' The labourer took Harry's other arm. 'Come on, miss, I'll help. Let's get into those woods—that's the only chance we've got against the mounted boys.'

Somehow, despite her hampering skirts, Janey managed to follow Harry and the labourer as they scrambled over a grey stone wall.

The first screams came as they began to run across the ploughed field that stretched between the farm and the wood. She glanced behind her. There were mounted men in the lane, slicing at the labourers with sabres, some using the flat of the blade, others the edge.

'Come on, Harry!' She increased her pace, cursing the heavy chalky soil that clung to her boots and petticoats, slowing her down, as she half-carried, half-dragged the frightened boy towards the shelter of the beech wood.

Glancing behind her, she saw men were streaming from the yard, running for the woods like herself, pausing now and again to shout defiance at the mounted men who had ridden into their midst, wielding swords against pitch-forks, firing muskets at men armed with nothing but stones.

If she had not seen it with her own eyes, she would not have thought it possible in England, she thought, as the keen air began to knife into her labouring lungs as she and Harry plunged on across the furrows.

'We'll give 'em a run for their money,' the grey-haired labourer greeted her from behind a beech tree as she threw herself and Harry flat upon the mossy ground at the edge of the wood as a musket ball whistled over her head. 'Horses won't be so much advantage to them here.'

'No, but—muskets will,' Janey said breathlessly, lifting her head to see men cantering across the ploughed field towards them, some waving sabres, and some whooping as if they were in the hunting field.

Her heart sank. There could not be a better recipe for disaster than frightened and angry labourers who did not have the sense to run away, and half the local young gentlemen out to play soldier.

The nearest horseman, in a scarlet and gold officer's uniform, was a good-looking young man, in a fair and florid way. She recognised him with a groan. Captain

Crowne, late of the Horseguards, and one of Annabel's admirers. He had dined often enough at Pettridges. And his solution to any complaints by the poor was to 'hang 'em or flog 'em'. Mercy was not among his more noticeable qualities and she doubted he would stop to distinguish between woman, child or labourer.

'Harry—' she caught the shivering boy's hand '—when I say go, I want you to get up and run with me as far into the woods as we can. We'll find our way through and get out the other side. Ready?' she asked him.

Harry nodded.

A second later they were running, ducking and diving between the trees as the first cavalrymen began to crash into the woods.

She ran almost blindly, her head ducked against the brambles and twigs that tugged at her hair and clothes.

Harry kept with her, keeping pace as she slithered down a bank and splashed across a small stream but, as they climbed up the far bank, he began to flag.

'Got a stitch in me side, miss,' he gasped. 'I got to stop for a bit.'

'You can't,' she gasped back, dragging him on. Behind she could hear the pounding of a horse's hooves, the splashing of its feet as it came through the stream.

But then Harry stumbled, and she knew it was useless. They could not outrun a horse.

Putting Harry behind her, she bent and snatched up a fallen bough. She knew enough of fighting to know that a sharp blow upon the horse's nose would cause it to shy away and spoil the rider's aim. The bough held high, she wheeled to face the horseman. And then, as she recognised him, a relief that was so intense that it made her weak at the knees swept through her.

'Mr Lindsay—oh, thank God!' She sat down abruptly upon the damp muddy ground beside Harry and tossed aside the bough.

'No,' he said, his voice as taut with anger as his white face. 'Thank Kate. She at least had the sense to do as her father told her. I found her sat in your gig, and she told me what you were about—that, I take it, is her errant brother?' He glanced down at Harry's small crouched figure.

She nodded, then, as the thought struck her like cold water, lifted her head. 'What are you doing here? You have not joined the Yeomanry in murdering defenceless men?'

'No!' he snapped as he swung down from his horse. 'Though I could easily be persuaded to do murder upon you!'

'Why?' She looked at him blankly.

'Why?' The air left his lungs with the rush of an explosion. 'Shall I tell you what I am doing here, Miss Hilton? I called early at Pettridges to see if you wished to ride and discovered that you, in your infinite wisdom, had decided to travel to Salisbury unescorted on a day when half the countryside is in revolt! And that the blasted Filmores had done nothing to stop you!

'I came after you as far as Hindon, where I was told by an ostler that you had turned back for Fonthill Gifford—and having followed you there I find you have run willy-nilly into the middle of bloodbath after some damn fool boy! And next I see you climbing over a wall and being chased across a ploughed field by that blood-thirsty hothead, Crowne!'

'Oh.' She got slowly to her feet and began to dust herself down. 'There is no need to shout. You are frightening Harry.'

'No need to shout!' he repeated heavily. 'That's the worst mêlée I've seen since Waterloo. There is a man lying dead back there, another with half his arm gone—I thought you were going to get yourself maimed or killed!'

'It would have saved you the trouble of murdering me,' she said tentatively. She had never seen a man quite as angry before, or as worried about her safety, she thought, her eyes very soft and dark as they sought his.

'True.' He exhaled audibly. And there was the merest glimmer of a smile upon his lips and a slight warming of his blue gaze as he looked at her. 'But don't tempt me, Janey Hilton.'

'You're not going to murder 'er! I won't let you!' Harry piped up suddenly, brandishing Janey's discarded bough.

'I'll give you sixpence if you are quiet,' he said, fixing Harry with a glare.

'All right.' Harry dropped the bough with alacrity. 'I won't say nothing.' He held out his grubby hand.

Jonathan fished in his blue coat pocket and dropped the silver coin into it.

'Sold for sixpence. You're not very good at choosing your knight errants, are you, Miss Hilton?' he said drily as their eyes met over Harry's head.

'Oh, I do not think I chose so very badly, Mr Lindsay,' she returned with equal dryness. 'You are a little late, but you are here.'

'I told you I am no damned Galahad,' he growled.

'Come on, let's get out of here before Crowne arrives and recognises you—or some other amateur soldier shoots us by accident. You look like a hoyden,' he added as his gaze travelled over her loosened hair hanging to her waist, and her muddied and torn grey pelisse.

'Then I suppose I had better behave like one,' she said mildly and, stepping forward, reached up to kiss him briefly upon his cheek. 'Thank you for coming to find me.'

'If you think to get around me like that, you won't, not this time,' he growled. And then, as her hazel eyes continued to hold his gaze steadily, he turned away suddenly to pick up Harry and dump him unceremoniously upon the saddle of his sweating grey and took the reins over its head so he could lead it.

'But,' he added, his stern face cracking suddenly into a grin, 'you may feel at liberty to try to do so upon another occasion, Miss Hilton.'

And then, as there was the crack of a musket and a scream of pain nearby, he sobered again. 'Come on—the sooner you are safely home, the better I shall like it.'

'So why this sudden desire to go to Salisbury?' he asked a little later when, the sounds of the fighting fading behind them, they slowed from a half-run to a walk, the grey plodding patiently behind them with Harry pretending to be a soldier upon its back.

'I wanted to see my solicitors, to ask if there was anything I could do to prevent Mr Filmore laying off men when it is so close to the time when I shall have control of the estate.'

'I see. . .' He sighed as his arm curled about her waist. 'You do not think this fracas might make him change his mind about using the threshing machines?'

'No. He thinks only of profit and nothing else.' Janey sighed.

'Then write to your solicitors,' he suggested. 'I will deliver it by hand for you tomorrow and wait for their answer.'

'You would do that for me?' She turned her head to look him in the eyes.

'I should do almost anything for you, Miss Hilton.' He smiled down at her, and her heart seemed to skip a beat. 'I thought you might have realised that by now.'

They walked on in silence and she let her head rest against his shoulder. It did not matter that she was muddy, cold and tired—even the riot did not seem to matter. She had never felt so happy in her life as she did at this moment with his arm about her, knowing he cared for her.

Chapter Ten

But as she stepped into the kitchen of Will Avery's grey stone cottage late the following evening, her spirits were far from buoyant. And her heart sank further as the ten men packed into the tiny room snatched off their caps as she greeted them, and she saw the hope in their eyes. A hope that died as she gave the smallest shake of her head.

'No luck then, miss?' Will Avery said heavily as he offered her the carved oak chair, black with age, which stood beside the fire.

'I am afraid not, Will,' she said as she sat down. 'I have just got an answer back from my solicitors. There is nothing I can do until I am twenty-one. I am so sorry.' she added as she saw the hopeless, desperate expressions upon the faces of the ten men Mr Filmore had let go. 'I have tried every argument I could think of to change Mr Filmore's mind, to no avail. And he says if any try and prevent him using the machines by violence he will have the Yeomanry out as they did yesterday at Pyt House.'

'Tha's it, then, I'll break their bloody machines—like they did yesterday and in Ansty,' one man said, his voice raw with anger. 'I'll break 'em into pieces and anyone who tries to stop me—and I don't care if I swing for it. What bloody difference is it going to make? I'd rather hang than watch Bess and the little 'uns starve—'

'Adam, there's a lady 'ere—' a grey-haired man muttered, shuffling his boots on the slate floor.

'It's all right, I quite understand,' Janey said quickly. 'If I were in your position, I know I should feel the same. But please, I beg you to do nothing to endanger yourselves—again—' she added. There were one or two familiar faces she had glimpsed in the mob the previous day. 'As soon as I inherit, I promise that you will have your old employment back and better wages.'

'We know that, miss, but what do we eat for the next five months?' another man said hopelessly. 'Wiltshire wages have always bin worse than Kent and the like, but lately it's bin even worse. None of us has got so much as a farthing put by, the children be half starved as it is.'

'I know,' she said despairingly, 'but there is nothing else I can do unless I marry before my birthday.'

'And there's not much chance of that, with your fiancé dead a twelvemonth,' a young man with dark brown curls said bluntly, 'unless that Lindsay fellow makes you an offer. Will said he's supposed to be the friend to the poor-speaking for us in the Parliament. Can't you persuade him, miss, tell him what good he'd be doing if he wed you?'

Janey stared at him, her heart skipping a beat. Marry Jonathan! She had not even allowed herself to think of it. He had made it clear enough his intentions towards her were hardly the honourable kind. And she had lived long enough in England to know that the sons of Earls did not marry the daughters of millhands, no matter how wealthy, unless they were in desperate need of funds, which Jonathan certainly was not.

And yet—after yesterday she was beginning to believe that he cared for her as well as desired her. So why not, why not ask him? She had not loved Edward, but she had been prepared to marry him to get control of the estate. So, could she not find the courage to ask a man whom she did love if he would marry her? What was there to lose if he refused?

'Tha's enough, Jethro,' Will put in sharply. 'None of this is Miss Hilton's fault, she's a lady, not one of your flibbertigibbets. You've no right to suggest anything of the kind. You make your apology right now.'

'It does not matter, Will—' Janey said, staring unseeingly at the black iron kettle which hissed gently as it hung upon its hook over the flames of the fire. There was everything to lose if she asked him and he refused, she thought sickly. It would be an end to their friendship, an end to her deepest, most secret hopes and dreams.

'It does,' said Will, giving Jethro a black look. 'Though it would help matters if we knew whether Mr Lindsay intends staying on at Southbrook—there's bound to be work if he does.'

'I know,' Janey replied, pulling herself out of her reverie. 'I shall be seeing Mr Lindsay on Saturday evening— if he is to stay on at Southbrook, I am sure he will want to take on some men. The threshing machines are not due at Pettridges Farm until Monday week. Please do nothing before then—I might be able to do something for the family men, at least.'

'Oh, yeah,' Jethro, the blunt young man, said sourly. 'Wait so you can get the Yeomanry out to stop us doing anything. Like sticks to like, especially when there be money in it.'

'That is unfair!' Janey replied fiercely. 'I do not think violence is the answer, but I should not betray you, or act against you. I have known what it is to be hungry, and what it is to watch your family die and be helpless to prevent it!'

'I'll believe that when I see you breaking one of their machines,' Jethro muttered. 'Playing Lady Bountiful is one thing—but risking your neck is another. You go back to your gentry friends, Miss Hilton, you don't belong 'ere.'

'Tha's enough, Jethro,' Will growled. 'Miss Hilton was at Pyt House yesterday, trying to stop Kate Cowley's brother from getting hurt. She's only trying to help us. She's never been anything but a friend to this village and you know it. You apologise to her now and treat her with the respect she deserves or you'll find yourself out of the door before those boots of yours touch the ground.'

'It does not matter, Will.' Janey sighed and stood up. 'Jethro is right in a way. If you are considering violent action, it is better I do not know of it. I had better go.'

Will showed her to the door and closed it behind them. 'Don't take what Jethro says too much to heart, miss. His sweetheart's in the family way; now her father's demanding to know how he's going to support her and the baby since he's got no place.'

'I know. Kate told me of his circumstances.' Janey sighed.

'Did her father get home safe, yesterday?' Will asked.

'Yes, thank heaven,' Janey said with feeling.

'Not like that poor devil Hardy, shot him dead like a dog they did—'

'Yes, poor man.' She frowned. 'If—if anything does happen, you will take care, won't you, Will?'

'I'll do me best, Miss Hilton,' he said. 'And don't you go risking yourself again any other way,' he added somberly. 'After that business at Pyt House yesterday, men are angry. It's not just Southbrook, things are bad everywhere. Half the men in the Knoyles, the Deverills and Mere aren't making enough to feed their families, either—and then there's this talk of bringing in cheap labour from the cities. Tha's making even those men who still have work unsettled. They can't feed their families on what they get now. If wages go any lower—' He broke off with an expressive shrug.

'I cannot think there is any truth in that rumour at least.' Janey sighed. 'Not even Mr Filmore would consider replacing a cowman or shepherd with a factory hand who does not know a cow's nose from its tail or the difference between a sheep and a ram, no matter what the saving. But you will try and stop them from doing anything too rash?' she added as they reached the gate at the end of the brick path.

'I'll try, but I can't promise,' Will said. 'Some of 'em are beyond reason. . .' He paused, his face splitting into a sudden unexpected grin as he opened the gate for her. 'But perhaps things aren't quite as hopeless as we think— looks like you got yourself an escort home again, miss. Afternoon, sir!' he called out cheerfully before turning away. Janey stared at the man upon the grey horse beside her gig, her heart skipping and leaping beneath her ribs as their gazes met and held.

She stood staring at him helplessly, something inside her melting as he swung down from his saddle, all lithe, lean grace, and came towards her.

'What are you doing here?' she said.

'I rather think that is my question,' he said a little tersely. 'I thought you promised me this afternoon you would go nowhere alone again.'

'I am not alone, Kate is with me,' she said glancing towards the gig and smiling a little as Kate, whose eyes had been out upon stalks, hastily looked away and pretended uninterest.

'Two women are little better than one.' He sighed. 'I cannot think what the Filmores were about to let you out again.'

'None of the local people would hurt me,' she replied with a half-smile, as she wondered what he would think if he knew how she had ridden across prairie and through forest with little more than her horse's surefootedness and speed as her protection from wild animal and Indian alike.

'It's not the local labourers that worry me,' he said as he reached out and tucked a stray strand of her honey-coloured hair into her bonnet.

She went still as his fingertip grazed her cheek. 'You—you don't believe this nonsense they are spouting about agents provocateurs?' she said a little unsteadily as his hand dropped back to his side and his blue gaze burned into her eyes. 'It is obvious why men are rioting—the machines are taking away their already meagre livelihood and forcing wages down further.'

'You are probably right.' He frowned. 'But as a favour to me, please do not go about alone? Not until—not until things are settled again. Promise me, Janey?'

'Very well,' she conceded with a smile, the way he said her name, and the concern in his eyes, warming her through like a flame.

He did care for her, he did—she was almost sure of it—almost sure enough to risk asking him if he would marry her. She took a deep breath, feeling herself start to shake inside at the thought.

'You're shivering,' he observed instantly. 'It is time you were home.'

Before she could even begin to frame the question in her own mind, he had taken her arm and handed her up into the gig and the moment was lost.

'I take it the news from the solicitors was not good?' he asked as he handed her the reins.

'No,' she said heavily. 'And I hate to think what will happen when the machines arrive at Pettridges Home Farm—'

'So do I.' He frowned again. 'This business is getting out of hand. There have been disturbances at forty places in the county within the last two days. And, I hear, at dozens of places in Hampshire and Dorset.'

'The whole thing could be stopped in a day or two, if only they would improve the wages a little and the provision for the poor.' Janey sighed as she picked up her whip.

'Perhaps,' he said as he remounted. 'I am not so sure. If the discontent reaches the towns, the government might find itself with a full-scale insurrection upon its hands.' He looked at her, as she was silent. 'Miss Hilton, if you hear of any plans for mischief, promise me you will tell me. If disciplined troops are brought in before anything happens, it can prevent people getting hurt.'

'I know.' She released the brake and flicked the whip over the skewbald pony's head. 'But I don't think the men trust even me enough to tell me of any plans, not any more, not after yesterday.'

'Well, whatever happens, promise me you will not get involved. I might not be there to rescue you next time.'

'I am hardly your responsibility,' she reminded him with a sideways glance.

'No?' His dark brows lifted as he met her gaze. 'Someone has to look after you, Miss Hilton; as the Filmores do not seem to consider it their duty, I see no alternative but to make it mine.'

'I am quite capable of looking after myself, Mr Lindsay,' she replied a little sharply, aware of Kate hanging upon every word. 'And you have no duty to me at all.'

'I suppose you are right, Miss Hilton; he replied with a smile from his saddle. 'But won't you indulge me, just a little?'

'I rather thought I already had,' she muttered as she flicked the whip over the horse's head, and sent the gig rattling forward down the stony lane.

'Not nearly enough.' He grinned at her as he brought his horse alongside.

And, as his wicked, laughing gaze met hers, she knew with sudden absolute certainty that this was the only man she wanted to spend her life with, the only man she would ever want.

Then suddenly, as he stared at her, his expression sobered. 'What did your solicitors say about the will? Who does get your fortune if you die before you inherit or before you marry?'

'They would not tell me,' she said. 'Apparently, my

grandfather left express instructions that that part of his will was to remain secret unless it was required. I think he meant to protect me from adventurers.'

'So no one but the solicitors know who would inherit if something happened to you.' He sighed with relief.

'Yes,' she said, and then laughed as she looked at him. 'You're not still thinking Piers is out to murder me, are you?'

'No.' He gave a slightly forced laugh. 'Of course not.'

'You're so lucky, miss.' Kate sighed as she helped Janey out of her many-caped green pelisse coat. 'Having a man like Mr Lindsay in love with you—'

Janey gave a mirthless chuckle. 'I am not at all sure he is in love with me, Kate.'

'Oh, miss, it's as plain as a pikestaff.' Kate hung up the coat to dry, ready for brushing. 'He's that smitten, he'd jump off a cliff if you told him to—riding all that way to Salisbury and back.' She said enviously, 'There's nothing he wouldn't do for you. I wish my Tom was half as keen.'

'I wish I was as sure of Mr Lindsay's affections as you are,' Janey said as she sat down in the chair beside her bedroom window. 'If I was sure of that. . .' The rest of the thought remained unvoiced as she stared out across the dusky park and saw the mounted figure cantering through the thickening mist. The horse, the rider in the dark coat and broad-brimmed hat, were totally familiar to her. . .

'No!' The word dragged out of her throat and she shut her eyes.

'Miss! Miss!' Kate came running across to her. 'What

is it? You're white as a sheet—' She stopped and blanched as she also looked out of the window.

'Mr Grey!' she gasped.

'You saw him, too?' Janey gave a sigh of relief and steeled herself to look out of the window again and saw only the empty park. 'I saw him as well.'

'It was his ghost!' Kate was aghast.

'No, don't be silly,' Janey said briskly, pulling herself together. 'It was nothing but a trick of the mist and the light. And please, Kate, don't mention it to anyone else—Mr and Mrs Filmore seem to think me weak in the head as it is.'

'Yes, and it would suit them all too well if you were,' Kate said, frowning as she looked out of the window into the mist. 'Yours wouldn't be the first fortune got that way, miss.'

'Not you as well, Kate,' Janey said in despair. 'Mr Lindsay is half-convinced the Filmores are plotting to have me "put away", if not worse.'

'You should take heed of him, miss. Did you never hear of that poor Henrietta Harcourt, miss? It were in all the papers. But I suppose it were just before you came,' Kate said. 'Her uncle bribed some doctors and had her put into the asylum so they might keep her money for themselves. It was only when her sister came back from India that the uncle was found out and she was released.'

'It sounds like something out of a novel, Kate.' Janey laughed.

'Maybe, but it happened, miss,' said Kate weightily. 'And I think you should be careful it don't happen to you.'

'I'll do my best,' Janey said placatingly as her maid returned a little huffily to her tasks. 'I shall do my best to behave with absolute decorum next time the good Doctor comes to dine.' Then, as a thought struck her, she turned. 'Get your cloak, Kate, we're going outside.'

Ten minutes later she and Kate stood staring at the soft turf of the park.

'That's the heaviest ghost I've ever heard of, Kate,' Janey said, frowning as she stared at the fresh hoofprints.

'Yes,' Kate agreed. 'Do you know what I think, miss? Someone is trying to frighten you out of your wits. Now I think of it, it wasn't Mr Grey I saw, it was a hat like his, a horse like his—'

'But who would do that—?' Janey began to say, shivering and pulling her hood closer about her face against the raw air.

They both spoke at once as they looked at each other.

'Piers!'

'Master Filmore!'

'I think the best thing to do is to ignore it,' Janey said after a moment. 'We'll let him think we did not see him. He'll probably try again tomorrow—'

'And the next day,' Kate chuckled.

'And the next.' Janey laughed. 'Let's hope for inclement weather, shall we, Kate?'

On Saturday evening, Janey stared into her pier glass, her stomach so full of butterflies that she felt sick. Preparations for the ball had meant that she had not seen Jonathan for three days. And the confidence she had begun to have about his feelings towards her had diminished beneath the barrage of Annabel's gossip about his past conquests, and the number of broken hearts he had left strewn in his wake.

If he had disdained to marry the daughters of Earls and Dukes alike, why would he consider plain Miss Hilton? A question Annabel had not hesitated to taunt her with every time Jonathan Lindsay called.

She took in a breath, and lifted her chin. Nothing ventured, nothing gained, she told herself, as she surveyed herself critically. Her gown was a foaming confection of white silk gauze and lace, with short puffed sleeves which began at the top of her arm, in line with the low heart-shaped neckline, leaving her throat and shoulders bare. The uppermost layer of gauze had scattered embroideries of gold thread that shimmered and glistened in the candlelight.

'Don't forget this, miss.' Kate came forward and fastened a wide white silk ribbon stitched to a pearl-encrusted buckle about the tiny waist, tying the two ends at the back in a bow.

'You don't think we have made it too short?' Janey said, smoothing back the front of the full rustling skirt to peer at the toes of her gold satin slippers, which she was unaccustomed to seeing.

'No, miss,' Kate assured her. 'Madame Tovee said it's the fashion now for the hem to sit upon the ankle. Now, if you'll just let me finish your hair.'

Janie stood patiently as Kate wound and pinned the knot of heavy gold on top of her head with pins decorated with delicate pearl flowers, and then carefully arranged a fall of loose ringlets at either side of her slender face.

'There,' said Kate happily, 'now you look like a princess in a fairy tale, miss.'

But I don't feel like one, thought Janey, as Kate carefully arranged a grey silk brocade cloak about her shoulders. Her reflection might look cool, remote, but inside she was shaking with nerves. How did you go about asking a man to marry you? Especially a man like Jonathan Lindsay—

'That's the carriage coming round, miss,' Kate said from the window. 'You'd better go down.'

'Yes.' Crossing the room to her tester bed, she picked up the gold and white reticule from where it lay upon the red counterpane and made her way slowly out of the room.

'Oh, do come on, Jane,' Annabel said tartly as Janey stepped off the last step of the flight of stairs into the panelled hall, where the Filmores were gathered in all their imposing finery. 'We've all been waiting for you, though I do not know why you are coming—you can hardly be expecting to dance when you are so lame.'

'Annabel,' Mrs Filmore said reprovingly with a toss of her scarlet and black plumed coiffure, which reminded Janey of the undertaker's horses. 'I am sure Jane will be far too sensible to make a spectacle of herself again. Now, come along, girls, into the carriage and do be careful not to crush your skirts, and you had better be careful of your hair when you are getting in, Annabel.'

Janey glanced at Annabel's hair, which was an elaborate arrangement of curls, false pieces and what looked like half a shrubbery of pink silk flowers and green leaves, adding at least four inches to Annabel's diminutive height.

'You should have borrowed Annabel's maid,' Mrs Filmore said as she followed Janey's awestruck gaze. 'The French are so clever with their hands. That girl of yours always manages to turn you out with a touch of the country convent about you.'

*   *   *

'What is it that makes women think they look attractive with half an ostrich, a ton of horsehair and a garden upon their head?' Jonathan said to Lord Derwent after they had greeted the Morrisons and the party from Fonthill and ushered them into the already-full ballroom.

'Don't ask me—most of 'em would wear a water pail if they thought it was the latest mode,' Lord Derwent said with a grin. And then, as he glanced down over the gilt balustrade into the hall, he smiled. 'Course, there are some who have more sense, like Miss Hilton.'

'She's here?' Jonathan's expression of bored indifference changed to a smile as he, too, looked down over the balustrade and saw Janey begin to climb the stairs in the Filmores' wake, several steps behind them, tall, slender and shimmering in her white and gold gown.

'Gets better-looking every time you see her, that one,' said Lord Derwent. 'There's something about her that you just can't help watching—moves like a thoroughbred.'

'If you have no serious intentions towards her, I should take it kindly if you would watch someone else,' Jonathan said quietly. 'She's mine, Perry.'

'Glad you realise it,' Lord Derwent murmured, then put on a bright smile as he greeted Mrs Filmore and Annabel effusively.

Janey climbed the last of the stairs at an ever slower pace, her knuckles white as her face as she gripped her reticule. After one snatched glance from the hall, she had not dared look at Jonathan.

She was not going to be able to do it, she thought. She could not just walk up to him and ask him to marry her.

'Oh—' She gave a gasp as she tripped upon the top step and all but fell.

But then her arm was caught, held, and she regained her balance.

'I knew it. I knew she would show us up,' Annabel muttered audibly to her mother.

But Janey barely heard her, as she found herself staring at Jonathan's snowy cravat and felt the warmth of his hand upon her arm, burning her skin.

'You really must stop prostrating yourself at my feet,' he said, his voice so warm, so affectionate, that she found the courage to look up.

He smiled down at her, and then his dark brows knit as he saw how pale she was, and felt how she was trembling.

'Are you all right? You did not hurt yourself?'

'No.' Her voice was a whisper.

'You're shaking.'

'I am nervous,' she stammered. 'I am not used to these occasions—I am not often invited.'

'I think you soon will be,' he said softly. 'Half the men here are already looking at you, so be sure to save me the first dance. You have no idea how much I have missed you these last three days—'

'Have you?' she said a little breathlessly, as the hope began to grow inside her that it would be all right after all.

'Jono! Look who we have with us! Is she not a sight for sore eyes?' a male voice said loudly from behind Janey.

Jonathan's hand clenched so suddenly and violently upon her arm that she had to bite back an exclamation. And then she saw the colour drain from his face, leaving his blue eyes blazing, brilliant.

'Susanna!' The name was hardly more than an exhalation.

Her insides turning to ice, Janey turned her head as

his hand dropped abruptly from her arm. Staring back at Jonathan from the midst of Sir Richard Hoare's party was a tall, queenly-looking woman, with pale green eyes, jet-black curls and a warm smile on her voluptuous mouth.

From her other side, Janie heard Lord Derwent swear softly beneath his breath.

'Well, Jono, have you forgotten me entirely?' The woman stepped forward in a rustle of purple silk, her hand outstretched, confident of her reception. 'You have not written to me in weeks.'

'I could never forget you, your grace.' There was an edge to Jonathan's voice that Janey had never heard before. She found herself staring as he picked up the languid white fingers and raised them slowly to his lips. And then, without knowing how, she knew quite suddenly, without any doubt at all, that he and this woman had been lovers, perhaps still were. She remained transfixed, stunned by a pain that was almost physical as she watched Jonathan's mouth curve into a smile.

The brunette's pale green eyes left Jonathan's face and flicked to Janey, and one finely plucked black brow lifted in amusement.

'I do not want to distract you from your guests.'

Jonathan turned slowly, and looked at Janey blankly.

He had forgotten her, Janey thought, forgotten her from the moment he had set eyes upon this elegant aristocratic woman, who was so obviously his perfect counterpart. She wheeled, a sudden lump in her throat that threatened to choke her as she fled into the noise and light of the ballroom.

There were people everywhere. A rippling churning sea of pale silks, lace, taffeta and glittering cut stones, with the dark coats of the men standing out like black rocks in the foam.

And not a single face she recognised. She could not even see the Filmores. At a signal from someone, the orchestra began to play a waltz. The floor around her emptied and she found herself standing alone in its centre. People were staring at her, wondering why she was alone. She walked hastily to the side, acutely conscious of the barely discernible limp that made her skirt dip and sway as she walked.

'Excuse me, excuse me—' Somehow she made her way through the press and found a chair against the wall beside two gossiping dowagers. She sat down, wishing she could sink into the floor as curious glances followed her.

'Susanna Spencer always was shameless,' the elderly woman nearest to her said. 'To have the nerve to come here tonight after she jilted him for old Sutton—well!'

'Quite,' the other woman agreed with a nod of her plumed head. 'Just look at her now! You would think it was him she was wed to.'

'I thank God daily that she is not,' said the first dowager. 'And I'd have thought Jonathan did, too, after six years.'

'I heard he still means to marry her, the moment Sutton is dead and she is free.'

'Piffle!' said the first dowager. 'Jonathan would never be such a fool, not even if he still loved her.'

'I should not be so sure,' the other said. 'Susanna Spencer came out of her cradle knowing how to turn any man's head.'

Feeling sick, Janey followed the direction of their gaze. The brunette was laughing, her beautiful head thrown back, emphasising the lushness of her white breasts, which were barely contained by the purple silk gown. And her elegant white hand lay possessively upon Jonathan's arm as they entered the ballroom. She looked away, staring down at her reticule. She had been so stupid, so full of foolish dreams and hopes—

'Lost your admirer, Jane?' Annabel's voice made her start. 'You did not really think that he would have eyes for anyone else now Susanna Spencer is here, did you? She is the only woman ever to touch his heart, everyone knows that.'

Everyone but me, Janey wanted to say. But she knew if she opened her mouth she would cry and make a complete fool of herself.

'Mama wishes you to join her upon the sofa at the far end,' Annabel continued. 'You'll have plenty of company—it's where all the wallflowers sit.'

'I'd rather stay here,' Janey forced out of her constricted throat.

'Oh, why can you never do as you are told!' Annabel snapped.

'Leave her,' the dowager snapped back at Annabel. 'You're not doing her any good. It is obvious she is out of sorts. Now, Miss—' She paused, glancing at Janey.

'Hilton,' supplied Annabel.

'Miss Hilton will be quite safe with us, will she not, Hermione? No doubt she is feeling a little shy,' the dowager said, snapping out her finely carved bone and lace fan and beginning to waft it to and fro.

'Are we going to dance or not?' The chinless young man standing behind Annabel sighed.

'I suppose so, come along.' Annabel flounced away in

a flutter of white and pink taffeta and blue lace.

'Thank you,' Janey said after a few minutes in which she struggled to regain her self-control.

'Think nothing of it,' the dowager said grandly. 'Never could stand the Filmores—unpleasant people, very unpleasant. Got some bad blood in them somewhere, I'll warrant. Now, lift that pretty chin up, m'dear. You're not the first heart to be broken by my grandson.'

'Your grandson?' Janey said, startled.

'Yes—' the dowager's wrinkled face split into a wicked grin '—I'm Lady Stalbridge and this is my sister, Lady Merwell. Now, do tell us all about yourself and how you know my grandson.'

Somewhat to her surprise, Janey found herself doing so. Even the circumstances of her first meeting with him amused Lady Stalbridge greatly.

'Yes, he can be quite the most arrogant of men at times, just like his grandfather—' she laughed '—but I don't think you could quite accuse him of being a dandy, his hair is always a little too unruly. And he saved your little arsonist, you say?'

'Yes.'

'He always was kind,' Lady Stalbridge said confidingly. 'Tries hard to hide it, of course, but I remember him taking on four stable lads once who were twice his size, all because they had kicked a stray dog. In tears, he was—'

'Thank you, Grandmama.' Janey went very still at the dry voice and found herself staring at the buttons upon Jonathan's dark blue coat.

'What d'you want here?' Lady Stalbridge asked. 'Thought you'd be dancing with that Spencer hussy.'

'If you are referring to the Duchess of Sutton, she is dancing with Lord Bath.'

'Dropped you for a title again,' his grandmother replied with a snort. 'That does not surprise me.'

'For your information, Grandmama, Miss Hilton has already promised me this dance.'

'Developing some taste at last,' Lady Stalbridge said. 'About time, boy.'

After a frosty glare at his grandmother, Jonathan extended his hand to Janey. 'Miss Hilton? Will you do me the pleasure?'

He was cool, aloof, formal, as he held out his hand to her. She did not know him like this, Janie thought, she did not know him at all.

'Will you do me the pleasure?' he repeated.

'I don't dance,' she said stiffly. She did not want to be in his arms. Did not want him to touch her and know that it meant nothing because he had only ever loved this Susanna Spencer and so obviously still did. 'I can't.'

'Nonsense,' said Lady Stalbridge, after glancing from her to her grandson. 'Anyone who moves as gracefully as you can dance. You go with him, m'dear, and give that woman a taste of her own medicine. That's what you've got in mind, Jono, ain't it?'

'You don't understand,' Janey began helplessly. 'My leg—I have not danced in a year.'

'I don't care,' Jonathan said, stooping to take her hands and pulling her unceremoniously to her feet. 'You are going to dance with me if I have to carry you around the floor.'

'All that money gone upon his education and he still forgets his manners.' His grandmother sighed heavily, earning herself a another furious glare from her grandson as he propelled Janey to the dance floor.

'Janey,' he said exasperatedly a few seconds later, 'we cannot dance if you insist on trying to be a sword's length away from me. Come here and tell me what the devil is wrong with you this evening.'

'There's nothing wrong with me,' she said miserably, her treacherous body melting and slipping into perfect step with his as he brought her closer.

'There is, I can feel it,' he said. 'Lord Derwent has not said anything to you?'

'Lord Derwent?' She looked up at him blankly. 'About what?'

'Nothing.' His expression relaxed. 'I would not hurt you for the world. You know that, don't you?'

'And the Duchess of Sutton—I suppose you would not hurt her either?' she said bitterly.

'So that's it—!' He laughed with relief. 'Feeling a little green about the gills, Janey?'

'Yes!' she said fiercely—the last thing she could bear at this moment was his teasing.

'You need not be.'

'No?' She tossed her head. 'You love her, you still want to marry her. But you would not marry me, not even if I asked you, would you?' Her voice faltered on the last two words, which had come out wistful rather than angry, as she met his gaze, and hoped against hope that he would tell her she was wrong.

'Is that a proposal, Janey?' He chuckled. 'I suppose I should have expected that you were the one woman who would not wait to be asked. This is very sudden, considering the alacrity with which you jumped out of the window last week. Has my grandmother put you up to it? I confess I am flattered, even if she did.'

He had not even taken her seriously, she thought with a mixture of rage and despair. But then, why should that surprise her? He had never had serious intentions towards her—never wanted to marry her as he had this Susanna Spencer!

'You need not be flattered,' she returned sharply. 'It is just that my lawyers said there was nothing I could do to prevent Mr Filmore bringing in the machines until either I am of age or I marry.'

'I see.' He laughed aloud. 'Only you, my sweet radical, would think you would persuade me to marry you on the grounds that it would keep men in employment.'

'That's not the only reason,' she said thickly. 'It is just that I thought, given the speech you made and the way you helped Jem, you might consider—'

'Sacrificing myself for the greater good.' His mouth twisted into a smile that did not reach his eyes. 'You've got the wrong man, Janey. The speech was a sham from beginning to end!' He sighed as he swung her around the corner of the floor. 'Something which I have been meaning to tell you for some time. I made it merely for a wager.'

'A wager! Upon such a subject!' She lifted disbelieving eyes to his face as she understood with sudden clarity Annabel and Piers's disdainful laughter. 'You mean the whole thing was a lie. How could you?'

'Probably because I am an unprincipled wretch who cares only for his own pleasure,' he said wryly, not meeting her gaze. 'I did try to warn you I am no Galahad, Miss Hilton.'

'I see,' she said flatly. 'And kissing me like you did, was that for a wager, too?'

He missed a step. 'Janey—'

'Oh, no.' She stopped dead as she read the answer in his eyes, heard it in his voice. 'It was, wasn't it? You—' Her voice cracked suddenly upon the last word and she tried to pull out of his grasp. 'It has all been a game to you.'

'Janey, Miss Hilton!' he hissed at her as he jerked her back into step. 'Filmore is watching us. Do you want to give him more evidence to suggest your mind is unbalanced?'

'What more evidence does he need when I have been stupid enough to believe you actually liked me—wanted me? Tell me, did they all know? Annabel, Piers—how they must have laughed.'

'No one knows—at least, only Perry, with whom I made the wager, and he will not tell anyone. In fact, he wished to call it off almost as soon as it was made—'

'And I am supposed to be grateful for that!' she snapped, the gold flecks in her hazel eyes blazing as brightly as the gold thread upon her dress in the candlelight.

'Janey, listen to me. I do like you.' He dragged her closer. 'A very great deal—it might have begun as a wager, but it was far more than that from the first moment I touched you. You must believe that.'

'I don't know what to believe,' she said bitterly. 'I thought you were different from the rest! I thought you cared about things—people—I thought perhaps you lo—' Her voice trailed off. She had to get away before she made a complete fool of herself.

She twisted out of his grasp, picked up her skirts and ran. Ran through the other dancers, out of the ballroom and down the broad sweep of stairs, past startled servants, across the hall and out of the house. Jonathan's spaniel, which had somehow found its way out of the gun room, followed her, barking at her heels, thinking it was a game.

She ran and ran, across the wet lawns, along the drive to the stable block.

'My carriage, please,' she blurted out to the first groom she encountered. 'The blue barouche with the bays—I want to go home.'

'Well,' said Lord Derwent as he stood upon the front steps of Southbrook House beside Jonathan and watched the lanterns of the barouche disappearing along the drive into the darkness, 'looks like you have just lost the wager, Jono.'

'It would seem so,' Jonathan said grittily.

'Oh, well, I don't suppose it matters now Susanna is here,' Lord Derwent said carefully. 'I gather old Sutton is on his deathbed and she will soon be free. That must be some consolation for losing Miss Hilton's affections.'

'Oh, yes,' Jonathan said with a ragged laugh. 'I have the undying devotion of a woman who left me at the altar, and who is willing to throw herself at me while her husband is upon his deathbed, by all accounts. My perfect match, wouldn't you say, Perry?'

'I did try to warn you,' Lord Derwent said with a sigh. 'And as for Susanna, I never thought she was the perfect match for you, nor did any of your friends.'

'Or your family,' Lady Stalbridge said crisply from behind, making them both wheel around. 'Now, tell me about Miss Hilton. I understand she is your neighbour. What's her background?'

'She is the granddaughter of an industrialist; her mother ran away with a millhand to the colonies,' Jonathan said tersely. 'Her grandfather brought her back to live upon the neighbouring estate after her parents' death.'

'Oh, what a pity,' Lady Stalbridge replied. 'I rather liked the look of her. Not such a simpering ninny as most of the young women one gets nowadays. But, of course, that makes her quite out of the question for you, Jonathan.'

'Out of the question for what?' her grandson asked belligerently.

'Marriage,' Lady Stalbridge replied blithely. 'You know the rules, Jonathan. Lindsays don't marry trade, never have.'

'I do not give a damn for the rules, Grandmother,' Jonathan declared. 'And who said anything about marriage?'

'Such passion, Jonathan,' his grandmother said reprovingly. 'You'd almost think you were in love with her.'

'I assure you I am not. I gave up such sentimental notions a long time ago.'

Lady Stalbridge and Lord Derwent exchanged glances as Jonathan stalked away.

'How is it that someone as intelligent as Jonathan can be such a dolt when it comes to his own feelings?' Lady Stalbridge shook her head.

'He never does think straight when Susanna is around,' Lord Derwent said, offering Lady Stalbridge his arm. 'A pity she had to arrive just now.'

'Yes,' said Lady Stalbridge, 'I rather think it is. Tell me, what do you think of this Miss Hilton?'

Chapter Eleven

'How nice,' Mrs Filmore announced happily at breakfast upon the Sunday morning. 'We are all invited to dine at Southbrook tomorrow evening. I knew you had made an impression upon Mr Lindsay, Annabel.'

'He only danced with me once, Mama,' Annabel said sourly. 'He had eyes for no one but Susanna Spencer. And, when he was with me, he kept making the most outrageous remarks about my hair.'

'If you ask me, he was so drunk he didn't know who he was dancing with half the time,' Piers drawled. 'Something, or perhaps I should say someone, seemed to have put him quite out of sorts.'

He glanced across the table at Janey, who was concentrating upon spreading the butter to the very corners of her toast. 'Shall you be coming to Southbrook to dine, my dearest coz? Or are you still suffering from the mysterious malady which caused your departure from the ball?'

'No. I am perfectly well, thank you, Piers,' Janey said coolly, determined that Annabel and Piers should never know how much Jonathan Lindsay had hurt her. 'Of course I shall go, if I am invited.'

'Oh, you are, my dear,' said Mrs Filmore, a note of incredulity in her voice as she read further in the note. 'Lady Stalbridge has specifically requested the pleasure of your company.'

'How kind of her,' Janey said woodenly. 'Are we to walk to church or ride this morning? It is such a bright morning—I rather think I shall walk.'

'Must we?' Annabel groaned. 'I have such a headache.'

'Shouldn't have let Captain Crowne fetch you quite so much "lemonade", should you?' her brother sneered.

'Shut up, Piers,' Annabel snapped. 'Or I will tell.'

'Oh, I shouldn't start revealing secrets, sis, dearest.' Piers gave his sister an unpleasant smile. 'You never know what might come out.'

'I am a trifle fatigued as well,' Mrs Filmore said. 'We will take the carriage. You may do as you wish, Jane.'

'Then I shall walk,' Janey said.

'Which way are you going?' Annabel asked.

'Through the lower meadow,' Janey answered.

'Oh, I should take the upper path,' Annabel suggested. 'The lower meadow is still very muddy.'

'But that means going through the covert—' Piers began to say.

'I am sure Jane will not mind that, she has such a penchant for walking through woods.' Annabel cut him off with a look.

'Thank you,' said Janey, more than a little startled by both brother and sister's helpfulness, 'I will.'

'Are you sure this is the right way, miss?' Kate asked Janey an hour or so later. 'It's ever so overgrown, you can hardly see where to put your feet.'

'I know,' Janey said, as she struggled to disentangle the billowing leg-of-mutton sleeve of her pelisse coat from a hawthorn twig. 'I think the going is easier over there to the left—Miss Filmore said her brother had said to be sure to keep to the left of the fallen ash.'

Freeing her sleeve, she plunged through the long dead grass and ferns. She had almost reached the shorter grass, which had been cropped by sheep, when there was a wrench upon her skirts and a bruising bang against her shins that brought her sprawling to the ground.

Kate, who was but a step or two behind her, screamed.

'What on earth—?' Janey began struggling to sit up and then her voice dwindled as she saw that what had snagged a great swathe of her skirts and brought her down was a gin trap.

She stared at the vicious iron jaws, the blood draining from her face, her mouth and throat going dry, and for a second she could not move for fear of the pain she expected to follow.

'It's a trap, miss, a mantrap,' Kate said shakily. 'Are you hurt, miss?'

Janey swallowed and forced herself to move her constricted legs. 'No, I can feel the iron against my skin, but it is only my skirts it has caught, not my legs.'

'Oh, thank the Lord,' said Kate, who had gone quite ashen. 'If it had been your leg—'

'Well, it wasn't,' Janey said with determined brightness, knowing she had come within an inch of disaster. The trap, which had bitten through layers of woollen pelisse coat and gown and cotton petticoats, would have sliced just as easily through flesh and bone. 'Now, see if you can help me get it apart.'

The two of them wrestled in vain with the jaws of the rusty trap for several minutes.

'It's no good,' Janey said breathlessly. 'We're just not strong enough to move it.'

'We're nearer to church than home. I'll get someone,' Kate said, getting to her feet. 'I'll be quick as I can.'

'Thank you,' Janey said, trying to shift herself into a more comfortable position upon the damp ground. 'But for the love of God, Kate, be careful where you step until you are on open ground, in case there are more of them.'

'Don't worry, miss, I will be,' Kate assured her. 'My grandfather bled to death in one of these accursed things.'

'Sir! Sir!'

Jonathan's horse went up upon its hind legs as Kate, bonnet flying on strings, and shawl flapping like a goose's wings, threw herself over a stile and on to the bridle path along which he was riding with Lord Derwent, Lady Stalbridge and the Duchess of Sutton.

'What the devil are you playing at?' Jonathan snapped.

'It's Miss Hilton,' Kate blurted out, her face almost as red as her hair from running. 'She's caught in a trap, sir, a mantrap. We were walking—'

'What?' The blood left Jonathan's face. 'Where?'

'Over the hill, sir, beyond those trees, but she's not—'

'Get help, Perry, the doctor—' Jonathan did not wait for the rest of Kate's explanation. Turning his horse's head, he backed it up against the other hedge that lined the narrow bridleway and then sent it forward in two bounding canter strides to jump the stile.

'While I go for Dr Hutton, can you find some men to get a hurdle or a gate?' Lord Derwent said to Lady Stalbridge and the Duchess as he kicked his horse forward.

'But she's not hurt, sir,' Kate said, catching at his rein. 'I was just about to tell him it was only her clothes that was caught. But the trap's so rusted we can't budge it.'

'Thank God for that,' Perry said with a sigh of relief, reining in again.

'Amen,' said Lady Stalbridge with a smile as she watched Jonathan's grey galloping at full stretch across the field. 'I think we'll leave him to it then, shall we, Derwent?'

'Perhaps we should go and offer assistance,' the Duchess drawled.

'Oh, no, there is no need for the rest of us to miss church, I am sure,' Lady Stalbridge said firmly. 'Jonathan will manage well enough, I am certain.'

'Yes, I dare say you are right,' the Duchess agreed a little acidly as she stared after the galloping grey. 'If he does not break his own neck in his haste to get to her.'

The bright sunshine of the early morning had given way to ominous-looking dark clouds. Huddled into her dark green pelisse coat, Janey drew up her knees as far as her constricted skirts would allow. It was, she thought, as she wrapped her arms about herself and let her head rest upon her knees, the last time she would listen to one of Annabel's helpful suggestions.

The rapid drumming of a horse's hooves made her lift her head a few minutes later.

She barely had time to recognise the rider as Jonathan before he had flung himself down from the back of his blowing and sweating horse and was beside her.

'Janey! Where are you hurt?' He was breathless, frantic almost, as he stripped off his riding gloves and tall hat and flung them aside. 'You must not move,' he said as he knelt down next to her and she twisted to look at him.

'I'm not hurt,' she said through chattering teeth. 'It's just my skirts and petticoats that are caught.'

'You're not hurt—' The breath left his lungs in an audible rush and the haggard look left his face. 'Thank God! You do not know what has gone through my head these last few minutes. I was expecting to find you bleeding to death with your leg smashed.'

'I'm just stuck, and cold,' she said, feeling a flicker of happiness amid the numbness she had felt inside since the previous night as she saw the relief in his eyes and upon his face. He *had* cared for her a little, then, she thought. It had not all been pretence. 'If you could get a branch or something, you can probably pry the jaws apart.'

'Of course—here—' he stripped off his topcoat and put it about her shoulders '—I won't be long.'

A few minutes later, after considerable effort on his part, she was free.

'Are you sure you are all right?' he asked as he helped her to her feet and drew her away from the gaping jaws of the trap.

'Perfectly—apart from a bruise or two,' she said, pulling her hands out of his. 'And just a little cold and wet. But the walk home will warm me soon enough. Please do not let me keep you longer from church.'

'Don't be silly. You cannot possibly think I should let you walk back alone after this. Come here.' He wrapped his top coat more closely about her shoulders, his hands lingering upon its edges as he drew it close under the small point of her chin. 'I know you are angry with me, and with every reason. But can we not be friends again? I shall not deceive you again, not upon any subject.'

'Friends?' Her voice quavered as his fingers brushed her jaw and they both went still for a moment. 'I am not sure that is possible.'

'No.' His eyes darkened as her gaze met with his. 'I suppose it would not be possible for you to forgive me for the wager?'

'No. And I understand the Duchess's husband is not expected to live more than a month,' she said, after a short silence in which they stared at one another without moving.

'So people say.' His hands lifted from the collar of the coat to cup her face.

'She is very beautiful,' she said thickly as his head bent beneath the broad brim of her black straw hat, which was beginning to soften in the rain.

'Yes,' he agreed as his mouth brushed over hers, featherlight.

'And you are still in love with her,' she blurted desperately against his cheek, wishing she had the strength, the will to pull away.

'So people tell me,' he murmured absently and kissed her again. A brief tender kiss that sent slivers of warmth through her chilled body.

'And she loves you,' she said raggedly as his mouth lifted from hers and his hands dropped to her shoulders and then her waist, drawing her closer.

'Perhaps,' he said slowly. 'One can never tell with Susanna, she does not wear her heart upon her sleeve as you do.'

'I don't!' she protested fiercely.

'I am afraid you do.' He sighed softly. 'Your feelings are always in your eyes—you'll never be able to play the game like Susanna and her kind.'

'I know that!' Her face crumpled suddenly beneath his gaze and for want of anywhere else to hide it, she buried her head upon his shoulder. 'I hate you!' she muttered against his waistcoat. 'I wish I had never met you, never touched you—'

'Oh, Janey, what am I do with you. . .?' he groaned and held her closer, neither of them noticing as his top coat slid off her narrow shoulders to the ground.

Love me, she wanted to say. Love me as I could so easily love you. But if she did, he would only laugh at her, laugh at her as he had when she had asked him to marry her.

'I am truly sorry about last night, Janey,' he said softly. 'I did not mean to be so brutal with my confessions. It was a shock seeing Susanna walk in through the door—'

'I don't want to know. Take me home, please.' She lifted her head, the brim of her hat catching upon his jaw as she did so. 'Now.'

'Only if you promise you will come to Southbrook tomorrow?' he said, distentangling himself from the hat and peering beneath its brim at her shadowed face.

'Anything. Just take me home, please.'

Without another word he picked her up and carried her over to his horse and lifted her on to the saddle. After a considerable amount of wrestling with her torn skirts and petticoats, which displayed rather more than was seemly of her pantaloons, she seated herself comfortably astride.

'Can you manage like that?' His brows lifted.

'I rode this way for the first sixteen years of my life, Mr Lindsay. There are not many horses broken to side-saddle on the frontier.'

'I suppose not.' He frowned as he glanced up at the darkening sky. 'I fear we are going to get rather wet.'

'If you get up behind me, we might be quicker,' she suggested. 'If you think your horse will survive the double load.'

'Oh, he'll stand it,' he said with a half-laugh. 'Whether I will,' he added a little raggedly as he picked up his coat, 'is another matter.'

Janey did not understand quite what he meant until he swung up behind her. There was only just room for the two of them in the saddle. She could feel his rock-hard body behind her from shoulder to ankle, his chest against her back, the front of his thighs to the back of hers beneath her rucked-up skirts. They could scarcely have been closer if they had been spoons in a drawer.

'You'll have to take your hat off, or it will poke my eyes out,' he said as he reached around her to pick up the reins and she remained utterly rigid and still.

'Oh, sorry.' She lifted her hands to her head, and unpinned the hat from her hair, which promptly slid out of its heavy knot to tumble down her back. 'Is that better?'

'Much,' he said, shifting the reins into one hand and rearranging the back of her skirts to his satisfaction. 'Comfortable?' he asked as he slipped his left arm loosely about her waist.

'Yes. Thank you.' She tried to remain rigid, tried to hold herself away from him as the horse began to walk. But it was hopeless. Her body had a will of its own, seeming to soften and merge into his lean hardness with every stride of the horse.

'You have beautiful hair,' he said after they had ridden in silence for a few minutes.

'Do I?' There was the faintest of tremors in her voice as she felt him rest his cheek against the back of her head. She wanted to turn. Turn and touch her lips to his skin, wanted it so much that it hurt physically.

'Yes. It is like silk—like your skin,' he said against her ear, the warmth of his breath making her skin prickle upon the nape of her neck. 'And it smells of lavender,' he said thickly a moment later.

'Does it?' She exhaled unevenly, her hands clenching upon the brim of her hat. 'You had best be careful—the trap is there,' she added in a rush.

'Yes,' he said, as he steered the grey carefully past the mantrap. 'You will not walk here again, will you?' he asked as he glanced down at the rusty metal and shuddered. 'The damned things should be outlawed.'

'Yes. I should not have come this way if Miss Filmore had not suggested it,' she agreed numbly, wondering how it was that she could make conversation when she felt as if it was her heart that had been crushed in the savage jaws of the trap. Last night she had been so certain she despised him, so certain she could give him up. And now—now, as he held her close, she was utterly confused. . .

'Miss Filmore suggested it?' His voice was as grim as the expression upon his face as his arm tightened about her waist. 'And no one objected? Surely Piers Filmore or his father must have known the keeper had set traps up here?'

'I doubt it. Neither Piers nor his father really take much interest in the running of the estate—' Her last word was a half-gasp as his hand slipped into the deep V-neck of her pelisse and his fingers fanned out over her ribs and she felt the warmth of his hand begin to seep through the fine wool of her gown.

'Don't they?' he said almost absently as his fingers began to stroke the soft undercurve of her breast. 'According to Richard Hoare, who was your grandfather's banker, Piers has been taking a great deal of interest in the affairs of the estate, or at least the financial arrangements.'

'I think he still hopes I will marry him when I have been upon the shelf long enough,' she answered breathlessly, her head tilting back against his shoulder as his fingers feathered upwards and he cupped her breast, circling its hardening tip with his thumb, sending ripple after ripple of liquid melting heat through her limbs.

'If he thinks you are likely to left on the shelf, he's a fool, Janey,' he whispered softly, his lips nuzzling aside a tress of hair and finding the little hollow behind her ear. 'But this is one accident too many. Something which I am going to make very clear indeed to Master Filmore and his father. And you, you are going to promise me that from now on you will take care never to be alone, never ride without checking your harness, and do not eat from any dish until someone else has. . .'

'I shall do more than that.' Her voice quavered a little as he reinforced the instruction by biting softly into her throat. 'My father gave me a pair of sleeve pistols on my fifteenth birthday, I'll keep them with me—'

'Sleeve pistols?' She heard the slight catch of his breath

and then he laughed. 'You are a constant surprise, my love, do you know that?'

'I am not your love,' she said raggedly as his lips kissed a path up the length of her neck to the point of her jawbone and her hat dropped unnoticed from her suddenly nerveless hands to be pulped beneath the grey's hooves. 'That was clear enough last night.'

'So clear that you asked me to marry you?'

'Like you said last night, we all make mis-takes.' Her voice caught and rose as his finger and thumb tightened upon the hardened nipple of her breast.

He laughed softly as a shudder went through her. 'Yes, I suppose we do. And I am beginning to think meeting you, Miss Hilton, was one of mine. My life was so much simpler before I saw you standing at that gate in the lane. I never used to think about anyone but myself.'

'I have not noticed the change.' She sighed, her eyes shutting as reality seemed to spiral down to the feel of his lips against her skin, the clever teasing caresses of his fingers.

'I saved Jem for you, did I not?' he murmured against her ear, nipping gently at its lobe.

'For the wrong reasons. It was to help you win your wager—wasn't it?' She struggled to hold on to reason.

'I lost the wager.'

'Lost it?' The words were little more than a whisper. 'But you got your kiss—'

'It wasn't just for a kiss,' he said succinctly.

For a moment she didn't understand. And then realisation dawned. She jerked upright, her eyes wide open.

'The wager was to seduce me!' She gasped in disbelief. 'Have you no—no shame—?'

'Not much.' She did not need to see his face, she heard the smile in his voice. 'About as much as you, I should say.'

'You—you—' She twisted half around to try and strike him but, as her gaze caught and clashed with his, she was lost. She did not even try and move as his mouth captured hers, did not even notice that the grey had come to halt, or that the clouds broke, and the rain soaked them within seconds. There was nothing but this—nothing but the bittersweet knowledge that he still wanted her, and she wanted him, even if he did love his beautiful Duchess.

It was the restiveness of the horse that brought them both to the realisation of the stinging rain that was running down their faces, their necks, even between their lips.

'You are the wickedest man I know,' she said breathlessly as he released her.

'Good,' he said unconcernedly, pulling her back against him again as he sent the grey forward again into a canter. 'Because I should hate to think what would happen to you if you met someone with fewer scruples than I.'

'I cannot think he exists,' she said with feeling. And then, after a minute or two, 'Just out of curiosity, what would you have won if—?'

'The full brother of last year's Derby winner.' He laughed. 'And he's almost certain to win next year. Why the devil I had to be afflicted with a conscience that morning upon the downs, I really don't know.'

'Are you sure it is not a temporary condition?' she asked, on some impulse which she did not entirely understand.

'If it was, we would not have passed that barn over

there,' he said grittily, taking the reins in both hands again and exhaling heavily.

'I don't see what conscience has to do with sheltering from the rain,' she said with deadpan innocence.

'Janey, if you and I were alone in that barn, we would not be sheltering from the rain.'

'No?' She smiled at the tightness in his voice.

'No. And the first time I make love to you, it is not going to be some rushed tumble in a barn,' he said shortly.

'You are so sure of me?' she said with a slightly choked laugh.

'Yes. I knew you would be mine the first time I touched you. I've never wanted any woman as much as I want you.'

'Not even your Duchess?' she said wearily as she leant into his body, and let her head tip back against his shoulder again, not caring about the rain falling upon her face.

'No. I wanted Susanna because every other man I knew did. That is how it began—the desire to compete and win. And then, after she jilted me, it was a matter of pride to win her back from her husband.'

'And now?' she asked unsteadily, knowing her happiness hinged upon his answer.

'Now—I just don't know,' he sighed. 'For six years I have been sure that she was the only woman I really wanted—and then I met you. And since then, I have been sure of nothing. I can't promise you anything, Janey, not yet—'

'I have not asked you for any promises.'

'Not in words, no,' he said softly, holding her closer to him. 'But you do with your eyes, Janey, every time you look at me.'

'I cannot help it,' she said, as she shut her eyes against the stinging rain.

'I know.' He dropped a kiss at the corner of her eyelid. 'No more than I can help wanting you.'

They rode the rest of the way to Pettridges in silence.

'Will you come in and get dry?' she asked tentatively as he brought his horse to a halt, not wanting to part from him.

'No, I must be getting back to Southbrook. Several people stayed over after the ball.'

'And the Duchess was one of them?'

'Yes,' he said, after a fractional hesitation. 'She was.'

'Oh, I see.'

'Do you?' He sighed as he swung down from the grey's back and lifted her after him. 'I very much doubt it. I am not at all sure I understand it myself. And if you are wondering, she slept in the east wing, and I slept in the west.'

'Oh.'

'Oh,' he mocked her softly.

'I had better go in,' she said awkwardly as he let go of her waist.

'Yes.' He gathered up his reins and put a foot in his near stirrup, and then turned to look at her again over his shoulder. 'Janey—'

'What?'

'Nothing,' he said, after a moment. 'But will you promise me that for the next week or so you will not take unnecessary risks of any kind—nothing that would give anyone an opportunity to harm you? There are a great many desperate men who, given sufficient incentive,

might be persuaded to strike at anything or anyone whom
they blame for their condition.'

'I told you, none of the local men would hurt me.'

'They might not be local—' he said soberly.

'If Captain Swing raises his head here, it will be because
of landlords like Mr Filmore, not because of any outsiders.' Janey sighed. 'But don't worry, I am not about
to take up machine breaking, even if my sympathies lie
with the labourers.'

'I am relieved to hear it.' He laughed as he mounted
the grey. 'You will come tomorrow, won't you?'

'Yes,' she said simply, knowing that neither wild horses
nor the Duchess of Sutton would keep her away.

'Miss, whatever have you been up to?' Mary, the housemaid, greeted Janey in the hall.

'I had an accident with a gin trap,' Janey said surveying
her reflection ruefully in one of the hall mirrors. Wet, her
hair was the colour of dark treacle, flowing down her
back, and her eyes looked enormous and dark in her pale
face. Her lips were swollen. She lifted a hand and touched
them, caught for a moment in a memory that made warmth
flow through her.

'A gin trap!' Mary looked at her horrified. 'Are you
all right?'

'Perfectly.' Janey's smile widened. 'It was only my
clothes that got damaged. Mr Lindsay came to my rescue
and brought me home, but we got caught in the rain.'

'Oh,' Mary said, in sudden understanding of the dreamy
look in Janey's eyes. 'Shall I have a hot bath drawn for
you, miss?'

'Please,' Janey said, her thoughts still on Jonathan and
what he had said about the Duchess. No promises, he had

said, *yet*. Her dreams hung on that one little word.

'Miss?'

'Yes, Mary?'

'I don't know quite how to say this, but Will was wondering if you had had any success with Mr Lindsay?'

'Not yet,' she replied slowly. 'Ask him to persuade the others to be patient just a little longer.'

'It's not going to be easy, miss,' Mary said worriedly. 'There's all sorts of wild rumours flying. They're even saying that men are going to be brought down from the mill towns in the Midlands to do the work at half the wages our lads were getting.'

'I am sure that's not true.' Janey shook her head. 'Weavers will never make shepherds and stockmen. But I'm doing my best, Mary,' she added with a slight wry smile. 'I promise you that.'

'So there you are, Jono,' Susanna said as she swept into the library at Southbrook and found Jonathan sitting in what was becoming his favourite leather chair, with his slippered feet resting upon the fender, and the liver and white spaniel upon his lap. 'I am beginning to think you are avoiding me.' She smiled at him, her ringleted head tilted prettily.

'Oh, pray, don't get up,' she said acidly after a moment in which he remained staring into the flames of the fire. 'I can see the morning's little adventure of playing Sir Lancelot to your colonial friend has quite tired you out.'

'What?' Jonathan started as Tess raised her head and gave a muffled possessive growl. 'Sorry, Susanna, I was miles away, wool gathering.'

'So I saw.' Susanna sighed as she sat down in the

opposite chair, and arranged the primrose yellow silk skirt of her gown gracefully. She frowned slightly as her gaze travelled from his tousled hair, to his loosely tied cravat, over his unbuttoned waistcoat and down to his slippered feet. 'You are becoming positively rusticated, Jono. You always used to be so well turned-out. That dog is moulting—'

'And you are as beautiful, as perfect as ever, Susanna,' he interrupted her, letting his eyes travel slowly downwards from the immaculate glossy black ringlets to the gown that clung to her full breasts and narrow waist. 'I thought marriage to such an old man might have changed you, but he has not made so much as scratch upon you, has he? But then, perhaps you have left your mark upon him—you always were something of a cat when roused.'

'That's enough, Jonathan!' The brunette got to her feet and strode to the fireplace. 'I endured your bitterness, your infantile attempt to make me jealous last night, because you were drunk—but now you do not even have that excuse!' Her voice had dropped a tone, become husky as she leant upon the mantel. 'Do you wish to make me unhappy?' There was the slightest of catches in her voice, a hint of a sob as she turned her head to glance at him over her shoulder with her slanted green eyes.

'Of course not.' He sighed.

'Then come here, tell me so.' She held out her arms to him.

'Susanna, you are married,' he said wearily as he stood up and took her hands.

'That has never proved an obstacle to you before, has it?' She smiled at him archly.

'People change.'

'I have not.' She moved closer to him, looking up from beneath long black lashes. 'And he does not care that we have been lovers—he never has, so long as we are discreet.'

'No,' he said succinctly, 'you have not changed. But I have. I have wasted six years of my life, waiting for you to decide that you had made an error of judgement—and now I know that I was the one who made the error.'

'But, Jono, he's ill—another month or two and I will be free! We can do all the things we had planned: go to Paris or Venice and live as man and wife until my year of mourning is up. Then we can come back here and marry—'

'Those were the things you planned,' he said quietly. 'I am not sure they were ever what I wanted.'

'You want to marry me, don't you?' She pouted at him, then she laughed. 'You know, I've never expected you to be a monk, Jonathan. Take the colonial girl to bed if it makes you happy, I shall not mind.'

His hands tightened on her wrist. 'That, Susanna, is exactly the problem. You really would not mind.'

'Oh, so I suppose you would rather I flew into a jealous rage like your virginal colonial friend did last night?' She laughed again and would have come close against him if he had not kept her at arm's length.

'Yes,' he said slowly, as he stared at her fashionably pale, discreetly powdered face, her darkened lips, and found himself remembering suddenly that Janey had freckles across the fine bridge of her nose and that her lips had tasted only of rain. And that when Janey looked at him, her eyes went soft and dark, not hard and glittering like two cut emeralds. 'I think I would prefer that—then

I might be able to believe that you actually cared for me once, Susanna.' He released her wrists abruptly.

'You know I care for you—'

'But not enough to have my child—'

She went ashen. 'How did you—?'

'Your husband wrote to me. He wanted me to know that it had been your decision alone to get rid of it, that he had not pressed you in any way. In fact, he would have been glad to acknowledge it as his heir. He thought I had a right to know—which is more, apparently, than you did!'

'It was the wrong time, Jono—I could not face the Season looking like a brood mare—we had Royalty to entertain.'

'Spare me the excuses, Susanna. Please. I do not think there is any more to say upon the subject—you have said it all. My carriage is at your disposal, whenever you wish to use it. I am sure Lord Bath would be delighted to have your company, if you cannot bring yourself to do your duty by your sick husband.'

'Jono—' the colour drained from Susanna's face '—are you sending me away?'

'I think that would be best, don't you?' he said coldly. 'Goodbye, Susanna. Please convey my wishes for his recovery to your husband, and my apologies. You have made fools of both of us.'

'Brown,' said Lord Derwent in a whisper, as the butler passed him in the hall carrying the tea tray, 'that carriage, was that—?'

'The Duchess of Sutton, m'lord,' said Brown, his bland face impassive.

'And when is she expected back?' Lady Stalbridge asked with a lot less reticence.

'Not for a very long time—' Brown paused for maximum effect '—if ever, I should say, m'lady.'

'Got rid of the hussy at last!' Lady Stalbridge gave Lord Derwent a slap upon the back which made Perry flinch. 'Now all we have to do, Derwent, is find him a suitable wife. He cannot, of course, be allowed to marry that colonial Miss Nobody!'

Lord Derwent and Brown both made involuntary shushing noises. 'The library door is open, my lady,' Lord Derwent said urgently.

'So!' Lady Stalbridge continued at full volume. 'My grandson knows that I should never permit him to marry trade, no matter how rich or pretty.'

'She is not pretty, she is beautiful,' Jonathan announced from the threshold of the library. 'And I have no plans to marry anyone, Grandmother. Is that clear?'

'Absolutely, dear boy,' Lady Stalbridge said, looking down her long hooked nose.

'I suppose you must be fretting to get back to Town?' Jonathan said hopefully. 'Lord Stalbridge will be missing you, no doubt.'

'Your grandfather will be at White's, swilling brandy and playing cards till dawn,' his grandmother snorted. 'I doubt he has even noticed my absence yet. And I have no immediate plans to return to Town, I rather like it here. It's so peaceful.'

'Was,' Jonathan muttered darkly beneath his breath.

'Might not be for long,' Lord Derwent said after exchanging a glance with Jonathan. 'The riots could well spread here, you know. Perhaps you would be better in Town.'

'My dear boy, I was visiting a cousin at Versailles when it was stormed by the mob in '89, so you do not think a few ploughboys with too much cider in 'em are going to frighten me, do you?' Lady Stalbridge sighed heavily. 'Oh, and by the way, Jonathan, I have invited Diana and her mother down for a few days. I knew Derwent would be pleased to see her. They'll arrive tomorrow.'

'Diana—' Perry groaned. 'She will expect me to propose.'

'Then you had better start practising pretty speeches or running, hadn't you, boy,' Lady Stalbridge said blithely. 'Now, Jono, what've you got in the stables that I can ride? I want to have a better look at this place of yours now it's stopped raining again.'

'I don't like this business of Miss Hilton and the Filmores,' Lord Derwent said to Jonathan as they strolled along the row of loose boxes, looking at the horses after Lady Stalbridge had ridden off with one of the grooms. 'The way they went on about Miss Hilton this morning at church, you'd have thought she threw herself into the trap on purpose. Not one of 'em showed an ounce of concern for her. And I almost got the impression they were disappointed she had survived it.'

'I do not like it either,' Jonathan said, 'but I have no firm evidence of any wrongdoing, Perry. Filmore seems to have stopped his intimations about her sanity since I warned him off. The girth, the trap can all be put down as accidents—'

'Like the collapse of the staircase in the Tower?'

Perry's fair brows lifted. 'Three accidents in the space of a year?'

'Yes,' Jonathan frowned. 'The first of which removed an inconvenient fiancé.'

'But surely they would not risk murder? Not the Filmores—I mean, they are one of the old families, they have money and land enough of their own,' Perry said.

'Not any more, according to Richard Hoare,' Jonathan replied as he stroked the nose of a bay mare absently. 'Apparently, old Filmore made some foolish investments and their Northumberland estate is mortgaged up to the hilt, and the young one has accumulated so many gambling debts, he dare not show his face in Town this Season.'

'I see.' Lord Derwent's frown increased as they walked on down the line of loose boxes. 'So what will you do? Go to the local magistrate?'

'He's a friend of Filmore.' Jonathan sighed and put out a hand to rub the nose of his grey as it whickered a greeting. He'll not act without firm evidence.'

'Mmm,' Perry agreed, 'I think the sooner we look at that Tower the better. Have to do it on the quiet, of course, since it's on Filmore's land.'

'Yes—perhaps next Sunday morning, while everyone is at church. I'll speak to Avery,' Jonathan said. 'And in the meantime, I intend to spend as much time in Miss Hilton's company as is possible. I want to try and keep the Filmores late at the table tonight—and then I'll press them to stay over. By the look of it there should be more rain tonight, so they'll probably accept.'

'Well, just make sure Miss Filmore's in the opposite wing to me,' Perry said gloomily. 'That young woman frightens me, and as for her mother—'

'Oh, don't worry, Diana will see them off.' Jonathan laughed.

'True.' Perry brightened. 'I suppose she should be here soon. Wonder if she'll let me have a ride on that new bay of hers?'

'Probably.' Jonathan grinned at him. 'I had the distinct impression she bought it as a wedding gift for you.'

Chapter Twelve

As Janey walked into the drawing-room at Southbrook Jonathan, who had had his back to her, turned. She stood quite still as his gaze blazed over her, from the coronet of braids upon the top of her head, to her bronze silk slippers, and then came back to her face, knowing with some deep female instinct that he would come to her, that he could not stay away, any more than she could from him.

'Miss Hilton.' He bowed over her hand, holding her fingers to his lips a moment longer than was strictly polite. 'I hope you are quite recovered from your soaking?'

'From the soaking, yes,' she said after a moment. 'I trust you did not suffer any ill effects?'

'Nothing but a sleepless night. I could not stop thinking about what might have happened.'

'I did not sleep well either,' she said, a faint colour rising in her cheeks.

'Do I take it camomile tea was not entirely efficacious?' he drawled, his tone sending a flood of heat racing through her body. 'We shall have to think of another remedy.'

'I have always thought camomile tea quite sufficient

235

for unmarried women,' Lady Stalbridge said drily from behind Janey's shoulder. 'Now, my dear, do tell me where you got that bronze taffeta. It suits you so well—and I wish to make a present of a dress length to a niece who is fair like you.'

It was only then that Janey realised Jonathan still had hold of her hand, and that the others were all staring at them. Hastily she pulled her fingers out of his and turned in a rustle of tawny silk to meet Lady Stalbridge's amused bright blue gaze

'She's gone,' said Lady Stalbridge succinctly, correctly interrupting Janey's surreptitious glance about the drawing-room as they made polite conversation about dress lengths. 'He sent her packing yesterday afternoon.'

Janey did not even try to pretend she did not know what the old lady was talking about. 'He sent the Duchess away,' she said slowly, her gaze flicking to Jonathan, who was greeting Mrs Filmore and Annabel politely.

'For ever, I think,' Lady Stalbridge said happily.

'For ever,' Janey echoed as Jonathan looked up and smiled at her.

'Thought that piece of news would bring some colour to your face.' Lady Stalbridge chuckled.

'Ah—you haven't met Lady Diana Patterson, have you?' she said as a chestnut-haired young woman, who was a little taller than Janey, strode into the room, a pair of fluffy grey puppies with enormous feet gambolling at her heels. Heels which Janey could not quite help noticing appeared to be somewhat incongruously encased in riding boots beneath the elegant blue silk gown.

'Knew I'd forgotten something,' Lady Diana said unconcernedly as she caught the direction of Janey's stare.

'Mama will have a fit. She was cross enough that I was late—I was trying to get Perry to use his legs properly on the bay—he's the laziest rider I know—'

'Lady Diana—Miss Hilton.' Lady Stalbridge made the introductions with a slight sigh, and then turned away, muttering something about being born in a stable, to answer an enquiry from Mrs Filmore.

'So, you're Miss Hilton. Perry wrote me all about you, says you'd have us all in a tumbril given half a chance.' Lady Diana grinned at Janey. 'Can't say I'd blame you. Oh—bad boy!' She tugged the hem of her gown out of one of the puppies' mouths, which then promptly turned its attention to the flounce on Janey's skirt.

'Just clout him if he's too much of a nuisance,' Lady Diana said blithely as Janey bent to disengage her skirt from the puppy's jaws.

'I trust you were referring to the puppy,' Jonathan said, as Janey straightened, holding the squirming puppy in her arms.

She smiled, feeling that instant jolt of her heart, her body that she had come to expect whenever he was close to her.

'Give the beast to me.' He took the puppy from her, his hand brushing the softness of her breasts as he did so, sending desire shearing through her with such force that she paled.

'Depends on who's being the nuisance, Jono.' Lady Diana's brown eyes sparkled as she glanced from Jonathan to Janey. 'From what Derwent told me, Miss Hilton should set about you with a horsewhip. Where is he, by the way? Hiding again, I suppose?'

'No,' said Lord Derwent huffily from behind her. 'Good evening, Lady Diana.'

'Derwent.' Lady Diana's glossy chestnut head was inclined in a careless nod. 'I'd be really grateful if we could get this marriage nonsense out of the way. There's a sale on at Tattersall's at the end of the week that I really want to go to and Mama's not going to let me go back to Town until you've proposed.'

'Tiresome of her,' Perry replied. 'What's in the sale?'

'Russell's greys and that bay of Wellesley's.'

'Begad! Wouldn't mind that myself. I'll come with you—if you'd like me to, that is?'

'Course I would, idiot.' Lady Diana sighed. 'Now, are you going to marry me, Perry?'

'Yes.'

'Good,' said Diana briskly. 'Let's go and tell Mama, shall we?'

'You really mean it?' Lord Derwent's face lit.

'Come on,' Jonathan said shortly to Janey, who was feeling somewhat embarrassed at being witness to what should, she felt, have been a rather more private moment. And more than a little envious of Diana's easy confidence. 'Help me get these damned dogs shut up, before their mother comes looking for them. Here, you take this one.'

'Their mother?' Her brows arched in enquiry.

'Diana's blasted wolfhound,' Jonathan explained as he steered Janey out of the drawing-room with his free hand. 'It's the size of a small horse and she takes it everywhere with her—ah—Brown, take these up to Lady Diana's room, will you?'

Taking the other puppy from Janey, he dumped the

writhing pair unceremoniously in the unimpressed Brown's arms.

'I rather like Lady Diana,' Janey said as Brown carried the puppies away, his stiff back expressing the measure of his disapproval.

'Diana?' He smiled as, after a glance over his shoulder into the drawing-room, he drew her to one side of the door. 'Yes, I thought you would like her. She's another woman who does and says exactly what she wishes.'

'Do you think I do?' she said in surprise.

'Yes,' he said, lifting a hand and smoothing a stray golden ringlet back into place upon her temple. 'For instance, just now, you have decided that you want to kiss me.'

'Have I?' Her mouth curved upwards at the corners and her heartbeat quickened.

'Yes,' he said as he put a hand upon her waist.

'Someone might see us,' she said as she tilted her face up to his.

'I don't care,' he said as their lips met. 'I do not care about anything but you. . .'

And neither do I, neither do I, Janey thought as she opened her mouth to his kiss and let her fingers slide into his silky black hair, holding him to her. The Duchess had gone and he was hers, at least for a little while and just maybe, for ever.

'Ahem!' It was a loud cough from Brown which brought them jerking apart some minutes later. 'Sir, there is a Captain Crowne requesting to see you and the other gentlemen. Apparently, the Yeomanry is to be called out—they fear another riot at Bourton Farm, on the Zeals road.'

'Oh, no,' said Janey, a cold sense of dread sweeping over her.

'Show him into the drawing-room,' Jonathan said brusquely, and then, taking Janey's arm, his voice softened. 'Come on, Miss Hilton, let us find out what your precious labourers are up to.'

'You may have your dinner, gentlemen, and there is no cause for alarm ladies,' Captain Crowne assured them a few minutes later as he stood beside the drawing-room fire, a glass of claret in his hand. 'The mob will take an hour or so to collect and another hour or two to walk the distance—'

'Then why do you not intervene now and prevent them from going?' Janey asked sharply.

'Because we want to catch them in the act and make an example, Miss Hilton.'

'Like you did at Pyt House, I suppose!' Janey said, ignoring the warning touch of Jonathan's fingertips upon her bare shoulder as he leant upon the back of the yellow silk sofa where she sat next to Lady Diana.

'Exactly! Give them a taste of a sabre and shot,' Captain Crowne said, smiling at her, oblivious to her disapproval. 'And take a few prisoners, of course, so they can be tried and properly punished. Then we should not get any more trouble in the district. And with luck there'll be a few less mouths for the parish to feed, what!' He laughed and looked about him, as if expecting approbation.

'Here, here,' intoned Mr Filmore.

'Sabres and muskets seems a bit much,' put in Lady Diana. 'I'd have thought a few cracks of a hunting whip would send 'em home fast enough. It's not as if they're likely to be armed, is it? And half the ones I've seen about here don't look as if they've the strength to be much trouble.'

'And exactly where has this mob come from?' Piers asked.

'All about, the Knoyles, Mere, Semley, even, I believe, some disaffected men from your own estate, Mr Filmore.'

'My estate,' Janey muttered.

'Yes,' Piers sneered at her. 'And now you see what gratitude you get for your cosseting of them.'

Janey ignored him, her attention focused upon Captain Crowne. 'You seem very well informed about their intentions, Captain. How do you know that it is not a peaceable protest?'

'Men do not go about peaceable protest upon an autumn midnight, Miss Hilton,' Captain Crowne replied. 'Now, you ladies must not worry your pretty heads about it. It will all be sorted out by morning.'

'You mean that men might be dead and injured by morning,' Janey retorted. 'Something which you could prevent if you wished it!'

'Dead!' Mrs Filmore groaned. 'I do believe I feel quite faint. We could all be murdered in our beds.'

'I doubt it,' Lady Stalbridge muttered derisively. 'Time to start worrying when they set up the guillotine upon the village green.'

'Quite.' Captain Crowne tossed off the rest of his wine. 'So, I can count upon all of you gentlemen? I know you and Lord Derwent are not members of the militia, Mr Lindsay, but may I count upon your assistance?'

'Of course. Be good to do a bit of sabre rattling again, won't it, Jono?' Lord Derwent said cheerfully.

'Yes,' Jonathan agreed after a moment's hesitation. 'Eleven o'clock at the Red Lion, you say?'

'Yes, we do not want them to know we are aware of their intentions,' Captain Crowne said. 'They should be well on their way by then.'

'How could you?' Janey said to Jonathan furiously, as he led her in to dine a few minutes later. 'How could you agree to be part of it? They are planning to send soldiers against men who have at most fired a rick or broken a machine—in all the riots in Hampshire, not one farmer or landowner has been touched, only property—can property really be worth more than lives?'

'In the eyes of the law, yes. In mine, no,' he replied tersely. 'Which is why I agreed, because if I am there, there is just a chance I might persuade them to avoid bloodshed. Though I don't hold out much hope,' he said grimly, 'not with hotheads like Crowne in charge. There are moments when I wish old Boney was still about—he'd have blunted that young man's ardour for killing.'

'I'm sorry,' she said. 'It is just that it makes me so angry because it is all so unnecessary. If people were just a little less greedy, less bent upon imposing progress on others at any cost—'

'You cannot turn back the clock.' He sighed as he pulled out her chair for her. 'The machines are here to stay, Janey. For every one that is broken, another ten will be made because there is money in it. Money for the manufacturers, money saved by the farmers.'

'I know,' she said bleakly. 'But, at the very least, the poor relief should be increased while men look for other work.'

'Speaking of which,' he said as he sat down beside her,

'I am thinking of restoring the old cotton mill at the edge of the estate.

'Hincks Mill?' She gave him a puzzled look. 'There is no money in cotton at present.'

'I'm going to convert it for silk. I understand there is a healthy market for ribbons. Miss Filmore alone should keep it going for a decade.'

She smiled, knowing he was making an effort to lift her spirits.

'You have decided to stay at Southbrook?'

'Yes. I intend to start taking on men next week. I wish now I had made the decision earlier. It might have prevented some of your people from being dragged into this affair tonight.'

'There has to be some way to stop it,' she said, sighing. 'There have been riots and protests since October. You would have thought the government would have stepped in by now with a solution.'

'The government has only one thing upon its mind and that is political reform. They are desperate to get the landowners upon their side at present and will do nothing to offend them.'

'I wish they would put as much effort into reforming the poor law,' she said bitterly. 'Representation for Birmingham will not feed men this winter!'

'No, but it might in time,' he said. 'The broader the representation, the more likely it is that the dominance of the landowners in Parliament will come to an end and there will better conditions for both labourers and factory workers.'

'But it will be too late.' She bit her lip.

'It might not turn out as badly as you think.'

'You don't believe that, do you?' she said as she looked at him.

'No,' he said after a moment. 'I think it is going to be a unpleasant mess and people on both sides are likely to get hurt.'

'You will take care,' Janey said later that evening as she stood upon the lantern-lit steps of Southbrook House, waiting for the carriage to be brought round.

'Don't worry.' Jonathan smiled at her as he adjusted his sword belt. 'I can't think the Almighty let me survive Waterloo to meet my doom in a rural brawl.'

'I suppose not.' She tried to smile back, but it did not reach her eyes.

'And you—I should have been happier if your party had agreed to stay here the night,' he said softly. 'You will make sure all the doors at Pettridges are locked and tell your horseman to keep watch at the stables.'

'Yes,' she said, 'but I cannot think they will come there.'

'Promise,' he said sternly. 'You can never be sure what a mob will do.'

'I promise I will see that all the doors are locked and the stables have a watchman,' she said, thinking that it was not a lie. She would see to it that all the doors were locked, it was just that she did not intend to be inside Pettridges Hall once they were.

The long case clock in the hall of Pettridges struck eleven as the door was opened to them.

'I think I shall take a glass of madeira before I retire,' Mrs Filmore said. 'It will help me sleep.'

'I will join you, Mama,' Annabel said, following her mother into the drawing room. 'Did you see what Lady Diana was wearing upon her feet! I think she is as crack-pated as Jane.'

Janey exhaled with relief that they had not invited her to join them. Picking up her skirts, she sped up the stairs to her bedchamber.

Kate, sitting in a chair beside the fire with mending in her lap, started and got to her feet as Janey entered.

'You need not have waited up,' Janey said. 'Go to bed, Kate, you look tired.'

'I could not sleep, miss. It's my father, I am so afraid he will get into trouble, miss.' Kate's good-natured face crumpled.

'Has he gone to Bourton House Farm?' Janey asked.

'Yes. How did you know, miss?' Kate said in alarm. 'It is supposed to be a secret.'

'It's about as secret as the names of Harriet Wilson's lovers!' Janey said tersely. 'Help me off with this, Kate, then find me my old riding clothes I brought with me from America.'

'What are you going to do, miss?' Kate said as she helped with the hooks of the bronze gown.

'I don't know,' Janey said. 'But I have to try and do something.'

Within a few minutes she was in the stables, dressed in a jacket and divided skirt of soft brushed leather, supple as cloth from much use. Snatching up a stable boy's discarded cap, she stuffed the long heavy braid of her hair into it, and led out Mr Filmore's fastest chaser.

'Here, you!' She heard Iggleston's shout as she leapt

from mounting block to saddle. There was no time to stop
and explain, not if she was to get to Bourton House before
the Yeomanry. She brought her legs against the chaser's
side and sent it flying forward out of the yard.

'Stop!' Iggleston's angry voice followed her. Janey
ignored him, and uttered a small prayer of thanks that
there was a full moon that lit the ground almost as well
as daylight as she galloped across the park, bent low upon
the chaser's neck. 'I hope you can jump,' she muttered
as they came up to the first hedge.

The horse steadied itself, and soared over, and she
breathed a sigh of relief. To go at this speed in this light
was dangerous enough on a good horse, but on a bad one
it would have been suicidal.

Field after field, hedge, ditch, wall passed in a silvery
blur as she concentrated simply on keeping the chaser
going as fast as was possible. For the last stretch, she
risked taking the road, aware all the time of the distant
drumming of the hooves of the Yeomanry clattering
behind her.

At the entrance to the yard of the home farm, she reined
in, slipped off the chaser's back and tethered it to the
gatepost. No one noticed her arrival. The yard was packed
with men, just as it had been at Pyt House. A heaving,
murmuring mass of men, carrying staves, hammers and
torches, whose faces were fierce and haggard in the flickering light of torches and lanterns.

Their attention was focused upon the men at the front,
who were in heated discussion with the men who worked
the Bourton House Farm and the tenant farmer, Mr
Coward, who by the sound of it had no intention of making
any concessions at all to the labourers.

Glancing about her, Janey could not see a single face she recognised. And for the first time, she felt afraid. A physical fear that made her want to turn and run. But she couldn't. She had to at least warn them that the Yeomanry were coming.

If she could only reach their leaders or find Will or one of the others she knew—tentatively, she began to push her way through the crowd. By the time she had lost her cap, been pushed back, and jostled roughly out of the way a dozen times, she knew it was hopeless. She was never going to get to the men at the front in time. A dark-haired man beside her frowned at her as she was caught in a pool of light from a lantern he carried. 'Be off with you, lass, this be no place for women—' He broke off, staring at her. 'Miss Hilton! What the devil do you be doing here?'

'John!' She recognised Will Avery's brother, the village cobbler, with a flood of relief, knowing he was an intelligent, level-headed man like his brother. 'The Yeomanry cavalry from Hindon are coming—' she blurted out. 'They will be here in minutes and are intent upon using force.'

'The Yeomanry—' John repeated and then swore.

'Perhaps soldiers, too, from Warminster,' Janey said despairingly. 'Listen. You can hear the hooves—'

'God save us! Get up there!' Picking her up in his great hands, he boosted her halfway up the side of one of the tall haystacks. Janey scrabbled and clawed her way over its sloping top to crouch at its summit. A moment later John was beside her, standing up, his feet planted firmly apart as if he stood upon solid ground. Silhouetted against the great silver disc of the moon, he cupped his hands to his mouth.

'Lads! Run, lads, run—the Yeomanry's out for blood again,' he shouted. Faces began to turn, to look up and there was a growing murmur of anger, alarm. 'Get out of here! Spread out, lads!'

There was a single crack like a whip, John's hands dropped suddenly from his face, reached out in an odd helpless gesture, and then he pitched forward liked a felled oak. He rolled once, twice, down the face of the stack and then plummeted to the ground. His body made a dull sickening thud as it crashed upon the cobbles, face down.

'No. . .' The moan came from Janey's mouth without her even being aware she had uttered it. 'Oh, no!'

For a fraction of a second there was absolute silence, a silence that was broken by the hiss of steel being drawn and an agonised bellow of fear and rage from the men in the yard. And then all was chaos. Crouched at the top of the stack, Janey could not bring herself to look as shouts and screams and the sound of musket fire filled the air.

She did not know how long she lay with her body pressed against the hay, her eyes shut—seconds? Minutes? She could not tell, or when she first realised something was burning.

She opened her eyes and lifted her head. Showers of red and orange sparks were shooting upwards into the star-studded blackness of the sky. And then, with a surge of panic, she realised the rick had been set alight.

She scrambled to her feet, coughing as the smoke bit into her lungs. She had to get down and quickly. She turned from one side to the other, seeking an escape, but the rick was ringed with flames now, crackling, roaring flames that leapt hungrily upwards.

It was some instinct, rather than hearing her scream, that made Jonathan look upward. Not believing what he saw, he rubbed his eyes with the back of his wrist, and then looked again at the blazing rick of hay.

And then he was running, running, pushing men aside, dodging horses and panic-stricken oxen alike. Snatching up a bill hook, he scrambled up a short ladder propped against the nearest rick to the one in flames.

Anchoring himself with one hand with the bill hook, he edged as near to the edge of the stack as he dared.

Janey didn't see him. She had lost him in the crowd and was turning helplessly, looking for a way down through the rising ring of flame. She would have to jump, jump onto the cobbles some twenty feet below—

'Janey!'

His shout brought her to a halt. She could barely discern his tall dark shape beyond the wall of flame leaping up before her eyes.

'Janey! You will have to jump across!'

'I can't,' she sobbed hoarsely, 'it's too far—too hot—'

'It isn't! I'll catch you! *Come on*!' he roared hoarsely as she hesitated. 'I'll catch you! Jump! Janey!'

It was the anguish in his voice as he screamed her name that cut through her terror; she gathered herself, took one running stride into the flames, and flung herself towards his outstretched hands.

She landed, her body half on the sloping roof of the other rick. She was slipping, slipping down into nothing. . . She opened her mouth to scream and then she felt the back of her buckskin jacket caught, and he was hauling her up by sheer brute strength. And then his arm

was around her, holding her so tightly she thought her
ribs would crack.

His feet slipped suddenly and, with an oath, he threw
himself backwards upon the slope of hay, taking her with
him. Grabbing the bill hook with his free hand, he arrested
their downward slide.

For several seconds she lay with her head against his
chest, aware of nothing but the vital, thudding beat of his
heart beneath her. Aware, only, that she was safe and that
she loved him. Loved him more than anything, more than
life, more than she feared fire or death.

'Janey,' he said raggedly, breathlessly, as he struggled
into a sitting position. 'We must move, this one will go
next—come on.'

Somehow, with the aid of the bill hook and his sheer
strength, they slithered and scrambled down the steep
sides of the rick until they reached the top of the short
ladder.

He caught as her as she almost fell off the last rung.

'Janey! Are you all right?' he demanded as he hugged
her close.

'Yes,' she lied. She felt sick and dizzy as she stared
down at John's body, which lay horribly still at the base
of the burning stack.

'He's dead—'

'Yes,' he said bleakly. 'There is nothing we can do for
him or half a dozen others, I fear. Come on—let us get
away from here before anyone sees you. If Filmore sees
you here like this, that will be all the evidence he needs
to suggest that you are not fit to take control of your own
affairs.'

He did not wait to say more, but ran across the yard, dragging her after him.

'Sir! Sir!' A lad of about fourteen accosted them, tears streaming down his smoke-darkened face. 'Please help me, sir, *please.*'

'Jake? What is it?' Janey recognised him as Mr Coward's ploughboy.

'It's the horses—Old Bess and Cassie and the rest of the team, they're in the barn and it's on fire and they won't come out. I've got to get them out, sir—Mr Coward's getting the cattle out of the byre.'

'Show me,' Jonathan said.

Jake pointed to a long, low, brick building whose roof was alight at one end, sending sparks shooting up into the star-studded blackness of the sky.

'Janey—get on my horse and stay out of trouble,' Jonathan said brusquely. 'Jake, you come with me.'

Janey watched him run across the yard, stripping off his coat as he sped towards the open barn doors from which smoke was already billowing.

Then taking off her jacket, she followed. The barn roof was alight, the beams blazing, and the smoke so dense it was almost impossible to see.

It was only the shrill screaming of the terrified horses that gave her the courage to go into the barn at all. She took a deep breath of the harsh night air and headed for the stalls, guided by the sound of stamping hooves and Jonathan's voice as he urged the horses out of their stalls.

A huge black shire came cantering out of the smoke, almost running her down, then another. Then she saw Jonathan, coughing, gagging, as he half-led, half-dragged out two more, their great heads blindfolded with his coat and shirt.

'Take these and get out of here!' he gasped at her. 'I'll help Jake with the others.'

She did as he said, thrusting her coat into his hands and grabbing the halters of the horses he held.

Somehow, by dint of bullying and coaxing, she got them to the door, where they needed no urging to get away from the barn, and jerked out of her hold to go careering across the yard and jump the gate like hunters, scattering men before them.

A moment later two more horses surged out, then Jake, his feet hardly touching the ground as the two horses he was leading reared and plunged, desperate to escape the crackling, roaring blaze behind them.

'Mr Lindsay,' she said to Jake, her heart turning to ice, 'where is he?'

'Went back for the missus's cob and the donkey,' Jake spluttered.

'Jonathan—no!' Her voice was a cracked whisper, not a scream, as she heard the crash of a beam falling, and half the roof fell in with an explosion of flame.

But then, a second later, out of the rolling clouds of smoke, she saw him leading a fat grey cob in one hand, a small, ancient-looking donkey in the other.

She ran to him, dodging the milling men, cattle and oxen that surged this way and that about the yard.

'I thought you were dead! If you ever do that to me again,' she croaked at him from her hoarse throat as she skidded to a halt in front of him, 'I will—I will—'

'Do what?' he rasped back as he released his charges. 'Shake me until my teeth rattle? That's exactly what I wanted to do to you when I saw you on that rick and then in that barn! Now perhaps you know how I feel when you persist in putting yourself in danger!'

The anger drained from her as she stared at him. She had not realised until this moment that he cared for her so much.

'I am sorry,' she whispered and put her arms about his neck, and kissed his smoke-blackened cheek. 'I will not be so foolish again.'

'Neither will I,' he growled as his arms closed about her and brought her close against his bare chest. 'I think I must be going insane, risking my life for a donkey, of all things. And it's your fault! A month or so ago I had a very well-ordered life. Morning calls, cards, the odd wager—never risking as much as a finger for anyone but myself and now—since I have met you—'

'I have caused you nothing but trouble,' she murmured as she rested her head against his shoulder, and luxuriated in his warmth, his strength. He was like a rock, she thought, her own particular rock in the midst of the swirling, milling maelstrom about them.

'Exactly.' He sighed and touched his lips to her smoky hair. 'But since you have the ill judgement to love me, I might forgive you.'

She went still. What point was there in denying it, when it was true?

'Come on,' he said softly. 'We're going home before we freeze to death and someone recognises you. Where the devil's my horse?'

Ten minutes later they were both up upon the grey, careering out of the mêlée away from the flames into the cool, welcome darkness.

'The horse I came on—' she began as they passed the gate where the chaser had been tethered but was no longer.

'Leave it, it is probably upon its way home by now.'

'I will not be able to get in for some hours,' she said. 'Mrs Filmore has the place locked up like a fortress—I shall have to wait for the kitchen maid to open the back door.'

'Then you had better come to Southbrook,' he said after a fractional hesitation. 'I am beginning to think that some fates cannot be avoided. . .'

Neither of them spoke again on the long cold ride back to Southbrook.

But she could feel the tension, the anticipation growing between them with each step of the grey, each contact between his smoky skin and the thin silk of her habit shirt.

'You could have been killed tonight—' he said as he lifted her down off the grey before Southbrook House.

'So might you.' She swayed forward, letting her forehead drop against his bare chest. He smelt of smoke and sweat, a quintessential male scent that made her want to put her lips to his cool, chilled skin.

His grip upon her shoulders softened and slid down to her elbows.

'You must be cold,' she said after a moment of utter stillness.

'Not when you touch me. . .' He breathed against her smoky hair. 'Never when you touch me—'

He caught her up suddenly in his arms, and she let her head fall against his shoulder as he carried her up the shallow white stone steps to the tall double doors. They would become lovers. It was inevitable. . .had been inevitable from the first moment they had touched.

The knowledge was there in the wide dark eyes of her reflection as they entered the candlelit hall and were greeted by their images, mirrored in the great gilt framed glasses which adorned the walls. And it was in his face, dark with smoke as he looked down at her, before his eyes too lifted to their entwined image in the glass.

'Zeus! Look at us. We look like savages!'

'Yes.' She stared at their reflection. There was something astonishingly intimate about seeing herself held in his bare arms, her smoke-darkened hair rippling over his shoulder. She had not realised until this moment quite how muscled his body was, how different to her own.

'If I was an honourable man, I should wake my grandmother and put you into her care,' he said slowly.

'And I suppose if I were a perfect lady, I should demand that you do exactly that,' she replied, a half-smile curving her mouth.

'Are you going to?' His eyes were almost as dark as the smoke that stained his face as he held her gaze in the glass.

'No.' Her quiet monosyllable seemed to echo to the very ceiling of the marble-lined hall.

He smiled. A slow, tender smile as he looked down into her eyes.

'You're determined to ruin my reputation, aren't you, Miss Hilton?'

'Yes.' She smiled back at him.

Shifting her weight in his arms, he carried her across the hall and up the two flights of blue-carpeted stairs, and into his dressing room, where he set her down gently upon a couch and picked up a folded rug from its foot and wrapped it around her. Picking up a bottle of brandy from the table beside her, he poured it into a glass and handed it to her.

'Drink it, you look exhausted,' he said as he pulled open an oak closet and took out a shirt and coat. Then, catching the surprised glance she gave him, he smiled. 'My horse—I can't leave him standing, much as I should like to—' he added, as he bent and kissed her briefly upon the mouth. 'I won't be long, I promise you.'

He was right. She was exhausted. The hectic ride across country, the horror of the scene in the farmyard, had left her utterly drained. She sipped her brandy, staring into the embers of the fire. It was shock, she supposed, that made the horrifying images of the night hover at the corners of her mind, refusing to be clarified, or put in any order. The only thing that she could remember with clarity was Jonathan's hands reaching out to her upon the other side of the flames. The note in his voice when he had shouted her name, the relief as his arms had closed around her—and the moment when she thought the roof of the barn had collapsed upon him. She had never been so afraid in her life, not even in the Tower—

It was on that thought that her eyes closed and the brandy glass tilted in her hand.

Chapter Thirteen

The dream began as it always did, with her walking along the track which led to the Tower at sunset. The sky was red and orange, vivid as flame behind the black bulk of the Tower. She did not want to go any further, did not want to go into the darkness of the Tower, but her feet kept rising and falling on the muddy, rutted track, carrying her up the hill, past Will Avery leading a plough team down to the village and his forge.

She stared at him, stared at the great grey horses, their manes and tails rippling in the breeze like seafoam. Help me, she wanted to say, but her mouth would not open, her tongue would not work. She could only walk. On and on, up the hill.

And then he was gone and there was her grandfather, standing beside the folly. He smiled at her and said something. Something she could not hear, but she knew he was wishing her luck for her wedding on the morrow. Except that he could not be there, because he was dead. He had died the week after her engagement was announced. She knew that, and yet she reached out to him, begging him for help. But then he was gone and her hand found only the door of the Tower.

The iron key was cold in her hand as she turned it in the lock. The door swung inward, pulling her into the near-total darkness. She felt for the wall; it was cool and damp beneath her hand as she began to climb, keeping her hand upon it as the staircase spiralled up and up, seeming to go on forever. And then at last she was at the top door; she pushed it and stepped out on to the top of the Tower.

And there was all Pettridges spread out before her: field after field, some ploughed, some fallow; the sweep of the woods, the trees turned to fire by the last rays of the setting sun; a sprinkling of cottages and a network of lanes, like silver ribbons leading away to the gentle slopes of the downs which nestled along the horizon like sleeping dogs.

It was beautiful. It was hers. And it did nothing to lift the weight from her heart, nothing to stop the cold creeping fear that swept over her even as the November mist rolled in and blotted out the horizon, rolled over her wet and cold. She could not see. She could only hear the voices.

Edward's voice and *hers*. . . laughing, murmuring, in the mist. She had to see, she had to—she leant over the parapet. They were there at the base of the Tower.

Edward. Edward in his sombre black coat and wide-brimmed hat. Edward, who had said he loved her. Edward and a woman, heavily cloaked, but so dreadfully familiar. She watched, her stomach churning as he embraced the woman passionately and she knew in an instant that he had never cared for her as he did this woman, never—it had all been lies.

Edward! She shouted but there was no sound. But he looked up. She saw his face contort with horror as she snatched off the pearl ring he had given her and sent it spinning and glittering down to the feet of the hooded woman.

'No!' His shout echoed all around her as she turned away and sought the door that led back into the Tower. It would not open. She tugged and tugged but it would not open. She could hear Edward's footsteps on the flagged floor of the tower, hear his frantic shouts.

'Jane! What are you doing here? Stay there!' His shouts echoed through the Tower as the door suddenly gave.

'Jane! *Stay there*!' He was almost screaming as she stepped on to the landing and put her hand upon the banister rail and looked down. He was staring up at her— his hands lifted as if in supplication, his face white in the last rays of the sun that arrowed through the open door.

'No!' he screamed.

And her scream merged with his, as the entire landing seemed suddenly to give way and she went plummeting down into the stairwell. Something hit her head, her leg and then there was such a jerk to her body that she thought she had hit the ground. Why wasn't she dead? She opened her eyes, not understanding.

And then she realised—what had seemed eternity had been no more than a split second. Her skirts had caught upon a broken creaking timber, slowing her fall, and she was hanging over another jagged timber like a rag doll. Edward was spreadeagled upon the floor below, pinned to the flagged floor by a vast oak beam, as neatly as one

of the butterflies that he so liked to collect was fastened
to a board.

He was dead. She knew that instinctively. And she did
not care. She could not feel anything except terror of the
void beneath her. She could not even scream for help as
she watched the woman bend over him, pull off her gloves
and throw them to one side as she shook him in a frantic,
useless attempt to rouse him.

She had been right, she thought dully. It was her. She
knew it even before the woman finally lifted her head,
her hood falling back from her silly, pretty face, which
was contorted with rage. Rage, not grief.

'Help me.' The words were a whisper, as the blood
trickled from the wound on her head into her mouth, and
the numbness in her leg gave way to agonising pain.

'Why?' The woman's voice sliced upwards like a blade.
'Why did you have to come today and not Sunday? You
have ruined everything! You always do!'

And then she was gone and the door was slammed,
leaving her in the darkness.

The empty darkness in which there was no noise but
the creak of the timber.

The timber beneath her waist gave suddenly and fell
with a bang and she jerked down, only to be stopped at
the extent of her skirts, hanging like a puppet from a string.

It was then that she screamed. And screamed until she
was hoarse and no sound came from her throat.

Today, not Sunday. Why did that matter? How long
before the fabric in her skirt tore? How long before someone would look for her? Today, not Sunday? The
questions turned in her pain-clouded mind as she hung
over the void. Her head hurt, her leg hurt. She did not

want to think. She dare not think about the creaking beam, or the thinness of the fabrics that made up her skirt and petticoats, or the unforgiving flagged floor so many feet below.

Today, not Sunday—the words revolved in her mind like a windmill. And then the answer came with bleak clarity as she drifted on the edge of consciousness. By Sunday she would have been Edward's wife—and he would have inherited everything. Edward had known the stairs were unsafe. Edward had known she came here every Sunday. He had meant her to die—all the time, he had meant her to die, and so had *she*.

She had always known inside that Edward had not loved her, known that *she* had despised her, but to think they had meant to kill her was like taking a step into an abyss. She shut her eyes, retreating into inner darkness. A darkness that was punctuated by men's shouts, and shearing pain. And then there was Will's kindly face, telling her she would be all right, and Piers saying she was a damned fool.

And then she was in her room, Kate fussing over her, ashen-faced, and then Kate was gone, and it was Annabel bending over her, smiling—offering a spoon—a spoon that Piers dashed out of Annabel's hand, his face scarlet with rage.

'Janey—Janey!'

She opened her eyes to find Jonathan kneeling beside her. 'You were having a nightmare.'

'Was I?' The dream had gone, back to the edges of her mind where she could not quite reach it.

'About the riot?' he asked softly, as he picked up the

empty brandy glass that had fallen from her fingers, and placed it upon a table.

'No.' She frowned and shivered, the dream leaving her, as it always did, with a nagging unease. 'It was about the Tower—I know I have dreamed it before, but I can remember so little of it when I wake.'

'It doesn't matter, you're safe now,' he said gently as he held out his arms to her. 'Come on, your bath is ready.'

'I think you are in greater need of one,' she said wryly as he helped her to her feet and she looked up into his distinctly grimy face.

'I thought we might share it.' He smiled at her, a slow tender smile that sent her pulse racing. 'I knew you would not wish to impose too much extra work upon the servants at this hour.'

'No, of course not.' She laughed a little shakily as he put his arm about her waist and led her through another door into a bedchamber, which was softly lit with candles and a blazing fire, in front of which was large wooden bath, lined with linen and steaming with fragrant warm water.

She swallowed as he halted her beside the fire, her mouth and throat suddenly dry as he began very gently to unbutton her soft shirt, his gaze never leaving hers as she stood absolutely still, her body so taut it hurt.

He slid the shirt from her shoulders, gliding it off her slender bare arms as if she were as fragile as porcelain and might break if he touched her too roughly. The soft silk pooled noiselessly upon the rug, as did her leather skirt.

'You are beautiful, Janey Hilton, so soft, so perfect,' he said. She looked at him a little uncertainly as his gaze burnt over her, heating her bare skin as much as the flames from the fire.

'So are you,' she said thickly, as he stripped off his breeches and she saw how lean he was, how honed and male. 'Perfect, I mean—not soft—'

'I should hope not,' he said drily with a lift of his black brows as her gaze dropped and then fled hastily upwards again.

'I don't know what I mean,' she said flusteredly, her cheeks burning with a heat that had nothing to do with her proximity to the fire. 'And I don't know what to do—well, not exactly—'

'Didn't they have baths on the frontier?' he teased and scooped her up in his arms, and before she had time even to react to the shocking contact of her skin against his, she found herself lying on top of him in the warm water.

'Not like this—mostly it was a cold river,' she said breathlessly as he began to sponge the smoke from her face, with the utmost gentleness. 'And you know I was not talking about baths.'

'Ah.' He smiled. 'Did you mean this?'

'Yes.' She sighed and shut her eyes as he kissed her, giving herself up to his mouth and hands and body without reservation. Nothing in her life had felt as right as this. . .

Or this, she thought later as they lay in his tester bed, wearing nothing but the candlelight, with her head upon his chest, and the warm weight of his arm wrapped about her waist. This was where she belonged.

She stretched lazily; her body ached in places, but her skin felt like satin against the crisp linen sheets and she felt beautiful and loved. So loved. . .even if he had not said it in so many words. And so safe. . .

'No regrets, Janey?' he asked softly, his black lashes lifting from his cheek.

'No.' She sighed as he shifted onto his side and began to stroke the curve of her hip. She would never regret this, not even if she never saw him again.

'Was this from the accident in the Tower?' he asked as he traced the faint silvery scar on her thigh with a fingertip.

'Yes.'

He hugged her closer. 'Will Avery told me something of it. You must have been terrified.'

'I cannot remember much of it. Just fragments here and there, like Will saying Edward was dead. . .' Her voice thinned, as she reached into the blackness at the edge of her mind where she was usually too afraid to go. 'They told me he was dead and all I felt was relief that I should not have to marry him.'

'You did not want to marry him?'

'No.'

'Then why did you agree to the betrothal?' he said, as he touched his lips to her throat and kissed her.

'I never really did,' she said slowly. 'Edward told me that my grandfather was ill, and that his dearest wish was to see me settled before he died. He said that to put Grandfather's mind at rest, it was the least I could do for him in exchange for everything he had given me. And then Edward explained how much good we could do for the village if we were married. . .and that if I were his wife I should not have to endure Mr Filmore as my guardian when my grandfather died.

'It seemed a good idea at first, but then I began to have doubts. . .sometimes, when Edward did not know I was there, he would say things that made me wonder if he thought any differently of me than the Filmores did—and although he said he loved me, I never felt he meant it. That's why I went to the Tower the evening before the wedding. I thought seeing the estate and knowing I could prevent Mr Filmore managing it might take away the doubts.'

'And did it?'

'No. It made no difference. When I thought of him kissing me, touching me—when he did not love me, nor I him—I knew I could not go through with it.'

'You did not go there to meet him?' His hand stilled upon her waist.

'No—' She shivered suddenly. 'He—he came later— I can't remember.'

'Good,' he growled gently against her ear as he held her close. 'Because I intend to make you forget Edward Grey ever existed.'

'You were going to take me home,' she reminded him even as her body melted into his. 'It must be nearly dawn—'

'Not yet.' He sighed and kissed her. 'Not yet, Janey.'

It was long past dawn when he woke to find her sleeping in his arms. He swore softly, thought for a moment of waking her and then decided against it. There were some fates which he had no desire to fight.

'Hello.' He smiled at her as she woke an hour or so later and looked at him with drowsy eyes.

'Mr Lindsay!'

'Yes.' He laughed at her momentary confusion. 'I think after last night you might call me Jonathan?'

'I might be persuaded.' She smiled, knowing from the tenderness in his eyes that nothing had changed. He still wanted her. Perhaps even loved her. . . She touched her lips to his stubbled chin, enjoying the rough texture, and his salty, male taste.

'Like this.' He turned his head and captured her mouth.

'Jono! Jono! Wake up!' Lord Derwent crashed into the room like a thunderbolt. 'Filmore is downstairs—says Miss Hilton is missing from her bed—'

His voice died and he went scarlet as Jonathan and Janey sat up, Janey clutching the sheet to her chin.

'Ah—Perry, you must be the first to congratulate us,' Jonathan drawled as he put his arm about Janey's shoulders, as cool, as collected as if they had been in the drawing-room. 'Miss Hilton has done me the honour of agreeing to become my wife.'

'Have I?' Janey stared at him. 'Jonathan, you don't have to do this.'

'Oh, yes, he does,' Perry said brightly. 'That's wonderful news, Miss Hilton—Lady Diana will be delighted. Sees you as a kindred spirit, you know.'

'Yes, well—you can kiss the bride later,' Jonathan said drily. 'Out, Perry—and not a word or—' He made a graphic gesture across his throat. 'I'll be down to see Filmore as soon as I am dressed.'

'You don't have to marry me,' Janey repeated as the door shut behind Perry and Jonathan pulled on his dressing-gown.

'Yes, I do.' He smiled at her and bent to drop a kiss upon her forehead. 'There is simply no alternative, given the circumstances—Perry is right. Besides which, I love you—didn't I tell you that last night?'

'No.' She gave a half-exasperated laugh as she looked at him and knew with a surge of joy he was telling the truth. 'Not in so many words.'

'Then I suppose I had better make amends.' He smiled at her and, dropping on to his knees, caught her hand and lifted it to his lips. 'I love you, Miss Hilton, I think I have loved you from the moment I first saw you, or at least the moment you stopped looking at me as if you wished to consign me to the guillotine. So, will you marry me?'

'Yes,' she answered, her face glowing. 'But are you sure? My father would have been the first to tell you he was no gentleman.'

'I do not give a damn what your father was. If he produced a daughter like you, Janey, then he was a gentleman in the only way that matters.' He leant forward to kiss her again. 'So the only obstacle I see is explaining to your guardian exactly what you are doing here.'

'We could say I went for an early morning ride on his chaser, took a fall and was brought here?' she suggested.

'You are positive genius,' he grinned at her.

'The only problem is my clothes,' she said, remembering the smoke-stained state of her riding skirt and habit shirt.

'Lady Diana will loan you something—you're much of a size and she will not blab. Now all we have to do is rehearse my speech to Filmore—since you're not twenty-one yet, I shall have to ask his permission.'

'Supposing he does not give it?' she said, the glow fading from her face.

'Then we shall elope to Gretna.' He laughed and kissed her again. 'Perhaps that is what we should do, anyway—

then we would not have to wait the three weeks for the banns.'

'Don't seem to have done much waiting as far as I can see,' came an acerbic female voice as the door opened a fraction again.

'Is there no privacy in this house?' he growled and headed to the door. 'What do you want, Grandmama?'

'Miss Hilton in the guest room, so we can put some gloss on whatever story you're planning to tell her guardian,' Lady Stalbridge said from around the door, pushing a dressing-robe into his hands. 'And don't try and tell me she is not in this house. I heard you come in last night.'

Jonathan sighed and tossed the dressing-robe to Janey. 'We'd better do as she says. I'll see you later, my love.'

'Congratulations!' Lady Diana greeted Janey cheerfully as she came into the guest room, followed by her maid carrying an armful of gowns, a wolfhound the approximate size and colour of a small donkey and the two puppies. 'You don't mind dogs, do you?' she said airily as she sat down upon the end of the half-tester bed, and the wolfhound bitch immediately jumped up beside her.

'No,' Janey said with a slight smile, turning from the window. 'Not in the least.'

'Didn't think you would.' Lady Diana smiled back at her as her maid calmly began to lay out gowns over a *découpage* screen.

'Jono said you'd had a fall from a horse this morning and needed to borrow a gown?' There was a slight question in her brown eyes.

'Something like that,' Janey replied, feeling herself blush.

Lady Diana laughed. 'Well, I for one don't care what you're doing here so early in the morning. Perry tells me you're to marry Jono and that's the best news I have heard in months. I'm so glad Jono's going to marry you. I've been terrified for years that old Sutton would die and he'd marry Susanna. She was all wrong for him, you know.'

'I am rather afraid that is what his family will say about me,' Janey said with a sigh.

'They won't—at least, not once they've met you,' Lady Diana said with what Janey was coming to realise was her usual bluntness. 'And you've already got Lady Stalbridge's approval, which is half the battle.'

'Have I?' Janey said, startled.

'Oh, yes. She's been going on at Jonathan since the ball about not marrying trade—knows him like the back of her hand, you see.'

'You mean that telling him he must not do something almost guarantees that he will.'

'Exactly!' Lady Diana laughed. 'I didn't realise you knew him so well already.'

'Two of a kind, I am afraid,' Janey replied a little ruefully.

'That's what Derwent wrote to me in a letter just after he first met you,' Lady Diana said. 'He said Jonathan had just met the woman he ought to marry, but he was not sure he realised it yet. Remarkably perspicacious for Perry—he does have his moments, even if he does like to play the fool.'

'Yes,' Janey said as she sat down upon the other corner of the bed and remembered exactly how Lord Derwent had been made aware of their engagement. 'And he is very kind.'

'Yes.' Lady Diana smiled fondly. 'Now let's sort you out a gown for facing up to Mr Filmore—what's it to be? Penitent and demure or brazen it out?'

Janey thought for a moment. Then she laughed. 'Brazen, definitely brazen. I am afraid Mr Filmore will never believe me as a penitent.'

'Right! Teresa—give Miss Hilton the cherry wool to try on,' Lady Diana ordered. 'And then attend to her hair for her,' she added as she got up. 'I hope to see you later, Miss Hilton. Good luck.'

Chapter Fourteen

'So what do you suggest I should have done, Piers? I took risk enough over the insurance upon those ricks for your sake!' Mr Filmore roared at his son later that day in the drawing-room of Pettridges Hall. 'Refuse him permission! Have her committed when he has made it clear enough he would have the hounds of hell at my heels if I try anything of the kind! We are ruined, and it is your fault alone—if you had left the tables alone, we would not be in this pickle.'

'Well, how was I to know he would want to marry her?' Piers said disgustedly, slumping into a chair. 'We made it clear enough what she is! The granddaughter of one jumped-up millhand and daughter of another, who is accustomed to eating in kitchens! A girl dragged up in a boarding house!'

'Dear God! You are such a fool!' Annabel said, throwing down her sketch book. 'She might have been that when she came here, but she acquired the manner of a lady better than you ever managed to appear a gentleman, though you were born to it! All you had to do was flatter her when she first came here—but no—you had to be your usual boorish self!'

'Don't damage your sketch book, dearest.' Mrs Filmore sighed, as Annabel stamped her foot upon it. 'You are so clever with your pen. That Leonardo you copied was hard to tell from the original.'

'Oh, yes, she's quite the little forger, aren't you, sis?' her brother hissed. 'And it wouldn't have suited you if I married her, would it?'

'What do you mean, Piers?' Mrs Filmore said mildly, looking up from her netting again.

'Nothing,' he said sullenly as his sister shot him a look.

'Shut up, Piers!' Annabel flared. 'You may spend the rest of your life as a pauper if you wish, but I am not going to!'

'That is enough!' Mr Filmore roared. 'If you cannot behave better, I suggest both of you go to your rooms and consider how you might ingratiate yourselves with Jane since, I assure you, her generosity will be our only hope of avoiding ruin.'

Outside, Janey hastily withdrew the hand she had just put upon the brass door handle and tiptoed back down the hall. So Jonathan's suspicions had been right. Mr Filmore had had designs upon her fortune, once she had made it clear there was no hope of her marrying Piers. She sighed. Three weeks of the Filmores' attempts to ingratiate themselves did not fill her with joy. But then she smiled—three weeks. In three weeks she would be Jonathan's wife and she could tell the Filmores to pack their bags and leave.

Lord Derwent had already intimated that he would be more than interested in renting Pettridges House after

Janey moved to Southbrook, as Lady Diana liked the look of the downs for exercising her horses. Her smile widened. She was looking forward to having the Lady Diana as a neighbour.

And with Jonathan's plans for his silk mill, and the improvements to both estates to be carried out, there would be plenty of work for the men and more prosperity for the whole village. And he had promised her he would help her build a proper school for the children. If it had not been for the riots, and John Avery's unnecessary death, she would have been almost perfectly happy.

'Well, one good thing,' Perry said late the following afternoon, as he and Jonathan strolled through the overgrown gardens of Southbrook house, 'if what Miss Hilton overheard is right, and old Filmore wanted to prove her insane, and Piers wanted to marry her, neither of 'em can have wanted her dead.'

'No,' Jonathan said slowly, a frown furrowing his brow. 'But there is still something about this whole business that makes me uneasy—something we have all missed.'

'Don't worry —you said yourself no one knows who would gain by her death—so what reason would anyone have to harm her now?'

'Yes, I suppose you are right—but I'd still like to take a look at that Tower. But I don't like to bother Avery— not until his brother is buried.'

'A bad business, that—'

'Yes, and it could have been avoided but for that hot-head, Crowne.' Jonathan sighed. 'He still thinks they have quelled the riots here with fear, whereas the only reason they have stopped is because every farmer in the district has made concessions. But even that's not enough. I'm beginning to think these Reform fellows are right. It is time for some changes in the way things are done. No one in England should starve—we're supposed to be the most advanced nation in the world, after all.'

Lord Derwent laughed.

'What are you laughing about?' Jonathan said, frowning as he bent and picked up a stick for Tess, who was bouncing at his heels.

'You. You're starting to sound like Miss Hilton, Jono. You're definitely in love. Never thought I'd see it.'

'Nor did I.' Jonathan grinned and threw the stick for Tess. 'And do you know, Perry, the odd thing is, I'm enjoying it.'

'Miss, there's another note come for you,' Kate said with a grin three days later. 'He'll have written the county out of paper soon.'

Janey laughed and took the note, which was addressed in the strong, slanting hand that was becoming so very familiar to her.

She broke the seal, and scanned the brief message, her smile broadening.

I MUST see you alone. Come to the waterfall at noon. All my love, Jonathan.

She took paper, pens and ink from her writing-box and wrote a swift note in reply, to the effect that she wanted nothing more than to see him alone and that she would be at the waterfall at noon. For the last three days, it had seemed everyone in the neighbourhood had wished to call with their congratulations, including the Norrises and the Huttons, who had been so effusive and different in their manner to her, and so sycophantic to Jonathan that Janey had been hard put not to laugh.

'I think I preferred them when they were fawning over the Filmores,' Jonathan had muttered darkly. 'At least then I wasn't expected to talk back to them.'

Still smiling, she handed her note to Kate and asked her to get one of the stable lads to take it over to Southbrook.

'What is it, Jono?' Lord Derwent asked as they came in from the garden and Jonathan, having read the note handed to him by Brown, went suddenly ashen.

'I don't know,' he said slowly. 'There is note here from Miss Hilton, saying she will meet me as arranged at the waterfall.'

'Well, that's nothing to be alarmed about, is it?' Perry laughed.

'No, except that I did not arrange the meeting,' Jonathan said grimly.

'Where are you going?' Perry said as Jonathan took to his heels.

'The waterfall,' Jonathan shouted back over his shoulder. 'There is something wrong, Perry, I know there is.'

A few minutes later, they were both running through the gardens.

The sun was already high in the bright clear winter sky when Janey reached the top of the cliff and looked down at the pool below. She shivered in the chill air and realised with a slight sense of disappointment that Jonathan had not arrived yet.

She took a step forward and then turned, a smile on

her lips as she heard a twig crack in the woods behind her. 'Jonathan—'

The greeting died on her lips as she recognised the figure stepping out of the trees with some surprise. 'Annabel? What brings you here?'

'You.' Annabel gave her childish little giggle. 'I am afraid I played a little trick upon you, Jane, I needed to get you alone. The note was from me.'

'You. . .' Janey stared at her, unease making her scalp prickle. All her instincts were screaming danger—danger of the most basic kind. 'But the note—the writing—'

'Was not at all difficult to copy.' Annabel smiled and stepped closer to her.

Janey retreated a half-step and then froze as Annabel pulled a pistol from her black fur muff. She stared at it. It was one of her sleeve pistols, which in her haste to meet Jonathan she had forgotten to bring with her.

'You left them on your dressing-table, which was very helpful of you, Jane.' Annabel smiled.

Janey ignored her, her attention now fastened upon the pearl ring Annabel wore upon her trigger finger.

She stared, seeing suddenly, as if in a picture, the woman bending to retrieve it after she had hurled it down at Edward's upturned face.

'It was you—it was you at the Tower.' Recollection came with swift and total clarity. 'You and Edward planned to kill me, didn't you?' she said, fighting against the panic she could feel growing inside her.

'So you have finally remembered. I was always afraid you might, though I would have denied everything, of course, and no one would have believed you anyway,' Annabel said calmly. 'You are right, of course. Edward and I had planned it all. We had met in Town, you see, but I could not possibly marry him when he had no money—'

'So you thought to get mine,' Janey said flatly.

'Yes. I did not see why Piers or Papa should have it all simply to pay off Piers's stupid gambling debts. It is so boring to be poor, Jane. But, of course, as usual, you had to ruin things by going to the Tower on the wrong day. I was very angry—I was very fond of Edward at the time. Not that it matters now—with your money I shall be able to do far better for myself.'

'You won't get my money, it goes to a trust.'

'No—' Annabel shook her carroty head '—after your death, a previously unknown codicil to your grandfather's will shall accidentally be discovered—in which everything is left to me, his beloved goddaughter. His handwriting is no more difficult to forge than Mr Lindsay's, you see.'

'I see.' Janey swallowed, her gaze fixed upon the barrel of the pistol, which had not wavered for a moment. 'But I am not dead, Annabel. And if you kill me, Jonathan will not rest until my murderer is found. He has suspicions enough of your father already.'

'Oh, *I* am not going to kill you. You are going to kill yourself by jumping from the cliff to drown in the pool— your coat is going to be found here upon the cliff top, neatly folded, and a note with it. A note in which you most touchingly make your farewells to this world and explain that you cannot abandon Mr Grey's memory by marrying another or be separated from him a moment longer.'

'Jonathan will never believe it,' Janey said fiercely.

'Why not? It will be in your handwriting.' Annabel

smiled. 'Take your coat off, Jane, I am getting cold standing here.'

'And if I do not—'

'Then I shall shoot you in the head—and the note will do just as well, though I should prefer it if you would jump. There is always the risk with a gunshot wound that someone may argue it was not self-inflicted.'

Janey undid the buttons of her coat as slowly as she dared. The one thing Annabel did not know was that she had replied to the forged note. Dear God, let her note have reached Jonathan, she prayed. If it had, then he might arrive here at any moment—

'Hurry up!' Annabel snapped, her face pale, but her grip upon the pistol still steady.

Janey shrugged off her coat and bent slowly to put it down. The ground was wet and muddy; there was not even a handful of dust and gravel to scoop up into Annabel's eyes. And the woods remained silent, empty. Jonathan might not even have received her note yet, she thought bleakly. If he had not been at home—

'Jump,' Annabel said coldly, cocking the pistol.

Janey turned and looked down, her heart pounding as she stared into the foaming water. Annabel did not know she could swim. It could be done, she told herself. She had seen it done by a Cheyenne, leaping from a fall higher than this to escape his pursuers. And she and Daniel had leapt from rocks and trees to swim in pools and creeks when she was a child.

But then she had not been wearing a gown and petticoats—if she got caught in the roll of water at the base of the fall—stop it, she told herself as she began to shake. She had to stay calm. If she panicked, she would die. At least it was a chance—and a chance was better than a bullet in the head.

After one last glance at the woods, she took a breath, pinched her nose and made two rapid strides and leapt as far out as she could, praying she would at least miss the rocks at the base of the fall.

It was like hitting stone, icy stone that shattered and closed over her with a roar as the force of her fall sent her down, and down, her skirts billowing up over her head like the petals of a flower. Oh, God—they were wrapping about her face and arms, she could see nothing—and then the air in her skirts took her upwards again towards the light. She broke the surface, coughing, spluttering, and then was tumbled over and over by the roaring water.

It was useless, she thought, as her head broke the surface a second time and she gasped in a breath, she could not even try to swim because of her stupid, stupid skirts. And then the water swept her down again, down and down into the darkness. Into the mercifully calm darkness, where the current tugged her skirts away from her head and arms. She still could not use her legs properly—but at least she could move her arms.

Go deep, a trapper had told her once, that's the only way out of a roll. Her lungs bursting, she dragged herself downward and forward in agonising strokes, praying that she was going away from the fall. She couldn't do it, she thought, as a redness seemed to explode behind her eyes, and her lungs felt as it they would burst. She had to breathe—she had to—she kicked her constricted legs frantically, and reached up with her hands towards the distant light and roaring noise. She had to breathe.

The roar was deafening as her head broke the surface. She had gone the wrong way, she thought, despairing, as the air sliced into her burning lungs like acid. And she had no strength left to fight the churning water—but it wasn't churning—it was calm. She was behind the fall, between the curtain of water and the cliff. There was rock no more than a yard or two away. A yard or two that was like a mile as she fought against the downward pull of her skirts, and the numbing, seductive cold that made her want to shut her eyes and give up.

And then her fingertips found the rock, found a hold. She managed to pull herself halfway out of the water, but then could do no more. She was too cold, her skirts too heavy, the rock too slippery with weed. She could not get any further up the rock. She was so cold, so very, very cold. She lay shivering, her face pressed to the shiny black rock, praying that Annabel would not come down to make sure she had drowned.

'My God!' Lord Derwent said in horror, some fifteen minutes later, as he stared at Janey's coat and read the note Jonathan had pushed into his hand. 'You don't think she has really taken her life?'

'No, I don't! Janey! Janey!'

It was Jonathan's scream of her name that brought Janey back from the brink of unconsciousness.

'Jonathan—' she breathed his name against the rock.

It was only as he called again and again that she realised he could not hear her or see her for the roaring, white sheet of water.

'I'm here,' she tried to shout, to move, but her body would not work properly.

And then suddenly, something was nudging her, licking her face, snuffling at her.

'Tess—' She half-groaned, half-sobbed the spaniel's name. 'Mark, Tess—mark, please—'

The spaniel started to bark, short, sharp shrill barks that reverberated against the cliff.

'Tess has found something—listen,' Perry said, his face as white as Jonathan's as he scanned the dark waters of the pool. 'Where the devil is the dog?'

'Behind the fall.' Jonathan was already running, his booted feet slipping and sliding on the wet rocks.

'Janey—don't be dead, Janey.' He groaned as he edged around the fall on a ledge of rock and saw her sprawled motionless upon the black rock, like a stranded mermaid, the hem of her gown still drifting on the cold dark water.

'I'm not—' she tried to say, tried to smile as he came into the range of her vision. But no sound came out of her blue lips, except the chatter of her teeth.

'It's all right, my love,' he said as he pulled her up into his arms and rocked her against the wonderful warmth of his chest. 'It's all right, you are safe now.'

She shut her eyes and let the darkness swallow her.

He was still there beside her, the following morning, or perhaps the morning after that; she was not sure what day it was when she opened her eyes again in the guest bedroom at Southbrook.

'Jonathan?' She tried to sit up and failed, finding herself as weak as a kitten.

'Just lie still and rest, my love.' He stroked her cheek with his finger.

'Annabel, she—'

'I know. She's been arrested. She cannot hurt you,' he said soothingly. 'Piers told me everything in an attempt to save his own neck. He arrived at Southbrook just after we found you. He knew all about Annabel and Edward Grey's liaison and had always had suspicions about the accident in the Tower—and then last week he found one of Annabel's practice copies of the codicil and realised she might try and harm you again. But I already guessed it the moment I read your note. Somehow I knew it was her—' His voice dwindled to a growl for a moment. 'And I knew, the moment I read it, what she had in mind—I have never run so fast in my life, Janey. And I was still too late. I thought I had lost you.'

'It's all right.' She reached up with her fingers to touch his face.

'Yes—' he caught her hand and held it to his lips '—everything is going to be all right now, I promise you.'

And he had kept his promise, she thought with a smile, some months later, as she stood beside a rather sheepish-looking, flower-bedecked Brutus in the late evening sunshine beside the now well-tended lawns of Southbrook and watched the children of the village race about between the long trestle tables laden with food and bedecked with garlands of greenery and flowers. It had been a good idea of his to have a harvest supper for all the tenants and their labourers.

'Happy?' Jonathan said softly, coming up behind her and putting a hand about her waist, which was just starting to thicken.

'Yes.' She smiled and leant her head against his shoulder. 'We must do this every year.'

'So long as I don't have to make speeches,' he pretended to grumble. 'I have to make enough of those in the House these days. I had no idea being a Reformer was going to be such hard work.'

'You are not wishing you had not crossed the floor to the Whigs?' she asked.

'No, my dear dangerous radical.' He smiled and kissed her. And then, sobering a little, he asked, 'Did you see the paper this morning?'

'No.'

'The ship the Filmores took for India after Annabel's trial—it was wrecked. There were no survivors.'

'Oh—that's awful,' Janey said and meant it. She had not liked the Filmores enough to feel grief, but she would not have wished such a fate upon anyone.

'Is it?' He looked at her quizzically.

She shrugged. 'I have everything I want, I should not have begrudged them their lives.'

'I do,' he said with feeling. 'In fact, I'd cheerfully have hung the lot of them—'

'No, you wouldn't,' she said with total confidence. 'You were as glad as I was that Annabel was judged insane and did not have to hang.'

'No, I was not, I'm no—'

'Galahad.' She smiled and sighed. 'I know, you are a wicked cynic who cares for nothing but your own pleasure. Now off you go and make your speech.'

'What speech?' he groaned.

'The one in reply to the children who are coming to thank you for your generosity with a special poem.'

'Must I? I hate being thanked—and I am not very good with children.'

'Then you had better start practising.' The little push she gave him was augmented by a hefty nudge in the back from Brutus's large black head.

'*Et tu, Brute*,' he muttered darkly at the horse before starting to walk towards the group of children. Then he halted in mid-stride and swung round to look at her.

'Janey? Do you mean—?'

'Yes,' she nodded, her heart soaring at the joy written on his face.

And then she was in his arms, being kissed so soundly that she entirely failed to notice Brutus had begun to chew contentedly upon the brim of her new wide-brimmed straw hat, and even when she did, she did not care. And neither did he.

REBECCA'S ROGUE

by

Paula Marshall

Dear Reader

  History and historical novels are full of stories about fortune-hunters who pursued rich women in order to marry them for their money. They are nearly always portrayed as villains, some major and some minor.

  In the world of the Regency if a young man who had expected to inherit money suddenly found himself penniless what other course was open to him? He was not trained to follow a profession and was too old to become an apprentice. He would be too poor to buy a commission in the Army and if he enlisted as a private soldier had little prospect of other than a miserable future. His one hope was a rich marriage, which was difficult if society discovered his lack of fortune and branded him a deceiving rogue.

  It was even worse if he were at all honourable since he might find pursuing rich women distasteful, but was condemned to indulge in it. I decided to write a romance sympathetic towards a man in such a sad predicament and so Will Shafto, my hero, was born. Aware of his true situation my heroine, Rebecca Rowallan, decides to marry him for her own convenience, but Fate, as usual, takes a hand in the game, and then… And then I hope that you enjoy reading Will and Rebecca's story as much as I enjoyed writing it.

Paula Marshall

Chapter One

1813

Will Shafto, his hat on the side of his handsome head, strode down Piccadilly, whistling merrily. The troubles which had haunted him since his early youth were over. Life lay fair before him. He had recently proposed marriage to Sarah Allenby, the woman of his dreams, and she—and her family—had accepted him.

That she was the woman of his dreams only because she was a great heiress, a golden dolly as rich as Croesus, and not because she was the youthfully charming beauty of the season who thought that it was her looks which had attracted him, troubled him not at all. The looks and the charm were a bonus for him, not a necessity.

For was she not—albeit unknowingly—about to rescue him from the Marshalsea, the debtor's prison which awaited him if he had failed to win her? The last decade spent struggling to appear rich and handsome on nothing a year, keeping himself afloat only by his wits, was behind him. He could truly be Shafto of Shafto Hall again, with all that that implied.

Oh, yes, the Hall could be repaired, the lands around it sold by his wastrel father might be bought back again and the Shafto family returned to its former glory. If the price were to be the sale of himself and his integrity to a woman whom he liked, but did not love, then so be it. He had his reasons, and so far as he was concerned they were good ones.

Moreover, many marriages between those of equal fortune were based on no more and no less than he was offering his heiress. He would be faithful to her, would be as good a husband as it was possible to be, particularly since she would be the means by which the Shaftos would be solvent again. Gratitude alone would keep him faithful.

He turned into the curtilage of the great palace in Piccadilly which a former Allenby had caused to be built in the Italian style of the early eighteenth century; a palace which would soon be his. He was visiting it in order to sign the marriage settlement which his lawyer, and those of the Allenbys, had been drawing up that morning.

Will stifled a grin at the thought of Josiah Wilmot, that clever shark of sharks, about the business of deceiving the Allenbys as to Will's true circumstances. The papers which he had been presenting to them appeared to show that Will was not only solvent, but magnificently so.

He was so lost in his dream that he did not notice the cold stare which the butler gave him, nor did the fact that he was shown into an ante-room, rather than the big drawing-room where he had always been welcomed on his earlier visits disturb him. He was still lost in his euphoric dream.

It gave him time to check his appearance in a Venetian glass mirror, to register that he was as well turned out as ever. His dark curls were brushed *á la* Brutus; his cravat was a spotless dream; his blue-black jacket was a perfect fit, as were his cream breeches and shiny black boots. He was not a vain man, but he was well aware that his looks and carriage were better than those of the common run.

Everything seemed to be in order. The butler returned to say, still cold, 'The family are ready to receive you now, sir.'

He was led down a black-and-white flagged corridor to a room which he had never entered before. On the way he passed a well-dressed young woman, with an obvious duenna in tow. The young woman responded to his obligatory bow with a stare as cold as the butler's. She was, he noted briefly—Will always made it his business to notice everything, one never knew when it might come in handy—of average height with a cold clever face in the ancient Greek mode. She was a beauty, but a severe one, with a straight nose, grey eyes and a high forehead below fashionably dressed chestnut hair.

The butler impatiently ushered him into a room where, instead of his beloved awaiting him, a group of men, all of them members of Sarah's family, were standing. Among them, Simpson, the Allenbys' lawyer, was an oddity in his decent black clothing, a crow among peacocks. The room was some sort of study where busts of antique philosophers were arranged along a high cornice.

At the far end of the room, behind the Allenbys, were two bruisers, instantly and unhappily recognisable to

Will as Bow Street Runners. Something was very wrong. He was soon to find out what it was.

John Allenby, Sarah's uncle and guardian, was the first to address him.

'You must, sir, being what and who you are, understand why we are receiving you after this fashion.'

Will decided to be brazen. It was the only thing left to him.

'No, indeed, sir. I am all at sea.' It was, perhaps, an unlucky phrase to use. John Allenby seized on it immediately.

'Would that you were, sir. Would that you were. Suffice it to say, as briefly as possible, that there can be no question of a marriage between you and my niece. Despite your own, and your lawyer's, lying assertions we have become aware, through the investigation undertaken by these men here—' and he waved at the two Runners '—that you are a penniless, landless fellow, heavily in debt.

'You are a rogue, sir, a miserable fortune-hunter, an adventurer of the worst kind. The ring you have bestowed upon my niece, and which lies on the desk before you, has not even been paid for. Your only income is less than two hundred pounds a year. Had we known of your true character and circumstances we should not have allowed you to speak to our niece, let alone propose marriage to her and be accepted.'

The world had fallen in on him. Will was like the man in the Eastern tale who, seated before a basket full of pottery, dreams of the fortune he will make by selling it, until, kicking his foot out in ecstasy, he knocks it over and breaks it all—and destroys his future.

The barefaced and insolent courage, which had sus-

tained him in the nine years since he had been left a
pauper at eighteen, did not desert him now.

'And your niece, sir? What does she have to say to
this dismissal of my suit? May I not speak to her?'

'What my niece may, or may not, desire is nothing to
you. She will obey her elders and betters and will not
be allowed to associate with you again. As we wish no
scandal to attach to her name through her unfortunate
connection with you we shall not bruit this business
about the world. You will leave at once, taking the ring
with you—and if you are so foolish as to argue this
matter, the Runners whom you see before you have their
orders to escort you to the door.'

Will made no move either to leave or to pick up the
ring from where it lay on the desk. Of all the dreadful
moments in his hard life this was perhaps the worst: a
public humiliation before men whom he had previously
thought of as his friends. He looked at Harry Fitzalan,
Sarah's cousin, who had introduced Will to her.

'And you, Harry?' he asked. 'You agree to this?'

John Allenby did not allow him to answer.

'Of course, seeing that it was his folly which brought
about ours in first allowing you into Allenby House and
then countenancing your courtship of our niece.'

There was nothing for it but to try to leave clutching
some shreds of dignity around him. Will bowed, and
turned to go before the bruisers removed him.

John Allenby called to his back in a jeering voice,
'Come, you are leaving behind your half-owned property,' and he threw the ring at Will's feet.

Will made no move to pick it up, but walked steadily
on his way to the door. He would neither defy the men
before him nor try to justify himself. Both courses of
action would be useless. He had been caught out in a

massive deception and he could only wonder what had caused Sarah's uncle to set the Runners on him. He was not a criminal, and had not associated with criminals, but if poverty were to be counted a crime in the eyes of the men who were judging him, then he was one.

Once at the door, and before he opened it, he turned again to hold his head high and say, in a distant, unmoved voice, 'I would have made her a better husband than any you are like to choose for her.'

It was, although he had no means of knowing it then, a prophetic statement which more than one present in the room had cause to remember. At the time John Allenby stared inimically at him. 'If you do not leave on the instant I shall order the Runners to throw you down the steps and into the street.'

Will inclined his head gravely. 'No need for that. You will present my compliments and my regrets to Sarah, Fitzalan. I know you to be a man of honour.'

Harry gazed miserably at him before biting his lip and shaking his head.

'So be it,' said Will, as his erstwhile friend denied him, and left. *He* had denied nothing, because everything that John Allenby had said about him was the truth.

And yet, not quite the truth.

Outside, in Piccadilly, the full horror of his circumstances struck Will hard. In the knowledge of his coming marriage he had borrowed money on it to outfit himself as a husband fit for such as Sarah Allenby. He had also laid out other monies, but not for himself, which would also now have to be repaid. He would not need to trouble about what the rest of society thought about him when the news of Sarah's jilting of him became public because he would be rotting in a debtor's prison.

His jaunty stride had declined to a tired amble, his head, for the first time in his life, hung low. He thus did not notice that a fashionable chaise with scarlet and gold armorials on its panelling was following him down Piccadilly. It stopped just outside Burlington House where a sturdy young footman sprang down from the box to accost him.

Will was so lost to everything that at first he did not respond to the footman's greeting and carried on walking in the direction of Hyde Park.

'Sir,' said the footman, 'my mistress would have a word with you. She is in the carriage there.'

'With me?' asked Will, bewildered at being spoken to by this stranger. 'With me?'

'If you are Mr Will Shafto, sir, then my mistress would talk with you for a moment.'

Will's gaze took in the man, the chaise, and the woman sitting in it. She was the severe young beauty whom he had seen at Allenby House. He walked over to the chaise. The woman lowered the glass panel in the door to put her head out and speak to him.

Seen close to, her looks were more classically severe than ever. She could well serve as a model for the goddess of wisdom, Athene herself, since she appeared to be on the point of handing out some unpalatable edict from on high. Will could only wonder why in the world she wished to speak to someone whom she must be aware was a disgraced adventurer—other than to reproach him, of course.

'Mr Will Shafto,' she said, and her voice was as cold as her face.

'Yes, I am he.'

'They have thrown you out of the house, I believe, and broken off your engagement to my cousin Sarah?'

'Is that a question?' said Will, a trifle nastily. 'Or a statement designed simply to put me down further?'

'Neither,' she replied, her lovely calm unruffled. 'I was merely making sure of my man.'

My man, indeed! What the devil did she mean by that? In no way was he her man—or anyone else's man for that matter.

'And I must introduce myself to you, seeing that we have not met before.' She continued, not a whit put out by his calculating stare, 'I am Rebecca Rowallan, and I am twice as rich as my cousin Sarah.'

'Congratulations and good day to you then, Miss Rowallan. And now, forgive me. I must be on my way. Not being an hundredth as rich as either of you, I have much to think about.'

'So you must, Mr Shafto, considering your changed circumstances. But, pray, do not rush away. I would wish to know two things. Where do you live? And may I visit you tomorrow morning at ten of the clock? I dislike doing business in the public streets.'

Of all strange things for her to say to him on this damnable day! Will finally lost his hard-won composure and gaped at her open-mouthed. The words were wrenched from him. 'What in the world for?'

'Not here, sir,' she answered him. She was as smooth and slippery as Lawyer Wilmot himself. 'I have just told you why, and I try never to repeat myself, but since your wits are a-wandering, for once, I will do so. I wish to do business with you. So, pray, tell me your address. Perhaps I had better reassure you that it will be to your advantage to receive me.'

Receive her? For what? And for what conceivable advantage to him? Surely it was her wits had gone awandering, not his.

'Ten, Duke Street,' he ground out. 'I have rooms there. On the first floor.'

Her beautiful eyebrows rose. 'Duke Street? Can you afford to live there?'

'Of course not. But needs must…'

'…when the devil drives. Yes, I know. I shall call at ten of the clock, remember. My companion, Mrs Grey, will be with me. We shall require no refreshments.'

Without waiting for an answer she called to the coachman, 'Drive on, James.'

Leaving Will staring after her as though she were an apparition ready to summon him to heaven or to hell.

Chapter Two

'No news from Josiah Wilmot, Gib?'

Gib Barry, Will's valet and man of all work, shook his head. 'None. I've not seen hair nor hide of him. But you know old Josh, he's so many irons in the fire he's probably on with the next one, now that yours is out of it and cooling.'

Will had been pacing around his drawing-room ever since he had reached home. Now he stood stockstill to stare out of the window.

'It's the end, Gib, you know that. Right up the River Tick, we are, and no mistake. If you wish to leave me to find employment elsewhere, I shall quite understand.'

'I know that. Faith, I've been your man since you were a lad—long enough to know what's what where you're concerned. But I like my billet here, and my little pension from the Army for my poorly leg means that all I need is a roof over my head. No, I'll not leave you, yet. No one else would be so considerate of a poor cripple.'

'But you will have to go soon, of course.' Will had begun his restless pacing again. 'For it cannot be long

before the duns haul me off to the Marshalsea and you'll
need to find another roof, this one having gone.'

'Wait and see, sir; wait and see is my motto. The
darkest hour is always before the dawn. Who knows
what tomorrow might bring?'

Such carefree optimism was beyond Will. Ruin had
been steadily creeping up on him for years until, meeting
Sarah Allenby, he thought that he had found salvation.
This very evening he had arranged to accompany her to
the Opera, but some other bright young spark would be
sitting beside her; knowing her, he doubted whether she
was giving Will Shafto another thought.

Her very shallowness had attracted him because it
meant that he would easily be able to satisfy her, make
her happy, but it also meant that she would not have
fought very hard to keep him. In the end, one man was
very like another to her, and she had chosen Will for his
bright good looks and his entertaining conversation as
much as for anything else.

If he had not truly loved her, then she certainly had
not, in any real sense, loved him.

His pride said, Go out and show yourself at one of
your clubs to prove that you are not set down by this
afternoon's work. His common sense said, What, and be
pointed and stared at as the man who was turned away
from Allenby House as an adventurer? He was sure that
more than one of the men present that afternoon would
talk of what had passed, regardless of John Allenby's
wishes that the matter be kept secret for Sarah's sake.

It was too good a piece of gossip to be kept quiet.
No, he would wait a few days before the brouhaha died
down. Not because he lacked courage, but if he were
once turned away from the fashionable haunts of young

men about town, he would be permanently ruined, never be received anywhere again, and he dared not risk that.

So, it was an early night for him.

Then it was an early rising the next morning and a manful attempt to eat Gib's good breakfast which, for once, tasted of the dust and ashes his life had become.

He could not even loll about comfortably in his dressing-gown for there was Miss Rebecca Rowallan to see, when he might find out what the deuce she wanted with him. He was glad that he had resisted the temptation to drink the night away for he was glumly sure that he needed a clear head to deal with her.

Gib dressed him as carefully as ever. He was not quite as glorious as he had been the previous afternoon, but glorious enough. For once Will did not examine himself in the mirror, taking Gib's word for it that he was entirely *comme il faut*. His face had become hateful to him. It was bad enough to play the fortune-hunter, but even worse to be exposed for doing so.

Miss Rowallan, he was not surprised to discover, was punctual to the very second. The small French clock on his mantelpiece was striking ten even as Gib announced her, and her attendant lady.

'Miss Rowallan has asked that her footman be allowed to wait in my kitchen, and so I have agreed,' Gib informed Will as he pointed the two ladies to a large French sofa.

Miss Rowallan, who was dressed in a demure morning gown of Quakerish grey with a white linen collar and cuffs, promptly seated herself, but her lady remained standing. Something which was explained almost immediately when Miss Rowallan, whilst drawing off her gloves, said sweetly, 'I must ask that Mrs Grey be allowed to join my footman. I prefer to speak to you alone, Mr Shafto.'

Will's eyebrows climbed—as did his servant's. He looked curiously at Mrs Grey, standing before him, her hands clasped, her expression mutinous, the perfect picture of a middle-aged duenna not being allowed to do her duty. It did not need saying, but everyone present thought it: no single young woman should ever be allowed to remain alone with a man. Particularly not with a young man.

'Is that what Mrs Grey wishes?' Will asked, more than ever intrigued by what Miss Rowallan had to say to him which her woman might not hear.

'No, it is not,' said Miss Rowallan calmly before Mrs Grey could answer him. 'But since I pay her wages she does my bidding, not I hers.'

The bitch! What a harsh thing to say before the woman herself—even if it were true.

'You are not afraid for your reputation then, madam? To be alone with me, I mean.' Will's tone was a trifle cutting, but that affected Miss Rowallan not at all. Her own reply was equally so.

'Who is to talk, Mr Shafto? Certainly not Mrs Grey nor, I believe, your man, whom I have reason to know is discretion itself where you are concerned. And if you were to make any such claim about my being here alone with you, who in the world would believe you—and not me?'

Who, indeed? The hard bitch had the right of it. He was discredited, was he not? Will shook his head to clear it. 'Very well, then, if that is what you wish.'

'That is what I wish. I will send for you, Amelia,' she told her companion, 'as soon as my private business with Mr Shafto is over. It should not take long.'

'There's a good fire in the kitchen, Mrs Grey, and some excellent tea,' Gib said encouragingly. 'Mr Shafto will only drink the best.'

This revelation of his reckless extravagance in view of his financial situation set Will internally wincing, but his guest appeared to take no notice of it at all. Her face changed not a whit.

Nor did Will's. He did not sit down, but moved to stand with his back to the window so that his face was in shadow. 'I am agog,' he said, 'to learn what private business you can possibly have with me.'

For the first time she smiled at him and her whole face was transformed and softened. For a brief moment he could see that she was related to the sweetly pretty Sarah—and then the resemblance was gone.

'The most private business of all,' she replied, without any form of preamble, 'for I have come to ask you to marry me.'

It was as well that Will's face was in shadow, for light would have shown that for a brief space he was thunderstruck.

He gave a short, harsh laugh.

'Marry you! Am I to understand that you are proposing to me? You must have known what passed at Allenby House yesterday afternoon and that I was rejected for being a penniless fortune-hunter.'

'Yes, I do know that, Mr Shafto. That was why I left. I did not wish to be present when you were interviewed, nor did I wish to undertake the unnecessary task of comforting my cousin for she needed no comforting. I have seen her more distressed when she lost her favourite doll.

'True, she wept a few obligatory tears when she learned that she was to lose you, but my Uncle Allenby comforted her by saying that with you well rid of she was sure to marry a Marquess, at least. That brightened her up wonderfully. I left her practising to be m'lady.'

'Well, *you* will never be m'lady, if you marry me,' returned Will shortly.

'True again, Mr Shafto. But you do appear to have a deal of common sense which most of the men around me lack.'

'Now, how can you know that?' wondered Will. 'Seeing that we have never met before.'

'Oh, I have seen a lot of you,' she said, almost carelessly, 'and heard much from Cousin Sarah and from Cousin Harry. From them both I have learned that beneath your charming manner you possess all the hard common sense which is missing in both of them.'

'And is it *your* common sense which has resulted in you proposing to me, a man you hardly know, and this not even Leap Year? You do know, Miss Rowallan, that it is not Leap Year?'

'Oh, I am well versed in the calendar, Mr Shafto, as I am in most matters not normally considered the province of the female sex. The law, for example. You must understand that my proposition is not a simple one. It comes attached to certain conditions which would be plainly set out in the marriage settlement.'

'It does, does it?' growled Will, who was beginning to think that there was something demeaning about being proposed to by a female.

Who and what did she think he was? A silly question, for she knew exactly what he was: a fortune-hunter. And had not almost her first remark to him been a declaration of her extreme wealth? Which should have told him something. He thought for a moment. For more than a moment.

'You are silent, Mr Shafto. You have not asked me what the conditions are.'

Her coolness, in view of the enormity of what she was saying and doing, was provoking. Will, normally a man whom little provoked, found it difficult to control himself.

'Because I am asking myself certain questions. For example, why, with all that money—twice Sarah's, you were careful to tell me yesterday afternoon—you are not buying yourself a Duke at the very least—if Sarah is considered to be worth a Marquess, that is?'

'I do not want a Duke, Mr Shafto. I am also well informed as to the marital eligibility of all the senior noblemen in England and a most unattractive lot they are. Particularly the Royal Dukes, who are both ugly and promiscuous. You, on the other hand, are most personable—if you will forgive me for saying so.

'But if I am to be allowed to usurp the man's prerogative by proposing to you, then I may also comment on your appearance, I hope, since it is commonplace for men to do that to the women whom they are trying to charm into marriage!'

Will closed his eyes. This was beyond anything. 'I am at sea,' he muttered for the second time in two days.

Miss Rowallan put her head on one side and, for once, looked at him almost coyly. 'A very apt thing for one called Shafto to say. You know the old song, ''Bobby Shafto''?'

'Too well,' said Will bitterly, wondering where this mad conversation was straying. 'But my hair is black, not yellow, and I have no silver buckles on my knee.'

'They are unfortunately out of fashion and not likely to return,' she agreed. 'But let us leave that, Mr Shafto. It is not to the point.'

Will bowed at her, 'Oh, by all means, let us get to the point. If there *is* one beyond your original proposal.'

Was she straying about in her conversation to wrong-foot him? Will had met some criminals and confidence tricksters who did exactly that to their victims. Was he her victim?

'If you marry me, Mr Shafto, it will be for my benefit rather than yours. A husband will give me protection, not only from adventurers, whom, unlike you, I cannot trust, but from relatives whom I cannot trust, either, and who seek to dominate me because I am a woman. You must understand that a single woman on her own, beyond a certain age, and under another, is an anomaly, and an anomaly to be preyed on.

'That being so, I am prepared to marry you if you will consent to have drawn up papers and settlements which will keep you from ever touching my fortune. Privately we shall draw up other agreements—to wit, that you will be my husband in name only, that this shall not be disclosed, and that, if at any time after a period of five years either of us wishes to end this purely business arrangement, we are free to do so.

'In return for your agreement to all these conditions I shall pay off your debts and allow you an income sufficient to appear in society as a gentleman worthy to be the husband of one as wealthy as myself.'

Will turned away from her, and offered her something which no gentleman should ever offer a lady: his back.

He stared unseeingly out of the window at Duke Street. He scarcely knew whether he had been complimented or insulted by such an offer. On the whole he felt...

He didn't know what he felt.

'Well, sir? Have you no answer for me?'

Will did not immediately show her his face. He said, speaking away from her, his voice harsh, 'You are trying to buy me.'

Nothing disturbed her lovely calm. It was intolerable that she should look like a perfect lady and say such unladylike things.

'But why should that trouble you? Were you not willing to sell yourself to my cousin, for, in effect, less?'

He swung round to drop on one knee before her, and say, his face savage, 'But that was *my* choice. This is yours.'

If Miss Rowallan was frightened at this sudden change of manner from someone so usually mild and self-controlled, she showed no sign of it.

'No,' she told him. 'It is still your choice. Think, you can say Yea, or Nay. No compulsion. And think also, if you say me Yea, then all your troubles will be over. Furthermore, if we do marry and then agree to part, I shall ensure that you will not go unrewarded.'

Oh, the temptation was great—greater, indeed, than she knew. But what sort of man would it make him if he agreed to do as she wished?

Will rose and said in a stifled voice, 'What makes you think that you can trust me? Why should I not fall on you, once we are married, and take my rights? For that matter, why should I not do so now—and then refuse to marry you? We are alone. Are you not very trusting—too trusting? After all, I am a rogue, am I not? That was decided yesterday afternoon.'

If he had thought to shake her, to frighten her, he had been mistaken. She remained as cool as ever.

'Yes, I believe that I can trust you. Last night I was told that you said that they could have done worse than allow you to marry Sarah. I believe that to be true. You may be a rogue, but I also believe that you are an honest rogue, and that, if we marry, you will be *my* rogue.'

Her rogue, indeed! The thought choked Will. It stiffened his resolve to refuse her.

'No, I won't. I reject your offer. I must have some honour left. To marry you in such a fashion would destroy my remaining self-respect.'

'I cannot see that in marrying me, you would be doing anything different from marrying Sarah. What's more I do not ask you to be celibate—I only ask you to be discreet.'

'How can you speak so?' Will was gazing at her almost in horror. 'And you a single woman!'

Miss Rowallan shook her head at him. 'I do not think that you know women very well, Mr Shafto. In that you are like most men.'

She rose. 'In a moment I shall ask you to ring for Mrs Grey. You may have refused me now, but I shall give you three days to think over my offer.'

He glared at her. 'I shall not change my mind. You must find another dupe.'

All that she replied to that was, 'We shall see. And now, Mr. Shafto, I think that it is time that you asked me to partake of the tea of which your man spoke. We must part as friends who might yet be more than friends.'

She was ice, she was steel and, marvelling at her, Will did as she bid and rang for Gib and Mrs Grey.

He could quite understand why she had not wanted her attendant lady to be present at their tête-à-tête!

Three days! Three days to decide whether or not to marry a woman whom he had disliked at first sight, and now disliked even more after he had the misfortune to know more of her. Beautiful she might be, but it was the beauty of the Gorgon who struck men stone dead. She was cunning and devious, no doubt about it, for how otherwise had she known that Gib would always be faithful to him?

Had there been two set of Runners shadowing him? No, he had not the slightest desire to lay a finger on her, could not imagine ever being roused by her... She must find another half-man to make a half-husband of.

Will was still fuming to himself later that day when Josiah Wilmot at last showed his worried face at 10, Duke Street.

'I had thought to see you before this, Josh. Much before this.'

Josh Wilmot heaved a mighty sigh. 'What point in that, Will? The matter was over and done with before you reached Allenby House. They were waiting for me when I was shown in. A whole cabal of them, sanctimonious faces and all. I was not even allowed to open my despatch box. They told me that they knew all about you—and me, too. They had put Runners on to us, they said, and the only things which prevented them from handing us both over to the law was that they could not discover that we had actually done anything criminal, and that they did not want the business to become an open scandal.'

'You might have warned me,' Will reproached him.

'Warned you! They kept me prisoner there until after you had come and gone. Confess it, Will, we were engaged in a nice little piece of flim-flam, pretending that you are richer than you are. After all, you are master of Shafto Hall, your family is an old and good one, and it is not criminal for you to be poor, nor to wish to marry a golden dolly. Many have done it before you. Bad luck for us that they found out before the wedding and not afterwards.'

'Bad luck for me, certainly,' agreed Will.

'True, and I've even worse news for you, which was why, as your good friend, I have come to see you to-night. Your paper, your bills, have been bought up by Jem Straw and before the week's end he will have you in the Marshalsea. Your little gallop is over. Get you away from London, if you can.'

'Back to the ruin which is Shafto Hall,' said Will wearily. 'At least in London I have managed to live, but what shall I do there?'

Josh Wilmot's honesty might be dubious, but his friendship for Will was not. He put an arm around his shoulders. 'Look you, Will, I would offer you a clerk's post in my office, pen-pushing, only I know that it would not answer because it would keep you—and *only* you.'

Will paced agitatedly about the room as a wild animal does when caged. He stopped to say, 'Were it not for that, for my other commitments, I would accept your offer. I am sick of the life I have been living and which circumstances have forced upon me. I have barely been keeping my head above water, waiting only for the flood which will overwhelm me—and which has now arrived.'

Josh shook his head. 'Have you no friend, no relatives who might help you?'

'None. For God's sake, Josh, what does a man do who has only been trained to be a gentleman and is fit for nothing else? I thought that marriage to Sarah would…'

He stopped abruptly and walked to the window, then turned to face Josh. He was in the same place, the same position which he had occupied when Rebecca Rowallan had made her monstrous proposition.

'Yes,' prompted Josh as Will stood there, as thunder-struck as he had been earlier. 'You were about to say?'

'Nothing…something.' Only, he thought, that Re-becca Rowallan was offering him salvation. Earlier in the day he had not been so completely on the ropes as he was now, with the prospect of the Marshalsea before him.

'Yes,' he exclaimed, striking one hand on the other. 'Yes, come hell, come the Devil, I'll do it. I was pre-pared to sell myself one way, so why not sell myself the other? She was right, damn her! Where's the difference? She gave me three days. God help me, I haven't needed one.'

Josh stared at him as though he had run mad.

'Eh, what's this, Will? Make sense, lad.'

Lad! Josh hadn't called him lad since they were boys together, not yet knowing how cruel the world might be to the poor and lowly.

'Don't ask me,' he said. 'But I have a way out. I'll not rot in the Marshalsea, Josh, and for old time's sake, I'll try to ensure that you have a decent life, too. Our hard times are over.'

'But how, Will, how?'

Will began to laugh, helplessly. 'I'm going to be mar-ried, Josh, to someone even richer than Sarah Allenby and this time there'll be no last-minute hitch. I hereby invite you to the wedding.'

He laughed all the harder at the sight of Josh's dropped jaw.

'Come, lose that Friday face, man. You shall be my lawyer again and my best man to stand at my side whilst the Allenbys watch me marry cousin Rebecca Rowal-lan.'

Josh took him by the shoulders. 'Look at me, Will, and speak the truth. Has worry driven you mad?'

'No, I'm not mad, Josh, far from it. You might even say that I'm suddenly driven sane. Tomorrow afternoon, as ever is, I shall be at your office to explain all.'

Josh could get nothing further from him by way of explanation, and went his way, shaking his head and muttering to himself about men driven witless by lack of money.

Left alone, Will sat down and began to plan what he might say to Miss Rebecca Rowallan on the morrow. Please God that she had not changed her mind!

Miss Rebecca Rowallan had not changed her mind. Not about her proposal nor about what Mr Will Shafto might choose to do. He was, she was sure, certain to agree to do what she wished when he had taken the time to consider her offer more carefully.

As he had suspected, she had put men on his trail to far more effect than the Allenbys had. She knew something of Will Shafto's life in London, of his lack of money, but little about the means by which he had managed to live on nothing a year. About his life in Northumberland she had learned nothing. The villagers had refused to talk to the man she had sent there. Some old and fierce loyalty made them silent when accosted by a chance-come stranger.

All that he could discover was that Mr Shafto senior had gambled everything away, shot himself, and that the family had left the Hall after his death.

'And that's all?' the man had asked. 'Is the old man's wife still alive? Has the present Mr Will Shafto no brothers or sisters?'

But he had gained nothing in reply beyond a terse, 'Nowt to do wi' you.'

No matter. Miss Rowallan had found out all that she needed to know. Mr Will Shafto was apparently alone in the world, and desperate. She was sure that he would visit her, if not this morning, then the next.

It was while she was seated in her drawing-room, waiting for him, that she had other visitors, two of them, arriving together. Mr Beaucourt and Mr Hedley Beaucourt, his son. She wished to see neither of them, but politeness demanded that she could not turn them away. They were family, after all, if only distant family, and Mr Beaucourt senior had been her guardian.

She rose to meet them, her manner as cool as ever.

'Mr Beaucourt,' she said in greeting, giving his son merely a distant nod.

'Oh, uncle, surely,' the father said, smiling, while the son tried to take her hand to kiss it. He failed. Somehow it eluded his grasp.

'Not quite,' Miss Rowallan told him gravely. 'You were merely brought up in the same household as my late mother, and are consequently no blood relation of mine.'

'Come, come, my dear. You refine too much on a relationship which allowed me to be your guardian.'

'Which you well know was none of my wish. Pray inform me why you have honoured me with this visit?'

Regretfully she sat down. It would be mannerless to keep them standing, but they must do so whilst she remained on her feet. She motioned them to sit, which they did with great flourishing of their tailcoats. Father and son both aspired to be part of the dandy set. Miss Rowallan was in another of her Quakerish gowns, a dull blue this time.

'You are in looks, cousin,' said Hedley, raising his quizzing glass to inspect her, 'but then, you always are.'

Miss Rowallan made him no answer, merely repeated her question as to their visit.

'Now, my dear, you know perfectly well why we are here.' Mr Beaucourt sounded reproachful. 'I have spoken to you of the matter often enough. You are twenty-five years old, a great heiress who has refused to take part in the Season until this year. You should be married. Nay, you must marry. You need a husband to manage your vast estates and affairs for you, and it was long the wish of your mother and I that you should marry my son Hedley.'

At the mention of his name Hedley rose and bowed. 'It is my wish also,' he said unnecessarily, having said the same thing many times before.

Miss Rowallan doubted whether her mother had ever wished any such thing. She had disliked Mr Beaucourt, who had only become her daughter's guardian because of the sudden death of her father's brother, after her parents' death in a coach accident. This had left no one of substance to be appointed in his place by the courts, except the man sitting before her, who, only moderately wealthy himself, had long plotted to marry his son to her.

She did not know which of them she disliked the more. The father, or the son. She smiled coldly at them. 'As I have informed you many times before, I have no mind to marry at all. Unless, of course, I find someone who attracts me so much that he makes marriage attractive, too.'

The elder Mr Beaucourt leaned forward and put a familiar hand on her knee. She removed it. No whit disturbed he continued. 'Now, now, my dear. We are well aware that you do not wish to entrust yourself and your fortune to anyone who might wish to exploit both it and you. But no such problem attaches itself to the proposal which I am about to make to you...'

He paused diplomatically. Undiplomatically, Miss Rowallan jumped into the silence.

'I believe, sir, that you have made it many times before. And, no, I must repeat again that I have no wish to marry your son—if that is what you are about to suggest.'

The elder Mr Beaucourt gave a melancholy sigh; the younger merely looked aggrieved and began to suck the silver knob on his cane agitatedly.

'My dear, you do not consider sufficiently what you are saying. You can trust us, for we have your best interests at heart, but as an unmarried young woman you are always at the risk of being taken in by a pretty face.'

He got no further. Miss Rowallan rose to her full height. 'This is the outside of enough, sir. You insult me. What can have given you such an absurd notion? May I say, in order to end your importunings once and for all, that if pretty faces are the problem, then I am in no danger from your son.'

Young Mr Beaucourt nearly swallowed his cane before choking out, 'Oh, I say, cousin. Steady on.'

'I am steady,' she announced, 'quite steady,' and her grim expression bore out her statement. 'Before we all say what we might live to regret, I think it better that you both leave, and do not come back until you have decided to cease pestering me to marry a man whom I do not like and cannot respect,' and she swept out of the room.

Both men were so taken aback that neither of them recovered sufficiently quickly to answer her in kind.

'I suppose,' whined the son, 'that in the circumstances we had better leave.'

'No such thing,' roared the father. 'I shall at once demand to see her again. Were it not for her money I would not wish to see you married to such a virago,' and he made for the door, followed by his complaining son.

They were met by the butler, who was followed by the largest footman either of them had ever seen. 'Madam has asked me to be certain that you leave at once,' he told them, his face quite straight. He continued suavely when Mr Beaucourt senior began to fume at him, as though forcibly removing gentlemen from the premises was an everyday thing, 'Or I cannot answer for the consequences.'

Nothing for it but to leave, thought Mr Beaucourt senior, while muttering morosely, 'I thought it a good sign that she saw us without her damned duenna, but I doubt if she would have been so downright had she been present. But this is not the last of it. No one speaks to me like that. No one.'

By now they were on the pavement, to see a hackney coach draw up from which stepped Mr Will Shafto, dressed with great elegance and carrying himself with his usual consummate ease. Passing them without acknowledgment other than a tip of his hat, he walked up the steps to Miss Rowallan's front door, to be welcomed by the butler who had just threatened to throw them out.

Father and son looked wildly at one another.

'Now what the devil is *he* doing here, paying calls in the morning?' said the father.

The son, who had taken up his cane again, decided not to suck it but to say instead, gloom written all over him, 'Perhaps he's the pretty face you said that she was sure to marry!'

Will Shafto was only half-aware of the two men who had preceded him. He had seen both of them about town and liked the look of neither of them. He had no notion that they were in any sense close to the woman he was about to meet, and who rose to greet him without so much as her duenna with her.

It was, then, to be another confidential meeting which boded well for him. Will made a mental note that if he were to marry the lady he would see that she employed a better dressmaker. The clothes she usually favoured did nothing either for her face or her figure. All that would have to change if she were to become Mrs Will Shafto.

He had had so many disappointments in life that he always used the conditional tenses when thinking about the future: something which he had failed to do when he had thought that he was on the point of marrying Sarah Allenby. He had made a mental resolve never to tempt Fate by doing such a thing again.

Nevertheless his spirits were buoyant and remained even more so when she graciously motioned him to a seat directly opposite to her.

'No need for you to stand, Mr Shafto, since by your appearance and the early hour at which you have arrived, I believe that you have come to give me an answer which I wish to hear.'

There! She was going straight to the point just like a man. No shilly-shallying, no missish drooping of the head, or touching of the handkerchief to the lips. No, everything was downright with her. Will stared at her in wonder and decided to answer her in kind—if blunt was what she wanted rather than tact, then he would oblige her.

'Indeed, Miss Rowallan, since you wish to buy me, then I am here to sell myself.'

She offered him the smile which briefly transformed her face. 'Oh, bravo, Mr Shafto. I see that we are both going to know exactly where we stand, and what we are about. It will save so much time, will it not, as well as a great deal of hurt feelings.'

'True,' returned Will. 'And since the marriage mart is what we are engaged in, then honesty ought to demand that we abide by market practices so that buyer and seller cannot later claim deceit.'

'I see that I have chosen my man well. And, Mr Shafto, you do understand that this is a purely business transaction? We shall be partners only in that sense, not in any other. The marriage will never be consummated.'

Oh, her frankness with him was strangely liberating! Will had spent a large part of his life in dealing in polite evasions—particularly where women were concerned—so that to meet with a woman with whom he could consistently talk brisk sense in plain language was like finding himself in an invigorating cold bath, not a steamy warm one.

'Yes, I understand that fully.' He decided to be as demeaning towards her as she was being towards him. 'Not to have to consummate the marriage will be a great relief to me, I assure you.'

'Excellent! That you do not find me at all attractive, I mean. That relieves my mind, too. We shall live happily together like a pair of old maids.'

'Or a pair of old bachelors,' added Will, joining in the game.

'Quite. We shall have no would-be amorous *rencontres* in corridors or bedrooms to worry about.'

'Perhaps the occasional meeting of minds in the library, instead?' was Will's counter to that.

'Oh, you read, Mr Shafto? That is a blessing I had not counted on. I had thought you quite given over to pleasure and the difficulties of being a fine gentlemen with no money to back you. Yes, I shall be happy to meet you in the library and discuss The Rights of Man—and Woman, too, perhaps. Have you read Miss Wollstonecraft's noble work?'

'No, but I am acquainted with Tom Paine, and Burke's answer to him.'

'Better and better. I anticipate a happy five years in which we shall both enrich our minds. All that remains to us is to set the lawyers to work. Do I take it that you will be employing your dubious friend Mr. Wilmot?'

'Of course, seeing that I am dubious, too… I have promised him that he may assist me at the wedding. If you agree to that, I shall be prepared to agree to all those whom you wish to invite.'

'Fair enough. It is going to be a pleasure to do business with you. Indeed, as a result of this meeting I am prepared to give you considerably more of a yearly allowance than I had originally planned. A result, I assure you, of your total lack of gentlemanly piff-paff when talking to a woman.'

'Oh, you can certainly rely on me to avoid gentlemanly piff-paff,' returned Will gravely. 'I only practise it when I talk to featherheaded women—and you are certainly not one of them!'

'Excellent, Mr Shafto, you reassure me. I do not think that I could long endure very much light-minded conversation. You will not, therefore, be surprised if the rest of our tête-à-tête is conducted along purely practical lines.'

'On the contrary,' said Will. 'I shall be most relieved.'

'Then you will not, I think, object if I suggest that we do not immediately inform society of our intention to marry. Bearing in mind what has just passed between you and my Allenby connection, I think it would be wise if we went through a reasonably lengthy pantomime in which you courted me assiduously, and I responded enthusiastically. Not straightway, perhaps, but on a rising note.

'Furthermore, to save precious time I think that we may begin this very evening. I understand that you were to have escorted my cousin Sarah to the Opera last night. Instead, with the three tickets I have purchased you may accompany myself and Mrs Grey to one of the best boxes tonight.'

Now this was pushing things on with a vengeance. Will did not suck his ivory-headed cane as young Mr. Beaucourt was in the habit of doing when wrong-footed.

Instead he countered rapidly with, 'Forgive me for quibbling a little, but will not attending such a public occasion together be an overhasty declaration of intent? When, after all, were we supposed to have met and become so fascinated with each other that you are willing to be seen out with me so soon after the…débâcle…of my engagement with Sarah?'

She had an answer for that as she appeared to have an answer for everything.

'Not over-hasty at all, Mr Shafto. We met, you must remember, at Lady Cowper's ball at the opening of the season, and since you were already involved with my cousin Sarah, you could not, as a man of honour, give way to the burning attraction which you immediately felt for me. Fortunately the Allenbys' untoward conduct towards you has given you an honourable release and you are now free to pursue me—gently and discreetly.'

Will rose and bowed extravagantly to her as a mark of respect for her lively mind as well as her lively tongue. 'Charmed to be described as a man of honour, I'm sure.'

He sat down again and resumed. 'But if I am to be a man of honour I must assure you that I have no memory of either having met you at Lady Cowper's ball, or contracting there such a burning passion for you as would excuse my over-hasty pursuit of you now that I am free again.'

'Then your memory, Mr Shafto—I do not think that I should yet call you Will—is at fault. Pray recall that after being introduced we danced together, and then, later, you joined me at supper and we discussed Tom Paine, rather than the ballgowns of my fellow heiresses. Come, come, my dear sir, you do not really suppose that anyone will remember exactly what took place at a ball some weeks ago. I find that most people are incapable of remembering what occurred at one the night before!'

For the first time she had dropped her solemn and icy manner and there was a touch of mischief in her face, which together with what she had just said set Will laughing.

Which caused her face to assume its basilisk set again so that he muttered, 'Forgive me. As a man of honour I must be solemnity itself when we discuss such important matters. Of course, I remember, but I believe that we discussed Lord Byron's latest work rather than Tom Paine. But I will defer to you if you remember otherwise.'

'You are an apt pupil, Mr Shafto. Tom Paine it was,

although I believe that you mentioned m'lord Byron in passing. Do I understand that you will therefore call for us this evening and escort us to the Opera?'

'You may, Miss Rowallan. It will be my pleasure. You would prefer me to be not too splendidly turned out. Something discreet, perhaps?'

'No, not at all. Be as splendid as you wish. I intend to be quietly elegant so that before we astonish the world with the news that we are to marry I may gradually become more and more the picture of a young woman whose appearance blossoms in response to the devoted attentions of a lover.'

Miss Rowallan ought to be writing for the Opera, not simply attending it, her imagination was so fertile, Will thought, but he did not yet know her sufficiently well to tell her so.

She rose. 'I take your silence to mean assent. I think that we have done enough plotting for today. On another occasion we shall decide in more detail how our future campaign is to be conducted.'

'One moment,' said Will, rising also. 'Are you prepared for the criticism which you will receive from all quarters when you are seen to be encouraging me?'

'Oh, indeed, Mr Shafto. Not only am I prepared for it, but it will give me the greatest pleasure to ignore it, knowing that no one will have the slightest notion of what we are about. That, in effect, I am exploiting you, not you me. It will add spice to all our meetings, will it not?'

Of all the brass-faced bitches he had ever met, Miss Rowallan was undoubtedly the acme, the very top of the tree. Will's regard for her was of genuine admiration for such raw courage from a woman alone in a world of men.

So moved was he that without thinking what he was doing he took her hand in his and kissed the palm of it reverently. The result of his hasty action astonished him. Miss Rowallan blushed a brilliant scarlet and snatched her hand back as though she had burned it.

'I had not meant to surprise you,' he came out with, for something needed to be said.

'Never fear, Mr Shafto,' she replied, her face a normal colour again. 'Any surprise will come from me, not you. After all, you were merely displaying the correct conduct of the lovelorn man—which in the context of our recent conversation is no surprise at all. *Au revoir,* then. We shall meet again later.'

It was his *congé,* and all the way back to Duke Street Will wondered what had provoked the blush and such a fierce reaction from the cold piece Miss Rowallan undoubtedly was.

Miss Rowallan knew. She had been fully in command of herself and him during all their meeting. But so far she and Will had not touched one another. All intercourse between them had been carried out at a distance.

And Will had surprised her by what he had done. She had not been ready for it, and she certainly had not been ready for the sensation which had shot through her when his warm lips had touched her cold palm. It had caused a *frisson* of pleasure to shoot through her such as she had never experienced before—and caused by such a slight thing, too.

She excused herself by saying that, whatever else, Will Shafto was an extremely handsome man, and perhaps that knowledge had caused the strong effect which had followed when he had touched her.

But other handsome men had kissed her hand without

her feeling anything at all so she could not but wonder at herself—and try to dismiss the memory from her mind.

With little success.

She was still wondering when Mrs Grey came in, her face an emblem of disapproval.

'He has gone?'

'Yes,' replied Miss Rowallan shortly, turning away.

'May I ask why he came? After all, we know him to be a rogue. I am surprised that you even received him.'

Miss Rowallan did not reveal that Will had come at her invitation. Instead she said after her usual icy fashion, 'He came to ask us to go to the Opera with him tonight.'

'And, of course, you refused.'

'On the contrary, I accepted for us both.'

'You cannot be serious—knowing of him what you do. Forgive me, but what will your cousin Sarah think of you taking him up?'

'My cousin Sarah is incapable of thinking, and even if she were, what she thinks is of no matter to me. She is not my keeper. I find Mr Will Shafto interesting and charming, and I trust that you will be civil to him whenever we meet. Is that understood?'

Mrs Grey's face was a picture. The heavens were falling in. She said feebly, 'You cannot be encouraging him?'

Miss Rowallan gave her attendant her best basilisk stare. 'And if I were, what then?' and she swept out of the room to signify that the conversation was at an end.

Chapter Three

For once, the attention of the audience at the Opera House was not on the stage, but on one of the boxes. For there, dressed as demurely as usual in unadorned white, sat England's greatest unmarried heiress, Miss Rebecca Rowallan, beside the dubious Mr Will Shafto, whose engagement to her cousin, Sarah Allenby, had been so sharply and so mysteriously called off.

If Miss Rowallan was aware of the furore she was creating, she gave no sign of it. Instead, she appeared to have no other interest than the music, paying little attention to Will Shafto who sat between her and an inwardly agitated Mrs Grey.

If Mr Shafto was agitated there was no sign of that either: quite the contrary. He was dressed *à point* all in black after the fashion established by Mr George Beau Brummell. His cravat was his and Gib's invention, being so elaborate that they had named it The Floral Dance. His black clothing possessed the advantage of distinguishing him from the rest of the *ton* who were dressed more gaudily, as well as enhancing the fineness of his physique and his features.

At the first interval Miss Rowallan suggested that he

might like to take a walk with her. Before he could so much as rise to offer her his arm, the box door opened and a number of her friends and relations entered, their faces arranged in various expressions of surprise and distaste.

They all converged on Miss Rowallan and ignored Will. He rose and stood by the door, ready to defend her if she became overset by their fiercely muttered disapproval of his presence.

John Allenby began first, hissing at her, 'Cousin Rebecca, I cannot believe that you are allowing that…scoundrel…to be your escort in a place as public as an Opera box.'

Miss Rowallan, as demure as her dress, opened her eyes wide, and murmured from behind the white lace fan which she had just raised, 'You would prefer him to escort me in private, perhaps? I scarcely think so. And, by the by, I would rather that you did not address me as cousin. You are no cousin of mine.'

'Miss Rowallan, then, and pray do not talk nonsense to me. I would prefer you to have nothing at all to do with him.'

Miss Rowallan yawned openly at him. 'Your preferences cut no ice with me, sir. You may be Miss Sarah Allenby's guardian: you are not mine.'

What John Allenby was saying was not originally meant to be overheard, but his voice had risen and Miss Rowallan was not troubling to lower hers so that Will— and the others present—could hear her every cutting word.

It was plain that Mr Allenby's supporters were as scandalised as he was both by Will's presence, and by her support of it. Will, however, was trying to suppress laughter at the spectacle of others beside himself being subject to Miss Rowallan's scarifying wit.

As John Allenby began to splutter at her, she lowered her fan and indicated to Will by a movement of her head that she wished him to leave them in order to promenade on his own.

He bowed in her direction and began to open the door. Whereat John Allenby acknowledged his presence for the first time and turned to thunder at him, 'You cowardly scoundrel, to leave the poor girl you are compromising to defend herself on her own!'

Before he could answer Miss Rowallan said sweetly, 'He leaves at my command, sir. And I am sure that he understands that I am perfectly capable of defending myself without his help.'

Will felt that he would indeed be the cowardly scoundrel he had been labelled if he said nothing, even though Miss Rowallan had defended him in her usual no-nonsense style.

He said in his best society drawl, 'Miss Rowallan is well aware that if at any time she needs my strong right arm, or my tongue, to defend her, they are both at her disposal. As it is, my lady's word is my command.'

He thought that John Allenby was about to drop dead of an apoplexy. Miss Rowallan, on the other hand, inclined her head prettily, saying in a voice as soft as silk, 'My thanks to you, Mr Shafto. You are as chivalrous as I had expected you to be. May I apologise to you for the rudeness of these people who call themselves my relatives. Wishing to save you pain I suggest that you leave me to deal with them and take the exercise which I am sure you require.'

Will opened his mouth to argue with her, but she

shook her head at him playfully, but meaningfully. She intended him to do as he was told.

And so he must: for he was there but to do as she commanded. He bowed again and made his way into the corridor where he found another group waiting to enter the box to speak to Miss Rowallan once the Allenby party left.

Among them was Harry Fitzalan who, on seeing Will, caught him by the arm, exclaiming, 'Will, old fellow, do not take it amiss that I did not defend you when the Allenbys turned you away. It was a cur's trick, I know, but my allowance depends on them, and a poor devil I should be without it. You do understand, I'm sure.'

Oh, yes, Will Shafto understood only too well. He also understood that Harry Fitzalan's idea of poverty was very different from his own. But he said nothing, merely clapped Harry on the back in return, and nodded his agreement that Harry was not to be condemned for letting a friend down.

'But what the devil are you up to now? What I don't understand,' Harry rushed on, 'is what you think that you are doing by escorting Beck Rowallan to such a public place as the Opera. And so soon after Sarah's jilting you.

'As for Beck, that cock won't fight, old fellow, we've all had a go there with no luck at all. The woman's an icicle, determined to be an old maid. You'll be wasting your time and money if you start chasing her, and you know you can't afford to waste either. Why not try to find some Cit's daughter who'd be only too pleased to marry a gentleman?'

This kind advice fell on Will like a ton of bricks, as the saying had it. First of all, he was furious to hear Miss Rowallan referred to so slightingly—something

which surprised him. Secondly, he was not Harry Fitzalan's old fellow, and thirdly he had tried chasing Cits'
daughters, only to discover their fathers were a deal
harder to pin down than Harry supposed, demanding
both station *and* money in exchange for their offspring.

Restraining himself with difficulty, and at the same
time beginning fully to understand what he was letting
both Miss Rowallan and himself in for once he had
agreed to her strange proposition, Will said, 'I'm grateful
for your kind thoughts, Harry, but pray allow me to be
the best judge of my own interests.'

Harry clapped him hard on the back again, saying
tactlessly, 'Only trying to help you, old fellow. Know
how you feel—well, not exactly, I've never been jilted
and thrown out of the house into the bargain, but who
knows? Need to marry money myself.'

Only because, although you have an allowance large
enough to solve my difficulties, you insist on gambling
it away, was Will's unkind thought on hearing that.

On stage the curtain had risen, the music had begun
and people were finding their way back to their seats.
Will became aware that the Allenbys were leaving Miss
Rowallan's box and that he was directly in their way.
By allowing Harry to corner him, he had nullified her
kind attempt to save him from insult by sending him
away from her box.

John Allenby marched up to him, frustration written
on his face. Will could only imagine what his supposed
beloved had been saying to him and his cohorts.

He stared fiercely at Will, exclaiming, 'I have told that
foolish young woman what a dishonest fortune-hunter
you are, but she refuses to listen to me. I would have
thought that what happened to you after you had been
cunning enough to entrap my niece, and been found out,

would have deterred you from engaging in such adventures in the future, but no! You immediately find another silly young woman to exploit. It all goes to show that women are unfit to be left in charge of their money without supervision… The empty-headed creature in there thinks that you are in love with her! Pah!'

He paused for breath. Behind him a chorus of 'Hear Hears', and 'Yes, indeeds', was supporting each unkind word he uttered.

'Have you quite finished, sir?' Will enquired politely. 'I must point out to you that it is only your age which prevents me from knocking you down immediately for insulting a defenceless young woman to the man who has so recently become aware of what a pearl she is. Pray allow me to pass before I forget myself. I have no wish to miss more of the entertainment than I need.'

He thought to himself that Miss Rowallan's brass-faced impudence must be catching, since he was busy practising it now. It was plain that John Allenby thought so, too.

'You are a fine pair,' he almost shouted. 'And were it not that the young woman needs my protection, I would consider that the best thing to teach her a lesson would be for her to be so unwise as to marry you…'

The man standing immediately behind him caught his shoulder. 'Come, Allenby,' he said, trying to keep his own voice as mild as possible. 'Do not allow yourself to bandy words with such scum as this. Leave him—and the lady—to their fate.'

'Bandy words?' returned Will, fine eyebrows raised. '*I* have not been bandying words. I have barely spoken, and then only to defend a lady's reputation.'

John Allenby lunged at him—to be held back by those around him. Harry Fitzalan, for once aroused from his usual languid torpor, exclaimed, 'I say, Uncle, not here. You don't want to create a scandal by brawling at the Opera, of all places. Not your style, at all.

'Will, old fellow, go and join Beck, I'll help to quieten Uncle Allenby down. Beck's not your responsibility now, Uncle, nor cousin Beaucort's either. She's her own mistress.'

Will did not hear John Allenby's response to that. He was too busy slipping back into the box where he found Miss Rowallan engrossed in the action on stage. She ignored him completely until the soprano's aria had finished when she turned her head to say calmly, 'I hope that you had a pleasant stroll, Mr Shafto. I fear things became rather lively in here, but all is quiet now.'

Mrs Grey, who had hitherto said nothing, suddenly exploded. 'How can you talk such nonsense, Rebecca? You know perfectly well that Mr John Allenby became quite impossible, and you were no better—no, you were worse. The whole theatre was staring at the pair of you. I wonder at you, Mr Shafto, for leaving Miss Rowallan to defend herself on her own.'

Miss Rowallan said sharply, 'He withdrew because I asked him to, Amelia. I did not wish him to be exposed to the insults of Mr Allenby, a man who calls himself my uncle, says that he wishes to protect me, and whose idea of protection is to marry me to Mr Hedley Beaucourt, who is a penniless cur.'

'Mr Shafto is penniless, too,' responded Mrs Grey miserably but truthfully, avoiding Will's eye as she spoke.

'But not a cur. Most emphatically, *not* a cur. I was informed that you frequent Jackson's rooms in Bond Street and that you spar with professional prizefighters, Mr Shafto.'

Oh, Miss Rowallan had employed only the finest to investigate him. Will had visited Gentleman Jackson's gym twice a week until his money had run low, and he still tried to keep himself in trim.

'That is true, Miss Rowallan, but not to the point, I fear. In Mr Allenby's eyes...' he began, only to be interrupted: Miss Rowallan had a fine line in interruptions.

'I am not interested in Mr Allenby's eyes, nor in his behaviour, and neither of them pleases me at all.'

She turned away from them both. 'And now if you would be so kind, let us pay attention to the music and forget what has passed. Cease to fidget, Amelia—and Mr Shafto, pray cease to smile. I cannot imagine what in the world you are finding to be amused about!'

Inexplicably the duns were holding off, or so Josh Wilmot came to tell him the day after the Opera. 'I was even informed that if Mr Will Shafto needed credit it would be supplied at a low interest.'

This was a surprise which Will had not expected. Unless the sight of him in Miss Rowallan's box had reached the duns and he was now considered a good prospect— if he married the lady, that was. Even so, he had to make sure that his friend was telling him the truth. Will never took anything on trust.

'Now, Josh, you are bamming me, surely.'

'No, Will, so if you need money, you have just to say the word.'

Yes, Will needed money, if only to be able to escort Miss Rowallan properly—and visit Jackson's gym again. He did not ask himself why he needed to do the latter, because he did not wish to answer himself correctly. Miss Rowallan had expressed admiration for his dabbling in the Fancy, as the boxing ring was known, and consequently Will was stirred to action again.

But he would not admit why.

He had promised to visit Miss Rowallan in the late afternoon so that they—or rather, she—could plot their next moves. He smiled ruefully to himself. She was firmly in the driving seat where matters between them were concerned, for he had to admit that at present he needed her more than she needed him and it was to his advantage to keep her happy.

But for all her shrewdness, and the hold over him which his poverty gave her, he was already determined that matters would be different once they were married. Oh, he was quite determined not to consummate the marriage, but he was equally determined to exert more power over their life together than she was allowing him in planning their future.

He gave Josh Wilmot *carte blanche* to arrange a further loan from the shark who was so eager to offer him one, secure in the knowledge that Miss Rowallan had promised to pay all his debts.

Consequently, when Will arrived at her home near Hyde Park that afternoon he was in a buoyant mood, ready to admire the lady's impudence and profit from it. He did wonder a little why she detested the Allenbys so much, but doubtless, later, she might tell him.

Miss Rowallan was, he saw immediately, dressed a little more stylishly than usual in a blue walking dress with lace inserts and a lower neck than usual, which allowed him to admire her creamy skin.

He was not to know that earlier that afternoon, as early as custom and good manners would permit, she had visited Lady Leominster, that great hostess and one-time mistress of the Prince Regent, to ask a favour of her.

Lady Leominster had been one of the curious at the Opera who had stared at the spectacle of the supposedly discredited Mr Will Shafto seated in Miss Rowallan's box. She was delighted to receive her privately—a signal honour—for being a great gossip, she was determined to glean something confidential about her visitor's relationship with Mr Shafto—which, of course, she would pass on.

Which was precisely why Miss Rowallan was visiting her. But it was not the only reason.

'So delighted to see you in such spirits, my dear,' Lady Leominster complimented her guest, immediately noting that Miss Rowallan's day wear was so much more voguish than that which she usually ventured out in. Was that Mr Shafto's influence? 'You have a particular reason for such an early visit, perhaps. In what manner may I assist you?'

She was nearly as frank as Miss Rowallan, and equally as devious. Miss Rowallan's smile would have been impressive on a crocodile.

'How like you, my dear Lady Leominster,' she gushed at her intended victim, 'to guess why I am here. I would ask a favour of you. Pray do not hesitate to refuse my request if it seems rather too particular. I shall quite understand.'

Inwardly bursting with curiosity, but outwardly calm, Lady Leominster riposted with, 'Until you make your request, my dear, I cannot know whether you are being too particular or not. I would be only too willing, you may be assured, to assist you, if I deem it politic to do so.'

Miss Rowallan put on a pretty air of diffidence which

would have had Mr Will Shafto grinning had he been
there to see anything so unlikely as a diffident Miss Rowallan.

'You have sent me an invitation to your ball this very
Friday. I wonder if you would be so good as to allow
me to bring a friend along with me. Mrs Grey will be
accompanying me, of course.'

'Of course,' echoed Lady Leominster, who thought
that she knew what was coming. She had rarely seen
Miss Rowallan so youthfully shy. She was plucking at
her shawl in the most *distraite* fashion.

Miss Rowallan decided at last to look Lady Leominster in the eye. 'I have recently become acquainted with
Mr Will Shafto, and find him a most delightful companion, so knowledgeable and witty. I was astonished to
discover that he could converse sensibly of Burke and
Tom Paine with me. Now that he is no longer engaged
to Miss Sarah Allenby, and is a free man again, I wonder
if you would be willing to allow him to escort me on
Friday. I think that you would find him as charming as
I do.'

After coming out with these last compromising sentences, Miss Rowallan looked down at her lap as though
acutely embarrassed at confessing to a *tendre* for Mr
Will Shafto. What she was really thinking was: judging
by the Lady's expression, I am reeling her in like a fish.
It will be all over the *ton* tonight that I am enamoured
of Mr Will Shafto to the degree that I am calling in
favours for him!

Lady Leominster leaned forward in her chair to say
confidentially, 'My dear, I shall be delighted to allow
him to escort you. You have been far too behindhand in
the matter of enjoying yourself. This is your first season,
is it not? I believe that I have seen the gentleman in

question on several occasions, but we have never been introduced. That must be remedied on Friday. Discusses Burke and Paine with you, does he? That sounds most impressive! Although I must confess that though I have heard somewhat of Burke, I know nothing of Tom Paine, but no matter.'

She paused, and asked something which seemed to her more to the point than Will's literary preferences.

'Does he dance?'

'Like an angel,' answered Miss Rowallan, who had not the slightest notion of whether Mr Will Shafto danced at all—some gentlemen did not—or whether he was accomplished in the art.

'Splendid, my dear, splendid. He will not lack for partners, nor will you, now that you have chosen to come out of your shell. You will partake of some Madeira before you leave, I trust? We have not, I confess, exactly been bosom bows, seeing that your Allenby connection favours the party of which Leominster does not approve—but we must remedy that.'

'I don't exactly favour my Allenby connection, either' admitted Miss Rowallan shyly, biting her lip, 'so there is a bond between us.'

'Exactly, and here comes Francis with the Madeira. We will drink to you and to Mr Will Shafto. After all, what matters it if he is penniless? You are not, and as a rich man may choose a girl for her looks, why should not you choose a man for his?'

So it was done. Miss Rowallan did not immediately inform Will of her manoeuvres on their behalf until she sent Mrs Grey away so that she and Will might talk confidentially.

'Lady Leominster,' she told him coolly, 'is London's biggest gossip and the news will be all over town by tomorrow that I am in deep water so far as you are concerned.'

Will marvelled at her all over again.

'I had understood that she was a tough nut to crack and rarely offers anyone favours. What nutcrackers did you employ to pierce her shell?'

Miss Rowallan smiled a secret smile. 'Oh, by my manner she thought me an innocent.'

Will began to laugh in spite of himself. 'Now why in the world would she think that?' he wondered.

'Because she sees what she wishes to see,' returned Miss Rowallan, her grey eyes as cold as the sea. 'Most people do, I find.'

Would she never cease to surprise him? 'Now that, Miss Rowallan,' he admitted, 'is true, but I had never met a woman who understood such a harsh truth until I met you.'

For once Miss Rowallan's smile was painful. 'Oh, Mr Shafto, to be an orphan and to be rich beyond the dreams of avarice is to learn many harsh truths about life.' She stopped to turn her face away from him before adding, 'And one learns them early, too.'

For the first time Will felt sympathy for her. Impulsively for him, for he was accustomed to calculate the effect of all his actions before he performed them, he leaned forward to take the hand which had been lying lax in her lap in his.

Why did he wish to comfort her? Comfort the woman who had always been so contemptuously dismissive of him, the man she was buying—as she was contemptuously dismissive of everyone. He did not know: he only knew that he wanted to stroke her pale hand and, by doing so, make her look at him again—with happiness written on her face.

He did not say 'There, there', he did not need to; his stroking fingers told their own story as they gently caressed the back of her hand.

Miss Rowallan slowly turned her head. For a moment of time of which neither of them could gauge the length, nothing was said. Her expression did not alter, nor did Will's. There was nothing sexual in what he was doing. On the contrary, it was similar to the action of a woman trying to soothe a hurt child.

And then, it was over. Miss Rowallan pulled her hand away, and her face, which had softened as Will had seen it soften once before, grew hard again.

'I see that you are a kind man, after all, Mr Shafto,' she told him emotionlessly, slowly withdrawing her cold hand from his warm one. 'But I do not need your kindness. It was not part of the bargain which we made, and which we agreed was to be a purely business one. Pray try to remember that. After all our hard work, I would not wish to cancel it and start again with someone else.'

She was ice, she was stone—as Harry Fitzalan had warned him. Yet the hand which she had spurned felt curiously empty. The fingers with which he had stroked her were suddenly deprived of the comfort which he had experienced in comforting her. Needless to say, this was a strange and new emotion for Will Shafto, too—to feel for another person. So new that he was quite overset.

What, to his eternal surprise, he was suddenly experiencing was an enormous pity for the lonely woman sitting opposite to him. What could have happened to her to stifle all the warmth and pleasant ease which a young woman of her age ought to be enjoying? Did Miss Rebecca Rowallan's *joie de vivre* solely come from putting down those around her as though they were enemies whom she needed to overcome? For a brief time he had felt her pain as though it was his own.

He said nothing of this, only, his voice desolate, 'I shall not forget your wishes in future, Miss Rowallan.' They were back to the beginning of their relationship again: that of a pair of merchants in the market place.

What he could not know was that Miss Rowallan, quite against her will, was remembering the warm sensations which had overcome her when Mr Shafto had first kissed her hand, and later had stroked it. She shook herself mentally. She must be sickening for something: yes, that was it!

Their masks resumed, they continued their conversation in its most practical mode. Will arranged the details of their visit to Lady Leominster's ball: Miss Rowallan informed him of his duties once they were there.

'You must conduct yourself towards me as though I have become the passion of your life,' she told him, 'but you will be discreet in your admiration of me—as I understand you were with Sarah. Should any of your friends—Harry Fitzalan, for instance—attempt to twit you about your sudden *tendre* for me, you will indignantly reject any suggestion that it is my money alone which attracts you. On the contrary, after your experience with Sarah Allenby, you regard it as a drawback.'

The fascinated Will could not stop himself from answering her, a wry smile on his face, 'In other words, I am to lie like a trooper!'

Levity, he found, would keep breaking in, particularly when the contrast between Miss Rowallan's demure appearance and the enormity of what she was constantly saying to him, became too great, so that he was compelled to answer her in kind.

As usual, nothing he could say shook her almost regal calm.

'Just so, Mr Shafto. I am delighted to find that you understand me perfectly. Now, I think that you should leave. We have been alone together quite long enough. Poor Mrs Grey will be quite beside herself—a condition in which she frequently finds herself since being employed by me. It is a great pity that she cannot know the truth of our situation, for it would ease her mind greatly to know that we have not the slightest intention of misbehaving ourselves after the fashion which she supposes.'

'True,' returned Will, rising and bowing. 'I find that our têtes-à-têtes together are of such a nature that all improper thoughts are quite driven from my head.'

Miss Rowallan did not inform him that it was not the condition of Mr Will Shafto's head which might trouble her, but that of quite another part of his anatomy. Such a remark would have been most improper!

And, why, in the name of everything that was commonsensical, should such a disgraceful thought have popped into *her* hitherto most well-ordered and maidenly mind?

'So, it's true, Will Shafto, you devil! You *are* after Miss Moneybags. Old Mother Leominster's been putting it all round town that Beck Rowallan is so smitten with you that she has even asked for you to be invited to her latest thrash so that you might act as her escort. Good luck to you so far as laying your hands on her tin is concerned, but you do have to take her to bed as well, you know.'

It was two mornings later. Will and Harry were in Gentleman Jackson's well-appointed gymnasium at 13,

Bond Street. The walls were decorated with boxing
prints designed to show the amateur what was what in
the ring. A weighing machine stood in one corner. Will
was dismayed to discover that since his last visit he had
risen above his best fighting weight.

He had arranged to spar with the Tottenham Tiger;
Harry, though, was merely one of a group which had
just arrived and which had come to see any fun there
might be on offer.

Will made no attempt to defend himself or Miss
Rowallan. Instead, he offered his friend a mysterious
smile, and continued to allow one of Jackson's orderlies
to lace up his boxing gloves whilst Harry roared on.

'Haven't see you here lately, old fellow. Decided to
get into trim again before the parson turns you off, are
you?'

'Haven't had the time or the tin to patronise Jackson's
lately.'

Harry put a finger by his nose. 'Moneylenders ready
to fund you now you're so near the Rowallan goldmine,
eh? But what will you do if the lady changes her mind?'

Will considered him as though from a great distance,
well aware that the men around them were waiting for
his answer.

'I don't think that Miss Rowallan changes her mind
very often,' was his cryptic reply.

'Aye,' laughed one of his hearers, 'that's her trouble—having a mind.'

This caused a roar of laughter and set everyone's
heads nodding in agreement. Will said mildly, 'I think
that we ought to respect the ladies by not indulging in
crass comment about them in private.'

Many heads nodded. Harry looked as though he might

be about to say more, but Jackson's arrival with the Tottenham Tiger in tow brought all gossip to a stop.

The Tiger was a big fellow, not as tall as Will, but broader and heavier. Like all the professional bruisers Jackson employed he had orders to let the gentlemen down easily: they were not employed to rearrange the young men's features.

He knew Will from of old, and knew that in his best fighting form he was one of the few who needed to be treated with respect. Before he touched gloves with him, he said drily, 'Not been training much lately, sir. Bit overweight, I see.'

Will gave a short laugh. 'I've come here to remedy that, Tiger, my friend. Don't hold off, I need the exercise.'

He was a little fitter than he thought. The Tiger needed to be wary, but was still able to pull his gentleman round the room. Jackson stood watching, occasionally saying sharply, 'Keep your guard up, sir.'

As the mock bout ended with Will puffing and blowing rather more than in the old days, Jackson took the trouble to say to him, 'Pity you're a gentleman, sir. I could have made a fighter of you. You'd have gone a long way.'

Privately he believed that Mr Will Shafto had a deal of spirit beneath his easy exterior. Will thought ruefully that if he had known Jackson in his penniless early twenties he might have taken his offer up. Successful bruisers could earn a comfortable living.

On the other hand, unsuccessful ones often ended up as paupers with deformed faces and bodies…

He touched gloves with the Tiger at the end and stepped back, sweating visibly, his white shirt clinging to his torso. Unnoticed by him in the heat of the bout,

Hedley Beaucourt had entered the gym and had been
watching him with feral eyes, willing the Tiger to plant
such a facer on him as would spoil Will's looks for good.

No such luck. One more count against Mr Will Shafto
was his athletic prowess. It wasn't fair; if everyone had
their rights, fortune-hunters ought to possess no social
or physical talents at all. It never occurred to Hedley
Beaucourt that both he and his father were also fortune-
hunters. They were Beaucourts, and that forgave all.

Consequently when Will, his gloves discarded, made
for the small room where customers towelled off and
changed into a clean dry shirt after their exertions he
found himself face to face with Mr Hedley Beaucourt.

Mr Beaucourt looked him up and down. 'Ah, Shafto,'
he said, his lip curling. 'I find you in your proper milieu:
a boxing booth. I wonder you never took it up. Not brave
enough, eh?'

Will chose not to answer him. He continued steadily
on his way. Mr Beaucourt caught him by the shoulder,
tried to turn him round, and failed.

'Look at me, damn you. I asked you a question.'

Will wrenched himself free. 'Which I chose not to
answer.'

He made to walk on. Mr Beaucourt snarled at his
back. 'I suppose that your only bravery is displayed
when you're alone with that silly bitch, Beck Rowallan.'

Will's reaction was purely instinctive and went
against all the advice which Miss Rowallan poured over
him whenever they met.

He swung round, saying, 'This will teach you to insult
a good woman,' and struck Hedley Beaucourt in his
ugly, leering face. The punch was not thrown with his
full power, but it was still strong enough to half-stun his

jeering opponent, and throw him back into the arms of those around him.

Sanity returned to Will as Harry Fitzalan and the Tiger pinioned him to prevent him from landing another blow on Mr Beaucourt, who was being helped to his feet by another of Jackson's bruisers.

'You can let go of me,' Will said stiffly. 'I shan't hit him again—unless he mentions her name again, that is.'

For some reason he could not call her Miss Rowallan, something which surprised him nearly as much as his sudden rush of anger on hearing her slandered.

'You shouldn't have hit an unarmed man without warning,' Mr Beaucourt snuffled at him, his handkerchief to his damaged and bleeding nose.

'Unarmed!' Will shot back. 'What arms am I carrying? I wasn't even wearing my gloves. And I warn you, if I hear that you have misnamed the lady again I shall call you out and you can face me when we are both carrying arms. As it is, I demand that you apologise to me or I'll call you out now!'

His inward reaction was not so brave, for he had no doubt that Miss Rowallan was going to be very cross with him when the news reached her that he had been involved in a brawl over her good name. She was likely to call their bargain off immediately. And what if she did…?

Will stopped this line of thought: it was too painful. He concentrated on staring at Mr Beaucourt, who was still whimpering something through his scarlet handkerchief. Harry and the Tiger, convinced that Will was now sane again, had released him.

'I'm waiting,' he said. 'I give you one minute to apologise, and if you don't I shall call you out.'

Mr Beaucourt knew when he was defeated. He snuffled something intelligible.

'Louder,' said Will. 'I can't hear you.'

Mr. Beaucourt looked desperately around him for support. Finding none, he muttered, 'I said that I'm aware that it was wrong of me to mention a lady's name in a place like this.'

'Don't insult Mr Jackson's establishment,' Will returned sternly. 'Simply admit that you were wrong to traduce a lady. And after that be sure that you don't try to blacken her name in public again, or, by God, I'll strike you again.'

Mr Beaucourt took his handkerchief away and babbled something which seemed to suggest that he had learned his lesson. He was not helped by being unhappily aware that, although many present thought that Will had gone a bit too far by striking him so hard, he had asked for it by what he had said of Miss Rowallan.

Honour was satisfied. Will turned away. He had probably dished himself for good—and his hopes for the future as well. And all for a woman who felt nothing for him—as he felt nothing for her.

If so, where had the rage come from?

Will became aware that it was Harry's turn to babble. 'Shouldn't like to get on the wrong side of you, Will. Always thought you were a mild fellow. Just now you looked exactly like the Tiger when he finished off the Tooting Terror, and no mistake.'

'Just leave it, Harry,' Will told him wearily. He was sure that his day of judgement would soon follow. Such a lovely piece of gossip would be all round the town in no time. The second juicy *on dit* about Will Shafto—no, the third—in a week.

What in the world would Miss Rowallan have to say to him when she learned that he had done exactly what she had told him not to do?

Chapter Four

'I thought, Mr Shafto, that I asked you to behave with decorum and discretion. You may imagine my astonishment, nay, shock, when Mrs Grey informed me of what had passed at Mr Jackson's gymnasium. Discreet you were not.'

'She would tell tales,' muttered Will. 'She couldn't wait to sneak to you, I suppose.'

Miss Rowallan serenely ignored him. 'I was not, I must say, sorry to learn that Mr Hedley Beaucourt received a bloody nose, I believe it is called. He has been asking to be rewarded with one for some time. No, what did distress me was that you chose to give it to him after all I have had to say to you.'

She didn't look distressed. On the contrary she was smiling.

'He insulted you. By name,' Will announced, deciding to go on the offensive. 'Before a pack of so-called gentlemen he questioned your honour—and mine. I couldn't let the insult to you pass, the one to me didn't matter.'

Miss Rowallan closed her beautiful eyes and lay back in her chair. She was, Will suddenly noticed, attired in a much more fetching turn-out than usual. Pale amethyst with pearls. Chaste, yet luxurious. Her glossy chestnut hair was dressed less austerely, too. Her tone, on the other hand, remained as austere as ever.

'I suppose,' she said at last, 'it's useless to ask you to be discreet. Gentlemen never are.'

No more than that? Will, who had fully expected that she would give him his *congé*, was a trifle unsettled on learning that she wasn't going to.

'*He* wasn't discreet—so how could I be? Your remarks ought more properly to be addressed to Mr Beaucourt, not to me.'

He expected another cool riposte, instead she asked him earnestly, 'Pray, what is it like at Mr Jackson's, Mr Shafto? What do you do there? Other than knock down offensive fools on my behalf?'

To say that Will was thrown by her rapid change of manner would be to understate matters.

'I work out, and then I spar with one of Mr Jackson's bruis— I mean, boxers. Sometimes with Mr Jackson himself.'

'Work out, Mr Shafto?'

'Exercise,' he said. 'To keep myself in trim. I've not been so much in trim lately.'

Miss Rowallan looked him up and down. Mr Will Shafto was wearing a deep blue jacket, cream trousers, a shirt and cravat of the purest white, and his hair was disposed in a fashionable Brutus cut. He looked a very tulip of fashion.

'Really, Mr Shafto? You do surprise me. You look very much in trim to me.'

Will decided to humour her. 'But I don't look very much in trim to a professional pugilist, Miss Rowallan. My wind is poor, for one thing.'

'Your wind, Mr Shafto?'

'Yes. I begin to huff and puff somewhat when I've been sparring for only a short time. The Tottenham Tiger would make short work of me and no mistake if we were in the ring together.'

'And are you likely to meet the Tottenham Tiger in the ring, Mr Shafto? Is that why your…wind…matters?'

By God, she was teasing him, no doubt of it. Because she had been speaking in her usual measured fashion he had thought that she was serious.

'You're bamming me,' he said, beginning to smile himself.

'So I am. I wondered when you would realise what I was doing. I am to suppose that boxing is one of the great mysteries which men perform in the absence of women, and I was somewhat curious about what it entails.'

'Dear Miss Rowallan,' said Will, unconsciously using an endearment to her for the first time, 'you might be surprised to learn that when boxing matches are held in the deep country—since they are illegal, you understand—a large number of women are often present who halloo on the champion of their choice and cheer each blow he lands.'

'Really, Mr Shafto? Yes, that does surprise me…' she paused '…I think. And now we ought to discuss our visit to Lady Leominster's tomorrow. I must insist that you refrain from knocking any one down for me there. Brawling at Jackson's is one thing—one quite expects it. Engaging in a mill at Leominster House, would, I am sure, be most ill seen.'

'You may depend upon me to behave myself,' Will assured her, relieved that being royally teased was all that he was going to suffer. 'I shall be as solemn as a bishop.'

'See to it, Mr Shafto, see to it, and now I will ring for Mrs Grey and tea. We must both look as grave as a pair of parsons when she arrives. I believe that she thought that I would show you the door, but we are too far along for that, Mr Shafto, are we not?'

The only possible answer was, 'Yes, indeed,' so Mr Shafto made it.

Mrs Grey, by her manner, made it quite plain that she disapproved of both her employer and the man whom she was so unaccountably favouring.

'A rogue,' she had said angrily to her best friend, Mrs Champion, who was Lady Leominster's chief attendant. 'He's nothing but a rogue. He was turned away by the Allenbys because they discovered that he was a penniless fortune-hunter, and now Miss Rowallan has nothing better to do than take him up. I had thought that she was the very acme of common sense, but no. I wonder at her, I really do.'

'She doesn't intend to marry him, surely!' exclaimed Mrs Champion as though she were speaking of Miss Rowallan catching the plague.

'Anything is possible,' admitted Mrs Grey mournfully, 'anything.'

So she glowered balefully at Will when Miss Rowallan was not looking at her, and Will smiled sweetly back at her in return. He did not blame her for her antagonism to him; in her place, he would have felt the same.

He had learned long ago in a hard school that more flies are caught by honey than by gall, as the saying had it, and he might yet win Mrs Grey over if he did not allow her to upset him.

She was still antagonistic, however, when he called for her and Miss Rowallan on Friday evening to escort them to Lady Leominster's ball. They were travelling in Miss Rowallan's carriage: she was well aware that Mr Shafto did not possess one of his own, and would not put him to the expense of hiring one.

'May I compliment you both on your appearance,' Will said after he had settled himself in the carriage opposite to the pair of them. Not was he being insincere. Miss Rowallan, superb in old rose and silver, was a vision of gauze and crêpe adorned with tea-roses made from silk. She was sporting her pearls and a large fan with a small mirror in its heart.

Mrs Grey was modest in pale blue. Her gown was elegance personified in its classic simplicity. Will thought that she must be in her middle thirties. He knew that she was a penniless widow of good family who needed a post with someone such as Miss Rowallan.

He handed them both out of the carriage, making little distinction between her or Miss Rowallan in the civilities which he offered to them. He walked between them up the great staircase at Leominster House to the landing where the Leominsters were receiving their guests.

He was immediately aware that their small party was a centre of interest. Eyes and whispers followed them. Lady Leominster herself made a great point of kissing Miss Rowallan on the cheek and welcoming Will warmly. Mrs Grey received only an indifferent nod.

The great thing, though, as he and Miss Rowallan well knew, was that Lady Leominster's enthusiastic reception of them meant that he would be accepted everywhere. She was a patroness of Almack's and one of society's greatest arbiters: her word was law. Had she turned Mr Will Shafto away, or spoken to him coldly, then it was likely that Miss Rowallan might have changed her mind about their bargain.

Many such as the Allenbys might have reservations about him, but now, provided he behaved with discretion, he was a made man.

'I had not thought him to be so handsome,' was the comment of more than one young lady, as well as many older ones. Miss Sarah Allenby, seated beside the middle-aged Marquess she was going to marry, could not help comparing his gross body and well-worn features with Will's athletic physique and his strikingly handsome face—to her new fiancé's detriment.

'I wonder,' said Mr Allenby to m'lord Marquess of Wingfield, 'that he dare show his face in decent society, but since the Leominster woman has chosen to favour him, then the rest of us are stuck with him, I suppose.'

His face darkened when he saw Will bend down to Miss Rowallan, who was seated on a chair beside him, in order to speak confidentially to her when she had drawn his attention by tapping him with her closed fan. 'The silly chit's run mad to encourage such a base fortune-hunter,' he muttered.

He was foolish enough to say this to Miss Rowallan a little later, when, temporarily deserted by Will—who had been taken off by Lady Leominster to be introduced to her nephew, Colonel Minster—she was consequently sitting alone with Mrs Grey.

She smiled sweetly at him and promptly trumped his ace by asking him if he would explain to her what the difference was between m'lord Wingfield, who was middle-aged and penniless, and was now betrothed to Sarah, and the equally penniless Mr Will Shafto.

'For,' said she demurely, 'the only difference I can see, apart, of course, from the Marquessate, is that Mr Shafto is a handsome young man, whilst m'lord is an ugly old one! Does fortune-hunting, as well as kissing, go by favour? Does the possession of a title make up for the lack of practically everything else in a man?'

'You forget yourself,' stammered Mr Allenby, purpling with rage. 'There is every difference between them. My only hope for you is that you are merely amusing yourself, and trying to annoy me, by taking him up so fervently—and will later amuse yourself by dropping *him.*'

Miss Rowallan fanned herself vigorously before replying, 'Oh, sir, you know that I never merely amuse myself. That is not my way. And I have not the slightest intention of dropping Mr Shafto. On the contrary, having caught him, I am thinking of taking him up permanently—if he will have me, that is.'

By ill—or possibly by good—luck, Mr Shafto arrived back at this moment, Lady Leominster on his arm. The Lady summed up the situation in a flash. She saw Miss Rowallan's control of the situation, Mr Allenby's jealous rage, and also took in the hovering Mr Hedley Beaucourt, who had been on his way to ask Miss Rowallan to join him on the dance floor.

Stirring any pot which needed it in order to ensure that society had a full complement of scandals and *on dits* to keep it happy was a speciality of hers. Particularly when, as now, she disliked one of her victims. The Allenbys, she considered, with all the benefit of a five-hundred-year-old title behind her, were a collection of parvenus whose money was mainly derived from trade—money which was but two generations away from its original creation, and therefore insufficient time had passed to allow it to be sanctified.

'I am returning Mr Shafto to you,' she carolled at Miss Rowallan, who had risen and bowed at her approach. 'You told me that he was handsome, you did not tell me that he was charming and clever.'

She turned to Mr Allenby, who was torn between glowering at Will and fawning on the Lady so that his facial expression was, to say the least, peculiar.

'You will, I am sure, agree with me that Miss Rowallan is most happy in her chosen companion tonight. I have been telling her how pleased I am to see that she has at last come out of her shell and is enjoying herself as befits a young lady of her station in life. She could have no better person to assist her in that task than Mr Shafto. They make such a handsome pair, do they not?'

What could Mr Allenby say? Miss Rowallan was smiling at him. Mr Shafto, the subject of more praise from the great ones of his world in one evening than he had received in the whole of his previous life, stood by looking as gravely composed as the bishop whom he had promised Miss Rowallan he would resemble.

He was inwardly amused at the grotesque spectacle of the obsequious snob whom he knew Mr John Allenby to be having to express his pleasure on meeting him and then being compelled to agree that Miss Rowallan could have no better companion.

He mumbled something which Lady Leominster chose to construe as consent, but the moment that she left them, still scattering benediction and imaginary posies around Miss Rowallan and Will, he turned on his heel and walked away.

Miss Rowallan raised her fan in order to laugh behind it, unseen. Her stratagems were working even more successfully than she had expected. It was plain that Lady Leominster had taken one look at Will and succumbed to his charms. Matters were moving along even better than she had dared to hope.

She could see young Mr Hedley Beaucourt hovering in the distance, hoping that Will would go away long enough for him to offer to take her on to the dance floor if he did so.

Will, amused by his roaring social success, but not to the degree that his head was turned, had also seen Mr Beaucourt. He bowed to Miss Rowallan, and as he straightened up, murmured, 'There is a gadfly hovering, Miss Rowallan. Would you care to dance with me so that you may be spared having to refuse him publicly?'

Miss Rowallan handed her fan to Mrs Grey, who was thinking that not only had Miss Rowallan run mad over Mr Will Shafto, but so had the rest of the world. She accepted the fan with a sigh and watched the pair of them make their way to join the quadrille which was about to begin.

It was sadly true that he and Miss Rowallan made a handsome couple. But was he not a rogue? And for all society's sudden endorsement of him, Will had only lived on its fringes before. Surely that acceptance was insufficient reason for Miss Rowallan to decide that she wanted to marry him? No doubt about it, she ought to marry one of her own kind.

The quadrille began. Will and Miss Rowallan bowed to one another before the intricacies of the dance took them away—only to reunite them before they parted again.

In one of its many variations Miss Rowallan met Sarah Allenby, whose fat Marquess was finding it difficult to keep up with the quadrille for all its slow stateliness.

'What are you doing with *him*?' Sarah hissed at her.

'Dancing,' replied Miss Rowallan sweetly.

'You know what I mean,' Sarah hissed at her again when next they met.

'Enjoying his company. You did,' added Miss Rowallan incontrovertibly.

This was one of those statements which does not possess an answer—or not one which can be made with any dignity.

'He was after my money,' Sarah said defiantly.

Miss Rowallan was all composure. 'Yes, I know. He's after mine.'

They parted again. The dance brought them side by side again. Miss Rowallan asked Sarah, her face puzzled, 'Does his title make up for his appearance?'

'I'm sure that I don't know what you mean,' was all she got back.

'Oh, yes, you do. At least my fortune-hunter is handsome and clever. Yours is ugly and stupid.'

This was to say the unsayable, even if it was truthful. Miss Rowallan had learned long ago that the truth is almost invariably unsayable in the kind of formal society to which she belonged. Telling it, as now, first gave her the most exquisite pleasure, and then made her feel sorry for having done so.

Sarah's eyes when next she passed her were full of tears. '*You* don't have relatives and a guardian to tell you what to do. I do. You're lucky.'

'Yes,' agreed Miss Rowallan. 'I'm sorry I twitted you, Sarah.'

But it was too late to repent—it always is.

Next there was Mr Will Shafto to deal with when the dance was over.

'What did you say to Sarah Allenby to distress her?' he asked. 'She was almost in tears.'

Miss Rowallan never lied. Well, hardly ever.

'I was unkind to her.'

Will looked at her. 'You shouldn't be, you know. She was happy with me. I made her laugh. Her Marquess won't. On the contrary, from what I hear of him, he'll make her cry. You should feel sorry for her.'

Miss Rowallan, for once, was almost defensive. 'She threw you over, and allowed her family to treat you cruelly.'

'It wasn't her wish,' Will said. 'She had no choice in the matter. Whilst you, *you* are free to do as you please.'

Not only was it what Sarah had told her, but he was rebuking her and they both knew it. If she chose to take offence… Will shrugged his shoulders.

Miss Rowallan recovered her fan from Mrs Grey and took refuge behind it to digest something which she had not known before. *Her* fortune-hunter was kind.

So the evening passed. Miss Rowallan made a point of confiding in Will behind her fan, and encouraging him to behave as though he were her devoted cavalier. She seemed, Will thought, a little gloomily, as much in command of herself as ever—more so, perhaps.

He was not to know that for the first time he had said something which had pierced the hard shell which Miss Rowallan had erected around her most inward self. She had thought that she was immune to either praise or blame—and most certainly immune to criticism from anyone.

But Will's gentle remarks about poor Sarah's sad condition and, by inference, her own unkindness, had made her uncomfortable, more particularly because she had regretted her remark herself. Such regret was new to her. More than that, he had made her understand that wit, carelessly used, could be too cruel a weapon when wielded against someone as helpless as poor Sarah Allenby.

For the first time for many years, Miss Rowallan examined herself, and did not like what she saw. And it was all Mr Shafto's fault, the rogue whom she had bought with her money, and who was no better than he should be.

Truly, life was strange when a rogue could bring tears into the eyes of a woman who had not cried since she was seventeen years old… Remorse, experienced after a long absence, is an uncomfortable companion. It whispered its sad message in Miss Rowallan's ear throughout the long evening and made it seem even longer.

Towards midnight that new and daring dance, the waltz, was played. Its daring lay in bringing the dancers in close contact with one another for the whole of its duration. That, and the exciting sensations roused in the bosoms of the performers.

For a woman to dance it with a man was to make a certain statement of involvement. Will had just escorted Miss Rowallan back from the supper room when its music began. Neither of them had eaten very much. Somehow in their odd situation it did not seem that it was quite the thing to be seen gorging themselves.

It did not occur to Will that the outwardly proper Miss Rowallan would wish to waltz with him, so he stood gracefully behind her chair and wished the evening were over. His surprise was great when she put a lace-gloved hand on his arm and whispered, 'I would, of all things, wish to dance this with you, Mr Shafto. Pray, I beg of you, invite me, so that all will be proper.'

Proper? For a maiden lady of mature years and so-far impeccable propriety to dance it with a person as dubious as he was? For a moment he was stunned, until he suddenly saw the light. It was simply a part of her campaign to persuade the *beau monde* that they were so smitten with each other that they were prepared to defy convention.

Will was suddenly all gallantry. He bowed low to her and said in a voice loud enough for those around them to hear him, 'My dear Miss Rowallan, will you do me the honour of dancing the waltz with me?'

Surrounded by shaking and disapproving heads, Miss Rowallan rose, handed her fan again to the aghast Mrs Grey, and shyly agreed to do so.

'I should like that of all things,' she whispered demurely, 'if you will not think me overbold for agreeing.'

'No, never,' murmured Will. 'However could I think such a thing of you, so charmingly modest and unforthcoming as you are!'

Considering everything, Miss Rowallan would have liked to kick his shins for making such a two-edged remark: an action which she had not performed since she had so rewarded an impudent boy cousin for trying to take liberties with her when she was fifteen. Instead, she felt compelled to hang her head a little, try not to blush—and walk on to the floor with him.

'I am afraid,' she whispered, 'that I have not performed the waltz with a gentleman before, only with a dancing mistress. You will be patient with me, I trust.'

'Oh, you already know that patience is my middle name,' retorted Will. 'And I also know how quick you are to learn.'

So saying, he took her into his arms, being careful to hold her at some little distance as he whirled her round the floor.

They knew that every avid eye was on them while they quartered the room with such infinite grace that it might have been supposed that they had been dancing together for years.

Was it that which was causing such odd tremors to run through Miss Rowallan's virgin body? The certainty that they were being watched?

Or was it being so near to Mr Will Shafto, so near that she could feel the warmth of him, not only of the strong hands which held her so gently, but of his whole body? She could smell the lemon in his hair dressing, and in the soap with which he had washed himself, as well as the aroma of something subtly masculine, quite unlike any scent which a woman gives off.

A scent which was uniquely male and which had always previously been distasteful to her, but which was now exciting quite another feeling in her breast. Except that it wasn't only Miss Rowallan's breast which was being affected. Her whole body was responding to him.

In all the plans which she had had for Mr Shafto, none of them included feeling any kind of emotion for him other than mild gratitude for his unfailing obedience to her wishes—as now. She chided herself. These new and strange feelings were most untoward and inconvenient and must at all costs be suppressed.

The problem was that, held in this intimate fashion, she was also becoming frighteningly aware of the sheer strength of him. It was as though she had been mercilessly baiting a mild pony only to discover that it was a stallion in his pride which she had been provoking!

This was yet another disturbing thought. Even more disturbing was to discover that, whilst experiencing these new and unwelcome impressions, she was apparently quite capable of performing the waltz without making a mistake—something which she had never accomplished with her instructress! Miss Rowallan was so surprised on realising this that she stumbled—to be kept on her feet by Mr Shafto's strong arms.

'Forgive me,' she quavered, finding herself at a loss with him for the first time in their acquaintance. 'I had not meant to be so clumsy.'

'Do not trouble yourself,' he told her. 'For a novice you are performing quite splendidly. All eyes are upon us.'

'For quite other reasons than our dancing ability, you must admit,' she announced tartly, recovering her balance and her *savoir-faire* at the same moment.

'That, too,' agreed Mr Will Shafto, who was having a few problems of his own now that he had Miss Rowallan in his arms for the first time.

Not only was she lighter on her feet than he had expected her to be, but she was so soft and tender in his arms, all her hard logic and severe self-command having disappeared from the moment that he had led her on to the floor.

Not only that, but she was wearing some subtle perfume which he had not encountered before. It was lightly floral, but with a certain spice added to it. Perhaps it was not a new perfume at all, but was eau-de-Miss Rowallan, as it were, instead of eau-de-toilette.

This thought was so erotic that it had the effect of rousing him, something which he had been firmly convinced that Miss Rowallan could never do! If her feelings for him in the dance were inappropriate and unwanted, Will felt the same about what she was unwittingly doing to him!

For one thing, dressed as he was in skintight breeches, it was a damned inconvenient state to be in. No wonder the waltz was described as sinful if this was what it did to you! He refused to believe that it was Miss Rowallan who was affecting him so strongly. No, it must be the music.

A conclusion which Miss Rowallan had also reached by the time that the dance had ended. They were both relieved that the entertainment which they had been providing was over.

'I should like to sit down now—and perhaps you could arrange for a footman to fetch me a glass of water.' She added in explanation, for one seemed to be needed, 'I have become a little overheated.'

So had Will, but water would not cure him. Not unless someone hurled a bucketful of it over him!

He bowed to her painfully, and thought of waterfalls, cascades of the stuff falling down into a vast pool, of swimming in it, shivering as he did so. This seemed to do the trick, and he tried not to look directly at her, even when he was handing her to her chair, and avoiding the reproachful eyes of Mrs Grey.

The water was duly ordered and arrived in a finely chased crystal glass carried on a silver tray by an obsequious footman. He was accompanied by Lady Leominster all of a-twitter.

'My dear Miss Rowallan, I do hope that this does not mean that you have been overdoing matters on your first major excursion into society. I vow that you and Mr Shafto were the most handsome couple on the floor. *That* is how the waltz should be done, I told Leominster, with airy grace, not in the clodhopping fashion that so many employ.'

Will bowed, amused. It was plain that whoever else disapproved of them, Lady Leominster was completely in his thrall. Miss Rowallan assured her that she was merely a little overheated, the waltz being rather more strenuous than the dances which she was used to.

'True, true,' agreed her ladyship. 'Leominster will have it that we are turning into savages by dancing two and two and not in a group. He says that we shall be performing on our own next—he will have his little joke, you know!'

Her hearers duly obliged her by laughing politely at it. Gratified, she left them, but not before she had made them promise that they would join her and her husband in their box at Drury Lane. 'A week from tonight, my dears.'

She did everything but wink complicitly at them, and if Miss Rowallan had wished not only to display Mr Shafto to the world as her cavalier, but also to have him accepted by society, that wish had been granted in the most public manner possible.

The Allenbys might roar as they like, Mr Hedley Beaucourt and his papa might sulk, Mrs Grey might deplore, but the deed was done. Miss Rebecca Rowallan and Mr Will Shafto were an accepted pair.

Chapter Five

Was he happy? Will did not know. He knew that he ought to be. He had at last achieved the goal which he had set himself. He was marrying wealth, if not high rank, and only he—and Miss Rowallan's senior lawyer, Mr Herriott—knew of the strings attached to his marriage.

Miss Rowallan's lawyers were thrashing out the financial details of the marriage settlement, with Josh Wilmot attending. Josh was surprised by the extent of Miss Rowallan's generosity over Will's allowance, but was not surprised by the conditions which hedged Will about in other ways. He knew nothing of the other settlement, privy only to Mr Herriott, Miss Rowallan and Will, which ensured that the marriage would be one in name only, and would not be consummated.

'You are sure that you wish this?' he had asked both of the parties when he had presented the document for them to sign. Both of them had earnestly assured him that such was their deepest desire. 'There will be no marriage without it,' Miss Rowallan announced firmly.

They had each decided that their sensations during the waltz had been something of an aberration, and had privately resolved that in future they would touch the other as little as possible. Only thus could they keep to their strange bargain.

'You could, of course, break this agreement if you both decided that that was what you wished,' Mr Herriott told them. Neither of them answered him, and he gave a great sigh.

He could understand Miss Rowallan protecting her money and property from Will's possibly predatory hands, but that she should also protect herself from Will's handsome person was quite another thing!

Finally, all the legal matters pertaining to their marriage were arranged—only its timing remained to be decided, and that would be when Miss Rowallan considered that Will had been accepted as her certain and future husband.

They remained the sensation of the Season. They were seen in the Leominsters' box at Drury Lane; they rode together in Hyde Park; visited Astley's Amphitheatre; boated on the Thames near Richmond where Miss Rowallan was exposed to Mr Shafto's athleticism again—and womanfully resisted its attractions.

Every great hostess invited them to their balls and receptions and even Almack's opened its doors to them—the final accolade. At which point Miss Rowallan decided that her campaign was over.

Nothing remained to them but to bring all speculation to an end and to marry, and it was Miss Rowallan who was ready to 'pop the question' as her kitchen staff had it, and not Mr Shafto as they all, quite naturally, supposed.

Will had not seen her for several days—he had business of his own to clear up, he had told her—but when

he walked into her drawing-room one sunny afternoon
he knew at once that she was about to make an announcement of some kind.

For all that she was a woman whom he told himself
firmly possessed no attractions for him, it was wonderful
how well he was coming to know her. He wondered
uneasily if she was coming to know him after the same
fashion. He hoped not.

She had motioned him to a seat opposite to her, sent
an unwilling Mrs Grey away and had begun by asking
him if they really needed to attend Lady Jersey's ball
that evening. He was only too willing to agree that they
didn't. Privately, for each did not confide in the other,
they were both growing bored with the empty round of
the High Season.

Will missed the country which, being penniless, he
could no longer afford to live in, and Miss Rowallan
missed her pretty home in the Yorkshire Dales and the
village where everyone knew her as someone quite different from the cold beauty who adorned the London
ballrooms.

There were times when she wondered how Will would
fit in with her uneventful rural existence, but at the moment all that concerned her was manoeuvring him into
agreeing to her marriage plans.

She had dressed herself with great care in a slightly
more frivolous turn-out than usual—something which
Will had already noticed. A high-waisted pale-green afternoon dress with cream lace insets, collars and cuffs
brought out the highlights in her chestnut hair, and flattered the cool porcelain of her complexion.

Mr Will Shafto would not be able to complain that
his future wife did not do him credit so far as her dress
sense was concerned. She listened to him gravely as he

agreed with her that balls and receptions were vastly overrated affairs.

'Unless, of course,' he ended, 'one is a Member of Parliament, or a patron of the arts, or like the Leominsters "count coup", as the North American Indians have it, every time that they arrange a function which outshines everyone else's in splendour.'

'Indeed,' said Miss Rowallan, and then continued without so much as drawing breath, 'I think, Mr Shafto, that it is time that you proposed to me.'

She had surprised him again.

'You do?' was all he managed.

'Oh, yes, indeed. And you must apply for a special licence at once so that we may be married as soon as possible.'

How was it that she so often managed to take his breath, as well as his sense away? Will liked to think that he was as blasé as a man might be, but beside Miss Rowallan he was a mere amateur in the game of oversetting others.

'I am crazed with love for you, you understand, and I am informed that persons in that condition commit the most impulsive acts.'

'They do?' Could one, Will asked himself, ever imagine Miss Rowallan committing any act which could conceivably be described as impulsive? She was surely reason itself, with logic as her goddess.

Miss Rowallan took his stunned silence for consent. 'Also, Mr Shafto, I think that it is time that I addressed you as Will, and that you saluted me as Rebecca.'

Mr Shafto took a small revenge. 'Not Beck, or Becky, then?'

'Indeed, not. I had rather you called me my love, only that seems a little excessive given our circumstances.'

Mr Shafto made an immediate resolution that if he ever wished to annoy Miss Rowallan he would most certainly address her as Beck. This mutinous thought gave him great pleasure.

Aloud he said, 'Perhaps it might be simpler if we called each other nothing at all—other than ''you'' if the occasion were sufficiently intimate.'

Miss Rowallan was not sure whether or not Mr Shafto was serious in proposing this, his face was so straight. She decided to ignore him and said graciously, 'Then that's settled, then.'

To his own surprise Will exclaimed, almost violently, 'No, it damned well is not! I haven't proposed to you, and I refuse to be fobbed off in this fashion. We must at least go through the forms. I may have sold myself to you for some purpose of yours which is obscure to me, but at least grant me some dignity in my servitude.'

He went down on one knee before her, seized her right hand roughly and said in a voice in which chagrin and self-mockery were finely blended, 'My dear Miss Rowallan, before your humble servant expires for thwarted love of you, pray do him the honour of agreeing to his proposal of marriage.'

Now he had her at a disadvantage. Miss Rowallan looked into his eyes, which were level with her own, and replied almost humbly, 'Forgive me if I took things for granted. I lacked tact, I fear.'

'Tact!' Will stood up. 'That is the least of it—Beck. But I forgive you.'

He was aware that he had lost his fine control and that, from being players in a sophisticated comedy, he and Miss Rowallan had become snared in something more dramatic.

He walked over to the window and looked down on

to the street. While they had been talking an organ grinder had set up his machine, had begun to play it, and his monkey had started its melancholy dance. Will knew exactly how the monkey felt. Beck Rowallan, he thought savagely, would make a splendid organ grinder and he her perfect monkey. He swung to face her.

'If you want to call this damned business off, and look for someone else,' he ground out, 'then say so now. I shall quite understand.'

Miss Rowallan was silent. Her expression had not changed. It was as inscrutable as ever. Her hands were lightly clasped together in her lap.

Will said nothing further. His back being to the light meant that his face was in shadow.

'No, Mr Shafto, you may not retreat so easily. We have a bargain, you and I. May I remind you that, without coercion, you have already signed the papers which dispose of your future for the next five years. For you, the bargain is a good one, whilst I am satisfied that in choosing you I have chosen well. No, I will not call this damned business off.'

Will bowed. 'I apologise,' he said stiffly, 'for using such language before you. It was not the act of a gentleman.'

Miss Rowallan's response was a little surprising. 'Oh, I have heard much worse than that, Will, and from a gentleman, too. If I promise not to demean you again, will you sit down so that we may discuss ways and means?'

It was more of an apology from her for her high-handedness than he might have expected, and Will accepted it as graciously as he could.

He resumed his seat, saying wryly, 'My dear Rebecca, our mutual apologies have convinced me that it is possible for us to continue without further acrimony. May I suggest that by uniting to deceive others we may enjoy ourselves in the knowledge that we know something which they don't.'

'Assuredly, Will,' and Beck laughed for the first time. 'I have spent much of my life in that happy situation and am greatly pleased to learn that I have chosen someone who will enjoy sharing it with me. Now, let us begin to make plans for the marriage which will shortly take place.'

Was he happy? Perhaps not. Will had a Friday face when he reached his rooms again. Gib opened his mouth to comment on it but, for some reason he could not have explained, he forbore.

Will ate an early supper and then retired to his bedroom, to emerge dressed in clothes of a kind worn by clerks and lowly functionaries—respectable but shabby. He had put on a porter's cap with a large peak.

'Thought you didn't need to trouble with all that any more—sir.' The sir was an afterthought.

'Probably not,' returned Will mildly. 'But I have a duty to perform—and the sooner the better.'

'Goin' out by the back way, are you?'

'Can't go by the front in this.' Will was brief.

'Be careful. Wouldn't do to get done over just when you're about to win the tontine of your life, sir.'

'If you mean by that I'm going to marry Miss Rowallan, then say so,' Will riposted.

'Miss Moneybags, then. She don't seem to be making you very happy—with respect, sir.'

'You've never shown me the slightest respect in the past, so don't pretend that you're starting to do so now.'

Will picked up a stick of the sort commonly used in

the country, stout and thick. 'You'll note that I'm taking heed of your warnings.'

Gib plucked Will by the sleeve as he walked out of the room. 'I meant what I said, young master. I know the hard time of it you've had. I don't want you to make it any harder on yourself by marrying this fine lady.'

Will disengaged himself gently. 'Believe me, Gib, if there were any other way of surviving, if it were only myself I had to think of, then my life would be very different. Now let me go, and if you can't give me your blessing, then don't grumble at me, either.'

He carried the memory of his servant's worried face to the shabby street where George Masserene ran a gaming hell for the lowly of London's varied world—who never met, and knew nothing of, its high society. It was up a dark alley and a burly porter stood at the door.

'Evening, Mr. Wilson,' he greeted Will.

'Evening, Jim. House busy tonight?'

'Aye. The master will be pleased to see you.'

The gatekeeper having been acknowledged, Will walked down some steps to find himself in a long low room, brilliantly lit, and filled with people.

Gaming tables were ranged down the middle of it. At the far end, in a poor imitation of the largesse available in London's richest gaming hells, stood a long table full of cheap food, wine and beer. A portly man, smoking a cigar, lounged by the open door of an office.

'Evening, Wilson. Made it this evening, have you? We're busy, as you see, good pickings, and later I've some accounts for you to go over for me.'

Will said, 'I'll run a table for you tonight, sir, but this is the last time I shall be coming. I've found a better, more secure position, a day job as well.'

George Masserene looked unhappy. 'I knew that you

were too good to last, Wilson. What's an honest man doin' here? I asked myself. If you give the books a last once-over before you go, I'll add a guinea to your pay.'

Will nodded agreement. No one at Masserene's knew who he really was. He had been a houseman there for almost two years, running a gaming table for three nights a week as well as keeping Masserene's books for him. He had also stood in on other nights.

When needed, he had acted as a strong man and had helped the porter to throw out those patrons who had become obstreperous when they lost. The pay had not been great but, as he had told an unhappy Gib, every little helped.

The job also had the advantage that it could be done at night, and not every night, leaving him free to play the gentleman and try to make his fortune at other times of the day. Now that he was to marry Miss Rowallan he no longer needed this small source of ready money.

He was surprised to find as he sat down to deal from his first pack of cards that he felt a certain sorrow at leaving. After all, he gave a good service to Masserene for his pay, and he was, as George had said, honest. He sought to defraud neither the punters nor the house, and in that sense he was almost unique.

It was, he told himself, with some inward sad amusement, exactly the same service as the one he was providing for Miss Rowallan.

Dawn saw him walking home, dog-tired. He had straightened out all of George's books for him before he had left, and in return George had added another half-guinea to his pay. 'If you ever need a job, Wilson, there's always one for you here. An honest man is a rare thing to find in London—especially in these quarters.'

This was another cause of sad amusement for a man who was so frequently despised as a barely honest fortune-hunter. What would George have thought if he had asked him to put his testimonial in writing so that he might show it as a proof of his integrity from a man who ran a gaming hell! His good memory and his mathematical ability Will took for granted. Neither of them was of much practical use to a poor gentleman.

He was turning into Duke Street when, by ill-chance, he encountered a party of young bloods on their way home after making a night of it at establishments better regarded than George's—if frequently less honest.

Among them was Harry Fitzalan, half-cut, but still able to stand. Will pulled his cap over his eyes, but even in his fuddled state Harry was acute enough to recognise Will by his body language rather than his face.

'Will?' he croaked. 'It is Will, isn't it? What the deuce are you doing in that get-up?'

Will had no need to answer, for Harry gave a great guffaw and clutched at the lapels of Will's dirty coat.

'No, old fellow,' he choked, 'don't tell me. Had to give Beck Rowallan the slip to get your oats, didn't you? Go somewhere where you weren't known, in case it got back to her. Don't worry, I won't peach on you. Mum's the word and all that. You'd do the same for me, I know.'

His companions had staggered past them. One of them turned round and howled at Harry, 'Don't get left behind, Fitzalan, by arguing with a filthy beggar. Throw him a few pence and have done.'

Harry put an unsteady finger by his nose and winked at Will. 'Here, take this,' he laughed, thrusting a florin into Will's hand. 'I'll not give you away. Neither now nor later.'

'Coming, coming,' he shouted to his cronies, and reeled up the road towards them, leaving Will to laugh ruefully and put his tip into the pocket which held his pay from George.

'All's grist to the poor man's mill,' he told himself. 'Harry will never know how welcome his largesse was to me!'

'It's true, then! He's proposed, and she's accepted. Beck Rowallan, of all people, to marry a pauper. I'd have thought nothing less than a Duke would have done for such a high-nosed piece of work.'

'They say that one of the Royal Dukes did propose, and gained nothing but a dusty answer.'

'Ah, but he doesn't look like Will Shafto when he strips off at Jackson's, does he?' and the pair of male gossips collapsed into knowing laughter.

Conversations such as this—more discreet when the ladies were discussing this unequal match—took place throughout London society when it became known that Beck Rowallan—she was rarely accorded the title of Miss—had accepted her rogue.

Sarah Allenby, already married to her Marquess and regretting it nightly, took a different view of the matter, but no-one asked her for her opinion, least of all her Allenby relatives.

It was fortunate for both parties that neither of them troubled much about what others thought of them—so long as they were being polite to them when they met face to face.

Beck, for so Will always thought of her, had never cared much for the opinions of others, and Will had learned in a hard school to put a brave face on life. Of the two he privately suffered the more—although he was never quite sure of his future wife's true thoughts.

Behind her carapace of hard indifference might beat a suffering heart but, if so, she never gave any sign of it to Will, or to anyone else. Now that the die had been cast, and marriage was near, dining or dancing, riding or boating, at the theatre or the opera, she offered everyone the same composed face which she had always shown them.

Will's trials were perhaps the harder since few ventured to say anything to his supposed beloved, but many of his circle of male friends were not averse to shoving him in the ribs and congratulating him for being such a lucky dog, or, as in Harry Fitzalan's case, commiserating with him yet again for having to get into bed with Beck Rowallan.

'Is the money worth it?' he demanded solemnly of Will at Jackson's one afternoon.

Will had been working out with the Tottenham Tiger and had been fighting him with a rare savagery as though they were truly in the ring together, gloves off and betting on. He turned a face on Harry which Harry had never seen before, so grim and dour it was. There was nothing of equable Will Shafto left in it.

'Cut it out, Harry,' he snarled, 'or I'll challenge *you* to take a turn in the ring with me. The *lady*—' and he dwelt on the word '—is going to be my wife. So that's enough. Don't mention her again unless you can do so with respect.'

Harry blinked at Will. 'Didn't mean any harm, old fellow. Not at all. No.' The prospect of entering the ring with the Will Shafto he had just seen held no attraction for him whatsoever.

Will turned away from Harry, still seething. His own guilt at marrying a woman he did not love, and could never bed, so that his marriage was a hollow sham, rode on his shoulders and was partly responsible for his savagery with Harry.

He worked it off by demanding another bout with the Tiger, who was beginning to wonder what ailed this gentleman. Will should be feeling pleased with life after netting such a golden dolly as Miss Rowallan was, rather than indulging himself in a fit of the dismals.

Afterwards Will felt better, even if he was drenched in sweat for his pains. One of the boys who acted as attendants on the society nobs who patronised Jackson's poured buckets of water over him until, feeling cleansed in soul as well as body, he roared 'Enough!'

Clothed again, he decided to visit his betrothed whom he had avoided for the last few days. They were to be married in a week, and after that he would be compelled to behave, in public at least, as though he were a loving husband.

In prospect this had not seemed difficult, but the nearer the day of reckoning drew, the more Will agonised over how he was going to manage his new life.

He was still agonising when he walked into Beck's drawing-room where he discovered, with some relief, that she already had another visitor.

In the armchair which he usually occupied sat an elderly straight-backed woman, or rather lady, for by her expression and her posture no one would ever call her anything else. She remained seated as Beck rose to greet him, and he responded by bending over her hand and kissing it.

'Will, I'm so happy to see you today. I have someone to whom I wish to introduce you. I don't believe that I have ever spoken to you of my distant relative, my cousin, or rather my aunt, Mrs Petronella Melville.'

Since Beck had never spoken to him of any relatives, distant or near, whom she wished Will to meet, Will could only nod assent and bow to the lady herself who responded by waving a gloved hand at him.

She was very much of the old school, raking Will from head to foot with her stern eyes. He concluded somewhat dismally that there was little doubt that she and Beck were related—they both had the same expression of severe authority.

She pulled off her glove and extended her hand, which Will assumed she wished to have kissed—and gratified her.

'So, you are the fortune-hunter whom my niece has decided to marry,' she barked at him. 'Let me have a good look at you, young man.'

She raised a quizzing glass the better to inspect him. Amused and intrigued, Will was grateful that he was turned out in the fullest fig and that although he had tied his cravat himself at Jackson's—or perhaps because he had—it was a discreetly modest affair, giving no indication that he was a member of the dandy set.

Inspection over, Aunt Petronella lowered her glass. 'Hmm,' she said. 'I see at once how you managed to charm my niece who, until now, I had thought to be the most sensible gal ever to be left in control of her own fate—which ain't saying much, to be sure. I had feared that the odour of loose fish would be strong about your person, but I own that now that I have met you, I am most pleasantly surprised.

'Rebecca tells me that you are a sensible fellow, too, and may be depended on not to fling her fortune away on the gaming tables. Is that true?'

This was barked at him in a sergeant-major's best voice. Will answered her with a lie which was not a lie.

'I assure you, madam, that I never gamble—that is not one of my failings.' Which was a true statement so far as it went—for at George Massarene's Will gambled with the house's money, never his own. Nor did he gamble in his proper person.

'Oh, so you do admit to failings, young man!'

Will bowed again. 'Under God, madam, we are all sinful men and women, and I do not claim to be different from the rest of my kind.'

Aunt Petronella turned to Beck, who was truly relieved at Will's clever and adroit handling of a woman who had a reputation as a dragon, and who, if she did not exactly eat those who displeased her, gave them the edge of a scarifying tongue.

'You are right, my dear. He's clever. Whether he's clever for you—or for himself—is another matter.'

Will answered her immediately. 'Since in a week's time, God willing, we shall be man and wife, which means that in the eyes of God and the law we shall have become one, then my cleverness must be as much for my wife as for myself.'

The old woman rewarded him with a crack of laughter, stood up and put out her hand. 'Let us shake on it, Master Will Shafto. For the moment I am pleased to recognise you, but beware…if I believe that you are exploiting my niece in any way, then you will have a formidable enemy in me.'

And that, thought Will, must be the joke of the year, seeing that in this situation the only person being exploited is myself!

But he said nothing, merely bowed again, sat down and proceeded to enjoy the old woman's forthright conversation. Opposite to him his proposed bride watched him, equally thoughtful. She was beginning to find depths in Mr Will Shafto which she had not believed existed.

At least he had managed to win over her formidable aunt. Beck had not informed her of the coming marriage, believing that she was safely hidden away in her draughty mansion in the Borders. Some interfering busy-body, however, had written her an excited letter giving her all the details of Beck and Will's courtship and their coming marriage.

At which the old lady had immediately ordered her horse and carriages to be harnessed and had set off for Honyngham House, her home on the Thames outside Richmond, to use all her influence with her niece to stop the marriage if she thought that Rebecca had been bamboozled by a bare-faced adventurer.

Instead, here she was smiling at Will and asking him in her usual forthright manner, 'And where, young man, do you and my niece propose to spend your honeymoon?'

Beck forestalled Will's answer by replying brightly, 'Why here, of course, Aunt. Where better?'

'Nonsense,' exclaimed her aunt, banging her stick on the ground. 'Of course you can't stay here! You will wish to be on your own, of that I'm sure, without prying eyes to gape at you.'

Before either Will or Beck could assure her that of all things they wished to remain in London, she said imperiously, 'I have it. I shall come to live here for your first fortnight and the pair of you must go to Honyngham! You will have the country, the river and the trees—and one of the best views in England from Richmond Hill. The situation is ideal. You will be quite

alone, but that does not matter, for I am sure that you
will wish for no one's company but your own.'

Privately appalled, both Will and Beck opened their
mouths to decline this honour, but Aunt Petronella was
having none of it.

'Stuff,' she declared robustly. 'Your modesty does
you both credit, but I know that you will thank me afterwards. For my part, I shall be happy to be able to join
in the Season from such a comfortable lodgement. Say
no more. I shall leave you shortly in order to return to
Honyngham as soon as possible, in order to ensure that
my staff makes everything ready for you.'

How to answer her? Will, his face firmly fixed in an
agreeable expression which bore no relationship to his
true feelings, was as dismayed as Beck at the prospect
of them being imprisoned in the country, unable to get
away from each other, and compelled to pretend to the
old battle-axe who was gazing benevolently at them that
all was for the best in the best of all possible worlds.

She would brook no denial; and since it was to their
joint advantage that the old woman smiled on their
union, they could not refuse to do as she asked. So far
as she was concerned it was a love-match, and everyone
knew that lovers wished to be alone together—particularly when they were first married.

Disillusionment might settle in later, but who cared
for that? She beamed at them, and though neither of
them had uttered a word she announced proudly, 'There,
that's settled. Now let us talk of the details of the marriage ceremony. Do I understand that you propose to be
married from here?'

Beck cursed the gossiping fool who had involved her

aunt in all her doings, but there was nothing for it but to agree with everything that she said—and contemplate the prospect of two weeks alone with Mr Will Shafto—something which she had not bargained for.

Chapter Six

'Have you taken leave of your senses, Petronella? I understand from Rebecca herself that you have given this disgraceful marriage your blessing.'

'Lord love you, John Allenby, I'm only too happy to see the poor girl married to someone. He may be a rogue after her money, but he's also presentable, well spoken, of a good family, and all my instincts inform me that he'll treat her well once they are married. Besides, I believe her fortune has been tied up so tightly by her lawyers that he'll have a devil of a job getting his hands on it.'

'Praise a fair day at night,' snorted John Allenby. 'She could have had anyone, anyone.'

'So she might. She might have made a fool of herself by marrying Hedley Beaucourt, something which you wanted for her, I'm told, and only the deity knows why you wished that—and he ain't telling. No, depend upon it, she has made a good choice. At least the children will be handsome, and that's one blessing.'

John Allenby lifted his eyes to heaven. It had always to be remembered that the old woman was a relic of the last century when manners and language were much coarser. And home truths were her speciality. She was now reproaching him for his niece Sarah's marriage.

'To marry the poor young gal to such an elderly roué was the outside of enough. What were you about, man? And because you were so dead set on acquiring a title, you didn't even tie her money up properly.'

'He wouldn't have married her if we had,' grudgingly admitted the man she was harrying.

'So it *was* his title you wanted. Heaven's above, man, you won't get rid of the stink of trade so easily. It takes more generations than two to wash away *that* odour. She was Mr Shafto's first choice, was she not? And you put a stop to the marriage? God grant that you don't regret what you've done. Young Shafto would have made her a far better husband.'

'You know nothing of him, or the matter,' exclaimed John Allenby, goaded beyond the prudence which dictated that he did not oppose her overmuch lest she leave her considerable fortune away from the family. 'I suppose you'll be at the wedding to lend it some respectability.'

'Wouldn't miss it,' exclaimed Aunt Petronella, banging her stick on the ground to emphasise each word she spoke, 'and you're not to worry about its respectability. The Bishop of Bath and Wells will officiate at the ceremony, and cousin John Ffolliot has promised to be present. Only too happy to see dear Rebecca caught at last. She'd better have married her head groom than no one at all, he told me, spinsterhood being such an unnatural state in his opinion.'

John Allenby closed his eyes and moaned inwardly. John Ffolliot was the Duke of Durness, a man so grand that he scarcely ever condescended to speak to anyone below the rank of Baron. But he was Petronella's cousin by marriage and rumour had it that he had once wished to marry her when he had been penniless Jack Ffolliot, and ten lives stood between him and the title.

Drink, disease, drownings and a carriage accident had carried them all away, but not before Petronella had been married off to a lowly, if rich, Baronet, so he had remained single, surrounded by a changing harem of ladies of easy virtue.

In old age he had got religion, or religion had got him—no one was quite sure which—and now he was as virtuous as he had once been vicious. For him to attend the wedding was to set the last—and greatest—seal on its respectability.

'I think that you have all taken leave of your senses,' was John Allenby's feeble riposte.

Petronella Melville stared at him coldly, and decided to change her will, leaving everything of which she was possessed to Will Shafto, who, whatever anyone else said, she judged to be a man as upright as any penniless gentleman could be.

Good, clever and sensible though her dear Rebecca Rowallan was, it was neither right nor proper that her husband should be condemned to be her permanent pensioner.

She would visit her lawyers the first thing in the morning, and no one, absolutely no one, was to know of her decision.

'A Bishop and a Duke? Have you run mad, Beck? I thought this was to be a simple ceremony.'

'And so it was until that idiot John Allenby wrote to Aunt Petronella to inform her of the marriage. She told me that he did so in order to try to persuade her to bring her influence to bear on me to stop it.

'Instead, it only took one look at you for her to succumb to your charms. So much so that she wishes this to be one of the weddings of the year—and is making sure that it will be. And please don't call me Beck!'

Will groaned. He had thought that they were going to have a quiet little ceremony, followed by an equally quiet little marriage. Instead, the whole business was turning into a version of Greenwich Fair, with only the tumblers and fire-eaters missing.

It put quite a different complexion on matters and if he had known this beforehand he would never have agreed to become entangled with Beck Rowallan at all. For some reason he could not think of her as Rebecca.

'I'm not happy, Beck. This is turning into a circus.'

'And I'm not happy, either,' exclaimed Rebecca spiritedly. 'What's more, Aunt Petronella is making a great to-do about you not having invited any of your relatives to be present.'

'I haven't got any relatives.' Will was equally spirited if not exactly truthful. He hadn't many and all of them lived far from London society and he particularly didn't want any of them to know of this marriage until it was over.

Worst of all, this whole brouhaha was making him question not only his behaviour, but Beck's.

'Why?' he asked abruptly. 'Why do you really want this odd marriage, Beck?'

She closed her eyes, and said, her voice weary, 'Why can you never remember to call me Rebecca? It's a small enough request to make.'

Will didn't know, so he couldn't tell her. Later, alone in his lodgings he concluded that it was the only way left to him of showing her that she couldn't dominate him completely. Everything else which she had demanded of him, he had agreed to without argument, so that to call her Beck against her will was to bring her down a little, a very little.

'Our first quarrel,' he told her. 'We have been so charmingly agreeable to one another I suppose that it's not surprising that it couldn't last. Most unnatural to be so constantly pleasant, do admit. And you haven't answered my question. Why?'

'You know why. Once I'm married, all the ceaseless bullying from those who think that they have some claim to control me will stop. I shall be safe. And once you are my husband it will be your duty to protect me from those who might wish to exploit me.'

'And who is to protect me, Beck? Tell me that?'

Unconsciously they had drawn nearer and nearer to one another so that very little space lay between them.

'Me—and my money,' she told him coldly and cruelly.

It was Will's turn to close his eyes when he heard this harsh pronouncement.

'And who is to protect *you*, when we are married? Are you not afraid that once the knot is tied I shall play Stony Bowes to your Countess of Strathmore?'

Will was referring to the marriage between Bowes, an adventurer, and the wealthy Countess to whom he had been so charming before marriage, but whom he had brutalised after it.

Beck shook her head. 'No, Will. I had you carefully watched. I know that you are quite unlike Stony Bowes. You would never hurt a woman.'

'Not even if she provoked me?' Will asked her softly. 'As you are doing now?'

He had brought them so close together that they were breast to breast, face to face, their breaths mingling.

Will wondered whether Beck's heart was thumping as hard as his was. He knew from experience that when a man and a woman engaged in violent argument strange consequences often followed. He was experiencing a strange consequence himself!

He wasn't sure whether he wanted to shake her or to overwhelm her with caresses. He wasn't sure which action would make her lose her unshakeable calm, and it was suddenly that which was troubling him, for he wasn't sure of anything.

No one, but no one, should be in such control of themselves. He imagined for one brief moment a Beck Rowallan who had lost her iron self-control. Would it be possible for her to shiver and moan beneath him, begging him to…to…?

Will blinked. He had, quite without willing it, closed his eyes, and now that they were open again he was astonished to discover that Beck and he were closer than ever, that her mouth was quivering and her eyes were slumberous.

Miss Rowallan with slumberous eyes! What a turn-up! Equally as surprising was this sudden lust for her which had him bending his head to kiss her mouth which had become so soft, was no longer firm, straight and forbidding.

He was going to kiss her, he was going to…he was going to do nothing, for there was a knock on the door so imperious that they sprang apart, staring at one another.

'Aunt Petronella!' exclaimed Beck, who did not know whether she was pleased or sorry at this haughty interruption. Something decidedly odd had been going on between her and Will. Something which she had not foreseen. 'It's Aunt Petronella. Only she would hammer on a door like that. If I don't answer her, she will be in without further warning.'

So she was. Her eyes gleamed and her mouth twitched before she said, her voice triumphant as she correctly read the expression on both their faces, 'Ah, love birds at last, I see. I thought that you were never going to get down to it!'

'Really, Aunt!' exclaimed Beck, for once at some loss to express herself with her usual logical clarity. 'What a thing to say!'

'Come, come, Beck,' said Will smoothly, not prepared to let an occasion pass which would enable him to catch his beloved on the hop as she had so often caught him. 'No need to deny what was so obvious. We were discussing our future together,' he explained, 'and matters became a little…confidential, didn't they, my love?'

He spoke as though they had been caught grappling together on the floor like a housemaid and a footman, fumed Beck inwardly. She opened her mouth to say something scathing but, catching the gleam in Will's eye and reading it correctly, she grasped that to do so might land her in further trouble from his ready tongue.

Besides, the old lady was so pleased to see her behaving like a woman passionately in love with her soon-to-be husband that it would be unkind to disillusion her—especially when that was the impression which she had been trying to create.

Beck simpered—what else could she do? Will almost choked at the sight—and at the same time felt a strange relief. She obviously loved the outrageous old woman—and here he had been thinking that she loved no one but Beck Rowallan.

Perhaps there was hope for both of them in this unequal marriage.

If so, Beck took pains to disillusion him as soon as Aunt Petronella left them alone again.

'Do not think that because it was necessary for us not to distress my aunt that anything has changed in the arrangement which I made with you, Mr Shafto. It hasn't.'

So, she was punishing him by not calling him Will.

'No, indeed,' he returned obligingly, 'and pray do not reproach me for following your orders. I was merely trying to persuade your aunt that this was truly the love match which you wish the world to believe it is.'

Beck interrupted him angrily. 'That is enough, sir. Do not try to bam me. You know perfectly well what you were about.'

It was disconcerting her mightily that Will was suddenly no longer her passive slave, but was choosing to wrongfoot and discomfort her at every turn. She had given a hostage to fortune which she had not intended when she had begun this masquerade and Will was showing her that, perfect gentleman though he might be, he was not above teasing her in situations in which she could not answer him without betraying their true relationship.

Of course, he had to behave like a passionate lover— for was not that the play which she had written for them? And despite her brave words it was too late to retreat. They were within a few days of the wedding.

Will saw the signs of a small surrender on her face, and pressed home his advantage. 'I trust,' he said, 'that you will allow me to escort you to Rundell and Bridges tomorrow. I wish to buy you a ring to mark our betrothal.'

It was truly the day on which Beck's tact was in abeyance. 'From the Court jewellers,' she exclaimed. 'Can you afford to do so? Perhaps—'

'If you are going to offer to lend me money to buy the ring,' Will announced through gritted teeth, 'then pray refrain. I have but little with which to indulge you—and myself—but that little is mine—and honestly earned.'

He was referring to the money which George Masserene had paid him before he had left his employment, but he could not say so. Beck realised her error at once and, wrongfooted again, began to apologise.

'Think nothing of it,' retorted Will, a trifle bitterly. 'It is quite understandable, given how much you are already endowing me with, that you should suppose I needed the money to buy you something which you could display with pride. I fear that what I might purchase would be too small and trifling, so perhaps we had better forget the matter.'

'No!' Beck's reply was rapid and heartfelt. She offered him a flag of truce at once. 'I assure you that that was not my reason for making such an offer. On the contrary, I shall now treasure any gift from you the more because it was truly you who have given it to me.'

It would be churlish to refuse her—and Will thought ruefully that, under the circumstances of their marriage, he had no excuse for displaying hurt pride.

'Very well,' he said. 'Tomorrow afternoon. I shall call for you at three.'

'Or,' Beck said, thinking to save him the expense of a cab, 'we could meet at the jewellers, and after that you could walk me home.'

Honour satisfied and hurt feelings forgotten, the following afternoon she and Will spent half an hour at the jewellers in Bond Street. The ring he chose for her was small but exquisite: a plain gold band with a small pearl set in it. And if the assistant who served them thought that it was an extremely modest present for a woman of such wealth, nothing he said betrayed the fact.

Instead he remarked as Will slipped the ring on Beck's finger, 'On madam's hand the ring possesses a chaste simplicity which far outshines a more gaudy offering.'

Beck held her hand up as he spoke and, as though regretting her ungraciousness of the day before, came out with the most spontaneous remark which she had ever made to Will. A remark which carried in its utterance the ring of truth.

'I am compelled to agree with you. Good taste and modesty frequently go hand in hand.'

The look which Will gave her carried its own reward. For the first time the pair of them experienced a little, a very little, of the emotion which a genuine pair of lovers might have felt.

But as, arm in arm, she and Will walked away from the jewellers, they were confronted by a shadow from his past...

George Masserene, feeling more successful than he had done for years, was walking along Bond Street. He was well aware that his shabby gentility ill accorded with the splendour of the men and women of London society around him.

As Will and Beck were jointly bowed out of Rundell and Bridges' he first registered them only as a pair of well-dressed lovers, or perhaps a husband and wife who had been indulging themselves. It was only when he was almost upon them that he remarked on the man's extraordinary likeness to his former employee, Wilson.

The nearer he got, the greater the likeness grew, until, on reaching them, he exclaimed, 'Why, Wilson, it is Wilson, is it not? I never thought to meet *you* here.'

Will had only one wish—that the heavens might open and swallow him up. He could see the avid curiosity on George's face, and could only imagine what Beck must be thinking.

He gave a light laugh, half-turned towards Beck and said, his face as serious as he could make it, 'My dear, allow me to introduce to you an acquaintance of mine, Mr George Masserene, with whom I recently completed some useful business transactions. I must present to you, George, my future wife, Miss Rebecca Rowallan. We are to be married in a few days.'

Beck curtsied, George bowed. Will continued desperately, 'I am sure, George, that you now understand why I cried off recently, and will not, for the present, be able to collaborate with you in any further ventures. My time is otherwise occupied.'

George Masserene was no fool. He had also heard tell of Miss Rebecca Rowallan and her fortune, and knew immediately that to reveal that Wilson—if that was his name, for he had seen Will wince when he had first spoken—would certainly not relish it being known that the 'business' of which he had spoken was his work as a professional gambler in a lowly gaming hell.

Better than that, he also thought that he knew that he might be able to benefit financially from this fortunate encounter, for surely Wilson would not wish his future bride to know how lowly a fortune-hunter he was.

Nor, it was to be assumed, would he wish his wealthy bride to know that he had been using another name.

George wished he knew what his real name was. He was unaware that Miss Rowallan would not care tuppence if she did learn of his involvement with George, or of his assumption of another name. For it was precisely because of his financial desperation that, to put it bluntly, she had bought him.

'Business transactions?' asked Beck sweetly. She had not for one moment been deceived by the scaly pair of rogues doing their deceptive dance around her. 'You interest me, Mr Masserene. Exactly what kind of business transactions? If a humble female may so ask?'

She looked anything but a humble female as she came out with this dangerous question.

George, whose imagination was not a lively one, looked wildly at Will, his mouth open. Will duly obliged by remarking airily, 'Oh, George and I have been plunging on the Stock Exchange, my love, in enterprises connected with the current war. My investment was modest—it allowed me to buy your ring—but George here is a devil of a fellow and netted much more, having risked more, of course.'

George, offered a lifeline, closed his mouth and murmured his assent to this unlikely statement. It would not pay him at the moment to give Will away.

Beck continued her pinpricking game, and offered him yet another lifeline—deliberately, for it amused her to play the pair of them as a picador might play with two lively, but confused, bulls.

'I am so happy to learn that my dear Mr Shafto has had such a useful partner. You must invite me to your counting house some time soon, Mr Masserene. I have never been inside one.'

She tapped Mr Shafto lightly on the arm and reproached him prettily. 'I wish you had told me of this before, Will. You know how interested I am in all matters financial! Pray arrange it soon, I beg of you.'

Oh, yes, Mr Will Shafto knew how interested his beloved was in money matters. He bared his teeth in a desperate grin at George, who, having been handed Wilson's real name on a plate—which was a plus—now had a minus to consider: he had no counting house. How the devil was Will Shafto going to wriggle out of that one?

And which was his real name? Wilson or Shafto?

Mr Will Shafto could, it appeared, wriggle out of anything. He clapped George on the shoulder, exclaiming, 'Yes, we must arrange it as soon as possible, old fellow—after you come back from your expedition to the north.'

Even for a rogue and consort of rogues like George Masserene, this latest bout of invention from Will was a little rich. He almost blurted out, 'What journey to the north?' but something in Will's steely eye stopped him.

That, and the sudden belief that the listening Miss Rebecca Rowallan might not be the total simpleton that she was pretending to be. George knew men and women, and knew that beneath their trappings—or lack of them—rich and poor were made of much the same stuff. He also knew from hard experience that women were by no means the fools which most men supposed them to be.

Did Wilson—or Will Shafto—know the true nature of the woman who was clinging to his arm so prettily? George never let the grass grow beneath his feet. He smelled danger. It was time to take his leave.

'I shall write to you, Shafto, when I return, giving you the latest news of our northern ventures,' he announced in his bluffest manner.

He bowed to Beck. 'Delighted to have made your acquaintance, madam. You're a lucky dog, Shafto, but I suppose you know that. I bid you both good day.' He strode away from them, whistling to himself.

Will heaved an inward sigh of relief at his departure. He was too forward, for Beck said in her best slightly mocking fashion, 'Do you consider yourself a lucky dog, Wilson? That was the name he called you by, I believe, before I kindly supplied him with your true one, was it not?'

'Now, Beck,' Will began.

'No, no,' she replied, laughing. 'Do not try to offer me an explanation of your involvement with Mr. Masserene, which I know before you make it will be as untrue as all the flim-flam with which you and he have just been trying to deceive me. I must admit, though, you make a more plausible liar than your friend.'

'He is not my friend,' Will offered loftily, 'merely a business acquaintance.'

'In a relationship in which he was most certainly your superior, judging by the tone which he adopted towards you before he grasped that you were not Wilson, and that I was a rich heiress, not some barque of frailty whom you were entertaining for the afternoon.'

Goaded, Will riposted, 'You ought not to speak of barques of frailty, Beck, even if you know what they are.'

Beck stopped, took her hand from his arm, faced him and in the most earnest voice which she had yet used to him, said, 'Will, I have not the slightest desire to know all the details of your life before we reached our agreement, so you need not make up any more Banbury tales to explain who and what that dubious gentleman was to you.

'As for visiting his counting house, I am sure by his

expression when you spoke of it that it does not exist, so we shall certainly not be visiting it. If he tries to blackmail you by threatening to reveal to me all your secrets if you do not pay money over to him, you may tell him to go to the devil because nothing that he might say of you would surprise me.'

There would come a day when Mrs Will Shafto would bitterly regret this confident statement, but at the time it was simply one more nail in the coffin of Will's disappearing independence.

He shook his head, and said nothing. What he thought was that he must never underestimate the woman whom he was to marry. More than that, Will had recently begun to feel a little tenderness for her, but she had trampled that untoward emotion to death beneath her elegantly shod feet as they walked along Piccadilly in the wake of George Masserene.

Chapter Seven

A quiet wedding! Well, Aunt Petronella had certainly knocked that idea on the head. Instead of a discreet little ceremony in the small room off the Grand Salon at Beck's home, a large crowd was gathered in the Grand Salon itself.

Most notable of all were the Bishop and the Duke of Durness who had come from his country home in Kent to, as he put it, 'bless the nuptials of my dear Petronella's niece.'

From the way in which he was carrying on, thought Will sardonically, it might have been thought that it was his nuptials with the aunt, rather than Will's with her niece, that were being celebrated.

The Allenbys were there in full force, again at the insistence of Aunt Petronella. 'You must not make too many enemies, child—you never know when you might want them to be your friends,' being her aunt's robust comment when Beck had demurred at the mere idea of inviting any one of them.

Will's supporters and relations were conspicuous by their absence. He had toyed with the wry notion of inviting George, but tempting though that notion was, he thought that it might be going a touch too far.

In the event he invited Harry Fitzalan and his crony Gilly Thornton, with whom Will had occasionally sparred at Jackson's, together with Josiah Wilmot with whom he had been at Oxford for a year when he was sixteen.

'Have you no relatives, young man?' Aunt Petronella had asked him severely, waving her stick at him like the wicked fairy in *Sleeping Beauty*.

'They all live in the north, madam, and the notice has been far too short for them to be able to attend.'

There was nothing that even Beck's indomitable aunt could say to that, so she said nothing.

Will did not inform her of the other reason why they were not present: that they would find the cost of visiting London beyond them. He had written to those nearest to him, saying that he was well, but had said nothing of his marriage. He would try to explain that later, at a more favourable date—if such a date ever arrived, that was.

Both Beck, quietly, and Aunt Petronella, noisily, had separately confirmed that Mr Will Shafto was truly the Mr. William Shafto of Shafto Hall in Northumberland through the good offices of Josiah Wilmot.

Josiah could scarce believe Will's good luck in bringing this match off. He looked around the brilliant company with awe: cringing before both the Bishop and the Duke.

'Have you told them at home of your grand marriage?' he whispered urgently to Will as they stood waiting for Beck to walk through the great double doors of the salon to be united with Will.

'No,' Will whispered back, equally urgently, 'and you are not to inform them, either.'

'But they will want to know why you are suddenly so flush—'

'That's all arranged,' Will whispered back, praying that no one was overhearing this intimate exchange. 'They believe that I have made money on the Stock Exchange. Now, leave it, Josh. My bride is almost with us.'

Sure enough, there she was. Josh gazed at her, awestruck. He had not believed that Beck Rowallan could look so beautiful when dressed with such charming simplicity.

She was wearing a classic high-waisted cream dress, with little in the way of frills and furbelows to ruin the purity of its line. A silver fillet was threaded through her hair. It was adorned only with a small posy of lilies of the valley made from silk.

Another silver fillet which bound her slender waist was also decorated with silk lilies of the valley. Her only jewellery was a rope of small pearls, a slender silver bracelet, and the modest ring which Will had bought for her.

So why did she look so completely altogether as Harry Fitzalan put it later? For the first time Harry actually envied Will, the lucky dog who was going to climb into bed with such a stunner. Why, she had lost that cold, forbidding expression which was enough to freeze a fellow. Her mouth was so soft it quivered, her eyes shone as though tears lay behind them, and as she entered the room she blushed the most delicate rosy-pink.

She's like a camellia, a very camellia, thought Harry, who had never before considered himself to be poetically inclined.

He was not the only person to be shocked by Beck's appearance. The bridegroom, who had believed that he could carry off this occasion without feeling anything but a mild inward amusement that he was getting married in such state to someone for whom he felt nothing, was surprised to discover that the sight of his bride was reviving in him all those untoward feelings which he thought Beck's recent coldness to him had suppressed.

How did she expect him to hold off, not to make her his true wife—to put it vulgarly, to bed her—when she turned up looking like that? 'Like that' being the exact image of the loving and tender woman whom Will Shafto would most like to have had for a wife, but had given up all hope that he ever would.

Good God! One might almost think that she was shy! Beck Rowallan shy? What an impossible thought. Either she was a consummate actress or the mere fact of getting married had created in her all the appropriate feelings for such an occasion.

Beck, as she entered, saw Will standing there, waiting for her, turned out immaculately in black silk, all his clothes perfect, and all of them fitting him perfectly. She felt her mouth quiver. For the first time the enormity of what she was about to do struck her. The man waiting for her, his face and body as perfect as his clothes, would, in a few short minutes, be her husband.

What had she done?

What was she doing?

She could not, would not, allow any man to touch her, either in love, or in hate, but the dreadful truth, a truth which she had been pushing to the back of her mind ever since she had first met him, was that Will was the only man whom she had ever met who possessed the power to make her forget her vows of eternal chastity.

No, she would not forget them, for he was nothing but a rogue. Had he not as coldbloodedly accepted her bargain as she had coldbloodedly proposed it? He was her rogue, Rebecca Rowallan's rogue; she must never forget that. A rogue who had never told her the truth about himself or his origins or the devious tricks he had got up to before he had proposed to Sarah Allenby, and, when that failed, had allowed himself to be bought by herself.

Ah, but had she told the truth about herself to him? And if she had not, did not that make her his equal in deceit?

All this while she processed down the room to face the Bishop, the smiling Duke, Aunt Petronella nodding her head approvingly, Harry Fitzalan staring at her, his mouth agape, the witless fool, and finally, Will himself who extended a hand to her.

For one dreadful moment when she took it Beck wanted to run. To run out of the room, to rush upstairs in order to jump into her chaste bed and pull the covers over her head and pretend she was still little Beck Rowallan who had yet to grow up and find how wicked the world was.

The moment passed. She gave Will a cool smile. He offered her a warm one: both, in their different ways were equally false. The Bishop started to read the marriage service in that special clerical voice all priests use, and the service began.

Neither of the principals was ever, for their different reasons, to remember much about it. The one thing which Will recalled was the phrase in the ceremony about marriage meaning forsaking all others, since it made him feel uncomfortable.

Beck lost everything. She moved in a dream, spoke

in a dream, and looked like a dream of loveliness. So much so that afterwards everyone there, like Harry, agreed that they had never before known how beautiful she was.

'Love,' bellowed the Duke when Aunt Petronella murmured her surprise in his ear at the wedding breakfast which followed the ceremony. 'Love always does that to a young woman, and to a feller, too. Depend upon it, this is a love match whatever anyone might think. Handsomest pair I ever saw, and no mistake. Worth marrying a fortune-hunter to get a feller who looked like that, I dare say.'

His bluff words floated out over the heads of all the guests. If anyone had thought that such home truths might visibly overset the bridegroom they were quite mistook, as Harry said later when reporting on how Will was 'turned off', as the slang saying had it.

Will laughed aloud, immediately raised his glass to the Duke and offered to toast him, 'For having the courage to say aloud what others were only thinking,' he told the Duke later when the meal was over.

'An honest rogue, I like that,' exclaimed the Duke. 'Look after her, my boy. My Peter'—he meant Aunt Petronella—'says that she's a deal more sensitive than she thinks she is. And no wonder when one knows what she went through when she was only a young lass—but no doubt she's told you of that.'

'No doubt,' echoed the amused Will, who had not the slightest idea of what the Duke was talking about, but was stowing away in his good memory what he had just heard.

'Enough!' commanded the Duke, who like many people was happy to speak his mind himself, but frequently counselled others against doing so. 'Here comes your good lady and she must not know that we have been talking of her. Wouldn't do. Strong minded, Peter says.'

Beck didn't look strong-minded. She looked as quietly modest and shy as a new young bride ought. And so Will told her.

'For the moment, yes,' she replied. 'I had no notion that I should feel quite so overwhelmed. I suspected that I might be—a little, perhaps—which was why I wanted a small and quiet ceremony.'

'All those prying eyes making one feel like an animal in a cage at Greenwich Fair,' offered Will.

'Exactly.' Beck had not expected to find him so perceptive. She was beginning to grasp that there was more to Will than his reputation, and the bargain he had agreed with her, might suggest.

They were given no time for further confidences which was, Will reflected, perhaps a pity. Instead they were torn apart by distant relatives who wished to speak to her of their mutual past and Will wandered off. For the first time he understood at what a disadvantage having none of his family present had put him. It left him very much the odd man out.

He walked over to a window embrasure and looked out at the garden, golden in the noonday sun. He was hidden by the curtains and so overheard something not meant for his ears. John Allenby was talking to a female Allenby cousin.

'Well,' he said, his voice heavy, 'it's done, for good or ill. I cannot but think it ill that she should marry a landless penniless man.'

'And of no family—or so I have heard say.'

'Then whoever told you that heard wrong. There's nothing odd about his family. He's Shafto, of Shafto Hall, no doubt of it. But his father lost everything gambling—hence the fortune-hunting. He's the last of his line, and there are, I understand, no near relatives. Someone said that his mother died not long after his father—and since she's not here I suppose that must be the truth. What I still don't understand is why Beck, who is supposed to be strong-minded, was so determined to marry him.'

'His looks?' ventured the cousin.

'If it were anyone but Beck I might agree with you. No, she's the coldest of cold fish. She's been so ever since Paul died. Now, if he'd lived she wouldn't be in a position to hand over the Rowallan fortune to a ne'er-do-well, for being the son he'd have inherited everything. Oh, she'd have had a nice little dowry, but nothing more. Not enough to tempt this fellow, I'll be bound.'

Will heard no more. They had evidently moved away. He abandoned his unsought and unwilling role of eavesdropper, moving through the crowd of smiling well-wishers. He suddenly wanted to find his bride. A bride who had possessed an elder brother of whom she had said nothing. But then, he hadn't told her everything, either.

What would he say to her when he found her? He didn't know. Something? Nothing?

He met Harry Fitzalan, who had an Allenby girl clinging to his arm and who greeted him with, 'Looking for Beck, old fellow? I think that she went down there with that old aunt of hers.' He pointed through the open double doors which led to the grand staircase.

'Probably getting into her duds to leave for Honyngham, you lucky dog. Never thought I'd say that.'

On an impulse Will followed Harry's pointing finger and made for the staircase himself. To do so he had to pass the small drawing-room whose door stood slightly

open. He was almost by it when he heard, coming
through it, muffled sobbing.

Beck? Surely not. It couldn't be Beck crying. But all
the same Will was suddenly overcome with dreadful
guilt. He couldn't think what for, except that if it were
Beck crying it almost certainly had something to do with
himself, and he ought to try to do something about it.

He pushed the door completely open and walked in.
'Beck?' he murmured. 'Beck? Is that you?'

Out of sight of the door, but visible when he walked
further into the room, a large armchair stood by the fireplace. A woman was huddled in it, her face pressed into
the cushions.

By her pale blue silk dress and her golden curls she
was plainly not Beck—and therefore no business of his.
Prudence dictated retreat, so Will retreated.

Too late. The woman reared up and turned a tear-
stained face towards him, to show him Sarah Allenby,
or rather, the Marchioness of Wingfield, as she now was.

All her pink and white prettiness had quite disappeared. Her face was blotched and stained with the
marks of heavy crying. She had, during the wedding
ceremony, been wearing a blue silk shawl, but that had
fallen away to reveal that her upper arms were covered
in bruises.

She took one look at Will before he could remove
himself, and ran forward to fling herself into his arms.
'Oh, Will, oh, Will,' she sobbed into his chest, ruining
his cravat and marking his elegant waistcoat.

'How could you have married her, of all people, so
soon after we were parted, when you knew how much I
loved you? Why did I not refuse to give you up? Why
did I consent instead to marry that...monster?'

Will tried to disengage himself, but failed. He nobly

refrained from pointing out that despite her great love for him, she had married her Marquess before he had so much as proposed to Beck. Unfortunately, the more he tried to hold her off, the more she clung to him, her sobbing becoming hysteria, her little shrieks becoming big ones.

The only way in which he could escape from her boa-constrictor grip was to knock her out with the kind of blow which he would have handed an opponent at Jackson's gym, an act which was quite beyond Will.

At the very moment when her shrieks were at their loudest and her struggles with him became frantic, the door opened and in came the Marquess of Wingfield looking for his wife.

To find her in Will's arms.

'You strumpet,' he howled, a word which Will had never before heard used except in a bad play. 'I've been looking for you everywhere in order to leave, and what do I find? That you're betraying me with Beck Rowallan's bridegroom. Wait until I get you home, m'lady, and you'll soon learn what it is to try to cuckold me. I shall give you such a lesson as you'll not forget.'

Will registered with wry amusement that Wingfield was not threatening him. He obviously knew of his physical prowess. Still trying to detach himself, Will said, as coolly as he could over Sarah's shoulder, 'By the state of your wife's arms and neck, Wingfield, you've already given your wife one more lesson than you should have done. You're a fool to think that I would try to deceive you with her on my wedding day.'

The Marquess ignored all of Will's rebuttal except that referring to his name. 'Hey, what's that? Did you call me Wingfield? Address your betters by their proper style, man. Just because you've tricked Beck Rowallan into marriage doesn't give you leave to be familiar with your superiors.'

Sarah, showing signs of recovery, and beginning to grasp that she had put Will at some disadvantage, stepped back, snuffling gently, and tried to appeal to her husband who ignored her.

Will was content to say, 'My superiors? Where are they, Wingfield? I'll not admit anyone to be that who strikes a woman.'

'Been bleating to him, have you, m'lady? I'll give you something to bleat for.'

'No, no,' cried Sarah. 'I didn't, I didn't. He guessed, that's all. It wasn't Will's fault.'

'I've a mind to call you out, Shafto—see if I don't.'

By now, to Will's horror, some of the guests, attracted by the noise, were finding their way into the room, to gaze entranced at the spectacle of the bridegroom being caught with another woman before he'd as much as gone on his honeymoon.

The Marquess swung on the newcomers who included the Duke of Durness.

'I found him alone with my wife—you may guess why—and he refused to address me properly when I taxed him with it.'

'Which offence was the greater?' asked the Duke politely. 'Bein' alone with your wife, or not calling you m'lord? It might affect the sentence we agree on for the offender.'

The Marquess glared at the Duke as though he could kill him. His silence gave Sarah her opportunity.

'There was no assignation, Duke. I was alone here for quite some time, feeling a trifle overset, when Mr Shafto came looking for his wife. I was asking him for comfort when my husband came in and misunderstood matters.'

'Is that true, Mr Shafto?' asked the Duke, who had obviously appointed himself judge and jury.

Will agreed that it was the truth. He could see John Allenby staring inimically at him.

The Marquess bellowed, 'He lies, damn him.'

The Duke stared at him. 'You are a trifle offensive, sir—even if you were being wronged, which I doubt. Lady Wingfield, pray approach me.'

Sarah, shaking, her face pale, did so.

The Duke said to her kindly, 'I do not wish to distress you, my dear, but you said that you had been crying for some time before Mr Shafto came in. Now I saw Mr Shafto leave the Grand Salon only a few minutes ago, and I would have followed him immediately, only I was detained.'

He took her face in his hand and tipped it towards him. 'I know what a crying woman looks like, and you have plainly been crying for quite some time—which is not the conduct of a woman who has arranged an assignation.'

He turned to the Marquess who was glowering at him.

'I fear that you misunderstood matters, Wingfield, which does not surprise me; you were never known for the sharpness of your wits. I suggest that you apologise to both injured parties if you wish to remain *persona grata* in any circles I frequent.'

This, Will and the others, understood to mean that the Marquess faced social extinction if he failed to comply with the Duke's order.

Grudgingly he did so.

'Now go home,' the Duke said, 'and comfort your wife, who appears to be more distressed than a new wife should be. Shafto, you will take my arm and allow me to escort you to the Grand Salon where I believe that your wife will shortly be arriving, ready for you to take her to Honyngham.'

Sarah threw an agonised glance at Will before she followed her crestfallen husband out of the room; a glance which the old Duke saw. Will was beginning to understand how shrewd he was and how little escaped him.

'You were lucky there, m'boy,' he told Will, not lowering his voice as he walked him along, and caring little that Sarah's Allenby relations were all around them.

'A flighty piece, always in the boughs, that one. None the less, you'd have made her a better husband than the brute she's been saddled with. You're much better off with Beck, you know. Not only is she richer, but she's a sound head and a good heart—if you can fight your way through the armour she wears to find it.'

Will hardly knew how to take this last statement. He was profoundly grateful to the old man for rescuing him from the predicament into which he had fallen through Sarah's ill-judged claim on his sympathy. On the other hand, he did not wish to antagonise Beck's relatives more than he had already done by marrying her.

'You do me too much honour, sir,' he managed.

The Duke snorted. 'Not at all, m'boy. Just telling the truth as I see it. Never could stand the man, gave me great pleasure to put him down. Ah, I see Beck's already waiting for you.'

So she was. She was wearing pale green silk now, and a bonnet of a deeper green which was adorned with cream ribbons. To Will's astonishment the look she threw him was an agonised one, a look which asked for support.

However, when she spoke it was to employ her usual

sharp manner to him. 'Goodness, Will, what was all the commotion about?'

Before he could answer her the Duke replied in stentorian tones, 'Never mind that, now, Beck.' He had adopted Will's nickname for her. 'All over, and your groom will tell you about it on the way to Honyngham—if he isn't employing his time in a more enjoyable fashion!' He rewarded them both with a giant wink.

'Haven't been to a wedding for years, so don't know the form. Peter tells me that I ought to throw rice over you, but damn that for a tale. Uncomfortable business sitting on rice. Off with you both,' he suddenly roared, 'and leave us to drink to your health until the moon comes up.'

'Now, Jack,' said Aunt Petronella who had suddenly materialised and was now busily playing the good fairy. 'Leave the young things alone. They don't need an old bachelor like you to tell them what's what.'

'And whose fault was it that I'm an old bachelor, eh, Peter? Should have run away with me, but too late now, water under the bridge.'

He leaned forward and gave Beck a smacking kiss on the cheek. 'Making up for lost time,' he said, and pushed Will at her.

'Blessings on you both,' he called after them to the amusement of the crowd of wedding guests who were just beginning to grasp what a true eccentric the Duke was.

'All the same,' Beck whispered in Will's ear when they walked through the great front door to the carriage waiting to take them to Honyngham, 'I really do insist that you tell me what you and Sarah Wingfield were about. Most odd that you and she should somehow be compromised on our wedding day.'

'You heard the Duke, my dear,' Will whispered back climbing into the carriage after her. 'Later, when we are well away, you shall have all the details of my supposed misdemeanour. Can you honestly believe that I should play the fool on our wedding day? Considering that you know how much I stand to lose by it.'

'True,' nodded Beck. 'But why is it that I have the oddest notion that you have frequently sailed close to the wind in the past—so why not in the present?'

'Well, I was never in the present with you before, Beck, and that being so, any desire I have to sail close to any wind, north, south, east or west, has completely left me, knowing how much you would deplore any such thing—you being the soul of straightforward truthfulness yourself in all your dealings with everyone.'

There was a terrible silence in the carriage. Will wondered whether he had gone too far. But his bride surprised him yet again.

She began to laugh, softly, before burying her face in the small lacy muff which Mrs Grey had given her in exchange for the wedding bouquet she had been carrying before she left for Honyngham.

'Oh, Will, you constantly surprise me! Every time I think that I have begun to know you, you do or say something which betrays that I don't.'

'Then, if I assure you that in the matter of poor Sarah I was completely innocent...' He paused.

'I shall believe you,' Beck returned. 'And why poor Sarah?' So Beck did not know everything. And this was something which she ought to know.

'He is already beating her,' Will said grimly.

'No!' Beck's face was white. She caught her breath. 'Can that really be true? So soon?'

For some reason the words 'so soon' annoyed Will profoundly.

'What can you mean by "so soon", Beck? Are you implying that after a decent interval it would be quite proper for Wingfield to set about his wife? Are you wondering whether or not you might have to fight me off?'

Beck's face grew paler still. 'Of course not. I knew that he had a reputation as a brute, but I had hoped that Sarah being so young and pretty after a fashion which men admire, unlike myself, he might have held off.'

'Held off?' Will shook his head, bemused. 'I saw the marks of his displeasure on her arms, Beck. And another thing, what can you mean by comparing yourself unfavourably with Sarah? Surely you must be aware that although your looks are quite unlike hers, many would think yours were superior.'

'Oh, please, Will.' Beck's voice was as frosty as she could make it. 'There is no need for you to curry favour with me by showering me with pointless flattery. You are not, after all, either in love with me, or my true husband. I know only too well that I do not in the least resemble what most men like.'

Could she possibly be speaking the truth? There was that in her voice which said that she was. Did she really not know how beautiful she was, after a fashion which made Sarah look pallid and characterless by comparison?

Evidently not, for Beck began speaking again. 'You will do as I ask, I am sure, and not raise the subject again. I am well aware that it is stupid of me to be pained by empty flattery, but since I am, and since we must live together in some amity, I must ask you to respect my wishes.'

Will looked out of the window rather than look at his

wife. How had she come to this pass? To think of herself as a plain woman, when she was a beautiful one? Was this the explanation of her ruthless approach to life which had resulted in her arranging for herself a cold-blooded marriage of convenience—something which most women strove to avoid? But not Rebecca Rowallan, now Beck Shafto, who unaccountably thought herself to be plain.

The Arcadian scenery of the Thames valley streamed by the coach window. The day had begun as a grey one, but once the sun had burned through, it had become both fine and fair. Would the sun in Beck's life ever dissolve the illusions under which she was living?

More to the point, could a man who had married her for his own ends forget himself and help her to find the happiness which was so obviously eluding her?

No! How could he, her self-confessed rogue, ever pretend that he could save her when he could not save himself?

But there was nothing to say that he could not try, was there?

Chapter Eight

Honyngham was beautiful. The house, all mellow rose and gold brick, stood back from the River Thames, but its gardens ran down to it. Will and Beck's rooms overlooked the river and a small quay where boats were moored.

Inside the house all was elegance and comfort. For one desperate moment when he was ushered into the entrance hall Will had found himself wishing that Beck was truly his wife and that they were going upstairs to consummate their marriage as soon as possible.

He checked himself. What was he thinking of? After all, it was surely only pity which he felt for Beck—and perhaps a touch of lust. Certainly not love, he told himself firmly, only to ask himself uneasily a little later when he looked out towards the river whether he was deceiving himself over that, in the same manner in which Beck was deceiving herself over her looks.

Because, at this very moment, he was wondering how he was going to spend the next fortnight alone with her without touching her! When he had first met her, she had been so cool and distant, so totally unlike the kind of woman he had always desired, that it had been easy to contemplate living with her in a loveless, unconsummated marriage.

No longer! The more he knew of her the more she had begun to attract him. Even her coldness, her severity, now seemed a challenge: a challenge to find the true woman beneath her austere façade.

Will shrugged his shoulders and began to turn away from the window. What he ought to be thinking of was how grateful he was to Fate that it had brought him a way out of the hell in which he had been living…

Two days ago, with the marriage settlements signed and all the financial details arranged, without telling Beck, he had gone to Coutts Bank, where each quarter she had arranged for a handsome sum of money to be paid into an account specially opened for him. It was his pay for agreeing to do as she wished and would ensure that he was able to present himself to the world as a monied man.

The clerk who had dealt with him had been all subservience. For some reason he had assumed that Will wished to transfer his account from whichever bank he used into this new one.

Will had rapidly disillusioned him.

'Indeed, no,' he had smiled. 'What I wish to arrange is something quite different. I have here a piece of paper with the address of a bank in a northern town and the name of a solicitor who holds an account there. I am authorising you to pay into his account each quarter sixty percent of the sum which will be placed in my name. I have given him the authority to transfer this money to the owner of a small estate which he manages, and I have here a letter from him accepting this duty and a copy of the agreement between us which will prove to you that this transaction is above board.'

The clerk read both the letter and the document. He looked closely at the name of the person to whom Will was acting as a benefactor and raised his eyebrows superciliously when he had done so.

Will leaned forward and took him negligently by his cravat, tightening his hand so that the clerk began to choke and splutter.

'Little man,' he said, 'you will not question what I wish to do with my money. You will carry out my orders—which are no business of yours—so long as my business is honest. Your bank claims total confidentiality for all its transactions, and if I discover that my confidence has been breached, I shall not hesitate to demand an interview with Mr Coutts himself.'

He paused, looking coldly at the clerk's purpling face.

'On second thoughts, you will take me to him now. That should ensure that my affairs are not gossiped of.'

He released the clerk who gasped at him, 'No need for that, sir. You may rest assured…'

'No, *you* will rest assured that you will take me to Mr Coutts. At once.'

It was done, and Will signed the banker's orders in Mr Coutts's presence. Mr Coutts made no demur about his somewhat odd request, and told Will that his business would remain confidential between the three of them.

Which did not prevent him, once Will had left, from picking up the papers before him and trying to make an educated guess at exactly what the fortunate Mr Will Shafto, who was marrying a great heiress, was about. He wondered briefly whether the new Mrs Will Shafto was aware of what her husband was doing with his princely allowance, before he returned to the task of running England's richest private bank…

Back in the present, Will shrugged again before taking

one last look through the window. There, strolling along
a gravel path which ran between two formal lawns, was
his new wife. She had changed from her travelling dress
into a simple pale grey gown with a Puritanic linen collar
and cuffs. She was carrying a white lace parasol to shield
her face from the sun and looked the picture of idle
contentment.

Once she gazed up at the windows. Will stepped back
so that she should not see him: it had not been his intention to spy on her. Rather he would join her.

Rapidly he ran down the stairs, shocked a little by his
desire to be with her, and by the thought of how difficult
it was going to be to keep his hands off her now that
they were truly alone.

Beck watched Will walk from the house. He was still
wearing his wedding clothes, and splendid he looked in
them. He was smiling.

He was her husband! Her husband!

Beck wanted to run, to hide, anything rather than be
with him. Alone. She had not bargained for this. She did
not know whether he frightened her, or attracted her. The
two sensations were so mixed together that all she could
think to do was to assume her frostiest face and manner.

'You are in a hurry, sir.'

'Always, on my wedding day.'

She did not want to be reminded of that, Will saw,
glumly.

'You are remembering our agreement, I trust?'

'How could I forget it?' Will riposted. 'It is written
on my heart.'

'As it is written on mine.'

'Have you a heart, madam wife, for anything to be
written on it?'

'My heart is no concern of yours, sir.'

So it was still war, even on their wedding day. Beck's eyes shot ice at him, not fire. Will was not to know that the icicles were an armour she had assumed in order to hold him off, for with him she was starting to find that her emotions were starting to rule her, and not her reason—which would never do.

He smiled at her again, though. Faint heart never won fair lady, the old saying had it, and whatever Will was, he was not faint-hearted. Had he been so he would have gone under long ago; the cruel world would have rolled over him and left him dead.

But he was not dead, he was very much alive. He had married a woman in cold blood, and now he wanted her in hot blood.

If Beck's plans were beginning to go awry in the face of their mutual attraction, so were Will's. It was no longer a question of a cold woman employing a hard rogue to play a trick on the world and, that trick played, then part.

The little god of love, Dan Cupid, who posed before them in stone in the middle of a bed of roses, his bow held high, its arrow missing since it was in flight, had taken a hand in the game.

The missing arrow had found not one target, but two, and the question was whether the pair of lovers who were walking by him could tear his arrow from their heart and ignore its potent message.

As though he were trying—and failing—Will pointed to the statue. 'There's a thing,' he said. 'His bow is empty; the arrow has gone to pierce the heart of someone fortunate. Who could that someone be, Beck?'

The look he turned on her was frank and free. If the arrow had pierced her heart, as he was trying to suggest, then so did that look. Answer him as that wounded heart told her, and she was lost.

Reason prevailed. 'Fortunate, or unfortunate, perhaps? Not all who love are happy. The songs that are sung of it tell of pain and suffering as much as fulfilment. Best perhaps not to heed Cupid—or the arrow.'

'"Tis better to have loved and lost,"' quoted Will, '"than never to have loved at all."'

'Oh, Shakespeare,' shrugged Beck dismissively, picking up the allusion. 'But can one trust poets?'

'Can one trust anyone?' countered Will. 'I think that perhaps we might trust...' he paused '...our hearts. I believe that that is what poets trust.'

'How foolish of them,' retorted Beck. 'The only safe thing to trust is our reason.'

Although the day was warm, Will shivered. Beck's tone was so implacable.

'What happened to you, Beck,' he asked her, 'to make you so unfeeling? I do not believe that you were born that way.'

She turned away from him, and stared past the smiling Cupid towards the house and the rising hills beyond, away from the river—and from Will.

'And you, Will? Why, being a rogue, are you yet so sentimental? Does not that make it difficult for you to succeed as a rogue?'

She had twice used the derogatory word rogue to hurt him, to keep him at a distance, Will was sure. Strangely, on another's lips the word might have wounded him, but hearing it from Beck failed to move him.

He laughed a little. 'Which shows, madam wife, how little you know of being a rogue! Sentiment, not true feeling, is one of our stock-in-trades. If I were, at this moment, being a rogue with you we should not be trading ideas, but I should be doing—this.'

Suddenly he swung towards her, took the parasol from her hands and tossed it away before taking her in his arms, and then laying his head on her startled breast.

'Oh, my heart's darling, see how you move me! I have only to be near you to forget everything.' He took her hand and pressed it to his chest. 'Feel how my heart beats—and know that it beats only for you. Lie with me, Beck, here under Apollo's chariot, the sun, and let us celebrate our love in the lists of Hymen now that we are married.'

Slowly, slowly, he began to lower her to the ground, murmuring the while, 'This, my sweet, is what you were made for. Let me love you, or condemn me to die, slain by the power of your eyes.'

Beck was overwhelmed by him, his masculine scent, the feeling of his powerful body, the strength of the arms which encircled her. She gasped—but not to refuse him. The fear which always consumed her whenever she was as near as this to a man had gone, as though it had never existed.

Without warning, Will briskly lifted her away from him, to stand free of her, murmuring, 'You see what I mean by a rogue's sentimentality, Beck? As good as a play, was it not? The lists of Hymen, indeed! See how a seducer chooses his words.'

What he did not tell her was how difficult it had been for him to release her: that his honeyed sentences had begun to affect him as well as her, that from mockery he had found himself moving on to true passion. Only the knowledge that this was not the time or the place to overcome her—for afterwards she would have thought that he had tricked her into submission to him—had stopped him from turning pretence into reality.

Will now knew that he wanted Beck to come to him freely and willingly, offering herself to him, rather than being half-coerced against her will.

As it was, Beck stared at him, her lips quivering. 'Oh, Will, you must not do that again. You were breaking all the rules to which we agreed before marriage.'

What really shocked her was to find how desolate she felt once Will had released her. It was as though the sun had gone in and the world was full of shadows again. Worse than that, she felt angry with him: for one glorious moment she had believed that he truly meant what he was saying to her. Only when the sense of excitement they had created was past had she become aware of their shoddiness.

On the other hand, what would a man who truly loved her say?

This particular man was picking up her parasol and handing it back to her. She was thanking him mechanically, and wondering how she was going to struggle through the next fortnight without accidentally committing herself to someone whom she ought to despise, seeing that she had chosen him for his mercenary nature.

No matter. She had spent the last eight years successfully living her solitary independent life, so sharing it for a short space with Will without giving way to him ought to be easy enough. But would it be? For the gods themselves must be laughing at her as they slowly broke down the barriers of fear and distaste for all men which she had erected around herself since she was seventeen years old.

Will Shafto was busy thinking the same thing about the gods—with a slight difference. If he truly loved her, then he must be resigned to sacrificing his love for her when this masquerade was over. The penniless wretch that he was must still retain enough honour not to hold on to the rich heiress, who would be sure to believe that he did so only because of her money, not because he loved her.

Unless, of course, he could persuade her otherwise.

Supper that evening set the pattern of their days together. They sat at each end of a long table with half a dozen servants waiting on them. Later they sat opposite to one another in a pretty drawing-room. Will read a book—one of the late Tobias Smollett's picaresque tales whose heroes somewhat resembled himself in the uncertain nature of their lives.

Beck embroidered. She had left Mrs Grey behind, so she was not there to act as a buffer. After a time she laid her embroidery down and began to play the pianoforte which stood at one end of the room.

She had been well taught and was a skilled executant. Listening to her, Will admitted morosely that she excelled in everything she attempted—and wondered why the knowledge of her many talents did not make her happy. That she was not truly happy, he was sure.

Shortly after ten o'clock, true to the resolution she had made earlier, Beck excused herself and retired to her room. This was the only time she had spoken to him since their conversation in the garden.

Loneliness encompassed Will. It had walked with him since his father's death when he had discovered that all that was left of a once-great fortune was a neglected house and the few acres of farmland around it.

Almost he was tempted to drink himself into oblivion, but since his father's ruin had partly been brought about by the bottle, as always, he resisted the temptation. Finally he went upstairs to his own room to be ministered to by Gib. Lying awake until the small hours, he wondered wryly what the servants at Honyngham were going to make of his strange marriage.

A week later when matters between himself and Beck had not changed, he found out. He was being helped to dress for the day by Gib, who had been eyeing him satirically for some days.

He was tying Will's cravat, and was taking a long time about it. At last he stood back, apparently to admire his handiwork, but when he began to speak it was of something quite different.

'They are laying bets in the servants' hall as to when, if ever, you intend to bed the missis,' he said bluntly. 'If you do know the date you could perhaps tell me—I wouldn't mind winning a few bob.'

'I wouldn't dream of it,' Will told him. 'It's neither their business, nor yours for that matter.'

'When I heard you were marrying her,' Gib continued, ignoring what Will had to say—a common habit of his, 'I wasn't exactly up in the boughs since I thought her a cold piece. I never thought that you were a cold piece, too. They allows as how you must be, but I said no, it wasn't your habit to go overmuch with the muslin sort, but you were a true man for all that. Don't fancy her now you're married, is that it?'

'Why,' said Will in exasperation, 'do I continue to employ a servant who speaks to me as though he were the master, not I? Tell me that.'

Gib was succinct. 'Because I remind you of better days when you were a hopeful lad and I wore a pretty uniform and you travelled in a chaise with the Shafto

arms on the door. Will she buy you a chaise with your
arms on it, d'you think? Not worthwhile having married
her if she don't. I'm supposing you wed her for her
money, but what I don't understand, nor the staff here
neither, is why *she* married you, if it weren't to get a
man in her bed, seeing as how that's all you're bringing
her. A bad bargain she's made of it, I must say—which
ain't her reputation.'

This earthy analysis of the state of his marriage would
have set Will laughing if it had been made about anyone
but himself. As it was he frowned, told Gib to hold his
tongue, and determined to speak to Beck. It would not
do to have all the servants in London gossiping about
their strange marriage.

It had been remiss of both of them not to arrange their
affairs so that such gossip could be avoided. He must
speak to Beck at once, and insist that as soon as possible
they do something to scotch it.

Beck broke her fast late that morning, and came into
the dining room looking pale. Will watched her drink
coffee before beginning his campaign, once he had ordered the servants attending them to leave the room.

'Madam and I can manage quite well without you,'
he had finished.

When they were alone Beck looked at him over the
rim of her coffee cup.

'Why did you do that, Will?'

'Because I wish to speak to you immediately about
something important. Our conduct towards one another
has become the gossip of the servants' hall.'

'Oh, is that all?'

This cavalier answer had Will springing to his feet
and walking the length of the long table to where she
sat staring coldly at him.

'All, madam wife, all? The servants are placing bets as to the date when we, to put it politely, consummate our marriage. They are well aware by our behaviour to one another, and by all the other evidence, that we have yet not done so. If you wish us to be the talk of the town, then so be it. Rest assured, however, that if we do nothing to silence them, then the next thing will be that your friends and enemies will be placing similar bets at White's. Do you really want that? The scandal would be enormous.'

Beck blushed. She put down her coffee cup before saying, 'You are telling me the truth, Will? This is not some ploy to get me into your bed?'

Will, tantalised for the past week by her nearness, enraged by his inability to do anything about it, and by her refusal to take him seriously, bent down and hissed at her, 'What in the world should make you think that I want you in my bed? No, I am simply asking you to join me in some masquerade, some pantomime to silence the gossips, by enabling someone in the servant's hall to win his or her bet and end the matter. We should have considered this possibility before we came to Honyngham and taken steps to avoid it.'

He straightened up and said savagely, 'On the other hand, if you don't mind your name being bandied about town and being the subject of lewd jokes in the clubs, then we can continue as we are.'

Beck had never seen Will truly angry before. He had always been equable, half mocking, at the worst, or stoically resigned. To her astonishment she found his anger exciting, even if a little frightening.

'You are right,' she said. 'I had forgotten the servants. And, of course, they would say nothing to me. Was it Gib?'

'Yes, it was Gib,' returned Will. 'He was trying to warn me in his rough way, and I shall not listen to any criticism of him from you about his role in the matter.'

'No, of course not.' Beck's tone was placatory. 'What do you suggest we do?'

'To begin with, Beck, you could try talking to me when the servants are with us. The occasional "dear", or "my love", would help, together with some of the small talk which newly married couples engage in such as, "Shall we go for a walk, my love?", or, "It is a fine day, let us go riding and take a picnic with us." Even, "I have a mind to retire early, if it pleases you."'

Beck coloured. 'I have been so busy holding you off I quite forgot how it would seem to outsiders.'

'Servants are not outsiders, Beck, they are insiders. They know more about us than we do. Try to remember that tonight when we walk up to bed together hand in hand, and you come to my room instead of shutting yourself in your own. And there is no need to trouble yourself about holding me off. I can hold myself off quite well.'

Will had not meant to be so savage with her, but the frustrations of the last week, nay, the last month were beginning to tell on him. Before that he had led a chaste life for some time because loveless affairs were not to his taste. If this put a strain on the young and athletic man he was, then so be it, but he had not bargained for the effect on him of having Beck constantly in the same room and sleeping under the same roof.

Gratifyingly she looked suitably chastised. Well, it would do madam good to learn that she was capable of making mistakes. It would also do her good to listen to him for a change.

Will had become aware, as a result of his hard life

over the last few years, of the reality which lay behind the glittering surface of the life of the *ton*. He knew that the fortunate few were sustained by an army of servants and flunkies of all kinds, who possessed few illusions about their masters, however outwardly servile they were to them in public.

And not only servants. There was also an army of people who swept the streets, who kept life safe and comfortable for Beck and her kind; who provided their pleasures, dressed them, ran the gaming hells, shops, theatres and the brothels which filled London.

Beck knew nothing of this. It was not her fault: it was the circumstances of her upbringing which ensured her ignorance. But since he had become penniless, Will had learned how hard life was for the many. He did not question the reasons for this—he was no reforming radical— but he simply knew that it was so and must be endured. It made him kind to Gib and able to understand George Masserene.

Nor must he be unkind to Beck, even if her face remained as stoic as ever, as though nothing said or done to her could distress her, for by her behaviour she was a victim, too.

'Come,' he said, smiling, and pulling her chair back for her to continue her breakfast. 'Let us be friends if we cannot be lovers or man and wife, and plan our campaign to confuse our silent watchers.'

It was an olive branch and Beck accepted it. She was beginning to learn that there was more to Will than a handsome face and a good body, and that if he was a rogue he was nevertheless a complex one, not simple as she had once thought.

But her next worry was how to face the coming night when, willy-nilly, they would be thrown together.

Inevitably supper was a fraught meal. For all her outward calm Mrs Will Shafto pecked at her food like an
overfed bird, and Mr Will Shafto, who was usually a
hearty trencherman, ate little more.

Bland-faced servants, grinning behind their servile
masks wondered what, as the butler said afterwards in
the servants' hall, 'was a-goin' on. More like they was
goin' to an execution than to bed.' He noted 'that the
master drank more than usual whilst the missis drank
nothing at all.'

Gib said nothing, not even when the under-footman
reported excitedly that 'they was a-goin' up to bed together, so they was, and he kissed her outside her bedroom door, whispered in her ear, and then, holding her
hand, led her into his room.'

'Tonight's the night, then,' chortled the butler, 'seein'
as how she told her maid she wouldn't need her this
evening.'

'Guess who's a-goin' to undress her, then?' sniggered
the youngest footman, to be silenced by the butler who
believed that all the best jokes should be his.

'None of that now, Wattie!'

'When do I get my winnings?' asked the pantry boy,
who had bet on this night being the night.

'Tomorrow, lad, tomorrow,' the butler told him. 'They
might change their minds—who knows? The bedchamber lass will tell us in the morning what was up the night
before.'

This last sally had the whole kitchen staff in convul-
sions of mirth so loud that it was a wonder that it did
not reach the master bedroom where Will sat in one
chair, and Beck in another on the other side of the room,
both of them fully clothed.

'Be reasonable, Beck,' Will was saying. 'You will

have to get into the bed with me, and we shall have to provide some evidence that we were in it together.'

He gave a short, nervous laugh. To his surprise he was finding this charade as disturbing as Beck did. Any notion he might have had that the pair of them would put the bed to its proper purpose was being rapidly dismissed by the sight of his wife's intractable expression. She sat in her chair as though she were waiting to be tried for a capital offence.

Reluctantly Beck rose. Earlier in the day she had carried into Will's room her night rail and dressing-gown, as well as her toilet water, a towel, slippers, and a little cap for her hair. She picked them up, looked woefully in his direction, and said, 'I shall change in your dressing room, of course, as you will.'

Will bowed. 'Of course,' he echoed.

But even as she spoke there was a knock on the bedroom door, and then, without waiting for Will's command, Gib walked in.

'Oh, sorry, sir, madam, forgive me.' He rewarded them both with a greasy, knowing smile before he left, Will's reproaches for his intrusion ringing in his ears.

Astonishingly, Beck began to laugh, and if there was hysteria in it, what of that? You could never, Will thought bemusedly, forecast how she would react to anything. Wiping her eyes, she said, 'Properly caught. That ought to silence the servants' hall.'

'Not immediately,' returned Will, whose spirits had risen remarkably in response to Beck's surprising acceptance of Gib's entrance. He must remember to tip him later. 'On the contrary, I should imagine that the whole place is abuzz by now. After all, they've been waiting for this for a week.'

He didn't add, 'As I have done.' But he thought it.

Beck suddenly reverted to her normal manner. The sight fascinated Will. It was as though a shutter had dropped. All the liveliness, the spontaneity of the true Beck whom Will believed hibernated behind her usual, frosty exterior disappeared in an instant.

Perhaps he would not need to tip Gib after all, was his melancholy conclusion. Like a sculptor chipping a beautiful statue out of a shapeless block of stone, he needed to find some lever, some tool which would enable him to free Beck from her self-imposed isolation.

She disappeared into the dressing-room without further ado, leaving Will to throw himself into a chair and gaze at the painted ceiling where two Cupids disported themselves above Venus and Mars, who were preparing to enjoy themselves in a way forbidden to him. His only consolation was that, fixed forever in paint, they had gone as far as they would ever go.

Which might also apply to him where Beck was concerned!

She emerged some little time later, demurely apparelled in a dressing-gown which revealed nothing. She might as well have been wearing a sack.

Will grimaced and, in his turn, retreated. Beck sat in the distant chair again; the one which was furthest from the intimidating bed. What would she do when he came back into the bedroom in his night rail?

More to the point, what would he do?

Involuntarily Beck began to shiver.

Time was doing strange things. First it moved so quickly that it left her gasping, and then so slowly that that, too, was disturbing, for it left her too much time to think.

As now when, despite herself, she was waiting to see what Will looked like when his splendid clothes were gone. The thought shocked her: she blinked and re-proached herself for such unseemly internal behaviour. He would, of course, do as she had done, and put on a dressing-gown which would muffle him, rather than, as his day clothes did, show off his splendid physique.

She was wrong.

When, at last, he came into the room again he was carrying his dressing-gown, and was wearing a white linen nightgown with a pie-frill collar which stood up around what Beck could plainly see was his newly-shaven face. His hair had fallen into unruly curls since Gib was not there to dress it. His feet were bare.

They were beautiful feet, long and shapely. Beck could not help herself; she stared at them. They made her feel quite odd. Now why should that be? Feet were feet, after all. Nothing exciting about them. Except that Will's feet were exciting her.

Unlike his face at which she dare not look. She looked instead at the dressing gown he was not wearing.

Will saw the look. He threw the gown on the bed.

'In case anyone else bursts in on us in order to find how far gone we are, it is better that we are not muffled up as though we were about to set off for a walk in the snow.'

'You mean that I am to take off my dressing-gown, too?' asked Beck, betraying agitation for the first time.

'Is that too great a sacrifice?' mocked Will gently. 'When you first approached me, did you not realise that it would inevitably and eventually come to this?'

By her face she had not.

'Oh, the world is coarse,' Will told her. 'It demands proof. It pushes its dirty fingers into our affairs. One thing that I did not say earlier was that it is essential that your enemies do not know the true state of affairs—they might use it against you.'

Now, as he well knew, this was pushing matters a little, but if he were to succeed, then push he must. Standing there, the light of the candle around her head like the halo of some saint in a Renaissance painting, Beck was temptation itself.

The odd thing about her was that she was so unaware of her powers of attraction. She truly believed the contrary, so truly that it would be difficult for any man to convince her otherwise.

'Beck,' he said as gently as he could, for he did not wish to frighten her. 'You must take off your dressing-gown and get into bed, and I will lie on top of it, on the counterpane. I promise not to touch you. When morning comes, while you are in the dressing-room, I will get into bed and make it look as though we spent the night there together. You understand me.'

Beck nodded, her face wry. She said hesitantly, for she could never have imagined before this night that she would mention such a thing to a man, 'Since I am virgin, and we are supposed to have consummated the marriage...' She let the sentence die out, for she saw by Will's face that he understood her.

'Yes,' he said. 'I know that this is not the Middle Ages, but we must provide visible proof of our marriage for the servants to cackle over. Never fear, I'll think of something before they come to examine the bed.'

Deviousness was his middle name, thought Beck, a trifle ungratefully, but she did as he had bid her, took off her dressing-gown and climbed into the big bed. She was careful to leave him plenty of room to lie by her on the prettily worked bedspread.

Will waited until she was comfortable before stretching out a hand to extinguish the one candle by the bed which he had left burning. Beck said urgently, 'No, not yet.'

She did not wish to be in the dark with him.

He nodded agreement before lying down beside her, his hands behind his head. Beck held her breath for a moment. Her tension must have shown for, looking at the ceiling Will murmured, 'Don't worry, Beck, I shan't jump on you. It's not my way.'

Of course, the real truth must be that she didn't tempt him, thought Beck resentfully. It was truly strange that part of her was frightened that he might try to seduce her now that they were sharing a bedroom, and the other part felt insulted if he didn't!

'Yes, I know.' She spoke in her usual crisp and matter-of-fact voice. So matter of fact that Will felt challenged. He reared up on one elbow and leaned over her, teasing her by saying naughtily, 'Don't be too sure of me, Beck. I might be trying to deceive you.'

He received his punishment straightaway. Beck reared up immediately, catching him in the face with the top of her head as she did so. Will let out an anguished 'Oof,' and reared back in his turn, putting a protective hand to his nose.

To Beck's horror, it came away covered in blood.

'Oh, God, Beck,' exclaimed Will, throwing himself back on the pillow as though he had been dealt a mortal injury. 'You've tapped my claret—which is more than Gentleman Jackson ever did!'

'No! Oh, Will, forgive me, I never meant to hurt you,' and then, 'Will, what on earth are you doing?' for he was sitting up again, leaning forward and rubbing his bleeding nose on the undersheet beside her.

'Splendid, Beck, couldn't be better. Sit on it and mark

your nightgown.' He leaned back again, laughing heartily.

Beck stared at him, and then understanding struck. 'Oh, yes. How fortunate. One of our worries quite solved.'

'At the expense of my nose,' said Will, closing his eyes and looking wounded, 'I have proved you virgin. That should make everyone in the servants' hall doubly happy. Firstly because it is visible proof of your innocence, and secondly because it is solid evidence of my manly prowess in the marriage bed. No man or woman could ask for more.'

This came out in such a self-satisfied fashion as though he had truly achieved what a husband ought to achieve on his wedding night that Beck, despite her misgivings about the situation in which she found herself, began to laugh.

'So happy my damaged nose amuses you, madam wife,' moaned Will provokingly.

'Not so damaged,' returned Beck briskly. 'It's stopped bleeding already.' Forgetting that she had promised herself not to move too close to him, she leaned forward to examine it. 'It doesn't seem to be swollen.'

The opportunity was too good to miss. Will caught her by the chin, and said, his blue eyes gleaming, 'Kiss it better, then?'

He had adopted a child's attitude and voice as he spoke, which had the effect of disarming Beck completely.

'Oh, you are ridiculous,' she said, laughing, momentarily forgetting all her fear of him, something which Will saw and immediately took advantage of.

He put his left arm around her shoulders and kissed the tip of her nose as delicately as he could, before withdrawing a little, and murmuring, 'Like that would be nice.'

Beck froze in his encircling arm, offering him the eyes and bodily stance of a trapped deer.

'No,' she told him. 'No, that was not in the bargain.'

'Not?' he queried his head on one side, mischief riding on his face.

Beck was in two minds again. One part of her wished to give way to him, the other, the stronger part, was afraid to do so. The ugly past reared its equally ugly head, and told her No.

'You know that it wasn't, Will. I made myself quite plain.'

'Now, that,' Will told her, releasing her, 'would be difficult. I never saw a woman who looked less plain.'

Beck, leaning back on her pillows, answered him fiercely. 'You are not to try to bam me, sir. I know what I am.'

'Wouldn't dream of bamming you,' retorted Will, 'and you do not know yourself—as I hope to prove one day.'

She gave him her back, safer so, for the sight of his tender, mocking face might yet undo her. 'Go to sleep, Will. We have done our duty and need not fear the morning.'

Will blew out the candle—to which Beck made no objection this time—saying to himself, 'No, Beck, I have not done my duty by you this time, but one day I promise you that I will.'

He rolled on to his back, believing that sleep would be long in coming, as did Beck, lying so tantalisingly near to him, but, to their mutual but not expressed surprise, sleep came quickly to them both.

Shared laughter had anaesthetised Beck, and relieved the tensions which Will suffered, and even their dreams were pleasant—although neither he nor she remembered much of them the following morning.

Chapter Nine

'Didn't bed her, did you, sir? For all that the pantry boy was s'posed to have won his bet.'

'Damn you, Gib, as I warned you at Honyngham, it's no affair of yours what my wife and I do.'

'Told your Pa I'd look after you just afore he died, din't I? Don't like to see you making a fool of yourself, sir, with that cold piece. My duty to your Pa to tell you so.'

'And damn you again, Gib, for putting your duty to a man who squandered a fortune, and left me and mine up the River Tick, before your duty to me. I'll thank you to be silent.'

They were back in London in Beck's mansion, the so-called honeymoon over and, for once, Will was being harsh with his servant. That Gib was right in what he said was one more irritant to a man who was beginning to regret the unequal bargain which he had made, whatever he was gaining by it.

Gib opened his mouth to say more, but was silenced by Will taking him by the shoulders and pushing him out of his bedroom. 'Not another word, Gib, or I shall lose my temper.'

'Niver knew as 'ow you'd got one 'til you married 'er,' grumbled Gib below his breath, safer so.

Oh, the rest of the servants might think that, at last, all was well between Mr and Mrs Shafto, but Gib knew that it wasn't. That haughty piece wasn't doing right by Master Will, that she wasn't, and if he didn't tell him so, who would?

Home truths from Gib were no new thing for Will. He had gone to sleep that night at Honyngham hoping that, come morning, there might be no need to trick anyone again, particularly his sharp-eyed servant.

Alas, he had awoken to find that Beck had risen from her bed and was sitting in an armchair facing him, in the armour of her dressing-gown and a frozen face. He had sighed and, sitting up, tried to coax her back into the better humour of the previous night by saying, 'Come back to bed, Beck. More comfortable than an armchair, I do assure you.'

She had shaken her head at him. 'No, Will. We only shared a bed last night to prevent gossip. The deed being done, we can go on as we were before.'

'You see no need to change your mind, then?'

Will looked so appealing, sitting there, his curls in a tangle, so strongly resembling a large choirboy in his white shirt with its frilly collar that Beck thought that one might almost expect him to begin singing a hymn— if it were not for that certain look in his eye.

Oh, how tempting that look was! How Beck resisted it she never knew. She told herself sternly to remember that he was her rogue, nothing more, there to do her bidding, and her bidding had not changed from the day she had first met him. Her face, as well as her voice, told him so.

Will knew when he was beaten. He would live to fight

another day—or night, and so he had reluctantly come to some sort of accommodation with Beck which allowed them to present to the world a façade of married love.

At least at Honyngham they had been on their own, and if there had been no excitement in their long days, then neither had there been any need to deceive an audience, but returning to London and its distractions had again altered the unsteady balance between them.

Gib's forthrightness that morning had upset Will more than he would have thought possible. Trying to wriggle himself into his fashionably tight breeches and jacket without his valet's assistance didn't help his temper overmuch, nor did the knowledge that he faced an afternoon visiting Beck's friends and relations.

After that he—and Beck—faced another ordeal for they were to spend the evening at Durness House where they would both be on show. Not a happy thought, given the Duke's propensity to generate a near riot either in his home or out of it.

No one, however, could have guessed at the contrary passions which were assailing both the Shaftos by looking at them as they ascended the stairs at Durness House off Piccadilly.

'Whatever else,' exclaimed Emily Cowper, to her lover, Henry Temple, Lord Palmerston, 'they make a handsome pair. Why did she marry him, though?'

'Probably for that very reason,' he drawled. His own nickname was Cupid, and he knew all the stratagems of the game of love.

He frowned as Will and Beck walked by them. 'Something wrong there,' he opined. 'God knows what. If it's scandalous we shall soon know.'

'D'you think so?' Emily Cowper turned to follow Will and Beck with avid eyes. 'Heard something, have you?'

'No,' he returned. 'Sense it, somehow. Tell you what, she's the odder one, not him. He's from a good family, they say, but no money. Perhaps that's what she wanted in exchange for her pile of tin.'

This shrewd remark set Emily laughing, until an old friend greeted her and the Shaftos were temporarily forgotten in an exchange of even livelier *on dits* about the affairs of the notorious Lord Byron who was also present. The Duke had naturally made sure that society's most scandalous member was present to give his guests something to talk about.

'And,' as Emily remarked cattily to Lady Jersey, 'I suppose we ought to be grateful that Lord Byron is spending his days this year in chasing women, rather than making revolutionary speeches in the House of Lords on behalf of the Luddites. It's bad enough that we are fighting the result of that kind of sentimentality in Europe without risking it here.'

'Really,' returned Sally Jersey vaguely, 'but pray enlighten me, who are the Luddites?'

Emily rolled her pretty eyes to heaven and informed Sally that they were handloom weavers who had lost their living because the Midlands manufacturers had introduced more efficient machines which needed less men to work them. Many of them lived on Lord Byron's estates near Newstead in Nottinghamshire. Sally was yawning before she had finished.

'Oh, that!' she said inelegantly. 'Why waste time on that? Tell me, is the extremely handsome man with Beck Rowallan the fortune-hunter she has just married? If so, I can quite understand why she did!' She raised an eyeglass to inspect him more closely.

'I shall ask Durness to introduce him to me at once,' and off she went to bully her host who, nothing loath, did just as she asked.

Will and Beck were both well aware of the gossip which they excited. Fortunately the Duke's patronage prevented it from becoming too malicious. He shook Will by the hand ostentatiously and gave Beck a smacking kiss. It always had to be remembered that he had learned his manners in the rougher days of the eighteenth century.

After that he peered at them through a magnifying glass at the end of a long silver chain to examine them more critically. 'Peaky,' he said to Beck. 'You look peaky, don't she, Peter? Married life being too much for you, hey?'

He punctuated this outrageous remark by giving Will a hard shove in the ribs. Aunt Petronella, who was acting as his hostess, thus addressed, announced forcefully, 'Really, Durness, you must remember that this is 1813, not 1778. That was not at all the thing to say.'

'No?' he queried. 'Just wanted to remind young Shafto here not to overdo things. No harm in that, surely?'

Will was amused to notice that his usually composed wife had flushed scarlet, and that those waiting their turn to be received by the Duke were tittering behind their hands.

On the whole, given their situation, the Duke was doing him and Beck a kindness in spreading the notion that they were so much in love that they couldn't keep their hands off one another.

'I shall take heed of your advice, Duke,' he said solemnly, 'and see that Mrs Shafto gets plenty of rest.'

'But not in bed, eh?' cackled the Duke, shoving Will

in the ribs again, and causing Aunt Petronella to close
her eyes in horror. 'But more of that later. There's a lot
of fools waiting behind you that I have to waste my time
doing the pretty to. Where in the world did you find
them all, Peter? Never mind, must do my duty, I suppose. Honour of a Durness and all that. Mind you take
notice of what I say, young Shafto.'

It was their *congé*. Will took his wife by the arm and
led her away, followed by amused eyes. 'Splendid,' he
whispered to Beck, 'absolutely splendid. If I'd paid him
to say all that about us, he couldn't have done better.'

'Really, Will,' Beck whispered back, agitated for
once. 'How can you talk so? He's made a raree show of
us for the rest of the evening.'

'Precisely. We need do or say nothing ourselves from
now on. The Duke has pronounced. He has told the
world that I am a satyr and you are my helpless nymph.'

He put his head on one side to examine her. 'By the
way, Beck, he has the right of it. You do look a bit
peaky. Why is that, d'you think? Is there something
lacking in your life which I could perhaps supply—thus
adding a little veracity to the Duke's despatch to the
nation about our marriage?'

How did Will manage to tickle the sense of humour
which Beck possessed but which she had spent so many
years suppressing? For, despite all her splendid resolu-
tions not to allow him to affect or influence her in any
way, Beck found herself laughing.

This was happening too often. She was about to tell
him so, sternly, when, unfortunately she looked squarely
at him and caught his dancing eyes—which set her off
again into the helpless giggles which she thought she
had left behind with her schooldays.

'Do confess, Beck. Given everything, is it not the

most splendid joke? That we shall be considered by everyone to be the exact opposite of what we are! Smile, my love. Look at me adoringly. Yes, just like that. Now raise your fan and hide your blushing face whilst I try to lead us towards a cooling drink which will help us to damp down our unruly passions.'

The trouble with Beck, thought Will, is that she hasn't enjoyed herself properly for years. One day, I shall find out why, and perhaps that will help me to breach the wall of ice which she has built around herself.

In the meantime, the more often I make her laugh, the more likely she is to give way to the unruly passion in which the Duke thinks I am already indulging—and what a day that will be.

In lieu of that, he fed Beck lemonade and ices, and it was perhaps a pity that whilst he was doing so Sarah Wingfield came up to them and stared at Will with great melancholy eyes.

The spasm of annoyance which ran through Beck as Sarah said mournfully to Will, 'I trust that my husband's foolishness towards you will not be allowed to spoil my friendship with you—and Cousin Rebecca, of course,' owed everything to unacknowledged jealousy and nothing to sweet reason.

Unacknowledged, because she did not care enough for Will—did she?—to be jealous of those females who sought to make some claim on his time and his attention. Particularly when, like Sarah, they hung on his every word and fluttered their eyes and their fans at him in an unspoken invitation to him.

She pre-empted Will's reply by saying briskly, 'Of course not, cousin. It is not your fault that your husband is a mannerless boor. On the other hand, it is hardly wise of you to spend overmuch time with us in public. Better by far to pay us an afternoon visit when he is otherwise engaged.'

Sarah's agreement was rapid. 'Oh, indeed, cousin. I will remember that. It is kind of you both to show me so much consideration. I bid you adieu.' She walked away before her husband could arrive to vent his displeasure on seeing her with the Shaftos.

'That was kind of you, Beck,' Will said, watching Sarah walk away from them. He was remembering the earlier occasion when Sarah had felt the edge of Beck's tongue.

'She looks so ill,' said Beck simply. 'I used to be jealous of her, she took life so lightly, but no longer. How could they marry her to that old roué?'

Instead of you was the unspoken end of her last sentence.

Will pondered a moment on Time's whirligig. One moment he had been down and Sarah had been up, but now the positions were reversed. No time to think of that, though. Beck must have her reward for taking pity on her cousin, so he suggested that she join him on the floor in the waltz.

Their appearance there gave the Duke another opportunity to crow at Aunt Petronella. 'Look at the lovebirds, Peter, and don't you try to tell me that Beck feels nothing for him. Just look at the face on her.'

Aunt Petronella, who had been worrying that her niece did not truly display what the poet called 'the lineaments of satisfied desire', was compelled to agree with him. Will was swinging his wife around the room with her eyes closed and her mouth smiling, so perhaps Beck was not so cold, after all.

Something which Beck was ruefully conceding herself. One of these days she was going to find herself giving way to Will—and what would that lead to? The kind of grief and shame which she had suffered once before when she had allowed her heart to rule her head.

Nevertheless it was pleasant to be in his arms while the music played and, later to know that she was being escorted by the room's most handsome man. Although, of course, the admirers of Lord Byron, who had leaned against the wall whilst the waltz was being danced, disapproving of it mightily—for the very reasons that Will was enjoying it—would have disputed that.

For Will it was becoming sweet torture to hold Beck in the dance and to know that that was all that was allowed to him. That later that night—or rather in the early morning—they would part outside her bedroom door to spend yet another night in their lonely beds…

'I've been thinking, Will.'

Beck had just walked into the study off the library where Will sat at a large desk writing a letter. He stopped when she came in, and had she not been so intent on what she had to say to him she would have noticed that he unobtrusively turned his writing paper over before rising to greet her.

He decided not to tell her that she thought too much. Instead he smiled and asked pleasantly, 'What is it, my dear?'

'Do you wish to stay in London much longer? The Season will shortly be ending, but I do not think that I wish to be in at its death. Something you once said leads me to believe that you prefer life in the country to the town. If so, why should we not go north to Inglebury next week? You do have some country clothes, but if not, then you could be outfitted suitably when we reach Yorkshire. The best cloth is made there, I'm told.'

Will carried out some quick calculations in his head. Yes, he probably had enough of his allowance left to be able to make himself as splendid as Beck's husband ought to be. She had already asked him why he had not used it to buy himself a curricle and pair, and he had been suitably evasive. He could scarcely tell her the truth about how he spent the majority of his allowance.

'To your ancestral home?' he queried.

He had not meant to mock her, but Beck perhaps thought that he had, for she replied quickly, 'Hardly ancestral! My grandfather, a successful millowner, who brought his only son up to be a gentleman, acquired it cheaply from a failed landowner. Does that qualify as ancestral?'

Will thought a moment. He had not realised that Beck felt defensive about her origins. He said, to amuse as much as to support her, 'My ancestral home was built by a freebooting pirate in the reign of Good Queen Bess. I'm not sure whether, in the great sum of things, that makes him better or worse than your grandfather. On the other hand, my own father threw away everything which came down to him from those times, except the house itself and a few acres around it.'

It was the first time that he had told Beck much about his origins. He wondered why he had done so and regretted it a little: the less she knew of him the better, given their temporary situation.

She said, and he thought that she meant it, 'We ought to visit it one day, perhaps.'

'Before we part?' he reminded her. 'It would take a fortune to restore it. I think not.' There were reasons why he did not want her there.

She made no answer other than, 'Then we are agreed.

We leave shortly—as soon as we have settled our affairs here.'

Will nodded.

Beck paused a moment, as if to say something more, decided not to, and giving him one of her rare smiles, left him to finish his letter.

To do what? To go where?

The semi-detached life they were living meant that they went their own ways—except when they going out into society. Will decided that when he had finished his letter he would take himself off to Jackson's and vent his frustration there on whoever was in attendance that day.

The Tiger, his friend, was absent: the Tooting Terror was present instead. His face, raddled with the effects of heavy drinking, lit up when he saw Will.

'Come for a mill?' he asked. He would dearly like to have the fine gentleman before him in the ring, stripped to the waist, without his gloves, and without having to show him the deference which Jackson expected of his employees. That would be a turn-up for the coddled beau who thought he knew what being a prizefighter meant. The Tiger was too gentle with him.

For his part, Will knew and resented the Terror's attitude to him, which was very different from that of the Tottenham Tiger. He was adept at reading the true feelings of the men and women around him, and the Terror's annoyance with him oozed from his every pore.

'Yes,' Will said. Marking the Terror's face might make up for the frustrations of his daily life. This was unfair of him, he knew, but he was also shrewd enough to be aware that he thought this way because of the Terror's barely hidden opinion of him.

'Fight with your shirt off?' asked the Terror. Now this was against the rules, but Jackson was absent at the Races that day and what the eye doesn't see the heart doesn't grieve, was always the Terror's motto.

'Why not?' Will shrugged.

'And bare knuckles, no gloves?'

'Why not?' said Will again, suddenly recklessness itself.

'Fight to the first knock down, eh—as though there was money in it?'

'Have you lost your mind, Shafto?' hissed Gilly Thornton who was one of the watchers, as Will agreed to this also. 'He'll kill you.'

'He can try,' Will shot back pulling his shirt over his head to reveal a heavily muscled torso which even had the Terror blinking a little.

The bout which followed was long and bloody. Will thought afterwards that he must have been mad to agree to it for his hands, without the gloves, were soon red raw, the knuckles damaged.

Harry Fitzalan, who had arrived just after it began, stood open-mouthed when he entered at the sight of Will mixing it, bare-knuckled, in the ring with the Terror.

'What the devil's going on?' he asked, and, 'Who's Will's second?'

'Only fighting to the first knock down so he don't need one,' answered Gilly, who had earlier queried Will's sanity, but now was more than a little awed that Will was still standing.

The Terror, Will soon discovered, was by no means the Tiger's equal, but he was a professional, up to every trick of the trade, and at first Will found that even to stay on his feet was almost too much for him. But the longer the bout lasted the more the Terror began to puff and blow, whilst Will, on the contrary, was in prime condition.

Thus at its beginning the Terror often had Will on the ropes, but the longer it lasted the more the balance of the fight began to change—until suddenly Will saw an opening.

He took it, to send the Terror crashing like a lightning-struck tree to the ground—and not before time, for his torso was showing the marks of the Terror's fists, and his knuckles were cut as the consequence of the blows he had been landing on the Terror.

'Mill over,' roared Harry, diving into the ring to throw a towel around Will's bruised and sweating shoulders. 'What the devil did you think you were up to, Will?'

'He annoyed me,' retorted Will inadequately, wondering like Harry what had got into him. He had little time for further thought, for suddenly Jackson himself—back early from the Races—was in the gym, his face like thunder. He had not seen the end of the bout, which had broken all the rules he had made for his patrons' safety, and he immediately assumed from the state of Will's face and body that he had been the loser.

'That's it,' he shouted furiously at the Terror. 'You know better than that, man. You'll not work for me again. You know perfectly well that you have to treat my gentlemen with respect, not maul them and knock them down.'

'No,' said Harry urgently. 'Will won the mill, not the Terror.'

Jackson stared at him. 'What? Never say so! I knew you were useful, Mr Shafto, but not as useful as that. But no matter. Rules are rules.'

This time it was Will who shouted 'No.' He could see the Terror's agonised face at the prospect of losing his means of making a living. 'It was my fault. I provoked him. You mustn't turn him away. He couldn't refuse a gentleman.'

Gilly Thornton, who had watched what had happened from the start, would have protested that this was untrue, but caught Will's fierce eye on him, and said nothing.

Jackson looked keenly at both men. At the Terror, bested by an amateur. At Will, who had shown more raw pluck than he would ever have expected of him.

'That's the truth?'

Both men nodded. Jackson knew that they were lying. He hesitated for a moment, then said shortly to the Terror, 'So be it. But if you ever do that again, man, I'll have you out in the street in five minutes. And you, Mr Shafto, you ought to know better.'

Will gave a painful cracked smile of pure delight. 'So I ought. As a cure for the blue devils, it might seem a bit extreme—but it worked.'

He walked over to where his coat lay and fetched a guinea from his pocket and handed it to the Terror.

'That's for the damage I did to your pride, not your body,' he said. 'We should never have agreed to do what we did, but men are men the world over, whatever their rank, as Mr Jackson well knows.'

The only thing which worried him was what Beck would say when she saw his bruised face and his damaged knuckles.

He needn't have troubled himself. She gave a wry smile when she met him in the entrance hall, catching him as he was trying to sneak upstairs in order to repair a little of the damage.

'There is an old saying,' she remarked sweetly as he gave her her wry smile back. '"Boys will be boys", so

I ought not to be surprised that men will be men. And I won't ask what you have been getting up to. I might not like the answer.'

'I took on the Tooting Terror, bare-knuckled.' Will had rapidly decided that with Beck honesty was usually the best policy.

Her eyebrows rose. 'Did you, indeed? Was that wise? He seems to have had a burning desire to rearrange your features.'

Will's smile was sardonic. 'So he did. Unfortunately, it was his features which came off second-best.'

There was something in his voice which Beck did not like. 'Why, Will, whatever possessed you? I shall never understand why men feel the need to fight and struggle with one another. He might have done you a serious hurt.'

'Well, he didn't.' Will was brusque. 'And now, if you will allow, I should like to go to my room to repair what damage he did do to me.'

It was the first time he had been brutally short with her. A mixture of sexual frustration and the punishment which the Terror's fists had inflicted on him, were taking a heavy toll.

Beck made a move in his direction as he walked by her...and then withdrew. She wanted to comfort him, for she sensed by his posture that he was in pain and needed comforting, but the habit of a lifetime was too strong.

Had she not retreated, had she followed her deepest, truest feelings, everything between them might have changed immediately and completely, for Will, as well as she, was vulnerable that night.

But, alas, the moment was lost. Before she could make another move he was up the stairs and walking to his room, calling for Gib—who was to add his reproaches to Beck's as he tried to relieve his master's aches and pains.

Nothing, though, could relieve Will's aching heart—or Beck's.

Chapter Ten

'Going home, are you?' commented Aunt Petronella. 'I would have thought you might see the Season out.'

'We decided against it.'

'You mean that *you* did,' replied Aunt Petronella bluntly. 'Durness will have it that you're a pair of love-birds, but I know better. He's a good young man, Rebecca. Why did you marry him if you were only going to torment him?'

Beck rose and walked to the window. 'I don't understand you, Aunt.'

'And *I* don't understand *you*, Rebecca Shafto. I thought at Durness's ball that you and he had come to an understanding. But I'm certain that you haven't, even though he puts a brave face on things. Your face is as cold as it ever was—which also tells a story.'

The old lady was too shrewd for her own, or anyone else's, good. A home truth about Will might silence her.

'Suppose I told you that he married me for my money?'

Her aunt snorted. 'Well, of course he did. He wasn't in a position to marry you if you hadn't any. It doesn't prevent him from loving you—and that's a bonus I am beginning to believe that you don't deserve.'

'And if I told you that he frequents Jackson's gym more than I consider wise?'

'Well, that's natural. Working off his frustrations, I suppose. In any case, you surely cannot wish that you had married a namby-pamby. Unless, of course, you wanted to run him ragged—as you have done everyone else connected with you.'

Beck closed her eyes. She opened them again to think that she and her aunt were birds of a feather. Birds who spoke their own mind and to the devil with everyone else.

'You forget that I was run ragged first,' she returned quietly, staring out of the window to see Will riding up the drive, Gib behind him in the undistinguished livery which was all that he would consent to wear.

'No, I haven't. But you can't live in the past forever. Let it go, Rebecca, before you allow it to destroy you—and him. I was a fool to let Durness slip away from me all those years ago. Don't you do the same.'

Will was dismounting, exchanging a joke with Gib and the groom who had come running up to lead his horse away. He had recovered some of his old jauntiness during the week which had followed the fight. Beck wished that she could feel jaunty. Perhaps if they went north together, away from the distractions of the town, they might come to know one another better.

She told her aunt so. Her aunt's reply was as brisk as ever. 'Only if you learn to value him—as I think that he values you. The more fool he.'

She stopped as Will entered. He bowed to Aunt Petronella, who rose and crossed the room to kiss him on the cheek as he did so.

Startled, he put up a hand to stroke the spot she had honoured. 'Goodness, Aunt, whatever would the Duke say if he knew that you were making love to me.'

'That it was time that someone did, I suppose,' was her dry answer. 'Do you really wish to go north with Rebecca in the middle of the Season?'

Will glanced over to his wife, who had resumed staring out of the window. So, Aunt Petronella was at outs with her, and by her first remark might be understanding far too much. Friendly Beck had changed to harsh Rebecca.

'If that is what she wishes and will make her happy, yes.'

Aunt Petronella sighed and was dry again. 'That will have to do, I suppose. Come and say goodbye to me before you leave—if you have time.'

'We go in a week,' Will said, for Beck remained silent, 'but we shall honour your request.'

'Good—and now I must leave you. The love-birds, as Durness insists on calling you, will want to be alone.'

'Now, what,' asked Will when she had gone, 'did your aunt mean by saying that in such a disbelieving fashion?'

'She knows,' replied Beck wearily, 'or has guessed, how matters truly stand between us, and she is reproaching me, not you, and is right to do so. But never fear. She will not talk.'

'Well, that's a relief.' Will was frank. He had decided not to oppose Beck over visiting her home, even if it did mean that he would lose Gib.

On being told that they were to travel to Inglebury in the near future, Gib had announced hardily, 'Well, that's that, then. I'll leave you to her. My brother-in-law has offered me a job as a man of all work whilst he looks after his thriving butcher's shop in Islington. I'll not go north again unless it's to Shafto Hall.'

'You'd leave me, Gib, would you? I need you—you're my last link to the old days.'

'No, you don't, Master Will. You've to make your own way now, and hanging on to me ain't helping you to do it. Oh, you've had a hard time, and getting your missis to see sense might be even harder—but you have to try.'

Nothing Will could say would move him. So, one of the servants in the second coach which would go north—the first holding Will and Beck—would be the young man, John Carter, whom Gib had already secretly trained to succeed him.

Beck, who rarely complained, was complaining. Her voice as she did so was as stoically calm as ever. 'I grow weary of this everlasting rain, and although I am not frightened of thunder, I cannot say that I like it.'

Even as she spoke a flash of lightning, followed by a crackling roll of thunder, lit up their carriage: the afternoon had grown nearly as dark as night.

Will leaned forward to offer comfort if it were necessary, but, as ever, Beck stared calmly at him. Only a slight quiver of the lips showed him that she was more disturbed by the storm raging overhead than she would ever admit. It seemed to have been with them ever since they had left London.

As though the weather had become their enemy, it had been raining hard and blowing a gale when Mr and Mrs Shafto had finally set off for Inglebury. Any hope that matters might improve as they left the supposedly warm south was dispelled by every cruel mile they travelled.

In good weather Will would have enjoyed seeing a

part of England which he had never previously visited, but heavy rain and unseasonable gales continued to make the journey miserable. It was as though the very heavens were weeping on their behalf.

Afterwards Will was to remember thinking that on this journey their marriage had almost reached breaking point; a belief reinforced by Beck's coldness towards him both in the coach and at every inn at which they stopped.

Beck was thinking the same thing. Her coldness was actually a form of defence, for she was fearful that if she once showed any sign of her growing affection for Will, she would be lost. She dare not call it love—for Beck Shafto could not love, could she?

They were making for Inglebury by way of Leicester and Nottingham before taking a post road north not far from Mansfield and Newstead Abbey, Lord Byron's home. Beck had taken this route many times before and preferred it to the Great North Road, which meant that she had to travel across country to her home by poor byways after Newark had been reached in order to avoid going out of her way through Lincoln.

When they reached Nottingham, Will had needed to find a coachman to replace their own who had fallen ill. His replacement was a surly, shabby fellow, one Job Cooper, but since he was the only man available he would have to do.

'After all,' Will had said to Beck when at last they set off again, having spent two nights in the city, not one, 'we are hardly likely to wish to converse with him overmuch, so his lack of manners is no great matter.'

'Nor his unwashed appearance,' added Beck, thinking of her own steady, well-mannered John in his spotless livery whom they had perforce left behind to follow them to Inglebury once he had recovered.

This latest storm, which had driven even Beck to voice her unhappiness, had begun to rage when the road took them through Sherwood Forest. Beck had told Will that, whilst it was not as good as the Great North Road, this stretch of it was better than most that they would travel over before they reached Inglebury. He was not finding it so.

'Might it not be wise to stop at The Hutt?' Will suggested as they jolted over yet another rut. The Hutt was a well-known hostelry on the Mansfield Road which the innkeeper had recommended to them if the weather became so bad that they felt that they could not go on.

Beck shook her head. 'The sooner that we are home the better. The storms cannot last much longer, I hope.'

'Nor will the coach if this goes on,' muttered Will. The road had become so bad that the coach had more than once been on the point of overturning. 'I thought that you said that this was a good road, Beck. It doesn't seem so. This is the roughest ride I have ever had.'

'It was in good condition when I came south in the spring,' Beck returned. She leaned forward to look out of the window—to discover that the darkness was not only due to the storm. They were travelling through a dense part of the forest which she had never seen before, on a road which was merely a track, and covered in ruts and great pools of water...

She turned a pale face on Will. 'We are not on the right road at all. We are on something not much better than a track to a farm! Somehow we have taken a wrong turning. We must tell the coachman so.'

Will swore beneath his breath, pulled down the window, and tried to shout to the coachman to tell him that they were on the wrong road and by some means should turn back. His efforts to make himself heard were made difficult by the noise of the rain, the frequent rolls of thunder, and the gusts of wind which carried his words away.

Either the coachman could not hear him, or more likely chose not to, for he continued driving down what was plainly an increasingly dangerous path.

Cursing again, Will looked back down the way they had come—to see no sign of their companion coach. Either it had broken down, or it had taken the right turn whilst theirs had taken the wrong one.

Neither supposition was attractive!

Will, his head and shoulders drenched, pulled himself back into the coach. He thought Beck was brave enough to hear the unpalatable truth.

'I believe that our coachman can hear me, but he chooses not to answer. I am sure that you are right and that we have lost our way. Our second carriage is not with us.'

He saw Beck's face pale. She said, still steady, 'Is there nothing that we can do?'

Will shook his head. 'Not until he chooses to stop. What troubles me is his refusal to answer. Neither of us liked the look of the fellow, but the landlord swore that he knew the route to Mansfield and from thence to Inglebury.'

'Perhaps he has lost his way in the rain,' Beck offered bravely.

Before Will could answer her the coach gave a lurch even more dangerous than before. So dangerous that it fell off the track altogether, to lodge slowly against one of the giant trees which bordered it.

Beck and Will slid sideways on to the floor. Beck

landed on top of him. Will held her gently for a moment
before he released her. He could feel her trembling.

'What now?' she asked him, still in the same cold
steady voice.

Even from Beck, Will had expected hysterics, reproaches, or tears. He had never admired her more. He
was not given long to do so for the door was wrenched
open by their driver.

'Out wi' the pair on you,' he shouted at them.

'What, in this rain?' Will said, staring at the pitiless
face the other offered them.

'Won't hurt you. We 'ave to stand it often enough.
Do as you're bid, and you'll not come to harm.'

To reinforce what he was saying he was waving a
blunderbuss at them.

'What is it?' asked Beck. She was behind Will and
could not see that the coachman was armed. 'He cannot
really mean us to get out into the rain, dressed as we
are.' She was wearing a light muslin dress, a cashmere
shawl, for the day was cold, and white kid slippers.

'Oh, but I do!' shouted the coachman, grinning evilly.
Seizing Will by the shoulder he pulled him out, and then,
whilst Will was gaining his balance, he leaned forward
to perform the same office for Beck.

Once they were both out in the open and shivering in
the pouring rain, they became aware that the coachman
was not alone. He had brought them to a clearing in the
forest. Facing them, standing in front of some rude huts
and hovels was a silent band of ragged men, women and
children. The men and boys were armed, either with
iron-tipped staves or large hammers, or with ancient
muskets which still looked lethal.

'Wh-wh-what?' stammered Beck, clutching at Will's
hand, not sure which she liked least: that she was rapidly

being soaked to the skin, or that she and Will were the target of the malevolent glares of the tattered crowd before them.

It was as though time had suddenly stopped and she and Will were the centrepiece of a ghastly tableau—a sensation which Will was also sharing.

And then it was over. Time started again. Their coachman shouted at the watching crowd, 'It's yours, my pretties. All yours. The coach alone will keep you in firewood for weeks, and there's money and clothes for you to share among you.'

In a second Beck and Will were engulfed by a crowd of screaming men and women who flung them aside to get at the treasures before them. Beck was hurled into the mud, but not before a skeletal woman had pulled the shawl from her shoulders.

Will, better able to protect himself, helped her to her feet as the looting of their coach began. Beck, her face a distorted mask of fear and cold combined, suddenly remembered the footman who had ridden behind them.

'Giles,' she cried at the coachman who had stayed behind to see that they did not run off, although where they could have run to was difficult to imagine. 'Giles, what have you done with Giles?'

'A knock on the head at the last stop disposed of him. We drove on without him. And now, behave yourselves. Don't try to run away. You're deep in Sherwood, and every man and woman's prey.'

His speech, Will noted, was more educated than that of the ragged looters. A large woman, stronger than the rest, had found the trunks holding their clothes in the boot at the back of the coach. She had lugged them on to the muddy ground and was throwing bonnets, petticoats, elegant Paris gowns, shawls and light kid shoes to the women around her.

One of the men had forced open Will's trunk and was holding up his fine shirts for admiration. To Will's surprise it was not a free-for-all: impromptu leaders were busy sharing out the finery so that no one was left without something.

One haggard woman, wearing Beck's best bonnet above her grimy rags, ran up to shake her fist at them and screamed something incomprehensible in a broad Nottinghamshire dialect at Beck and Will before she hurried back lest she lose her share of the loot.

Will's pistol and his fowling piece were swiftly discovered—but there was no sharing there. The coachman, who seemed to be their leader, was presented with them.

The coach was stripped of everything: even the cushions were thrown out to be carried triumphantly away by running boys. The numerous leather straps, both inside and outside the coach, were cut free and handed out. The coach doors were ripped from their hinges and two men ran with them through the trees towards distant hovels, barely visible in the pouring rain.

The brass lamps were carefully removed and placed in a large sack. Will was later told that they were taken off to be sold at Mansfield market. One blessing was that the cases containing Beck's jewellery were in the other coach under Mrs Grey's care. It had presumably fallen behind them, taken the right road, and no one would be aware that they had disappeared until Mansfield was reached.

'Watch, my beauties,' gloated the coachman, 'and see how the things which you take for granted are treasured by those who go without them.'

Neither Will nor Beck could speak—Beck because

fear had her in its grip, and Will because he did not deem it politic. Besides, he was too busy wondering desperately if there was anything which he could do to save them from the dangerous predicament in which they found themselves.

He felt Beck tug at his sleeve when the coachman's attention was drawn away from them. He was busy organising a party of men armed with hatchets who were arguing about how best to cut up the carcass of the coach for firewood. Its wheels had already been removed, and were being stripped by a brawny man with the muscles and appearance of a blacksmith.

'Will,' she whispered, 'who are these men and women? I had no notion that such wretched creatures existed in England.'

'They are,' he told her, 'framebreakers, that is hand-loom weavers who have lost the means of making a living because the new machines have made the ones they own out of date. The manufacturers can make more money by installing the new ones—thus putting them out of work. They are known as Luddites when they band together to smash the new machines and attack the manufacturers who have robbed them of their livelihood.'

Beck, like Sally Jersey at the Duke of Durness's reception, was about to ask him why they were called Luddites and why they were living in the forest when the coachman, having settled the dispute over the destruction of the coach, returned and overheard them.

'You can stop mumbling between yourselves. I'll not have you plotting and planning.'

To Will's horror, Beck, who had begun to accept her plight, was now ready to argue with her captor in her usual brisk fashion. 'We are not fools. We weren't plotting and planning anything, or trying to run away—a more stupid suggestion I have never heard. I asked my husband if he knew who you are and why you have attacked and robbed us. He said you were Luddites.'

Will's relief was great when their captor, instead of rebuking Beck, appeared on the contrary to admire her spirit.

She was wet to the skin, her hair had come loose and water was dripping from it on to her shoulders. She was standing ankle-deep in mud, had watched her clothes and other possessions shared out among a pack of women whom she must regard as harpies and was still able to stare haughtily at him.

'Why, missis, you're a pluck'd 'un, so you are. Well, time will tell if you'll still be as proud-stomached when you've lived among us for a few days while we decide what to do with you.' He gave an odd laugh. 'Captain Ned Ludd's our leader, missis—or so some say.'

Beck could not be the only one showing gallantry. Will said in his most winning manner, 'Once this rain stops you could take us back to where the forest track began and set us on the way to Mansfield. Someone would be sure to see us and offer us assistance.'

The coachman thrust his face into Will's. 'D'ye take me for a fool, Mester Whativer-your-name-is? And then you'd go to the authorities, so you would, and lead them here.'

'I could promise not to.' Will was still trying to use his charm on the monster before him.

'And what would your promise be worth, mester? Word of a gentleman, you would say, but I'm not a gentleman, so most like you wouldn't keep your word to me. No, here you stay, until our man comes from Nottingham to advise us on what to do wi' you.'

One of the brawnier man carrying a large hatchet on his shoulder came up to them, saying to the coachman, 'I vote to cut their throats straightway. Dead men don't talk, Job.'

'Aye and those who make them dead most often hang, Jem.'

'I'll take that risk, Job.'

'It's not just you taking that risk, it's all on us what would suffer. No, wait until Mester Henson comes. 'Twas him what gave me the wink about the coach. The lady here is passing rich, he said.'

'Then 'ow about demanding a ransom for 'em?' Jem was eager to make the most of their captives. He surveyed the ruin of Beck's clothes and appearance, and said doubtfully, 'She don't look rich to me.'

'Use your noddle, Jem. We'd niver get away wi' that. They'd have the sojers on us like lightning, so they would. No, best this way, Henson said, seein' as how they'll have disappeared mysterious-like, with none to guess where they are, so there'll be none to track us down.'

'They'll blame Ned Ludd most like—and they'll be right,' sniggered Jem, before walking away to join a bedraggled woman and two dirty children who were loaded down with loot.

Beck had begun to shiver uncontrollably from a combination of the cold, the rain and the shock of their capture. Will, forgetting all prudence, said impatiently, 'How long are you going to keep us standing in the pouring rain before you allow us to shelter? My wife is not dressed for this weather. She is shaking with cold and has not eaten since breakfast. Common humanity should make you show a little pity for her.'

'Oh, aye,' retorted Job. 'A little rain won't harm her—

and as for missing her food, why, that means she'll be the same as all the women and bairns here. We live on short commons and no mistake.

'But not tomorrow—tomorrow we go to Mansfield market with the guineas from your coach and buy us enough for a feast day. 'Twon't hurt your missis to go without today—and perhaps tomorrow. Cool her temper down most like.'

Before Will could stop her Beck burst out with, 'Oh, no, it won't cool my temper down. I'm sorry for your women and children, but it is not my fault that they are starving.'

'No?' Job raised his brows. 'Is that so, missis? Why, Mester Henson allows as how your grand-daddy began life as a millowner in Yorkshire. Tell me, how many men and women starved so that he might make his fortune?'

'None,' said Beck spiritedly. 'He was a merciful master. But even if he weren't, it is no reason for you to leave me standing in the rain.'

By the end of this forthright defence she could scarcely speak for shivering. Job stared at her in admiration and horror mixed. 'I'll say one thing for you, lass, you're not the mardy sort. Does she speak like this to you, mester?' he asked Will. 'If she did, and she were mine, I'd take a stick to her, so I would.'

'Would you now?' said Will solemnly. 'Best not tell her so!'

To Beck's indignation both men laughed together companionably, shaking their heads over the vagaries of women, their class differences temporarily forgotten.

But only temporarily.

Job shook his head at them both. ''Tis true that you're

passing wet. You can shelter in old Mother Cayless's hut for the time being.'

He looked around him. 'Bob,' he called to a man who was busy sawing the panels of their coach into pieces suitable for the fire, 'take them to Ma Cayless's. They can shelter there for the time being.'

Bob, still sawing, shouted back, 'She'll not be best pleased when she comes back from birthing Lizzie Orton's babby to find them cluttering up t'place.'

'Then she'll have to lump it, won't she?' Job roared at him.

With sad amusement Will noted that Job's democratic beliefs disappeared when it came to managing the affairs of the landless men and women of the forest. Like Beck he allowed his tongue to run away with him.

'You're not taking a vote on it, then?' he enquired politely as Bob led him and Beck towards the largest of the makeshift dwellings in the small clearing. 'Just issuing an order?'

Job glared suspiciously at him. 'Makin' fun of me, are you, mester?'

'Not at all.' Will was still reckless. 'I just wanted to see revolutionary radicalism in action. Jacobin beliefs have always interested me.'

He thought Job was about to strike him. Then his captor threw his head back and laughed.

'By Gow, Bob, we've snared a right pair here and no mistake! You're well matched with your shrew of a wife for all your mild looks, mester. I wish you joy of one another. Get a move on, Bob, I want to be out of the rain meself. And Bob, you can have the Mester's fine coat for your pains.'

Ma Cayless's hut consisted of one room and was dark and smelly. There was an empty primitive fireplace at one end, but no chimney. The smoke from the fire when it was lit could only find vent through a hole in the thatched roof. The floor was a dirt one on which a straw palliasse rested, with a battered trunk at its bottom which presumably held its owner's clothes.

Two stools, another small table and a wash-stand holding a cracked china bowl, a jug, and a candlestick were ranged along one wall. A bigger table on which stood some rough crockery and a knife, fork and spoon stood in the middle of the room and made up the tally of the room's furniture.

Daylight came in through the open door: there were no windows. It was apparent that anyone living in the hut carried on most of their business out of doors.

Will walked over to the table and picked up the knife. It was so blunt it would scarce cut butter, and would be of no use to a man and a woman seeking some sort of weapon to help them escape.

Beck sat herself down on one of the stools after looking around the room for some clean cloth with which to dry herself. In vain: a piece of ragged towelling was thrown down by the hearth next to a small pail holding coals and wood obviously cut from the surrounding trees. Alas, it was black with grime. Beck stared at it and shuddered.

Not only was the interior of the hut dark, but it was also cold. Will was relatively warmly dressed, even though he had lost his coat and was only in his shirt-sleeves. His breeches protected him, and he still had his boots so that he was by no means as wet as poor Beck in her thin muslin gown and her light kid slippers.

But he wasn't to keep his boots for long, nor Beck her slippers. He had scarcely had time to seat himself

on the stool by Beck before Job came in with a fresh
demand.

'Off wi' your shoes and boots, the both on you. You'll
not be able to run far wi'out 'em. Besides, I've a mind
for a good pair of boots and we're much of a size.'

Briefly Will considered suggesting that they fight one
another for them, but rejected the idea immediately. He
was in no position to bargain about anything, and he
must do nothing to make Beck's situation any more uncomfortable than it already was. He must protect her as
well as he could.

So it was goodbye to boots and slippers. Beck looked
ruefully at her feet in their torn stockings, and tried to
offer some consolation to Will.

'If we were to escape, it might be easier for us in the
mud without slippers or boots. On the other hand, since
we have no notion where we are, it would be difficult
to know exactly in which direction to go if we did manage to get away.'

Will stared at her, bemused. She never ceased to surprise him. When he had first met her he had thought of
her as a simple bully, but he might have known that
there was nothing simple about Beck. Her stiff-backed,
stiff-knecked attitude to life was sustaining her now. The
raw courage of her staggered him. She might be wrong
about how easy it was to walk without shoes, but at least
she had given the matter some thought.

'How do you propose that we escape, Beck?'

She shook her head, and said, 'I don't know. I shall
have to think about it. Do you have any useful suggestions to make, Will?'

'At the moment, no. To begin with, Job will have
undoubtedly put a guard outside the hut. All the men we
have seen so far are armed in one way or another. We

have, as you said, no idea where we are, other than that we are somewhere in Sherwood Forest, between Mansfield and Nottingham, perhaps not far from Newstead, Lord Byron's home. It is likely that these are not the only squatters in the Forest—even if the others aren't Luddites.'

Whilst he was speaking Beck had risen from her stool and walked to the door to peer out into the rain which had slacked a little. He heard her talking to someone—the guard, no doubt. He closed his eyes. Whatever would she do next? Her fearlessness, admirable though it might be, was dangerous given their situation.

He opened his eyes to find that she had returned. 'You were quite right, Will. There is a guard outside. I asked him where we were and he said hell. I told him that, all things considered, that was a good answer. He told me that I talked too much.'

'And so you do,' retorted the goaded Will. 'I don't think that you understand the danger we are in.'

She traded him glare for glare. 'Of course I do. But I refuse to sit down and wail about it. That would not benefit either of us. Tell me, when do you think that Mrs Grey and the others in the second coach will realise that we are missing?'

Will thought for a moment before answering. 'Not when they reach Mansfield, unfortunately. They will assume that they have fallen a long way behind us and that, arriving there early, we continued our journey to Chesterfield without changing our horses. When they find that we never reached Chesterfield they will probably think that we lost our way, and, to avoid the storm, stayed overnight somewhere else before making for Chesterfield.

'I'm afraid that it's highly likely that it will be midday

tomorrow before they grasp that we have disappeared. And even then they may carry on to Inglebury, believing that we have simply gone ahead of them at full speed.'

For the first time Beck's brave front shivered a little. 'Never say so, Will. But, of course, you are right.'

Will had been honest with her because he thought that she was courageous enough to be told the truth. He cursed himself a little, and then as she firmed her mouth, and blinked at him before resuming her stoic face, he knew that he had done the right thing.

'I'll think about possible escape, Beck, I promise you, but don't be too hopeful.'

'They hate us, don't they?' she said simply. 'Because we are rich. That is what frightens me. You called them Luddites. I had heard of framebreakers, and even of Luddites—but why that particular name?'

'They are supposed to have a secret leader named Captain Ned Ludd—but it's very likely that he's a myth like Robin Hood, who also roamed Sherwood as an outlaw in the reign of Richard I. They have settled in the Forest as squatters because they have lost their homes. Lord Byron made a speech about them in the House of Lords asking that they be helped, but we are in the middle of a major war and authority sees them as expensive nuisances.'

Not for the first time Will surprised Beck by the depth of his knowledge. He was also behaving as she would expect him to. If she had not moaned and wailed and complained, neither had he. Like her he was weighing up their options, and if they did not seem too hopeful he was not allowing that fact to daunt him over much.

'But they have little children,' she said sadly, 'and no money to feed them—which is why they robbed us. I pity them, Will. Do you find that odd of me? Of course,

I cannot condone what they have done to us, but I can understand why they did it. In their place I should do the same.'

And that was true Beck, and it was why he loved her. Here, in this miserable hovel, as she sat opposite to him, drenched, her delicate beauty extinguished, her spirit was as unextinguished as ever. Will fiercely asked God not to allow her to be treated after a fashion which would extinguish it forever.

'We must not do anything stupid,' he said at last, 'for that would be worse than doing nothing.' Something with which Beck wholeheartedly agreed. She told him so.

He came over to her and took her hands in his. 'That's my brave girl. You must not be too brave, too foolhardy. You understand me?'

Yes, she did, and told him so. Moved by everything which had happened to them and her stoic acceptance of it, Will took her in his arms to comfort her. For the first time Beck offered him no resistance. At last they stood heart to heart, breast to breast, as a man and wife should. Will stooped a little to join his lips to hers…

And then a harsh voice broke in on them.

'Ain't Job Cooper got owt better to do than use me 'ome as a prison for you, and make me share Janet Thurman's dirty hut?'

It was Ma Cayless, come to lament the loss of what was hers, and to reproach them for being the cause of her losing it.

Their improbable moment of rapport was broken. Improbable because neither of them could have foreseen that they might come together as captives held in a squalid hut deep in a dense forest far from everything that they knew and loved.

Chapter Eleven

'I never thought a hunk of black bread and cheese and a tin mug of water would taste so sweet,' Beck told Will, as she tore ravenously at the bread, forgetting her manners in her hunger.

'That's because we haven't eaten for nearly twelve hours,' said Will who was also enjoying his harsh fare, being more used to it.

They were sitting in the open doorway. The rain had stopped and a weak sun, almost on the point of setting, had come out. Their captors were enjoying a better meal. They had roasted joints of venison, cut from a deer which one of them had killed with his ancient musket. Several rabbits and some pigeons made up their bill of fare. They had not feasted so well for months.

The scent of their cooking was making Beck's mouth water. They had not been offered any of the meat, for as Job had said earlier, 'Do you both good to starve a bit—as we often have to.'

'You know that you could be hanged or transported for poaching the deer—and the rabbits,' Will had said quietly when Job had given them their short commons on one tin plate.

'What's that to us, mester, when we'd starve else? Sherwood Forest and its animals should belong to all on us, not just the lucky few. You be the thieves, not us.'

Will had no wish to debate political morality with their captors. He thought wryly that he had lived for many years on a knife edge where, if he made a mistake, he would descend into the underworld of poverty in which so many lived. Marriage to Beck had saved him from that, but the people around him had no such means of escape.

Shortly before their evening meal was ready to eat the men who had been sent to Mansfield to buy ale returned with several barrels of it. They broached it immediately and began to drink heavily. The clearing rang with their noise. Will took Beck by the hand and led her back into the hut, shutting the door on the saturnalia outside.

'Safer so,' he said. 'Pray God they leave us alone.'

Some of the more reckless, flown with drink, wished to have some fun with their captives, but Job had insisted that they should not be harmed or unduly harassed until Mester Henson came from Nottingham to advise on how they should be dealt with. After much grumbling they unwillingly gave in to his wishes.

Inside the hut Beck said sharply, 'I hope that they saved some of the money to buy food for the children and have not spent it all on drink.'

'For God's sake, don't tell them so,' ordered Will. 'We must try to placate them, not annoy them.'

He was so agitated that when he took her by the hand and said, 'Promise me, Beck, that in future you will say as little as possible,' she nodded her agreement.

'But it goes against the grain, Will,' she said earnestly, 'now that I have seen the poor children who have been living on short commons for so long.'

Her concern for the little ones showed Will another side of her. Because she was so astringent in speech and manner he had often wondered what sort of mother she would make, but he now knew that she would be a loving one.

When Ma Cayless had finally arrived to disturb them Beck had seen at once that the woman was tired after long attendance on a difficult birth and had made no sharp answer to her, but had, surprisingly, apologised for their presence in her home. Which, considering that they were only in her hut at all because they had been ordered there, Will thought was a bit rich.

He watched Beck busy herself about the squalid room. She wet her handkerchief and tried to clean herself a little. She made no open objection when she had to leave the hut to answer the call of nature in some nearby greenery, even though one of the sharp-faced women insisted on going with her lest she take the opportunity to try to run away.

When darkness fell she lit the one candle, and came to sit by him on the stool, saying gravely, 'I fear that we shall have to share the palliasse, Will, there is nothing for it.'

'Is that an invitation, Beck,' he asked her, 'and if so, to what?'

'To sleep,' she returned with all her normal austerity of speech. 'What else! I am tired to the bone, and I suspect that you are, too.'

'Yes,' he agreed gravely. He could scarcely tell her that, tired though he was, the sight of her as she quietly accepted her fate without complaint was rousing him more than she had ever done when she had been dressed in her finery and in command of all around her.

She was a woman in a thousand, and she was his wife.

Come what may, he would protect her, and she might, he feared, soon need his protection. Sheltered as she had been all her life, it had apparently not occurred to her that rape was a definite possibility—a possibility that did not bear thinking of.

More than one of the men had eyed her delicate beauty—still visible beneath her mistreatment—with lustful eyes.

They lay down at last on the bed of straw in the corner of the hut. Hunger and exhaustion claimed them both. Once, Will put out a hand to take Beck's as they lay side by side, and she hung on to it as though it were a lifeline.

Her small hand was cold in his warm one. After a little time he felt her begin to shiver uncontrollably. Will rose on his elbow, and asked, 'Beck, what is it? Are you ill?'

She was silent. He wondered if she had heard him. Presently she answered him in a whisper. 'Not ill, but I'm so cold. I can't seem to get warm. My dress is still damp, and my feet...' Her voice trailed off.

Love, lust and pity fought for dominance in Will. He moved towards her. 'Let me put my arms around you and try to warm you, Beck. I promise not to do anything untoward.'

He thought that she was going to say 'no' in her usual vigorous fashion, but suddenly she gave a little cry and turned in his direction so that he was able to draw her to him and hold her close. To his secret delight she lay on his chest as sweetly and confidingly as a little bird.

'Put your feet between my legs, Beck. Yes, like that. If that doesn't warm them, nothing will.'

He had made the offer although he believed that she might certainly refuse him, but she did not. Instead she did as he had bid her, and they lay entwined together like an old married couple.

She could have no notion of how her nearness, and her growing warmth, were beginning to affect him. He told his treacherous body to behave itself. Only a brute would force himself on her after the awful experiences of the day. But exhaustion claimed her and Will felt Beck's breathing alter as she slowly fell asleep. Her trust humbled him. He kissed her damp hair gently, and wondered whether sleep would come to him as easily as it had come to her.

Outside the noise of the impromptu celebration continued for a little longer, to be followed by the sound of owls hooting. Inside, Beck held close to him as though in the aftermath of love, Will at last fell asleep.

'Where am I?'

Beck had woken up to find herself being held in someone's arms.

Will! It was Will who had his arms around her as though he would never let her go. What in the world had happened last night?

Had he? Had she? Had they?

She asked herself Where am I? again because she was certainly not in any bed or bedroom she had ever been in before. Painful memory flooded back. She sat up and looked wildly around the ill-furnished hovel.

No, they had not...most definitely not. Her last memory was of Will holding her in his arms to warm her, and the comfort which that had given her. He had behaved like a perfect gentleman, exactly as she would have wished him to do.

So why did a tiny *frisson* of disappointment shoot through her?

Beck looked down at him, to find him still sleeping. In the semi-dark of the hut—for someone had opened the door a little, doubtless to check that they were still there and had not, by some magic, escaped—his sleeping face looked stern and strong. It resembled not at all Will's usual amiable and smiling mask. Which was the true man? Or was he, like most humans, composed of many parts, as Beck knew herself to be?

The dark stubble on his chin reminded her that Will usually shaved twice a day and had not been able to the night before. Without her willing it, her hand crept out to stroke his jaw, to feel there not smoothness, but strength. Even as her fingertips touched his face he gave a great sigh—and woke.

Like lightning his hand shot out to grasp hers fiercely. 'Who's that?' he muttered, sitting up and opening his eyes to find Beck's near to his own.

'Oh, it's you, Beck. I feared—I don't know what I feared. Did you sleep at all?'

Beck withdrew, claiming her hand back, wondering what mad impulse had led her to wish to caress him while he slept.

'Surprisingly I did. I suppose that I was tired.'

'Exhausted, rather.' Will rose, yawned and stretched. His fine shirt was rumpled and dirty; his buff-coloured breeches also bore the marks of rain and mud. Beck wondered ruefully what she looked like: she rapidly concluded that in the great sum of things it did not matter.

She rose herself. Her whole body ached after a night spent on an uncomfortable bed quite unlike any in which she had slept before. Like Will she stretched—which might be unladylike but made her feel better.

'I'm hungry,' she said. She could never remember having felt so hungry before.

'Not surprising,' said Will, 'since it's more than twenty-four hours since we last ate a decent meal. But it would be policy to starve us. Firstly because going without food would make us feel low, and secondly because we should be too weak to run away.'

'Run!' exclaimed Beck, walking to the door to find that the day was turning fine and that yesterday's rain seemed to have disappeared. 'At the moment I feel that a brisk walk would be beyond me.'

She stretched out a shoeless foot. To her horror the sunlight revealed great holes in her stockings. While she was lamenting their ruin the door was pushed further open without so much as a 'by your leave', and another tin plate was thrust at her.

'Breakfast,' growled the slatternly woman who had brought it. 'And there's a jug of water outside.'

Breakfast! Both Will and Beck stared disbelievingly at several slices of black bread and a small hunk of elderly cheese.

'I shall never complain about my food again,' sighed Beck as she devoured the meagre fare before her. 'Can this be what these poor folk have been living on?'

'Yes,' said Will. 'At the best of times their diet is not a rich one, to say the least. But these last few years it has declined even further. Unless they poached the game in these parts—which if they were caught would mean that they would hang—or ambushed and looted the wagons carrying grain to the surrounding villages, they would starve to death.'

Beck shuddered. 'Never say so.' For the first time in her comfortable life she was being brought up against the stark realities of the world of the very poor. Realities of which Will was well aware.

'It follows,' he said soberly, 'that we must say and do nothing to annoy them. Our very lives may depend on it.'

Beck tried to remember this as the day wore on. They were allowed out into the open, but it was plain that they were being given little chance to escape. Curious eyes followed them everywhere. In the late afternoon one of the grimy children, a little girl, ran up to Beck to show her her rag doll.

Beck was seated at the time on a large branch of one of the trees which the Luddites had cut down, either to provide firewood or to build the huts. The child handed her toy to Beck, looking up at her as she did so and saying 'Pretty lady.'

Beck wasn't sure whether the little girl meant by this the doll or herself. She felt far from pretty, and though the doll bore little resemblance to the splendid ones which she had once owned, she dutifully admired it. Its hair was made from coarse brown thread and its eyes were small black boot buttons.

She had scarcely taken it from the child and begun to rock and sing to it when the child's mother, a woman who might once have been pretty before starvation had left its mark on her, darted up and snatched it from her.

'Leave the kid be,' she said, as though Beck had been trying to kidnap her little one. 'She's nowt to do wi' you.'

The little girl put her finger in her mouth and, pointing at Beck, said again, 'Pretty lady.'

Her mother shook the little girl hard, took her by the hand and ran her into one of the huts as though Beck had the plague, but not before shouting, 'And so she should be, she's allus had enough to eat. Well, she knows now what it's like to go wi'out.'

Which was true enough. Beck's stomach was making distressful noises, and it was little consolation that Will's was in the same case.

Job came up to them where they sat watching their captors gnaw greedily at the cold meat left over from the previous evening's feast. They were eating white bread and butter with it: delicacies bought with the money looted from the coach. Beck and Will had been gifted with black bread again.

Job eyed Beck with insolent admiration. 'Aye,' he said, in imitation of the little girl, 'you was pretty yesterday, missis. Not so pretty today, p'raps, but you'll do.' He turned his attention to Will. 'You look a little less dapper today, too, mester.'

Will nodded. 'True. What concerns me is what you propose to do with us. You can scarcely wish to keep us here permanently. If you let us go, we could promise not to betray where, or who you are. Our lives would be a good exchange for the coach and its contents.'

Job shook his head, 'That's not for me to say. The man from Nottingham runs matters for us. He should be here by tomorrow—and then we'll see. Until then you'll have to hold yer hosses.'

'Have you done this before?' asked Will, apparently innocently.

Job guffawed. 'That would be telling.' He rewarded Beck with another leer which set her shivering again, and had Will clenching his fists impotently. He knew that she was in real danger, but guessed that Job would not touch either of them until 'the man from Nottingham' arrived.

In later years both of them remembered the grim week which they spent with the Luddites as having seemed endless. For Will, the worst aspect of it was the enforced inactivity as the days went by without the master of their fate arriving. His beard grew, and Beck, to her great surprise, found that it made him look more handsome than ever, like a rakish pirate in an old oil painting.

In the privacy of their hut he astonished Beck by going through a series of exercises. He filled the pail with stones and earth and lifted it above his head. He performed simple gymnastic tricks which he had learned at Gentleman Jackson's salon. Out in the open he amused her and their captors by jumping up to grasp a tree branch with both hands in order to carry out a series of acrobatic exercises of the kind which Beck had seen performed in a circus—and this despite only being sustained by their meagre fair.

Not so meagre after the first few days. Because they behaved themselves, although Beck was hard put not to use her sharp tongue on their captors, they were given more to eat. Venison scraps, and a few early plums filched from the orchard of a local farmer, arrived on the tin plate together with the occasional slice of buttered wheaten bread as well as the inevitable cheese.

'Don't want you falling sick, so's we have to look after you,' announced Job ungraciously.

Beck earned their respect by picking up the little girl who had called her 'Pretty Lady' when she fell over in front of her and grazed her knee badly. She promptly bound the cut with a strip from her cotton under-petticoat. Slowly some of the women began to talk to her when they realised that she was no complaining and idle fine lady, but instead uncomplainingly did her share of work in the impromptu camp.

At night she and Will lay companionably on their straw bed, talking as though they had been friends for years. Beck discovered that Will had an excellent memory and could quote whole chunks of poetry and drama, imitating Kemble and his fellow actors. He did not tell Beck that he had spent one summer before he came to London earning a little money by joining a company of strolling players.

Night by night, they drew nearer and nearer to one another, both physically and mentally. Beck was beginning to lose her obvious fear of men so that Will could only hope that, here in the forest, far from civilisation and the stiff formalities of society, he might achieve what he could not have done in the town. Make Beck his true wife.

And then, one morning, as Beck sat before their hut, mending a tear in the little girl's only frock, there was a great commotion.

The 'man from Nottingham' had arrived.

Chapter Twelve

Will had had no real notion of what the Luddites'
leader might look like. If asked, he would have said that
he supposed him to be both large and imposing in order
to be able to control the unruly mob which had captured
them. Instead he turned out to be a small man with a
thin clever face, dressed like a superior clerk.

One thing was plain: he had never starved, and Will
noted that his boots were good and that the horse he
rode was not an inferior nag. Everyone ran up to greet
him and to ask for the latest news. Had the government
decided to give way and help them?

The newcomer shook his head and said shortly, 'As
you might expect, they are offering us nothing.'

This brought a torrent of angry words from Job and
shouts and curses from the rest. The newcomer said
nothing more, simply dismounted and taking Job by the
arm led him away, speaking to him earnestly and privately.

During their discussion Job frequently looked over to
where Beck sat, with Will standing by her protectively.
Will was left in no doubt that he and Beck were the
principal subjects of their urgent consultation. Presently,

their conference over, Job called for everyone's attention. 'The Mester wishes to speak to you all.'

This brought cheers and cries of 'Hush' until 'the Mester', as Job named him, stood on a stool so that all might see and hear him before he began to address them in a speech which would have had them rioting in the streets had they been in a town and not in the depths of a forest.

'Brothers and sisters' he called them as he reminded them of their grievances, of their helplessness, and of the need for them to make ready for the great day when, like the French, they would rise in revolt, execute the tyrant king and all the representatives of 'old corruption', by which he meant the Government.

Will had seen and heard radicals speak before, but seldom one who looked so mild and was so effective a demagogue. He had seen prints of the French Revolutionary Robespierre, and read his speeches, and was reminded irresistibly of him. The Luddites' leader was both clever and cunning and this was the man who was to determine his and Beck's fate!

Every now and then the Mester stopped to allow his audience to cheer him—particularly when he promised them that the day would come when they would rise against their oppressors, loot and fire Nottingham Castle and the homes of the rich so that they might be the ones who would dine off silver plate, sleep between silk sheets and rule in the place of their former masters.

Beck's face grew paler as he spoke. And when, his speech over, he walked towards them through the ragged throng who shook his hand, clapped him on the back, and if they were women, kissed him, she clutched at Will's hand for support.

He grasped it tightly and said, his voice earnest, 'Go into the hut, Beck. I wish to talk to this man alone.'

'No, Will. I do not wish…'

He took both her hands and looked deep into her eyes. 'Beck, when we were married you swore to love, honour and obey me. So far you have done none of these things. This is the first time I have asked you to obey me, and I have good reasons for doing so. I promise to tell you all that passes between us. Now, do as I ask, for my only wish is to protect you.'

Beck's lip quivered. He looked so stern and harsh, not like Will at all. She relinquished his hand and replied, meekly for her, 'Very well, Will, but you must take care, too.'

'That I promise you.' He bent down and kissed her. 'Do this for me, Beck.'

He watched her walk into the hut before turning to face what might be their doom. The man before him said coolly, 'I gather Job has been foolish enough to tell you my name.'

'If you are Gravenor Henson,' replied Will, equally cool, 'yes.'

Henson smiled. 'You must understand that that makes matters a little more difficult to resolve.'

'So I would think. I remember your name as one of the so-called moderate leaders of the framework knitters who gave evidence before Parliament recently.'

Henson's thin eyebrows rose. 'Do you, indeed, Mr Shafto? Then you will grasp why it might not be politic for me to allow you to be released. Ned Ludd is an invention, but I am not. My life would be in your hands if we freed you.'

'As mine is in yours,' replied Will. 'And you hold all the best cards in this game.'

'A great change for you, I do admit,' agreed Henson smoothly, 'seeing that in the past you and your kind have always controlled the lives of these poor hard-working folk around you—and precious little you allowed them in return for keeping you in idleness.'

'You mistake, Mr Henson.' Will's voice was firm and steady. 'I am not a mine owner, a manufacturer, nor yet a gentleman who is the lord of thousands of acres and the poor labourers who work them. I have never exploited anybody.'

Henson laughed in his face. 'That's as maybe, and so speaks the fine gentleman whom, I am informed, married a rich woman for her money. You've never done an honest day's work in your life, have you, sir?'

The sir came out derisively. Will refused to be set down although Henson's accusations stung cruelly because they were partly true.

'This is beside the point. I would wish to relieve the sufferings of my wife. At least allow her to be returned to her home and friends even at the expense of doing your worst with me.'

Henson said, 'I do believe you mean that, Mr Shafto. But I have two problems so far as your wife is concerned. Job has taken a fancy to her. Indeed, if it were not that he is more frightened of me than of the law, he would already have killed you and taken your wife as his doxy. He says that she is a spirited piece whom it would be a pleasure to tame. Also, if we freed your wife, as a spirited piece she would run straight to the authorities and inform on all of us.

'Now Job has already asked me to grant him your wife and your death, but I confess that it goes against my principles to agree to what he wishes. I find rape and murder distasteful. On the other hand, alive and free you are both a danger to us all.'

'We could promise not to inform on you,' Will offered. 'I would give you my word as a gentleman to say nothing, and I know that my wife would agree. She has been distressed by the sight of the starving women and children and would not wish to do anything further to hurt them.'

Henson continued as though Will had not spoken. 'A further problem is that it would not be wise for me to overrule Job too often. You see my dilemma, Mr Shafto, I am sure. Now, I have a solution which would have the merit of giving you a chance of freedom and also of providing a little entertainment for these poor folk here. I think that I can persuade Job to agree to what I wish. I wonder if you would be so willing?'

What in the world could the man be proposing? Could he trust a fellow who ranted of revolution one moment, and in the next assured one of his dislike of rape and murder? Truly, he would be another Robespierre if the English Revolution ever came. On the other hand it would be wise to hear what he had to offer.

'In the old days of chivalry, Mr Shafto, I am told that a knight would cheerfully fight anyone or anything on behalf of his lady. Now, we cannot stage a tournament or a joust, but we could arrange it so that you could take part in a prizefight against one of our local bruisers. I am told that gentlemen of your kidney engage in a little amateur boxing to stave off boredom in your idleness.

'If you were so fortunate as to defeat the champion of my folk then we could engage to let you and your wife go free on promise of your silence. On the other hand, if you lost, then I would regretfully be compelled to hand your wife over to Job and you to your executioners. Which would also be the consequence if you refused to fight for your lady.

'The choice is yours, Mr Shafto.'

Will's head was whirling. He managed to say, 'But if I were to win, could I trust you to keep your promise? And if we are to have a boxing match why should I not fight Job?'

'Ah, Mr Shafto, but as you are your lady's champion, so is our bruiser, Job's. That makes you equal.'

'And I have not eaten properly this last week.'

'A misfortune, I agree, but we could put the match off for two days and fatten you up a little. As for trusting us—that is your problem, not mine.'

Will put out his hand. 'Then let us shake on it. But what my wife will have to say about this does not bear thinking of.'

Henson became almost human. He grinned. 'Being a spirited piece, a great deal, I dare say.'

Which, as Will knew, was exactly what followed.

'So that was why you wanted me out of the way, Will. So that you could engage in some hare-brained piece of gentlemanly piff-paff. I don't want to become Job's doxy at the expense of your life. I would rather die with you.'

'You are, like Henson and all his crew, assuming that this yokel will beat me. He's probably some over-muscled blacksmith who knows nothing of the Fancy. And I had no notion that Henson would propose anything so unlikely.'

'And if he is a proper bruiser, Will, what then?'

He kissed her. 'Then we go down fighting.'

Beck said sternly, 'I shall slit my wrists with a bodkin, Will, if you lose…or…or…something, rather than allow that odious man to lay a finger on me.'

'So, you will let me fight?'

What could she say to him but, 'I believe that we are doomed either way, so I agree that we do not wish them to think that we are cowardly lackwits.'

'And they are going to fatten me up for two days to make the fight fairer.'

Beck's look at him was a stern one. 'Was that the bribe they offered you, Will, in order to get their fun?'

'Good God,' exploded Will, and then he saw that, improbably, given everything, she was quizzing him. Her gallantry in the face of death and dishonour never ceased to amaze him.

Nevertheless his principal worry was what might happen to her if he lost to Henson and Job's champion and she was left alone to fight her own battles. In the meantime, all that he could do was prepare for the coming match—and pray that he won and Henson kept his word…

One consequence of Will's extra food was that he slept more easily until the morning of the day of the fight when he woke with the dawn. He left the hut to find that most of the men and women had risen, too. Like them he washed his face and hands in the nearby stream.

His beard had grown mightily, giving him the stern look which Beck had remarked on. He would be fighting bare-knuckled and bare-chested. Henson had sent two men to collect the bruiser and bring him and his supporters to the forest.

Their man was from Hucknall, Job had told Will, grinning; his name was Black Jack, and he had some reputation already and hoped soon to be able to go to London to try his luck there.

So Will's opponent was no lumbering over-muscled blacksmith, but a young fellow of his own age who would undoubtedly have some professional skills. It was to be hoped that he was no better than the Tooting Terror or he would have a real struggle on his hands.

The fight would last more than one round, too, and Will had never engaged in a long one. He wondered what advice Jackson would give him. Usually, even among folk as poor as the Luddites, vigorous betting on a prizefight's outcome took place, but none of them gave Will a chance so no money was being wagered.

Except by one little man, Charley Norton, always known as Charley Wag, who had been a tailor in Mansfield until he had lost his job and taken refuge in the forest when his money ran out. He had been a second to one of the fighters from Nottingham who had made their name in London and he had kept a beady eye on Will's acrobatics.

After the fight had been announced he had sidled up to Will one afternoon and asked him to make a muscle with his arm. Will had obliged him and the little man had whispered in his croaking voice, 'I allows as 'ow you might be useful in the ring, young feller. I knows a fighter when I see 'im. You've got the look.'

Will laughed shortly. 'I'm a gentleman amateur, that's all.' He wanted his opponent to underrate him.

'Aye, so you says. But I'll 'ave a little money on you all the same.'

Charley Wag must have been waiting for him that morning for he came up to Will saying confidentially, 'You'll want seconds, young sir. I'll stand in for one, and Bill Pyke will be the other. Not that he's bet on you. He reckons as how he's too fly for that. Time will tell, says I.'

Will nodded and yawned. Time was speeding up for him. He had noticed that before in his life: that when one dreaded something time went rapidly whilst desired events in the future were slow in coming.

'This man, Black Jack,' he asked, 'has he arrived yet?'

'Aye, last night. Mester Henson brought him. He stands to win a deal of blunt if he beats you, else he'd not have come.'

By blunt he meant money. Will knew all the cant of boxing, and that because he was a gentleman he would be mocked by the spectators as a *nib sprig*, a gentleman amateur, ready to be slaughtered by any bruiser who cared to take him on.

'I'll find you a pair of shoes,' Wag offered. 'You can't fight barefoot. Jack knows all the tricks—he'd jump on your toes and break 'em, no doubt about it. And you'd best watch that haymaker right of his, it's like a hammer and done for mor'n one man. Nigh killed his last opponent, that he did.'

Beck arrived in time to hear this last cheerful piece of news delivered in Wag's sepulchral voice.

'No,' she said in her most determined mode. 'No, if that's the case I shan't agree to this, Will.'

'Too late,' he told her, 'and Charley Wag is only trying to help me, not frighten me.'

Beck was acid. 'Well, he certainly frightened me!' But she said no more, for she could see that Will was not to be moved.

The fight was to be held in the afternoon, and from early morning folk from the surrounding villages streamed in. Only the gentry were missing, for the mill was being kept a secret from them. The Luddites were supported by villagers who lived near to Sherwood Forest, which meant that the authorities were never able to find their hiding places, nor would anyone inform on them.

Wag and his friends erected an impromptu ring in one of the forest's clearings, using tree branches rather than the usual posts. Beck noted wryly that the so-called ring was actually a square. It was big enough to hold the boxers, their seconds and two umpires, one of whom was Henson.

'To see fair play,' he told Will.

Black Jack, surrounded by his supporters was introduced to Will just before the mill began, Will having only Charley Wag and Bill Pyke on his side. Jack was all that Will feared that he might be. He was Will's equal in height and weight and looked like the blacksmith's assistant he had been before he became a member of the Fancy.

He thrust a giant fist at Will and, grinning insolently, tried to crush Will's hand with it. 'May the best man win,' he growled after such a fashion that Will knew that Jack considered himself to be that man and that the fight was already won.

Charley Wag, officious and delighted to be at the centre of things, helped Will strip off his once-fine shirt, now dirty and stained, and laced on to his feet a pair of light shoes which fitted him well enough. Any fear that Will might have felt at what he was about to do was banished by the knowledge that Jack was only fighting for money. He was fighting for Beck's honour and for his life, and therefore must not lose. But if he did, he must lose with honour for that was all that would be left for him.

Jack, readied by his seconds, narrowed his eyes a little when he saw Will's torso which was not that of an effete dandy. He had come to the forest believing that he was going to earn his blunt easily. He still knew that he would win, but perhaps not quite so painlessly as he had thought.

Everyone in the large crowd was eager for the match to begin. Everyone but Beck. Will had told her to stay away, but Job was having none of that. She was to stand by his side, at the very edge of the ring, and watch her husband being hammered. Every blow he suffered would tell her that she would soon be in Job's bed.

He took a grim pleasure in explaining the rules of the Fancy to her. There was no set number of rounds to a boxing match. A round lasted until they wrestled each other to the ground, when both men retired to be looked after by their seconds. If either of them was not ready to fight again in a stipulated time, then he was deemed to have lost. If at any time his seconds declared he was not fit to continue, he had lost.

If the opponents were roughly equal the match could thus be a long one. 'And the longer it goes on, the worse your man will suffer,' Job told her gleefully.

'Then I shan't watch,' announced Beck defiantly, putting her hands before her eyes.

Job tore them away. 'Oh, yes, you will, missis! Do that again and I'll give you such a blow as you won't forget in a hurry.' Nothing for it but to do as he bid her. Beck was torn in two. If Will won, then they would be free again—if Henson kept his word. But at what a price! And it was plain that the crowd considered that Jack would have a walkover, as the saying went.

Henson and the other umpire entered the ring after Black Jack and Will, and explained the rules to them and their seconds. Will and Jack touched hands again. Henson and his fellow stood back, and the fight was on.

Immediately the noise was ferocious. Women, as well

as men, cheered Black Jack on. Presently, though, when it became obvious that Will was an opponent to be respected, and that the fight might be longer than expected, the noise died down a little.

Beck clenched her own fists. Once, in a silence brought about by the sight of Will hammering Jack rather than the other way round, she found herself shouting, 'Come on, Will, hit him again.' Some of the spectators near her stared at her in astonishment. Beck would have stared at herself if she could. Whatever had possessed her, that she should make such a spectacle of herself? Living wild in the forest was obviously beginning to change her.

After several rounds the fight became more serious in that both men showed signs of the punishing blows which had been exchanged. Will landed a punch on Jack's mouth which set it bleeding. Jack did the same for Will's eyebrow. Jack trampled on Will's feet. Will did awful things to Jack's left arm. The spectators became restless. Things were not going as they should. Henson's fellow umpire tried to cheat Will over the timekeeping between the rounds. Henson would have none of it. He had given Will his word that the fight would be a fair one.

Beck's hands were now in her mouth. As Will staggered away from Jack, narrowly dodging a crucifying haymaker, she leapt to her feet and shrieked at Henson, 'Stop it, I'll agree to anything if you will only stop it. I don't want Will hurt any more.'

Charley Wag rounded on her from inside the ring. 'Shut yer gob, missis. Yer man's winnin'.'

Will winning? It did not look like it from the punishment he had taken. Only the two men in the ring knew how finely the match was balanced. If he had been spar-

ring with Jack in the Gentleman's salon in London, Will
knew that he would have beaten him easily. But this was
no situation set up for a gentleman's diversion, this was
the real, cruel thing, with every dirty trick in the bruisers' book being used.

Nevertheless, he thought that if he could only stay on
his feet he would win, for Jack, tiring himself, was growing impatient. A lucky blow from either man could end
the contest in a second.

Will decided on trickery. He would pretend that he
was weaker than he was, though God knew that he felt
weak enough. He began to stagger and to breathe
heavily, dropping his poor bleeding fists a little. Black
Jack, eager to end a match that was very different from
the one which he had expected, saw his man, as he
thought, faltering and darted in for the kill. He would
deliver the haymaker which was gaining him such a reputation and consign this damned dancing gentleman amateur to oblivion.

In he came in the false belief that his opponent was
so weak that he did not need the careful guard he had
been keeping. Going in to deliver his haymaker, he left
his whole left side open and Will, seeing his opportunity,
summoned up the rags of his strength, and did for Jack
with his right. The effort had him seeing stars and perilously near to falling over himself.

Jack, though, had already fallen, to lie prone before
him. His seconds ran to him to try to revive him. Charley
Wag and Bill Pyke caught Will and dragged him to his
corner where they supported him on their knees. Charley
had a bucket of water and a cloth with which he began
to wipe Will's face.

A deathly silence followed Black Jack's fall. It was
broken when Henson and his fellow, consulting their

watches, announced Will as the winner, seeing that the other man was unable to continue within the stated time.

The fight was over.

Someone shouted 'Huzzah for the *nib sprig*. He's done for Jack right royally,' and the very men and women who had hoped that Jack might do for Will, now cheered Will instead because, improbably, he had done for Jack. And they recognised raw courage when they saw it.

Will, dazed, bruised and bleeding, knew only one thing. That, whatever happened next, he had fought for Beck and won. His seconds helped him out of the ring. Henson said something to him about Black Jack. Will croaked back, 'Tell him not to trouble himself to go to London.'

Charley Wag was shouting to all those in the crowd who had risked their money on Black Jack and now owed him. Even Job looked respectfully at Will—but never mind that. Someone, one of his previous tormentors, took Will's bruised and bleeding paw and shook it vigorously. He hardly felt the pain. That would come later.

And there was Beck, waiting for him.

He tried to smile at her, but his mouth was too swollen and painful. Her eyes were huge and there were tears in them. She put out her hands as though to embrace him, but now that she was near to him she could see the bruises and the burn marks from Black Jack's blows plain upon his face and body. One eye was black and his right hand was swollen. The knuckles of both his hands were raw and bleeding.

She gulped, then said softly, 'Oh, Will...' Leaning forward, she kissed him tenderly on an unmarked patch below his left breast. It was a gesture of affection mixed with pride so unforced that Will closed his eyes before muttering, 'Now, Beck, do not unman me.'

She looked up at him and sparked in her usual brisk fashion, 'Now, Will, how should I do that when Black Jack couldn't?'

Henson, who stood by him, gave a crack of laughter. 'By God, Will Shafto, you've a right game filly there!'

'I know,' croaked Will.

The crowd around them which had roared at Henson's quip now parted to allow Black Jack, who was on his feet again, to approach Will.

'We haven't shaken hands,' he said, his voice as muted as Will's. 'I never thought a Johnny Raw of an amateur would lay me low. I'll lay odds you were taught by a master—but your pluck's all your own.'

'Jackson,' said Will, who was gradually recovering and now stood free of his seconds and Henson. 'The Gentleman himself taught me. I never thought I'd need to put his lessons to use.'

He paused. 'You may not wish to hear this, but I'd advise you to ply your trade in the provinces. London's not for you. You'd have your brains beaten out of your head by those who would make mincemeat of me.'

Black Jack lowered his head sadly, to lift it again to say, 'So I suppose—but that doesn't alter what you did. Shake hands then, and all's fair and square between us.'

Will took the proffered hand and shook it. 'I hope they paid you well.'

Jack's grin was rueful. 'Aye, but not so well as they would if I'd beaten you.'

They laughed together, amazing Beck, who wondered how it was that two men who had been grimly intent on stunning the other could so soon afterwards be enjoying a joke together! She would never understand men—but to be fair to them, would men ever understand women?

Will broke into her thoughts. 'Come, Beck,' he said. 'If Mr Henson keeps his word to us, we should be preparing ourselves to leave.'

Henson replied stiffly, 'If I give anyone my word, Mr Shafto, I keep it. But I think that it would be better if you rested here for the next day at least. Otherwise you will scarcely be fit for the long walk you will need to make to find safety and a way home. Charley Wag will drive you in his cart to the road out of the forest. After that you must make your own way. It would not be safe for any of our people to be seen with you.'

'No,' Will said to this suggestion.

But Beck said 'Yes' in her most determined voice. 'You cannot walk far in your present condition, Will, and I trust Mr Henson not to keep us here any longer than is necessary.'

Will was tired to the bone and only wished to lie down, so he gave way, but not before he had assured Henson that in exchange for their lives he would not betray the Luddites' whereabouts. He suspected from something Charley Wag had said that, once he and Beck were gone, they would take no chances but would move to a distant part of the forest where they had another temporary home.

He allowed Beck to lead him to their hut where he lay upon their poor bed and ultimately dreamed strange dreams full of blood and pain, only redeemed by an occasional glimpse of Beck smiling at him and stretching up to kiss him, oh, so gently, on the chest.

Chapter Thirteen

'These shoes don't fit me very well, but I suppose that they are better than nothing if we have to walk a long way tomorrow.'

At Henson's request one of the women had given Beck a pair of her own cast-offs, kept for rough work, so that she might not have to leave the camp barefoot. Will had been allowed to retain those he had been given for the fight. They were sitting in their hut on the following evening. Will's success had brought him a certain popularity. More than one rough fellow had told him earnestly that if that was what he could do whilst he was a gentleman, then if he had trained to be a bruiser, no one could have stopped him.

Will thought that they overestimated Black Jack's prowess, but he did not tell them so. He was greatly recovered, although still sore, and his black eye was inflamed and angry.

But he was affable Will again, friendly and charming to everyone. Beck had washed his face for him, and tried to trim his beard with a pair of scissors. Razors were in short supply in the Luddite camp so he still looked more like a piratical villain than the gentleman he was.

Beck, putting the shoes on one side, came to sit by him on the dirt floor. 'Will,' she said softly, 'I've never really thanked you for what you did for me yesterday. Then you weren't fit to exchange pleasantries with anyone, and today we've been busy preparing to leave.'

Will said, 'Oh, Beck, I only did what a man of honour should. Try to protect my wife, and in doing so, protect myself as well.'

'But at such expense.' She leaned forward to stroke his face on the left side away from his damaged eye. 'You know that I didn't want you to fight that man, and while you did I nearly ran mad, but I only gave way once to my fears and asked Henson to stop it.' She paused. 'And, oh, Will, once I forgot myself.'

Will took her stroking hand in his and kissed its palm. 'Tell me, Beck, how did you do that?'

'Well, all the women were shrieking at Jack to hit you, so when you hit him, I screamed at you, "Come on, Will, hit him again." I scarcely knew myself.' She hid her blushing face in his chest.

Her reward was a laugh. Will dropped her hand so that he might use both of his to cradle her face in his two hands.

'Was I your champion, Beck? Was I?'

'Yes, Will, you were.' She lifted her head to look at him. 'It was scarcely the act of a lady, Will.'

'Ah, but yesterday, Beck, I wasn't a gentleman and you weren't a lady.'

'And today?'

'Today we are what we wish to be,' and slowly, slowly, Will lowered his mouth on to hers.

Here in the forest, anonymous, her unhappy past a distant thing, Beck did not resist him. It was truly as though she were someone else.

Her own hands went up to circle his neck as she vigorously kissed him back. Still holding her head with his left, damaged hand, Will dropped his right one to run it down her body in order to stroke her left breast.

Beck gave a little cry—but did not stop him. She had no wish to stop him. The kiss went on and on and slowly, slowly, Will lowered her on to the bed.

Again he met with no resistance—only cooperation. Was it gratitude for having saved her from Job which moved her, or was it love? No matter. Now was not the time for such needless introspection. Now was the time when the demanding body took over from the questing mind.

He stripped Beck of her scanty clothing; she helped him out of his bloodstained breeches and his grimy shirt so that they lay as close together as a man and woman might before the act of union itself.

And, for whatever reason, she was ready for him at last: her acid tongue and her busy mind both forgotten, as he had forgotten all the reasons why he should not be doing this. He kissed her everywhere, celebrating parts of Beck which she could never have imagined being kissed by any man, until at last she writhed and cried beneath him for consummation.

At first he wanted to be gentle with her, as much for the sake of his own bruised and battered body as for her virginity, but passion drove him on. Once he looked down at her face, also transformed by passion, all her cold command blown away by the wind of their loving, and muttered, beneath his breath so that she could not hear him, 'Oh, how I love and worship thee, my beautiful termagant who cheered me on when I was sore beset.'

For he had heard Beck's frantic shout of encouragement and it had helped to spur him on to his victory over Jack—and over her, as she lay helpless before him, begging for she knew not what.

There, in the rude hut in the depths of the forest, far from the comfort and luxury to which they were both accustomed, Will and Beck consummated the marriage which they had both vowed never to consummate. Even as he breached her virginity she urged him on as she had done in the fight—only the words she used were different—'Oh, yes, Will, yes!'

Afterwards they lay quiet together, Beck cradled against the broad chest which she had kissed in his moment of victory. Presently she slept. If he had hurt her as he made her his, she said nothing of it to him. Before she had fallen asleep she had kissed him on the cheek, saying, 'Oh, thank you, Will, thank you,' as simply as though she were a child who had been given a particularly pleasant sweet.

Quintessential Beck, Will thought to himself before he, too, let sleep claim him, wondering as it did so how she would greet him on the morrow when her head would rule her actions again, and not her heart.

He need not have worried. Beck was up before him, dressing herself for the day in the gown which she had perforce worn ever since their capture. It was stained and torn. Her hair had grown a little so she had tied it back with a short piece of yarn begged from one of the women who had befriended her once it became plain that she was no whining fine lady. Her refusal to be idle had earned her their grudging respect.

She had, indeed, spent much of her time in captivity mending and altering the clothes of the many small children who ran about the camp. Nothing, she found, was ever thrown away: clothes were handed down through the family and then passed on to another until, at length, they fell to pieces.

Carefully though she might dress herself, Beck knew that she looked more like a beggarwoman than the Mrs Will Shafto who, in London, had never been seen other than perfectly turned out.

Her toilet over, she turned to find Will, propped up on one arm, smiling at her. She blushed, and hid her face from him by the simple expedient of bending down as though to inspect her shoes. Her whole body was a testament to last night's loving. Not only did it feel thrillingly alive, but it had aches and pains in peculiar places which she had scarcely known existed before the previous evening.

'Beck,' Will said softly, 'forgive me for last night. I was carried away.'

Forgive him? Why should she forgive him for having been the cause of such pleasure? Dismal reality burst in on Beck. Oh, he must be referring to the bargain which they had broken. Did he regret having broken it?

More to the point, did she?

She stared coldly at him. 'It's a little late for repentance, don't you think?'

Will, who had foolishly assumed that she would understand that he was referring to the haste with which he had deflowered her, not realising that she would interpret what he said as regret for having made love to her, felt as though she had thrown cold water over him.

So they were back to their previous relationship of cool tolerance of one another. He jumped out of bed quite forgetting that he was naked. 'No, Beck. Repentance was not in my mind at all. Celebration, rather.'

Beck stared at the first completely naked man whom

she had ever seen. She had thought Will magnificent
when he was only naked from the waist up, but now that
she was gifted with the sight of a male body as impressive as the nude Greek statues which decorated her various homes she had no words left with which to admire
him.

The sight of his long powerful legs and his equally
powerful sex were doing strange things to Beck. She
gulped, looked away from him, and said, her voice shaking a little, 'You really ought to get dressed, Will. It
would be wise to make an early start.'

Belatedly Will became aware of his naked condition.
He considered an apology, rejected it. Beck was facing
him again, and her expression, whether she knew it or
not, could only have been described as excited and anticipatory. He advanced on her, smiling.

Beck stood her ground. She gave an excited little cry
when he reached her and took her in his arms. His
arousal was plain as he did so.

'Again, Beck, again?' he whispered in her ear.

'Someone might come in,' she gasped.

'Not at this hour of the morning.'

'Won't it tire us—before we set out, I mean?'

'Invigorate us, rather,' Will whispered breathlessly,
bearing her down to the bed. 'Don't waste time talking.'

Beck didn't. And somehow, because she was terrified
that someone might break in on them, it was even more
exciting and her pleasure was far more powerful than it
had been on the previous night—and so she told him.

They lay entangled on the makeshift bed. Will said,
'That was what I meant earlier. You were virgin last
night, and I was sorry for the haste with which I took
you. This morning, now...'

Beck put a finger on his lips. 'No apologies. I could

have stopped you both last night and this morning—and I didn't. Now, we really must get dressed.'

She was so matter of fact that she almost set him laughing.

Nevertheless Will did as he was told. The woman who brought their breakfast arrived just as he was pulling his breeches on. She smirked knowingly at him, and at Beck who was busy rearranging herself.

'Summat good for you,' she told them. 'The Mester says as how you'll need it. You've a long walk ahead of you when Charley Wag drops you off.'

And so Charley told them when he drove up in his cart to where they stood with Henson and Job who was still protesting that it was a mistake to let them go.

'I gave my word,' Henson said, 'and they have given theirs. And I don't want murder and rape on my hands. It's not a risk I'm prepared to take. And, Job, you're not to go chasing after them—you hear me?'

Job nodded sullen agreement, and watched Charley Wag drive off with Beck and Will before heaving a great sigh and going off to help the rest strike camp. Even if their recent captives broke their word and informed on them, the authorities would have great difficulty in tracking them down.

Charley Wag took them to the end of the byway—down which Job had driven them into the forest nearly a fortnight ago—before he stopped the cart, saving them at least a mile of their long walk.

'Which is no more than you deserve after the way you fought Black Jack. Follow this byway until you come to the turnpike and walk along that until you reach the first village. Good luck to you both. You're a brave feller, and your lass is a good plucked 'un, too. I know you'll not peach on us.'

Will scrambled out of the cart and handed Beck down. They watched Charley Wag turn his cart round and drive back in the direction from which they had come. As he disappeared into the trees Will took Beck's hand in his.

'Come,' he said. 'We have a long way to go.'

He was right. The sun was up, there was no breeze, and it rapidly grew very hot. Perspiration dewed Beck's brow and what had seemed a short distance when they were riding in the coach was a long one when they were walking. Her shoes hurt her, but she did not complain.

They came to a stream which ran by the side of the rough track. Will knelt down and drank from it and bade Beck do the same. Then he tore a strip off the tail of his shirt, wetted it and made Beck put it round her neck. Despite her stoicism he could see that she was suffering from the heat and, by the gingerly way she walking, it was likely that her feet were blistered.

Neither of them spoke much until, with a sigh of relief, they reached the turnpike where walking was easier.

'Not far now,' Will told her. 'There is a village called Ashworth nearby, and there we shall find succour. We must make for the inn, tell our tale, and ask for help.'

Nearby seemed a long way to walk, but shortly after mid-day they reached the first cottages on the edge of Ashworth. Salvation was near. Beck straightened up, held her head high and took her hand out of Will's. Soon, she thought, soon they would be on their way to Inglebury again.

There were men and women going about their work on the road which ran through the village, and they stared curiously at the two ragged strangers. One man, well-dressed, gave them a cold glare, and walked into a

large house which stood next to the inn. Will took
Beck's hand again.

'Not far, now,' he said.

But he spoke too soon. Behind them the well-dressed
man had emerged from the house and was walking rapidly towards them, accompanied by a beadle.

They reached Beck and Will when they were a few
short paces from safety.

'Do your duty,' cried the well-dressed man.

The beadle put a hand on Will's shoulder. 'Come with
me, young feller, and your doxy, too. We don't allow
beggars in our village. Mr Earnshaw here is a friend of
the magistrate, and we shall take you to him instanter!'

'No,' said Will, 'we are not beggars. This lady—' and
he waved a hand at Beck '—is my wife, and we have
been captured...'

He was silenced by a blow across the shoulders from
the beadle's staff.

'Don't try to gammon me, young feller. I know your
sort...' and he made to strike Will with his staff again.

He was interrupted by Beck who, her face a mask of
fury, shouted rather than said, 'Stop that at once. He is
telling you the truth. He is my husband, Mr Will Shafto,
and I am his wife, who was Miss Rowallan of Inglebury,
near Sheffield and we were...'

She said no more, for the beadle seized her and put a
hand over her mouth to silence her. Will would have
gone to her rescue but a group of villagers, attracted by
all this unwonted excitement had come up and, obeying
the beadle's shouted instructions, seized hold of him,
too.

'Tricksters,' said Mr Earnshaw severely. 'I've met
their kind before. Take them to Sir Charles immediately,

and he'll see that they're whipped back to the village they have fled from before they become a charge on us.'

It was useless to struggle. 'Do as they say,' Will told Beck wearily. 'We can't stop them and Sir Charles might prove more reasonable than a pack of yokels and a self-important fool.'

He knew that he should not have said anything quite so provoking, but he was nearing the end of his strength. Even so, he was not prepared for the blow across the face which nearly felled him. Beck, sobbing, tried to go to him, but was swept along by the villagers, the beadle and Mr Earnshaw, along the road, up the drive to Sir Charles's fine house where he was about to go into the dining room to eat an early dinner...

Sir Charles Ashworth was large, middle-aged and hungry. He wanted his dinner, having missed his luncheon. The news that Earnshaw, that fussy busybody, had brought him yet another pair of wretches to deal with before he could eat it did not please him.

It pleased him even less when the wretches were pushed into the library where, as JP, he handed out law and judgement. A more ragged pair of rapscallions it had seldom been his misfortune to see.

Will, catching sight of himself and Beck in a long mirror in the hall, would have agreed with him. Ten days in the Luddite encampment had turned him and Beck into persons indistinguishable in appearance from the poor folk among whom they had lived. He was dirty, bearded, and his clothing was both filthy and ragged: Beck, hobbling in her ill-fitting shoes, was little better. He could almost forgive Earnshaw for his misjudgement of them.

But surely all that he and Beck needed to do was to

explain their predicament to this country squire and they would be free again. He misjudged his man. Sir Charles was not stupid but he was set in his ways and, what was worse, had no imagination.

To begin with he would not allow Will to speak. When he tried to explain who they were he bellowed, 'Silence, fellow, and do not speak until you are bid. Earnshaw, pray explain how you came upon this pair of vagrants.'

Nothing loath Earnshaw began his tale of how he had come across them in the village street.

'And what were they doing there, sir? Were they begging?'

'They had not yet begun to do so, but I had no doubt that that was their intent.'

Will, angered, said, 'Nonsense. We were on our way to the inn when we were stopped by…' but Sir Charles did not allow him to finish.

'Be silent, fellow,' he roared, 'or I'll have you gagged.' He turned to Earnshaw. 'Did you have them searched before you brought them here?'

'Aye. The beadle searched them in case they had stolen property on them.'

'And had they?'

'No, Sir Charles, but they had no money either, so they could not have been making for the inn.'

Beck, furious at their mistreatment, called out, 'If you would only allow us to explain…'

Sir Charles cut her off in mid-statement. 'Silence, woman, or I'll have the scold's bridle put upon you. Go on, Earnshaw.'

'That's all. I've no doubt that they would have made for the inn when they had finished begging.'

'Difficult when we hadn't even begun, and didn't intend to,' remarked Beck in her most acid tones.

Something in her manner of speech prevented Sir
Charles from threatening her again. He was about to
question her when the door opened and a fashionably
dressed gentleman came in.

He put up his glass to examine the assembled company before saying in a languid voice, 'What the devil's
happened to dinner, Charles? Never say you're having
to dispense justice while the mutton grows cold.'

Will stared at the newcomer, that ass, Gilly Thornton,
whom he had last seen in Jackson's rooms in Bond
Street and had now been sent by heaven to save him—
and a more unlikely saviour he could not think of.

'Gilly Thornton,' he said, 'tell these fools who I am.'

Gilly peered at him uncertainly. 'I know the voice,
but I'm dem'd sure I've never known anyone who
looked like you!'

Will roared at him. 'For God's sake, Gilly, if you
don't recognise an old friend when you see him, at least
tell me that you recognise my wife!'

'Beck?' drawled Gilly. He raised his quizzing glass
again to stare at her. 'Beck, what the devil are you doing
in that get-up, and Will, what in the world are you playing at in yours?'

Everyone in the library stared at Gilly.

Sir Charles said in a dazed voice, 'Do you know these
people, Thornton?'

'Know them? I should say I do. It's my old friend
Will Shafto and his wife. But what they're doin' here in
fancy dress is beyond me. Is this some sort of joke,
Will?'

'Of course it's not a joke, and if Sir Charles will
kindly send the tipstaff and his idiot master away, I shall

be only too happy to explain how we come to be in this get-up and hauled before Sir Charles as beggars.'

Gilly Thornton turned an unexpectedly shrewd eye on them both. 'Quite right, old fellow, but before you do anything in the explainin' line someone should do something for poor Beck. She looks as though she's about to faint any moment.'

Everyone turned to look at her. He was right. Beck's eyes were closed and she was swaying gently on her feet. What no one knew was that she had decided to put an end to all this nonsense by practising, for once, some of the female artifices which she had previously despised.

On hearing Gilly's exclamation she let out a small moan and began to fall sideways towards Will. As she had expected every man in the room immediately experienced a rush of guilty compunction over their ungallant behaviour towards a gentlewoman.

Sir Charles stared at her, shamefaced, and exclaimed, 'Good God.'

Gilly, more acute, cried, 'Catch her, Will.'

Mr Earnshaw, astounded by this turn of events, goggled his bemusement, and the beadle whimpered, beginning to fear for his job now that he had mistakenly insulted and struck two members of the gentry—a class on whom he normally fawned.

Will, by far the most practical man present, surprised by Beck's sudden collapse when only a few moments ago she had been her usual charmingly truculent self, immediately seized the opportunity which she had offered him to break the tension in the room.

He scooped her up, and turning on Sir Charles, bellowed at him, 'She needs rest and a decent bed. She hasn't slept or eaten properly for over a week.'

Sir Charles recovered his normal character of a man chivalrous and courteous to all women—provided they were of gentle birth.

'Of course, of course.' He bellowed in his turn, at the gaping footmen who stood at the door, secretly all agog at this untoward commotion in Sir Charles's library. 'Fetch m'lady, the butler and the housekeeper—on the double.'

Beck decided to improve the shining hour. 'A bath,' she quavered, and in case no one took the hint, 'and some clean clothes.'

'Of course, of course, dear madam,' repeated the hapless Sir Charles. 'Pray forgive me my previous discourtesy, forgive all of us…' and he glared at Earnshaw who had landed him in this pickle '…but, of course, we could not have guessed…'

'I did my best to explain,' Will offered from the sofa on which he now sat, cradling Beck, 'but I was forcibly prevented…'

He looked down at her. Her face was turned away from the embarrassed company. She opened her eyes, gave him a wink and then closed them again to the accompaniment of yet another tortured moan. Will was hard put not to laugh. Oh, the naughty, clever doxy! She had succeeded—as usual—in putting everyone in the wrong.

The arrival of Lady Ashworth, the butler and the housekeeper resulted in Beck being carried off to be petted, bathed, found clean garments, fed and generally, as she later told Will, succoured.

As for Will, he was left, still in his dirt, to tell his tale of woe with suitable exclamations of mingled anger and sympathy from everyone except the beadle who had been sent home.

Sir Charles was pacing the library, enraged. When Will had finished, he said with great satisfaction, 'Well, the best thing about this sorry business, Shafto, is that you will be able to lead us to where these wretches are hiding in the forest and put an end to their rebellion.'

Will put on a long face. 'Alas, Sir Charles,' he said earnestly and untruthfully, 'neither my wife nor I have the slightest notion where we were taken. We were captured in the recent storm, after our coach was driven down a byway. In the dark and the confusion which followed we completely lost our bearings. When they released us, we were blindfolded, put in a cart and driven towards the turnpike road in what I am sure was a different direction.

'I also gathered from what was said that the Luddites intended to move camp, as they put it, once we were freed, in case either of us might be able to reveal their whereabouts.'

On hearing this all present, except Gilly Thornton and Will, gave vent to their anger. Sir Charles said abruptly, 'And by the look of your eye, Shafto, you were mistreated. I should think that you'd like to see the whole pack of them hanged or transported.'

Will remembered the starving women and children and the desperation of their fathers, husbands and brothers. He looked around Sir Charles's comfortable library, and thought of the excellent meal which was undoubtedly waiting for them all. He could not condone what had been done to him and Beck, but he could understand why it had been done.

'And their leader,' continued Sir Charles, 'this fellow Ludd, did you come across him?'

Will shook his head. 'No, Sir Charles, nor anyone like him.' Which was true so far as it went, seeing that Henson was not at all like the roaring captain of men Ned Ludd was supposed to be. But Henson had saved both him and Beck on condition of his silence, and having given his word, and remembering the suffering which he had seen, Will intended to keep it.

Only Gilly Thornton, that frequenter of Jackson's salon, now revealed as Sir Charles's brother-in law, looked sideways at Will once he had been shaved, washed and dressed in decent clothing, and drawled quietly at him, 'What bruiser gave you that black eye and damaged lip, Will, and why?'

So Gilly was shrewder than most gave him credit for. Will laughed and replied, 'A man has to do strange things when he is in the hands of those who hate him, Gilly. I'll only say this, and for your ears alone—thank God I took my practise with the Gentleman seriously.'

'And what does your opponent look like, Will?'

'Worse than I do—and that is the end of the matter. Beck and I are safe and sound again, and wish to forget what has passed since we were dragged from our coach in the pouring rain.'

Will lied. He could not forget, nor did he wish to. Even as he ate Sir Charles's reheated mutton and drank his good port he had at the back of his mind those less fortunate than himself—who had counted himself unfortunate. But he now knew that, in comparison with those among whom he had briefly lived, he was blessed beyond words.

What was worse, his pursuit of heiresses, and his marriage to Beck, seemed the actions of one who was less than a man. That he had come to love Beck was beside the point if all that he had to offer her was the possession of a rogue without honour.

He had been truly a man when he had fought Black

Jack for her, but what would he be if he sank back into the life which he had been living before the Luddites had dragged him from the coach?

The fine food he was eating was as ashes in his mouth because the price he was paying for it was too high.

Chapter Fourteen

'What is it, Will? What's wrong?' For ever since they had returned to London he had been not joyful at their return to normal life, but sombre and withdrawn, quite unlike the man who had made such ardent love to her during the last night of their captivity.

'Nothing,' he said. 'Nothing.' A reply which was not truthful and which did not deceive Beck, but she could get nothing further from him.

They had returned to their London home by a road which did not lead through Sherwood Forest. Beck had sent word to Inglebury for Mrs Grey and her staff to remain there until she came north again in a few weeks' time. London suddenly seemed a haven of peace to her. Will agreed, almost absently, as he had agreed to everything since they had arrived at Ashworth.

Ironically, on the afternoon of the very day on which they had arrived at Ashworth—too late to save them from humiliation—Sir Charles had received a letter from the Lord Lieutenant of Yorkshire asking him to make a search for Mr and Mrs Shafto who had disappeared, with their coach, somewhere between Nottinghamshire and Yorkshire.

The Lord Lieutenant had been alerted by Mrs Grey, who had been in a fever of anxiety once she had discovered that Will and Beck were missing. As Will had supposed, those in the second coach assumed that they had taken a different route in the storm.

It was unfortunate that Beck's courses began at Ashworth so that she and Will were prevented from making love again, just at the very moment when Will might have found in their mutual passion an answer to his problems.

The main one was that he no longer felt that he could continue to be simply Beck's appendage. The more he knew that he loved her, the less he felt inclined to be someone who had no real role to play in her life. Nor did he wish to live off her without giving anything to her in return. In his present position he was nothing more than the stallion whose only purpose was to service the mare.

And all this as a result of fighting Black Jack and listening to Henson's taunts about his never having done a real day's work in his life.

The difficult thing was to tell Beck how he felt, for he was certain that her own feelings of insecurity would result in her seeing his attempts to free himself from bondage, as it were, as an attack on her. Their night of passion in the Luddite camp had made it harder for Will to reach a decision which would hurt her, but what he really feared was that whatever he decided, he would end up by doing so.

Regardless of that, somehow he needed to prove himself. Fighting Black Jack, and winning had been one thing, but it had been done in hot blood. Taking charge of his own destiny would be another and even more terrible thing to be done, and it could not be accomplished in the heat of the moment.

It would mean leaving her.

The more Will thought about it the worse he felt.

He recalled the poem written by the seventeenth-century poet, Richard Lovelace, 'On Going to the Wars', in which he wrote as he left his love, 'I could not love thee, dear, so much, loved I not honour more.'

That exactly described his feelings towards Beck. The more he loved her, the more unworthy he felt. He saw himself as a parasite, nothing more, living on her bounty. Oddly enough, he had not experienced this particular sensation very strongly until after he had made love to her. He had felt then that he was unworthy of her, that she deserved better than having for a husband someone who had married her for her money—even though she had proposed to him, and not the other way round.

In honour he should have refused her. The difficulty was that in the forest by fighting Black Jack he had found his honour again, and having done so he could no longer continue as Rebecca's rogue. Because he had nothing to offer her but his honour, he must free her and himself from their unequal bargain.

It would break his heart to leave her, but he could take nothing further from her, instead, he must give her something: her freedom, and the opportunity to love someone more worthy than himself. He was certain that in the forest she had given herself to him out of gratitude, not love.

He sat down at the escritoire in his room one morning shortly after they reached London and wrote two letters. One was to Coutts Bank, cancelling the quarterly draft which he had caused to be sent north, saying that he would no longer be receiving any allowance from his wife.

The second, and the hardest, was to Beck. She must not know where he was going, only that he had gone.

'My dearest love,' he began, for that was what she had become. 'When you read this I shall be far away. Because I love you, I can no longer continue to live on your bounty. In the Forest I defended you like a man, and now, though it breaks my heart to leave you, I must play a man's part and free you to live and to love someone who deserves you more than I ever can. I must try to support myself by my own efforts and live an honourable life.

'To this end I must break the bargain which we agreed to: a bargain to which I should never have consented. You may believe that it is dishonourable of me, having made it, to break it, but it is less dishonourable than if I continued to hold us to it. I can no longer be Rebecca's rogue because it prevents me from being Beck's honourable husband.

'My heart's darling, believe that this inequality between us would, in the end, come between any chance of our enjoying a happy marriage, and that you should be happy is the one wish of Will Shafto.'

He sealed it, and when he had packed a small bag containing only sufficient clothing for the journey to his new life, he placed it on the writing desk in Beck's room before leaving the house, where he had found love, if not complete happiness with her, by a side entrance so that no one was aware of his departure.

Once in the street he walked briskly toward the inn yard where the coaches left for the north.

Beck had been out visiting her Aunt Petronella. Will had pleaded a headache and the old lady had been disappointed by his absence. She was one of the few people to whom Beck had told the true story of their kidnapping and of Will's fight for her honour with the professional bruiser from Hucknall.

She was a little surprised when she returned in the early evening to find that he was not in. She retired to her room, and called for her maid to dress her in something informal for an evening at home. Her courses had ended and she felt a *frisson* of delight at the notion of celebrating that event by inviting Will into her bed.

Unfortunately the footman who brought the teaboard to her room upon her return thoughtlessly placed it over Will's letter, so that it was not until some little time later that Beck, now growing worried over his continued absence, found it.

She had already asked the butler if he knew where his master had gone, only to receive the reply that he was not aware that Mr Shafto had left the house—something which the footmen on duty confirmed.

This was most unlike Will. He had always been punctilious in informing her of his whereabouts—in complete contrast with her cousin Sarah's husband who came and went without regard for his wife.

It was only when, growing distracted, she sat down at her writing desk that she came across Will's letter, which had been pushed almost out of sight when the footman carelessly retrieved the teaboard.

Where could he be? And why was he writing to her? For she knew Will's hand at once. Agitated, Beck broke the seal and read his letter. For a moment she could scarcely understand it. He could not have left her, he could not, when they had so recently celebrated their marriage and sealed it in love after he had defended her so nobly.

And what was this talk of honour? Oh, men's notion of honour was something which Beck had never understood, and now she understood it less than ever. How could he say that he loved her, and then leave her, claiming that he did so in the cause of honour?

He had written that his heart was broken, but what about her poor heart? Was he not breaking hers by writing this…this…sorry rigmarole? The letter lay crumpled in her disbelieving hand. Shaking, Beck opened it out and read it again.

This time she read it slowly. Read the words which told her of his unhappiness about his position in her life which had come to a head after he had fought Black Jack. Beck's fight was with the tears which demanded to overwhelm her; but she would not cry, she would not.

Instead, silently she invoked the heavens. The man whom she had coldbloodedly chosen to marry for her own ends had left her for his, and improbably, her heart was broken, for though he had told her to live and to love again, her heart was irretrievably given to her rogue, who had decided to be a rogue no longer.

And she had not the slightest notion where he might have gone, or what she could do to find him and get him back again. She might try to tell herself that she did not care whether she ever saw him again, but it would be a lie.

In the meantime she would tell no one that he had deserted her, while she tried to track him down so that she might throw this letter in his face and call him a rogue in truth!

Beck could not keep Will's disappearance a secret for ever. The servants knew that he had walked out of the house and had not returned, and Beck's absence from the social scene which she and Will had graced, was soon commented on. It was Aunt Petronella who first confronted Beck with her suspicions soon after Beck had employed an ex-Bow Street Runner to find out everything he could about Will's life before she had married him, and where he might have fled to when he had left her.

Aunt Petronella arrived in full fantastic fig, having just refused to marry the Duke of Durness for the fourth time. She had been arguing with herself as to whether she ought to accept him if he ever asked her again, when it occurred to her that it was time for her to pin Beck down over what had become of Will.

Beck, when she received her aunt, looked very much as she always did. Cool and in control of herself. This had the effect of annoying Aunt Petronella mightily—she might, at the very least, have had the decency to betray a little distress at the loss of her husband. She would, Aunt Petronella thought acidly, have shown more emotion if she had lost a parlourmaid!

In this she did Beck an injustice. She had no notion of what it was costing Beck to retain her usual composure. Aunt Petronella grimly decided that she would do her best to destroy it.

'Well, what have you done with him?' she began, all aggression.

'Done with what or with whom, Aunt P.?' replied Beck, full of bland innocence.

'Come, come, my girl, you know perfectly well what I mean. Where has Will gone? And has he gone for good after saving you from unimaginable insult in your recent captivity?'

'I am not your girl, Aunt P. And where Will has gone is as much a mystery to me as to you.'

'Not my girl, eh? Too true—I fear that you are no-body's girl and like to remain so. What did you do to him? Drive him away with your nasty tongue? If so, you are a fool—something which I never previously thought you.'

To her horror Beck's eyes filled with tears. She was near to breaking point: a state which she had resisted for the past week.

'On the contrary, Aunt, we had never been so happy as we were before he left—or so it seemed to me.'

'Oh, I do beg leave to doubt that, Beck. Why did you think so? Was he truly happy? Happy men do not leave their homes and wives without warning.'

'He seemed a trifle distrait, it's true, but nothing more.'

'There must have been something more, and you were too busy, I suppose, playing the iron maiden to notice it.'

The tears were really determined to fall. Beck, in a vain attempt to stave them off, said savagely, 'I'm not an iron maiden, Aunt. Indeed, I'll have you know I'm not a maiden at all…'

There it was, out, and she had not meant to confess it!

Aunt Petronella shook her bedizened head. 'Bedded you at last, did he? Was it too much for you—or him? Found he didn't love you, perhaps, and being your lackey was thus too much. Left without a message, did he—just cut line?'

That did it! Did it royally, in fact. Beck gave a loud cry and flung herself down on the sofa. 'Nothing of the sort,' she sobbed into the cushions. 'He wrote me a letter saying that he loved me and that was why he was leaving me—of all the stupid things! Oh…oh…oh…'

Now the sobs came thick and fast. Aunt Petronella— as she had intended—had finally undone her niece. But having done so, she regretted her handiwork, for she sat down by Beck, took her in her arms and rocked her until the sobs slowly died down.

Beck rested her head against her aunt's breast like a child who had come home to her mother to be comforted.

'There, there,' said her aunt, tenderness succeeding asperity. 'Tell me the truth, Beck, and you will feel better. Do you love him, after all, truly love him, after telling yourself you never would? More to the point, did you ever *tell* the poor fellow that you loved him?'

Beck's answer was a sniffle and a shake of the head. 'Not in so many words. I thought that he must know that I loved him—after…' She could not bring herself to tell her aunt of their one glorious night together in the woods.

Aunt Petronella, ever practical, handed her a handkerchief. 'Blow your nose, child, and tell me what he said in his letter.'

'That he loved me,' confessed Beck over the handkerchief, 'but that his honour would not allow him to continue as we were with him living off me. His honour, Aunt! Are all men mad that they talk of honour so much?'

'I told you that he was a good man, Beck, and so he has proved. He needed to be told of your love. They're different from us, you know, they demand proof. I can only suppose that fighting for you settled something for him in the way of honour. Men do prize honour, Beck, however much we women may think it a bauble. It gives their lives a point which bearing children gives to us. We must not scoff at it, even if we don't understand it.'

'I don't understand anything,' wailed Beck, 'and for this to happen just when I realised that I loved him so much…' The sobs began again, louder and deeper than ever.

'Stop that,' commanded Aunt Petronella sternly. 'At once! Do you want him back again? If so, you must try to find him, not sit here behaving like a ninnyhammer—most unlike you.'

'I *am* trying to find him,' retorted Beck, showing a little of her normal fighting spirit. 'I have hired a man who was a Runner for that very purpose. He is coming to report to me later this afternoon. My lawyer recommended him to me. He says he is a very tiger for tracking people down.'

'Poor Will,' murmured Aunt Petronella, smiling, 'what chance has he of escaping you with both you and the Runner after him?'

'This is not a joke, Aunt,' Beck said, deploying her aunt's handkerchief as a sponge to wipe up her tears. 'On the contrary.'

'Indeed not, but crying won't help, either, even though it comforts me to see that you are human, after all. There have been times when I doubted it.'

Beck sat up straight. 'Mock me, Aunt. I deserve it. For I did not truly know how much Will had come to mean to me until I lost him.'

'Oh, that is frequently the case,' offered Aunt Petronella cheerfully. 'Took him for granted, didn't you? No one likes that. Now, tell me where you think that he might have gone. I could perhaps be of service there.'

Beck dried her eyes and, her manner composed again, she moved away from her aunt and folded her hands in her lap. 'He could be hiding in London, or he may have gone north to his old home. But I doubt that he has done the latter. The lawyer tells me that Shafto Hall is so derelict that no one has lived there for many years. So I have ordered my man to begin by making enquiries around London.'

'And he is due here this afternoon? May I remain until after you have finished your business with him? You will, of course, wish to speak to him alone.'

'Of course, and of course, you may stay. I must tidy myself a little. It would not do for him to find me like this. You will excuse me if I retire to my room and ring for my maid. I shall see him in the study so you may wait here. I shall order the butler to bring you the tea-board.'

Amused, Aunt Petronella watched Beck recover her usual coolly competent self. But now she knew that, beneath it, Beck suffered and bled like the rest of humanity, and that being so, there was hope for her and Will.

'You will be pleased to learn, madam, that I have news for you of Mr Shafto's life in London which I trust might prove helpful, though I have not succeeded in locating the gentleman himself. No one confesses to having seen him since he returned to London with you.'

Jack White, the ex-Runner—for he had retired from his profession to work for Beck's lawyer, Mr Herriott—was a biggish man with a strong face and a body to match. He spoke after a peculiar fashion, mixing slang and good English together, peppered with legal phrases doubtless garnered from his acquaintance with the trials of those whom he had caught.

He fished a notebook out of an inner pocket of his loose grey overcoat which he had insisted on retaining.

'You may be aware of some of what I am about to tell you, so forgive me if I am instructing you in what you already know, but you told me to reveal everything which I discovered whether it be good or ill.

'Mr Shafto was a poor man when he married you. He had a small income, sufficient to keep him in a little comfort, but he seemed, I learned, to be perpetually short of money, although he never gambled. I began by questioning his lawyer friend, Josh Wilmot.' He did not tell Beck that he had actually leaned on Josh heavily in order to get her this information.

'It seems that Mr Shafto did not draw all his income from the bank for his own use, but sent the majority of it away. Mr Wilmot claimed not to know to whom it went. I think that he was speaking the truth. This left your husband on extremely short commons. He supplemented what was left of his income by a variety of means, thus enabling him to appear reasonably well monied in society.

'He took on a series of positions in the evenings, principally with a man named George Masserene who runs a cheap gaming house. He acted there as his chief croupier, occasional bouncer and made up his books. He also kept the books of a number of tradesmen and shopkeepers who could not afford professional help. Mr Masserene told me that Mr Shafto had a gift for numbers and that he was sorry to lose him when he married you.'

Masserene? George Masserene? Beck remembered meeting him in Piccadilly soon after her marriage to Will and the extremely odd conversation which had followed.

'You are sure of this?' Her question was really unnecessary, she knew, but the knowledge that Will had worked hard in the evenings to keep himself afloat was difficult to believe, remembering the usual carefree face he presented to society on those nights on which he was not working.

'Quite sure, madam. I also traced his valet, Gilbert Barry, always known as Gib. He's a right close-mouthed fellow and no mistake. He allowed as how he had not seen his master since he had left his service, and I am inclined to believe him.'

He did not tell Beck that Gib had thrown his head back and laughed after having guessed that Beck wanted Will traced because he had left her.

'You've made my day, that you have. He'd do nowt good for himself until he'd either thrown her shackles off him or had decided to master her, one or the other. Come to his senses at last, has he? I niver believed that she cared tuppence for him.'

Looking at the white-faced woman before him, the Runner thought that Gib might be wrong. She was suffering, no doubt about it, and suffering meant that she cared. But it was no business of his, or Gib's, and so he continued his report.

'Besides Wilmot, I spoke to his other friends, including those who joined him at Jackson's Saloon in Bond Street—and to Jackson himself. None of them admitted to having seen him recently. Jackson said one curious thing: that he had heard that Mr Shafto had taken on a professional bruiser in a match recently, and had beaten him. Did you know that, madam? Any point in following it up?'

Beck shook her head. 'I don't think so. I knew that he had fought a bruiser, and won, but I don't believe that Will would ever wish to be a member of the Fancy. Not his line at all.'

'Well, that's that, Mrs Shafto. Unless you have any other information which you haven't given me yet. I doubt me whether your man is in London—or if he is, no one is telling. You allowed as how he might be in the north. That's a large area of ground—can you narrow it down a little?'

It was Beck's turn to shake her head. 'Leave it with me while I make some enquiries of my own. If I think of anything useful I will tell Mr Herriott to get in touch with you again. In the meantime he will pay you for the work which you have already done for me, and for which I thank you.'

She was a gracious lady whatever the jealous servant, Gib, thought of her. Why would a man wish to leave her? But White knew as well as anyone that the true inward nature of any marriage is a thing known to few beside the principals themselves.

He bowed his way out. Beck sighed and went to tell Aunt Petronella what her man had found out about Will, in particular the information that Will had been earning a hard and painful living before he had married her.

'Which does not surprise me,' said her aunt robustly. 'I always said that he was honourable. What I don't understand, knowing him, is why he never went for a soldier—perhaps he couldn't afford to buy a commission?'

'Now, what do I do next?' asked Beck, a trifle miserably.

'Think of anything odd about Will's behaviour which might prove helpful. You lived with him long enough to know if he said or did anything untoward which might need explaining.'

Beck was morose. 'Everything about Will's conduct needs explaining. For instance, what did he do with his income? The Runner said that he didn't spend it. Why not? Where did it go? There's a mystery if you like, given that disposing of it left him nearly penniless and needing to take on a series of odd jobs such as few gentlemen would expect to engage in.'

Both women sat silent for a time before Beck rang for more tea. It might stimulate thinking.

Aunt Petronella said thoughtfully, 'I never understood why Will didn't buy himself a carriage with the handsome allowance you gave him. For that matter he didn't even spend it on a horse, or refurbish his wardrobe overmuch.'

Beck looked at her, her memory beginning to tell her something she had almost forgotten. 'I asked Will why he didn't buy a carriage—he said that he was thinking about it. So, what did he do with his allowance? Coutts informed me that it was always spent by the end of the quarter.'

She paused, said slowly, 'Do you suppose it was going the same way as the other income of which White spoke?'

Aunt Petronella nodded. 'A reasonable assumption. But does it take us any further on?'

Beck sat silent for a moment. She was having a dreadful thought which she dare not pass on to her aunt. Could it be that Will was already married when he had married her? Did he have a wife and family dependent on him somewhere—and had he disappeared in order to rejoin them?

She shuddered at the mere idea, and to banish it began to speak slowly and deliberately. 'You asked me if there was anything odd about Will's behaviour before he disappeared and I have told you all that I can think of.'

'I suppose that you could ask Coutts if Will was sending the money on to someone by banker's draft—perhaps the same someone as before.'

Beck shook her head. 'Can you believe that, under

these odd circumstances, Will did other than ask Coutts for confidentiality? And, if so, Mr Coutts would almost certainly not give me any information.'

'You could always try, Beck. After all, you could tell him of your sad circumstance and he might then relent.'

'I doubt it, Aunt. But before I visit Coutts Bank I shall visit Josh Wilmot and George Masserene. Both of them knew Will before I did and they might be more willing to talk to me than to Mr White.'

Aunt Petronella rose and kissed Beck. 'Bravo, my dear. Far better than grieving, you must admit, to go out and about and try to find your honourable man.'

Beck thought a minute before speaking. 'That depends on how honourable Will's reason was for passing on the major part of his income and my allowance.'

'Indeed. But, however painful the reason might prove to be, you have a duty to continue your search. And the duty is not only to yourself, but to Will.'

'Agreed.' And Beck threw her arms about Aunt Petronella and kissed her. For a moment the two women clung together, wordless. Aunt Petronella could never remember a time when her niece had offered her spontaneous affection. Adversity is a great teacher, she thought, and kissed Beck again before leaving her.

Josh Wilmot was so cagey that Beck could get nothing from him. 'Disappeared, has he,' he said. 'My commiserations, Mrs Shafto. Will's a good fellow. I've not the slightest notion where he has gone. Afraid I can't help you there.'

He smiled at her. Beck said coolly, 'Mr White informed me that you told him that Will sent the greater part of his income to a secret address.'

'Indeed. He had a small amount of money left him by

a maiden aunt in the form of an annuity, and he gave away the major part of it. But he did not ask me to perform the business for him. He drew a sum of money each quarter and disposed of it himself. So I cannot help you there, I am afraid.'

Was he speaking the truth? Beck was not sure. But it was plain that he would tell her nothing further.

Josh added, kindly for him, 'You see, Beck, he didn't want anyone to know where the money was going. Not even me. He banked it at Coutts, I do know. But, I'm afraid that if Will asked for confidentiality, Coutts would not pass any information on to you. Against their house rules.'

It was a dead end. Beck thanked him and drove on to the address for George Masserene which White had given to her. He lived in a small villa in one of the modest streets which were being built in north London. Fortune favoured Beck for he was at home: he and his wife and four children ranging in age from five to fourteen.

On arrival a small tweeny showed her into a room furnished in lower-middle-class comfort. It was apparent that George Masserene made a useful income, not a large one.

He came in, smiling. 'Mrs Will Shafto, we have met before, have we not?' He looked around him. 'Will not with you, eh?'

Beck explained. George heaved a great sigh and repeated what Josh Wilmot had told her. 'I've no idea where Will might have gone. I've no idea where he came from either. Only that he was a gent down on his luck— until he married you, of course. Clever and honest, was Will. I could only wish there were more like him!'

'He never spoke to you of his family, and where they might be found, Mr Masserene?'

'He was from the north, he said once, and to be honest Mrs Shafto, in my line of business one doesn't question people about their origins overmuch. Doesn't do, you understand. Will wanted his private life private, and that was that.'

All that Josh Wilmot and George Masserene, and the shopkeepers around the corner whose books Will had kept could offer Beck was a series of testimonials about Will's hard work and his transparent honesty. Gratifying though this was, it offered no clues to Will's current whereabouts.

She told Aunt Petronella and the Duke as much later that evening. All that now remained was for her to visit Coutts Bank, ask for the great man himself and, if he refused to reveal to whom Will was passing on the majority of his money, consider another journey north.

'I'm told that Shafto Hall in Northumberland is a ruin, which leaves me the rest of the district to comb—no small task!'

The Duke said, quietly reasonable for once, 'Unfortunately, I know nothing of his family, other than that his father gambled everything away. They were the last of their line. His mother's family cut her off when she married Shafto, and I'm told that she died some years ago. Report has it that he has nothing left at all in the way of relatives. A dead end, I fear. I asked my old friend Gascoigne if he knew where Will might have gone, but he's as ignorant as the rest of us.'

'How can a man disappear in the England of 1813?' queried Beck. She sank her head in her hands.

Aunt Petronella comforted her. 'Never despair, my

child. Go to Coutts. He can only refuse—but he might not.'

'It is virtually all that is left to me,' sighed Beck sadly. Secretly she was beginning to wonder whether she wanted an answer. Might it not be better, in the long run, to let Will go rather than uncover his secret life?

She could not. For better or for worse, she loved him, and loved him all the more fiercely because she had never expected to love again. At all costs she must know what had happened to him.

And if, once she found him, it was simply to say goodbye to him, because he could never be hers, then that was better than living forever without knowing where he had gone and without allowing her to say farewell to him before he had left her.

She put his letter into her bag and arranged to visit Coutts Bank on the morrow.

Chapter Fifteen

Beck had the status of a great lady in the world of 1813 and Thomas Coutts and his minions treated her as such. She was shown into the bank's parlour where sherry wine and ratafia biscuits awaited Coutts's most honoured clients. Mr Coutts rose and bowed to her.

'What may I do for you, Mrs Shafto?' he asked her after offering her the sherry which Beck refused.

'You may have heard,' Beck said stiffly, for it was painful for her to say it, 'that my husband, Mr Will Shafto, has left me. Unfortunately I do not know where he has gone, and for a variety of reasons, some of them financial, I wish to trace him. I believe that you can help me.'

'No, I was not aware of your husband's departure, and I commiserate with you on it. I will do my best to assist you, if assistance is, indeed, possible.'

Beck leaned forward, her face earnest. 'As you know, Mr Coutts, on marriage I made my husband an allowance, paid quarterly through your bank. I have reason to believe that he spent little of it, but, instead, paid most of it by Banker's draft into the account of another person. If I knew who that person was, and where they lived, I might be able to trace him. I would not ask this information of you were it not that I have exhausted every other avenue which might lead me to him. You are truly my last resort.'

Whilst she was speaking Mr Coutts's face grew more and more melancholy. 'Alas, Mrs Shafto, you ask of me an impossibility. Mr Shafto particularly requested that this transaction remain a secret between himself and the bank, and signed a document to that very purpose. It grieves me to tell you this, but you know as well as I that I cannot breach such a confidence once made.'

'Even,' faltered Beck, 'if to do so might relieve suffering and distress on the part of the person who asks?'

'Mrs Shafto, even if the Regent himself made such a demand of me I could not satisfy him. My word is my bond, and without that my business and that of others, would be at risk. There can be no exceptions. May I add that I deeply regret having to disappoint you.'

Beck would have liked to tell him that his deep regrets cut no ice with her, but for once, held her tongue. It was pointless to make an enemy of a man who was, after all, only carrying out what was asked of him. She allowed him to show her to her carriage and promised to inform him if Mr Shafto should return.

'For,' he said, 'I formed a favourable opinion of him, which, forgive me for saying so, considering his reputation, surprised me a little.'

Another testimonial for Will, thought Beck bitterly. He seems to have behaved well towards everyone but myself!

And what do I do now?

She was still asking herself that question later on that evening. She had sent her supper away uneaten: the sight of it made her feel sick. Although the day was hot she had ordered a fire to be made for she found herself shivering, and even its flames failed to warm her.

She tried to read a novel, but could not, for the future stretched before her dark and friendless. She picked up *The Morning Post* and tried to read that, but could not. She was about to ring for the butler to bring the teaboard in, tea being always recommended for the distressed, when he arrived to tell her that 'There is a person waiting in the entrance hall, madam. He has asked to be allowed to speak to you. He says that he has some information for you which you will be gratified to receive. He says that the matter is urgent.'

'Pray what sort of a person? Does he seem respectable?'

'Most respectable. He has the aspect of a clerk. He says that his name is Smith.'

'Then show him in at once.'

Will! Could he conceivably know something about Will, for that was the only news which could possibly gratify her these days?

The butler ushered Mr Smith in. He was a man of medium height, medium appearance, and medium clothing. Beck could see why the butler thought him a clerk. He was dressed in plain black with a spotless but simple white stock. He bowed in her direction when he entered.

He looked at the butler, who had retreated to the door, and said under his breath, 'Is it possible for me to speak to you alone, Mrs Shafto?'

Beck instructed the butler to leave, which he did after offering her a speaking glance of disapproval.

'What do you have to tell me, sir? The butler said that you were most urgent in your manner.'

'Indeed. I must begin by informing you that I work at Coutts Bank and that I can provide you with information regarding your husband's dealings with the bank. Information which Mr Coutts refused to divulge. For a consideration I would be prepared to offer it to you. You must understand that it is I who deal with your husband's account. This transaction must remain secret between us, for I have no wish to be turned away should it become known that I have breached confidentiality.

'But it seemed wrong to me that a wife should not be aware of her husband's affairs when that knowledge might help her to trace his whereabouts.'

He sniffed and looked pious. 'I could not endure to think of your sufferings, Mrs Shafto, when I had the power to relieve them.'

Beck wished that she could like the man before her. But it did not matter whether she liked him or loathed him if he could lead her to Will.

'How much do you want?' she asked coldly.

Smith—if that were his name—looked surprised. He had met few women who spoke and behaved as bluntly as a man.

'If you could see your way to fifty pounds, perhaps.'

'You are modest, Mr. Smith.' Beck was still blunt. 'Tell me what you know and if it is worth more, then you shall have more. If not, then I will give you less.'

'As you wish. You asked to whom Mr Shafto made regular quarterly payments from his account. A banker's draft was sent to a solicitor by the name of Milburn in the town of Burnside in Northumberland. The draft was made out to a Mrs Will Shafto.'

The room swam before Beck's eyes. All her worst fears had been realised. Will had a wife hidden away, and she, she was the victim of a bigamist who had made her his whore to get at her money and send it to another woman! Why had he left her? Had honour, as he claimed, suddenly overcome him, or had he left because he wished to return to the woman whom he truly loved and for whom he had lied and thieved.

Oh, the monster! If she had begun this search by wishing to find Will so that she could tell him how much she loved him, she would continue it in order to find him and gain her revenge! She would make him wish that he had never been born, the man who had deceived everyone by making them think that he was both brave and honourable!

She suddenly realised that Smith was speaking, his voice anxious.

'Mrs Shafto, Mrs Shafto, are you ill? Shall I ring for your maid?'

Beck sat up straight. 'Of course I am not ill. Far from it. I am well for the first time in months. And for your pains I shall double the money for which you asked. I can give you fifty pounds now and you may have another fifty from the butler if you return in a week's time.'

She went to her escritoire and, unlocking a drawer, took out a purseful of sovereigns and almost flung it at him. 'I do not wish to see you again, understand me?'

'Oh, yes, madam. I shall return in a week. You are most kind.'

'Kind! Kind! I have forgotten the meaning of the word. Take your thirty pieces of silver with you, and enjoy it more than the man you have imitated did.'

She swung round and left the room at once, leaving Smith to gape after her. All that Beck could think of was that, haste, post-haste, she must pack at once, order the carriage to be made ready and set off for Burnside as soon as she and John Coachman had found out where the damned place was.

In the meantime she wrenched from her finger the ring

which her faithless husband had given her and which she had treasured because he had told her that he had bought it with his money, not hers.

Had that been a lie, too?

No matter, she would soon confront him with his lies in the bolthole to which he had scuttled. And when she got there she would set such a mine under cheating Will Shafto as would blow him to hell and beyond—wherever that might be.

Beck's second journey to the north was not so eventful as her first, but was more exasperating. She took only a small staff with her: her lady's maid, Kitty Jackson, who travelled in the coach with her, two footmen standing at the back, and an outrider who arrived early at the posthouses where they stayed overnight to make sure that everything was made ready before she arrived.

She and Will had dispensed with one on their fated journey to Inglebury, something which they had both acknowledged later had been a mistake. Neither of them had wished to travel in overmuch pomp, but Beck, as a woman on her own in a treacherous world, felt that this time she could not have too many strong men about her.

The journey was exasperating because it seemed to take place so slowly. Beck wished that she had not left Mrs Grey at Inglebury, to look after it until she and Will returned later in the year. She would have been someone to talk to. Kitty was so overwhelmed by being alone with her mistress that she could scarcely do more than blush and agree with everything Beck said.

Now and again Beck looked down at Will's ring which, for some reason she did not understand, she had replaced on her finger in the middle of the night before she had left London. She had been unable to sleep: the look on his face when he had given it to her swam into her mind every time she turned her pillow over or tried to compose herself.

At last, to try to exorcise it, she had risen, slipped the ring on again—and sleep had come immediately, as it had done on the night when they had made love. Her own weakness disgusted her when, in the morning, she had not the heart to discard it again.

All the justification that she could offer herself was that it was the one thing of his which was truly hers and no one else's—if she could believe him, that was.

Beck's odyssey took her up the Great North Road, avoiding the Midlands and Sherwood Forest, since this particular route would take them almost to Burnside which Beck had discovered to be a small town not far from Shafto Hall. Which, of course, was not surprising.

Several days' hard driving brought them to Alnwick in the late evening. Beck had reserved a suite of rooms at the White Swan, the principal coaching inn there. Burnside was some five miles distant, on a byway. She felt that she needed a hearty meal and a good night's sleep in a comfortable bed before she confronted her faithless husband.

Only she could not sleep. She rose shortly after midnight to draw the bedroom curtains and gaze up at the moon, the goddess Diana's lamp, the virgin goddess whom she had forsaken when she had allowed Will to make love to her.

Which was, Beck knew, not a completely accurate description of what had happened on that fateful night. She shuddered at the memory, but whether with fear, anger, or frustrated desire at the prospect that he would never make love to her again, she did not know.

Reason told her that it was possible that her long journey might be nothing but a wild goose chase: that Will was not at Burnside, but some place else where she might never find him.

But something, Beck knew not what, was telling her that he was not far away, and that by the time the sun set on the next day she would meet the other, the legal Mrs Shafto.

Her first port of call the following morning was at Mr Milburn's office in Burnside. The town was situated almost at the end of the byway and was typical of those which she had passed through on her journey north. Its small houses were of stone. There was a little market place with a cross in the centre. Behind it loomed greyblue hills. The people who walked in the narrow streets were dark and suspicious looking.

Mr Milburn's office was soon found. It was the most imposing building in Burnside. Pasted on the wall beside the door was a large notice offering for sale the lands near Shafto Hall, once part of the Shafto estate, but now in the possession of John Whately, Esquire, who wished to sell them.

The clerk who received Beck in his small office conveyed to her his regrets that Mr Milburn was away in Newcastle, representing a client who had been accused of sheep stealing. The fields around Burnside, Beck had already noted, were full of them.

'Then perhaps you may be able to assist me.' Beck had already decided that she would not ask for Will's whereabouts since it was not certain that he had fled to Burnside. Instead she asked, her voice as sweet as she could make it, since she did not wish to earn a refusal by appearing to be an enemy of the woman, 'I am trying to trace a Mrs William Shafto who, I am informed, is a resident of Burnside.'

'Oh,' said the clerk, 'that is easily done. You did not need Mr Milburn's presence in order to learn *that*. Mrs Shafto *was* a resident of Burnside, she rented a small cottage facing the market place, but latterly she has gone to live at the Home Farm.'

'The Home Farm?'

'Ah, you are a stranger in the district. The Home Farm is all that is left of the land around Shafto Hall which used to belong to the Shafto family. The byway ends there, so if you wish to visit Mrs Shafto you will be able to travel down it in your carriage. Is there anything I can do to assist you further?'

Beck had no intention of letting anyone know of the true purpose of her visit.

She rose, picking up her reticule and her bonnet which she had taken off on entering the office. ''No, I thank you, sir. You have already told me all I wish to know.'

Oh, what a lie that was! Her real wish had been that the whole thing had been a fiction promoted by Coutts's clerk to relieve her of her money. Instead she found herself being pointed in the direction of a very real Mrs Shafto.

The clerk followed her to the door, giving her further directions as to where the Home Farm might be found. 'Am I to inform Mr Milburn of your visit?' were his final words.

'Oh, no, indeed not. The matter was concluded when you directed me to the Home Farm.'

The clerk stood in the bow window of his master's office wondering who the fine lady might be who had come with such a simple request. He had been so overwhelmed by her beauty, her toilette—Beck had dressed herself most carefully in her deep blue walking gown with fine lace trimmings—that he had quite forgotten to ask her for her name.

Mr Milburn would not be best pleased with him on hearing that he had committed such a *faux pas*—but then, she had told him not to trouble his master, so he would not.

The longest part of Beck's journey to find Will was the last mile from the little town to the lane which led to the Home Farm.

She stepped out of her carriage, bidding the coachman wait for her. She could see the small farmhouse through a stand of trees which screened it from the lane and the byway which led to it. Beyond the house she could see more fields full of sheep, and some that were given over to wheat and were awaiting the harvest, which was reaped later here than in the warm south. To reach the house she had to cross a farmyard where a collie dog glared at her from his kennel.

The farmhouse had two bow windows at the front and a small porch in which some flowering plants stood in pots on a low ledge. The knocker was of brass and shaped like an imp. She lifted it and rapped sharply on the door. For some moments nothing happened, then the door opened and a large red-faced woman in a black stuff dress and a very white apron stood facing her.

'Yes, Mam?'

Well, by her age and her appearance she was certainly not Will's wife—which was oddly comforting.

'I am informed that a Mrs Will Shafto lives here...'

She got no further, the woman cut her off.

'Aye, that be so. Well?'

'I wonder if I might have a word with her?'

'And who may you be that wants a word with the missis?'

Foolishly, as she now realised, Beck had not considered what she might say in answer to such a question. She did not wish to confess that she was Will's supposed wife if Will were not here.

'I am Miss Rowallan,' she said, for if Will could deceive her, then she was entitled to deceive this other Mrs Shafto. 'I have just visited Mr Milburn who has sent me to you.'

'From Mr Milburn? Come in and wait a moment, hinny, afore I ask the missis if she be willing to see you.'

She opened the door wide and Beck stepped into a small entrance hall with a red-tiled floor of the kind commonly seen in farmhouse kitchens. A warming pan and some dried flowers hung on one whitewashed wall.

The woman disappeared through a rough door made of oak planks and decorated with a wrought iron handle. Beck could hear voices.

Presently the woman reappeared. 'The missis will see you. She's in the kitchen—it's the only downstairs room fit to live in, ye ken, until the house is improved. This way.'

Beck followed her through the door and into a passage from which a staircase rose to the upper storey. Facing them was another oak-planked door which the woman opened, saying, 'Here y'are, missis.'

Beck walked through it, the woman retreating to leave her alone with the kitchen's occupants. The kitchen was large and warm. A fire burned in a huge grate which had a cast-iron spit before it, and a hook from which hung a large cauldron. Brass and copper pans stood on shelves around the room. In the middle of the floor was a well-scrubbed table on which someone—the large woman?—had been making bread.

Seated by the fire was a pretty young woman, a shawl around her shoulders, and a blanket covering her legs. She had some sewing in her hand and a work table by her side. Walking towards her, and waving her hand for Beck to seat herself in a Windsor chair facing the hearth, was a tall, middle-aged woman who bore the traces of great beauty now overworn by age and suffering.

'I am Mrs William Shafto,' she said in a cultured voice. 'I understand from Jinny that you wish to speak to me.'

Chapter Sixteen

Beck stared at her. This was Mrs William Shafto? This woman who, by her age and appearance, could not possibly be Will's wife. It was a wild goose chase that she had embarked on after all.

Mrs Shafto said quietly, 'You seem surprised.'

Beck nodded, swallowed and said in a stifled voice, 'I had understood you to be a much younger woman.'

Mrs Shafto shook her head. 'Alas, no. I am the only Mrs William Shafto in these parts. This,' she added, waving a hand at the young woman by the fire, 'is my daughter, Emily. You will excuse her if she does not rise to greet you. She has been crippled since birth which, as you see, does not prevent her from being useful.'

Emily smiled at her mother and the dazed Beck in response to this tribute, and quietly continued with her work, which was turning an aged sheet.

'Pray will you not sit, Miss Rowallan. I believe that was the name Jinny gave me? Forgive me if I say that you look tired and I would not be inhospitable. I shall ask Jinny to brew us some tea and butter us some bannocks.'

Her legs failing her, Beck sat down. This was all so

different from her expectations that she had no notion of what she might say next, since all that she had intended to say seemed so inapposite. Where was Will? And where was the wife which she had supposed him to be harbouring here?

She looked around the homely room and came out with, 'I had heard that you once lived at Shafto Hall. Mr Milburn's clerk said that you had been residing in Burnside, but had recently moved into the Home Farm.'

'That is true, Miss Rowallan. Forgive me, but may I ask what is the purpose of your visit? It cannot be to learn of my housing arrangements.'

This pleasantly sardonic statement delivered by Mrs Shafto as she sat down in an armchair opposite her daughter reminded Beck so strongly of Will that her brain began to work again, and she knew exactly who the woman before her, and the pretty crippled girl, were.

This, then, was the Mrs Shafto to whom Will had sent most of his income and the allowance which she had made over to him as part of the marriage settlement. He had done so in order to maintain not a mistress, nor a wife, but his penniless mother and his crippled younger sister. He had plainly not told them that he was married, for Mrs Shafto had not recognised her name. Nor had he told them how he had acquired the extra money which he had been sending to them—and had now abandoned.

But where was Will?

Did his mother know of his whereabouts? She certainly appeared to know nothing of his London life.

Even as Beck gathered herself to speak, to ask if they knew where Will might be found, she heard footsteps and voices outside the kitchen door which led to the farmyard.

Her heart sank. This must be the farmer who was responsible for the upkeep of the fields through which she had driven. The door opened and a man in the rough clothing of a working farmer stepped through the door.

The man was Will.

Time, which had, for Beck, been running first fast and then slow, now stopped altogether. No one else seemed to notice. She blinked and time started again.

Mrs Shafto said happily, 'Ah, there you are, Will, most opportune. Perhaps you might be able to help our visitor, Miss Rowallan, who has come to find a Mrs Will Shafto…'

Will's eyebrows rose. 'Has she, indeed? You didn't really need to travel as far as Burnside to find her, did you, Beck?'

Mrs Shafto said, surprised, 'You know Miss Rowallan, then, Will?'

'Indeed I do, mother. In every sense of the word. She is my wife, Mrs Will Shafto.'

Beck licked her lips. She had been far too busy taking in Will's transformation from London dandy to working northern farmer to consider what she might usefully say next. She looked wildly from Will's grave face to his mother's.

Mrs Shafto's showed a mixture of surprise, puzzlement and growing reproach. Her daughter had given a little exclamation and dropped her sewing to the floor from which it was plain that she was unable to retrieve it.

Unable to look Mrs Shafto in the eye after her unmasking, especially when she said unhappily, 'You never told us that you were married, Will,' Beck moved forward, and bent down to pick up the sheet in order to hand it back to Will's sister.

Emily whispered 'Thank you,' and then asked, 'Are you *truly* Will's wife?'

Beck straightened up. 'Yes, truly.'

'Then why did you say that your name was Miss Rowallan?'

'Exactly.' This was Mrs Shafto, her voice now frosty.

Will said nothing, but leaned against the whitewashed wall beside an embroidered sampler declaring hopefully, 'God bless our happy home.'

'Because that was my name, and…' She must say it, she must. 'I was not sure that I was truly Mrs Will Shafto when I found out that a Mrs Will Shafto appeared to live at Burnside.'

'But why did you think that? Will has just told us that he married you.' Mrs Shafto's puzzlement had become extreme.

All of Beck's usual defences against life and its many difficulties were impossible to deploy here. She could not use her sharp tongue, her ability to wound and to control against these two poor women, whose simple goodness was so patent, and who were staring at her rich and sophisticated self in bewilderment.

Spite and wicked vice she could deal with and overcome, but virtue disarmed her. She was suddenly as defenceless as they. And Will was not helping her.

Time ticked by. No one spoke. The fire crackled in the hearth. Emily resumed her sewing. Will's mother sank into an armchair. Will said, sardonically, 'Quiet, Beck? Most unlike you.'

Beck looked around the room. Something inside her snapped. She dropped her head and said in a broken voice, 'Please, Will, help me. Tell me why…' She got no further. She had come here prepared to rail at him, to reproach him for his faithlessness, to mock at the woman for whom he had betrayed her, to have her revenge on him and instead she had found... What?

'Why did you leave me,' burst from her of its own accord, 'when I love you and you said that you loved me. Why? Why? You wrote of honour. Where was the honour in that? To leave me without telling me where you were going.'

On hearing the words 'I love you', Will levered himself off the wall. He began to walk towards her. Beck gave a stifled moan, held out her hands to him, then, her face crumpling, she turned on her heel and ran out of the kitchen.

Mrs Shafto rose to her feet and cried at Will in an accusing voice, 'She was your wife, and you left her, Will, without telling her where you were going. How could you?'

Will, who had almost reached the door, looked at the accusing faces of his mother and sister. How could he explain his apparently callous behaviour to them: the mother and sister who had worshiped him because by some means he had kept them from the almshouse—nay, from the workhouse—to which his father's fecklessness, and then his death, had doomed them.

He was suddenly as frantic as Beck. 'I'll explain everything later, Mother. I must go after her. I can't lose her now.' Without further ado, he, too, ran out of the kitchen. By the time he was in the lane he could see Beck running ahead of him, her skirts lifted to give her greater speed.

He must catch her because she had said, at the last, that she loved him. Why had he been so sure that she cared so little for him that his leaving her would not hurt her so much as it surely had?

More, the one thing which he had not foreseen—

which he should have done—was that somehow she would discover that, through Coutts, he had been sending money to his mother, Mrs Will Shafto, and would instantly assume that this Mrs Shafto must be his wife—which made her—what?

Beck had reached the gate which divided the farm from the lane. Before her was the carriage which would take her away from this place where she had shamed herself. She, who never lied, had lied—and had been royally caught out.

She heard Will pounding along behind her. He must not catch her. He had lied to her when he had written that he loved her. He had lied about his mother and his sister. As a consequence she had assumed all the wrong things about the Mrs Shafto whom he had been supporting.

She was so lost to everything that she was unaware that she was sobbing as she ran, that the tears were running down her face, and were blinding her. She scarcely felt Will catch her up, put a hand on her shoulder to swing her round—to see the ruin which Beck Shafto had become, and all because she had fallen in love with her rogue.

Who was not really a rogue at all, but a man who had been supporting two poor women to the limit of his ability and his endurance. He had lived on the edge of ruin for years in order to keep them from the workhouse, and rather than deck himself out, buy a curricle and gamble with the allowance she had made over to him, he had sent the bulk of it to them to ease their hard lives a little.

She should have had the wit to see that the man she had come to know and love would never have deceived her so cruelly, would never have married her if he had a wife already. The magnitude of her misunderstanding of him overwhelmed her.

'Oh, Beck, what have I done to you?' burst from Will. He tried to comfort her but his very touch seemed to complete her undoing. She had paled, her eyelids had fluttered: she was plainly about to faint. 'Oh, my dearest heart, let me hold you and never let you go. What a pitiful fool I was to desert you.'

Beck heard him as from a great distance. She summoned up the tatters of the strength of mind which had sustained her all her life.

'No, Will,' she managed at last into his rough jacket. 'I was a fool, a wicked fool, to believe that you could have left me because you already had a wife. But I had become so used to betrayal...' She fought back tears.

'Oh, Will.' It seemed to be all that she could say. 'What are we to do?'

'We could go back to the farm and explain ourselves, perhaps.'

'Not yet. I could not face your mother and sister, yet. Oh, why did you not tell me of them? I could have helped them so much.'

Will held her away from him. 'My love, that is part of the problem, my problem, something of which we must speak together before we can resume our marriage. You cannot make matters better simply by doling out your money as the fancy takes you. And, yes, I can see it would be a kindness to all of us if we don't go back immediately. I must be honest with Mother and Emily, after I have talked with you.

'If I had known that you loved me so deeply I would have talked to you before, not left you. But not knowing that, I thought that the kindest thing I could do was to leave you and allow you to start a new life without me.'

Instead of reassuring her, as it was meant to do, Beck's sobs redoubled. 'But I don't want a new life without you. I want my old one—or no life at all. I knew that I loved you when we were prisoners in the forest and I didn't want you to fight that man for me because I couldn't bear to see you hurt. And when you made love to me afterwards, I was in heaven.'

Will was to reflect afterwards on the sad misunderstandings which could part men and women. For the moment he was content to hold Beck to him and stroke her gently until she quietened. He wondered what in the world her watching coachman was making of them!

As Beck hiccuped her way into calmness again he said, 'Let us take a walk together as an old married couple should. Not far from here is Shafto Hall. I could show it to you—ruins are all the fashion nowadays, are they not? Though I cannot promise you a ghost.'

This poor joke brought a watery smile to Beck's face.

'I wouldn't expect a ghost in the summer, Will.'

'I can promise you a dog, though, Beck.' Will put two fingers to his mouth and gave a most ungentlemanlylike whistle, whereupon the collie whom Beck had seen earlier came running out of the farmyard towards them.

On reaching Will it lay on its stomach in submissive fashion, looking up at him with adoring eyes.

'This is Pilot, a working dog. He is not, I fear, a pretty lap dog. I cannot picture you with a lap dog, Beck, I think that Pilot is more your style. He will let you stroke him providing you are gentle. The man who was my tenant here is teaching me not only how to farm, but also how to use Pilot to work with the sheep, before he retires into a contented old age on the only cottage left on the remnant of my father's estates, where he has gone to live since I brought my mother and sister to the Home Farm.'

He could not have thought of a better diversion, one more calculated to dry Beck's tears. She bent down and stroked Pilot, who now transferred his affection to her.

'Pilot may walk with us, Beck, if you wish.'

'I do wish, Will.' She had taken a handkerchief from her reticule and was drying her eyes. 'And you may tell me what made you come here to learn to be a farmer— and why you left me.'

'Yes, I owe you that. Forgive me, Beck, I have been a selfish brute—'

Beck leaned forward and put her fingers on his lips. 'No, Will, if we continue to reproach ourselves for the past we shall never come to terms with the present and, hopefully, the future.'

Will took Beck's arm, and snapped his fingers at Pilot who promptly rose and trotted obediently at his heels. 'This is the way to the Hall. It lies beyond the trees you see before you. There was a drive to it from the byway, but it has become overgrown through neglect. We can walk quite comfortably along its remains, though, and sit on what is left of the terrace.'

Shafto Hall, Beck discovered, was a redbrick building dating back to Tudor times which had been very beautiful before it had decayed into near ruin. Will led Beck to a broken stone bench on a terrace behind the house which overlooked a long slope towards a distant stream. Beyond that were fields dotted with still more sheep, happily grazing.

'I wish I were a sheep,' said Beck as she sat down beside Will, Pilot at their feet. 'Just think how pleasant it would be to have no worries, no notion of the future nor the past, just the delight of grazing in the sun without troubling about where the next meal is coming from.'

'Ah,' said Will naughtily, 'but think what a sheep's destination is, Beck. The slaughterhouse and your plate!'

'But the sheep doesn't know that,' replied Beck incontrovertibly, 'and it is our knowing things which causes us so much unhappiness, is it not?'

'But it causes us so much pleasure, too. Remember our happy night in Sherwood Forest?'

Beck looked earnestly into his face. 'Of course I do. And remembering it makes it even more difficult for me to understand why you left me as you did.'

'I'll try to explain myself. I will say in my defence that I didn't know that you loved me. I thought that night arose out of your gratitude to me for saving you from Job. You never said otherwise, never breathed a word of love to me. Why not, Beck?'

. Beck looked away from him and twisted her hands together. 'I can't, Will. I daren't. My life until I met you had taught me a harsh lesson: that I was unloved because I was unworthy. And when, once, long ago, I dared to love, everything went horribly wrong, so I told myself I would never care for anyone again, or, if I did, I would never admit it.'

Her last words were uttered in a voice so low that Will had to strain to hear them. He took her hand in his and saw that she was still wearing the ring which he had given her. The sight of it gave him hope that they might yet have a future together.

'Tell me,' he said at last. 'Tell me what happened to you, Beck, to make you afraid of life and love. The telling might heal you since keeping silent hasn't helped.'

'You will think me foolish...'

'Never that, Beck, never that. Whatever you are, you are not foolish. You may look away from me as you speak if that would make the telling easier.'

So she did—and the words came tumbling out and the hurts of the long-dead years came into the light again, and, as Will had said, the telling brought relief.

'I was not the eldest child. I had a brother, Paul, born some five years before me. I was a disappointment because my father never wanted daughters, only sons to help him to run his business and the lands he was busily buying. He saw himself as the founder of a new noble family. To his great chagrin my mother was sickly and never managed to bear another living child. She was constantly ailing.

'And then Paul was killed when we were out riding together. I will never forget what my father said when I reached home.

'"If one of you had to fall off your horse, why wasn't it you? Why was your brother taken and not you?" He never forgave me for that, nor for the knowledge that whilst I was a good horsewoman, Paul hated horses— he was frightened of them—and the accident happened because of his fear. My father had the horse shot that Paul had been riding, although the grooms with us when the accident happened told him that it was not the horse's fault. Really, it was my father's for he was insistent that Paul learned to ride.

'My mother died soon afterwards as a result of yet another attempt to bear him a son. He said that she and I had been his curse, and he married again as soon as he decently could. But my stepmother was no more fortunate than my mother and, what was worse, she hated me and fed my father's dislike of me.

'You cannot imagine how lonely and unloved I was.

When I was seventeen my father hired a new footman, the son of a yeoman farmer who had had a grammar-school education. He was very handsome. I had seen very few handsome young men, for my father refused to take an interest in me, seeing that he was still trying for a son. Besides, he resented having to supply me with the kind of dowry which would be expected from a man of his wealth. Absolutely everything must go to the son he still hoped to have.

'Robert—for that was the young man's name—and I were thrown together. He talked to me. He said that he felt sorry for me, and I think that I fell in love with him because he was the first person to treat me kindly. What he really felt for me I shall never know. Father said afterwards that Robert hoped that having seduced me and run away with me, he would be bought off. I've no idea whether or not that was the truth. Robert said that he would take me to Gretna, marry me, and then we should go and live on his farm. Now I can see what a foolish plan that was, but then—

'Then I was in heaven because someone really loved me and I loved him. My father always believed that Robert had seduced me, but he had not. He was oddly respectful towards me, as though he could never forget that I was the master's daughter.

'But we never reached Gretna, indeed, we never even left Inglebury House, which was where we were living then. Robert foolishly gossiped about our plans to one of the grooms who went and told my father. We were caught leaving the house.

'You may imagine the scene which followed. Robert was turned away. I never saw him again. My father condemned me to a suite of rooms in the attic where I was allowed to see only female servants. Ironically, my stepmother, who was increasing at the time, bore my father a son shortly afterwards but he only lived for a week.

'Like my mother she became an invalid. The doctor said that she must never bear another child, it would kill her. She died shortly before he did, so I became my father's heir; he could never forgive me for that. He called me his plain stick who had not had the decency to be born a son. He constantly compared me unkindly with my beautiful cousin, Sarah Allenby.

'I was certain that he would disinherit me, but he had quarrelled bitterly with his sister Allenby, my aunt, and wrote in his will that the only reason he was leaving me everything was because I still bore his name—and was the last of our line.

'Our line! My grandfather began life as a poor weaver who took advantage of the changes taking place in the woollen industry in his youth to make a large fortune, but my father always spoke as though we had the blood of Earls in our veins.

'After his death I became Hedley Beaucourt's ward because my father had said that the Allenbys were not to have the guardianship of me. Hedley Beaucourt and the Allenbys badgered me to make the kind of grand marriage which they later arranged for Sarah. I fought them off as best I could until I came of age, and I am so happy that I did because Sarah…poor Sarah…' She began to cry again, so Will held her close to him and stroked her chestnut mane until she had recovered herself a little.

'Oh, Will, poor Sarah! Just before I travelled north to find you—and your supposed wife—Aunt Petronella told me that Sarah had been found unconscious and injured in the home which her uncle had bought for her and Wingfield. Wingfield had beaten her senseless and disappeared. He probably thought that he had killed her. He also hurt Sarah's maid who had tried to protect her...

'And then I remembered that I was told what you had said to the Allenbys when they stopped your marriage to Sarah—that you would have treated her kindly... And I thought of how kind you had been to me—until you disappeared.'

Beck stopped. Everything which she had held inside of her for years had poured out like water from an un-stopped bottle. She quivered and trembled in Will's arms, for when she finished speaking he gathered her to him to comfort her—and his merest touch was enough to set her longing for him to do so much more than simply touch her.

She looked up at him for she had something important to tell him. 'You do understand me, don't you? Why I couldn't say "I love you" until I saw you in the kitchen just now. I was so overwhelmed that the words flew from me.'

'Understand you? Of course I do and I love you and admire you for your bravery, my dearest.' Will under-stood at last of what the Duke of Durness had been speaking on their wedding day when he had referred to Beck's sufferings in the past.

'I can say "I love you, Will" and because I can do so, you must tell me why you thought that your honour demanded that you leave me. What I find difficult to believe is that honour had anything to do with the matter, but Aunt Peter says that women will never understand what men mean by honour so perhaps you had better not try!'

She paused for a moment before murmuring thought-fully, 'I love you, Will. Every time I say it, it becomes easier the next time. You will grow quite bored with hearing it.' Mischief in her eyes, she challenged him, 'Now you, Will.'

Will leaned back, still holding her, although like Beck, he was finding that he was longing to do so much more with her than that. But loving must come later when all the misunderstandings which lay between them were cleared out of the way.

He owed it to her to be as frank with her as she had been with him so that they could forget the unhappy past and start life anew, and put the baggage of shame and suffering behind them.

'I can't say that my childhood was unhappy because it wasn't. My father hadn't yet sunk completely into the morass into which drink and gambling had led him. I had—or thought I had—the world before me. And then my father committed suicide when I was eighteen and we, my mother, my sister and I, found that he had left us virtually nothing. Everything had gone to pay his gambling debts except the Home Farm and the few acres around it.

'Oh, we knew that the Hall was falling into ruin, but my father was always telling us that next year he would have it repaired, but next year never came. Before he died I was beginning to understand that something must be wrong, but even then I could not have guessed at the magnitude of our ruin.

'My mother and sister were left with nothing but the small rent from the Home Farm. Shortly before my father shot himself an old aunt left me an annuity and I was able to pass on most of that to her and Emily, just enough to allow them to live in straitened circumstances in upper rooms in a house in Burnside, the village which the Shaftos had owned from time immemorial.

'The worst thing was that I had been trained to be

simply a gentleman living on his acres and his rents, nothing more. I had no profession by which I could earn money to support myself and my two dependents. I was little better than an odd-job man, falling in and out of debt and picking up bits and scraps of employment in order to keep myself, as well as Mother and Emily, out of the gutter. One summer I even joined a band of strolling players—with some success—but the life did not attract me.

'If I had not had Mother and Emily to support I would have signed on as a soldier in the ranks—for I could not afford a commission—but I could not leave them in a situation barely beyond starvation.

'Now you see why I was so desirous to marry a rich wife. Marrying you was their salvation as much as mine. I can only suppose that you found I was here by bullying out of Coutts Bank the fact that I was sending money to a Mrs Shafto in the north—and immediately jumped to the conclusion that I already had a wife, since it was commonly supposed that I was alone in the world.

'What I had not bargained for was not only that the more I knew you, the more I came to love you, but that I soon discovered that I was not cut out to be a kept man: Rebecca's rogue, a man without honour, content to live on a woman without giving her anything in return.

'What finally made me face the truth about myself was fighting Black Jack for you. I had behaved honourably in doing so, but once we were back in society I was again a man without a true occupation, simply someone whom you had married for your convenience.

'If I had known that you loved me I would not have left you as I did, but I would have tried to explain to you then that I must have some reason for living, for accepting your money without giving you anything real in return. So I came back to Burnside to see whether after renouncing everything you had given to me I would be able to keep Mother, Emily and myself in reasonable comfort by learning to run the Home Farm, so that when my tenant retired I could take over from him. I was astonished to discover that hard though it was, I liked the life. I have found a point and purpose in it which I have never known before.

'The work may be hard and menial but it is honourable and I need make no apology for doing it. If we are to save our marriage, Beck, it must be on the understanding that I have some worthwhile occupation. I could not ask you to be a poor farmer's wife, that would not be fair—'

He did not finish for Beck interrupted him eagerly. 'I could restore the Hall, Will, and buy back some of the lands around it. I learned today that they were for sale. And we could improve the farm so that we could live there until the Hall is habitable again. And you can manage Inglebury for me as well. Mr Carter, my agent, is growing old.'

Will shook his head. 'It will not be enough, Beck, for you to shower me with your bounty. We must become partners, only spending our money after joint consultation. If we are to restore the Hall it will have to be done slowly by us, to our taste, and not by an army of workmen from outside whilst we fritter and idle our life away in pointless pleasure.

'I should like to visit London occasionally, but I would not wish to make living there a major part of our lives. I want to be a country squire, living on my acres like Coke of Norfolk does, farming my own land, not simply taking rent from the true workers on it whilst I do nothing.'

Beck sat silent for a moment. She bent down to scratch Pilot gently behind the ears before raising her head and looking earnestly at Will. 'I'm sure you are right to wish that you should be more than an absentee landowner living idle in London.

'I think that I, too, should have an occupation. Mine could be supervising the Hall's restoration and its refurnishing. If Bess of Hardwick nearly three hundred years ago could be a true chatelaine of her husband's lands and possessions, why should I not be? The farmer should have a working wife, after all. I cannot bake or brew, but I can run a great house as I have proved at Inglebury, and the Hall would provide a real challenge for me as learning to be both farmer and agent would for you.'

Will kissed her again, real affection in his voice. 'There speaks my managing Beck! No, I don't object to you managing things—so long as you don't manage me, but leave me something of my own.'

'But you would let me manage our children, Will?' This came out shyly.

'Of course, although when the boys grow up, they would become my responsibility—as the girls would be yours.'

'Boys, Will? Girls? How many children do you plan on having?'

'As many as you wish, Beck. The Hall is big enough for any number, and so is Inglebury, I understand.'

'Any number?' Beck was thoughtful. 'And we haven't even started.'

Will tightened his arms about her. 'What do you mean by that, Beck?'

'Well, we are not getting any younger, Will, are we?

And apart from that night together in the forest we have lived together like a monk and a nun—which is not exactly the way to start a family, now is it?'

'Oh, Beck,' said Will, showering little kisses on her face and neck. 'I might have known that you would be as frank and free a lover as you are in everything else in life. How do you propose that we remedy this sad situation?'

She hid her face in his chest before muttering in a voice so low that he could scarcely hear her, 'Well, we are alone, and not like to be interrupted, and oh, Will, I have missed you so, and I thought that…' Her voice ran out.

'Thought what?'

'That you would never hold me in your arms again. Love me, Will.'

'Now, Beck, now? Whatever will Pilot think?'

'Oh, I had forgotten Pilot.' Her expression was so sorrowful that Will began to laugh. 'No need to worry. I can send Pilot home. Listen,' and he gave a series of whistles which had Pilot on his feet again, his ears pricking.

'Home, boy, home,' said Will, giving a longer whistle after the word home.

Obediently Pilot turned and began to trot briskly in the direction of the farm. 'You see how obedient he is, Beck. Will you be as obedient a wife to me as he is a dog?'

'Only if you agree to be as kind to me as I promise to be to you.'

'Agreed.' Will turned to take her in his arms and lower her on to the grass at their feet, something which he had wished to do from the moment when they had left the farm behind them.

'Oh!' Beck struggled to a sitting position. 'Whatever will your mother and sister think if Pilot returns home without us?'

'That I have sent him ahead.'

'And you will explain to them later something of what went wrong between us?'

'A little, Beck.' He was unfastening his breeches flap, 'but if you don't lie down with me soon I shall think that you have changed your mind about the large family with which you propose to bless me.'

'Oh, I will bless you before that, Will.'

And so she did, there in the open, far from the haunts of men, lying in Will's arms, the sun shining above them, the sheep grazing below, and the birds calling and wheeling in the blue sky.

They were passion's children, and their loving was all the sweeter because it was delayed, and because neither of them had ever dared to hope that they would find the one twin soul with whom they might unite. And afterwards when they were two again, they would carry the memory of being one with them to ease life's burdens.

So Will told Beck when they were lying in each other's arms afterwards. 'I have a confession to make,' he said, 'one which I hope you will not use against me.'

'I would never use anything against you, Will. In future I shall try not to judge anyone, or anything, too hastily. What is it?'

'This. I think that when I left you, always, at the back of my mind, was the thought that, knowing you, if you truly loved me you would be prepared to track me to the polar wastes and beyond to get me back again. Is that what you did, Beck?'

She smiled up at him.

'I didn't track you to the polar wastes, Will, that

wasn't necessary, even if Northumberland is colder than London. But I must confess to employing a Runner, cross-questioning Josh Wilmot and George Masserene and bribing a clerk at Coutts' Bank.'

Will's shout of laughter was a joyful one. 'Oh, that's my wife all over, that's my Beck. Come and have your reward for your perseverance and your determination.'

'Then you're not cross with me, Will, for tracking you down?'

'Cross with you? Of course I'm not cross, and here's your punishment—or your reward—whichever you like to call it.'

With that he bent to kiss her, and one thing led to another so that they celebrated their reunion all over again, only desisting when the sun began to fall down the sky.

Later, much later, the other Mrs Shafto, standing at the window waiting for her son and his wife to return, and guessing what might be delaying them, saw Will walk into the farmyard, his arm around a flushed and smiling Beck.

'Here they come,' she said to Emily, who, her face anxious, was also awaiting her brother's return.

'Oh, Mother, is all well between them, do you think?'

Mrs Shafto watched Will bend his head to kiss Beck when they reached Pilot's kennel.

'Very well, my dear. If his wife drove all the way to Northumberland after him, and he was willing to sink his pride in order to run after her to keep her, then I cannot doubt that, somehow or other, they will find a way to live together happily.'

Beck and Will, now hand in hand, all their misunderstandings behind them, were in full agreement that they would face the pleasures—and the occasional pains—of married life together. Rebecca and her rogue had come home at last.

* * * * *

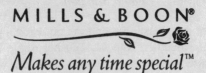
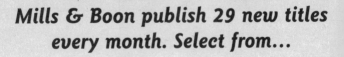